W9-CBA-758

Praise for the Lord of the Isles series

Mistress of the Catacombs

"World building, characterization, and systems of magic . . . are all so well conceived that the saga continues to be Drake's most ambitious work to date."   —*Booklist*

"The fourth volume of Drake's ambitious high-fantasy saga, Lord of the Isles . . . [is] a worthwhile continuation of what is emerging as the author's most important work."

—*Publishers Weekly*

Servant of the Dragon

"A thrilling read. . . . A solid addition to the series."—*Starlog*

"Drake [has a] talent for creating personable characters driven by their loyalty to one another to achieve great deeds."   —*Library Journal*

Queen of Demons

"From the start, Drake's characters took on a life of their own, and the magic system and culture are interestingly different, drawn from the religion of Sumer and other aspects of the classical world. The series' distinctive qualities are even more apparent in this second volume. . . . The strong color and characters keep this consistently entertaining."

—*Locus*

"The world building and characterization here are among Drake's best, and the magic is well thought out. Drake clearly has embarked on a fantasy saga as big as Eddings', Jordan's, and Goodkind's and as eminently worth reading."

—*Booklist*

Lord of the Isles

"True brilliance is as rare as a perfect diamond or a super-nova. *Lord of the Isles* is truly brilliant. We are in at the birth of a classic. . . . There is a lot of fantasy out there, but there is only one *Lord of the Isles*." —Morgan Llywelyn

"This epic has everything that serious fantasy readers demand—heroic action, mysterious magical forces, strange beasts, ghosts, sorcerers, and good writing . . . Drake's characters generally are credible and well-drawn. To add authenticity, Drake researched ancient magic and used actual spells." —*Tampa Tribune & Times*

"A marvelous page-turner, and an enchanting masterpiece of epic fantasy." —*Dragon*

MISTRESS
of the
CATACOMBS

TOR BOOKS BY DAVID DRAKE

MISTRESS

of the

CATACOMBS

David Drake

TOR®
fantasy

A TOM DOHERTY ASSOCIATES BOOK
NEW YORK

NOTE: If you purchased this book without a cover you should be aware that this book is stolen property. It was reported as "unsold and destroyed" to the publisher, and neither the author nor the publisher has received any payment for this "stripped book."

This is a work of fiction. All the characters and events portrayed in this book are either products of the author's imagination or are used fictitiously.

MISTRESS OF THE CATACOMBS

Copyright © 2001 by David Drake

All rights reserved, including the right to reproduce this book, or portions thereof, in any form.

A Tor Book
Published by Tom Doherty Associates, LLC
175 Fifth Avenue
New York, NY 10010

www.tor.com

Tor® is a registered trademark of Tom Doherty Associates, LLC.

ISBN: 0-812-57540-7
Library of Congress Catalog Card Number: 2001034700

First edition: September 2001
First mass market edition: August 2002

Printed in the United States of America

0 9 8 7 6 5 4 3 2 1

To Randy Long,
who's not only been a friend for many years but who also
acted as my son's coach when he started bodybuilding—
a task for which I would've been hopelessly inadequate.

Acknowledgments

For many years now Dan Breen has been reading the rough drafts of my prose and making it better. *Mistress of the Catacombs* is the latest beneficiary of his attention.

I didn't, for a wonder, blow up another computer while writing this novel. Nevertheless, my wife, Jo, found me a backup and my son Jonathan set it up for me. (Mark Van Name and Allyn Vogel, who I believe have been cited for computer help in every book of mine for the past decade, will doubtless be back in the next one.)

Many friends provided this or that bit of information which will show up in the text of *Mistress*. Thanks very much to everyone who helped. Two whose contribution was even more considerable are Karen Zimmerman, my webmaster, and Sandra Miesel.

Stephanie Lane, my liaison with the machinery of Tor, is a continuing delight to work with. Contact with Stephanie is clear and pleasant, and she invariably follows up her end of whatever business.

And, finally, I owe many debts to historians and to other fiction writers. Readers who are familiar with the work of Clark Ashton Smith will realize that I owe him in particular. Readers who *aren't* familiar with Smith should correct that gap in their education at their earliest convenience.

Author's Note

The common religion of the Isles is based on Sumerian cult and ritual. That is, the Lady equates with Inanna; her consort the Shepherd equates with Dumuzi; and the Sister fills the place of Ereshkigal, Queen of the Underworld.

Religion in the Isles (and generally, except perhaps in fantasy fiction) is separate from magic. The magic in *Mistress of the Catacombs* is based on the practice of the Mediterranean Basin in Classical times. The wellspring was mostly Egyptian, but there were admixtures from many other cultures (particularly the Jewish). What I've referred to as "words of power" are formally *voces mysticae*, words in the language of the demiurges who act as intercessors between humanity and the Gods.

I don't myself believe in magic, Classical or otherwise, but I know that reality doesn't always conform to my opinion of what it should be. Just to be on the safe side, I prefer not to pronounce the *voces mysticae* aloud.

As in the past, I've used Classical authors as part of the cultural underpinning of the Isles. Pendill is Ovid, who's given me much pleasure over the years and has also educated me as a writer; Tincer is Tacitus, about whom I would say the same; and I was thinking of Gildas by the reference to Ascoin. I suppose a writer can learn from everything he reads, but I do hope that less of Gildas stuck than others.

—Dave Drake
—david-drake.com

the ISLES

LAUT

ORNIFAL

ATARA

KEPULAKECIL

BIGHT

CHARAX

Sea

TELUT

PARE

KANBESA

SIRIMAT

SERES

reefs

DALOPO

BOWWKAN

EHH '98

Dramatis Personae

PREVIOUSLY INTRODUCED

ATTAPER: Chief of the Blood Eagles, the royal bodyguard regiment.

CARUS: Last and greatest ruler of the Old Kingdom; dead a thousand years, but a laughing, hardhanded ghost in Prince Garric's mind.

CASHEL: Ilna's brother, Garric's friend, and Sharina's fiancé; a stronger man than any who've tried conclusions with him thus far.

CHALCUS: A sailor, pirate, and red-handed killer; a friend of Ilna.

GARRIC: A peasant and scholar, now Prince and real ruler of the Isles.

ILNA: A skilled weaver, now returned from hell with inhuman powers.

LERDOC: The ambitious and powerful Count of Blaise.

LIANE: Garric's amanuensis; his guide to present-day politics; and his lover.

MEROTA: Ilna's ward; nine-year-old girl with a penchant for singing inappropriate songs.

ROYHAS: Chancellor of the Isles.

SHARINA: Garric's sister and alter ego, but a person in her own right.

TENOCTRIS: A wizard saved from the wreck of the Old Kingdom; less powerful than most wizards, but more skilled than any other.

WALDRON: A warrior and aristrocrat, commander of the royal army.

NEW CHARACTERS

ALECTO: A young wizard from a far place—and a very savage one.

ECHEA: A wizard, savior of Laut in ancient times.

ECHEON: A wizard, tyrant of Laut in future times.

ECHEUS: A wizard, ruler of Laut in present times.

GAR: A youth who might have been Garric's double, had a lizard not bitten into his skull.

METRA: A wizard; companion and advisor to Lady Tilphosa.

METRON: A wizard; companion and advisor to Lord Thalemos.

METRUS: A wizard with a taste for antiquities.

THALEMOS: A descendant of the Earls of Laut.

TILPHOSA: An orphan raised by the Children of the Mistress; the intended bride of Lord Thalemos.

TINT: A beastgirl and friend to Gar; a pet and drudge for bandits calling themselves the Brethren.

VASCAY: Leader of the Brethren.

Chapter One

The spy, a stocky shipping agent named Hordred, looked at Garric and Liane with haunted eyes as he whispered what he knew of the planned secession of several western islands. His restless gaze flicked about the room with the randomness of a squirrel surprised on the ground.

"There's priests in it too," Hordred said. "They call themselves Moon Wisdom and have ceremonies in the Temple of Our Lady of the Moon in Donelle. It's not just prayers and temple tithes, though. This is . . ."

He swallowed. Liane had found Hordred through associates of her late father, a far-travelled merchant before his wizardry first ruined, then killed him. In the normal course of things the agent must have been a man well able to take care of himself. A falling block might as easily have been the cause of his broken nose as a rival's cudgel, but the scar on his right forearm had to have been left by a knife. Mere physical threats wouldn't have frightened Hordred into his present state.

"I think there's something real," he said. He stared at his own hard-clasped hands on the patterned wood before him. "Something that comes in . . . dreams."

They sat at a round cedarwood table in a small conference room, part of Prince Garric's private section of the palace compound. A row of louvers just below the tile roof let in air and muted light, but no one could see those inside. Members of the royal bodyguard regiment, the Blood Eagles, stood unobtrusively in the surrounding gardens. Garric had told the guard commander not to let anyone pass while he and Liane interviewed their visitor; therefore, no one *would* pass, not even Valence III, though he was in name still the King of the Isles.

"In *your* dreams, Master Hordred?" Liane said to jolt the spy out of his grim silence. "What is it that you see?"

Hordred looked up in bleak desperation. "I don't *know*, mistress!" he said. "There's not really anything, it's all gray. I'm dreaming, but it's just gray; only I know there's things there reaching for me and I'll never see them because they're gray like everything else. And then I wake up."

"You're safe now, Master Hordred," Garric said, hoping to sound reassuring. He reached out, touching the spy's hand with the tips of his strong, tanned fingers. "You can stay here in the palace if you like, or you can go to any of the royal estates on Ornifal if you think you'd be less conspicuous out of the capital. The conspirators won't bother you here."

In Garric's mind, the spirit of his ancestor King Carus scowled like a cliff confronting the tide. "*And if I could put my sword through a few necks,*" the king's ghost said, "*the Confederacy of the West wouldn't bother anyone. Except maybe dogs fighting over the carrion.*"

Carus grinned, reverting to the cheerful expression he most often wore. "*But I know, lad, cutting throats isn't your way; and maybe if my sword hadn't made so many martyrs, things would've turned out better in my own day.*"

Carus had been the greatest as well as the last ruler of the Old Kingdom. When he and the royal fleet sank in a wizard's cataclysm, the Isles had shattered into chaos and despair. A thousand years hadn't been enough to return the kingdom to the peace and stability it had known in the age before the Collapse, and forces gathering now threatened to crush what remained into dust and blood.

Not if I can help it! thought Garric.

"*Not if we can help it!*" echoed the ghost.

"I'm not afraid of their bravos!" Hordred snapped. In the angry response, Garric caught a glimpse of the man he must usually have been: tough and self-reliant, able to handle himself in a fight and well aware of the fact.

Relaxing with a conscious effort, Hordred continued, "I wrote down the strength of the forces gathering on Tisamur and the names of as many leaders as I could find. That's in the books I gave you."

He cocked an eyebrow at Liane; she nodded back. Hordred continued, "There's contingents from Haft and Cordin, but the real danger's in the mercenaries the leaders've been hiring from all over the Isles."

Garric's face went hard. His formal title now was Prince Garric of Haft, Adopted Son and Heir Presumptive to Valence III, King of the Isles. What he really was . . . one of the things he really was . . . was Garric, the nineteen-year-old son of Reise the innkeeper in Barca's Hamlet on the east coast of Haft. The only contact Barca's Hamlet and the borough around it had with the outside world was the Sheep Fair every fall and in summer the Tithe Procession, when priests from Carcosa on the west coast rolled images of the Lady and the Shepherd through the countryside and collected what was due the temple.

Garric was a peasant from Haft—and he was also the real ruler of the Isles, though the authority of the central government didn't really stretch far from the capital here in Valles on Ornifal. If he didn't put down this Confederacy of the West promptly, he wouldn't rule his birthplace even in name.

"The notes are in Serian shipping code," Hordred added. "Can you read that?"

"Yes, of course," Liane said, touching the travelling desk in which she'd placed Hordred's notebooks. They looked like ordinary accounts, thin sheets of birchwood bound in fours with hinges of coarse twine. The inner faces were covered in a crabbed script written in oak-gall ink.

"I should've stopped there," the spy muttered, sounding both angry and frightened. He clasped his hands again unconsciously. "I thought, 'Let's see what the cult's part in it is. Let's learn about Moon Wisdom.'"

He swallowed. "I got into one of the ceremonies," he went on, his voice dropping back to a whisper. "There were over a hundred people in the temple, some of them from as far away as Ornifal. They each had a symbol stamped on their forehead in cinnabar, a spider. I made a stamp for myself and nobody noticed anything wrong. But . . ."

Hordred fell silent again. Garric moistened his lips with his tongue, and prompted, "What went on at the ceremony, Master Hordred?"

The spy shook his head, trying to make sense of his memories. "We chanted a prayer to the Mistress of the Moon," he said. "I didn't know the words, but I could follow well enough."

"Chanted words of power?" Liane asked, her face and voice sharper than they had been a moment before. She understood that wizardry was neither good nor bad in it-self; like a sword, the power depended on the purpose—and the skill—of the wizard using it. But Liane would never forget the night that her wizard father had prepared to sacrifice her for purposes *he* had thought good.

"No, no," said Hordred to his writhing hands. "Just or-dinary speech, a hymn like you might hear at any Tennight ceremony if you're the sort who wastes his time in tem-ples. Only something happened, I don't know what. I could feel something. And I thought I saw something in the air in the middle of the room, but there wasn't anything there except gray. Nothing!"

He clenched his right fist as though to bang the table, but his arm trembled and he lowered his hand instead.

"There wasn't anything there, but it's been with me ever since. Whenever I go to sleep."

Garric stood. The discussion made him uncomfortable. He was as religious as any other youth in Barca's Hamlet. He dedicated a crumb and a sip of beer to the Lady and her consort at most meals, and once a year he'd offered a flat cheese of ewe's milk to Duzi, the roughly carved stone on the hill overlooking the meadows south of the hamlet. Duzi watched over sheep and the poor men who watched *them*; and if he did not, if Duzi was only the scars of time on rock, well . . . a cheese wasn't much to spend on a hope of help in trouble.

But this business of temples and the powers called down by them—this was wizardry or worse, and no place for ordinary mortals. Becoming king hadn't made Garric any less mortal, but he knew that this was a matter for kings regardless.

He grinned. There was a time that Garric or-Reise had imagined that nothing could be more unpleasant and frustrating than herding sheep caught in a sudden thunderstorm. Prince Garric knew his slightly younger self had been wrong.

"Master Hordred," he said, "I've called a meeting of my council to discuss the conspiracy. You needn't be present—"

Not every member of the council loved Garric, but each councillor knew his own survival and the best chance for the Isles to survive depended on Garric's success. Even so, Liane had insisted that as few people as possible know the face of this spy or the other agents she had hired.

Garric accepted her judgment, as he did on most matters where Liane felt strongly and he did not. A boy from Barca's Hamlet didn't have the special skills needed to gather intelligence from across the kingdom's scattered islands.

"—but I'd like you to remain here for the time being

in case we have further questions for you afterward. There are cushions if you want to sleep—"

He nodded to the built-in benches. The walls were wainscoted to the height of a seated man's shoulders and frescoed above with scenes from pine forests like those of Northern Ornifal.

"—and I can have food and drink brought in if you choose. You'll be well guarded, of course."

"Sleep!" Hordred said. "I could sleep on broken lava, I'm so tired. If I dared!"

"You're in Valles now," Garric said. "You're as safe as I am myself. Or Lady Liane."

Hordred looked up at him, then toward Liane as she rose also. "Am I?" the spy said. He laughed bitterly. "I suppose I am at that. Well, it doesn't matter, I've *got* to sleep."

Liane had been taking notes of Hordred's information with a small brush in a vellum chapbook. Even though she was merely going with Garric to a larger bungalow ten paces distant, she placed her notes in the uppermost tray of the desk and locked it with a four-ward key.

"Yes, well . . ." Garric said. "We'll see you soon, Master Hordred. On my honor, the kingdom won't forget the risk you ran for its safety."

As Garric opened the door for Liane, who carried the desk, he heard Hordred mutter, "I should've known better than to go into the temple. I thought it was just priests with a new trick to put money in their purses, but it's wizards' work or worse!"

"*There's no safety for anyone in the kingdom,*" said the wizard-slain king in Garric's mind, "*while there's wizards above the ground!*"

Carus was wrong in his blanket condemnation: without the aid of the wizard Tenoctris, Garric and the Isles would have been doomed long since. But Garric remembered the desperation in Hordred's eyes, and he knew that there was more than just prejudice to support King Carus' opinion.

Cashel or-Kenset walked down the crowded street beside Tenoctris, protecting the birdlike little woman without really thinking about it. Tenoctris didn't seem frail any more than a wren does to somebody like Cashel, who'd often watched those sprightly, tuneful little creatures. But she was old, seventy years or so; and small; and a woman.

Cashel himself was none of those things. People who watched where they were going didn't barge into him. In a busy city like Valles, there were always those who didn't watch. They bounced back from Cashel's shoulder or the arm holding his quarterstaff, placed for the moment in front of the old wizard.

"Huh!" said Tenoctris, stopping before the open front of a shop selling used metalwork. Nearest the street were bronze bedsteads with verdigrised statues farther inside. Cashel knew that people paid good money for art, but time had eaten these figures to greenish lumps, with here a torso, there something recognizable as a horse's head. Smaller—and therefore more easily stolen—items were racked against the back wall.

Tenoctris pointed to an octagonal pewter bowl, racked on its side so that passersby could see the niello symbols on the interior. She said, "Look at that, Cashel. I wonder how it got here?"

Cashel couldn't read or write beyond picking his own name out with care, but he recognized the flowing black marks as letters in the Old Script. Scholars, Garric and his sister Sharina included because their father Reise had taught them, could read the Old Script, but the only people who wrote that way now were wizards when they drew words of power for their incantations.

Cashel gripped his staff a little tighter. Wizards were

just people. Tenoctris was a wizard, and she was a lot like the grandmother who'd raised him and Ilna when their father brought them home with no word—ever—of who their mother might be.

But there were wizards who thought their power let them push other people around. Cashel had met that sort too; and they'd all been wrong when they'd thought they could push Cashel or anybody Cashel happened to have put himself in front of at the time.

The shopkeeper noticed Tenoctris' interest and got up from his stool. He was a balding man with a wispy goatee who reminded Cashel far more of a weasel than anybody so fat should've done.

"You have excellent taste, madam," the fellow said. He lifted the bowl from its place and brought it toward them through the maze of corroded metal. "This is a genuine Old Kingdom antique, the prized possession of a noble family here in Valles. Only their present distressed circumstances persuaded them to part with it."

"It's a great deal older than that," Tenoctris said sharply. "This came from the grave of a priest of the Mistress, either on Tisamur or just possibly on Laut. There would have been a lid as well."

"I'm sure I can find madam a craftsman who can make any sort of lid madam wishes," the proprietor said, still smiling. "The workmanship is quite exquisite, is it not? And such a remarkable state of preservation."

Cashel blinked. The fellow was responding to what Tenoctris said, but he wasn't *listening* to her.

Tenoctris backed and raised her hand as the proprietor offered her the bowl. "No, I don't want to touch it!" she said. "You wouldn't either, if you had good sense. It held the priest's brain. The sort of thoughts that a priest of the Mistress might have aren't for sane humans—or humans at all, I'd say. Melt it down! Can't you feel the power in it?"

Cashel couldn't see swirls of power the way Tenoctris said she did, tangles that clung to objects the way foam boils below the rocks in a fast-flowing stream, but he knew when they were there. Things used by wizards in their art held some of their power ever after; prayer permeated the stones of a temple; and scenes of blood and death held stains much deeper than those of the fluids that leaked from corpses.

The pewter bowl created a sort of pressure like that of air gone still before a storm. It didn't frighten Cashel any more than a storm would, but it was something to be wary of. Unconsciously, he shifted his grip on the hickory quarterstaff that he'd shaped with his own hands as a boy and had carried ever since.

The shopkeeper blinked and looked at the bowl in his hands. Cashel wondered if the fellow really saw the object. More likely it gleamed in his mind like a stack of silver pieces or even gold Sheaf-and-Scepters.

"Well, then," the man said in the same oily voice as before. "Perhaps madam would care to see some candlesticks from the palace of King Carus himself, preserved in the collection of a noble family linked by blood to the ancient royal house?"

"Come, Cashel," Tenoctris said, turning abruptly and continuing down the street with quick, short steps.

After a moment, she sighed and slowed to a pace more proper for an old woman and a youth accustomed to walking with sheep. She said, "In my own day I didn't get out into the world enough to realize how ignorant most people were, but I'm sure it was no better then."

Tenoctris had washed up on the shore of Barca's Hamlet one morning, thrown there by a storm not of wind but of wizardry. She said she'd been wrenched from the age a thousand years before, when King Carus ruled and the Isles were unified for the last time in their history.

"Well, people can't know about everything," Cashel

said, calm as he usually was. "I don't know about much of anything at all, Tenoctris. Except sheep."

He grinned. He'd have given his quarterstaff a spin for the pleasure of it, except that the street was far too crowded. Seven feet of hickory take up a lot of room, especially when the hands of a youth as strong as Cashel were whirling them.

They passed a shop which sold new and used bedding: coarse wool covers to be stuffed with straw for folk with just enough money to sleep on a mattress rather than the rush floor; close-woven linen that their betters would fill with feathers; and blankets, coverlets, and bed-curtains to suit any taste or purse. Tenoctris didn't give the wares even a glance.

"Was the bowl what you were looking for?" Cashel asked. He was glad to escort Tenoctris through the city—though he didn't mind the palace, there wasn't anything for him to do there—but he was sure that the old wizard had more in mind than a change of scene for herself.

Tenoctris hadn't explained, probably because it hadn't crossed her mind to. Cashel was used to doing things simply because somebody asked him, but this seemed a good time to say something. He guessed he was about as curious as the next fellow, but he'd learned that a lot of times it was better to just keep his eyes open than to ask and be lied to—or be given a flip answer, the sort of joke people tossed at the dumb orphan kid.

Cashel's fingers tightened very slightly again. They hadn't laughed at him much since he got his growth, though.

"What?" said Tenoctris. It'd taken her mind a moment to come up from the depths of whatever mental sea it swam in. "Oh, dear, I don't think so, Cashel. But I'm not really sure. I did a guidance spell because there's something nagging at me, and it directed me here. I think."

She gave him an apologetic grin. "I'm not a very powerful wizard, you know," she said. "Even in times like these, when there's so much power everywhere."

Tenoctris had explained that every thousand years there was more of the sort of power that wizards used. In those times wizards could do far more than in the past, and generally far more than they'd intended. It was a peak like that which ended the Old Kingdom; and the forces were rising again.

Cashel and the wizard reached a building site from which the remains of the former brick-and-wattle structure had mostly been cleared. Though heavy construction wagons weren't allowed in Valles during daylight hours, the stacks of freshly cut stone for the new foundation blocked part of the street.

Cashel paused, letting a group of housewives pass from the other direction with baskets full of greens bought in the produce market a little nearer the river. He could've pushed through the congestion easily enough, but he and Tenoctris weren't in any kind of hurry.

On the building site, men were already at work on the kiln which would provide lime for the cement; it was better to burn it there than to transport so dangerous a load through the city, with the chance of losing it to a sudden rainstorm besides. Piled as high as the quarried blocks was a load of broken limestone and marble to feed the kiln. Some of the bigger pieces had been ships' ballast at one time; those were dark and still slimy from bilgewater.

The housewives passed; Tenoctris started forward, then stopped when she realized that Cashel was staring at the rubble. She said, "Cashel?"

Cashel's skin prickled, the same sort of feeling as when he got too much sun when plowing in early spring. There was something about the stones. . . . Holding his staff out for balance in his left hand, he clambered onto the pile.

Several of the workmen glanced toward Cashel, but nobody shouted at him. He wasn't doing any harm by climbing around on a pile of rock, so only the urge of people to boss other people would've led them to speak. Cashel was too big for that to seem a good idea, even to a half dozen burly workmen.

Tenoctris watched intently, but she didn't say anything that might have distracted Cashel from whatever he was doing. Cashel grinned. He didn't know what he was doing either, just that there was something about these chunks of stone that made his senses prick up. It was the way you could feel there was something wrong with your sheep, even before ewes ran out of the woods blatting because one of their sisters had managed to catch her neck in the fork of a sapling.

"Here!" Cashel said in triumph. He used his free hand and his staff's iron-shod tip to pry a piece of marble out of a litter of limestone gravel.

"Hey! What's that you're doing up there?" called the foreman of the building crew, a squat man of thirty with a bushy moustache and biceps that would've looked well on a man of twice the size. The other workmen watched in interest, glad for an excuse to stop work and hopeful that there'd be more entertainment to come.

"I'm looking at your rock," Cashel said. The crew wouldn't own the building materials, but he guessed they'd still be willing to sell a chunk for the price of a round of ale. "This piece here."

He hefted it, noticing the foreman's eyes narrow. It was the torso of a statue, meant originally for a woman, Cashel guessed, though he couldn't swear to much in the shape the piece was now. The marble had weathered and worse, been buried in a forest where rotting leaves had blackened it and eaten at the surface during every rainstorm. In some places white foam had boiled from cancerous pits in the stone. A soaking in a ship's bilge had added final indignities.

Though the block was of no obvious interest—even to

Cashel, except for the tingling it raised in him—it was still stone and weighed as much as a man of ordinary size. The foreman knew that and understood what it meant that Cashel held it easily in one hand.

"I want to buy it from you," Cashel said. "I'll pay you a, a . . ."

He didn't know what name a silver coin had. In Barca's Hamlet there was mostly bronze and little enough of that, except during the Sheep Fair, when merchants and drovers came down the road from Carcosa. Ornifal used different coins; and though Cashel now carried a purseful of them on a cord around his neck, they weren't something he paid a lot of attention to.

"A silver piece!" he said, getting the idea out well enough. That'd buy a jar of wine that the whole crew could share at any of the open-fronted cookshops in this quarter of the city.

"For what?" cried a workman in amazement.

"Let's see his money," said another, slipping his masonry chisel into a pocket in his leather apron.

"What is it you want it for?" the foreman asked, scowling like thunder. He was confused and because of that a little angry. He walked forward.

Instead of answering—because he didn't have an answer, just a feeling—Cashel said, "Tenoctris, will you pay the man for me? I, ah . . ."

To pull out his purse and open it, Cashel would have to use both hands. He didn't want to let go of either his staff or the piece of statue until he'd gotten to a place where he had more friends than he did here.

"Yes, of course," Tenoctris said. She carried a small purse in the sleeve of her silk brocade robe. She squeezed a coin through the loosened ties, then held it up so that sunlight winked on the silver in the sight of all the workmen; then she gave it to the foreman.

"Deal?" said Cashel from his perch above the others.

"Deal, by the Lady!" said one of the workmen. "For that you can carry off the whole pile and we'll tell the boss the rats ate it."

The foreman rang the coin against the head of the hammer in his belt. It sang with the bright note of silver rather than something duller and leaden.

"Deal," he said, still a little doubtful. He spat in his palm and held it out to Tenoctris. She stared at the man blankly.

Cashel stepped down from the mound of rubble with the care required by bad footing and the weight he carried. "Shake his hand on the deal, Tenoctris," he said. "Ah, if you wouldn't mind?"

"Of course," said the old woman, nodding to Cashel in gratitude for having explained how you sealed a bargain. Nobles probably did it different. Tenoctris was of a noble house; though from what she'd said, in her lifetime they hadn't had money even by the standards of Barca's Hamlet. Still, she took the foreman's hand gracefully like an adult humoring a child and let him shake hers up and down.

Cashel cleared his throat. "Ah, Tenoctris?" he said. "I'd like to be getting back to the—"

Cashel's tongue stuck. He'd dressed this morning as he would have back in the borough, in woolen overtunic and undertunic. The garments were peasant's wear, though smartly cut and of the best quality—as they were bound to be, since his sister Ilna had woven and sewn the cloth. Nobody in the Isles, maybe nobody in all time, could do more with fabrics than Ilna could.

Tenoctris was in silk, but her robe was neither new nor stylish. The two of them would pass for a noblewoman fallen on hard times and the sort of rustic servant such a lady could afford. That was fine, but Cashel didn't want to use the word "palace" here and cause all sorts of fuss and excitement.

"To go home, I mean," he said instead.

"Yes, of course," Tenoctris repeated. She turned, getting her bearings with a skill that a countryman like Cashel couldn't match in this warren of streets. "I think if we go . . ."

A few of the passersby had stopped to see what was going on. Cashel and Tenoctris weren't doing anything more exciting than hens did in a farmyard, but it was a little different from the usual. There were people in Valles—and everywhere Cashel had been in his life—who'd rather watch others work than do something themselves.

Through them came a clean-shaven heavyset man, not a youth but still younger than his baldness made him appear. He wore a tunic of tightly woven wool, black with a stripe of bleached white slashing diagonally across the front. His face was set. He wasn't exactly angry, but he looked ready to snap into anger if something balked him.

"You there!" he said to the foreman. "Are you in charge? I want to buy this pile of stone. I'll pay—"

The workmen's eyes shifted from the newcomer to Cashel and Tenoctris. Cashel made a wry face, but he'd learned young that some days bad luck was the only kind of luck you were going to have.

Cashel squatted and set the block of stone between his feet rather than drop it on the cobblestones. Then he rose again, holding his staff with both hands and waiting for whatever might come next.

The newcomer's glance followed the workmen's; he looked at the piece of statue, then raised his eyes to Cashel's. "I believe you have some property of mine, my man," he said. His tone held a thin skin of politeness over fury. "I'll take it now, if you please."

"It's not yours," Cashel said. Tenoctris had stepped behind him, but he didn't know just where. He hoped she'd be clear if things started to happen, as they might. "I bought it, fair and more than fair."

"Yes, well," said the stranger, looking over Cashel appraisingly. He reached into the folds of his twisted silk sash. "I'll buy it from you, then."

"No," said Cashel, his voice husky. His hands were going to start trembling soon if he didn't do something, either spin the quarterstaff into the stranger's face or pick up the statue and run.

The stranger's hand came out of the sash with three broad, thin pieces of gold. He fanned them into the light between his thumb and two well-manicured fingers. "Look at this, my man," he said. "Yours for a bit of old stone."

"No," Cashel said. There was going to be trouble if Cashel didn't move away, but he couldn't leave the stone, and he didn't want to be holding it if the stranger came at him with a knife.

Instead of attacking, the stranger swept the spread of coins under the foreman's nose. "Bring me the piece of marble," he said, pitching his voice so that all the workmen could hear, "and these are yours. Twice this, a gold piece for each man!"

The foreman scowled his forehead into even deeper ridges than before. The gangling, scar-faced workman beside him snatched a pole from the bundles of scaffolding and stepped forward. "Ansie, Blemm . . ." he called in a matter-of-fact voice. "All you guys. That's enough money to set us up for life."

"Right!" said the foreman, reaching for his hammer.

Cashel stepped forward, driving the tip of his quarterstaff into the foreman's gut. The fellow saw it coming and tried to jump back. He wasn't fast enough, but the move may have saved his life. The iron-shod hickory flung him into the kiln, spewing his breakfast of bread sopped in wine lees, but it didn't punch through the muscle walls as it could've done if Cashel was really trying.

The stranger had ducked behind the stack of quarry-stone. Cashel ignored him and the shouting spectators both. It might be that a section of the City Watch would arrive, but Cashel doubted that. He sure wasn't trusting his safety and Tenoctris to that hope.

The workman with the pole swung at Cashel. The bamboo would've made a decent weapon if the fellow'd known what he was doing, but he didn't. Cashel blocked the stroke with the ferrule nearer his body, then spun the other end into the workman's side. He heard ribs crack.

Two of the men who'd been hesitating when things started to happen now backpedaled. Another had pulled out his chisel to use as a sword; he flung it as a dart instead. The heavy bronze tool caught Cashel on the right shoulder, a solid blow but not a dangerous one because the edge was sharpened to split rock rather than to shave wood.

Cashel grunted with anger and stepped forward, recovering the staff so that both his hands gripped the wood at the balance. The workman squealed and dodged behind the partner who held a heavy maul up in the air like a torch.

The fellow with the maul couldn't have been more open to a stroke from the quarterstaff if he'd turned his back and begged to be hit. Didn't anybody in Valles know how to fight? Cashel rapped him where he gripped the helve, breaking fingers on both hands and flinging the maul into a cart hard enough to tip it over.

Cashel kicked the screaming man he'd just crippled out of the way and went after the fellow who'd thrown the chisel at him. That one was scrambling off by now. Most times Cashel would've left him be; but his shoulder throbbed, and he knew that except for the bulges of muscle there he'd have had a broken collarbone.

The workman tripped on his leather apron and skidded into the stack of scaffolding. Cashel raised his staff for a straight-arm thrust that would've been fatal—then grimaced and instead gripped the apron's neck loop with his right hand to jerk the fellow upright.

"You like to throw things, do you?" Cashel bellowed. The workman's eyes were screwed shut: he couldn't change whatever was coming, but he didn't have to watch it.

Cashel straightened his arm and put his shoulders in it too, hurling the fellow over the basement excavation to slide through debris at the back of the lot. The man's arms and legs were moving before his body came to a halt. He hopped over a mound of dirt saved for backfill and continued running.

There was a blue flash from the other side of the pile of quarrystone. The stranger who'd started the trouble sprang into view with a shriek. His robe was on fire. Instead of the grudging, halfhearted flames Cashel expected from wool, these were vivid and tinged with the same blue as the flash: wizardlight.

The stranger bolted down the street, tugging his garments off as he ran. Spectators lurched out of his way, pushing a path violently through their fellows the way they'd have done to escape a runaway horse—

Or maybe more violently yet. Wizardry scared lots of people worse than death did.

Tenoctris stood alone at the edge of the street, swaying and so weak she was about to fall over. Cashel, gasping with his own efforts, stumbled to his older friend and put his arm around her. His shoulder hurt as badly as it had the day Scolla's ill-tempered lead ox had flung its head around while Cashel was trying to yoke it.

"Are you all right, Tenoctris?" Cashel asked, speaking the words between one deep breath and the next. "You did a spell to send the fellow off, is that it?"

He'd split the back of his undertunic when his shoulders bunched; it looked like he'd broken his sash too. Well, it hadn't been a proper bout where he'd have had time to get ready.

"I interfered with his own spell," Tenoctris said, panting

like a snared rabbit. Cashel had seen before now the wonders that wizards could do; but it took real effort to guide their powers, as sure as it did to use a quarterstaff the way Cashel used one.

Still clinging to Cashel's arm, Tenoctris hobbled around the stack of squared blocks. Spectators kneeling in the dirt there scattered like startled quail, looking over their shoulders at the old woman. Cashel guessed that the stranger had dropped the gold he'd offered. People in this district weren't going to let a gold coin go to waste, no matter how much wizards frightened them.

Tenoctris pointed to symbols drawn on the ground where the stranger had been hiding. "He was going to send dust into your eyes, Cashel," she said. "I just opened his circle of protection before he'd directed the stroke."

Cashel felt a surge of warmth for the old wizard. Tenoctris was quick to say that she had very little power; but she knew things, knew what she was doing, and generally knew what other wizards were doing better than they did. Cashel trusted Tenoctris the way he trusted his own ability to put an axe into a tree trunk where he meant it to go.

Strength was fine, but control was a better thing if you had to have only one.

"What's this made of, do you suppose?" Tenoctris said in surprise. She bent closer to the greenish-yellow rod lying beside the symbol the stranger had drawn with it. It was his athame, abandoned like the coins when he fled— and to a wizard, far more valuable than that gold. "It looks like the shell of an insect. A very large insect."

Cashel reached toward it with a bare toe. He could see the blurred texture of the soil through the athame, as though it was a sheet of mica.

"No, I don't think we'd better touch it," Tenoctris said, moving her slippered foot to block Cashel's. She scuffed the athame sideways, onto the cobblestones. "The wagons tonight will grind it to powder; I suspect that's the best choice. And I'll burn this slipper when we've gotten home."

"Let's be doing that now," Cashel said, looking behind him for the chunk of statue he'd forgotten during the fight. Quite a fool he'd feel if somebody'd made off with it . . . but they hadn't, nobody would. It was an ugly, awkward piece of stone whose only use was for burning into the living white fire of quicklime; but it was Cashel's piece now for sure.

"Will you be able to carry it yourself?" Tenoctris asked. "I mean, you must be tired from . . . ?"

Cashel grinned. "Guess I'll manage," he said as he lifted the block, using his knees instead of his back for leverage. "The harder thing's going to be figuring out what to do with it now that I've got it, but maybe Sharina will have an idea."

And because he was thinking of Sharina, he grinned even broader.

Ilna os-Kenset's fingers wove with a speed and skill that any woman on the island of Ornifal would have envied, but her mind wasn't on her work. In this fine weather she'd set her loom in the bungalow's courtyard, walled off from the rest of the palace. Bees buzzed about the flowers; birds chirped and pecked and fluttered for food among the plantings. Ilna didn't pay them much attention either, except to note that they were just as quarrelsome and snappish as they'd been back in Barca's Hamlet.

Not long ago Ilna had been the orphan girl who supported herself and her brother Cashel by skill and by working so hard even by the standards of a rural village that everyone marveled at her. She was a woman that everybody respected and nobody liked; nobody, or very few.

Sharina had liked her, even then; and she thought Garric liked her as well.

Ilna's fingers moved: opening the shed, feeding through the shuttle, and closing the shed again with the certainty of water pouring through the spillway of the ancient tide mill that had been her grandfather's. The pattern of the cloth she wove suggested a woodland at sunset, all buffs and browns and blacks shading into one another.

Today Ilna worked in naturally colored wools, her usual choice. She could have used silk, coarse hemp, or hard-drawn copper wire, and had the same effect on those who viewed the fabric. She'd always been a skilled weaver; since she returned from Hell, her skill had become inhuman.

Her fingers wove. She'd paid with her soul for the power to rule others in the way that evil would have her rule them. She'd been freed from the evil that came from outside her, but Ilna knew her heart well enough to be sure that the home-grown variety was sufficient to ruin more lives than even a city the size of Valles held.

If she let it, which she would not..

The garden was peaceful but not silent. At the quarter hour, criers called the time across the palace compound from the water clock near the center. Occasionally servants laughed and chattered as they passed along the path on the other side of the back wall, and in the bungalow's atrium a music mistress was giving Lady Merota bos-Roriman her voice lesson.

The child—Merota was nine—had a clear voice and an instinct for craftsmanship. Ilna found her lessons as pleasant as a wren's warble, even when they involved nothing but repetitions of the scales.

Ilna was weaving a thin baize, almost a gauze. Even in its partial state it gave anyone who viewed it a sense of peace and tranquility. If Ilna wished—and once she had wished, had *done*—the same threads could have roused those who saw them to lust or fear or fury. The patterns of the cloth, the patterns of a man's life—the pattern of the cosmos itself—all were connected.

Anything Ilna wanted was hers for the taking. Anything at all; and she smiled with wry self-disgust because she didn't *know* what she wanted.

Once not so very long ago she'd wanted to be the wife of Garric, the innkeeper's son. He was Prince Garric now, but so great was Ilna's power that she could have him nonetheless.

The shuttle clattered across the loom; Ilna's smile grew harder still. She'd done things in the past that she'd be paying for throughout the future, no matter how long she lived; but she hadn't done *that* thing, and today she wasn't even sure she still wanted to.

Ilna os-Kenset, the orphan who couldn't read or write, didn't belong on a throne beside the King of the Isles; nor did Garric belong in a little place like Barca's Hamlet, for all that he'd been raised there with no reason to expect he'd ever travel farther than Carcosa on the other side of Haft. Garric was fit to be king, and a noblewoman like Liane bos-Benliman was a fit companion for him. As for Ilna—

Merota began "Once There Was a Servant Girl"—a song Ilna 'had heard before, but not from the child, and certainly not at the request of Lady Stolla, the music mistress. Ilna smiled, this time with a gentler sort of humor.

"*Early one evening a sailor came to me,*" Merota sang, "*and that was the start of all my misery.*"

Chalcus had a tenor voice every bit as fine as Merota's high soprano. He was a sailor when Ilna and the child met him, as skilled at that trade as any soul else on the ship— though Chalcus would've been the first to say it was no honor to be first among that crew of thumb-fingered nobodies.

"*At sea without a woman for forty months or more ...*" Merota sang.

"Lady Merota!" cried Lady Stolla, a decayed gentle-woman, as prim as she was proper, and clearly horrified to realize the thrust of the child's performance.

"*There wasn't any need to ask . . .*" Merota continued. Her birth was better than Stolla's as those who cared about such things judged it, and she wasn't about to let the older woman decide for her what a lady might choose to sing.

"*. . . what he was looking for!*"

Ilna sniffed. She was Merota's legal guardian now—one orphan caring for another. Despite that, Stolla persisted in treating Ilna as a jumped-up governess or perhaps a maid; and if the music mistress chose to be embarrassed, well, Ilna wouldn't pretend to be sorry about that.

Her face grew harder. Ilna wouldn't *pretend* to anything.

Instead of going on with the next verse, Merota squealed cheerfully, and cried, "Chalcus!"

"And how's one of the two most lovely ladies in all Valles?" replied the cheerful, lilting voice of the man who must just have arrived at the bungalow.

Ilna rose from her loom and went to greet her visitor: a man of middle height with a broad chest and muscles that appeared flat until effort made them bunch. There was generally a smile on Chalcus' lips, the curve of it echoing that of the inward-sharpened sword thrust through his sash.

Ilna herself smiled less often than Chalcus did, at least as an expression of good humor; but she was smiling now.

Princess Sharina of Haft spent most of her public life wearing the formal garb of an Ornifal aristocrat while receiving deputations from the provinces in place of her brother Garric. Thanks be to the Lady, there was no need of such rigid, stifling state at this meeting of the royal council—the real, working government of the kingdom.

Having said that, the dozen or so heads of the civil and

military departments were all aristocrats. In Barca's Hamlet, casual dress meant an undertunic alone—worn without a sash on a summer day like this. Here the civilian councillors wore court robes of silk brocade with a sash, while their military colleagues replaced the sash with a sword belt bearing an empty scabbard. The Blood Eagles didn't allow anyone but themselves to enter Garric's presence armed, and the chief of the Blood Eagles—Attaper bor-Atilan—accepted the limitation himself to avoid friction with Lord Waldron, the equally highborn head of the army.

Sharina stifled a wan smile. To avoid worse friction, rather; Waldron, thirty years Attaper's senior, believed in his heart that he himself should be king. He was at best on stiff terms with Attaper, who didn't bother to put a diplomatic gloss on his disagreement with that opinion.

"There's more to this 'Confederacy of the West' than hick rulers on Haft, Cordin, and Tisamur deciding they want to secede from the kingdom," said Chancellor Royhas, seated at Garric's right hand.

"Begging your pardon sir and lady"—Royhas nodded to Garric and Sharina, a cursory apology for the implied slur against the island of their birth—"but all the force of those islands isn't enough to delay the royal army any longer than it takes to sail there."

"They've got more force," said Attaper forcefully. "They're hiring mercenaries. We knew that even before this latest spy came back with the numbers."

"They still couldn't stand against us," Waldron snapped, though it didn't seem to Sharina that Attaper had suggested otherwise.

"And that's why I say there's more to it than just these three islands!" Royhas said. "Why, they scarcely know they're part of the kingdom as it is. When's the last time enough taxes came out of Carcosa to pay the salary of an underclerk here in Valles?"

"They may be concerned about the future," said Lord Tadai. "We—by which I mean Prince Garric—have given Ornifal a real government for the first time in generations. They may realize that in time, we—"

The plump, wealthy nobleman had been royal treasurer until his rivalry with Royhas meant one or the other had to go for the sake of the kingdom. He'd accepted his removal with the good grace of a patriot and a man of great intelligence, but no one would deny him a seat on the council so long as he remained in Valles.

He nodded to Garric in smiling—but real—homage.

"—will unify the whole kingdom again, and they'll no longer be able to apply their own notions of justice and tax policy."

"Count Lascarg never thought beyond trying to keep Carcosa quiet and spending the revenues of the estates that he took over when the previous rulers of Haft died," Garric said with harsh assurance. "Died in riots it was his duty to put down as commander of the Household Troops. *His* foresight isn't behind this secession."

Sharina nodded, in agreement and in understanding for her brother's bitterness. The parents who raised them, Reise and Lora, had served the former Count and Countess of Haft until the night of the fatal riots; that much she and Garric had known since childhood. Only during the disruptions of the past months had they learned the other half of the story: that Count Niard was Sharina's father, and that Garric was the child born to Countess Tera, who traced her ancestry back to King Carus and the royal line of the Old Kingdom.

Niard had been an Ornifal noble, which explained for the first time Sharina's blond hair and slender height. She'd always felt something of an outsider among the darker, stockier folk of Barca's Hamlet, but she'd still been shocked to learn the truth.

"They're getting money from outside," said Attaper,

leaning forward with his hands clasped before him on the burl walnut tabletop. "The wages of the mercenaries gathering on Tisamur run to more than the revenues of all three rulers combined. And the troops *are* being paid—they're not staying on in hope of future loot."

"The Earl of Sandrakkan's behind it!" said Lord Waldron. "That's the only place the money could come from. Earl Wildulf doesn't dare face us directly, so he's setting up this confederacy as a stalking horse to see what we'll do!"

Waldron was an active, passionate man who was rarely comfortable sitting down. Now he rose so abruptly that his chair clattered over behind him. Normally a servant waited behind a seated noble, but Garric—though in truth Liane, Sharina suspected—had instituted a policy of greater privacy during discussions of such moment.

The noise startled everybody, even Waldron, who grimaced and tried to pick the chair up. He got the legs tangled in the robe of Lady Vartola, Priestess of the Temple of the Lady of Succor, and today representing religious interests before the council.

Sharina sprang to her feet and stepped around Vartola. Waldron was about to fling the chair into the paneled wall in fury. She took it from him. With the skill of one who'd been serving in an inn before she could read, Sharina set the chair upright again and gestured Waldron into it. The old warrior obeyed, his hard face maroon with embarrassment.

Sharina sat down also. She kept from smiling, but only with difficulty.

"I believe Lord Waldron has the right idea," said Pterlion bor-Palial, the new treasurer, "but he's wrong about the source. The money's coming from Blaise, not Sandrakkan."

He stopped, waiting with a smug smile to be asked why he was sure. The treasurer was a clever man, but rather too fond of *showing* how clever he was instead of just getting on with the job.

"Explain," said Garric, his sharpness wiping the satisfaction from Pterlion's face. "And in the future, Lord Pterlion, please recall that there are no fools at these council meetings—and no time for foolishness either."

"That would be a good idea," said Lord Waldron, glowering as though he'd prefer to rip the treasurer's throat out with his teeth instead of using a sword on the fellow. "A very good idea."

Pterlion grinned in embarrassment. "Yes, ah, Prince Garric," he said. "Ah. There are two items of evidence. Merchants coming from Cordin and particularly Tisamur are paying their port duties in Blaise coinage, much of it fresh-minted—and, I might add, with more lead than silver in the bullion. Whereas reports from Blaise itself indicate that trade is suffering because of a lack of currency on the island. Lerdoc, Count of Blaise, is behind this secession."

"I never thought Wildulf had the sophistication to mount a plan like this," Tadai agreed, tenting his fingers before him. "Successfully, at any rate."

"They haven't succeeded," said Garric. "They won't succeed. And thank you, Lord Pterlion. Knowing where the trouble started will make it easier to end it."

"I want to know about this Moon Wisdom you mentioned," Lady Vartola said in a rasping wheeze. She was the color of old bone and so thin that Sharina wondered if she had a wasting disease. There was nothing wrong with Vartola's mind, however, save that she focused it wholly on the betterment of her temple rather than the common good of the kingdom. "Are they usurping ownership of temple property?"

Garric glanced over his shoulder. Liane's formal position was amanuensis to Prince Garric, so she wasn't qualified to sit at the council table proper. Instead she waited at Garric's right elbow, her lap desk open and her fingers ready to withdraw whichever scroll or codex might be required.

"We don't have direct information on that as yet," Liane said without bothering to consult the records this time. "The evidence suggests that may be the case."

Sharina's mind ticked back over a file of appointments already in her schedule for the next two weeks. For the most part they involved providing a high-ranking ear to which aggrieved citizens could complain: salt merchants protesting the new tariff on their product, the clothmakers' guild demanding higher tariffs on silk from Seres, and a thousand variations on the theme of what the government was doing wrong.

Occasionally there was an exception. For example—

"An assistant inspector of temple lands has returned recently from Tisamur," Sharina said, loudly enough to cut through Admiral Zettin's question about the confederacy's naval forces. When everyone was looking at her she continued, "He's been demanding an audience with Prince Garric—"

Royhas snorted angrily at such presumption in a junior member of a department tangentially under his direction.

"—and gathered enough support from his superiors to be shunted to me, whenever I manage to get around to him," she continued. "I'll see him this afternoon."

A thought struck her. She added, "Unless you *would* like to see him yourself, Garric?"

He looked at Liane, who gave a tiny shake of her head. "No," Garric said. "But I will want to know what you learn, Sharina. This Moon Wisdom may be more than—"

He glanced at the priestess. "Than a scheme by opportunists to defraud the temple of its proper revenues," he concluded. Only the slightest hesitation suggested that he'd intended to say something a little different from the words that actually came out.

Garric stood, ending the meeting. "Lords Waldron, Attaper, and Zettin," he said, "I'll need a report on the current readiness of the forces you command. By the end of the day, if you please."

He turned his eyes to the Chancellor. In the same tone of command, so different from anything Sharina had heard from her brother's lips during the years they grew up together on Haft, he continued, "Lord Royhas, I want all the information we have on the property and perquisites of the individual rulers of this confederacy. I realize that—"

Someone nearby shrieked like a hog nose-clamped for slaughter.

"What's that?" bellowed someone else, a guard because during the meeting nobody else was permitted near this building and the smaller one adjacent, where her brother had interviewed a spy. "What's the matter in there!"

Garric was the first to the door and out it, drawing the sword that he alone wore in the council. Attaper and Waldron had the same instinct to run toward trouble, but Garric was younger and already standing.

Another scream.... Sharina followed Attaper, leaping over the chair Garric had flung aside as he moved. Waldron was at the other end of the room, fighting his way through civilians who'd risen also but weren't as quick to learn for themselves what was causing such terror.

The pair of Blood Eagles posted at the door of the smaller conference room were banging their fists on it, apparently trying to get the attention of the man inside. He had other things on his mind, to the degree that fear let him think at all.

"Break it down!" Garric shouted. Before the guards could act, he slammed his own right bootheel into the latchplate. Sharina knew her brother wasn't Cashel for strength, but nobody who'd seen Garric lift free a bogged ewe would doubt he was a powerful man by most standards.

The bronze catch inside flew out of its staples. Garric

rebounded from the impact, so the guards burst into the room ahead of him.

The spy, his face contorted, was wrestling with nothing at all. And yet there must be *something*, because both the man's feet were off the floor. . . .

A Blood Eagle thrust his spear past the spy's ear; the steel point met only air. His partner dropped his weapon and tried to grapple with the screaming man.

The spy vanished with a sort of twisting motion, like the last of the foam being slung from the rim of a washbasin. There was an odd odor; it reminded Sharina of the way a stone might smell in the dead of winter.

For a moment she thought she could still hear the screams; then they too vanished.

Chapter Two

S wing me on your arm again, Chalcus!" Merota demanded. "I want to go all the way over this time!"

Ilna didn't let her face react. In the sailor's presence the girl was sometimes either younger than her nine years or very much more mature.

"And so we shall," said Chalcus, glancing up at the square funnel that slanted rainwater from the roof into the pool here in the center of the entrance hall. "In the garden, though, for you're growing to such a fine woman that I fear your heels would smudge the ceiling."

He gestured the women ahead of him and out the south doorway, adding a little bow to Ilna. "And then," he continued in the same cheerful lilt, "you'll go back to your room and the lessons I've no doubt your tutors have set you. Mistress Ilna and I will speak alone after that."

They stepped past the loom, covered for the moment. In Chalcus' company, Ilna took in the colors and sounds of the brick-walled court, the richness that she generally ignored because it had nothing to do with her work.

Five generations in the past, Duke Valgard of Ornifal ruled the neighboring islands outright and claimed with as much justice as any other could to be King of the Isles. Valles was the kingdom's greatest metropolis then, while the palace compound housed thousands and was a city in its own right.

Those times were over, but workmen were restoring the buildings and grounds at the same rapid tempo as Garric rebuilt the government itself. The bungalow Ilna shared with Cashel, and now Merota, was meant for a senior gardener. It was a detached structure rather than part of a barracks housing the families of twenty clerks or servants, but it was neither spacious nor expensively decorated.

Ilna had chosen the residence herself, mostly for the garden courtyard that gave her good light on clear days. Even that was a needless luxury: *she* could weave in the dark with perfect assurance. The chamberlain—he'd been replaced since then—had tried to insist that someone of Lady Ilna's stature *must* have more luxurious accommodations.

Ilna's expression at the memory could have cut glass. There were many things that Ilna os-Kenset felt she must do, but none of those duties were imposed by others.

Chalcus extended his left arm, bare except for its scars. He wore as usual only a single short-sleeved tunic. Because he was in money, the present garment was of linen dyed with first-pressing indigo. The hem and sleeves were embroidered in gold thread, and the sash was of fine black silk.

He wore it with a swagger; but then, Chalcus did everything with a swagger.

Merota gripped the sailor's thick wrist and forearm. She

jumped, and Chalcus added a little toss, giving the girl the boost she needed to go over, shrilling delight as her tunics flapped like flags in a storm.

"Why do you always swing her with your left arm, Master Chalcus?" Ilna asked suddenly. He'd said he was here to have a private interview with her. One result of the discussion could be that they'd never see each other again.

"Swing me again, Chalcus!" Merota said.

Chalcus hugged the child to his left side, but it was Ilna he faced with a broad grin. "Indeed, what would happen if some ill-wisher sprang from the lemon balm there—"

He nodded to the bed of herbs with tiny white flowers. None of the stems were as tall as Ilna's knee.

"—and my sword arm was all tangled with a lovely woman, eh?"

Chalcus wasn't wearing a sword, and the short curved dagger thrust through his sash was no bigger than the knife every man in a rural village carried for routine tasks. The steel of the blade, however, was as incomparably better than that of knives forged by travelling blacksmiths as Chalcus himself was superior to the common run of sailors.

"Then you'd kill him with your left hand!" Merota said, giggling.

Chalcus looked down at her. "Aye, perhaps I would at that, child," he said. "Now leave us, if you will."

Instead of arguing as Ilna had half expected the girl would do—expected until she heard the tone Chalcus used this time—Merota said, "Yes, Chalcus."

She turned and curtsied to Ilna. "Mistress Ilna," she said, then reentered the bungalow at a swift but ladylike pace.

Chalcus bent away from Ilna as though to smell the purple-tendriled mint along the east wall. "I've been thinking over where I might go next, mistress," he said.

"There's little use for my sort in a place like Valles, you know."

He turned and smiled at her. "You've a fine crop of herbs growing here," he added in the same negligent tone. "Those who you cook for are lucky folk indeed."

Ilna allowed no servants in the bungalow, though with the child's tutors traipsing in and out there was work enough to keep the place in proper order. Ilna hadn't met the cook or maid yet who performed to her standards; and in truth, even if such a paragon appeared, Ilna wouldn't want to share *her* dwelling with a servant.

"The garden's well enough," Ilna said. "If I were to stay here, I'd want a dovecote, though. I've never liked chickens running around my ankles."

What did Chalcus expect her to say? *Her!* Did he think Ilna os-Kenset would beg?

Instead of speaking, Chalcus took out his dagger and spun it from hand to hand. He caught it each time by the point, then spun it back.

"I wonder, mistress . . ." he said as though to the shimmering steel. The blade was slightly curved and sharp for a finger's length along the reverse edge. "If you were on a ship about to sink, would you save the tall man . . . or the short man. . . ."

There was a rhythm to the blade, as crisp and regular as the dance of Ilna's shuttle across her loom. She found she was holding her breath; she grimaced angrily.

". . . perhaps a middle-sized man like myself?"

The dagger slipped back into its scabbard as surely as water finds the drain hole. Chalcus met her gaze. His lips smiled, but his eyes did not.

"I don't like ships, Master Chalcus," she said, chipping her words out like hatchet strokes. "The last time I was aboard one, there was a crew of a hundred but only one *man:* you yourself, as you well know."

Ilna turned away, wishing she believed enough in the

Gods that she could curse and not feel she was being a hypocrite. "Master Chalcus," she said to the man behind her, "I regret to say that I don't know my own mind. Or perhaps I do, and I don't have the courage to act on it."

"Ah," said Chalcus, an acknowledgment in a tone stripped of all implication. "Well, mistress, I haven't met the person whose courage I'd trust further than I would your own. We'll talk again before we act, either of us."

Ilna spun to face him. "Chalcus," she said, "there are things I've done—"

"Aye!" he said, the barked syllable breaking off her confession. "And I have done things as well, mistress. But we won't have that conversation ever, you and I, for we each already know the truth the other knows. Now, go to your loom and settle your mind—"

He did know her; not that Ilna had doubted that before.

"—while I chat with your guards and perhaps open a jar of wine. In a while we'll talk about what we will do, leaving the past to take care of itself. Eh?"

Chalcus smiled; and he kissed her, which no one before in this life had done, and he swaggered back into the house calling to the pair of Blood Eagles at the entrance. Chalcus the sailor; Chalcus the pirate and bloody-handed killer.

Ilna swept the cover from her loom and resumed her work, pouring her soul into the pattern her fingers wove.

Chalcus the man.

Ilna's fingers played the threads without her conscious consideration while her mind grappled with questions that were beyond any human's certain grasp. A spindle of rich brown yarn was nearly empty. She replaced it with a full spindle, and as she did her eyes glanced over the fabric she'd woven.

To another it was merely a pattern of subtle hues and textures, an image that made the person who viewed it a little calmer, a little more happy. What Ilna saw in the muted shades . . .

She slid from her stool and strode into the bungalow's central hall. She heard the sailor from the porch beyond, his voice lilting a complex joke to the pair of guards on duty. Even at this moment Ilna found herself hoping that Merota wasn't listening in also.

"Chalcus!" she called. "Garric will be in the water garden. We've got to warn him. Now!"

She swept out the front door. The Blood Eagles stiffened to attention; Chalcus by contrast looked as supple as the long silken cord around Ilna's waist, a sash for now and a noose at need.

Ilna wasn't much of a runner, but she broke into a trot. This *accursed* palace was bigger than the whole of Barca's Hamlet, and she didn't know the terrain nearly as well.

Chalcus was just as quick and agile on dry land as on shipboard. He swung along beside her. The only sign that he too felt the tension was the way his left hand reached down to steady the curved sword that he wasn't wearing at the moment.

Chalcus didn't ask what the danger was, only grinned at her as they ran through a tunnel of pleached ironwoods. Maybe he didn't care.

What Ilna saw in her fabric was Garric frozen in a cavern. Around him, holding him so there was no escape, were the eight legs of a huge female spider.

And her mandibles were poised to suck Garric's life out.

"A quarter past the seventh hour!" said the crier standing like a colorful statue on his podium beside the flagstoned pathway. As Sharina waited for Garric, she glanced through the columns of the pergola toward the call. The servant turned his eyes aside so that he wouldn't seem to be spying on Prince Garric and his companions even though it was his job to call the time in their direction.

On hot days Garric often worked in this corner of the

compound with its tall hedges and fountains. Now he bent over the table, signing short parchment documents one at a time as Liane put them before him. A gaggle of aides and runners waited against need just outside the pergola, and a dozen Blood Eagles stood just beyond.

Half the guards were turned outward, watching for threats which might lurk among the structures and plantings; the other six kept their eyes on those inside the pergola. Sharina smiled sadly. It wouldn't occur to Garric to worry that his sister might try to assassinate him; it wouldn't occur to a Blood Eagle not to worry.

Fountains on each of three superimposed terraces splashed and gurgled as they fed a stream running in a channel of cut stone. The landscaping was as old as the palace compound, but recent repairs meant that some blocks of the soft volcanic rock were clean though most wore beards of moss that wobbled in the gentle current.

An ascetic-looking man in sea-green silk knelt on the other side of the streamhead, apparently in prayer. He was a stranger to Sharina but from his dress not a servant.

Garric finished the last of the patents and looked up; his eyes followed Sharina's. "That's the ruler of Laut," he said. "My next meeting." He shook his head in frustrated wonder. "I'm supposed to be talking to him now."

"Echeus, the Intercessor of Laut," said Liane, amplifying Garric's statement rather than correcting him. She filed the sheaf of completed documents and closed her little desk. "I'll ready the next group for your signature while you're with Echeus; those will be the judicial appointments for the three Ataras."

"Garric, if this isn't a good time—" Sharina said, a little irritated despite herself. She knew the demands on her brother's time, but the only reason she was here now was that he'd said he wanted to hear about Moon Wisdom as soon as possible.

Her brother raised his hands. "Sharina, without the

weight you take off me, and the organization Liane provides . . ." he said. He covered Liane's hand on the table; she turned it palm up and squeezed back fiercely.

"Without those things," Garric went on, "the kingdom could better run itself than be in the muddle I'd make of it. I don't mean to complain about the part of the job that's left for me."

He nodded, putting an end to the apology. "Now," he said crisply, fully King of the Isles in tone and manner, "tell me about Tisamur and Moon Wisdom."

"The Inspector of Temple Lands has only three Assessors under him . . ." Sharina said. "For some reason he decided to send one to Tisamur."

"His wife has property there," Liane murmured. "Well, perhaps that's fortunate."

"I talked to the Assessor, Kidwal bos-Kidrian," Sharina said. "I believe she's a trustworthy witness."

Kidwal was a young woman from the minor nobility; smart, well educated, and very plain. It'd seemed to Sharina that the barely suppressed anger in Kidwal's presentation was more a reaction to life in general than at her difficulty in getting anybody to take action on her present report.

"She says that the regular temples on Tisamur, at least those within several days' journey from Donelle"—the island's capital—"are either deserted or 've been surrendered to Moon Wisdom. Most of the priests and temple functionaries have joined the new cult, though a few have gone into lay businesses or are living on their personal wealth."

"Moon Wisdom confiscated temple *lands*?" Garric said, frowning. "Is the . . . who is the ruler, a count? Is he behind this?"

"A Council of Elders governs Tisamur," Liane said. She touched her desk but didn't need to open it to withdraw a reference. "Wealthy individuals; all of them landholders, though many depend on trade for most of their income."

"Moon Wisdom is the government now," Sharina said. "It's not imposed by force, it seems to be what people want. Lady Kidwal says she wasn't attacked even though she'd arrived openly without concealing her, well, duties. But those she questioned were derisive."

Sharina paused to recall the assessor's precise wording, letting her eyes follow the barn swallows darting above the water. She could see several mud nests plastered to the underside of the three-arched bridge crossing the artificial stream. Most of the meandering channel was narrow enough to step across, but the architect had provided a lotus-fringed pool so that the bridge didn't look absurd.

"She said," Sharina continued, "that one former Elder told her, 'Whoever saw the Lady, except as a statue being pulled by purse-snatchers in priestly robes? But I've seen *our* Gods, and so have many others.' And everyone listening nodded agreement."

"Did he say what these Gods looked like?" Garric asked, pressing the knuckles of his fists together. Liane looked particularly intent also. Sharina guessed they'd learned more from the vanished Hordred than they'd had time to pass on to her.

"No," Sharina said. "Kidwal asked a number of citizens, in Donelle and also outside the city. That was the only question that seemed to disturb them."

Sharina cleared her throat. "There's one thing more," she said. "Kidwal was permitted to go where she pleased—not into the temple during services, but apart from that. She could talk to anyone, and she doesn't think she was watched or followed. She says very clearly that she wasn't threatened in any way."

"Go on," Garric said. His expression was still but not calm. When Garric was in this—mood? But it was more than a mood—he seemed less like the brother she'd grown up with than he did a great cat, waiting for prey to come a few steps closer.

"Despite all that," Sharina said, "Lady Kidwal was frightened. Frightened enough to convince her chief to get her an appointment with me."

She swallowed. "Frightened enough to frighten me, Garric," she concluded.

Garric stood and braced his hands against one of the crossbeams supporting the pergola's roof. He bunched the muscles of his shoulders and thighs, straining upward to work the stiffness out of them. Echeus, waiting across the stream, turned toward the group in the pergola for the first time. He didn't get to his feet yet.

"Hordred frightened me as well, Sharina," Garric said. He grinned wryly at her. "That was before we saw him disappear."

He turned his head, and added, "Liane, can this Intercessor wait while I talk to Lady Kidwal myself?"

"I'll meet with him if you like, Garric," Sharina offered. "If it's just a formal audience, that is. But I really don't believe that Kidwal knows any more than she told me and I've passed on to you. It's what she feels that's important, and she can't give a reason for that."

"There are reports from Laut that something . . . odd is going on there also," Liane said. "The Intercessor's coming to see you could be an opportunity to learn what he wants, if not necessarily what he plans."

Sharina's eyes narrowed very slightly. Liane was too polite to give Garric a direct order, but she was ordering him nonetheless. Still, it was for his good and the kingdom's, of that Sharina was sure.

"All right," Garric said. He hitched up his sword belt so that the heavy weapon rode more comfortably. "I'll talk to Echeus."

Echeus rose also, tossing a glitter of powder into the stream before he started toward Garric. The men would meet in the middle of the bridge unless one stopped for the other to join him.

Two guards tried to precede Garric; he gestured them back with a curt command. The undercaptain in charge of the detachment eyed the Intercessor's aged dignity. He frowned, but he didn't argue the issue of safety with his sovereign.

Movement from the side drew Sharina's attention. Escorted by another group of Blood Eagles, Tenoctris and Cashel were returning from their foray into the city.

Cashel waved his quarterstaff in greeting. On his left shoulder he carried a lump of stone. From the way his ripped tunics fluttered loose, he'd been to considerable effort getting it.

Sharina smiled as she walked out of the pergola to meet her friends. Cashel's presence was a wall of security. For the first time since she'd seen Hordred vanish screaming, Sharina felt safe.

Dragonflies and swallows whizzed over the sluggish stream, but they didn't get all the insects. When Garric stepped from sunlight into the shade cast by poplars near the water, a mosquito keened close to his left ear. He swatted, hoping to drive it away if not kill it.

In Garric's mind, King Carus chuckled, and said, *"There's more honesty in blackflies than in courtiers, lad. The bugs are just as quick to suck the blood of a shepherd as a prince."*

Garric smiled. If he closed his eyes, he could imagine that he was herding sheep near the marshes fringing Pattern Creek. Mosquito bites weren't something he'd ever have thought would make him feel nostalgic.

The Intercessor came from the other direction at a stately pace. Garric frowned, wondering who Echeus interceded with. Probably he interceded *for* the people of Laut or at least claimed to do so.

Reise had given his children a classical education which couldn't have been bettered by one of the academies in Valles or Erdin on Sandrakkan. Unlike Liane, however, who *had* attended one of those academies, Garric and Sharina knew little more about current events than did any other peasant from Haft.

Garric smiled again. His education taught him that "prince" meant "first." It was an honest claim, if not a humble one.

Again Carus guffawed. *"Princes don't have to be humble,"* he said, hooking his thumbs in his swordbelt and flaring his fingers. Carus was such a vibrant presence in Garric's mind that Garric had to keep reminding himself that others didn't see the ancient monarch—who had drowned a thousand years in the past.

The hump of the arching bridge hid Echeus from Garric when they were on the opposite approaches, though both men were tall. Garric looked over his shoulder. His detachment of Blood Eagles followed at a respectful distance. In the pergola, Liane and Sharina greeted Tenoctris and Cashel. They were looking at a rock—a small boulder—on the table. Whatever had Tenoctris found this time?

Echeus rose into view, step by step. He was an imposing figure: spare rather than powerful, but surrounded with an aura of enormous dignity. Garric had the impression of a person whose time scale was that of an oak, or possibly of the crag of a mountain.

"Lord Echeus?" he said when they were within a double pace, right toe to right toe, of one another.

Echeus stopped and bowed slightly. "Thank you for meeting me, Prince Garric," he said in a thin, hoarse voice.

Unexpectedly Echeus turned and looked over the bridge

coping. "What is that in the water, do you suppose?" he said.

Garric peered into the pool. A few leaves rotated slowly on the surface; at one stone edge glistened a mass of frog eggs. In the water directly under the central arch on which Garric stood—

For a moment, Garric thought he saw his reflection and that of the bridge he stood on. The reflected stonework was covered with lush, broad-leafed vegetation like nothing that grew on Ornifal, though, and the figure looking at him from the pool was—

"*Get back!*" King Carus shouted.

Too late. There was a flash of vivid red light like nothing in the natural world. The reflected figure was toppling upward, and Garric was falling toward it.

They merged at the surface of the water. There was a crash like the cosmos splitting—

And Garric was alone in his mind.

"Set it here," Liane suggested, waving Cashel to the table under the pergola.

He eyed the surface doubtfully before he set the statue there, but she was right about it being sturdy enough. Though small, the table was polished granite and at least as solid as the plinth the statue must originally have stood on. Cashel placed his burden with his usual care so that it didn't roll off; stone scrunched on stone.

Sharina hugged him. "Cashel," she said, "I was just thinking how lucky I am to have you. You make me feel safe."

Cashel blushed. *In front of everybody!* He was even prouder than he was embarrassed, but he was so embarrassed he couldn't breathe for a moment.

"I'm all black from the stone," he said in a hoarse voice.

He raised his hands; they were smudged with the residue of decaying marble.

"Cashel . . ." said Tenoctris, scrubbing at the block with the hem of her robe. Cashel was enough Ilna's brother to cringe at such a use of a fine silk garment. "Look at this! I hadn't noticed."

The statue's right arm, apparently raised, was broken off at the shoulder, but the left hand had been placed on its girdle. The marble fourth finger wore a real ring, a ruby on a simple gold band. While Cashel carried the statue, he'd flaked away the crust of corroded stone which had been covering the jewel.

"It's a pretty little thing, isn't it?" Cashel said. He waited for Tenoctris to tell him what to do. Instead she turned away from the statue to stare abstractedly toward the fountains in the near distance.

"Tenoctris?" he said.

Ignoring him, she took a bamboo sliver from her right sleeve. She knelt and began to scribe on the gritty stone floor with it.

Many wizards used athames of exotic materials for their spells; the tool gained power each time it twisted the forces of the cosmos to the wizard's will. Tenoctris instead picked a simple twig or split of wood, casting each make-shift wand away after one use. She said that no one could be sure of what they were doing if they practiced their art with an object in whose fabric they'd overlaid and braided past wizardry.

Tenoctris claimed she wasn't a powerful wizard. Probably she was correct—it wasn't a matter Cashel could judge. But she was a very, very careful wizard; and in the past that care had saved her and the Isles as well, to Cashel's certain knowledge.

Sharina and Liane were watching him expectantly. "Go on, Cashel," Sharina said. "It's yours."

With a grin of acknowledgment, Cashel gripped the ring

between his left thumb and forefinger and gave it a twist. He didn't expect it to come loose—not unless he used more strength than he planned to, anyway—but it turned easily.

Still wondering, he pulled. The ring slipped free in a cloud of powdered lime; Cashel sneezed.

"I wonder why someone put a ring on—" Liane said, bending slightly for a better look at the circlet in Cashel's hand.

Tenoctris looked up from the simple triangle of words in the Old Script which she'd traced in the grit. "Garric!" she cried. "Cashel, stop him!"

"Garric!" Cashel bellowed, but he was already in motion. Garric stood on the bridge arch near a well-dressed stranger, looking down at the pool. Tenoctris couldn't shout loudly enough for him to hear her.

Cashel burst out of the pergola at a dead run, holding his staff crossways and close to his body. He didn't call again because he'd popped the ring in his mouth for safe-keeping. In common with most poor folk, that's where he'd generally carried the few coins he came by until he paid them out again. Faced with a sudden crisis, he treated the ring the same way out of reflex.

Red wizardlight flashed, unmistakable even in the bright sun. For a moment the ruby glare shone through the ancient stone of the bridge. Even after the initial flash, a rosy haze hung over the water.

Garric toppled forward, over the railing and into the glow. He fell like a half-filled wineskin, limply unconscious. One of the Blood Eagles at the foot of the bridge immediately jumped into the pool—and sank.

The water was a good deal deeper than landscaping required. From the way it clouded as the soldier flailed desperately, the bottom was gluey muck like that of a marsh. The man was in half-armor: thirty pounds of steel, leather, and blackened bronze since he hadn't even taken the time to unstrap his helmet. No amount of strength and goodwill was going to enable a man with no more fat than a rutting stag to swim while wearing that load.

Cashel wasn't going to be able to swim either: he was afraid of the water, so he'd never learned how. He was still afraid; that didn't make any difference now.

The distinguished-looking stranger who'd been talking to Garric raised his hands palms upward. Two Blood Eagles grabbed his wrists and forced him down on his knees. The fellow didn't resist, not that it would have done him any good.

Cashel jumped as far out as he could get, the way he would've tried to cross a stream in spate. He landed feet first, legs pumping, as he sank through water and wizard-light. Holding his quarterstaff out to the side where he wouldn't slap Garric with it, he thrashed his way forward. He couldn't see properly. It had gotten dark, and salt stung his eyes.

The staff was hickory and floated despite its iron ferrules. With luck it was long enough to touch bottom; if not, Cashel hoped to hold it out so that a soldier at the margin of the pool could seize it before he and Garric sank.

And if not that either, well, he'd tried.

The wind screamed. For an instant Cashel thought he heard Sharina call his name, but the gale carried her voice away.

Cashel's left hand caught fabric and closed on it. A lightning bolt lit the sky and reflected from the white frothing surf in which he struggled. More lightning slashed cloud to cloud. The shore was fifty double paces ahead of him, and an undertow was trying pull him out.

Cashel didn't know where he was, but that could wait till there was more leisure. The person he dragged with him wasn't Garric; when the white flashes quivered from an upturned face, he saw he held a girl of more or less his age. Her expression was set but not panicky. She grabbed his sash with both hands.

Cashel set his quarterstaff on the firm holding behind him, then lumbered several steps forward on the thrust of the next wave. The girl managed to get her feet down and help, though when the water started to stream back she fluttered like a flag in a windstorm.

Cashel dug his staff in and waited, then resumed his march as a comber boiled over him and his burden. He didn't know what was happening, but he knew what he had to do; that was all that mattered.

The reversing wave twisted him sideways. Over his left shoulder he saw a ship breaking up in the lightning-lit darkness. The surf sprang as high as the mast trucks from the fangs of a reef. More human figures struggled in the water, though it was hard to tell them from other flotsam in the blue-white glitter from the sky.

The current released him. Cashel and the girl strode forward, moving faster because the sea was no more than knee deep now. The girl lost her footing at the ebb, but Cashel continued to plod on. She pulled herself up on his sash, then scrambled the last few steps without his support.

Cashel heard a long, deep cry from out to sea. He turned, feeling wobbly. The effort of the last minutes had caught up with him now that he had time to be exhausted. He thought the sound was wind howling in the cavity of the ship as a hatch carried away and gave it passage; but he was wrong.

A reptile raised its wedge-shaped head from the breakers beyond the reef. Lightning gave its wet scales the sheen of opals. Then, with a sideways lurch seaward, the long body vanished again.

The girl had collapsed on the sandy beach. Cashel picked her up by an arm and staggered a few steps farther inland to where they'd be beyond even the strongest of the waves.

Cashel spat the ring into the wash-leather purse he wore on a cord around his neck. His fingers were numb. His whole body was numb.

He'd build an altar to the Shepherd in thanks for his safety; but later. A little later.

Chapter Three

Garric hit the water facefirst. He wasn't unconscious, just numb, as though he'd been drugged.

The shock and splash freed him. His throat had tightened for a shout when he looked into the pool; the sound turned into a choking gurgle from a mouth filled with water and leaves.

By reflex Garric's arms brought his head up with a breaststroke. He and Sharina both swam like otters, a skill that few of their neighbors in Barca's Hamlet had learned—not even the fishermen who took their dories out beyond the sight of land and every day risked an unexpected storm.

Leaf mold stained the water black. Great branches interlaced overhead, their lush foliage hiding all but speckles of the bright blue sky. He'd fallen from a ruined building into a meandering stream; the bank before him was completely overgrown.

His *body* didn't feel right!

A female figure leaped to the cornice from which he'd fallen, shrieking, "Gar! What happen?"

He could understand her, but he shouldn't have been able to because she wasn't human. Not fully human, at any rate: she was one of the hairy half-men of Bight. "Tint save you!" she cried, and she dived into the water beside him.

"I'm all right!" Garric said, but that wasn't true—though he wasn't at risk of drowning, he could swim as well as he ever could. His arms were a deeper tan than they'd ever been except at the end of a summer's plowing; these last few months of living as a prince rather than a peasant had left him as pale as someone with a swarthy Haft complexion ever got.

He was alone; King Carus no longer shared his mind as a constant companion and advisor. Garric clutched for the ancient coronation medal that should hang around his neck. There was nothing, not even a tunic; he was naked except for a breechclout of fabric as coarse as sacking.

Memories flooded in. They weren't Garric or-Reise's memories. *Wedge-shaped jaws the size of a bread oven closing on his head—*

There was a moment of disorientation as stunning as the shock that had paralyzed Garric on the bridge railing. His face slipped into the water.

Fingers strong enough to bend iron gripped his right shoulder and lifted him. "Tint save you!" the beastgirl screamed in his ear. "Tint save you!"

Tint paddled strongly for the bank from which he'd fallen. Garric stroked with his left arm, but he didn't try to break the beastgirl's grip on the other. He wasn't sure he could.

The stream's current was sluggish, but it had carried them past the ruins as Garric spluttered. The ornate building had ten feet of frontage on the water and was about that height despite the ruined condition of the cornice where he'd been standing, but it was only five or six feet wide. It was an altar, or perhaps a monument, where statues had once sheltered beneath porches at either end. Thick vegetation hid any structures that might have been placed nearby.

A root was twisted over the bank. Tint caught it with her free hand and brought a gnarled, hairy leg up so that a prehensile foot could double her grip.

Garric put his legs down, expecting to touch bottom. Instead he stubbed his toe on the channel's masonry wall. He'd have gone under again had not the beastgirl raised him up like a sack of grain and deposited him on the bank.

She sprang up beside him and squatted on all fours. Her legs bent more naturally into that posture than they did when she stood upright.

"Tint *save*," she announced proudly. "Gar safe."

"Thank you, Tint," Garric said. The image of jaws closing on his head was still the most vivid of the new memories, though unfamiliar human figures also shuffled hazily through his mind. Most often the figures were shouting at him, striking at him, or kicking him the way some men would kick a dog.

Garric's belly muscles tensed over a cold lump. *He* wouldn't kick a dog; and nobody would kick him, unless they were trying to learn whether Garric could break their leg with his bare hands. Garric figured he probably could, if he were angry enough.

But the jaws . . .

Seawolves, giant marine lizards whose legs were little more than flippers to steer the beasts through the water, sometimes came ashore near Barca's Hamlet to prey on the flocks. Garric had killed seawolves, and once a seawolf had seized his leg and very nearly killed him.

He touched his calf. His body would bear the scars of those long fangs for the rest of its life, but *this* body did not. The muscles were rock hard, if anything stronger than Garric's own, but he no longer wore the form to which he had been born.

"Gar?" said the beastgirl nervously, sensing Garric's feeling of trapped horror.

"It's all right, Tint," he said, hoping he sounded reassuring. He stood up. There was nothing wrong with this body; it just wasn't his own.

There was nothing wrong with this *body*, but the mind that had used to wear it—

Garric raised his index fingers to his temples, probing gently. He found what he expected: a line of indentations on either side where the jaws of a huge seawolf had closed, driving its fangs deep into the bone. Into the bone, and into the brain beneath.

It was a wonder that Gar's body had survived a mauling like that. His mind had not survived.

"Gar, what wrong?" Tint said, standing also. Fully erect, she only came to the middle of Garric's chest. She began grooming him with her fingers. His scalp was as shaggy as a ram's fleece in winter, and now he had an unkempt beard as well.

"Nothing's wrong, Tint," Garric said, staring in bleak despair at the jungle of palmetto and larger trees choking the landscape around him. He saw squared stones under the network of surface roots supporting a large magnolia; as he'd guessed, there were extensive ruins in the vicinity.

"Nothing's wrong that you can help with," he added.

And very possibly no one could help. No one in whatever world this was.

As he sat above the tide line, Cashel ran a swatch of raw wool slowly over his quarterstaff. In part he was polishing the hickory, but mostly he used the familiar task to settle his mind. He carried the pad of wool under his belt. It'd sloshed through the breakers with him, but the fibers' coat of lanolin kept them free from salt water.

The girl was coming around. Cashel had wrung out his sodden outer tunic and rolled it into a pillow for her. The beach was mostly sandy, but there were rocks in it.

"Mistress . . .". the girl murmured. Her left hand closed

on the amulet hanging from her neck by a silver chain.

The storm had broken up; the remaining clouds scudded across expanses of clear sky. Cashel had already looked at the amulet by the light of the stars and the waxing moon: a lens of rock crystal whose silver mounting mimicked a spider lying on the disk and encircling it with her legs.

It wasn't something Cashel would have wanted to wear; but then, nobody was asking him to.

The girl sat up sharply. "Are we safe?" she said, peering at Cashel. She knuckled her eyes, trying to rub away the salt that blurred her vision. "Are you one of the sailors?"

"I think we're safe enough," Cashel said. He sounded hoarse, and his stomach felt queasy; he must have swallowed seawater while he was fighting the surf, though he didn't remember it now. "I'm not a sailor, but there's other fellows here with us. I guess some of them may be sailors."

The light wasn't good enough to tell much, and Cashel didn't have the energy to go about meeting strangers in a place so new to him. Debris from the ship, human as well as cordage and timber, littered the beach. Not all the bodies were alive, of course, but some of them were starting to move.

"Ah," Cashel said. "My name's Cashel or-Kenset."

The girl was quickly regaining her composure. She touched the ground lightly, apparently judging whether her muscles had recovered enough from her struggle to shore that she could stand up again.

They hadn't; she didn't try. "I'm Lady Tilphosa bos-Pholial," she said with dignity. "Are we on Laut, Master Cashel?"

Cashel frowned. "Laut?" he said. "I don't think so, ah, Lady Tilphosa. But I'm not from around here either."

Up the beach had grounded a great wooden lump, either the ship's dinghy or a portion of the hull; one end rose and sank in the pull of the surf. A ball of blue light flickered beside the wreckage, then rolled a ghostly course down the sand toward Cashel and the girl.

Cashel hadn't been planning to move for a while yet. He decided he would after all, rising to his feet in a smooth motion. He gave his quarterstaff a trial spin. Funny how something like that brought his strength back better than a day's rest.

"Master Cashel!" the girl called. "What's the matter?"

"The light coming this way," Cashel said. "That's wizard's work."

He stepped forward to keep Tilphosa clear of the staff if he had to move quickly. Cashel and his seven feet of iron-shod hickory took up a lot of room.

The ball of light was the size of a man's head. It half floated, half bounced; never quite touching the ground, but never rising a hand's breadth above it. It was a blue haze just bright enough to show the texture of the pebble-strewn sand it crossed.

"It's all right, Cashel," the girl said. She grunted softly as she stood. "That's just Metra trying to find me."

"Lady Tilphosa!" called another female voice from the shelter of the wreck. "Are you all right?"

"I'm all right, Metra!" the girl said. She started up the beach, wobbling for the first few steps but then getting full control of her legs. The glowing ball dissolved like a shadow in sunlight.

Cashel followed, grimacing because he'd been worried about something that wasn't a threat after all. Still . . . he slanted his quarterstaff across his chest instead of leaning it on his shoulder as he walked. Metra might not be a danger, but there was danger enough in this place: the great serpent writhing out beyond the breakers for one.

Coming toward them was a youngish woman, in her early twenties perhaps. She was plump, dark-haired, and wore a black robe slashed white across the front. The garment was much the worse for the abuse it had taken during the wreck.

Cashel's eyes narrowed. The light wasn't good, but the woman looked a lot like the fellow who'd set the workmen on him this morning.

"Lady Tilphosa!" the woman said. "Thank the Mistress you're safe!"

Tilphosa embraced her, and said, "Yes, She saved me through the agency of Master Cashel here. Cashel, this is Metra, Daughter of the Mistress. She's an acolyte at the Temple of the Lady, Mistress of the Moon, in Donelle— and accompanies me as advisor until the marriage."

"I'm Lady Tilphosa's guardian," Metra said in a distinctly cool tone as she appraised Cashel. "Who are you, sir?"

"I'm Cashel," Cashel responded, setting his feet a little wider. His voice was growing hoarse again, but his bath in seawater was no longer the cause. "I'm from Barca's Hamlet. Do you have an older brother, lady? The sort of guy who thinks if he can't buy what he wants, he'll buy toughs to take it for him?"

"What?" said Metra in surprise. "I have three sisters, two stillborn and one died as an infant. What are you talking about?"

She held a knife-shaped thing covered with symbols in the Old Script. It was a wizard's tool, an athame. Well, Cashel already knew Metra was a wizard, even if she claimed to be a priestess besides.

"I met a man in Valles," Cashel said, still harsh but now embarrassed again; this time by the women's identical expressions of puzzlement. "He looked like you. And he was dressed like you, too."

Metra lifted her chin in a gesture of denial. "I know nothing of Valles," she said curtly. "As for my robe, it's what the Children of the Mistress wear. Perhaps another of us has journeyed to Valles, but he wasn't a relative of mine."

Her eyes locked with Cashel's again. "Now, sir," she said, "tell us what *you're* doing here."

"I'm not sure," Cashel said, wishing that he didn't feel so defensive. Other survivors were moving in groups. Light winked; not wizardry this time but an honest bonfire kindled with handfuls of dry grass and fed with pandanus stems. "I went to help a friend who'd fallen into a pond, and then I was here."

"Where is 'here'?" Metra demanded. "Are we on Laut?"

One of the men around the fire stood up. In a loud voice he called into the darkness, "Did the priestess get to shore? Get her over here if she did! I want to talk to her."

One of his companions called in an equally loud voice, "*I* don't want to talk to her. If there's any justice, she's feeding that demon snake that wrecked us. You know it was because of her!"

Metra turned toward the fire, her lips forming a hard line. Her expression reminded Cashel again of the fellow who'd tried to take the statue from him in Valles. She didn't speak.

The sky had continued to clear. Cashel could recognize most of the constellations, but they didn't look quite right. The space between the Calves was too wide, and the feet of the Huntsman were above the Drinking Cup instead of below the way they should've been.

Metra's eyes focused again on Cashel. "Well?" she said. "*Are* we on Laut?"

"He says he's a stranger too," Tilphosa said, frustrated and a little angry because of her advisor's attitude. "Metra, he saved my life. He pulled me from the sea!"

Cashel cleared his throat. "I was in Valles," he said. "Something . . . brought me here. I don't know what."

"You're a wizard?" Metra said. She took a half step back and made an obscure movement with the athame. A splutter of blue wizardlight picked out the symbol the point had drawn in the air. "You *are* a wizard!"

"Cashel?" said Tilphosa in surprise, raising her eyes to look at him.

"I'm *not*," Cashel said. He'd growled, and he didn't mean to. He planted his staff firmly in front of him and twisted it as if he was trying to screw the ferrule into the gritty soil. "I'm not a wizard, but I've been told . . . Well, sometimes stuff happens when I'm around, that's all."

Cashel didn't want to think about what he was. He'd done fine being a shepherd and a man folks in the borough called on for heavy lifting. That's all he wanted to be: normal.

He sighed. The world had never much cared what Cashel wanted. This business was just another example of that.

"Mistress Metra!" bawled the leader of the men around the bonfire. "If you're alive, get over here or may the Sister take me if you don't wind up back in the sea!"

The fire was drawing the survivors together. Sailors from farther down the beach straggled by, eyeing the two women and Cashel as they passed.

"That's Captain Mounix calling," Tilphosa said. It was obvious that in a few moments someone would tell the captain that Metra was standing close by.

"Do you want me to go along when you talk to them?" Cashel said. He swung his staff level and brushed the ferrule clean with the hem of his inner tunic. He felt calm again, both because the subject had changed and because it looked like he'd have a chance to do something he understood.

"To handle them?" Metra sneered. "No, I'll take care of those fools myself."

"We're going to Laut because I'm betrothed to Prince Thalemos," Tilphosa said, in explanation but with a hint of understandable pride. "He's the ruler of Laut."

"Thalemos?" said Cashel. "I thought the ruler was named Echeus. I just saw him in Valles, talking to Garric."

Metra had started for the bonfire, but she was still close enough to hear Cashel's words. She turned sharply, holding the athame in a fashion that reminded Cashel it was a weapon—though not a material one.

"What did you say?" she demanded. "What do you know of Echea?"

"Echeus," Cashel corrected. His hands slid apart on the shaft of the quarterstaff, one to either side of the center, where they were ready to make it spin and strike. "And I don't know anything about him, lady, just that he was talking to my friend Garric."

There was a moment's tense silence. Tilphosa put her hand on Cashel's forearm. "Echea was an enemy of ours," she said calmly. "An enemy of the Mistress, really. But she's dead now. You're sure of that, aren't you, Metra?"

"I was sure," the priestess said, with slight emphasis on "was." "You saw someone named Echeus in Valles, you say? Was he the wizard who sent you here?"

Cashel made an angry gesture with his right hand, then gripped his quarterstaff again. "I don't know who put me here," he said. "I don't know where I am."

Instead of shouting, Captain Mounix crunched over the sand toward Metra and her companions. Most of the gathered survivors came with him.

Cashel looked up at the skewed constellations. "Who's the King of the Isles?" he said. "Do you know?"

"The king?" Tilphosa repeated. "Why, King Carus, of course. Who did you think it was?"

The arriving sailors saved Cashel from answering that question.

Chapter Four

Sharina held back instead of plunging into the water ahead of Cashel as she could easily have done. There wasn't time to discuss plans, and having someone Cashel's size land on top of her flailing a quarterstaff wouldn't help the trouble. She knew Cashel couldn't swim, but she trusted him to do the right thing by instinct.

Now Cashel leaped with all his considerable strength, a graceful arc despite him looking like a broad-jumper rather than a diver. Garric sprawled limp, sinking slowly on the weight of his sword.

Cashel should have landed next to him; Sharina paused on the mossy coping stones, waiting for a splash like that of a boulder dropping in the sea. Instead, Cashel vanished the way water soaks into hot sand.

The look of the pond changed. Sharina hadn't noticed the rosy haze over the water until now, when it disappeared.

Garric was still sinking. Several guards were dragging Echeus from the bridge. One had jumped into the pool, and others looked ready to follow him. Wearing armor, they wouldn't be able to swim any better than Cashel, and Sharina had no reason at all to trust *their* judgment.

Sharina made a clean dive. The water was shockingly cold—she'd forgotten that it had bubbled from the spring-fed fountains only fifty paces away. She reached under and caught the front of her brother's gold-embroidered collar. Her grip rolled Garric's face out of the water as they broke the surface.

Sharina kicked despite her hampering garments and

stroked for the shore with her free hand. She wished she'd taken a moment to remove the court robe, though it didn't matter much.

She didn't let herself think about Cashel. Tenoctris could explain or—

But anyway, Sharina couldn't let herself think about it now.

One of the soldiers on the margin held out his javelin so his fellow floundering in the water could grab it behind the point and be dragged to safety. Voices all around babbled. Several Blood Eagles lifted Garric away from Sharina with the care owed a priceless treasure; they laid him on the grass.

Sharina grimaced. She didn't need help getting out of the water, but she had to swim two paces down the coping to clear the out-turned hobnails of the soldiers bending over her brother. The pool was deeper than she was tall, and the several feet of mud on the stone bottom didn't help matters.

A few minutes ago this corner of the palace had seemed as sparsely inhabited as a stretch of plowland. Now scores of soldiers, servants, and officials descended from all directions. Most of them were shouting.

Garric lay belly down on the grass, his face to the side. Blood Eagles surrounded him; one was making a clumsy attempt at artificial respiration.

Sharina slipped between a pair of black-clad soldiers to her brother's side. A Blood Eagle grabbed her shoulder. She turned her head back, and snarled, "No, you cur!" as though he'd touched her importunately as she served in her father's inn.

"Princess!" the soldier blurted. "My pardon!" He snapped his head around to face the gathering crowd.

"Here, let me have him!" Sharina said to the fellow massaging Garric's back muscles in apparent hope of restoring the victim's breathing. Garric's chest rose and fell without help, though the deep, shuddering nature of those breaths showed that something was wrong.

Garric's eyes opened. For a moment his expression was blank; then—

Sharina couldn't have said what the change was. She only knew that the soul behind those eyes wasn't her brother's.

Blood Eagles returned from the bridge to the circle of their fellows, holding Echeus. The Intercessor wore the expression of calm dignity appropriate to a gentleman buffeted by circumstances.

Garric put a hand on the grass and lifted his torso, coughing up a swallow of pond water. He looked at Sharina, saw her stricken horror, and smiled. "It's all right," he whispered. "It'll be all right."

Lord Attaper, the commander of the Blood Eagles, pushed through the crowd of jabbering civilians. His tunic was short—military-style—but it was embroidered in gold and purple, and he didn't wear armor.

"What's happened to the prince?" Attaper said in a tightly controlled voice. He asked the way he would have demanded word of a flanking attack sure to overwhelm his line. Attaper's left hand was on the ivory pommel of his sword, holding it tight for a charm.

"We got him!" said one of the guards holding Echeus. "This is the guy who—"

The soldier stopped. He didn't know what had happened; and since he'd been watching when Garric fell, he knew that Echeus hadn't been within arm's length of the prince.

Eyes turned to the Intercessor. "Prince Garric greeted me on the bridge," Echeus said. He spoke in a high tenor, not an unpleasant voice but thinner than the man's bearing suggested. "I replied, and his eyes suddenly turned up. I'm afraid the prince may have had a fit. Before I could catch him, he'd toppled into the water."

Garric reached toward Sharina; their eyes met again. She took his hand, supporting him as he rose dripping to his feet. A Blood Eagle tried to help; Garric angrily shook him away. He looked at Echeus.

"Are you all right, your majesty?" Attaper said. The guard commander had faced death a dozen times without quailing, but he was frightened now.

Sharina understood the grim logic in Attaper's mind. If Garric died, Attaper had failed in his duty. And if Garric died, the Isles would crash into ruin.

Echeus looked at Attaper and pitched his voice for the gathering crowd, as though Garric himself weren't present. He said, "From the expression I saw as the prince fell, I'm afraid he may have lost his mind. Occasionally even a youth like the prince may have a stroke and—"

"No, traitor," Garric said. The words came from his mouth, but they weren't in the voice of the brother Sharina had grown up with. Garric's right hand closed on the grip of his long sword. "I *haven't* lost my mind, despite your wizard tricks!"

"Your majesty?" Attaper said. The guards holding Echeus stepped back instinctively. Echeus opened his mouth but he seemed to be too startled to speak further.

Garric drew his sword with a smooth motion that continued as a long cut. Water danced from the shimmering edge.

"No!" the Intercessor shouted, trying too late to leap back. The sharp steel caught him on the right side of the neck and continued through. Echeus' head spun away, wearing a startled expression; his body crumpled where it stood.

Garric's powerful arm carried the blade on for another several feet of arc. Now it slung drops of bright blood.

* * *

Ilna watched Garric's arm and sword come around in a backhand stroke without a quiver or waste motion. The green-clad stranger's head leaped away; his vivid blood spurted higher than where his hair had been in the time his head was still attached.

"Now *there's* a man who knows his work!" said Chalcus, voicing Ilna's thought as well. She was too much a craftsman not to focus first on the skill of what she'd just seen, regardless of the act itself.

The act—the killing—didn't touch her. Ilna didn't know the man whose body sagged on the other side of the little stream, but she didn't worry that Garric would have killed someone who didn't need killing.

Ilna herself, on the other hand . . . Well, she hoped she'd learned from the mistakes she'd made in the past, but that didn't change the fact she'd made them.

For a moment Ilna didn't understand Chalcus' posture. The sailor was poised in a near crouch, his hands slightly raised with the palms outward. He saw her glance and crooked a grin, still concentrating on the scene before him.

Chalcus is showing that his hands are empty. That he's not the next threat the killer across the water should deal with. A sign of respect, from one craftsman to another. . . .

Garric knelt, his head raised and alert. He gripped the dead man's sleeve and jerked *hard*. Ilna knew Garric was strong, but not even he could tear silk brocade barehanded.

The shoulder stitching popped. Garric rose, wiping his swordblade with the swatch of lustrous fabric. Ilna winced.

The single swift blow had silenced the crowd, those on Garric's side of the stream as well as those near Ilna who'd gotten a better view of what had really happened. Garric looked around like a hawk on its kill, his eyes suddenly lighting on Ilna—across the channel but only a few paces away. For an instant her heart leaped at what she saw in his gaze—for an instant, no more.

"Garric?" said Sharina, motionless where she'd been when her brother stepped forward into his cut. To move would have been to risk not only being maimed but also getting in the way. Ilna had seen only danger in the pattern she wove, not this quick slaughter. Sharina and the others here in the garden knew even less of what was going on.

Tenoctris, healthy but hobbled by old age, made her way from the gazebo to where the others gathered about Garric and the corpse. The Blood Eagles of the wizard's escort had abandoned her at the threat to Garric; now, angrily abashed, they opened a path for her through the spectators. Garric saw her and nodded.

"Princess Sharina," he said in a ringing voice. "Lady Liane—and you, Lady Tenoctris, you for I *must* have you. We'll meet now in the small council room, we alone. Attaper, keep all others out!"

"Garric?" called Ilna.

She lifted her inner tunic knee high to jump the artificial stream. Chalcus, seeing more or sensing more, put a hand of restraint on her shoulder.

"Not her!" Garric snarled to his guard commander.

He looked at Ilna again. His sword, so sure a moment before when it took off the stranger's head, began to tremble in his hand.

"Mistress," Garric said in a voice that Ilna had never heard from her old friend's lips, "I will speak with you, I promise that. But not now, not yet."

He turned his back to Ilna and started to walk away.

Ilna brought out the hank of short cords she kept in her left sleeve against need. Her fingers started to knot them.

She felt nothing at all. Looking at herself from the outside, she saw her eyes focused on the back of the man she had grown up loving. They were pits of black hellfire.

* * *

Rainwater had pooled in a stone paver hollowed by the feet of men long dead. Garric used the natural mirror to examine the face he now wore. It was more familiar than not—the features he'd grown used to from birth, though framed with shaggy hair. The dark brunet locks had grown in white where the seawolf's fangs had punched dimples in his skull.

"Gar, we hunt lizards?" Tint asked. The beastgirl dabbed her hand out and back, clearly wishing to groom Garric but afraid to touch him in what she thought was his present strange mood. "Lizards in stones here."

Garric looked at his companion. "Tint, do you understand what I say?" he said. "When I talk like this?"

The beastgirl spoke in clicks and grunts. Though Garric—Gar—heard the sounds as speech, his tongue and palate could no more reproduce them than Tint's long, narrow jaw could form normal human words.

Tint shrugged and scratched the back of her scalp. "Tint hear," she said, sounding a little bored. "Tint hear other men too, but they not hear Tint."

Scowling, she added, "Tint not *like* other men!"

Garric stood, looking around him again. Not only were these ruins old, they'd been long in use before the forest re-covered them. There was nothing remarkable about the architecture to connect the ruins with any description he'd read in an ancient author. He could be on Ornifal, though he doubted it; or even somewhere on Haft.

"Gar, we hunt lizards?" Tint repeated, shifting nervously from one foot to the other. "Only—snakes in stones too."

She shuddered. "Snake Island!" she said. She hugged herself and looked longingly at Garric. "We go away! We take ring to other men and go away, Gar?"

Garric looked at her sharply. "What other men?" he asked. "How did we come here, Tint?"

She shrugged again. "Vascay's tribe," she said. "Our

tribe. They take us on hollow log to Snake Island, hunt for ring for wizard. Other men not smell ring and not hear Tint."

She dropped to all fours again and turned her head quickly from side to side, taking in her surroundings. "Bad place," she said. "Many snakes!"

Garric thought about Tint's words as he listened to the forest. Besides the chirps and trilling that would've passed unnoticed in the borough's common woodland, something shrieked every few minutes like a cat in a bonfire. Garric supposed it was a bird, but it'd get on his nerves if he had to listen to it for long.

He could guess from Gar's hazy memories what the beastgirl meant by "Vascay's tribe": a band of twenty or more men, all armed beyond what was normal for honest folk. Some had eye patches and several were missing limbs.

Most of the gang had cuffed or kicked Gar in the past. A few of them seemed to have done so every time the half-witted youth came within reach.

"Tint," he said, "can you show me where the ring is? If we find the ring, maybe we'll be able to leave this island."

At the moment the only thing Garric was sure of was that his relationship with the tribe—the gang of bandits, he supposed—was going to be different from the one that they'd had with Gar. Bringing in the object the gang was searching for would be at least a good start toward that change.

"Tint show," the beastgirl said with another shrug. "Stone wears ring. Tint smell stone."

Tint set off through the forest, moving roughly parallel to the watercourse. Garric started after her. He caught at once in a kind of bamboo with back-curved hooks on the edges of the leaves.

"Gar come?" Tint called, already hidden by the foliage. "Come, Gar!"

"Wait!" Garric snapped. The leaves' grip left dotted rows of blood, on his forearms and along his ribs. He had to get down onto all fours to pass the bamboo; he didn't dare try circling the stand because it seemed to cover the whole area of a courtyard building which had collapsed into a mound of brick and stone in past ages.

He sighed. He'd wondered what the calluses on Gar's knuckles came from. Now he knew.

Most of Gar's fuzzy memories were of fears and beatings, not the ordinary business of his days. As best Garric could determine, Tint and the half-wit served Vascay's band as something between unpaid servants and ill-treated pets. They carried water, fed the fire, and were allowed to eat scraps from the gang's own meals as well as scavenge for themselves.

It wasn't a bad life, really—for an animal. Garric's face hardened at the thought.

Tint came back to Garric before he reached where she'd been waiting. The beastgirl's irritation had become renewed solicitousness: she couldn't imagine what had caused the change in her friend.

Garric smiled with a touch of humor. He couldn't imagine either, though he guessed that the Intercessor of Laut could explain it.

When at Echeus' direction Garric had looked into the pool, he'd seen something in the instant before Gar's reflection appeared in place of his own. A pattern had formed in bits of glittering flotsam carried down on the stream from where Echeus had knelt. Tint's calling this place Snake Island had helped Garric identify the remembered objects: they'd been snake scales.

The ruins, though extensive, appeared to be of a palace complex rather than a city. The buildings had ornamental façades, and the walls were sheathed with marble over brick cores. Much of the damage was deliberate: time and the forest had only buried the ruin brought by human assault.

Tint brought Garric to ruins that were both cruder and more recent. Blocks and column barrels from the original palace had been piled into a wall which had enclosed a dozen huts or so.

Fire had swept this later hamlet as well, blackening the stones before they fell again to rubble. The mound was now covered by moss and a fungus that sent up small orange balls, ready to puff out their spores if touched.

There'd only been the one patch of bamboo, but pine trees of some sort branched frequently into hedges of spikes hidden in the softer-leafed vegetation. The soil around this later settlement was too soggy to support brush above knee height, let alone trees. Garric straightened from the crouch he'd been in most of the way through the forest and strode toward the jumbled ruin.

Tint shrieked and bounded in front of him, baring her teeth in terror. "No, Gar!" she said, hopping up and down on all fours. "Gar die! Gar die!"

Garric froze, splaying his hands at his side to calm his companion. "I'm not moving, Tint," he said quietly. "Tell me what the danger is."

"Mushroom kill!" Tint said. She pawed at Garric, not really trying to move him back but miming a further signal of danger. "Gar touch mushroom, Gar die!"

The beastgirl made a theatrical sweep of her hand, indicating the puffballs' bright nodules. Her arm, covered in coarse reddish-gold hair, was as long as Garric's own.

Garric nodded his understanding. Even in the borough there were poison mushrooms. This was the first time he'd run into a species whose spores were dangerous, but already he trusted the beastgirl's woodcraft as implicitly as he did Tenoctris' judgment on wizardry.

"How do we—" he said.

Beneath Tint's pointing hand was a vine with leaves as broad as a watermelon's. A stem suddenly rustled. The beastgirl glanced at the ground, then froze.

"Tint?" said Garric. He touched her shoulder. She was trembling like a tuft of goosedown. He looked past her, bending forward to bring his eyes to the angle of hers.

A snake coiled beneath the vine. Its head was a wedge as broad as Garric's fist, its mottled body as thick as his forearm. He couldn't tell how long the serpent was: ten feet, twelve feet, perhaps even longer. Certainly it was long enough to strike Tint where she stood in frozen panic.

The snake's tail quivered, making a dry rustle against the leaves. Its head rose minusculely, weaving slightly with the tension of muscles compressing. The beastgirl whimpered, "Hoo . . . hoo . . . hoo. . . ."

"Jump back, Tint," Garric whispered. He'd seen her spring fifteen feet from a standing start; that would carry her clear of the snake before it could strike.

But not this time: Tint was too frightened to move. Garric wasn't sure she even heard his voice. His right hand, concealed behind the beastgirl's body, tugged loose the knot of his breechclout.

The snake's tail blurred again. Most serpents slither away if given the opportunity; not this one. Its ridged underside was the color of hot sulfur. As its fangs unfolded, a drop of venom glinted on the tip of each.

Garric leaped past Tint's left side, carrying the fluttering length of his breechclout with him. If he'd had time to tie a stone in the cloth for weight, he'd have thrown it instead; there wasn't any time.

The snake struck. It was quicker even than Garric had feared, sinking its long fangs in the wool with an audible *clop* of air. Garric twisted, catching the snake beneath the head with both hands. He'd rather have run, but he couldn't have gotten up from his sprawl before the snake struck again, this time into his thigh or torso.

Now Tint jumped, first away and then back like a toad bouncing between the walls of a ditch as it tries to flee a sudden motion. She screamed.

The snake's body writhed about Garric's right arm. The creature was strong, probably stronger than he was, but it couldn't get a fulcrum that would allow it to wrench itself out of his grasp. He could feel the scales' keel ridges cutting into his callused palms.

"Tint!" Garric shouted. He'd come down hard, slamming his left side on a chunk of rubble that bruised him badly if it hadn't broken a rib. Pain crackled through him like lightning hitting the sea. "Help me!"

The beastgirl capered and squealed. The snake was trying to stab its fangs down into Garric's forearm. Its long tail curled, slapping Garric across the eyes.

"Duzi!" he shouted, lashing hysterically. The snake's back popped. Garric flung the creature from him, horrified by the memory of his fear of a moment before.

The snake continued to twist, but now spasmodically. Its jaws opened and closed without force; its eyes were glazing.

Garric stood up slowly, rubbing his side. He'd have a bruise; nothing worse than that. He saw his breechclout among the vines where the struggle had flung it. Venom had soaked through a patch the size of his palm. He left the coarse woolen where it was; it hadn't been much of a garment to begin with.

"Gar good?" Tint said, creeping to his side and stroking him. "Gar good!"

Garric brushed the beastgirl's hand away. She couldn't overcome a fear like that any better than an effort of will would enable her to breathe water; but Garric remembered with revulsion how nearly the serpent had come to squirming its dry suppleness from his unaided grip. . . .

"Show me where the ring is, Tint," Garric said in a

husky voice. "That's all I want from you. Find me the ring."

Sharina followed as Garric entered the meeting room; he moved like a caged cat, still holding the sword bare in his hand.

She'd been concerned since he fell into the pool. Now she was beginning to feel a sick horror.

Garric paced to the other side of the round table, only then turning to face the three women he'd summoned. Liane was helping Tenoctris; Sharina met his eyes directly.

Garric swiped the wad of silk again over the tip of his blade; the steel was already spotless. In an odd tone he said, "The way he jumped, I was afraid I'd caught him in the jaw. Nothing bites a sword edge as bad as hacking at a fellow's teeth."

"Garric," said Sharina. "What's wrong?"

Garric shot the sword home into its scabbard without looking at what he was doing. That smooth, ringing motion took as much skill as threading a needle in the dark.

"What's wrong?" he said. "I'm not Garric, milady— that's what's wrong! That *wizard*—"

His face contorted; he snarled out the word as though it were "father-slayer" or a worse term yet.

"—snatched away your brother's mind and replaced it with the mind of some drooling moron from the Sister knows where!"

The man who looked like the brother Sharina had known for nineteen years glared at the birds frescoed in a band between the ceiling moldings and the lowered casements, then met her eyes. Again Sharina had the feeling she watched a trapped animal.

Tenoctris slid from her backless ivory chair and settled onto the terrazzo floor. With the writing brush and a small inkhorn she'd taken from her sleeve, she was drawing a six-sided figure.

"This so-clever Intercessor thought he'd leave the Isles leaderless because the prince's body was barely able to feed itself," the man said, grinning at Sharina in a way that could've been Garric after all. "What he didn't know . . ."

He reached under his tunics and came out with his fist around the medallion hanging there from a neck thong. He went on, ". . . is that Garric hadn't been alone in his skull. There's a half-wit boy whimpering in here with me, wondering what's going on; but I'm the one wearing Garric's body, not him."

Smiling still broader, he opened his hand to display his own image on the worn gold disk. "My name is Carus," he said. "A thousand years ago, I was King of the Isles."

A spark of blue light, vivid but minute, glittered in the center of the figure Tenoctris had drawn over the irregular pattern of the stone chips. It snapped with the quick certainty of a gadfly toward the man speaking, but vanished before it touched him—and before his hand had more than gripped the sword again.

Tenoctris swayed. Liane was closer; she reached out to steady the old woman before Sharina could bend to do the same. Wizardry was hard work, especially for someone whose knowledge was much greater than her power.

"Yes," Tenoctris said as she rose with Liane's help. She smiled faintly. "You *are* Carus."

The man—Carus—let out a long, shuddering breath. "Lady Tenoctris . . ." he said. He paused, averting his eyes for a moment. He squeezed the pommel of his great sword so fiercely that his knuckles mottled white and red.

"Lady Tenoctris," Carus resumed, looking down at her with an utterly humorless smile, "I would do, *will* do, everything I can to preserve the kingdom until my descendent Garric returns to his rightful place. I will even take a wizard as my advisor and confidant, though I'd prefer to thrust my hand in the fire."

He released his sword hilt and worked the incipient cramp out of it, his grin this time an honest one if wry.

"But milady?" he resumed with an undertone of earnestness beneath the banter. "Please don't strain my determination again. I'd regret the reflex that took the head off your shoulders if you sent another of your spells at me when I wasn't expecting it."

To Sharina's surprise, Tenoctris offered a curtsy. "Your majesty," she said, "I'm an old woman who's spent much time with books and none until recently with men of war. I treated you as a question to be answered, not a person; I apologize for the disrespect. If it happens again, you have my leave to behead me."

Carus bellowed with laughter and stepped around the small table. Liane jumped, but not quickly enough; Carus caught her by the shoulders and lifted her out of the way with a cheerful lack of ceremony.

He offered Tenoctris his hands, palms up. "I watched through Garric's eyes ever since you came ashore in this age," he said. "I saw you"—he glanced around, including Liane and Sharina in his statement—"*all* of you save the kingdom when it would otherwise have gone down to a worse smash than in my day, for all Garric and I alone could have done to save it. I know your goodness; and more, I know you're necessary. But . . . by the Shepherd, milady, please don't startle me if you can avoid it. Eh?"

Tenoctris laid her delicate hands on those Carus now wore: large and long-fingered, with calluses on the right palm from Garric's sword practice. "Done," she said.

"Your highness?" said Liane, her voice calm but her expression wholly unreadable. "Why would the Intercessor of Laut have wished to remove Garric? Sandrakkan and Blaise might think they could rival Ornifal for the kingship, but surely not Laut."

Carus shrugged, then grinned broadly as he stepped away from Tenoctris. "He had some wizard reason, I'd suppose," he said. "Nothing that a man like me could fathom. But Liane, all of you: in the past you said, 'Garric' when you spoke to the fellow wearing this flesh, and 'your highness' only on formal occasions. When we're alone together, I'm just Carus. And you're Liane, Tenoctris, and Sharina. All right?"

"All right, Carus," Sharina said, and Tenoctris echoed, "Yes, yes, of course."

Liane nodded instead of speaking. Her expression remained guarded for a moment. At last she forced a smile, and said, "Yes, of course. I'm sorry, this has been a . . ."

Liane's mood broke in a trill of laughter. "I was going to say it was a shock to me," she said. "But not so great as it was to you, I realize. I'll be all right."

"Right, then, right," Carus said. He'd become less tense after blurting his real identity, but this was a man who preferred the open air to the inside of a building. "To business, then."

He looked at the women, grinning. He wasn't her brother, but Sharina found him as easy to trust as she did Garric and Cashel.

"The business is," Carus said, "that the kingdom needs Garric to hold it together. The Ornifal nobles will follow him—and the common people, they'd walk over a cliff if he told them to, the most of them."

"Ornifal isn't the Isles," Liane said, quietly, but speaking to hear the king's response.

"No, and it never will be," Carus said with enough edge to his tone to show that he knew he was being tested. "King Garric *will* rule the united—the reunited—kingdom, though—on my honor!"

He paused, relaxing his face into the smile of moments before. Nobody looking at Carus could doubt that this was an older man than the youth who'd worn the flesh only minutes before. "The rulers of the other islands won't bow to Garric yet, but even now they respect him enough to be careful. The way Lerdoc's using the Confederacy of the West for a stalking horse proves that. Not so, milady?"

Carus leaned across the small table. He'd have chucked Liane under the chin if she hadn't jerked back in amazement. Tenoctris watched the byplay with the mild interest she might have shown for finches fluttering about a sunflower.

Carus straightened, and continued, "So long as all but a few think Garric's hand is still on the reins of the kingdom, we'll have time—you'll have time, w-wiz . . . Tenoctris, that is. Time to bring him back in all truth."

"You can pass for my brother," Sharina said. "You *are* Garric, in body at least."

"Aye, and I've looked through Garric's eyes in the months since he began wearing this," Carus said. He waggled the medallion, then dropped it back beneath his tunics. "I have Garric's memories besides."

"You know everything Garric knew?" Sharina said.

"No," said Carus. "But I know everything he *remembered*. He's forgotten a lot of things, everybody does. But I'm not going to be tripped up because somebody greets me on the street and I don't know he's Cog or Varsel who had the goose that followed him into the tavern every evening at sundown. Where the problem's going to be, though . . ."

Carus grimaced. He touched the wall where painted birds perched on a painted trellis in the painted sunshine. He looked like a trapped cat again.

"You see," he went on softly, "it's not what Garric's done that'll trip me up, it's the things he'll be asked to do. I'll have to make the choices a king makes, handle usurpers in the kingdom and quarrels in the council. I've *been* king, ladies; friends, I mean."

He slammed his balled right fist into his left palm with a *crack!* like nearby lightning.

"Been king and failed at it!" Carus said. "I thought all virtue lay in quickness, but sometimes I should have waited; I flew hot when things happened that I should've let pass, the first time they happened anyhow."

He grinned, an expression as common to Carus' spirit as it was to Garric's face—but forced this time, almost tentative. "And I hated wizards the way some men hate spiders," Carus said. "Hated wizards and feared them, my friends, and so I let wizardry bring the kingdom down. I had no one to help me against the dangers that my sword couldn't cure."

Sharina put her hand on Tenoctris' shoulder. "You've a wizard to help you now—"

Tenoctris nodded crisply. "For what my help is worth," she said.

"It's been worth the kingdom's salvation in the past," Carus said. He touched his cheekbone with his finger. "As I've seen through these eyes."

"And I know my brother relied on Liane's advice regarding both the court and the kingdom," Sharina went on. "In addition to what the royal council suggested."

"Liane's advice and your own," Carus said. "Yes, I know that, and I'm relying on you to help me as well. But your first business, friend Tenoctris, must be to retrieve Garric so that I can go back to being only another of the prince's advisors."

He shook his head ruefully, and added, "Echeus isn't the first man whose head I took off in anger when he might better have lived to answer some questions. I regret that stroke, for all that I wish somebody'd taken him out of this world a few hours earlier and saved me trouble."

Tenoctris stood. "I think the Intercessor will give me some idea of what he was about," she said. "His brain's still fresh, you see. If I may be excused, ah, Carus?"

The ancient king winced as though the reference to necromancy had been a knife in his stomach. "Yes, milady, do what you must do," he said. "So long as I don't have to watch—"

His face hardened. "Though I'd do that if I must," he said. "For the kingdom's sake, even that."

"There'll be no need," Tenoctris said as she started for the door. "Though perhaps Ilna will help me?"

She made the words a question. Carus nodded. He was neither smiling nor grim but . . . *something*. "Yes," he said, "and I've business with her Master Chalcus next. Pray get Ilna to help. And whoever else you wish—that has the stomach for it!"

Sharina and Liane rose to go out with Tenoctris. Carus raised a finger for attention. "Sharina?" he said. "I'd like you to stay during my interview with Chalcus. I think . . . it will be a more quiet affair, perhaps, with a young woman present."

Sharina smiled. "Yes," she said as she settled back on the ivory stool. "I can see that it might be."

Liane was fiddling with a latch of her travelling desk so that she had an excuse not to meet Carus' eyes. She said, "Ah . . . your, that is *Carus*, you said that you watched everything that Garric . . . ?"

"If I said that," Carus said, "then I lied, milady. Anything that may have passed between you and Prince Garric privately remains private. And you'll hear no other story from these lips though I die for it."

With a great laugh, he added, "Dying's a matter I've experience with too, you'll remember," he said. "And in the end, I proved better at it than I did at kingship."

Still laughing, he escorted Liane and Tenoctris to the door, one on either arm.

*   *   *

The morning sun was so low behind Cashel that the island shadowed the reef on which Tilphosa's ship had broken up. The wind had dropped still further; foam outlined the rocks, but there was no high-dashing spray as he'd seen at the height of the storm.

Barca's Hamlet was on the east coast of Haft. Until a few months ago, it wouldn't have crossed Cashel's mind that you could look at the sea and not be looking east.

"Master Cashel?" Tilphosa said. "What are we going to do now?"

Cashel turned, frowning. It was a good question, one he'd been turning over in the back of his mind, but he didn't see why the girl seated on a lava block would be asking him.

"What's your wizard say?" he said. He frowned still deeper. Personally, he wouldn't trust Captain Mounix's judgment much farther than he would that of sottish Kellard or-Same back in the borough, but Tilphosa had boarded the fellow's ship. Maybe she felt otherwise. "Or the captain, I suppose."

"Metra's doing an incantation," Tilphosa said, gesturing toward a stand of palms where a piece of salvaged sailcloth was rigged as a screen. A puff of orange smoke rose above the fabric and dissipated in the breeze. "She wants to learn whether our wreck was chance or if Echea struck at us from beyond the grave."

She didn't mention Mounix; her opinion of the captain must be pretty close to Cashel's own.

"That big snake wasn't a common thing," Cashel said, looking seaward again. The water shimmered like jewels now that the sun had risen farther. "Not where I come from, anyway."

Tilphosa shrugged. "In these times it could have been chance," she said. "The forces that turn the cosmos are peaking, you see. That's why I'm being sent to wed Prince Thalemos now and bring about the return of the Mistress to rule the world . . . but Chaos has power also, and creatures of Chaos can be met anywhere."

Cashel noticed the matter-of-fact way Tilphosa discussed wizardry and the powers wizards controlled or tried to control. She sounded like a peasant discussing the risk of a bad winter: potentially disastrous, but nothing unnatural in her scheme of things.

About two double handsful of the crew had survived the wreck. They were combing the black-sand beach sullenly, dragging the more interesting bits of flotsam above the tide line to where tree ferns grew among lobelias and geraniums the size of shrubs.

When the sailors looked toward the screen around the wizard, they scowled. Occasionally Cashel caught them looking at him and Tilphosa with much the same expression—until his eye fell on them.

Cashel smiled. He guessed he'd be doing something wrong if this lot liked him.

Captain Mounix was examining the ship's dinghy, still keel up on the beach. With him were two of his particular cronies: a tall but cadaverous fellow named Costas, and a runt with a fringe of red hair who went by "Hook," probably because he'd lost the outer three fingers from his left hand.

Cashel had done enough woodworking that he might have had something useful to say about the dinghy's condition, but he didn't suppose the captain wanted his company any more than Cashel wanted the captain's. Joining the beachcombers was an even less appealing prospect.

"I guess I'll take a look around the island," Cashel said. "I'd like to find a stream or a spring, anyway."

Rain had pooled in a basin of rock just above the tide line. Cashel had drunk from it—Tilphosa was more squeamish than thirsty, at least while the darkness was still cool—but found the water brackish from windblown spray. The lush vegetation inland meant there was likely better available.

"Ah . . ." Cashel added, balancing his quarterstaff as he thought. He'd just as soon not leave the girl alone with these sailors—or with her wizard Metra, if it came to that. "Would you like to come?"

Cashel felt responsible for Tilphosa the way he'd feel for anybody who needed the sort of help he could give them. Folks in the borough stuck together, pretty much. A peasant's life was hard enough even when neighbor helped neighbor.

Tilphosa nodded curtly. "Yes," she said. "When I look at the sea, I remember the dragon coming toward us. Metra's wizardry kept it from pulling the ship under, but it drove us onto the rocks. I thought I was going to drown."

She flashed Cashel an embarrassed grin.

"You weren't going to drown," Cashel muttered. He looked at the captain, then toward the screen around the wizard and her dealings. Smoke rose from the enclosure again, this time a soft magenta. "Right, the ground rises enough to be worth following. We can always find our way back by striking for the shore."

He started into the tree ferns—a mistake. It was easy to push through the shoulder-high fronds, but they hid from sight the frequent head-sized chunks of lava littering the ground. The second time Cashel tripped, he shifted their route into the mixture of gnarled shrubs. There were woody-stemmed varieties of geraniums, violets, and even buttercups.

Cashel had taken to wearing sturdy sandals to walk the stone pavements of Valles. They came in handy here; the soil, though obviously rich, was thickly sown with sharp-edged pebbles from the same volcanic rock that the sea had ground to sand to form the beach.

"Who's this Echea you're worried about?" Cashel asked. He was curious; and besides, it was better for the girl to talk than brood. Because he was using his staff to hold vegetation aside, Tilphosa could follow closely without being slapped by stems that he'd released.

"A great wizard," Tilphosa said. "An enemy of the Mistress. She cut a jewel—or two jewels, rather. Their patterns combined will bring back the Mistress."

Cashel slipped through a gap between the stems of a tree begonia. Another man, certainly another man Cashel's size, would have needed an axe to hack through the tangles. Cashel got along well with wood. He'd always been able to judge the grain of the branch under his shaping knife or where he should cut to drop a tree in a particular line. The same talent helped him here.

In his mind he moved around the girl's words the way he'd handle chunks of fieldstone for a wall. Not every piece would fit in every place, but generally if you shifted slabs this way and that, you'd come up with something that looked as tight as mason's work.

A lot of times Cashel could also puzzle through a statement that didn't make sense when he first heard it. This wasn't one of those times.

He said, "If Echea was against your Mistress—"

When he first met her, Cashel had thought Tilphosa meant "the Mistress" the way Sharina would say "the Lady": the Queen of Heaven whose mate was the Shepherd. He wasn't sure of that anymore.

"—then why did she make jewels that will, ah, help her?"

He could hear water, but in forest like this you couldn't get any direction from sound. The trunks twisted the gurgling around till it could've come from anywhere. Still, if he hadn't heard it before and he did now, then they were likely getting closer.

"The pattern only exists once in all eternity," Tilphosa explained. "By forming it and then hiding the pieces, Echea keeps the Mistress from returning."

Climbing through this undergrowth was hard work for her, even with Cashel choosing the path and holding aside the big stems. After each few words, Tilphosa whooshed out a breath and drew in a fresh one before continuing.

"But when Thalemos and I marry, our rings will hold the two jewels. The Mistress will reenter the world!"

"Ah," said Cashel. He didn't believe that or disbelieve it. The Great Gods didn't have much to do with the world Cashel lived in. "I guess you've got books that tell you this?"

They'd reached a beech tree whose base was farther across than Cashel's own height. The trunk had split a generation ago; half had fallen, but the remainder was sprouting new growth.

Wings the length of a child's arm clattered as creatures roosting in the upper branches launched themselves into the sky. The girl cried out, but the fliers were going the other way. They weren't birds, and peering through the small leaves, Cashel wasn't sure they were bats either.

"Let's hold here for a bit," Cashel said, not that he was winded. Tilphosa hadn't complained, but he saw now that the soles of her high-laced shoes were thin suede. They were meant for carpeting, not this pebble-strewn soil.

She nodded gratefully, sinking onto the fallen half of the trunk to take the weight off her feet. The spongy, mushroom-covered wood couldn't do much to harm tunics that had come through a shipwreck.

"The Mistress sends dreams to her worshippers," Tilphosa said when she'd gotten her breath. "The priests see them most clearly, of course, but we all can feel her will. I *know* the truth of what I've said, because I've felt it myself."

"Ah," Cashel said, nodding. He didn't have anything to say about that. He'd learned young that you'd do better to argue with a sheep than with somebody who knows the Truth.

Another stand of ferns nearly concealed a limestone out-crop. He'd thought shadows thrown by the fronds caused the faint shimmer on the stone. Now, maybe because he was sitting still and looking in any direction except Til-phosa's face, Cashel saw that the water he'd been looking for was seeping between rock layers.

"We've found—" he said, rising from the log.

"Cashel, what's that?" the girl asked sharply. Then she said, "That's gold!"

She pointed to a bed of plants with sword-shaped leaves and feathery crimson flowers. Twisted among their thin stems was a tracery of metal—gold, just as Tilphosa had said.

The water could wait. Cashel checked his quarterstaff with his right, then his left hand, reflexively making sure that the shaft hadn't gotten splinters or sticky patches while helping him through the foliage. He moved forward, holding the staff slantwise before him.

"Are these pipes?" Tilphosa said. "No, they can't be—it's just a framework, isn't it?"

"I don't know what it is," Cashel said. "What it was."

The forest's trunks and branches wove through a fabric of tubes ranging from thumb-sized to as thin as Sharina's blond hairs. Cashel pushed into the vegetation with careful deliberation, measuring the length of the thing: a handful of double paces, four times as long as Cashel was tall. The tubes connected several pods of the same shining metal. The largest of them was the size of a small canoe, smooth-skinned and featureless.

The thing had hit the ground crushingly hard. The im-pact wrapped the nearer end around the outcrop, even gouging the rock in a few places. The top and back had flexed forward on their own inertia, warping the structure out of its original spindle shape.

Cashel looked up. It'd fallen here; fallen from *where*,

he couldn't guess. Waves could pick a boat up and fling it inland. Or again . . .

Whatever the cause, it had happened a very long time ago.

"I guess it could be a frame," Cashel said aloud. "Gold lasts when other things rot away or rust."

Tilphosa had followed Cashel along the crumpled tracery. With a careful lack of emotion, she said, "Then it would be quite old."

With the end of his staff, Cashel tapped a tube broken at the impact. His ferrule woke a musical chime from the gold. "See the root?" he said.

"Oh," said the girl. "Of course."

Another fallen beech, larger even than the half-ruined one, had sent surface roots over the tube. In human terms the life span of a tree like that would be measured by generations.

Cashel looked again at the tube and frowned. His iron butt cap hadn't scratched the metal. As soft as gold was . . .

He knelt and drew his knife from its wooden sheath. It had been made with ram's horn scales and a straight, single-edged blade by Akhita the Smith, travelling through the borough on his circuit; Barca's Hamlet was too small to support a resident blacksmith.

Akhita had forged the blade from the same iron he used to shoe horses, but he'd hardened it with a fast quench. It wasn't fancy, but it did well for digging a stone from an ox's hoof, slicing bread at dinner, and all the scores of other tasks a peasant needed a knife for.

The edge should have notched gold. It didn't; not this gold.

"Let's get back to the others," Cashel said, straightening. He put his knife away so he had both hands for his quarterstaff. He didn't think of a knife as a weapon; not that he needed a weapon here, not for any reasons he could point to. "We'll tell them about the water."

And they'd learn about the gold, too; but Cashel wasn't sure he'd mention that.

He and Tilphosa started back the way they'd come, moving faster from familiarity with the route and because they knew where they were going. Both of them wanted to be away from whatever it was that had smashed up there on the knoll.

"In ancient times, there were beings whose ships flew through the air," Tilphosa said. "The scriptures say."

"I wouldn't know about that," Cashel said grimly. He wondered what scriptures she meant, but he didn't ask. "I can't read."

He led on the descent as he had on the climb: if the girl slipped, he was there to catch her . . . and if he slipped, well, she wasn't in the way to get hurt.

"Cashel?" she said. "Are you sure we're going the right direction?"

"We're a little to the side of how we came up," he explained. "The clay here doesn't have so many chunks of lava in it to trip over. We'll come out on the other side of the point south of where we started, but we can walk along the beach to get back."

Through the last screen of tree ferns, Cashel heard several men shouting. One called, "Captain Mounix! Everybody! Get over here now!"

"What's the matter?" Tilphosa said in a tense, controlled voice at Cashel's shoulder.

"Stay close," he muttered. He held his staff crossways before him and crushed down the feathery fronds as he stepped onto the sand.

Three sailors stood around a fourth figure sprawled at the tide line. More crewmen were clambering over the rocky spine of the headland to join them; the captain was among the newcomers.

"What is it?" Mounix called. "Sister take you if you're just shouting to exercise your lungs!"

He carried a short, curve-bladed sword unsheathed. Costas accompanied him with a bow, while Hook had a cudgel made from a length of spar.

"Well, look for yourself then!" snarled the sailor.

A quick glance showed Cashel all he needed to see of the torn corpse. It'd been a girl Tilphosa's age or thereabouts before something clawed her chest open and devoured her heart and lungs.

Tilphosa gasped but didn't scream. She had a right to scream. "That's my maid Matone!" she said. "I thought she'd drowned."

"No," said Cashel. The girl had been alive when she was ripped open; otherwise, there wouldn't have been so much blood. It must have happened during the night, though: the carrion was already starting to smell.

"What did this?" Mounix bellowed. "What hellspawn lives on this accursed island?"

Cashel turned to face the wall of vegetation. Unless they were luckier than he expected, they were going to learn the answer to the captain's question the hard way.

Chapter Five

Fingers closed on the pattern Ilna was knotting. She jerked back, confused by the contact and not really aware of her immediate surroundings.

The fingers were stronger than her own. They snatched the cords from her, crumpling the half-done curse . . . for curse it was, certain condemnation to the bleakest levels of Hell for the victim and for Ilna herself.

Her mind opened onto present existence. Chalcus faced her, holding her eyes as his fingers picked apart her knots with a seaman's skill.

"Don't do this thing, dear one," Chalcus said calmly.

With the fury of a hornet, Ilna shouted, "Do you wish to spend forever with crows pecking your liver, little man! Do you doubt I can do *that*?"

"I well know what you're capable of doing; to me or to any man, dear heart," Chalcus said. He reduced the pattern to individual cords and stroked them alongside one another on his callused palm. "In good time you'll be able to do whatever you choose; but not just now. And not, I hope, in this way."

He tilted his hand and dropped the hank of cords back into hers.

Merota had joined them, still wearing the single thin tunic in which she took her lessons. Ilna frowned. *The girl knew better than to come out in public in such a scandalous state of undress!*

Ilna breathed deeply. Her legs were trembling; for a moment she wasn't sure the big muscles of her thighs would continue to hold her. Chalcus held out his left forearm for her to grab the way she would have gripped a railing. She took it and felt her body return to normal.

"You saw what he did to me," Ilna said, her eyes on the ground. Seeing that Merota had grounded her again in a world where duty constrained Ilna os-Kenset more straitly than ever chains did a prisoner. It was a safe world, a world she knew well enough to feel comfortable in. There was nothing Ilna feared more than herself and the things she might do if unconfined.

And there was nothing she regretted more than the things she *had* done when she put her skills at evil's service and was governed only by anger and her own cold logic.

"I heard him," said Chalcus. "I've left men lying in their

guts for less, dear one. But not you, not that way."

"I'm sorry," Ilna whispered. "I was so angry that I wasn't . . ."

She laughed, surprising herself but not—from his expression—Chalcus. "I was so angry that I *was* myself," she corrected herself. "And that's a thing I try not to be very often."

Ilna reached toward the silent Merota and, holding the girl, hugged Chalcus as well. There was as little give to his flesh as there was to a brick wall. Merota squeezed back fiercely.

They stepped apart. Chalcus eyed the small building now ringed by Blood Eagles, the conference room into which Garric had disappeared with the three women. The other women.

"Dearest . . . ?" he said in a bantering tone. At any other time Ilna would have snapped at him for the word, but not now. "Don't ever use your art to kill someone you care for. Use that little knife you carry, if you must. Or better—"

He grinned at her. There was no expression at all in his gray eyes.

"—use me. It's a thing I've a talent for."

The crowd of civilians across the watercourse was beginning to break up into lesser groupings. Each pair or handful chattered among itself as people went off to tell others about the wonders they'd witnessed—and likely, from Ilna's experience of human beings, telling about many things they *hadn't* witnessed.

Ilna brushed the thought aside, angry at herself for what she'd tried to do. "No," she said. "I'm not so great a fool as that; at least when my friends see to it that I've time to think. Garric's a clever man and a wise one. He'll have had a good reason for whatever he chose to do."

"Ilna?" Merota said, perfectly the lady now despite her garb and hair tousled from running. "You saw Garric being threatened, and now he's acting funny. Couldn't that be because of the danger you saw?"

Ilna looked at the girl coolly. "You were listening to me and Chalcus when you should have been about your lessons," she said. She paused, then continued, "And a good thing, too, since you've obviously got better sense than I do."

Her eyes met those of Chalcus again. "You both do," she said.

"Do you care to wait here, Mistress Ilna," Chalcus said. "Or shall we—"

The door of the conference room opened. Tenoctris shuffled out, looked across the narrow stream, and said, "Ilna? Would you help me with a task, please? It may help us find your brother."

"Of course," said Ilna, hiking up her tunic skirts and jumping the channel. Spectators still in the neighborhood watched with renewed interest.

Garric came out of the building with Liane on his arm. Liane stepped away, glancing toward Ilna. Ilna froze where she'd landed.

Garric acknowledged Ilna with a nod, then put his fists on his hips and stood arms akimbo.

"Master Chalcus?" he called. "Will you talk with me now? Liane can take care of Lady Merota, for neither our business nor that of Tenoctris and Mistress Ilna is anything they should trouble themselves with."

Chalcus looked at Merota. "Go on, Chalcus!" the girl said. "Liane and I will sit in the bower there"—she nodded to the ivy-covered frame of withies near the terrace of fountains—"and discuss Celondre's poetry."

She giggled, suddenly a child again. "Or something."

Ilna gave the sailor a brief lift of her chin in assent. She didn't know what was going on, but that wasn't a new experience for her.

"I'll be right glad to join you, prince," said Chalcus,

hopping the stream without seeming to prepare for the leap. "Indeed, I think we've matters to discuss."

He sauntered toward Garric, grinning broadly when he saw the Blood Eagles tense at his approach. The officer in command leaned toward Garric, who waved him away with a curt syllable. Garric held the conference room door for Chalcus, then entered behind him and closed it.

Ilna sighed. Part of her wanted to squat here on the turf and see what her patterns told her, but no doubt she'd learn in good time. For now she'd help Tenoctris.

She smiled coldly. It was her duty, after all.

Tint crept up to the fallen structure, pausing midway to turn and stroke Garric nervously. He grimaced but didn't let reflex jerk him back in disgust. The beastgirl had been frightened even before the snake; she was proceeding now only because Garric demanded that she do so. It wasn't much to ask that Garric let her take a little reassurance in his presence.

The palms and jagged-leafed philodendrons which shaded the boggy clearing were so motionless in the still air that Garric had the feeling he'd stepped through the frame of a painting rather than being part of a real setting. There was a chittering and sudden swift motion behind him; his heart leaped. A flock of bright yellow finches burst through the foliage and wheeled away again as suddenly.

"Stone and ring here, Gar," Tint said, pointing to a corner of the ruin. "Under wall. You dig from side, not touch mushrooms."

She hadn't started at all when the birds fluttered past. They were harmless, after all. . . .

Garric smiled faintly and patted Tint's shoulder; she licked his hand. That was disconcerting, but it no longer irritated him.

He looked at the fallen wall. The orange puffballs grew only on the stones, bright blotches that punctuated the mosses and the original gray surface. If the builders had buried a statue as part of a foundation course to keep the new structure from sinking into the bog, Garric ought to be able to reach it by tunneling into the soft soil.

If it was there. And if it had the ring.

"Tint," Garric said, "how do you know the statue you smell is the one that has the ring?"

The beastgirl shrugged. "Men find stone feet," she said, gesturing back the way she'd brought Garric. "Writing on stone. Vascay say, 'Find rest of statue.' Stone under there smell same as stone feet."

She scratched the middle of her back absently, a multijointed motion that startled Garric almost as much as the finches had. "Gold with stone," Tint added. "Maybe ring, maybe not ring."

Garric probed the ground with his finger. Water gleamed in low spots in the soil, drowning even the moss. He didn't see how Tint could actually *smell* objects through that, let alone discriminate between particular veins of marble and types of metal.

But it was easier to believe that than to imagine the beastgirl either wanting to lie to him or having enough intelligence to carry it off. "Then I'll dig," Garric said.

It struck him suddenly that he had no tools or clothing whatever. Granted the ground was soft . . .

Garric looked around, chose a palm sapling whose trunk was only two fingers broad, and pulled it upward. It came easily, but the mat of surface roots at the end would make a better broom than a digging implement. Maybe he could chop or crush the staff into some sort of point?

"Tint," he said, "do you see a rock with a sharp edge? I want to cut the roots off this tree."

Instead of answering, Tint took the sapling and put the end in her mouth; her lips curled back. The beastgirl's eyeteeth would have shamed any dog Garric had seen, but now he realized that her long jaw held the molars of a horse besides.

She crunched down hard, twisted the stem with her hands, and spat out a wad of fibers. "Tint fix," she said proudly as she handed back the staff.

"Thank you, Tint," Garric said. He bent to his task, thrusting his pole into the soil at a flat angle and scooping it aside. His new body—Gar's body—was stronger than Garric's own had been when he was in top shape at the end of harvest and threshing.

But he wasn't stronger than Tint, for all that the beast-girl weighed barely half what he did. Gar's memories were too chaotic to tell Garric how he and Tint had met. It seemed that the bandit gang had gathered them up separately, but Garric wasn't sure the brain-damaged youth could have survived without Tint's sharper senses and clear, if limited, intellect.

The palm trunk was too flexible to be a perfect dibble, but the ground was so soft that Garric made good headway nonetheless. The end of the pole almost immediately rapped stone beneath the lowest visible layer. He kept prodding inward and thrusting the spoil sideways. Tint, though she wouldn't help dig, scooped the muck out of his way with her long hands.

This piece of the foundation was a statue's torso, all right. The raised right arm was now broken off. The left rested on the figure's waist. When Garric saw the hand, he set the pole aside and rubbed the marble clear with a philodendron leaf.

The fourth finger had been carved in the round; it was broken at the first joint. On the stub, under a layer of mud and corroded stone, was a gold ring set with a small sapphire. Garric twisted it free without difficulty.

He sloshed off the dirt in a puddle, then rubbed off the rest of the lime crust with his thumb before holding the ring up to a shaft of light. Tint leaned against him, trembling and making little clicking noises with her teeth. She didn't seem to be frightened, just excited.

Garric tried the simple band on his little finger; it would have been loose, but not very loose. The jewel, though small, had been faceted with great skill.

"I wonder who the fellow was," he said. The statue's face was too worn to have features; without the carven sword belt, Garric wouldn't even have been sure the subject was male.

"Thalemos," said Tint unexpectedly.

Garric looked at her in surprise. She edged sideways, afraid he was going to hit her. "Gar?" she said nervously.

"I'm just curious how you know who he was," Garric said. The name wasn't one he remembered hearing before. "I'm not angry, Tint."

He hoped the sudden hardness of his lips didn't frighten the beastgirl further. Her reaction reminded him of the life she'd lived with the bandit gang . . . and brought back some of Gar's memories as well.

Tint crouched close again, rubbing Garric with her hands and neck. "Vascay see stone feet by house," she explained. "Rub stone with finger, then shout, 'Thalemos! Find rest of statue!' Men dig around house, but no smell stone. Tint smell stone!"

Sure, the bandits had found the base of the statue carved with the name of the subject portrayed. They'd have looked nearby and even dug in the ground, but even if they'd guessed that later comers had carried the torso off they couldn't possibly have found it here under a later ruin.

She looked up at Garric. "Gar like Tint?" she said.

"I like you very much, Tint," Garric said. "Without you, we wouldn't ever have found the ring."

He patted her shoulder while he thought. "I guess," he said, "we need to find Master Vascay. To meet Master

Vascay, though he may not think so at first."

Garric considered carrying the ring on his finger, but he decided not to. It wasn't so much that the ring gave him a bad feeling, but there *was* something odd about it. Garric didn't understand a lot of what had been happening; he didn't care to increase his contact with strangeness.

Besides, he'd never worn jewelry, either as peasant or as prince. Holding the ring between his left thumb and forefinger, Garric said, "You'll have to lead me, Tint. I don't know the way."

The beastgirl twisted her head up and back to look at Garric in concern. "It's all right," he said reassuringly. "I'm fine, Tint. I just don't know some of the things I used to know before I fell in the water."

Tint dropped onto all fours, her normal travelling position. As she did so, a tall man with his beard bound into three tails stepped through the palm thicket. He wore a leathern jackshirt studded with rivets for additional protection; from his bandolier hung three daggers and a long, curved sword.

Tint hunched and bared her teeth. Gar's memory gave the man a name: Ceto. He was a swaggerer who thought himself a handsome fellow despite a scarred cheek and the two toes missing from the left foot visible through his hobnailed sandals.

Ceto was the sort of man you sometimes met among the bodyguards whom merchants brought to Barca's Hamlet for the Sheep Fair. Garric smiled with one side of his mouth. He'd met the type, and he'd occasionally had to throw one out of the inn. He could do something similar with Ceto if he had to.

"What are you monkeys doing here?" Ceto demanded. He sounded angry, but angry the way you'd be to find a dog sniffing the stewpot. "You're supposed to be foraging! Heigh yourselves up those nut trees by the camp!"

"We're headed back to the camp, Ceto," Garric said,

speaking with the insouciant precision of an educated man dealing with an inferior. "We have something to show Vascay."

Light winked from the sapphire. Ceto, striding toward Garric and Tint, noticed the ring and stared. He hadn't listened to Garric, let alone noticed a change from Gar's demeanor.

"What do you have there?" he demanded. "By the Sister! Let me have that!"

"I think it'll be safe with—" Garric said. Ceto hit him in the pit of the stomach.

Garric doubled up, his lungs paralyzed and his brain screaming for air. All he could hear was Tint's terrified chirps and the white roar of pain.

Ceto kicked him in the head with a hobnailed foot. White drained to blackness, taking Garric's mind with it.

Cashel pushed through a lobelia thicket, thrusting his staff into the clay of slope behind him for a brace; Tilphosa clung to his sash as she'd done as they came through the surf. The spring and the twisted framework were as they'd left them an hour earlier.

"We're there," Cashel said, stepping aside so that Metra and Captain Mounix could make their way to the top, panting. Cashel might have offered them the alternative of the gentler slope where the lava nodules complicated the footing, but he'd decided that he didn't care about their opinion. It was enough that he'd agreed to guide them back here.

Tilphosa had come along without comment. She'd taken off her red-leather slippers; that was another reason Cashel had chosen the less stony route.

"May the Lady bless my eyes!" Mounix cried. "That's gold, or I'm a virgin!"

He started forward. Metra cried, "Wait! Let me examine it before you tear it apart."

Mounix ignored her. Cashel caught the neck of the captain's tunic and pulled him back with a startled grunt. Costas, laboring along well to the rear, cried, "What is it? Where's the gold?"

"Let the wizard work her spell," Cashel said quietly to the captain's furious scowl. "Then you can do what you please, so far as I'm concerned."

Tilphosa lifted her chin in agreement. "I don't want anything from this island," she said. "It's a place of ill omen."

"You don't have to tell me about ill omen," Mounix growled. He relaxed; Cashel let go of his tunic. "I saw what happened to your maid, didn't I?"

He'd sheathed his curved sword because he needed both hands for the climb; he drew it again now. Cashel had met swordsmen. Mounix wasn't one.

Costas joined them, saying nothing. He nocked one of his three arrows in the waxed string of his bow.

Metra sat on the nose of the outcrop where only lichen grew. The crumpled golden framework lay before and beside her. Instead of scraping figures onto the rock, she took out a square of white silk embroidered with symbols in red. She began to murmur an incantation, her ruddy copper athame dipping and rising above each syllable in turn.

Mounix grimaced and turned his back. "Sister take all this!" he muttered. "But if she can send whatever it was that ate the girl back to the Underworld, she can talk to a thousand demons for all I care."

"When we get off this island," Cashel said, "it won't matter what it is that lives here. The boat looked like it came through the storm pretty well. Can't we leave in it?"

"The dinghy, you mean?" Mounix said with a sneer of disgust. "Not like it is now, not if we want to get everybody aboard and take food and water for them. I guess that doesn't matter to you, since you're not with us, right?"

"We're all strangers here," said Cashel. "I figured we'd stick together for the time being."

"Master Cashel will accompany me, captain," Tilphosa said coldly. "Will you be building another ship, then?"

Light—red wizardlight—shimmered in the thicket where the framework lay. Metra raised her voice enough that the others could hear, ". . . *iorbeth neuthi* . . ."

When Mounix heard the words of power, he snarled, "Sister take her!" under his breath. He was one of the people who lost all their courage in the face of wizardry; though it didn't seem to Cashel that the captain was particularly brave on a good day.

Costas didn't seem to be bothered. "It's easier than that," he said. "We'll just build up the gunnels of the dinghy so that we can load her deeper. We've got enough timbers salvaged from the wreck we can do that easy. Right, captain?"

"Yeah, we can do that," Mounix said. "I've got the crew working on it now. That's why I left Hook behind, to get going on the job. He's the ship's carpenter."

The air in front of Metra squealed; the sound didn't come from the wizard's throat. Red light coalesced into something almost solid, the way butter forms in a churn.

Metra lowered the athame and slumped backward. She'd have fallen if Cashel hadn't reached out to support her; he carried the wizard back a double pace.

She'd managed to hold on to her athame, but Cashel bent to pick up the embroidered silk with two fingers of the hand holding his staff. He didn't much like Metra, but he'd so often helped Tenoctris that caring for a wizard exhausted from working her art had become second nature to him.

The rosy light expanded. Cashel couldn't judge its size; without any seeming change, what had been a globe became instead a hole into another place. A spindle-shaped object of ivory and mother-of-pearl floated on its side over a forest of giant horsetails and trees with limbs like green whips.

"Is that a ship?" Costas said, squinting at the vision. "What kind of a ship *is* that? It's flying!"

Captain Mounix glanced over his shoulder, then turned his head again with a look of thunderous misery. He sliced at a shrub with his sword. His blade cut into the wood, then sprang back.

"The Third Race was able to fly, according to Asterican scriptures," Tilphosa said quietly. She was composed: frightened but facing her fear.

Cashel didn't know who the Astericans were, let alone the Third Race. "Did they live around here?" he asked. Though he didn't really know where "here" was.

Metra had regained enough control of her limbs to stand without Cashel's help. She slid the athame under her sash. Cashel offered the silken document. She took it from him without thanks and folded the square into a tight bundle before replacing it in her sleeve.

Tilphosa looked at Cashel. "The world was very different then," she said. "According to scripture. The Isles didn't exist."

Cashel frowned, trying to imagine how the Isles could *not* exist. It was like hearing that there was no sky.

"The Third Race weren't men," Tilphosa added. "According to scripture."

The vessel's hull began to glow with soft pastels that weren't just the sheen of the mother-of-pearl. The ship rose straight up, then sailed toward the horizon at gathering speed. Though the evening air was warm, Cashel felt a chill along his spine.

The vision ended—or the window closed?—soundlessly. In its place was the brushwood thicket where incorruptible metal sparkled.

"How old is the boat you just showed us, Mistress Metra?" Cashel asked. He squatted down for a closer look at part of the framework sticking clear of the undergrowth. He didn't touch it.

"You couldn't understand," Metra said with a shrug. Turning to Mounix, she said, "Captain, you can do what you please now. I have no further use for this trash."

Tilphosa gave the priestess an appraising look; while not actively hostile, there was no affection in it either. To Cashel she said, "It would be very old, Cashel. If it was from the Third Race, it was older than we have words to describe. A year wasn't the same thing when the Third Race lived."

Mounix and his henchman were listening to the girl also. The captain spat, then said, "Let's get back to the shore. It's getting late, and I don't want to be caught around this thing in the dark."

"But how about the gold, captain?" Costas demanded. He rotated his arrow and held it against the bowstaff instead of ready for use. "Aren't we going to take it with us? Some, I mean."

Mounix started down the slope. "You do what you please, Costas," he said. "I don't want any part of that thing."

"I'll go in front of you like before," Cashel told the girl. Metra started to speak, then decided not to. Cashel guessed the wizard was going to ask him to help her as well, but she figured he'd give her a short answer because of the way she'd been acting toward him.

Cashel smiled faintly. Sure, he'd help Metra the same as he'd help most anybody. He couldn't change how other people were, but he didn't let them change how he behaved either.

Mounix was moving faster than Cashel cared to do on this slope. There was some reason—it *would* be dark soon; dawn and nightfall were more sudden in this place than Cashel was used to. Cashel guessed the captain was afraid of more than darkness, though.

On the outcrop, metal chimed as Costas tried to break off pieces of the gold. He'd have his work cut out for him: the tubes were hard enough that iron didn't scratch them and so tough that mostly they'd bent instead of breaking when the boat smashed into the rocks.

"Metra?" Tilphosa said. She spoke without turning her head but in a clear tone so that the woman following could hear. "What did your dreams tell you? Does the wreckage up there have anything to do with why we wrecked on this island?"

Cashel caught several geranium stems in his left hand. "Watch this," he warned those behind him. "The clay's slick here."

The soil anchored roots solidly, though. Even Cashel's weight with Tilphosa's added hadn't threatened to pull out any of the bushes he'd used for support on the way up.

"Captain?" Costas called from some distance above them. "I'm coming, captain. Which way are you?"

Mounix didn't answer; he might not even have heard. "We've gone this way, Costas!" Cashel shouted. He knew what it was like to be alone in a strange place . . . and this island was stranger than most.

"Metra?" Tilphosa repeated more sharply.

Metra spoke in a tired murmur. Tilphosa said, "I can't hear you. Please speak up."

It struck Cashel that the girl was—or anyway felt she was—of a higher station than the wizard. Cashel had spent most of his life as a poor orphan, so for the most part he'd been on the wrong side of that division.

It was kind of interesting to see how it worked from the top, so to speak. He hadn't told a stranger that he was Tilphosa's guardian; and maybe by now Metra was wishing she hadn't done that either.

"This island, this *place*," Metra said, "has always been a focus for Chaos. When the powers that work the cosmos rise, as they're rising now, the tendency toward . . . bad luck, call it, grows stronger. We were caught by that, and so was the vessel that crashed on the peak. But at an earlier time."

A lot earlier. Sharina would understand it better, though Cashel didn't guess it made much real difference. He wished Sharina was here, though.

He could hear men's voices ahead of them, and the slope was leveling out. "We're getting close," he said. He turned his head, and repeated loudly, "We've reached the shore, Costas!"

Tilphosa let go of Cashel's belt; they walked together through the palms fringing the sand. Captain Mounix stood with half a dozen of his crew, talking in angry frustration. Cashel heard him say, "By the Lady, Hook! If you don't have the dinghy ready to take us all away before tomorrow midday, I'll take her with enough men to work her and leave you here!"

Sunset lighted the beach, but the inland jungle was jet-black save for orange and pink tinges to the topmost foliage.

"Costas!" Cashel called. "This way!"

A terrible scream split the night—and stopped. Mounix fumbled as he tried to draw his sword. Several of the sailors ran toward the dinghy, then paused uncertainly.

Cashel stepped toward the forest. "No, Cashel!" Tilphosa said.

He halted. She was right. In the darkness he couldn't have found where the scream came from.

And from the way it had broken off, there wasn't a thing anybody could do for Costas now anyway.

Sharina watched past Carus' right shoulder as Ilna's close-coupled friend swaggered toward the conference room with a grin for the Blood Eagles. She murmured, "Will you be wearing your sword when you interview him, Carus?"

The king—and Sharina didn't know how anyone could mistake the face for her brother's, for all that the physical features were the same—glanced at her and smiled minutely. "I'd insult him if I took it off, girl," he said. "That one isn't afraid of my sword—or my temper, either one. Though I think he respects them both."

He faced Chalcus again. Out of the corner of his mouth, he added, "But I'll keep my temper on a checkrein; and you'll be here to tell me if I'm out of line, will you not?"

"Yes," said Sharina. She grinned. "Of course."

The guard officer snapped a command; two of his men stepped shoulder to shoulder across Chalcus' path.

"Your dagger, please, sir!" said the officer loudly, his back stiff, and turned to Carus. He pointed to the weapon in Chalcus' sash.

Carus frowned. "Captain Deghan—" he began.

"Your majesty, on my *oath* I won't let him by while he carries that blade!" the guard officer said.

Chalcus looked past the two Blood Eagles. He cocked an eyebrow at Carus, then handed his sheathed dagger to the officer without deigning to look at him.

"Shall I give him my belt as well, my brave lad?" he asked Carus. "Many a man's been throttled with a leather strap, you know."

"I'll take the knife, Captain Deghan," Carus said. He held out his left hand, palm upward.

Deghan—young for a captain in the Blood Eagles, in his early twenties—turned, trying to control the emotions skating across his face. "Yes, your majesty," he said; all he could say, on his oath.

He placed the curved weapon in Carus' hand. The sheath and hilt were both tin, decorated in black niello with symbols that looked like writing—though not in a script that Sharina recognized.

"Sorry for the rigmarole, Master Chalcus," Carus said, gesturing the sailor into the conference room. Sharina stepped back to let the men enter. "There's wine on the sideboard, and I suppose we can find food if you need it."

He drew the hilt and sheath a finger's breadth apart to look at the steel, then clicked the blade home. He said, "A nice piece, though I don't fancy curved blades myself," and gave the weapon back to Chalcus. Nodding to Captain Deghan, Carus closed himself in with Sharina and the sailor.

"You've a good pack of hounds there," Chalcus said, tossing his head slightly to indicate the black-armored guards on the other side of the door. He slid the sheath into the folds of his sash and walked to the sideboard.

"Aye," said Carus, walking to the other side of the table. "But sometimes I wonder which of us serves the other."

Chalcus laughed, an infectious sound that made Sharina realize how little laughter there was in the palace. Little of it in the presence of great ladies like the Princess Sharina, at any rate.

"Oh, I don't think there's really much doubt, is there?" Chalcus said. "When it matters to you."

Two carafes of etched glass stood on the sideboard, one full of deep red wine and the other with a lemon-colored fluid. A mixing bowl, drinking cups, and a larger vat of water with a ladle—all of the same pattern as the carafes—were ranged tastefully behind them.

Chalcus raised the red wine and said, watching Carus, "And this is such a vintage as the poets sing of, is it not? Sunlight pressed from grapes, a nectar fit for the Lady to offer the Shepherd in their bower?"

Carus shrugged. "I suppose," he said. "You'd have to ask somebody who cared."

"And if I cared, I would," Chalcus said agreeably. He swigged from the mouth of the carafe to make his point, then set it down on the sideboard again. "So if we're not to talk of wine, what is it that you brought me here to discuss, then?"

Carus put his palms on the table and leaned his weight onto them. "Would you care to go to Tisamur, Master Chalcus?" he asked; his tone challenging, though playful rather than hostile. "Lady Merota has wide holdings there, granted her by the crown to replace the wealth she lost when her parents were murdered."

Chalcus raised an eyebrow.

Carus grinned. "No, she doesn't know it yet," he said. "But it's true regardless . . . will be true as soon as I've talked to Royhas, anyway. You and Mistress Ilna would pass unnoticed travelling as the child's servants, of course."

"Would we indeed?" Chalcus murmured. His left hand reached for the wine again, then withdrew; his eyes never left Carus' face. "But you haven't discussed this with Mistress Ilna. Why is that?"

Carus straightened, lacing his fingers together before him. He was watchful; not tense, exactly, but as controlled as an archer throwing his weight onto his left arm to bend a bow. Across the room, Chalcus' posture was identical.

Sharina remained motionless. She understood now why Carus wanted her here. Though neither Chalcus nor Carus acknowledged Sharina even by a glance, her presence was a reminder of civilized behavior to men who were only by courtesy civilized.

"Master Chalcus . . ." Carus said.

" 'Chalcus' will do," he interrupted. "Or 'sailor' . . . or such name as you choose, soldier, for I've had my share and more of different ones."

"Chalcus, then," Carus said with a smile rather than a scowl at the baiting. "I know you wouldn't—and couldn't—force Ilna to your will; but I'm sure as well that she won't go to Tisamur if you refuse. I want you both on Tisamur; and I want her especially, because there's wizardry in that place and worse from the reports I've gotten."

Chalcus laughed. "You know a thing I don't, then," he said. Sharina thought she heard bitterness underlying the banter, but it was hard to be sure.

Chalcus took the carafe again, but this time filled a goblet—straight, no water to mix it—and drank it down. He wiped his mouth with the back of his left hand and looked appraisingly at Carus.

"Well?" said the king. He was smiling; with humor, but a sort of humor Sharina found more disturbing than most men's rage. "Will you go to Tisamur, sailor?"

"You don't think duty would carry Ilna to Tisamur, whatever I said or said against, soldier?" Chalcus snapped.

Carus walked to the other end of the sideboard and splashed some of the white wine into a goblet. He dipped a double measure of water into the wine, then smiled over at Chalcus.

"If I had the power to convince Ilna that it was her duty to carry a child into such danger," Carus said with an edgy lilt not so very different from the sailor's tone, "then I'd be the greatest of wizards, would I not? What I *do* believe is that if I tell her that Merota is willing to go for duty's sake, and you—"

"For duty?" Chalcus said, his voice louder than before. "Will you say that, soldier?"

"And you for the sake of adventure," said Carus, calm and more nearly relaxed than ever since the moment he called Chalcus to him. "And for duty as well, I think, though I won't push the point with a red-handed pirate . . . if I can say those two things, then perhaps Ilna will go despite her concern for the child, eh?"

Chalcus fluttered a smile, the normal humor of his expression alternating with something as bleak as the gray steel of his dagger blade. "Aye, she might," he said. "I don't doubt you read her as well as I can, friend soldier."

He stared for a moment at Carus, then said, "If it's a wizard you need on Tisamur, you could send Lady Tenoctris. Not so?"

"Tsk!" Carus said between his teeth. "Sharina has a knife as long as my forearm, does she not?"

For a moment the present world became a flat, colorless backdrop to Sharina's vision of Nonnus the Hermit: her protector, her friend; and at the end, her savior at the cost of his own life. Sharina had his memory—and she had the long, heavy knife that had served Nonnus and other hunters from Pewle Island for tool and weapon as needed.

Sharina had used the knife also; for both purposes.

"Nonnus," she prayed in an unformed whisper, "may the Lady shelter you with Her mercy. And may She shelter me as well."

"Aye," said Chalcus with an appraising glance at her. "She has a Pewle knife, that's so."

"Which she would use again at need," said Carus. "Shall I send her out on purpose to give hard strokes, then, sailor? I have Attaper and his hounds for that, do I not? And perhaps I have you."

He smiled; Chalcus smiled back. Neither man spoke for a moment.

"There's hard wizard strokes to be given on Tisamur, sailor," Carus said softly, almost whispering. "Who better should I send? Who better *is* there?"

Chalcus laughed cheerfully. He poured himself more wine; this time he chose to cut it. As he lifted the ladle a second time from the water vat he said banteringly, "Prince Garric is a bold young man and a clever one besides. . . ."

He straightened, holding the goblet in his left hand. Instead of drinking, he fixed his eyes on Carus. His lips smiled, but his eyes did not.

"Prince Garric is all those things," Chalcus continued, "but he'd not be making a plan so heedless of the lives of a young child and a childhood friend. Who made this plan . . . soldier?"

Carus crossed his arms before him. "I'm not heedless, sailor . . ." he said. The emotion wasn't on the surface of his words, but Sharina heard it bubbling beneath them. "But a general who won't risk his troops when needful will lose them all when there was no need. And as for who made the plan—I did. My name's Carus. I'm not here by my own will; but seeing that I *am* here, I won't sit on my hands and let the kingdom go smash for want of a ruler."

"Are you indeed?" said Chalcus, and he sipped his wine. "Are you indeed."

He set down the goblet. "May I tell her?" he said, nodding toward the door.

"Yes," said Carus. "Or I will, if you prefer."

Chalcus shrugged. "I'll take care of it," he said with a wry smile.

The smile broadened into a bark of laughter. "Well, soldier," Chalcus continued, "I'm not one to sit on my hands either. If Mistress Ilna chooses to go to Tisamur, why, I wouldn't mind going back. I was only a lad the last time I was there."

"And you think the survivors have forgotten by now?" Carus said, strait-faced.

"Who says there were survivors, soldier boy?" Chalcus replied.

Sharina watched as the men clasped arms, laughing like demons. They understood one another, those two.

And might the Lady protect her—Sharina understood them also.

Chapter Six

Garric's skin burned. He was bathed in white light and it *burned*. Consciousness returned with the suddenness of a casement closing; with it came pain.

That was all right. Garric had hurt before, and this time the anger coursing through him burned all other feelings to cinders. He opened his eyes.

The foliage of the palms from which Ceto appeared were still quivering; the bandit must just have brushed his way through on his way back to the camp. Garric was far too coldly angry to rush off after him; he needed to get control of himself first. *Then* he'd take care of Ceto.

Tint was jumping frantically, making clicking sounds with her teeth. She saw Garric move and started to lift him.

"Hey!" Garric gasped. "Don't do that!"

"Gar!" Tint cried, the first actual word that'd come from her mouth since he awakened. She sprang into a clump of hibiscus. Voice fading with the distance, she called, "Tint fix ear!"

Garric could breathe again, though the pit of his stomach was numb with a jagged circle of pain around it. Ceto's punch might have cracked a rib.

He dabbed his ear; his fingers came away bloody. The hobnails had caught the tip, though the damage didn't seem to be serious.

Garric knelt, then rose to his feet as the beastgirl reappeared with a wad of . . . of spiderweb! "Tint fix ear," she repeated, motioning him to bend down.

He obeyed, feeling a moment of vertigo that cleared at

once. Instead of wiping his ear, Tint licked him with a tongue that seemed almost prehensile. Garric didn't jump away because the beastgirl was holding him by the shoulders. Only when the wound was clean did she press the spider silk over the wound.

"Tint fix!" she repeated. The silk stayed where she'd placed it, glued by its own adhesive.

Garric took a deep breath. His ribs still hurt, but nothing was broken.

He grinned at his companion. "All right, Tint," he said. "Now take me back to the camp. So that I can fix Ceto."

Sharina watched Chalcus leave the conference room; he moved with the grace of a dancer—which he might be—or a swordsman, which she knew he was. Captain Deghan relaxed visibly to see Carus standing in the doorway unharmed.

Carus glanced back at Sharina. "Shall we—" he said.

"Shut the door please," Sharina said. Her stomach was tight; mention of the Pewle knife and her memory of Nonnus made her able to ask a question when ingrained courtesy would have kept her silent. "For a moment."

Carus turned, nodded to Deghan, and closed the door again. When he faced Sharina he was expressionless, watchful. "All right," he said.

"Why won't you see Ilna?" she said.

"I told—"

"I heard what you told Chalcus!" Sharina said. "I can see the logic; so could Garric, and I think he'd have done the same—for all a sailor's doubts. People in Barca's Hamlet have to make hard choices every fall if they expect to survive the Hungry Time the next spring. But you haven't answered *my* question."

Carus' grin was brief and false. He walked to the sideboard and poured himself wine, using the carafe of red and the goblet closest to him—the one Chalcus had left behind. He didn't mix water with the wine.

"When I was . . ." he said to the far wall. "In the flesh, say; alive, I don't care what you call it."

He set the goblet down untasted and met Sharina's eyes. "When I was a *man*, Sharina, I knew a lot of women," he said. "I liked them well enough, and some I liked a good deal. But there was one . . ."

Carus reached for the wine, then snatched his hand back and snarled, "Sister take it! And may the Sister take *me* if I'm so great a coward that I won't talk about her!"

"Carus . . . ?" Sharina said. She didn't know what she wanted to say next, except that she wished she hadn't spoken before. "I don't need . . . You don't have to tell me anything."

The king's passing reference to the knife had opened an old wound, but he'd had a reason. Sharina no longer believed she'd had a reason for her question, at least not one that was worth the pain it gave her companion.

"Don't I, girl?" Carus said. He managed a gust of his usual laughter. "Perhaps not, but I'll tell you anyway. There was a girl, a woman, named Brichese bos-Brediman; from Cordin, noble of course but from a family no wealthier than yours in Barca's Hamlet despite the title."

He shrugged. "I loved her," he said. "And she died, because I didn't save her . . . or couldn't save her. . . . Or perhaps you could say because I didn't choose to save her. And that was all a thousand years ago. She'd be dead now in any case and none of that would matter. Except—"

Carus grinned. "You know," he said, "I sometimes think that the Lady . . . or Fate, if the philosophers are right when they say the Great Gods don't exist . . . that whoever rules men has a sense of humor. Your friend Ilna is as close to being my Brichese as ever twins were born. In body, but in spirit as well."

Sharina's face went blank. "Ah," she said. "I see now."

"It was hard enough when I watched through your brother's eyes and heard through his ears," the king said. He sipped the wine, drinking without the desperation that had driven his urge a few moments before. "Now that I'm wearing this body instead of being a guest in it, I thought . . ."

He laughed and finished the wine. "I thought it'd be best for everybody," he said, "if I put temptation out of the way."

"Yes," said Sharina. She breathed a sigh of relief. If Carus had been a different man, Ilna and the kingdom both would face a future that would be even more dangerous than what loomed today.

"Let's go out to the others," she said, crooking her arm to be taken by the man wearing her brother's body. "I want to see what Tenoctris has learned about Garric."

Fear twisted her gut. She immediately hid it beneath a smile.

"And Cashel," Sharina added; and then lied. "Though I'm sure Cashel will never meet any danger that *he* can't manage."

Tenoctris had decided to use the marble bench on one side of the artificial grotto as a table. Ilna watched while the wizard adjusted the strips of parchment that she'd written on and placed around the edges of two smoldering braziers. Along the grotto's back wall water trickled from lead pipes into a channel leading out into the garden, past the squad of Blood Eagles facing stolidly away from the wizard.

Beards of moss grew on the wall beneath the pipes. A similar dark smudge spread down the front of the bench. Echeus' severed head sat upright between the braziers. Blood still leaked from its neck.

Tenoctris stepped back, breathing quickly. "There," she said. "That should be all right. Now where did I put—"

"I have your wand," Ilna said, holding out the split of bamboo the wizard had chosen for this incantation. "And your stool is set up right here."

"Ah," said Tenoctris. "Yes, of course."

She sat carefully, gathering the hem of her robe so that it didn't collapse the folding ivory stool Ilna had placed facing Echeus. She glanced up at Ilna. "I'm sorry," she said. "I'm nervous because of what I'm about to do."

Ilna shrugged. "But you'll do it anyway," she said. "That's all that matters, not what it costs."

She smiled wryly at the older woman. "That's what I tell myself, anyway," she added.

Tenoctris grinned. "Yes, of course," she said. "And I'm sure you're right."

She faced forward, focusing on a point in eternity rather than on the head in front of her. Echeus had died with his eyes open and a look of surprise on his face. The eyes had glazed and the stiffness of death was sharpening the expression into a demonic grimace.

The parchment crinkled in the slow fire; by becoming black ash, the words of power executed themselves in coils of smoke. Tenoctris tapped the air silently for a moment, then said in rhythm with her wand, "*Oh maosaio naraeeaeaa. . . .*"

With every syllable Tenoctris spoke, the rising smoke quivered. Ilna saw hints of glowing color in the thin columns. There was a pattern to them, something her brain couldn't grasp but her soul almost could.

"*Arubibao thumo imsiu . . .*" the wizard said. "*Oulatsila moula imsiu. . . .*"

Ilna, Tenoctris, and the severed head were alone in a grotto carved out of the cosmos, not just a man-made hill. The entrance and the guards outside had vanished. The only light was from glowing smoke that wove new patterns in the fabric of space and time.

"*Ae eiouo soumarta max akarba. . . .*" No longer words spoken by a human but rather the thunder of the cosmos.

Echeus' eyes were expanding, or else Ilna was looking into another world which those eyes had seen. Gray, softly gleaming . . . utterly evil.

"*Chraie zozan ekmet prhe satra!*"

A world: a world draped in gray silk, webs swathing rocks and trees—and everywhere those who had woven the webs, watching through jewel-hard unwinking multiple eyes. A world of spiders the size of dogs, the size of sheep. Spiders waiting: expressionless, emotionless; as cold as the void between worlds.

Spiders who had woven patterns of inhuman perfection, and who were weaving one further pattern that Ilna could almost understand. Indeed, she *could* under—

The gray hellworld shrank into itself, vanishing like a snowflake caught in an open hand. Ilna staggered, but the instinct of duty caused her to grab Tenoctris and hold the old wizard firmly before she could slip off her stool. She seemed skeletally frail within her silken robe.

The grotto stank of charred flesh: parchment was no more than sheep gut, after all. The strips had burned to ash and Echeus' head was only a body part, already flushing with the purple tinge of decay.

A haze of gray smoke filtered the sunlight entering through the entrance, but it still made a bright contrast to the place Ilna's mind had just visited. She lifted Tenoctris as she'd carry an injured child and stepped outside.

"Ma'am?" said the leader of the guards. "Is she—"

"She's all right," Ilna said.

"I'm all right," Tenoctris echoed weakly, "I'm just tired."

The Blood Eagles shifted their stance, uncertain whether they ought to be helping the women or simply preventing the approach of intruders. There was no one within fifty paces of the grotto except for the larger detachment of guards around the conference room where Garric and Chalcus spoke.

Ilna felt the older woman gather her strength, then straighten her legs. When Ilna was sure, she let go except to keep one arm crooked where Tenoctris could hold on to it.

"Tenoctris, did you see it?" Ilna whispered. "That *place*?"

Garric . . . Ilna remembered she'd felt murderous passion when Garric turned his back on her less than an hour before. She was purged of that now. Nothing humans did was worth anger, not when one had seen Hell wrapped in webs of finest silk.

"Yes, I saw it," Tenoctris said. "I don't know what it means, but now that I have a starting place I think I can learn."

"That was what Echeus was trying to bring about?" Ilna said. She'd meant to whisper, but for once control failed her. She let her loathing loose in her rising tone. "*That* was why he attacked Garric?"

Tenoctris took a deep breath. Now at last she appeared to have recovered from the ordeal of her art—and perhaps from the shock of what her art had shown her.

She stepped back and managed a wan smile for Ilna. "No," she said. "Echeus wasn't trying to create that . . . world, that path for the future to follow."

Tenoctris drew in another breath; her smile failed her.

"What we saw was a vision of what Echeus feared most," the old wizard explained. "Echeus attacked Garric to *prevent* that future from occurring."

Cashel sat with his back to a coral head thrusting up from the beach. He made no more sound or movement than the rock behind him, but he was fully alert.

The sailors' several driftwood campfires had burned down to coals. Occasionally a salt crystal spluttered into transparent pastel flame, but for the most part the fireglow sank slowly toward the darkness of the surrounding night.

Cashel waited the way he'd watched over flocks when he knew danger threatened. Captain Mounix had set guards, but Cashel didn't believe anybody had relieved the first watch. The shipwreck had disturbed the crew's structure, and the terrible slayings had put paid to what discipline remained.

There would be no more slayings. Cashel smiled. Not unless the killer got through him first, anyway.

The surf rumbled on the reef, drowning with its low note the many lesser night sounds. When Cashel took his place the tide had been going out; now it was returning. Occasionally waves splashed against the base of the coral head. Most of the survivors were sprawled on the sand up at the tide line. Cashel had chosen this location because he wanted to cover as much of the encampment as possible, though in darkness he couldn't see his companions.

Just inland of Cashel's position, Lady Tilphosa slept under a sailcloth shelter for privacy. Metra lay nearby but outside the shelter. Cashel hadn't asked them to stay close, though he would've done so if Tilphosa hadn't volunteered that she wanted to sleep nearby for protection.

Another wave hit the coral, spraying high enough that drops spattered Cashel. Arms of water reached around from both sides, hissing and foaming; one wet Cashel's tunic before sinking into the sand.

It'd be dawn soon. He'd move when the sky brightened, maybe even get some sleep of his own. Until then, well, he'd been wet before.

Cashel felt a presence in the night; he tensed.

It wasn't anything he could've described to another person, unless they were folks who'd felt this sort of thing themselves. *Something was threatening his flock. . . .*

There was movement though not a shape against the palmettos and screw pines. It was at the head of the trail Cashel had broken, going uphill to the spring. That was what he'd expected, though he hadn't been conscious of his belief until the event confirmed it.

He rose in one silent, fluid motion. Cashel was deliberate in all things, but no one who'd seen him act during a crisis thought he was clumsy. He started toward the shadow. It was now drifting in the direction of a campfire which had settled to a shimmer of heat.

Cashel moved in a near shuffle, his feet lifting barely above the surface of the sand. He angled his approach to put himself between the intruder and the gap in the vegetation from which it had come.

It was very near to dawn, though the constellations were distorted enough that Cashel couldn't say if the sky would begin to lighten in one handful of minutes or two handsful. Certainly no more than two.

One of the sailors lay a little farther from the dead fire than his companions did. The intruder sprang the remaining distance to him while Cashel was just beyond his staff's reach.

"Hi!" Cashel shouted, and jumped himself, whirling the quarterstaff in a full-armed slash.

Quick as Cashel was, the intruder proved quicker. It had snatched its chosen victim from the sand in the eyeblink before Cashel moved. Now it hurled the sailor away and ducked beneath the whistling blow.

The sailor was screaming. His companions sat up, shouting in fear; men at the other fires cried out also. Cashel skidded on the sand, recovering his staff with both hands at the balance to defend himself from the intruder's counterstroke.

Instead the shadow—it was still no more than a shadow, though Cashel was nearly on top of it—bounded for the jungle in a graceless, low-slung motion. It covered ground like a scorpion jumping. Cashel couldn't cut it off before it vanished into the vegetation.

That was all right. Cashel knew where it was going, or anyway thought he did.

A bow twanged from the direction of the southernmost campfire. Cashel didn't hear the whistle of an arrow, so maybe the archer wasn't aiming toward him after all.

Cashel plunged into the forest, slanting his staff before him to extend the line of his right forearm. His left hand was free to clutch or fend away.

"Cashel, wait!" Tilphosa called. "Wait for daylight!"

Cashel kept going. When he'd come this way during daylight he'd blundered into trees while watching his footing and had slipped if he kept his eyes on the trees. Now he moved through the darkness as easily as a puff of smoke. He had a countryman's feel for a path once trodden, but more than that was working tonight: he was on the trail of the creature which as long as it lived would threaten those under Cashel's protection.

Surefooted Cashel might be, but he crashed through the undergrowth like a bull in a thicket. He couldn't hear the thing he was chasing, and there was at least a chance that it'd pick its spot and turn on him.

He wasn't worried. He wanted to get his hands on the thing—the sooner, the better. He couldn't in his heart believe that it was a real danger to a man who was alert and unafraid.

The sky grew paler through the broadly splayed leaves of the begonias. It was still some minutes short of sunrise, but false dawn brightened the heavens if not the ground beneath. Cashel no longer needed to climb on instinct: gnarled trunks stood out from one another and from the background. He was close to the outcrop where the airship lay wrecked. He paused to decide how he'd negotiate the last dozen paces of steep hillside.

As he stood silent, he heard movement down the slope

behind him. *Was there a pack of them, surrounding him before they struck?*

Farther back still he heard Metra call, "Lady Tilphosa! Stop!"

Cashel smiled. Tilphosa'd said she'd stay close to him for protection tonight. He hadn't expected her to follow him up here, but maybe she wasn't showing such bad judgment.

The chime of gold on gold rang softly through the night. Cashel sighed in relieved anticipation. He'd been afraid that his quarry would keep running instead of going to ground. A shepherd learns to get along in the woods, but he doesn't become a tracker.

He started climbing to the crag and spring, slipping a little on the slick, steep clay. Funny. It'd been easier to lope through the night than it was to make this last short way under a pink-gray sky. The immediacy was past, though the job that remained might be hard enough.

"Cashel?" Tilphosa called from not far below him. "I'm coming up! It's me, Tilphosa."

She was smart enough to know how Cashel might react to being startled just now. Tilphosa was smart enough, period.

After his breathing slowed, Cashel could hear water dripping down into the basin of the spring. Dawn had awakened creatures to squawk and warble, unseen because of distance and the foliage.

The airboat's skeleton lay as Cashel had left it. So far as he could see, Costas hadn't been able to mark the flint-hard gold. The sailor's body lay at the edge of the spring, his chest ripped open and emptied. Costas' eyes stared at the dawn.

"I'm coming, Cashel," Tilphosa said, blurting the words out between gasps. "It's me behind you."

The girl clambered onto the ridge as she spoke. Cashel

turned slightly so that he could see her without losing sight of the wreck.

Thorns or a sharp branch had torn Tilphosa's tunic. A line of dried blood crossed her right cheek to the lobe of her ear. She didn't have Cashel's instinct for the darkness, but she'd come anyway.

In her right hand Tilphosa clutched a chisel she must have taken from Hook's tool chest. The shaft was hardwood, but the fluted blade was steel and sharp enough to shave with.

"You took a chance," Cashel said, but his tone was approving. "I guess there isn't anywhere a lot safer around here, though."

"Yes, well, I wasn't going to stay down there without you," Tilphosa said. Her quick breaths whistled, but she made a point of not opening her mouth to pant like a dog. "Did it get away?"

"I don't think so," Cashel said. He looked around him carefully to be sure that nothing, no *thing*, waited in ambush. Then he pushed into the lobelias with his staff slanted forward, this time in both hands.

"Cashel?" said the girl. She'd stayed far enough back to be clear if he and the quarterstaff had to spin suddenly. "Do you know what it is? Is it a man?"

"We'll know in a little bit," Cashel said, his voice a growl as he concentrated on what was in front of him.

Three larger swellings grew from the tubing like seedpods hanging on a trumpet vine. One was near the bow. The impact had crushed it open. Roots twisted about it, and a line of ants crawled in and out of its protection.

Cashel moved on, each time testing the ground with his toes before putting his foot down. At any moment his legs might need to anchor a smashing blow of his quarterstaff. . . .

He heard rustling and the crackle of a branch behind

him. "Lady Tilphosa!" Metra wheezed. "Where are you, lady?"

"Keep her out of the way!" Cashel said. He trusted Tilphosa's judgment, but he didn't trust anything at all about her attendant wizard.

The two women talked in quick, irritated voices, but Cashel needn't worry about that now. He'd reached the second pod, this one about the size of a goatskin water bag. It dangled in the air, half-wrapped in the skein of tubes that supported it. The pod's weight had pulled the hard gold into a cat's cradle, folding and flattening the tubes without breaking them.

The third pod was egg-shaped and larger than a man. Loam, the detritus of centuries of leaves and fallen branches, mounded around it. The softly gleaming upper surfaces reflected growing daylight; the smooth metal was not only untarnished but clear of the litter which covered the surrounding soil.

Cashel eyed the pod, watchful for any change in it. After a time—he couldn't have said how long, a length of time he found appropriate—he rapped the cold metal with the outstretched tip of his quarterstaff. It rang hollowly at the touch of the ferrule, a sweetly musical sound. It was the same note that Cashel had heard as he chased his quarry in this direction.

Cashel eyed his surroundings, sure now of what he needed but not quite certain he was going to find it here. Tilphosa waited, still-faced and obviously nervous, just back of the crumpled framework. She raised her eyebrows in question when Cashel glanced at her, but she didn't speak. Maybe she was afraid of breaking his concentration.

Metra sat behind Tilphosa, her athame bobbing like a chicken gobbling corn. She'd spread another silk square, this one black with symbols—different symbols from those of the other day, Cashel supposed—in red. Clever of the wizard to change colors so that she wouldn't grab the wrong pattern in haste.

Cashel saw what he needed, a torso-sized chunk of limestone separated from the rest of the outcrop. Moss outlined the fracture, probably the result of the airboat's crash.

Could the creature hear him? Could it understand speech even if it *did* hear?

"It's all right," he said to Tilphosa. He smiled. "Just keep that chisel ready. I'm going to have to put my staff down for a bit."

She probably thought he was being reassuring. He truly *was* glad she was here with a weapon.

Cashel backed, then sidled, carefully, to the block. After watching the pod intently for some moments more—just in case it decided to open—he leaned his quarterstaff into the angle where two gold tubes joined seamlessly.

He squatted, gripping opposite sides of the block and shifting it slightly to make sure it would give. It did. Because the soil was so thin over the outcrop he didn't have to worry about trees. He didn't want to trip and lose his balance when he was carrying a stone as heavy as a young bull.

Cashel breathed deeply—once, twice, and again. "Now!" he shouted—to the stone, to himself, it didn't matter—and jerked the block free. As it crunched away from the outcrop, Cashel straightened his knees. Stiff-legged, his hands adjusting the block minutely to balance it as he moved, he walked toward the pod.

The blood roared in his ears. He couldn't hear outside sounds, not even the thump of his heels on the ground step after step, but he felt the words of Metra's incantation. Her art was affecting the cosmos through which Cashel moved. . . .

He couldn't look down: his spine was perfectly vertical to accept the weight it now bore. The pod was a golden shimmer through the red haze throbbing with his pulse.

"Now!" Cashel repeated. He swung his missile down, tilting his whole body when the stone's path had slanted clear of him.

Cashel fell forward, following the missile. The block hit corner foremost in the center of the smooth curve. Metal bonged, splitting before the massive stone rolled off to the left and wobbled crazily several paces downhill before a stand of lobelias halted it.

Cashel struggled to his feet. Tilphosa grabbed his arm to lift. She was more trouble than help, but he didn't have enough breath to send her away. Anyhow, he appreciated the thought.

Metra pushed through the brush, looking as wobbly as Cashel felt. She tried to slide her athame back under her sash, but the effort of her art had robbed her of the necessary coordination. Her eyes were fixed on the ruptured pod.

"Get her *back*," Cashel whispered hoarsely. Tilphosa handed him his quarterstaff—that *was* a help—and caught Metra around the shoulders. She held the wizard easily; and would, Cashel was pretty sure, even if the other woman weren't already exhausted.

As Cashel himself was, but strength came flooding back now that he was on his feet again. His whole body had locked into a series of mortise-and-tenon joints in order to support the block of stone. Now he was himself again, Cashel or-Kenset, moving with the graceful deliberation of thick cream flowing.

The stone had dented the pod over a surface the size of a wash basket, but the split in the center was no longer than Cashel's hand and too narrow to reach through. The impact had sprung the hidden catch that locked the pod into a featureless whole, however: the top stood away from the bottom half over most of the oval seam.

Cashel shifted his grip on the quarterstaff, poising it so

that he could punch a ferrule forward like a spear. He stretched out his right foot, then lifted the lid with a quick jerk of his toes.

In shadow, the figure lying within could have passed for a man: the jaws were a little longer, the brow flat; the eyes set too far to the side and bulging more than a human's would. The creature's skin had a faint green cast and a pebbled surface with fine scales on the backs of the hands.

Faint though the morning light was, when the lid opened the creature gave a squeal of agony and covered its face with its four-fingered hands. It stank: the blood and bits of human tissue that smeared its head and clawed hands were rotting. A pendant hanging from a neck chain was the creature's only clothing or adornment.

Cashel stabbed his staff down, crushing the creature's hands and skull together. The ferrule rang with a muffled note on the bottom of the pod. The creature's back arched; it writhed, flinging its legs out of the capsule where it had laired.

Gasping more with revulsion than effort, Cashel stepped back. Tilphosa touched his arm, letting him know where she was. She peered past him to the interior of the pod.

"Duzi, stand at my side," Cashel whispered. A palm tree growing down the hill leaned over him. He ripped a frond from it and scrubbed furiously, cleaning blood and brains from his quarterstaff. "Duzi, help the one who guards your flock."

Metra edged past. Tilphosa caught her arm. "Let her go," Cashel muttered. "I'm done with that now."

The almost-human body still twitched. It was smaller than it'd seemed in the darkness, the size of a girl in her early teens. The teeth were no more impressive than a man's, and the claws on the fingers were more like a dog's than the big cat Cashel had imagined from the corpses.

Savagery and bestial strength, not weapons, had torn the victims apart.

That wouldn't happen again. Cashel didn't know what the creature was or why it killed the way it did—but he'd stopped it.

Metra bent over the corpse and lifted the pendant. Cashel had thought it was metal. Raised so that light fell on it, he realized it was transparent and shimmered like the fire opals which nobles from Shengy wore when they visited Garric's court.

"The Talisman of See-Char!" the wizard cried. "It wasn't a myth after all! Relonia really did see it in her questing dreams!"

"What is it, Metra?" Tilphosa said. Her voice was calm but a little louder than it need have been to be heard. She'd stuck the chisel under her sash, but as she spoke her fingers stroked the use-polished pommel.

Metra pulled the chain over the creature's shattered head. It didn't seem to bother her to touch the congealing ruin. She held the pendant out at arm's length and turned it to view from every angle.

"It's what kept him alive," she said. "He must have been a great wizard. Perhaps he was fleeing the cataclysm that wiped out the remainder of the Third Race when his vessel crashed here. The amulet is a thing of wonderful power."

"Did all of them kill this way?" Cashel asked. "All the Third Race, I mean."

As he spoke, the flesh blackened and sloughed from the corpse. The shinbones separated, pulled from the thighs by their own weight; they fell to the leaf mold around the pod. The bones themselves crumbled first to dust, then less than dust. A faint black slime remained to color the golden cavity.

"What?" said Metra with the angry irritation of someone interrupted by what they think is a stupid question. "No, of course not, they were more advanced than we are in many respects. The amulet could keep him alive, but it wouldn't dull his hunger. Over the years, the centuries . . ."

She smiled at Cashel, looking down on his peasant simplicity from the height of her sophisticated wisdom. "Well, after all," she said, "there wouldn't have been anything for him to eat except other castaways, would there?"

"Ah," said Cashel.

"Metra, put that amulet back in the coffin and leave it," Tilphosa said with a grimace of disgust. "I don't think it's a good thing to have, however valuable it may be."

"Don't act like a child!" snapped the wizard. "With the Talisman of See-Char we'll be able to——"

Cashel reached out and closed his fist over the dangling amulet. It felt greasy, as though the stone was a heavy liquid.

"Tilphosa's right," he said. "We're not going to have this around."

"Who are you to tell me what to do, you barbarian?" the wizard shouted. She held on to the chain. Cashel lifted his arm until Metra dangled by her hand.

"Metra!" Tilphosa said. "Let go at once!"

The chain didn't break, but Metra whimpered and let go when the thin metal had lacerated her palm beyond bearing. She tried to grab it again, but Cashel body-checked her with a thrust of his hip.

"I'm the man who killed the thing wearing it," he said in a low growl.

He dropped the amulet onto bare stone. Tilphosa caught the wizard as she crawled toward it. Cashel brought the butt of his staff down in a short, sharp blow, the same way he'd smashed the creature's skull. The amulet exploded into powder.

"Now," Cashel said, "let's get back to the others."

* * *

Gar's senses were even sharper than the ones Garric was used to. He smelled the campfire fifty double paces before he reached their encampment, and he smelled the scattered garbage and human excrement almost as quickly.

Garric wrinkled his nose in disgust, less from the stench itself than what it said about the gang he was joining. The tanyard in Barca's Hamlet, where Halmat and later his son cured hides with dung, was downwind from the rest of the community. Vascay's band didn't bother with such niceties.

Garric stepped into the natural clearing where the band camped. Tarpaulins were strung for shelter from the frequent rains. Smoke from the cookfire clumped in the humid air. A pudgy fellow stirred the stewpot hanging from a rod placed between wooden forks.

Ceto stood in a midst of half a dozen men. One of them held a horn that had probably once belonged to a noble's coachman: the etchings on the curved brass tube were filled with silver and gold. He raised it and blew a long, deep note calling in other members of the band.

A pair of giant fig trees had shaded out all lesser growth save for ferns and seedlings with trunks only the diameter of a finger. The bandits had chopped away some of the palely hopeful saplings and were using others as drying racks for soaked clothes and bedding.

"Gar?" chirped Tint, still in the clump of elephant ears growing at the edge of the clearing. "Gar not be hurt? Gar?"

Nobody noticed Garric until he whipped a canvas ground sheet off the bush it was draped on and wrapped it around his waist. Tunics hung not far away, but Garric needed to cover himself more than he cared about the style of his garment. He knew that being naked would put him at a greater disadvantage than being unarmed did.

"Hey, monkey boy!" called the cook, sweating profusely despite being stripped to a breechclout. "Get some more wood, and make it dry this time! That punk you came back with last time isn't worth the trouble to toss it on the fire!"

Ceto didn't look around, but the peg-legged older fellow he was showing the sapphire ring to did. He carried too much of his weight around his waistline, but he still had the shoulders of a powerful man. The two knives thrust under his orange-silk sash had simple, serviceable blades . . . but they'd been forged from steel, not iron, and their bone scales were yellowed by frequent use.

Garric would have recognized the leader, Vascay, even without Gar's memory. The other men were mostly bigger, younger, and more heavily armed, but *this* fellow was in charge.

Garric noticed the glance; he nodded in response. Vascay made no overt reaction, not even a raised eyebrow, but his face tightened minusculely above his grizzled, short-cropped beard.

The brain-damaged Gar wouldn't have met another man's eyes. Garric shrugged mentally. Well, the whole band would learn shortly that things had changed.

"You've got my ring there, Ceto," Garric said in a clear voice. "I'll take it back now, if you please."

Ceto turned in amazement which changed swiftly to anger. He folded his right hand over the ring, protecting it at the cost of preventing him from drawing his sword. He reached for a dagger in his bandolier. Garric's left hand caught the bandit's wrist.

"Hey, what's got into Gar?" cried the fat cook. The horn was bringing more men out of the forest. They were calling too, curious about why they'd been summoned.

Ceto tried—vainly—to free his knife hand. He snarled, "Sister take you, you—"

Garric punched him in the pit of the stomach, between the flapping halves of his armored vest. Ceto's face went white; his legs wobbled, and he sank to his knees.

Garric was breathing hard. His whole body shuddered with awareness of what he'd done and the dangers in what might come next. Ceto had tensed his belly muscles against the blow he saw coming, but Gar's arm had the strength of a mallet.

"Watch he doesn't bite!" a bandit shouted. "Is he foaming at the mouth?"

Garric started to unfold the fingers of Ceto's right fist. Vascay touched the back of Garric's hand, and said, "I'll take care of the ring."

Garric was ready to flare out in any direction. "I found—" he said, straightening in a surge of fury.

"Hold him," Vascay said. Men grabbed Garric's arms from behind. Tint was chattering on the edge of the encampment.

Garric hunched down and brought his arms forward, swinging the men holding him against one another. The fellow to Garric's left shouted as he lost his grip. Other bandits grabbed Garric, tearing away his makeshift garment. He went over backward in a pile of men.

"I said hold him, Sister take you!" Vascay shouted. "I didn't say kick him, Ademos! Now settle down all of you!"

Garric said, "All right, all right," and let himself relax. Two men were holding either arm. Several were on his legs though he couldn't see them because of the fellow sprawled across his torso.

Vascay looked down with a bland smile. He held the ring between thumb and finger of his left hand; the sapphire was a glitter too small to have color.

"Let him up, then," Vascay said to the men holding Garric. "He's ready to behave."

Ceto had put both his hands on the ground. He was trying to rise, but he still couldn't breathe properly. His face was twisted, and his lips formed curses that he lacked the strength to utter.

"But boss?" said the man with the horn, one of those on Garric's arms. "He's gone mad, hasn't he?"

Vascay glanced back at Ceto, his expression friendly in a mild fashion and his eyes as hard as chips of jasper. He'd hooked his right hand negligently into his sash where it half covered a knife hilt.

"I'm not mad," Garric said, trying to get his breathing under control. "I'm just not in a good humor. But yes, I'll behave."

"What's going on?" asked one of a pair of latecomers just arrived from the forest.

His companion cried, "Hey, Vascay! Is that what we come for? The ring, I mean?"

Vascay thrust his boot out—not quite a kick, but a thump that got the attention of the man on Garric's torso. "I said, let him up, Halophus," he said. He didn't raise his voice, but the mild previous tone was beginning to congeal into something much harder. "Toster, Hame—all of you. Let him *up*."

The bandits released Garric, grunting as they got to their feet. The stubby redhead who'd been holding Garric's right ankle scrambled away. That would be Ademos. He was the one who'd just kicked Garric; a frequent sport of his when poor Gar wore this flesh.

That was a matter for another time. Garric sat up, set a foot behind him, and stood with his arms crossed in front of his chest, a show of coordination that he correctly assumed Vascay would notice.

He bent to retrieve the ground sheet. Vascay stepped on a corner of the canvas, pinning it to the ground, and instead tossed Garric a tunic draped over a guyline anchoring an overhead tarp. "Try one of mine," Vascay said. "It ought to fit."

He grinned, and added, "The way the weight's distributed is a little different, of course."

The tunic was close-woven linen with vertical stripes of

brown and cream; a well-made, attractive garment which indeed did fit Garric as well as anything in the palace wardrobe. He raised it, bunched, above his head, then slipped it quickly down to cover him. Under the circumstances, he didn't want either to cover his eyes or bind his arms any longer than necessary.

Vascay chuckled. "Nobody's going to stick you while you're dressing, boy," he said.

"By the Sister!" snarled Ceto, finally on his feet. He reached for his sword. "*I'm* going to stick him any way he comes!"

"That's not how we do things here, Brother Ceto," Vascay said calmly. "We're civilized men, remember, driven to our present straits by a tyrant's exactions rather than our own vicious natures."

Ceto snarled a curse. Garric tensed to jump. The chine of Ceto's swordblade sang against the lip of the scabbard as he drew it.

"Ceto!" said Vascay.

He was smiling. His knives were in his hands: the left one held low with the edge upward for a disemboweling stroke, the right one beside his ear ready to throw, blade vertical and the hilt in Vascay's palm.

"Rules, Brother Ceto," Vascay said, mildly again. None of the other bandits had drawn their weapons; some were deliberately holding their hands out where they could be seen to be empty. "We don't fight among ourselves, remember?"

"Gar's not one of us!" Ceto snarled; he slammed his sword back in its sheath, however. "He's an animal!"

Garric took a deep breath. He didn't know what the situation he'd stepped into was, but he knew there was one. The politics of this band were probably less complex than those of the royal council, but the sanctions for mistakes were likely to be quicker and more final.

"Captain Vascay," he said, giving the leader a half nod,

half bow. "Tint and I found the ring we're here searching for. Ceto robbed us."

Toster was nearly as tall as Garric and much heavier; only part of his weight was fat. "What is this?" he asked in puzzlement. "What's Gar doing talking like that?"

"When Ceto kicked me in the head . . ." Garric said, raising his finger to his bruised temple. It struck him that Gar's unkempt bush of hair might have prevented a cracked skull in all truth. "I regained my faculties."

"The animal tried to take the ring away from me after I'd found it," Ceto said. "I knocked him down—and I'll do it again, Vascay, whether you like it or not!"

Garric waited silently. In his experience, you didn't threaten a man like Vascay. If you wound up with that sort as an enemy, you'd best deal with him quickly—and not turn your back until you had.

Instead of speaking, Vascay stepped backward, a movement that allowed him to keep both Ceto and Garric in his field of view at the same time. His knives were back in his sash, but Garric had seen how quickly they appeared when Vascay chose.

"Well, Gar," the chieftain said cheerfully, "then you'll understand when I tell you that I'm not a captain. I'm merely Brother Vascay, a member of the band and its spokesman only so long as the majority wills it. Is that not so, brethren?"

"*We* all know that, Vascay!" Ceto said. "Sometimes I wonder if you remember it, though."

The others didn't speak. Their attention was uneasy; their eyes moved from Ceto to Vascay, sometimes pausing to consider the person who'd been Gar when he went into the jungle this morning.

"So, Gar," Vascay said calmly, "you say you found the ring—"

Which had vanished somewhere onto Vascay's person during the same series of movements that brought out the knives ready to kill. Conjurors came regularly to the Sheep Fair, but Garric had never seen one as quick with his hands as Vascay.

"—and Ceto took it from you?"

"Tint led me to the ring," Garric said, looking over his shoulder. "I dug it out."

Tint had come into the clearing when the shouting died down, but she ducked away from Garric's glance. He wouldn't have believed it was possible to hide behind the tuft of ferns into which the beastgirl disappeared.

"How come Gar's talking like that?" Toster repeated plaintively. "He can't be Gar."

Garric kept Toster at the corner of his eye. He and Vascay—who were probably opposite poles of the band's intellectual spectrum—were the only members who fully grasped the truth. Unlike the others, those two knew they weren't dealing with dim-witted Gar. The big man wasn't hostile, and Vascay seemed more positive than not, but they were potentially dangerous.

"Why do you talk to that animal?" Ceto demanded. "It doesn't matter what Gar says, he's a—"

"Arguments between Brethren," Vascay interrupted, "are judged by the Ball of Truth. We'll have the trial now."

He gestured to a wooden chest resting on blocks beneath the nearby tarpaulin. It looked to Garric like a sea locker, though its floral decoration was of a much higher order than the chip carvings of dolphins and mermaids that graced most sailors' chests.

"What do you mean a trial?" Ceto said.

"Hey, it's just Gar," said Ademos, as puzzled as Ceto and almost as worried about what was going on. "Trials are for brothers, not monkeys."

"Shall we cap each other's quotations from Celondre, Ademos?" Garric said in a cutting tone. " '*The same chance that joins the wolf and the lamb....*' Or do you have a different favorite poet?"

"What?" said Ademos. "What's he *talking* about?"

Garric smiled coldly, though maybe it was a shame that Ademos hadn't turned out to be a scholar. A contest of verses would be one way to prove to the band that Garric's claim wasn't the maundering of a monkey boy. In his mind he completed the tag, "... *makes you my enemy.*"

But Vascay was preparing to prove matters in a different fashion. He squatted and opened the chest without using a key, keeping his eyes on Ceto. His left hand darted within and came out with a red ball the size of a hickory nut.

"Which will you have, Ceto?" Vascay asked as he stood upright again. "Will you tell your story first, or will you hold the Ball of Truth after Brother Gar has spoken his version?"

"He's not a brother, he's an *animal,*" Ceto said, apparently hoping that repetition would give his statement an effect it'd so far lacked. "You can't make me go through a trial with an animal!"

A bird shrieked in the canopy, responding to Ceto's rising tone. Another of its kind answered from a distance.

"Unless we all vote to change our laws," said Vascay, holding out the red bead, "that's just what we'll do, Brother Ceto. Which do you choose, that Gar takes the ball first or that you do?"

"He doesn't talk like an animal," Toster said. "He talks better'n me."

"Yeah, the Ball of Truth," said Hame, a short, bandy-legged fellow whose ears had been notched—for theft, Garric supposed; though, looking on the band with civilized eyes, they didn't seem to be the illiterate bravos he'd expected. Several of them, Hame for one, were city dwellers by their appearance.

"All right, give him the ball and watch him spit his lies up!" Ceto snarled. "I don't care!"

Gar might have been present at previous trials, but if so the experience had passed through his ruined brain like rain fallen on parched sand. Garric didn't know what was going on—

But he *did* know he had Vascay on his side. The peg-legged chieftain touched his hands together, transferring the red bead from his left to his right. He held it toward Garric, and said, "Put the Ball of Truth under your tongue, Brother Gar. Speak your story, and if you lie the words will poison you."

"I'm not lying," said Garric.

"Then you'll hand the ball to Brother Ceto, and he'll do the same," Vascay said equably. "A man who tells the truth has nothing to fear from the ball."

He looked around the circle of watchful men. The whole band was present, twenty or so. Many of them were mutilated, like Hame and Vascay himself.

"I still don't know about this truth stuff, Vascay," Ademos muttered, his eyes jerking side to side without lighting on the man to whom he spoke. "I know what you say, but I don't see how a little ball knows who's lying."

"With you, Ademos," said Hame, "it's whenever your mouth's open."

"Stuff it!" said Ademos. He kept his hands carefully clear of his weapons. "Stuff you, Hame!"

"I served a saintly hermit in my youth," Vascay said, reinforcing the story he'd obviously told often in the past—and incidentally informing Garric for the first time. "The Ball of Truth was his legacy to me. Not wizardry but faith gives it the power to see men's souls, Brother Ademos."

"Get on with it," Ceto snarled. "Just get on with it!"

"Yes," said Garric. He took the red bead from Vascay. "Let's do that."

It was surprisingly light, more like wood than the stone he'd expected. The surface was hard but slightly pitted.

"Be brief, Brother Gar," Vascay said. "And on your life, tell the truth."

Vascay nodded expressionlessly. Garric put the bead under his tongue.

"I dug the ring out of the ground," Garric said. The lump under his tongue slurred his words. He could feel the bead starting to dissolve. "Ceto sucker-punched me and stole the ring."

He spat the bead into his left palm. He couldn't see any change except the glister of saliva, but he knew it had begun to come apart.

"Your turn now, Brother Ceto," said Vascay. "Give him the Ball of Truth, Gar."

Garric's belly muscles were tight. His tongue worked, trying to decide what the taste in his mouth was. It was dry, limy, and nondescript. Apparently harmless, but there was *some* trick connected with the business.

"Here, Ceto," Garric said, stretching his left arm out to full length so that he didn't have to approach the other man. The bead gleamed in the center of his upturned palm.

"I don't have to do this!" Ceto said, turning his head side to side like a beast at bay.

"It's your turn, Ceto," Toster said. The big man carried an axe with a long helve, a weapon that in hands like his could smash through any armor a man could wear and still be able to walk. He raised the axe slightly, holding it slanted across his body. "Take the ball."

"Sister drag you *all* down," Ceto muttered. He snatched the bead from Garric, hesitated a moment, and popped it into his mouth.

"*I* found the ring myself and—" he said. His face went white, then flushed red. He spat the bead onto the ground, then gagged up a mouthful of phlegm and saliva.

"You tried to poison me, Vascay!" Ceto shouted. He

whipped out his curved sword in a slashing arc. "I'll send your soul to Hell!"

The other members of the band backed away. Ceto was a powerful man, and the long sword was a particularly dangerous weapon in the hands of somebody too angry to worry about self-preservation.

Instead of drawing his knives, Vascay hopped sideways to put the cookfire between him and Ceto. He nodded to Garric with a sardonic grin. "Brother Gar," he said, "your opponent doesn't accept the verdict of the Ball of Truth. What do you say?"

Ceto whirled toward Garric, raising his sword. Garric gripped the near end of the rod supporting the soup and jerked it toward him. The pot tipped into the fire, hissing and fuming. Garric backed a step, judging his new weapon's weight and balance as Ceto came on.

The rod was iron, five feet long and thumb-thick beneath the scale and rust. By reflex Garric slid his left hand toward the center the way he would've gripped a quarterstaff.

A quarterstaff hadn't been holding a stewpot over a fire for the past several hours. There was a sizzle and a *greasy* feeling in Garric's fingertips. Grateful for Gar's calluses, he jerked his hand back to the end where the iron was cool enough to be safe.

Ceto slashed down at Garric. Garric raised the rod crosswise, blocking the stroke in a shower of sparks. The blade bit deep enough not to skid, but it'd take a stronger man than Ceto to hack through so thick a rod with a sword.

Garric heaved the rod up, lifting Ceto's sword arm with it. While Ceto was extended, Garric kicked him in the gut, near the spot where his punch had landed. Ceto *woof*ed and doubled up, drawing both arms close to his sides.

Garric stepped back, judged his distance, and brought the rod around in a whistling sideways stroke. Ceto tried to raise his sword. The rod flung it away and thumped into the bandit's skull.

Ceto sprawled onto his left side, bleeding brightly from the pressure cut in his scalp. The sword spun end over end—Ademos jumped out of the way with a squeal—and stuck in the ground. It sang angrily until it had damped itself to silence.

Garric stabbed his rod into the dirt at his feet and rested some of his weight on it. He sucked in great gasping breaths, wavering slightly because his blood still raced with readiness to fight or flee.

To fight: Garric or-Reise wasn't running anywhere.

Smiling faintly, Vascay walked around the spluttering fire and pulled Ceto's sword from the ground. He held it up at a slant, peering along the edge. Garric could see from where he stood that there was a dent where his rod parried the blade, but the edge hadn't broken away. The smith had started with good steel, then cooled it slowly to a working temper instead of the brittle hardness suitable only for razors and fools.

Vascay swept his glance around the circle of his fellows, turning his body slightly so that he eyed each man squarely. Ademos and a few others looked away, but nobody spoke.

"Ceto didn't accept the verdict of the Ball of Truth," Vascay said; not shouting, but an open challenge to anyone who might disagree. He stared at Ademos, whose head was turned sideways as though he were fascinated by the bromeliads growing from the trunks of the great figs. "Does anybody want to take up where he left off?"

Garric had his breath back and his pulse under control. He straightened and lifted the rod again. The iron had cooled enough he could hold it by the balance now.

Tint came out of the ferns and crept to his side. She was whimpering. Garric reached down and rubbed her scalp, but he didn't take his eyes off the gang's leader.

"That's what I'd hoped," Vascay said with a broader smile. He walked to Garric and rotated the sword in his hand, offering him the hilt.

"Here you go, Brother Gar," he said. "Finish the oath-breaker and take the scabbard as well."

Garric took the sword. He'd never handled a curved blade before, so he was glad to find that this one, at least, balanced perfectly in his hand.

"He can live," Garric said. Ceto was unconscious and breathing in a ragged snore. "I won't kill a man in cold blood."

"Well, that does credit to your upbringing, brother," Vascay said. He bent and undid the two-tongued buckle of Ceto's heavy belt, then jerked it clear and tossed it to Garric. "You and I will take a skin of wine to a quiet place and discuss matters now, shall we?"

"Yes, all right," said Garric. Other members of the band nodded or murmured approval under their breath, even Ademos.

"Fine," said Vascay. He bent again and cut Ceto's throat from ear to ear. Blood like that of a slaughtered hog spewed out. *There was no bowl of meal here to soak it up for black pudding. . . .*

"My upbringing, on the other hand . . ." Vascay said. He let out a full-throated laugh.

Chapter Seven

Vascay settled on a boulder whose angles had been smoothed by the freshets that swept the channel during every heavy rain; he gestured Garric to a similar slab which sloped to face his own. The stream was now only a milky gurgle at their feet. Fern fronds and the hard green foliage of large-leaf philodendrons spread overhead.

Garric eased himself onto the rock. It felt clammy through his tunic, but everything in the forest was.

The seat Vascay had chosen for himself was less comfortable than Garric's broader slab, but it was also a hand's breadth higher. Garric grinned knowingly—upward—at the chieftain.

Vascay laughed and sucked wine from the stoneware bottle—a sip only, just enough to show it was safe. He offered the bottle to Garric. "Now, my friend," he said. "Why don't you tell me who you really are?"

Garric's mouth had tasted foul ever since the fight with Ceto. He took a swig of wine, sloshed it over his cheeks and tongue, and spat it out. Then he bent and dipped a palmful of water from the stream. It had a milky tinge, but it tasted clean and cold.

He met Vascay's waiting eyes. "Ceto kicked me in the head," he said. "I regained my memory."

"I see the bruise," Vascay said pleasantly. "But Gar didn't start remembering a poet dead for two thousand years. I was a schoolteacher before this"—he tapped his wooden leg—"and the rest of my problems with the Intercessor's tax men, and I could only spout half a dozen tags from Celondre. I say again, who are you?"

Two thousand years! Celondre had been one of the greatest poets of the Old Kingdom—but that was only a thousand years before Garric's day. Echeus had sent Garric's mind not only to a strange place but to a distant time.

"I'm Prince Garric of Haft," Garric said deliberately, watching for any change in Vascay's expression. "If the 'Intercessor' you're talking about is Echeus of Laut, then we share an enemy. I think he's the one who . . ."

Garric flicked his free hand in a circle, searching for the right word. He couldn't find it.

"Who sent me here," he said, close enough for Vascay

to understand as much as Garric himself did.

The camp was within easy bowshot if the jungle hadn't intervened, but the rest of the band could have been on the moon for all the sign there was from where Garric sat. Every few steps in this green maze put you in a separate world.

Tint hunched on the bank nearby, shivering but otherwise motionless. She stared fixedly at a liana which trailed crookedly across the stream. Garric followed the line of her eyes in puzzlement till he realized that the liana was unusually thick for part of its length. A python mottled brown on green lay on the vine; perhaps sleeping, perhaps waiting for prey to pass beneath it.

"I'll take the wine," Vascay said. He drank, deeply this time, and rested the bottle on his thigh. His lips smiled very tightly as he looked Garric up and down.

"Prince Garric of Haft," Vascay said musingly. "The last ruler of the New Kingdom. He died in battle on Tisamur, fighting the Count of Blaise. After his death and the destruction of both great armies, the Archai swept over the Isles. Only Laut was preserved, by the power of the Intercessor."

He drank again. Handing the bottle back to Garric, he added with a wry grin, "That's the way we tell the story on Laut, at any rate."

Garric shrugged. "I don't know how I came here," he said. "I only know that I *am* Garric, though the body I'm in is Gar's."

He drank. Wine was an imported luxury on Haft. Reise kept bottles on hand for visitors during the Sheep Fair, but his family and the other residents of Barca's Hamlet drank the bitter beer he brewed with locally grown germander.

This bottle had a wreath impressed into the clay before firing, showing that the vintner was proud enough of his product to make it identifiable. It was all a matter of what you were used to, though; to Garric the drink had a nasty aftertaste.

He wasn't sure he was going to like being a member of a bandit gang a thousand years after his own time; but, like the wine, it was what he had at the moment.

Instead of responding immediately, Vascay pursed his lips and eyed the fabric of leaves overhanging the stream while he thought. After a moment he grinned again at Garric, and said, "The question now is what to do with you, eh?"

"That isn't how I'd phrase the question," Garric said, "but I'll let it stand for now. Tell me how you worked the ball. Poisoning Ceto and not me, I mean."

Vascay laughed. "You don't believe I cared for a saintly hermit, my friend?" he said. "Indeed, I did just that."

His face changed minusculely; Vascay's lips still smiled, but he was no longer the jolly plump man. "That had nothing to do with Ceto, of course," he said. "It wasn't poison, just a wash of alum. Some beads have the alum on the outside, some under a thin layer of hard biscuit."

Garric considered what he'd just been told. "You didn't know that Ceto was lying," he said. "You didn't *care* whether he was lying or not."

Vascay chuckled. "Well, friend," he said, "let's just say that I've had my eye on Ceto for some time. He was getting a little too big to wear the cap I'd given him, so when you came along, well . . ."

He turned his hands palms up in a gesture that only context made clear.

The buttress roots of the giant tree behind Vascay were wrinkled like a rooster's wattles, brown and gray and gray-brown. One of the folds formed a cup large enough to hold a firkin of beer. Garric suddenly realized that the pair of specks glittering on the rim weren't black-capped mushrooms but rather the eyes of another snake coiled in the hollow. There were a *lot* of snakes in this place.

"How did you know I'd be able to handle Ceto?" Garric said quietly. He already knew the answer; he was asking to hear the way Vascay responded.

"I didn't, to be honest," said Vascay—honestly, which was what Garric needed to know. "But I'd seen you face Ceto, and I'd seen the way you moved. I'd have bet on you, friend . . . and if I'd lost my money, well, you wouldn't have been much good for the job, would you?"

"Go on," said Garric. Snakes weren't the only thing cold-blooded in this place, but Garric had learned how cold a prince had to be many times. He could imagine that was true as well for a bandit chief.

"If you're a prince from another time," Vascay said, crooking his finger for the wine again, "and even if you're not—"

He smiled, but only partly in humor. The words were an open warning that Vascay was willing to accept Garric's story, but that belief was a different thing from acceptance.

"—you may not understand our situation on Laut."

"This is Laut?" Garric interjected. Neither he nor Carus in his own time had visited Laut. Liane would know more about the island, but—Garric felt his gut tighten—she wasn't here.

"This is Serpent's Isle, just off the south coast of Laut," Vascay said. "A place no one ever goes by choice, eh? Unless they've a very good reason."

He tapped his wooden leg again. "My reason, *our* reason," he went on, "is that Lord Thalemos has hired us to find a ring of power on Serpent's Isle. Thalemos has a wizard advisor who tells him that the ring will bring down Echeon the Tyrant and reopen Laut to the world beyond."

Vascay closed his left hand into a fist. When he reopened it, the sapphire ring winked on his little finger.

"That ring?" Garric said. "The one I found."

"So I hope and believe, my friend," the chieftain agreed.

Vascay closed and reopened his hand; the ring vanished again. "I keep in practice," he said softly. "You can never tell when you'll need the skill. Today, for example."

He met Garric's eyes squarely. "There's a lot I can do through sleight of hand," he said, "and a few things I can do with my knives as well; but Ceto would've become a real problem for me if you hadn't"—Vascay's hand duplicated the questing circle that Garric's had made a moment before—"appeared when you did."

He held out the wine. When Garric's hand touched his on the bottle, Vascay added, "I need someone like you as my deputy, Garric. The man I can trust to do what I'd do every time . . . only maybe better, some of the time, because he's got the stronger arm."

Garric drank, paused, and drank more. The wine's astringency was what his mouth needed, and the aftertaste didn't seem so unpleasant now.

"You think I'd make a good bandit, Master Vascay?" he asked. "Perhaps so, but I don't have a taste for the work. We'll part after we return to the mainland."

Garric leaned forward very slightly. "Unless you have different ideas on the matter," he said. He wondered whether he'd have been quite so ready to carry out the threat implicit in his words if his red-handed ancestor Carus hadn't shared his mind for these past months.

Vascay burst into full-throated laughter. "Unless I choose to threaten the fellow I just watched use a rusty spit to put down the best swordsman among the Brethren, you mean?" he said. "No, no, I won't do that, friend Garric."

He gestured for the wine, but instead of drinking immediately he gave Garric a hard smile over the bottle. "And you're right, we're bandits," he said. "But we wouldn't have been, most of us, if honest men could live on Laut under the Intercessor. *I* wouldn't have been."

Vascay drank. His hands trembled slightly, and his

smile when he lowered the bottle was sour with the thoughts behind it.

"We're not saints, Garric," he said. "We'll rob anybody with money—but that's pretty generally the Intercessor's agents and his friends. We're here now on Serpent's Isle"—he too leaned forward, his face as hard as Garric's had been shortly before—"which has the name of being cursed, and where Kelbat or-Haysa died of snakebite before we'd been ashore an hour. Not for the money Metron is offering but because of what he plans to do. Thalemos' ancestors were Earls of Laut before the wizard Echeus set himself up as Intercessor before the end of the New Kingdom. The present Intercessor, Echeon, has ruled alone for the past hundred years; the greatest wizard and the worst tyrant of the line. But Metron says he can put Thalemos on the throne in Echeon's place with the help of this—"

The stone on his little finger winked blue fire.

"—ring."

Garric frowned. "Is Echeon immortal?" he asked.

The chieftain shrugged. "He hasn't changed in a hundred years," he said. "From the way he guards himself, no, he's not immortal, but it may be that he'll never die naturally. Which wouldn't be a problem if I ever got within arm's length of him, I promise you, or if any of the Brethren did."

Vascay laughed again, relaxing visibly. "But as I said, friend," he said, "we weren't saints most of us to start out with, and our tempers didn't change for the better when Echeon's tax gatherers broke us. I could use—we Brethren all could use—your mind and your sword arm; and you'd be better to have *family*, let's say, when you learn the realities of Laut. Even if your brothers are outlaws."

"Fairly said," said Garric, relaxing with a degree of surprise at how tense he himself had been a moment before. Vascay was too smart to want to be on the wrong side of

Garric, fair enough. But Garric had seen Vascay—and Vascay's knife—in action, and . . .

Garric grinned.

"Eh?" said Vascay.

"A friend of mine named Carus," explained Garric, "would've said that close in a man with a knife had an advantage over a man with a sword. Might have. But I don't guess I'll ever learn for sure."

Vascay spread his hands on his knees. "Listen, lad," he said, grimly serious. "If you please, you can leave now or the moment the boat touches the shore of Laut, without my let or hindrance. But there's no safety for any honest man on Laut, so unless you're going to offer your services to the Intercessor . . . ?"

He grinned, but there was a hint of real question in his eyes. It vanished when Garric shook his head in fierce denial.

"Right, I didn't think so," said Vascay. "If you're not going to do that, then stay with us for at least a time. And if you stay long enough to help bring down the Intercessor . . ."

Fierce joy unexpectedly transfigured the bandit's face. "If we can do that," he said, "I'll count my leg well lost."

He slapped the peg leg with his hand with a sharp *rap-rap*: fingers against wood, and wood against the rock in which it rested.

"By the Lady, my friend," Vascay said harshly. "If we can bring down Echeon, then I don't mind if they hang me the moment after. Truly I do not."

Garric frowned. "You talk as though there's only Laut, Master Vascay," he said. "I grant it's your home, but if things are so bad—why don't you leave for another isle?"

Vascay frowned in surprise that came close to anger; then his face cleared. "I forgot it was Prince Garric from the New Kingdom who was asking," he said. "Echeon's a wizard, you see. Those who venture into the seas at the horizon from Laut, coming or going, are run down by the galleys manned by Echeon's Protectors of the Peace."

He grinned harshly. "And sunk, and all drowned with no more trial than the crabs give them," he added. "Nobody enters Laut or goes more than a league beyond the shore and lives. Some claim that the Intercessor uses his wizard arts to bring lightnings down on fleets too great for his Protectors to deal with, but I wouldn't know. I doubt there've been any such fleets in the Isles since Prince Garric died and the Archai brought down the New Kingdom a thousand years ago."

There was more than humor in Vascay's smile; but there was humor also.

"If no one can enter Laut . . ." said Garric, weighing cautiously the words he'd listened to, "then how did Thalemos' advisor get here from Tisamur? Metron."

"Aye, Metron," Vascay said. "With a purse full of gold and a tongue full of promises. His art brought him, I suppose."

"Could he be an agent of Echeon's?" Garric pressed. "Tricking you and others like you into coming out where he can snap you up?"

Vascay laughed bitterly. "You're a prince indeed, aren't you, friend Garric?" he said. "You think like a prince, at any rate."

The bandit's face hardened. "Aye," he said. "That could be; I've thought it, though it's not a thing I'd say to the other Brethren, you understand. But I took the chance regardless, because it's the only chance on offer that *might* bring down the tyrant."

Garric nodded. "I see," he said.

What would Carus do in this place? Take the risk of supporting Thalemos, probably. And yet, how much of a risk was that compared to the other choices? What else could he do but wander Laut as a lone vagabond . . . with a beastgirl in tow?

Garric glanced at Tint. She felt his eyes and met them, still shivering with fear of the snakes all about her. He couldn't very well leave Tint to her fate, any more than he could stay here on Serpent's Isle as an alternative to trying his luck on the mainland of Laut.

Garric smiled at the bandit chieftain. The expression warmed him, so he let it spread more broadly across his face.

"All right, Master Vascay," he said. "This past year I've found myself filling many jobs I wasn't raised to. For a time, at least, I'll try my hand at being a bandit and a rebel."

Vascay leaned forward and clasped forearms with Garric. "Be a good enough rebel, my friend," Vascay said, "and we can all of us give up being bandits. Welcome to the Brethren!"

Cashel shielded his eyes with a hand and squinted besides; the noon sun gave the bay a brassy sheen that'd make the back of his head hurt if he wasn't careful. The water was so still that the reef formed a ragged black line instead of tossing spray.

"It'll be a good time to go out," he said to Tilphosa, who sat beside him. Her legs were crossed, right knee over left knee, and her hands were clasped over them tightly. "Past the reef, I mean."

They'd have to row, of course; the sail the crewmen had rigged to the new mast—the wreck's former main spar—hung as limp as the fronds of the palms at the tide line. That didn't matter to Tilphosa one way or the other, of course.

Cashel dried his hands on his tunic. "I wouldn't mind doing some real work," he said. "Rowing would feel good."

Metra was working her art in a space Cashel had cleared

among the ferns. The sailcloth screen she'd used earlier was now part of the pinnace's kit. Metra didn't want the sailors watching her and maybe getting in the way—and the sailors, like most people, didn't like to be around wizardry.

Cashel didn't mind wizardry, but he was just as glad not to have to see Metra. He didn't like her or trust her, either one.

"But you lifted that huge rock," Tilphosa said, drawn out of her brown study by Cashel's words. "Surely that was work, even for you."

"That was a job, all right," Cashel said. He paused while his mind sifted words to find the ones that'd explain. "But all that, killing the cannibal in its coffin . . . that's kinda what I'd like to clear out of my mind, do you see?"

He gave her a smile. He didn't suppose Tilphosa would understand, but she wasn't the sort to sneer because "nothing that dumb ox Cashel says is worth listening to" like some folks in the borough whispered.

Tilphosa smiled back, but her expression chilled suddenly. She lowered her eyes to the ground and hunched her shoulders.

"I want to be off this island," the girl whispered. Her clasped hands trembled, and for a moment Cashel was afraid she was going to cry. "I'd start swimming if I didn't think they were going to have the boat ready soon. They will, won't they?"

Tilphosa raised her eyes to the dinghy. A dozen sailors clustered about it, putting on what Cashel too thought were the finishing touches under Hook's direction. They'd raised the sidewalls with boards from the wreck's decking and had fitted the mast, turning a boat into a pinnace.

"Right, it shouldn't be long," Cashel said. He didn't try to sound especially hearty; if Tilphosa hadn't learned by now that Cashel meant the things he said, there wasn't much point in tricking her into believing him. Funny that she'd been so, well, *solid* when it really was dangerous. Now that the thing in the gold coffin was dead—and it surely was dead—she was letting her nerves get to her.

Tilphosa resumed staring morosely at the ground. The sailors were rigging a rudder—the dinghy had been steered with the oars—and hadn't started loading the stores of food and water yet, so it'd be a while longer.

Cashel cleared his throat, and said, "Can you tell me about this Thalemos you're going to marry, mistress? I don't know anything about Laut. I, ah, come from Haft."

The truth was, up to a few months ago Cashel hadn't known any more about Count Lascarg in Carcosa, the capital of Haft, than he had about whoever ruled Laut. Folks from Barca's Hamlet didn't travel much, and the merchants who came to buy sheep and wool didn't give much idea of the wider world they moved in.

Tilphosa looked at him and smiled unexpectedly. "Thanks," she said, "for trying to distract me. But if you really want to hear about my marriage . . . ?"

"Sure," Cashel said, watching a speck above the western horizon. "Now that I'm getting a chance to learn new things, I figure I oughtn't to waste it."

The speck was an albatross, he figured, though he couldn't be sure at this distance. Even the seagulls seemed to keep away from here. He'd never guessed that gulls cared about anything but finding the next beakful to send down to a belly that was never full.

"There's really some mystery about it," Tilphosa said, lowering her voice slightly. The sailors by the pinnace were too far away to hear anyway, but it was toward the jungle where Metra was working that the girl's eyes turned. She grinned at Cashel, already herself again. "A mystery from me, at any rate. I think Metra . . ."

She shrugged. Cashel nodded understanding.

"My parents died when I was too young to remember even their faces," Tilphosa said. "They were lost at sea. I

. . . well, I've never liked the sea, but there wasn't any choice if I was to get to Laut, was there?"

"Someday maybe you'll meet my sister Ilna," Cashel said. "You'd get along, I guess. You'd get along with all my friends."

Tilphosa frowned. "Because they're afraid of the sea?" she said.

"Not that," said Cashel. "Because they do things whether they're scared to do them or not."

He smiled softly, remembering Ilna and Garric and especially Sharina, lovely Sharina, with her musical laugh.

"But what about you, Cashel?" Tilphosa asked. "You do things even if you're afraid, don't you?"

Cashel shrugged. "I guess I would," he said. "But the only things I've found to worry about are, you know, not doing a good enough job."

His lips pursed. He wondered if he sounded like he was bragging. It wasn't like that, he was just trying to explain how he felt.

"Well, anyway," Tilphosa went on, "I became a ward of the Temple of Our Lady of the Moon in Donelle. The priests saw to it that I was educated as a proper lady. They didn't make me a priest myself, though. I know no more about the rituals of the Mistress than any householder on Tisamur does."

Cashel nodded to show that he'd heard. On Haft the priests chanted hymns to the Great Gods on major festivals; ordinary folk just bowed and paid their tithes; paid a tithe of what the temple officials could prove in their assessment rolls, anyhow. It sounded like things were different on Tisamur. At least—

"You always say 'the Mistress,'" Cashel said, turning to meet the girl's eyes. "It *is* the Lady you mean, right?"

Tilphosa frowned slightly. "Well . . ." she said. "It's hard to explain, Cashel. The Mistress, the lunar aspect of the Lady, is real. I mean . . ."

She looked over her shoulder with a hooded expression, checking to be sure that Metra was still at her work out of sight. "We don't have an image of the Mistress in our temple in Donelle," Tilphosa said in a lowered voice. "She comes in the visions when worshippers gather in the sanctuary at night to pray; and She comes in dreams to the specially devout. The Mistress isn't a statue of wood or stone like the Lady in other temples."

Captain Mounix was satisfied with the way the rudder hung, though Hook had taken a rasp from his tool chest and was softening the edges of the hinge-pin. The rest of the men began loading the pinnace from the stores piled to either side.

Mounix glanced toward Cashel, but he didn't call. Most times Cashel would've gone to help without thinking about it, but there were too many sailors for the job already: three handsful of them, besides Mounix himself and Hook. They worked like they were as ready to leave this place as Tilphosa was.

Cashel smiled. He wouldn't mind getting away himself, though he wasn't sure he was going to like Laut any better. Well, by now he'd been a lot of different places and he'd managed to do all right in all of them.

"And that's what happened, you see," Tilphosa continued, watching the final preparations with greedy eyes. "The Mistress told Her Children in dreams that I should marry Thalemos of Laut so that She can return to rule the world. So, well, here we are."

She smiled at Cashel, then looked over her shoulder again. Her expression became guarded again.

"I've never met Prince Thalemos," she said softly. "And I'm not even sure he knows I'm coming to Laut to marry him. But the Mistress knows all; Her will be done."

"Girl!" called Captain Mounix, though his eyes were on Cashel rather than Tilphosa. "You better bring your wizard if she expects to leave with us!"

"Let her stay!" shouted a sailor from the other side of the pinnace, mostly hidden by his fellows.

"I'll get her," Cashel said quietly, but Tilphosa stood with him as he rose.

They started off toward Metra's clearing. Before they entered the trees, Cashel glanced back to make perfectly certain that the sailors wouldn't be able to launch the pinnace before he and the women could return. There were farmers in the borough who'd cheat you of anything they thought they could get away with; they'd trained Cashel, so he was ready to deal with Mounix and his men.

"Did you have any say in the business, mis . . . ah, Tilphosa?" Cashel asked. "Mistress" was what he'd ordinarily call a woman when concern made him formal, but he didn't like the sound of the word here.

Bent fronds marked the trail, but enough of the vegetation had sprung straight again that he walked in front of the girl. "I mean, what you're doing doesn't sound like, like something I'd want to do."

Tilphosa laughed and touched his shoulder from behind. "I appreciate what you're saying, Cashel," she said, "but you don't understand what it is to have a real God, the Mistress Herself, order you to do something."

Through the foliage ahead Cashel heard Metra's voice hoarsely chanting. His skin prickled.

"Mistress Metra!" he called to give warning. "We're coming to fetch you back to leave!"

Then, softly over his shoulder, he added, "No, Lady Tilphosa, I don't know what it would be like to have a real God order me to do something."

Cashel wasn't sure that Tilphosa knew either, though she thought she did. Well, he'd deal with his part of the job the best way he could, whatever it turned out to be.

He pushed through the ferns; Metra was trying to rise, but wizardry had robbed her legs of strength. "You take her gear, Tilphosa," Cashel said. He shifted his staff to his left hand and bent to pick Metra up whether she wanted that or not.

Cashel wasn't one to waste time arguing when a job had to be done.

"Chalcus is coming!" Merota said, hopping up from where she sat opposite Ilna on the horseshoe bench under a grape arbor. She started to run toward the conference room but caught herself before her legs moved. "Ilna, can I . . . ?"

Ilna felt a thrill of anticipation. It didn't reach her face, of course, and her fingers continued the knotwork she was using to busy them.

"Yes, of course," she said. The words weren't fully out of her mouth before Merota was racing across the lawn toward Chalcus. He'd just passed through the cordon of guards with a joke and laughter.

Ilna's almost-smile—about as close as she ever came to a smile, she supposed—hardened before it reached her lips. Though Chalcus moved with his usual lithe grace, Ilna recognized the tension beneath the grin he flashed her.

Tenoctris waited just outside the cordon of Blood Eagles, resting some of her weight on Liane's arm. Garric spoke from the doorway; the two women joined him and Sharina in the conference room. Just before closing the door, he gave Ilna a look she couldn't read.

She continued to knot wool into fabric on her lap. Ilna didn't carry a loom with her, but she always had skeins of yarn. Work didn't occupy her mind, but the rote exercise provided a foundation of support that settled her when otherwise she would . . .

Would be unsettled, leave it at that. Not even Ilna os-Kenset could in perfect calm view the gray web-draped Hell Tenoctris had drawn from Echeus' mind.

Ilna thought of the spiders whose unwinking multiple eyes stared as if they saw her through the curtain of wizardry. Well, let them stare; she had her work.

The fabric lengthened. Ilna didn't have to look at it to know that anyone who did would feel the touch of sunlight on the ancient stonework of the mill in Barca's Hamlet. There was hard work and hard living in the borough, as there was everywhere in this world for a poor orphan. But the sun endured, and the mill endured, and Ilna had endured also.

It wasn't the most cheerful gift to offer those viewing the fabric, but Ilna didn't believe there was a better one. Especially for a viewer whom spiders might be watching.

Ilna didn't need to be in the conference room; Tenoctris alone could tell Garric what they'd seen in the dead man's eyes. Perhaps the old wizard could even explain it, though she'd seemed as much at a loss as Ilna was.

Ilna's fingers continued to knot the yarn, turning the vision of Hell into a pattern of repose and gentle pleasure. She was making the world a better place by *that* much; a trivial thing in the long run, but—Ilna grinned coldly—in the long run they'd all be dead.

Merota flung herself toward the sailor; he scooped her up in his arms. Ilna had expected that, but she was surprised when—instead of striding directly over to the bench where Ilna waited—Chalcus set the girl on the platform of a sundial several paces away. He stood before Merota, holding her hands and talking earnestly.

Ilna deliberately turned her head and studied the grape leaves behind her. Small ants tended herds of aphids along the curling shoots.

Ilna felt a surge of bitter desperation: she had as much kinship with those insects as she did with the human beings around her. Garric had turned her away, and now Chalcus chatted with the child instead of—

"Mistress Ilna . . . ?" he said, unexpectedly close.

Ilna spun around, flustered despite herself. She'd grown accustomed to Chalcus announcing himself with a whistled tune; and of course his soft-soled boots made no sound on the turf. . . .

Merota remained standing beside the sundial, wide-eyed and nervously stiff as she watched them. "She won't wander," Chalcus said, half-turning his head to indicate the girl. "I told her you and I must talk without her, mistress"—he smiled, though not as broadly as at most times—"and she agreed, though without pleasure. So that now I can speak with you about matters that give me no pleasure either."

Ilna folded the knotwork ribbon and put it in her sleeve. She took out a few lengths of twine to occupy her fingers in its place.

"Speak, then," she said. Her own smile was as cold as the winter sky.

"Your friend Garric's mind was raped away by the wizard you saw killed," the sailor said baldly. He squatted so that she needn't look up to meet his eyes. "The fellow who looks through his eyes now says he's a friend to the Isles and to Garric . . . which I believe. But he's a very hard man, that one, my dear. There's nothing he wouldn't do if he thought the choice were failure."

"A change indeed from Garric," said Ilna calmly. She took Chalcus' words as fact, the way she'd have expected hers to be accepted in a similar case. "Not so very different from present company though, perhaps."

"Aye," said Chalcus with a flash of the old humor. "Not different at all. But when he asks you and me to go to Tisamur with young Lady Merota to conceal our purpose, then you must know that it isn't Garric who weighed the risks to the child before he spoke."

"I see," said Ilna. With a flash of relief she understood why Chalcus had paused to chat with Merota before he came to where she sat. "The girl has agreed, of course?"

"The girl thinks she'd be safe in the heart of the Underworld with you and me to guard her, dear one," the sailor said softly. "She would not, and I've told her she would not; but she won't believe me."

"What does the one who isn't Garric expect us to do on Tisamur?" Ilna said, filing the response to consider later if at all. She suspected that Merota understood more than Chalcus thought she did, but she didn't suppose that mattered.

"There's wizardry besides rebellion there, he thinks," Chalcus said. "That one—"

He'd never given a name to the one in Garric's body.

"—doesn't need help with rebels and sword strokes, but wizards are another matter. A matter for you, he thinks."

"And you think, Master Chalcus?" Ilna said with a faint smile.

"I've seen that one use his sword, dear one," he said. The term didn't grate on her ears as it sometimes had. "I trust his skill as I would trust my own. And I've seen you work as well. None will stand against you, of that I'm as sure as I'm sure—"

Chalcus laughed; fully alive, fully himself again. "As sure as I am that I'll stand by you," he concluded.

Ilna sniffed. "Yes," she said, "*that* at least I'm sure of."

Tisamur was only a name to her. She'd woven for buyers trafficking to the powerful islands of the north: Sandrakkan, Blaise, and even as far as Ornifal. All of them based their fashions on the mode in Valles.

Ilna's lips twisted in a grim smile. The nobles of other islands might not recognize Prince Garric as their overlord, but Garric's court formed their taste in dress.

She looked at Chalcus, watching his face settle into a neutral expression as he waited for her to speak. Merota remained the set distance away, shifting from foot to foot because she was too young to have learned how to hide her nervousness. The child was afraid that Ilna would refuse to let her voyage to Tisamur because of the danger.

"Yes, all right," Ilna said, pleased by the flicker of surprise in Chalcus' eyes. She'd thought of questioning him about Tisamur first, letting him wait and worry about her response the way he and Garric and all of them had forced her to wait.

That would have been petty. Ilna wasn't petty—when she caught herself and mastered her nature, at least. Mastering her nature allowed her to avoid being so many other things, worse things. On a good day.

"I'd thought—" said Chalcus; and stopped himself, for they both knew what he'd thought. There was nothing to be gained by going over that ground. "I'll tell the chancellor—or would you care to, mistress? That one"—a quick nod toward the closed conference room—"says he's transferring properties to Lady Merota, which she'll be visiting to take stock."

"A reasonable plan," Ilna said calmly. "I'll let you talk to Royhas. I've found that people don't listen to me unless . . ."

She smiled, an expression as grim as a set of manacles. "Until, I should say," she continued, "I force them to."

She glanced down at the pattern her fingers had just tied in the twine. She picked it out again. "And on a good day," she said, "I don't like to do that."

"Aye, I'll do that," said Chalcus. He rose as though about to summon Merota; again he paused, and said, "The coasts of Tisamur are much like what you'll find anywhere in the Isles. Fishing villages, coasting ports; a little more clannish and reserved than Shengy, say, but not in a bad way. Donelle's the only real city, and maybe Brange on the north coast. Inland . . ."

Chalcus' left index finger stroked the place the horn hilt of his incurved sword would ride if he were wearing it. "Inland," he said, "away from the river valleys . . . there's stories that come out."

He laughed, but the sound wasn't wholly convincing. "There's stories everywhere," he said, "stories about the place I grew up even, and they're mostly as empty as the foam on a jack of ale."

"But sometimes the stories are true," Ilna said, completing the thought Chalcus was skirting.

"Aye, that's been my experience," he said, grateful for the interjection. "I know nothing about Moon Wisdom, dearest, but in the hills of Tisamur they're said to worship many things besides the Great Gods. It may be that Moon Wisdom is one of those, come down to the coasts and the cities."

Ilna's eyes narrowed slightly. She'd seen Chalcus face wizards with no more fear than he'd have shown for so many swordsmen . . . but for all his profane irreligion, he feared the Gods.

"I see," she said aloud. "I gather the plan is that we travel as Merota's servants?"

"Aye, if you're willing," Chalcus said, clearly more comfortable with the change of subject.

"And why wouldn't I be willing?" Ilna snapped. "I'm not too good for any honest work!"

She heard the outrage in her voice, paused, and gave Chalcus a wry smile. "Sorry," she said. "With so much in the world to be upset over, that was a foolish concern. Even for me on what seems to be a foolish day. And if you'd asked me were I willing to *have* a servant, then you'd have gotten a different answer."

She stood. "I'll see to packing," she said. "My own clothing won't take long, but Lady Merota bos-Roriman will no doubt have greater requirements."

"Dear one?" Chalcus said, saw her face harden, and went on, "Mistress Ilna, then. A question before we part, if you please: why did you agree so easily?"

Ilna quirked a smile. "Why am I not worried about the danger to Merota?" she asked. "I am, Master Chalcus; I'm very much afraid."

The smile faded. "But I saw a thing in a dead man's

eyes just now, and I'm more afraid of that."

She stretched out an arm in summons. Merota, bubbling with excitement, came racing toward her two protectors.

"Because if that vision comes to pass," Ilna said quietly, "there'll be no safety, for a child or for anyone, in all this world."

Sharina heard a shout from the king sleeping in the inner room of the suite. She got to her feet without stumbling and took the lighted candle from the alcove which shaded its gleam to a soft glow fanning across the floor. She was still half-asleep, but an innkeeper's daughter learns to cope with crises in the darkness.

She pushed through the curtain of carved wooden beads across the doorway connecting to the master bedroom. Garric—Carus—thrashed on the bed, wrestling with the feather-stuffed mattress. His face was contorted. As Sharina entered he shouted again in wordless fury.

"Carus!" Sharina said, wondering if the guards could overhear them. There were Blood Eagles in the corridor and in the grounds below Garric's second-story living quarters, she didn't want them bursting in. She couldn't guess what Carus might say in his nightmare. "Your majesty!"

The wall above the cherrywood wainscoting was frescoed with images showing the march of the seasons in the countryside. It was part of the room's original decorations, though workmen had repaired the fallen plaster when Prince Garric chose the suite for himself.

Ordinarily the scenes were cheerful if a little idealized to someone who knew the realities of peasant life. The painted snow lay on the ground at the turn of the year; real snow drove down, with intervals of sleet which locked the stubble beneath a coat of ice that hooves couldn't chip away. The painted dancers at the harvest festival were bright-eyed instead of logy with fatigue and beer. And in the painted world, the animals were clean, even the oxen who'd just come in from the field. Regardless, Garric and Sharina both had found them a pleasant reminder of a world they'd never be a part of again.

The candle had sunk to a blue glow about the wick as Sharina moved. Now it flared and guttered, distorting the frieze into presences worse than shadow. *Almost* Sharina could feel tendrils reaching for her from the spaces beyond the plastered wall.

Almost, or possibly . . .

"Carus!" she said. She dropped the candle onto the brass bedside tale and grasped the king's wrist with her strong right hand. "Wake up!"

Carus lunged upward like a dolphin jumping, awake and seated upright in bed in the same instant. He gripped Sharina as though she were a spar he'd caught while drowning. His eyes were wide, and his jaws were set in a rictus of fury.

His breath slowed. "Thank you, milady," he said in a husky whisper. His arms released her; his fingers had bruised her forearm when he'd twisted in her grasp.

He grinned faintly. "Call Tenoctris in while I get some clothes on, will you? Or I can—"

"No," said Sharina, leaving the candle as she padded back through the anteroom where she'd been sleeping. She picked up a light cape and draped it over her tunic before she opened the door to the corridor.

The Blood Eagles on guard had heard, all right; several had drawn their swords. All looked tense, though two kept their eyes on the corridor in either direction while the others waited for Sharina to explain the reason for the cries.

"The prince had a bad dream," Sharina said curtly. "One of you bring Tenoctris to us, please. She's in the—"

"Chaigon, go get her," said the officer in a breastplate with silvered engravings. A rangy swordsman padded off at a quick pace toward the adjacent suite where Tenoctris slept tonight. In deference to the sleep of those they protected, the Blood Eagles on interior guard wore soft-soled sandals rather than hobnailed boots.

"We know where the wizard is, princess," the officer said, polite but not afraid for doing a thing quickly instead of waiting for needless elaboration.

"Yes, I see," Sharina agreed. She turned back into the suite, saying over her shoulder, "Send her through immediately when she arrives. If you please."

Carus had pulled on an outer tunic and the high boots he'd added to Garric's wardrobe. As Sharina entered, the king was wrapping the double tongue of his sword belt around the belt proper. He saw her eye it.

"No, I don't think I'll be using a sword tonight," he said with a smile of embarrassment. "But I decided that I liked the weight of it to . . ."

He shrugged.

Instead of finishing that thought, Carus looked at a corner of the room, and said in a quiet, rigidly controlled voice, "I knew I was dreaming, Sharina, but I wasn't able to wake up. Until you pulled me up out of the dream. And even then I wasn't sure I was going to reach the surface until I was there."

"The room felt . . . I guess *cold* when I came in," Sharina said. The temperature was normal now, and the frieze had returned to being flat and inoffensive. The young mother was fluffing the covers around her baby, not smothering it with a pillow as a trick of the light had made it seem a moment before. . . .

The anteroom where Sharina'd slept was meant for a servant. Normally Liane would have been there while Sharina had her own separate bungalow, but for the time being the two of them had exchanged accommodation.

The change was at Carus' suggestion, but Liane had leaped at it with an audible gasp of relief.

There was a bustle in the corridor. "Go on through, Lady Tenoctris," the officer called in a loud voice. "We'll close the door behind you."

Carus stepped into the anteroom with his hands outstretched to greet the wizard and support her if she needed it. Sharina grinned at the care the soldiers took to communicate their intentions without giving offense. She sobered when she thought of the danger-filled void that those men—she didn't know a single one by name—faced. The soldiers didn't know whether indigestion or a monster from the deepest pit of Hell had caused the man they guarded to cry out.

Neither did Sharina, of course, but she and her friends at least had the chance to learn. The soldiers would remain in ignorance, most likely forever—but possibly until only an instant before some hellspawn struck them down.

Tenoctris, looking as sprightly as a sparrow, came in. She didn't need the support of Carus' arm, though he carried her satchel of paraphernalia. Behind them the outer door closed with heavy finality; the guards were putting a material barrier between themselves and the wizardry they expected—feared—would take place within.

"You said you had a nightmare," Tenoctris said, surveying the room with quick jerks of her head instead of a sweeping glance. "What exactly did you see?"

She sat on the floor abruptly; Sharina caught and helped her the last of the way as the older woman paused in midmotion. Carus passed the satchel to Sharina, who placed it before Tenoctris.

"I didn't really see anything," Carus said. He had control of himself again; he spoke reflectively, casting his mind back to retrieve the details of the experience. "I felt as if I was deep underwater. Something held me, pulled me down, but I couldn't touch it when I tried to."

He cleared his throat. "I was drowning," he said. To Sharina's amazement, there was real humor in the king's smile. "Drowning again, I mean. Only this time I don't think I'd have seen daylight again. Not even in a thousand years, through another man's eyes."

The floor was a woodland mosaic. In the slight present illumination the trees and creatures were shadows on shadow, with the only real contrast the splotches of white plaster: temporary patches filling places where the tesserae had fallen out.

Tenoctris took a writing brush and a pot of cinnabar from her satchel, then outlined a simple triangle over a stag with unlikely antlers. "Could you see anything?" she asked as she began writing words of power in the Old Script along the sides of the figure. "Or was it just blackness?"

"I couldn't see anything," said Carus. He scowled reflexively at what the wizard was doing, then caught Sharina's glance and smiled in wry self-deprecation. "But it wasn't black, it was gray."

Tenoctris tapped the three sides of her figure with her bamboo sliver, then began to intone the words under her breath. Air within the triangle blurred the way it might over a field on a summer day.

"Gray like what Hordred saw," Sharina said. "Didn't see."

"Yeah, that's what I was thinking about while I was down there," Carus agreed. "Wherever 'there' was. And after watching what happened to him, I can't doubt that something really was after Hordred in that grayness."

Tenoctris flung her wand aside and sagged. Sharina caught her before her head hit the floor.

"Wait," Tenoctris said. She straightened, then deliberately smudged the symbols with the sleeve of her robe. Red pigment smeared into the fine silk brocade.

Sharina winced, wondering what Ilna would say if she'd seen that. Perhaps nothing: Ilna was ruthlessly pragmatic herself, and Tenoctris would have a good reason for whatever she did.

"I didn't want to leave that where someone might accidentally pronounce it," the wizard said, now allowing the younger woman to help her up. "It was a simple location spell, but it started to go deeper than I thought was safe."

"Deeper?" said Carus.

"Spells have a weight of their own," Tenoctris said, settling herself onto an ivory chair. Its legs crossed in an X before curving upward to form the arms. All the surfaces had been chased with a pattern of vines and snakes. "I thought it would point me to a place in the present, Laut, perhaps, or Tisamur. Instead it began racing toward an end so distant that I was afraid it might carry me with it."

She quirked a smile, but the slight trembling of her hands was not merely from physical reaction. Carus squatted beside her, cocking his sword with one hand so that the scabbard's chape didn't rap on the floor. His other hand closed gently over those of Tenoctris.

"Carry you far in time?" Sharina asked. She thought of the cataclysm that had flung the old wizard a thousand years to this age.

"Carry me to the Underworld," Tenoctris said. For a moment she didn't move or even blink. "Carry me to Hell, Sharina."

Carus rose, patting the old woman's shoulder. "We can't have that," he said, his tone quietly cheerful. "If I need to sleep only in daylight, well—"

"Hordred was asleep in daylight," Sharina said sharply. "The last time."

"Then—" said Carus, louder yet and grasping his sword hilt.

"There's another way," said Tenoctris. The others looked at her.

"Go on," said Carus, opening his right hand. Sharina

felt a surge of relief; she hadn't seen any good result coming from the desperation she knew the ancient king felt even more strongly than she did.

"If Ilna is amenable," Tenoctris said, "I can put her in a trance and send her soul to follow the visitation back to its source. I don't think it would even be difficult for her. Though of course there's some danger."

Sharina shrugged. "Ilna would do anything to help," she said. "Any of us will."

"Send me," said Carus. His smile had a tinge of ruthlessness—if the expression wasn't simple cruelty instead. "This is my fight, after all."

"It's all our fight!" Tenoctris said with unusual force. "It's the fight of everyone alive and everyone who hopes to be born."

Her expression softened. "Of course you'd all go," she added, "but you'd never find the way. It's not what you *would* do but what you can. Ilna can follow the pattern to its source, I'm sure."

"And *I'm* sure," said King Carus, "that I'll know what to do when somebody shows me where to strike."

He laughed in fierce anticipation, his right hand on his sword. The candleflame guttered at the violence of his joy.

Chapter Eight

The guards accompanying Sharina and Ilna couldn't help marching in step. The clash of their boots on the flagstone walkway leading to Garric's apartments sounded like construction work on a large scale. It was a harsh sound, and maybe for that reason Sharina felt nervous.

She took her friend's hand, and said, "I wish Cashel were here."

Ilna looked at her with her usual lack of expression. "I do too," she said, "but I've never known my brother to start a job he didn't finish. I expect he'll do the same this time, whatever the job is."

She squeezed Sharina's hand firmly, then released it. Barely audible over the hobnails' ringing hammer strokes she added, "Does Tenoctris think the same thing that made Cashel disappear is attacking Garric also?"

Does she know Garric is gone? Sharina wondered. She opened her mouth to explain, then choked off the words. That was for Carus to say if Chalcus hadn't.

"I don't know," Sharina said. "I don't think she does, but we don't know very much at all."

Then, because of the previous realization, she went on, "Does your friend Chalcus stay within the palace?"

The building Garric had chosen for his apartments was larger than most of the residences within the compound, though still smaller than the town houses of the city's wealthy merchants. By now Valles had grown up to the south and southeast walls of the palace, but the two were still separate communities.

When the Dukes of Ornifal took the title of Kings of the Isles four hundred years ago, they sequestered a huge tract north of the city proper. They walled it and built therein scores of separate structures, ranging from open gazebos to barracks for the clerks, guards, and domestics of the palace staff.

"Generally he does, I believe," Ilna said, her eyes straight ahead. The muscles were tight over her cheekbones, but you didn't have to be a childhood friend like Sharina to know that Ilna was tense most of the time. "I don't know precisely where, but I believe he's found himself accommodations with the unmarried guards."

She cleared her throat, and added, "Tonight, *last* night—"

Dawn was turning the east-facing upper façade of Garric's residence pink.

"—he said he'd be going down to the port to find passage to Tisamur for the three of us."

Turning to meet Sharina's eyes, Ilna said, "I keep house for Merota and my brother. But not for Master Chalcus."

Knee-high cypresses lined the walk to either side. During a generation of neglect the original plantings had evolved into a tangle of undergrowth. When Garric revived the monarchy, the newly enlarged staff of groundskeepers had cleared away the mass as their first priority, but it would be years before these replacements grew into landscaping fit for the majesty of the Kingdom of the Isles.

Sharina smiled wanly.

It would also be years before the Kingdom of the Isles grew back into something truly majestic.

The officer of their guard exchanged passwords with the colleague who commanded the detachment at the entrance to the residence. Sharina saw her friend's lips tighten in something just short of a sneer for the workings of bureaucracy, whether military or civilian.

Ilna caught Sharina's glance and met it with a wry smile. "I'm not very good at getting along with other people," she said. "As you know. Fortunately, there are tasks that a person can do alone."

Ilna smile hardened into something an enemy would find frightening. "And some that have to be done alone, I gather," she said. Then, turning her face forward again, she asked, "Will the prince be here? When I go off to where Tenoctris sends me?"

Sharina licked her lips before answering, also looking toward the building. "I think it'll be just you and me with Tenoctris," she said, "but I really don't know."

She didn't understand—had never understood—the way

her friend's mind worked, but she knew Ilna was in pain. She reached out to link hands again, briefly.

A palace servant could've brought Ilna to the prince's residence, but it was more than for courtesy that Sharina had gone herself. Tenoctris didn't need help with her preparations, and besides—Sharina had wanted to get out of the building for a time. Even after Carus woke and the chill dissipated, a feeling, a touch of something slimy, had seemed to remain.

After Sharina left to fetch her friend, someone had opened the mullioned windows of the upper story. Carus looked out, waved a formal salute, and then went back inside. Quite aside from how the king felt about a woman who'd looked like, *been* like Ilna, Sharina supposed his distaste for wizardry would keep him from joining the three women during the planned incantation.

"I believe they'll let us in now," Ilna said as though she hadn't noticed the man at the window above them. "Back in, so far as you're concerned."

"I was daydreaming," Sharina apologized as she started forward. But what had happened to Hordred wasn't a dream.

The porch was a semicircle whose tiled roof was supported by four simple pillars. The double doors were wood. Royhas had wanted to replace them with bronze. Garric had refused, but the chancellor had gotten his way in part by attaching a bronze appliqué of linked rings, the symbol of the royal house of Haft during the Old Kingdom, in the center of both leaves.

And now King Carus, the last member of that house, ruled here in fact. . . . Aloud, more to herself than to her friend, Sharina said, "I'm going to have to watch myself. Everything seems like an omen to me now!"

"That must be very uncomfortable," Ilna said with a minuscule smile. "I've found the present to provide more than enough difficulty by itself."

The anteroom was meant for show. The coffered ceiling was the full height of the building, with the curving staircase to the private suites a seeming afterthought along the right side.

The walls had been recently redecorated. The fanciful painted arches and porticos of the earlier style were reduced to red lines on a cream background, framing a winged messenger to one side and a sea nymph on the other. To Sharina the design looked skimpy, but she noticed Ilna eye it with obvious appreciation.

"They'll be upstairs, ladies," said one of the guards stationed here. He looked uncomfortable.

Sharina's sturdy sandals—her feet weren't hardened to the city's stone pavements, and she didn't limit her walking to carpets where court slippers were appropriate—slapped on the stair treads. Attaper had insisted there be soldiers around Prince Garric during every moment. They hadn't saved Garric from the Intercessor's attack, nor were they any present help to the man now wearing Garric's flesh.

"Tasks for each of us," Ilna repeated with grim pleasure. She must have been thinking the same thing as Sharina.

A passage skirting the anteroom connected the north and south corridors; the occupant could choose a room to suit the season and personal taste. Garric's quarters were to the right, where the windows of the main bedroom looked east.

Sharina smiled faintly. It was as close as one could come in a palace to the garret room of the inn where her brother had slept until everything changed.

"Your highness, Lady Tenoctris is inside!" called the leader of the squad outside the open door. He and most of his men flattened against the corridor wall as the women passed.

One fellow, middle-aged and bearing the scars of hard

service, tapped his helmet visor to Ilna in salute, and said, "You going to sort 'em out, ma'am?"

"I'll do what I can, Osnan," Ilna said. Her tone was noncommittal, but the glance she gave the soldier was—for her—affectionate.

"Then they don't have a chance!" the guard said, stepping past his squad leader to close the door behind the women. Through the panel Sharina heard him say to his fellows, "Mistress Ilna won't leave enough to bury, boys. You'll see!"

As they walked through to the master bedroom, Ilna said in an undertone, "Osnan was a guard at my bungalow for a few weeks. I think he's as much afraid of wizards as the rest of them, but he appears to trust me."

Sharina laughed and hugged her friend. "So does everyone who knows you, Ilna," she said.

The heavy bronze headboard of Garric's bed was chased with scenes illustrating the courtship of the Lady by the Shepherd and—on the footboard—the Lady's descent into the Underworld. It'd been pulled out from the wall, and the canopy had been removed. The room looked much larger though it still contained clothes chests, a table, chairs, and several lampstands—an unusual amount of furniture.

A lighted brazier stood between the eastern windows. It'd been brought in since Sharina left.

A section of fresco had fallen away sometime in the past. The plaster had been patched but merely distempered instead of being fully repainted.

Garric had sketched a votive figure in charcoal on the plain surface. A stranger would have thought it was a drawing of the Shepherd, but Sharina recognized her brother's much simpler intent: this was Duzi, the little God of shepherds like Garric, who tended flocks around Barca's Hamlet. The bed-curtains would have concealed it until now.

Tenoctris stood and gave the younger women a bright smile. "Your timing's perfect," she said. "I've just finished with the preparations."

She beamed down at the floor. She'd drawn a circle around the bed—that was why it'd been moved out—with powdered lime, then used the pot of vermilion to draw around it in the Old Script.

Tenoctris stoppered the vermilion and set it on the circular table with the rest of her paraphernalia. There couldn't be much left, even though she'd written the characters too small to be read from any distance.

The flames of the multiple lamps paled as dawn came through the windows. The rosy softness still hid as much as it displayed.

"Ilna, Sharina's told you what I'd like you to do?" Tenoctris said. As she spoke, her eyes traced her preparations in quick motions. Another person would have seemed nervous, but the old wizard was simply showing her normal, sparrowlike intensity.

Ilna shrugged. "You're to put me in a trance," she said. "You'll send my mind—"

"Your soul," Tenoctris corrected.

"My soul, then, to a dreamworld," Ilna said. "There I'm to follow a path of some sort and come back to tell you what I've found."

"I didn't know how to describe what she was to do," Sharina said apologetically. "I don't really understand about that part."

Tenoctris flashed a smile. "Nor do I," she admitted. "Amalgasis and Princess Querilon both described the process very clearly, but those are things I've read, not experienced. I hope—I trust—that the pattern will be clear to one of Ilna's abilities."

"A soldier named Osnan shares your confidence," Ilna said, her tone too dry for even Sharina to be sure whether she was joking. "You want me on the bed?"

"Yes," said Tenoctris. "And if you wouldn't mind, I'd like you to chew some lettuce cake first. To help you relax."

"I need all the help I can to do that," Ilna said, this time with a faint smile. "Whatever you think is best."

Sharina shaved the cake of narcotic with the great knife she wore under her cape tonight. It was the knife she'd gotten from Nonnus, the healer for Barca's Hamlet and the surrounding borough; it was while helping him that Sharina had learned to judge a dose of lettuce cake and other basics of the healing art.

Ilna pinched up the drug and swallowed it, making a wry face. "Let's get on with it, then," she said. She sat on the edge of the bed, then slid into the center and lay flat.

Sharina rarely thought of her friend as small, but Ilna looked tiny in the center of the pale blue coverlet. Her weight wasn't enough to make the ropes supporting the mattress creak.

Sharina backed against the wall. Behind her was a scene of happy peasants shearing sheep in springtime. She pressed her shoulders against the plaster and thought of other times.

"*Malaas athiaskirtho,*" Tenoctris chanted. "*Nuchie uellaphonta steseon. . . .*"

She tossed a pinch of powder onto the brazier. It flared white with a smokeless crackle.

"*Kalak othi lampsoure . . .*" the wizard continued.

The room was growing cold again. Sharina waited, her eyes turned toward the sunrise and her hands clasped on the hilt of the Pewle knife.

Eight sailors astern of Cashel worked an oar apiece, while he sat where the bow narrowed and rowed with two. He lifted his oarblades and carried the looms forward with his arms and whole torso to prepare for another stroke. The sun was low behind him and would set within half an hour.

"Land!" said Tilphosa, standing ahead of Cashel in the far bow. "Under that cloud on the horizon!"

"Yes, by the Lady!" cried Hook, rising to his feet in the stern beside the captain. As the ship's only surviving officers, they'd been trading off with the tiller throughout the hot, windless day. "Real land this time, not another cursed reef!"

The oarsmen were at the thwarts to bow and stern. Stores and baggage saved from the wreck filled the middle of the pinnace; Metra and the off-duty crewmen perched on it however they might. The wizard can't have been comfortable, but the sailors gave her plenty of room.

Tilphosa hadn't wanted to risk how she'd have been treated in the close quarters of the ship's belly. She'd chosen to place herself with Cashel sitting between her and all the others aboard. The pinnace had been under oars the whole way from the islet where they'd wrecked, so the bow never lifted high enough to smack spray over her. Even if they'd been spanking along on a strong wind, Cashel guessed the girl would've made the same choice— and been wise to.

A breeze—the first since dawn—ruffled the sea, then filled the limp sail. The pinnace heeled slightly to starboard. Sailors looked up with bare interest.

"Well, get it trimmed, damn you!" Captain Mounix shouted. "Posal and Kortin, tighten the lee brails! Don't you have eyes?"

Two sailors grabbed lines and began to shorten them, obedient but not enthusiastic. The men seemed cowed, but whether by the wreck itself or events on the islet Cashel couldn't say; he hadn't known them before the trouble. Cashel wasn't the sort to think ill of folks he didn't really know, but he was pretty sure his sister Ilna would've said they weren't any great shakes ever in their lives.

Cashel pulled his oars aboard through the rowlocks

twisted from cordage and crossed the shafts before him. He rubbed his palms together, then checked them. He didn't row often even when he lived in Barca's Hamlet, but the calluses he'd developed from other tasks had protected him today.

"Hey you!" Hook called. "Farmer! Nobody told you to ship your oars!"

"No," Cashel said. "You didn't."

Another man might've argued that he'd done as much as any two of the sailors during the long, brutal day. Cashel didn't bother. There were people who could give orders that he'd obey, but none of them were aboard the pinnace.

The sailors were bringing their oars aboard also. The breeze continued to freshen, so rowing was pointless even if Cashel hadn't wanted to turn toward the land. He squinted, hoping he'd see something that'd make the shore look more attractive.

"I thought there'd be more than just wilderness," Tilphosa said. "If we've really found Laut, I mean."

"I don't know about Laut," said Cashel. "This is a big place, anyhow."

He paused, letting the shifting light and the pinnace's motion confirm what he'd suspected. "Anyway, there's a building on that headland," he said. "It could be a temple, I think. A little one."

"Wizard, where is this that we've fetched up?" Mounix snapped. "Hook, take the tiller, will you? Where's the cities you told us about?"

"I don't know," said Metra, turning from her view of the shore to look back at the captain. "When we reach land, perhaps I'll be able to learn more. Through my art."

She spoke deliberately, using the words as a weapon to threaten and silence Mounix. Cashel was sure that the crew hadn't known Metra was a wizard as well as a priestess when they'd signed on for the voyage.

"Cashel?" Tilphosa said quietly. "This morning, were you thinking about the sea serpent that wrecked us on that terrible island?"

He shrugged. "I thought about it," he said, drawing his quarterstaff up from where he'd stored it along the boat's side. "I'd never seen one before, though, and I don't expect to see another one anytime soon."

The staff's iron butt caps already had a light coating of rust. Cashel drew out his wad of raw wool and began to polish first the metal, then the hickory itself.

"But what if it had been *sent*?" the girl asked. "It could've still been waiting for us."

"Well . . ." said Cashel as he continued his task. It relaxed him, even if he hadn't needed to do it for the staff's sake. "*I* didn't plan to spend the rest of my life in that place, mistress. I guess if the snake had showed up again, I'd have tried to do something about it."

"Yes, I suppose you would have," said Tilphosa. She giggled. For a moment Cashel thought she was getting hysterical. After reflection, he still wasn't sure she wasn't.

The tide was going out, though low water wouldn't be till well into the first watch of the night. A narrow beach sloped gently to a limestone escarpment never more than two or three double paces high. There was vegetation on the rocks, ordinary woodland from what Cashel could tell in the dimming light. The one stone building was either a small temple or a tomb made to look like one.

"Well, it doesn't seem like much," Cashel said, "but we ought to get a night's sleep. In the morning, we can go look for your Prince Thalemos or somebody who knows about him."

The shore was rushing up at a surprising rate. Mounix called orders that meant more to the crew than they did to Cashel. With a rattle of brails, several men hauled the sail up to a quarter of its original area. They were going to chance grounding without unstepping the mast, though.

"We could've used some of this breeze at midday when it was so hot," Cashel said, but it wasn't a real complaint. No peasant expected the weather to do the thing that best suited him.

The shore was already in darkness, but arcs of white foam outlined the waves' highest reach. Mounix had the tiller to starboard, bringing them in at a slant that would ease the impact.

"Get out quick when we ground," Cashel said as he judged where the pinnace would touch. "The less weight in the bow, the better."

He slid his quarterstaff back for Tilphosa to take. "And hold this for me," he added. "Ah, if you would, I mean."

It bothered Cashel when he wasn't always polite when he was working on a problem. Things weren't happening so fast at the moment that he couldn't ask properly instead of just ordering the girl around.

"You men in the bow!" Mounix called. "Get ready to drag us up the beach when we ground!"

"I have the staff, Cashel," Tilphosa said clearly. She gripped it in both hands, putting just enough pressure on the hickory to assure Cashel that he could safely release it.

"I'm ready!" Cashel said, though the other forward oarsmen didn't bother to reply. Mounix waved a sour acknowledgment to him.

Metra sat on the pile of canvas over the storage jars amidships, her expression unreadable. Her eyes met Cashel's; she was watching him and Tilphosa, not the land. Cashel nodded the way he'd have done with a chance-met neighbor he didn't care for, then returned his attention to the shore.

The keel grated, then bumped momentarily harder as Cashel vaulted the port side. To his surprise Tilphosa was in the shoaling water just as quickly, but she'd judged his intent and leaped out to starboard so that she wouldn't be in his way. She scampered through the foam and up the beach with the staff crosswise before her. It was more weight for a slight-built girl than Cashel had realized.

Cashel had his own job, though. The pinnace heeled toward him. He gripped the gunwale and his port oar at the rowlock, then strained forward.

The furled sail thumped down amidships, raising an angry shout from Metra. Cashel smiled faintly. The wizard hadn't been quite under the sail and spar when Hook released them, but she was close enough to have been surprised. That was all right with Cashel.

Another wave curled up the sand. With the weight out of the far bow and the water lifting, the keel broke free from the trench it'd dug. Cashel strode forward, dragging the pinnace three short paces up before the wave sucked back. The sailors were tumbling out also; with their help the keel slid on several paces more before sticking where only the tide could lift it farther.

Two sailors staggered inland with the anchor, a section of ironwood trunk. The prongs of two branches had been cut to form flukes and a ball of lead was cast above the forks for weight. The men carried it to the edge of the escarpment and set it as firmly as they could. It wasn't a safe tether—the sand wouldn't hold the flukes—but it'd do till someone ran a line around the trunk of a tree above.

It was growing dark. Tilphosa's face and the smooth, pale shaft of the quarterstaff were blurs against the weathered limestone. Cashel sloshed toward her, stepping over the anchor cable on his way.

He heard a sailor mutter something; he didn't turn to make something of it. Most of Cashel's life people had been calling him a dumb ox or some variation on the notion. Knocking people down wouldn't make them think he was any smarter, so he didn't bother.

"Cashel," the girl said as she handed him his staff, "I

don't want to stay with the sailors tonight. Do we have to?"

Cashel ran his hands over the wood, checking it by reflex. "I don't guess so," he said. "I've got food in my wallet, enough for both of us. Biscuit, cheese, and a bottle of water is all, though. They'll probably heat up a fish stew, you know. Well, salt fish."

"I don't care," said the girl. "I heard the men carrying the anchor talking. They want to go back home, and they think if I'm with them, they'll be safe from Metra."

Some of the sailors were unloading the pinnace, but a good number of them had clustered around Mounix and Hook near the vessel's prow. Their voices were lower than honest men would have needed to use, and their heads turned frequently in the direction of Cashel and the girl.

He couldn't see their features. The sun was down, and the cliff threw a hard shadow over the beach.

"Let's see what the temple's like," Cashel said. "It's got a roof, anyhow."

Storm-tossed waves had undercut the escarpment. Tilphosa was standing at a place where the limestone had collapsed into a slope of sorts—steep and irregular, but good enough even in the dim light. It wasn't more than twice his height where they stood; well, maybe a little more.

Cashel expected to have to help the girl, but she turned immediately and started up using her hands as well as feet. She wasn't as agile as Sharina would've been, but there wasn't any doubt about her being willing.

Cashel waited for Tilphosa to crawl onto flat ground, then clambered to join her, using his staff as a brace. Metra, identifiable from the bleached white slash across her outer tunic, walked northward up the beach. She was carrying the satchel of silk brocade which held the implements of her art.

"Cashel?" Tilphosa said quietly. "I don't think . . ."

She licked her lips, her eyes following the other woman's progress. In a hollow, distant enough to be concealed from the pinnace, Metra squatted and began to draw on the damp sand.

"I knew the Children of the Mistress weren't telling me everything about my marriage," Tilphosa said. "But now I'm not sure that the things they did tell me were all true. If Prince Thalemos is a great and powerful leader, shouldn't there be more than—"

She gestured toward the temple. Cashel had been wrong about the roof. It looked all right from below, but up close to the side he could see that several trusses had fallen and taken the tiles with them.

"—this?"

"We'll know more by daylight," Cashel said. "And after a good night's sleep."

He led the girl the rest of the way to the temple. It was only ten double paces, but it was pretty steep in the darkness. He tapped the end of his staff ahead of him; they didn't want to go over the edge of the cliff.

The sailors had climbed the escarpment also. They were shouting to one another, though Cashel couldn't make out what they were talking about. He heard Hook's saw rasping, and also the sound of chopping from several places.

Firewood, he guessed, but his eyes narrowed. There was only one small hatchet in the carpenter's tool chest, so they must be using the adze and probably the captain's sword as well. That seemed a lot of effort when there were plenty of fallen branches available. You didn't have to cut wood to length for an open fire.

Cashel rubbed his staff absently again. He wasn't sure he'd be sleeping tonight after all, though he wasn't the sort to borrow trouble that might never come.

The temple was small, but the masonry was well finished, and there'd been lots of carvings on the triangular front of the porch roof. They'd weathered badly, so Cashel didn't guess he'd be able to tell much even by daylight.

He walked into the nave. The God's image was gone, though the base remained. There was no writing on it.

The moon was rising out of the sea, painting a white road across the water. Cashel could see pretty well, but he found the light didn't make him feel . . . comfortable, he guessed he'd say. Full moons always made a herd restless, so maybe that was his problem.

"Look at this reredos!" Tilphosa said. "This is marvelous!"

There'd been a thin wall made from a single sheet of pale stone behind where the statue had stood, dividing the public part of the temple from the back where the priests stored things. It'd split and later fallen to pieces on the floor, probably when the roof right above it collapsed. Tilphosa was bending over a triangular piece, one of the larger fragments.

Cashel stepped closer. He'd have guessed that the girl was talking about something he couldn't see from where he stood in the doorway, but it turned out a reredos was the stone screen itself.

"The sculptor was illustrating the *Demonomachia*, the Battle of Demons," Tilphosa explained, easing to the side to keep from blocking the light as she pointed with a slim white finger. Sure enough, the public side of the wall was as full of carved figures as an ungrazed meadow is of dandelions. "See? Have you ever seen art so involving?"

"Yes," said Cashel. "But I guess I don't know how you mean the word."

Cashel knew his sister's fabrics, not only the arras she'd woven as a votive to hang behind the statue of the Protecting Shepherd in Valles but also the lesser drapes and ribbons that carried no image at all when you first glanced at them. Ilna *made* people feel things. This was just carved stone.

And it wasn't what Cashel called pretty carving, either.

Six-limbed monsters, generally standing upright on the hind pair but sometimes on the bottom four legs, fought with monsters that walked like men but had the heads and tails of lizards. They weren't animals, either: they were using swords and spears, and as best Cashel could tell in the light they wore armor besides.

"The guy who did it knew his business, though," Cashel said, hoping that he didn't sound grudging. Tilphosa obviously liked the thing, and the fact he didn't was no reason to spoil her happiness.

"Pendill describes the battle," the girl said. She was excited about the carving, picking up one piece after another to see how they fit together. "In his *Changes*, not the *Love Lyrics*, of course. But look at this, Cashel!"

Tilphosa started to hold out another slab, then changed her mind and got to her feet again. "Here, where the light is better," she said as she went back onto the porch.

Cashel smiled faintly. The expression felt good; he hadn't been smiling as much as he ought to since he'd gone into the palace pond and wound up here. This wasn't anything he understood, much less cared about, but it was giving the girl a lot of pleasure.

"This is the Queen of the Archai," Tilphosa said, tilting the stone in one hand so that it caught the light the right way. "But you see, she's not an Archa. She's human!"

"Right, I see that," Cashel said. The fragment had been lying facedown so the carving was as sharp as you could ask. It was a woman all right, her right arm raised and her left hand stuck out like she was signalling somebody to stop.

He squinted and bent closer. "What's that on her head?" he asked. "Does she have horns?"

"Cashel, I think she's meant for the Mistress!" Tilphosa said. She touched her silver-mounted crystal pendant. "In Her guise as the Lady of the Moon, you see!"

Cashel didn't see, not really, but he was glad for the

girl to be so excited. "I wish Sharina was here," he said. "She'd understand better than I do."

Tilphosa lowered the stone but didn't look up for a moment. "Sharina is your wife, Cashel?" she asked.

"What?" said Cashel. The smile that had blossomed across his face when he thought of Sharina now faded slowly.

"Well, not that," he continued, turning over in his mind how he ought to explain. Deciding that the simplest way was best—at least for Cashel or-Kenset, and probably for more people than tried it—he said, "I love her, though. And I think she loves me."

"Let's sit down, shall we?" said Tilphosa, walking out to the second of the four pillars holding up the porch. She seated herself with a graceful motion.

Cashel butted the quarterstaff on the littered floor beside the third pillar and lowered himself carefully, controlling the motion by his grip on the staff. He angled his legs onto the temple's three-stepped base so that while facing the girl he could watch Metra on the beach below as well.

"Do you miss your Sharina, Cashel?" Tilphosa said.

"Well, I miss talking to her," he said, frowning as he tried to understand the question. "But I don't . . ."

He balanced the staff across his lap and shrugged. "Tilphosa," he said, "she's not really gone, you know. She's always with me, and I know that when I get back to Valles or wherever she is, she'll be there. Do you see?"

Tilphosa didn't, he could tell that from the carefully neutral expression on her face. Well, they'd both managed to puzzle the other tonight by talking about things the other didn't understand.

He looked down at Metra. The wizard had drawn her symbols across at least three double paces of wet sand. They were in a line rather than a closed figure the way Cashel had seen these things done in the past. Metra walked behind them, turning when she reached the end and starting back.

He could hear her chanting, but he couldn't tell what the words were. She wasn't using her athame, but on every third step she tossed a pinch of glittering dust toward the words in the sand.

"I wonder if I'll feel that way about Thalemos," Tilphosa said, her face turned out to sea. She was looking at the moon or the path it drew on the water. "I've never even seen a picture of him. He's supposed to be exactly my age, but . . ."

She shrugged. "Laut isn't like what I was told," she said, "so I don't know if Thalemos or anything else is."

"Tilphosa?" said Cashel. He pointed with his staff. "Do you know what Metra's doing there?"

The girl leaned forward, then shifted the way she was sitting so that she could see around the pillar. She said nothing for a moment, then turned to Cashel with worried eyes.

"Cashel?" she said. "When Metra was in the woods this morning, before we boarded the boat—could she have gone back to the top of the hill where you killed the thing?"

Cashel stroked his staff as he considered. "I guess she could've," he said. "There was time enough, and she knew the way. I wasn't paying any attention to her."

"Because I wonder . . ." Tilphosa said. "If she went back for the amulet the thing was wearing."

"There's no amulet, Tilphosa," Cashel said. He spoke calmly, just as if he didn't know the girl had watched him grind it to dust. Maybe she'd gotten too much sun on the pinnace? "I smashed it, remember?"

"Yes, I know you smashed it," Tilphosa said with a little of the sharpness that Cashel had carefully kept out of *his* voice. "But that didn't make it vanish—or its power either,

I'm afraid. What do you suppose Metra is dusting onto her words of power?"

She grimaced. "Oh, I'm sorry, Cashel!" she blurted before he could speak. "I'm just mad at myself for not thinking of that before it was too late. It's not your fault."

"I don't know that it's too late, either," Cashel said, rising to his feet like an ox. He shrugged his whole body, loosening the muscles for what he might have to do after he went down and rubbed Metra's symbols out of existence.

"Cashel," Tilphosa said, not loudly but with a hint of urgency. She was looking inland around the north corner of the temple.

Cashel, his staff held close along his side, stepped past to look for himself. Sailors were coming through the woods toward the temple in groups of three or four men, each with a lighted pine knot for a torch.

"Mounix!" Cashel said. "I don't need your company tonight. We'll talk in the morning, if you think you need to."

"Stand aside, farmer!" Hook called. "You don't need to get hurt, but it won't bother us if you do."

He carried a sapling with a chisel lashed to the end to make it a spear. Other sailors had spears tipped with the belt knives that had been their only weapons when they landed, or sections of branch shaped into cudgels. Mounix had his sword out, but he let his carpenter do the talking.

"I'm not standing aside," Cashel said. "And you're not getting past me either, Hook."

He knew there were sailors to the south side of the building where he couldn't see them; there was no chance of getting to the shore the way he and Tilphosa had come up. As for trying to climb straight down at night from where he and Tilphosa stood at the highest part of the cliff, he'd likely break his neck even without sailors dropping rocks on his head.

There wouldn't be much gain to being down on the sand. And besides, he didn't feel like running.

"We're not going to hurt the girl!" a sailor said. "We just want her with us while we go back to Tisamur where we belong. The wizard stays here, and the girl comes with us so we're sure she doesn't send anything after us!"

Tilphosa had stepped sideways into the nave, where the sailors couldn't see her until they came around the front. She fingered her crystal pendant and watched Cashel with wide-open eyes.

"I told you no!" said Cashel. Tilphosa gasped at the volume of his growling bellow. "If I need to crack heads, I'll do that. It won't be the first time!"

The dozen men Cashel could see from where he stood had reached the back of the temple. He risked a glance to the side; torchlight flickered around the southern edge of the masonry, showing that the rest of the crew were close to being able to rush him from behind.

"Get inside," he snarled to Tilphosa. There'd been a door through the back wall to the storage room, but half the roof had collapsed across it. Beams and broken tiles blocked the opening. Given time, the sailors could clear a passage, but Cashel didn't guess they'd try that for a while.

"We're coming for you, farmer!" Hook shouted.

The girl had obediently moved to the center of the nave. She nodded when Cashel's eyes glanced across her. She'd picked up a jagged piece of the screening wall, small enough to throw but big enough to hurt if it hit somebody.

Cashel placed himself in the middle of the opening, just back of the porch. It was some three times as wide as he was tall, about the right width to give him free play with the quarterstaff but not let the sailors get around him to the sides. The raised steps gave him an advantage too.

Sailors edged into sight on both sides, staying close to the cliff edge until they were sure where Cashel stood. One of them waggled his torch between two pillars, then jumped back. A fool's trick, a nervous fool's trick.

Cashel started to spin his quarterstaff slowly before him, waiting for the moment one of the gang milling in front of the temple would get up the courage to rush him. He was a lot better at this kind of fight than any of the sailors dreamed of being, but there was a right herd of them.

"We're coming!" Hook repeated, holding his spear by the butt instead of the balance to make it reach longer.

"Then come!" growled Cashel.

A heavyset sailor with a club bounded up the temple steps. Cashel's staff struck—half spin, half thrust—and broke the man's knee as the rest of them came on.

Red wizardlight mushroomed from the beach below. It wrapped the ruins of the temple, and the stones began to change.

"No like water, Gar," Tint whimpered. "Gar, take Tint to land? Tint smell land close."

"We'll be ashore soon, Tint," Garric said, seated in the fishing boat's stern with the beastgirl hunched against his legs like a hound frightened by thunder. "We're just looking for the place to land."

"Shut that monkey up," snarled an oarsman, "or by the Lady she goes over the side!"

The vessel the Brethren had stolen for the voyage was undecked but broad and beamy. There was a mast step amidships, but Vascay had decided they'd row instead. "You can see a sail for a long ways," he'd explained when Garric raised an eyebrow on first seeing the boat.

"Gently . . ." Garric said. It took him a moment to dredge the man's name from Gar's damaged memory. "Alcomm. We'll all be happier when we get to shore."

The sun had set an hour before. The air was cooler, but rowing an uncertain course in the darkness was more uncomfortable than the glare of sunlight reflected from the calm sea. Except for Hakken, a fisherman before his wife had gone off with one of the Intercessor's officers, the bandits were landsmen.

A few households in Barca's Hamlet supported themselves by fishing. Garric had pulled an oar on occasion himself, though never one as long as the sweeps of this Laut craft which the men sculled standing.

"Aimal," called Vascay to the lookout, standing with a foot braced on the stempost and a comrade holding his belt for safety. "Can you see anything?"

"There's lights, Vascay," Aimal said. "Hearthfires through a window, or maybe shepherds on the hillsides. I can't tell any more than that there's lights."

"We've got to go in," a man in the belly of the boat said. He wasn't being belligerent; just tired and maybe frustrated. "We can't hang around out here till dawn. The Protectors'll see us sure and wonder what we were doing out all night."

"Yeah, we drifted bugger knows how far in the midchannel," said another bandit. "Best to get ashore any which place and head for Durassa overland when we figure out where we're at."

Vascay squinted at the shore, then looked up at the sky. The stars were bright points in the clear night, but even the most skilled navigators—none of whom were aboard *this* vessel—could draw only direction, not location, from them.

He sighed and cocked an eyebrow to Garric. Garric nodded minutely in agreement.

"Aye," said Vascay, cramping the steering oar to head the boat toward shore. "Put your backs in it, boys. And keep your eyes open in the bow. We don't want to run up on the private dock of one of Echeon's cronies."

The vessel had four sweeps, each worked by a single man; they creaked as the oarsmen leaned into them. Metal chinked and whispered as the others readied their weapons.

Garric drew his new sword a hand's breadth out of the scabbard, then let it slip back with a faint chime. It moved freely.

Vascay lifted a bundle of three short javelins from the boat's bottom, leaning them points up against the gunwale beside him. He caught Garric's eye and shrugged.

"Take the tiller, lad," he muttered. "One of us needs to be in the bow, and you've got your dog to care for."

Garric gripped the steering oar's crossjack as the chieftain took the javelins in his left hand. He ducked under Alcomm's sweep, and called in a loud voice, "Make way, brothers! I'm coming forward."

Garric craned his neck to see past his poised fellows. The shore was rocky, and there was no beach at all.

"We'll break her ribs if we come in here, Vascay!" a man warned nervously. "We're *leagues* east of where we ought to be! This must be somewhere in Haislip Parish, not Matunus."

"Then we'll stave her in, Hakken," Vascay snapped. "The District Clerk we stole her from isn't any friend of mine or of any decent man. And as for a few leagues, I'd rather walk them than row."

"Aye!" Alcomm grunted as he put his back into his oar.

"Ready yourself!" Aimal warned.

Garric laid the fingers of his left hand between the shoulders of the whimpering beastgirl. "We're going to land now, Tint," he said. "There'll be a scrape—"

They ground into the rocks with the crash of a door being broken down. All the men lurched forward, Garric included. The impact was much worse than he'd expected. The boat wasn't moving fast, but it was so heavy that it took a great deal of stopping.

Garric would've sprawled into Alcomm's oarpost if Tint hadn't held him firmly while bracing herself with a three-limbed grip on the boat's ribs. So much for taking care of the poor animal. . . .

Men carrying their personal gear jumped to the shore with more haste than grace. The crumpled bow was filling, but the boat wasn't properly aground; sinking, it started to slide backward into deeper water. Hakken cursed and threw a bight around one of the taller rocks as his fellows splashed past him.

As the last of the bandits splashed into the bow, Garric said to the beastgirl crouching at his feet, "All right, Tint, let's go—"

Tint leaped to shore in a single twenty-foot movement, as smooth as a cat. She whirled, and chattered, "Come, Gar! Come quick!"

The bow had settled to the bottom with only a hand's breadth of the hull above water; the stern continued to fill. Garric hefted the blanket roll with his belongings and hopped onto the port gunwale. It was no great trick for him to walk to land dry-footed.

Ceto's clothes fit Garric. None of the Brethren quarreled when Vascay awarded the entire kit to "Gar," who'd regained his faculties, though he gathered that normally the whole gang would share in the division. Garric didn't mind wearing a dead man's clothes, though he had chosen not to take the shirt Ceto had on when Vascay let his life out in a gush of blood.

Tint fawned on Garric when he stepped to a rock, then jumped to shore. The band had gathered around Vascay, looking into night and muttering.

"That's the high road, there past the trees," Hame said. "Many a time I hiked it while my sister was alive in Durassa."

The shore was a rising waste ground of rock and coarse, prickly bushes. A line of poplars grew fifty feet inland, straggling in both directions to where they were lost in night and the hills. A farmhouse was silhouetted on the eastern horizon; an ox moaned, but there were no lights.

Vascay nodded; the band trotted forward, forming a loose line abreast without need for discussion. Vascay was on the left flank, so Garric fell in on the right.

"Aye, it's the high road!" Hame repeated with satisfaction.

So it might be—and a better road than Barca's Hamlet had known since the fall of the Old Kingdom—but it was years since the track had last been gravelled. Twin ruts showed there was wagon traffic, but Garric couldn't imagine anything but walkers and pack mules using it during the rain.

"There'll be patrols, like enough," a man said, looking at the road doubtfully.

"Not at this hour," another said. "Look at how high the Phoenix is."

Garric followed the line of the bandit's pointing arm. The constellation was the one he'd learned to call the Goat Horns in Barca's Hamlet.

"We're deep in the second watch by now. The Protectors of the Peace like their sleep as much as honest men do. They won't ride again till dawn."

"We still dassn't take the high road," said the first man—Blesfund, Garric saw now as the speaker's head turned. " 'Tain't safe."

"We've no choice," Vascay decided abruptly. "There's no place to lay up near here, not the whole lot of us, and we've got to get to Lord Thalemos' estate by daybreak. Prada, go on ahead to scout. We'll give you two furlongs' lead. I'll take your sword and you carry one of these javelins. That way if you run into the Protectors, you're just a traveller who needed to be in Durassa at daylight."

"Why me?" muttered Prada, a lanky, sad-looking fellow at the best of times. He unbuckled his sword, though—a wide-bladed, square-tipped weapon like no other Garric had seen—and traded it to Vascay for the javelin.

"Somebody'll spell you in a while," Vascay said.

Prada grimaced but started trudging down the road. With his pack and the javelin over his shoulder, he really did look like a traveller who'd decided to keep on through the night. Garric suspected—and Prada almost certainly knew—that regardless, the Intercessor's patrols would sweep up anyone they caught out at night.

"Get out of the middle of the road," Vascay said mildly to his band. He gestured.

Obediently the band moved into the shadow of a poplar, each man squatting or stretching his muscles, according to his individual taste. Tint crept on all fours along the rock-strewn slope toward the sea. Occasionally her hand shot out and snatched something into her mouth. Once the prey squeaked before the beastgirl's molars crunched down.

Prada reached the farmhouse and started down the other side of the hill. The road seemed to curve as well.

"Gar, keep him in sight," Vascay ordered. "The rest of us will follow you."

"Right," said Garric. He rose, hitched his sword belt to settle it more comfortably, and strode down the dusty track after the scout.

Tint gave a squeak of alarm and bounded to his side. Men laughed, and somebody muttered, "I still don't believe Gar coming around the way he's done. I swear I don't."

"We leave Vascay now, Gar?" the beastgirl asked. She didn't sound concerned, just curious. She ambled along the road on all fours most of the time, but every few paces she rose to her hind legs and scanned her surroundings. Her flat nostrils flared.

"No," Garric said, "we're just watching Prada so that if the Intercessor's patrols catch him we can warn the others. Vascay and the others will come behind us."

Tint scratched herself between the shoulder blades with

a long-fingered hand. "Tint tired," she said. "We sleep soon, Gar?"

"Probably not till almost dawn," Garric said. "I'm sorry, Tint."

He could use some sleep too. He'd had two shifts on the sweeps, but it hadn't been a hard day so far as work went.

Lord Thalemos—or his advisor, Metron—had hired Vascay's band because they were willing to go. They didn't have any particular expertise at searching for a ring on a deserted islet some distance from Laut.

It wasn't until he'd boarded the stolen fishing boat that morning that Garric had realized almost the whole crew were landsmen as surely as he was himself. Garric had faced worse dangers than setting off in an open boat with men who barely knew how to row, but the hours of constant low-level tension had wrung him out worse than the same time spent digging a drainage ditch would've done.

Garric walked briskly to keep Prada in sight. The full moon gave good light, but the poplars frequently hid the scout on the winding road.

Garric and Tint neared the farmstead to the right of the road. A waist-high drystone wall set the foreyard off from the highway—to keep out animals being driven to market in the city, Garric guessed, rather than to keep the household's own stock in. The house was stone like the wall and had a thatched roof, but the large barn was of frame construction. It slumped sideways; the boards gapped and seemed never to have been whitewashed.

Pigs grunted from the pen at the back of the yard; the sharp, bitter stench of hog manure had already announced their presence. There wasn't a dog, though, which was surprising.

Tint stopped and gripped Garric's thigh. Her fingers were painful. "Gar!" she said. "Men behind wall! Men hurt us!"

"How do you—" Garric said.

He swallowed the rest of what would've been a stupid question. Tint's senses were sharper than his, as she'd proved several times in their brief acquaintance. Besides, now that she'd warned him, Garric could smell horses. A farm like this plowed with oxen, not horses which had to be fed grain.

The corner of the farmyard was fifty feet ahead—an easy spear throw, and no distance at all if those waiting in ambush had bows. Since they had horses as well . . .

"Walk on," he murmured to Tint, but he only took one more pace before he stopped to look at the sole of his bare foot as though he'd picked up a thorn. By bending over he could see that Vascay and the others were only a hundred feet behind him. He was simply the relay; Prada was expected to spring any ambush.

If the ambushers were mounted, then the bandits who survived the first volley of arrows would be run down as surely as the sun rises; which it would not, for them, ever again.

"Hey, Vascay!" Garric called. He stood straight and waved toward the gang. "Come up here, will you? There's something funny out to sea!"

Hame started forward, then paused when he saw his fellows had stopped where they were. Garric's call was unexpected, and in a bandit's life the unexpected was usually bad news.

"Gar, we run!" Tint whimpered, tugging his left hand hard. "Many many men hide by wall!"

Garric gently disengaged her. There was no use asking the beastgirl exactly how many ambushers there were— six? A hundred?—because she couldn't count. Besides, the number didn't matter because no matter how many there were . . .

"Come along, Sister take you!" Vascay growled. "Didn't you hear the boy?"

He sauntered up the road, one javelin point down in his left hand. The other missile was in his right hand but behind his back, as though he were scratching himself behind the shoulder blades with the butt; it was unobtrusively cocked to throw. After a further moment's hesitation, the rest of the gang followed.

Garric waited as they approached, smiling broadly. "I noticed it when I was getting a thorn out of my foot," he said in a loud voice. He was only half-turned, so that though he was speaking to Vascay, he had the farmstead in the corner of his eye. "Come here, and I'll show you."

"So, lad?" Vascay said as he walked to touching distance. He continued to scratch his back; his eyes flicked about him the way sunlight dances from running water.

"*Don't* look around," Garric said quietly. "There's a band of men behind the wall; they'll jump us any moment. They've got horses, so our only hope is to go for them first."

"They can't be waiting for us!" Ademos said. "*We* didn't know where we were going to fetch up on Laut. Nobody could've set an ambush here."

"Gar, we run!" Tint demanded.

Garric was ice-cold and trembling; he wasn't consciously frightened, but the emotion racing through his veins had its own logic. "Let me borrow this," he said, taking the javelin from Vascay's left hand. The shaft was thumb-thick and three feet long, with a short fluted head and a length of cord tied just above midpoint to stabilize the missile when thrown.

"This don't make any sense!" Ademos said. "They *can't* be laying for us, it don't make sense!"

"Let's get 'em!" Garric shouted in the clear, carrying voice he'd learned from Carus for ruling troops. He turned and charged the farmstead, cocking the javelin back as he ran.

"Blazes!" a bandit squealed. "He's gone nuts a—"

Armed men stood up behind the stone wall, two at first and then a score. Garric loosed the javelin with the skill he'd learned hunting squirrels as a boy with similar weapons. The strength of Gar's right arm was behind the cast.

The first man to stand was the officer whose silver gorget gleamed in the moonlight. The javelin thumped into his breastbone, sinking to the knotted cord. The officer flopped over backward, his orders frozen in his throat by the shock of death.

"Carus and the Isles!" Garric screamed as he drew his long sword.

An archer went down with Vascay's remaining javelin in the eye. He'd started to draw his bow; the arrow wobbled into the dirt when his fingers spasmed open. Several others of those behind the wall had bows, but the dying man was the only one who'd been alert enough to respond instantly.

There were twenty Protectors along the wall. There must be others in the barn with the horses, but those didn't realize yet what was happening.

"Carus!" Garric repeated, whirling his sword in a moonlit circle. He knew from experience—his own and that of Carus before him—how frightening a ten-foot arc of edged steel looked when it was coming at you. The bandits' only hope of survival—*Garric's* only hope of survival—was to startle the ambushers so completely that they didn't react until their would-be prey was among them.

He wasn't quite successful.

An archer drew his arrow to the head while Garric was still ten feet from the wall. Both the Protector's eyes were open. He aimed at Garric's midriff, but the arrow's lift at the moment of release would take it through his heart.

The ambushers wore close-fitting iron caps, not real helms, and breastplates of quilted linen. Except for the archers they carried six-foot spears with a knob instead of spike on the butt; the latter would make a useful baton for crowd control. Echeon's Protectors were more closely akin to the City Patrols who policed Valles than they were to the Royal Army of the Isles. The bandits, most of whom had real swords instead of the long knives the Protectors carried, were armed as well or better than the ambushers.

But one arrow would be enough to end Garric's existence, in this time and probably all time. Still running, he tensed himself to receive the missile—

Tint bounded past in the same sort of flat leap that had carried her to shore. Her long jaws closed on the archer's throat as they tumbled backward together. The man didn't have time to scream.

Garric bounded to the top of the wall, slashing to right and left. His edge cut deep into the forearm a Protector flung up reflexively to cover his face; the back of Garric's curved blade wasn't sharpened, but it rang on the skullcap of the fellow short-gripping his spear to jab at the sword-swinging demon who towered over him. The Protector staggered sideways, sprawling onto the wall; his cap fell off. Vascay, swift despite his peg leg, beheaded him. Prada's sword turned out to be serviceable after all.

Except for Vascay the bandits had been almost as surprised by events as the Protectors were, but they reacted with the desperate suddenness of men who'd long been hunted. Several hurled javelins as they rushed the wall. The hail of missiles dropped two more ambushers, and others ducked or flinched away. The Protectors' knobbed spears couldn't be thrown, so they'd lost the initiative even before the bandits closed.

Blesfund squealed as he took an arrow and doubled up. The archer tried to nock another, then turned to flee. Toster jumped the wall and sank his axe—an ordinary forester's tool—helve deep in the Protector's back. He jerked the axe head free with casual ease.

The barn door opened. A Protector stood there, one

hand on the door and the other holding a horse's bridle. He stared bug-eyed at the carnage: most of his fellows were down, and the few still upright were trying to run.

"Don't let 'em break out!" Garric said. He ran toward the barn, raising his bloody sword. He was gasping for breath.

"Shepherd guard me!" the Protector cried. The javelin Vascay had retrieved from a dead man's eye socket took him in the hip joint; the point had bent so that the missile didn't fly true, but it was true enough. He fell over screaming.

A man already mounted spurred his horse out of the barn, trampling his comrade. His spear jabbed at Garric. Garric hunched and chopped the rider's left knee as he passed. The fellow toppled over his horse's right shoulder as it shied because of the reek of fresh blood.

Garric started into the barn, then jerked back to safety. The interior was full of horses, pitching and kicking in terror. With the door open they forced their way out two abreast. A powerful roan gelding struck the jamb with his shoulder and knocked it askew, causing the sagging structure to lean still farther.

"Catch the horses!" Vascay called. "By the Lady, we'll ride to Durassa tonight on the Intercessor's bounty!"

The last of the animals, a flea-bitten gray, plunged into the courtyard dragging a Protector whose left hand was tangled in the reins. The horse circled, trying to free itself from its living anchor.

Garric grabbed the beast's headstall and held it steady. He pointed his sword at the Protector's face, and shouted, "How many of you are there in the barn?"

"Mercy!" the man cried, lying on his back with his hand lifted in the reins. "No more, nobody more, just three of us!"

"Here's the mercy you lot gave my sister," Hame said.

He set one of the Protectors' own spears against the man's breastbone.

"Don't!" said Garric.

Vascay took Garric's right wrist, his sword wrist, in a grip that would grow firmer if it needed to. "Aye, boy," he said. "We must. And Hame would anyway, with good reason."

Hame leaned his chest against the spear's knobbed butt, driving the point through the man and deep in the ground beneath. The Protector thrashed wildly, then went limp.

Garric turned his head. He'd seen worse, and he understood the kind of reason Hame might have had, but . . .

He let go of the gray's harness. Somebody else could hold the beast—or not, he didn't care.

One of the Protectors had been wearing a short cloak. Garric pulled it off the body and wiped his sword. There was a nick in the belly of his blade; he'd have to polish it out with a stone. His first victim wore a wristlet in the shape of a curling snake; the sword had struck one of the ornament's ruby eyes.

"That's a rare bit of luck, isn't it, brethren?" Vascay said in a satisfied voice. "Mount up and let's get going. Oh, and Toster—lead one of the extras for Prada when we catch up with him."

"Gar safe?" Tint asked, rising on her hind legs to stroke Garric's neck.

"Gar is fine," Garric said. If he'd had anything in his stomach, he'd have thrown it up, from reaction and from the slaughterhouse stench.

"I'm fine, Tint," he said, squeezing tight the beastgirl whose warning had saved all their lives. "Thanks to you we're all fine."

Tint purred contentedly as she licked her muzzle. Her bloody muzzle.

*   *   *

Ilna stood above her body, though the only reason she recognized the still figure on the bed was that it wore her clothing: a bleached inner tunic beneath a heavier garment of blue yarn with a gray pattern woven, not embroidered, into the hem. Her own work, of course, so that was her body as well: slim but sturdy, not willowy—that was a word they used for tall blondes like Sharina—but showing the supple strength of a hickory switch.

Mirrors of polished metal were for rich folk. In Barca's Hamlet, girls filled buckets and looked at themselves in the water's reflection; but not Ilna, she'd never cared about that. . . .

She was surprised to see how attractive her face was. The cheekbones, *her* cheekbones, were visible instead of being cushioned by fat; flecks of gold floated in the depths of her brown eyes; her lips were severe and thinner than some might choose, but in all ways they suited Ilna herself.

She sniffed. She supposed it was all right to be vain about your body when you weren't wearing it anymore.

Tenoctris sat—had collapsed, more properly—on her ivory-legged chair; she looked utterly drained. Sharina stood close behind the older woman, supporting her by holding one forearm and the opposite shoulder. They both looked with concern toward the waxen figure on the bed. Despite the smoke of the charred parchment, the edges and colors of the scene were vivid to Ilna's present eyes.

But her business wasn't in the room where her body lay, nor even in this world. A gray curtain hung around her. She stepped toward it, walking through a corner of the bed.

The grayness resisted for a moment; the curtain wasn't a fabric but rather a blurring of light and of all proper existence. Ilna grimaced sourly—the touch reminded her of putting her hand on a slug's trail in the dark—but pushed on through.

That was her responsibility, after all. What was there in a decent person's life besides carrying out her responsibilities?

The grayness closed around Ilna. She swallowed and continued walking. She'd been in this place, this clammy gray limbo, before. That time the way back to the waking world had led through Hell, and Ilna had brought a portion of Hell back with her. Tenoctris would never have sent a friend back to *that* place, but Tenoctris hadn't, couldn't, walk this route herself.

Ilna took the hank of cords out of her sleeve and began knotting them. She had no pattern in mind, but it gave her fingers something to do as she walked and stared into a self-lit emptiness, a place without shape or color or hope.

As the pieces of cord joined into fabric, a line of jagged darkness drove a schism through the gray. Ilna walked toward it, without confidence or even hope. She would face her future as she faced all things, without complaint or flinching. If that future meant this place, this *non*-place, for all eternity, then so be it.

She stepped into the crevice in the gray, and through it, into a world of color again. This wasn't the waking world Ilna had departed a seeming lifetime ago: the hues were washed out like those of vegetable dyes left in the sun, and when Ilna tried to touch the oak beside her, her hand passed through the bark with only the slightest resistance.

That didn't matter. This was *a* world, even if it wasn't hers.

Breathing deeply, she stood among the trees on top of a hill otherwise grassy. On one horizon—the sky was bright but there was no sun, so she couldn't tell directions—rose the hulking stone forms of great buildings, spires and cylinders and domed roofs carried on pillars. The movement along the ramp circling the outside of a tower was a line of human beings climbing it; at this distance they were ant-sized.

In a swale below Ilna, two chastely dressed women talked with what would have been a man—he was nude, so that wasn't in doubt—if he'd had a human head instead of a stag's. Ilna thought first he was wearing a mask, but the beast's pinched-in skull was narrower than a man's.

The stag-man extended a hand. One of the women took it tentatively. They turned and walked together toward a nearby glade. After a moment, the other woman followed them.

Ilna's lips tightened, but it was nothing to do with her. Tenoctris told her there would be a track somewhere. . . .

Yes, of course; and quite obvious when she looked for it. A discontinuity trailed across the landscape—across this world, moreover, because the sky itself showed the same distortion. It was an absence and bunching, like the damage caused by pulling a single thread from a fabric.

In the middle distance, a procession of humans mounted on beasts Ilna had never seen or imagined came riding across the strain mark. There were hogs the size of oxen, horses with the hind parts of lions, and a thing like a goat that walked hunched over on two legs—but saddled and ridden by a nude woman as lushly beautiful as Syf, the goddess of love, whose image harlots wanted woven into their scarves.

Ilna grinned coldly. The customer can request any design she pleases; but the weaver refused some requests as *she* pleased.

The riders talked cheerfully among themselves. They didn't seem to notice the discontinuity as they approached, but when each crossed it he or she fell silent for a time. A man plucking a harp made from antelope horns fumbled his instrument and almost dropped it.

They passed out of sight behind a hill. One of the women had brought a curved brass horn to her lips several times as she rode along, but Ilna heard neither the horn call nor the voices some of the others raised in song. So far as Ilna was concerned, this place was as silent as the bottom of a frozen millpond.

She started off, following the distortion. It struck her that whatever had warped this world might be unpleasant company to meet. Tenoctris hadn't seemed to think that was likely; and if it happened, well, they'd see what came next.

Ilna smiled faintly. Her fingers were knotting another pattern, this time one she understood very well. If she met the thing, then it too might find it was in unpleasant company.

She continued in the direction of the strain. Her legs moved normally, but instead of feeling the touch of springy turf she found herself on a path circling a lake when her foot came down.

The water was so clear that only the ripples quivering from ivory boats shaped like fallen leaves showed that there was a surface. Couples and trios sat in the boats; a handsome older woman poled one while a youth smiled at her from a cushion in the bow, but the other vessels merely drifted.

A group of severe-looking bearded men stood on the shore a few feet away, talking among themselves with a solemnity obvious even without Ilna being able to hear them. One stared fiercely in her direction; she frowned and waved a hand toward him. He turned, having composed his mind, and resumed the discussion with his fellows.

So. She could see but not hear the inhabitants of this place, and they couldn't even see her.

The chasm in the world stretched across a distant building that looked as if it was teased from meringue. It was decorated with fanciful wings, puffs, and feathers of alternating pink and blue. A naked man was dancing on the tip of one of the flares; a bird, easily the size of the man, watched him with the solemn dignity which he so completely lacked.

Ilna's nose wrinkled. She stepped forward, wondering what would happen if she found herself within the dreadful structure. It disturbed her, and not merely because it was tasteless.

Ilna was used to tastelessness, after all. She'd now lived in cities as well as the countryside where she was born. She'd found people were generally the same anywhere, and even more generally without taste or decency—judged by Ilna's standards, of course, but she lived by those standards and saw no reason she shouldn't judge others by them also.

Her foot came down in a forest. Near her a stocky man with unkempt hair drew figures and symbols on a slab of rock, using his finger for a stylus and lees dipped from a wine cup for ink. He wore a calm, distracted look; Ilna suspected that he still wouldn't have seen her if they'd been fully in the same world.

Ilna understood that kind of focus. She practiced it herself, after all.

Tenoctris had called this place "the dreamworld." It wasn't what Ilna thought of dreams being filled with, but perhaps that was because she herself dreamed rarely and those few times were always unhappy.

The strain mark passed through the kneeling man's bare right foot. His big toe twitched to a rhythm controlled by the shimmer of the discontinuity, but his gaze never faltered and his finger continued to draw. With a nod of approval, Ilna strode on.

She was in a darkness lit by the fires of devastation. A city burned on the skyline. Its structures were silhouetted and picked out by flames leaping from roofs and through the windows.

A slender bridge arched between buildings. The figure crossing it was human or might have been, using a long pole to balance. The exercise seemed pointless as both ends of the bridge blazed like a rich man's hearth in the winter, but the figure struggled on.

Ilna smiled without humor. She'd never dreamed that particular dream, but she understood the mind from which it sprang.

She walked on. How far was she to go? Until she'd found an answer, she supposed. She could only hope that she'd recognize what Tenoctris had sent her after. Since the old wizard hadn't known what the thing was, Ilna might wander this landscape until she chose to turn back, having failed.

She smiled again, even more harshly. She might well fail, but she wouldn't turn back.

She stepped into the boggy lowlands that fringed a river. Eyes peered through the reeds toward her, then vanished in a muddy bubble that popped silently. Did the things that weren't human—the things that lived in this place that dreamers visited—see what the dreamers' eyes did not?

Ilna took another step; she flinched despite herself when she found herself in a wasteland. The ground had been baked till it cracked. A few woody-stemmed plants twisted from it, their gray-green leaves wrapped into tight bundles in hope of better times. There'd been a creek large enough to be crossed by an arched stone bridge, but the channel was now so dry that a dust devil swirled briefly over the silt-blanketed rocks.

To Ilna's right was a round tower; a fortress, perhaps, or a prison. The gate leaves were open; an iron grate had slipped halfway down from its slot above the passage, then skewed and stuck. Ilna saw no sign of life, either in the structure or the surrounding landscape it was meant to dominate.

On the dust-blown path between the bridge and the tower stood a wagon carrying a large iron cauldron. The skeleton of a horse lay between the wagon poles; the beast's flesh and all but a few brass studs of the harness had wasted away.

The strain in this world's fabric ended at the mouth of the cauldron.

Ilna looked about her, seeing nothing more than she'd seen the last time she looked around. She glanced at the knotted pattern in her hands, nodded, and took a step. This time she remained in the same landscape, just a little closer to the wagon.

The tailboard lay on the ground; it had shrunk out of the mortise meant to hold it. Ilna stepped onto the wagon bed, paused, and looked into the cauldron.

Instead of rusty iron she saw below her the interior of a temple. A group of priests wearing robes of white-slashed black chanted around a pool which reflected the full moon.

"Thank the Sister!" called a voice behind Ilna. She whirled to see a girl dressed in animal skins running toward the wagon. "That goat I sacrificed to Her has saved me after all!"

Chapter Nine

Ilna glared reflexively at the newcomer. The Great Gods weren't a part of Ilna's world; the only truths *she* knew were those formed on her loom and in her heart. For those who did believe and worship, though, a sacrifice to the Queen of the Underworld meant they had turned in directions Ilna did not.

"You're still in the waking world, aren't you?" said the girl. Her voice was thin and hollow, as if she was speaking up through the pipes feeding a cistern. "You can't hide from me so you needn't try. I can't see you clearly, but you won't be able to get away now that I've found you."

She was no more than Ilna's modest height, but her large breasts and broad hips meant the two women were unlikely ever to be confused. Carried openly in the newcomer's hand was a bronze knife with a long, leaf-shaped blade.

Ilna glanced at the cords she held and deliberately placed them back in her sleeve. "Can you hear me?" she asked in a cold voice. "If you can, then hear me when I say that I'm Ilna os-Kenset, and I'm not in the habit of running away. Who are you and what do you want with me?"

The girl squatted on her haunches beside the wagon and began to draw on the hard-baked dirt with her dagger point. "I'm Alecto," she said, without looking up. "And what I want from you is to get away from the Pack."

Ilna's eyes narrowed, first at the tone and then still further as she took in the girl's appearance. Alecto's clothing was savage beyond doubt, but it wasn't crude. The short wolfskin cape, the only cover for her torso, was well sewn and closed at the throat with a pin of gold and garnets, and the ivory pins in her hair were subtly carved. Her kilt was of deer hide, tanned and bleached to the shade of cream. Judging from the way it bunched over the girl's knees, the leather was butter soft.

The kilt had a sinuous line of decoration made with porcupine quills, chosen for thickness and color. Ilna didn't remember ever seeing a more able piece of embroidery, though the pattern—or rather, what the pattern suggested to *her*—made her lip curl.

Alecto had sketched a many-pointed star and was now drawing words around the outer angles. It didn't take someone with Ilna's eye for patterns to make the connection between this wizard and whatever was attacking Garric. "The Pack you're afraid of," she said. "You loosed them, and they've turned on you?"

The girl leaped to her feet, switching her grip on the dagger so that she held it as a weapon rather than an awkward stylus. "That's a lie!" she shouted. "I was just trying to frighten Brasus. I didn't let the Pack out! Brasus wasn't worth *that,* and besides, I'm not such a fool."

Her face changed. "Faugh!" she said, shaking her head as she squatted again. "I can't imagine anybody letting the Pack out, but somebody did . . . and I came across them because of what *I* was looking for."

She resumed drawing. Ilna could hear the *skritch* of Alecto's bronze on the hard soil, though, like the girl's voice, it was muted by a distance not of space.

"And all right, I took more of a risk than I should've for Brasus, I see that now," Alecto muttered as she wrote. "I should just've laughed and let him go back to his wife. *I* can find men, the Sister knows!"

Ilna's nose twitched again. She wondered if Alecto could see her expression. Well, it wasn't Ilna's place to correct the tramp. . . .

"You expect the Pack to come here after you, then?" she asked instead. Without Ilna noticing what they were doing, her hands had brought the hank of cords out of her sleeve again.

Alecto looked up from her work with a cruel sneer. "Worried?" she said. "Well, you needn't be. They won't touch you while you're in the waking world, not unless they're set on you. I came too close to their lair, though, because I didn't realize that anybody'd be stupid enough to let them loose . . . but they had."

"I didn't say I was worried," Ilna said, wishing that this slut didn't have such a remarkable talent for irritating her. "I asked if this Pack was coming after you. Coming here, that is, since this is where you are."

"I won't be for long, thanks to you, Ilna os-Kenset," the

girl said. "Never fear, we'll be in the waking world long before they arrive. I couldn't get back by the portal I'd made because that'd mean going through the Pack. I wouldn't have made it."

Alecto looked up with an expression that Ilna had seen once before on a rabbit paralyzed by a serpent's gaze. "Nobody'd make it!" she said. "But it doesn't matter, because it's not going to happen."

Alecto sliced carefully into the ball of her thumb and squeezed a drop of blood into the circle. "No choice in this desert," she muttered.

She began chanting, tapping out the words of power with the point of her dagger. Unlike most of the athames Ilna had seen in the hands of wizards, Alecto's was a perfectly serviceable weapon and had obviously been used as such.

Ilna looked into the cauldron again. The scene had changed. The temple's interior was empty, now. The rectangular pool in the center reflected the sun, which must be squarely overhead, streaming through a roof opening that Ilna couldn't see.

She wondered if she was visible to someone in the temple looking upward. Probably not, since her own reflection didn't appear in the pool.

Alecto's voice was growing louder; it seemed to be coming from all directions. Ilna straightened and glared at the wild woman. Dust devils began to spin around the wagon, six of them sunwise and the seventh widdershins.

Ilna sniffed. It was time she returned to the palace and Tenoctris. She could describe the temple and the chorus of priests; there didn't seem any further benefit to hanging around here. She supposed if she followed the schism in the same fashion as she'd come to this place, it would bring her back.

She tried to step down from the wagon. Her body didn't move. Her muscles weren't paralyzed, but they strained uselessly as though her limbs were stuck in blocks of stone.

Ilna's fingers twisted cords into a pattern. It was desperately hard work, but not even the power that held her now could prevent her from working her own art.

The bright baking sky grew darker. Alecto's voice thundered from the heavens. Ilna could no longer see the dust devils. She felt a wind tugging at the sleeves of her tunic.

"Alecto!" she shouted, but she couldn't hear her own voice over the scream of the wind.

Ilna's world dissolved into a flow of downward-rushing color. Alecto stood before her, her face triumphant and the bronze dagger raised skyward. They whirled together, then landed feetfirst on a stone floor hard enough to send them both sprawling.

Ilna rose to her hands and knees. It was night, and she was at the edge of a pool in a circular room. A double row of columns supported the domed ceiling; above the pool was an opening, an oculus as she'd heard Liane refer to a similar structure.

She and Alecto were in the place Ilna had viewed in the cauldron. They were in the temple from which a nightmare had been sent to trouble Garric's sleep.

Alecto had dropped her dagger when she hit the floor. She snatched it into her hand again before she stood up.

"You utter fool!" Ilna said.

Chanting voices echoed through the temple's entrance passage, the only way in or out of the room. The priests were returning.

Sharina tried to concentrate on the mural. Before her was a scene of herdsmen with long poles driving brindled cattle back from mountain pastures in autumn; the trees had already begun to lose their leaves.

Barca's Hamlet was sheep country. They raised cattle

in the highlands of Northern Haft, but those regions had been as far away as the moon when Sharina was growing up.

Merchants and drovers came to the borough from Sandrakkan, Blaise, and even Ornifal during the Sheep Fair. Nobody came from the north of the island, though. The folk there had their own markets and their own customs. If they bought wool, they did so from factors in Carcosa when they drove their herds to market in the capital.

Sharina thought about Ilna lying on the bed in waxen silence, of Cashel vanished without a trace, and Garric's body walking and talking under the control of a mind not his. She hugged herself and wondered if she were going to cry.

She turned, planning to ask Tenoctris—again—how long it'd been since Ilna had gone into her trance. The old woman sat on her backless chair, reading from a small parchment codex. She looked up with a smile when she felt Sharina's eyes, but Sharina waved her back to her book.

There wasn't anything to say. It had been however long it had been—not really very long; and it would be however long it was. Tenoctris couldn't say more, and if she was managing to lose herself in reading, all the better.

Garric would have had a book also, though Sharina doubted whether he'd have been able to concentrate on his beloved Celondre. What was the man who wore Garric's flesh doing now? King Carus wasn't a reader, of that she was sure.

The mural's next panel was of men piling hay on a wagon with long forks. Two oxen waited in the traces, grazing contentedly on the tufts a small girl held out for them. Women with double-sided rakes—the wooden pegs extended above and below the crossbar, an unfamiliar style to Sharina—gathered more hay from among the stubble. The mower sat in the shade of an apple tree, sharpening his scythe with a wooden rod dipped first in tallow and then in sand, just as mowers did in the borough.

Half the scene was familiar, half as strange to Sharina's childhood as the customs of townsfolk here in Valles. Either way she felt alien and alone, out of place and unable to help her threatened friends.

Sharina stroked the black horn scales of the Pewle knife she'd inherited from Nonnus. Today for her there was more comfort in that weapon than in pictures of happy peasants or in all the great literature she and Garric had been introduced to by their father. That was a terrible thing.

But still, she had the knife. She smiled faintly.

The outer door opened. Sharina whirled; Garric—not Garric, *Carus*—entered and slammed it shut behind him. Now by daylight Sharina noticed that the panel's covering of blue-dyed leather was tooled in delicate floral patterns. She'd been sleeping in the outer room for two nights and hadn't previously noticed the door's decoration.

Carus entered the main room. Garric was as graceful as any athletic young man; the man in his body walked like a great cat.

He nodded to the figure on the bed. "How is she?" he asked in a tone that could be mistaken for calm. He hooked his thumbs under his sword belt.

Tenoctris closed her codex without marking the place. She set it back within the satchel standing open on the floor beside her.

"The preparations went well," she said. She braced her hands on the chair arms as if to rise; Carus waved her back with a hard face that was just short of exasperation. This wasn't a man who had any interest in form or what he considered foolishness.

Tenoctris sank down gratefully again. She said, "The rest is up to Ilna. I expect her to succeed if that's within human abilities."

She paused and smiled. "Or even if it isn't," she said.

"I expect that too," said Carus tonelessly. His hand reached for the pommel of his sword but jerked back again as if the polished steel knob were hot. Instead he paced.

"I thought I'd stay away till it was all over," he said in a conversational voice. "Maybe not see her even then. Let her go to Tisamur with Merota and with her pirate and never think of her anymore. Except that I couldn't."

Faster than Sharina could see, Carus slammed the base of his fist into the wall. The thump wasn't loud—the concrete masonry was a hand's breadth thick, even here on the second floor—but the plaster sheathing flaked off in a radius of several inches from the center of the blow.

"If you like . . ." Tenoctris said carefully, "I can arrange for us to see what Ilna herself is seeing. Ah, not clearly that is, but—"

"Can you?" cried the king, no longer even pretending to be calm. "That is . . ."

He caught hold of himself, flashed Sharina his old smile, and knelt to rest his big hands on the wizard's, crossed in her lap. "Of course you can do what you say, Tenoctris," Carus said. "But can you do it without effort that might unfit you for work you have to do in the near future? Because I'm well aware I'm being foolish, and I needn't be coddled by my friends."

The old wizard's laugh reminded Sharina that Tenoctris had once been a girl, and that Garric was a handsome youth. She smiled and corrected herself: Garric was a handsome youth. The same flesh around Carus' soul was no longer quite youthful but was handsome in a very different fashion.

"Effort yes," said Tenoctris, "but not a serious risk in these days when the weakest wizard has powers that only the great ones of a generation before could manage. We'll need something shiny. Can we send out for a mirror?"

Carus stood and grinned. He drew his dagger and held

it so that the long polished blade sent sunlight dancing across the room. "Will this do?" he asked.

"Admirably!" Tenoctris said, taking the weapon by the hilt. She examined it, cocking the blade at an angle. To Sharina the edge looked sharp enough to cut the very light.

"Especially for Ilna, I believe," the wizard murmured in satisfaction. "I think she'd appreciate the symbolism."

She stood without difficulty and bent over the figure on the bed, holding the dagger down at her side. She laid the tips of her right index and middle fingers against Ilna's throat, then nodded.

"Yes, all right," Tenoctris said, straightening. "Sharina, will you . . . no. Your highness, will *you* hold this so that the surface reflects Ilna's eyes toward the wall there?"

She gestured. "Above the painting, I mean," she said. "Hold the blade so that if Ilna were looking, she'd see wall reflected in the blade. That's what I mean."

Carus nodded. He took the dagger back and brought it into position with only a glance at the girl's still form. "Go ahead," he said.

Tenoctris seated herself on the floor. "It's really quite simple," she murmured, tugging a split of bamboo from the small bundle she carried in her satchel. "I don't need a figure for the incantation, the rosette here will do. The portal's already open, after all. . . ."

She closed her eyes momentarily and settled her breathing. Then, stroking her temporary wand over the eight-sided figure joining four cartouches of the mosaic, she said, "*Basumia oiakintho phametamathathas!*"

A face sprang into life on the blank wall. Sharina hadn't expected anything to happen so suddenly. She'd been watching her friend on the bed, but the change at the corner of her eye made her whip her head around.

The face was a woman's, blurred but recognizable like a fresco painted while the plaster was too wet. She was probably young and certainly savage, whether or not the

spots on her cheeks were the tattoos they appeared to be.
Her mouth moved to shout.

The image of light vanished. Carus cried out in a voice
of despair and fury.

"What . . . ?" said Sharina, turning.

And knew what had caused the king to shout. The bed
was empty. Ilna's slight weight had dimpled the coverlet;
nothing more remained of her in this room or this world.

"By the *Lady*," Hakken moaned as he rode along behind
Garric and Vascay. "If the Protectors caught us, they
wouldn't hurt me worse 'n this saddle's doing. If I had to
do it again, I'd say tie me to the cursed nag's tail and drag
me along behind!"

"It's not much farther," Vascay said. "Pretty quick we'll
all have a chance to get outside a quart or two of Lord
Thalemos' wine, Hakken."

They'd skirted Durassa proper to reach their employer's
estate northeast of the city. The past mile of road had been
bordered to either side by vines growing in the shade of
great elms whose leaves kept sunlight from blasting the
tender grapes. So far as Garric could tell, the plantings
were all part of a single estate. If Lord Thalemos owned
it, he was a wealthy man indeed.

"They can curse the horses all they like," Vascay murmured to Garric, "but going on four feet has gained us
back the time we lost by not being navigators. There's no
way we'd have hiked this far before daylight."

Tint vaulted onto Garric's pillion again, making his
mount whicker and bunch. Garric lifted the reins to keep
the horse from bolting, though the beastgirl had startled
him as well.

"Soon we sleep, Gar?" she said. "Sleep *soon*."

"Not long, Tint," Garric said. "Now stay quiet, do you
hear? Just sit quiet."

He was bone tired and the *scrunch* of his sword into that first Protector's forearm still grated in his mind. His nerves were worn by the beastgirl's refusal to ride a horse alone and her frequent jumping up and down behind him. There were extra mounts, so Garric—heavier than most men—could shift at intervals between horses. Even so, Tint's additional eighty pounds were more than an animal should have to bear.

"Saved our lives, though, didn't she?" said Vascay, correctly reading the anger in Garric's stiff expression.

Garric smiled and relaxed. "So she did," he said. "She's like a child, but in some ways a very clever child."

He reached behind him left-handed and patted the beastgirl's shaggy buttock. She whimpered with pleasure.

Garric wasn't the horseman his ancestor Carus had been, but the experience he'd gained during the past few months with the king in his mind had enabled him to ride the ten miles from the ambush site without difficulty. Vascay was almost as good—the peg leg didn't handicap him in this any more than it did in any other fashion Garric had noticed—and others of the bandits were at least competent horsemen.

Half the band, though—well, Garric had seen grain sacks with as much business in the saddle. Still, as Vascay had said, they'd gotten where they were going. The stiffness—and bruises, for the men who'd repeatedly fallen—wouldn't be a problem after a day and a few good meals.

"The entrance drive's just beyond those willows," Vascay said. "There'll be a gatehouse and a watchman."

He clucked and prodded his horse's ribs with his iron-banded peg. It complained but quickened its pace slightly.

Garric grimaced and nudged his gelding with his heels. He wasn't sure it'd obey—and loaded as it was, he wouldn't blame the poor beast if it simply continued to plod along. To his pleased surprise the horse broke into a shambling trot, drawn by Vascay's mount and perhaps hope of getting Garric off his back. He and the chieftain rounded the curve together.

The gatehouse was there, but empty. A real gate would've been pointless since the estate was unwalled, but there was a turnpike to halt those entering by road. The shaft lay on the ground, broken off at the post instead of being swung out of the way; intruders had chosen to emphasize their power and their hostility.

Vascay and Garric drew up, side by side in the moonlit road. The chieftain had slipped his javelins butt first down the top of the high boot on his remaining leg. He pulled one out and balanced it in his palm.

"Tint!" said Garric in a hoarse whisper. "Are enemies waiting for us?"

"No men here, Gar," the beastgirl said. She slipped from the saddle. "House, Gar! We sleep in house?"

The rest of the gang was riding up behind them; though, judging from the cursing, Hakken had fallen off in the road again. Garric had touched the hilt of his sword; he deliberately released it.

"Not just yet, Tint," he said. "We've got things to learn before we sleep tonight."

"Hey, what's going on?" Ademos demanded. "Isn't this the place?"

"It's the place," said Vascay quietly, "but somebody's been here before us. The Protectors, I'd judge. They were waiting for us to land, and they'd already been here."

"Well, you knew the Intercessor was a wizard," Garric said. He supposed his voice sounded cold, but the facts were obvious enough when he came to think about them. The time and place of their landing had been predicted, as only a wizard could do. But—

"Since you say Metron is a wizard powerful enough to enter Laut from Tisamur," he continued aloud, "then he may have kept Lord Thalemos safe from the Intercessor's men. Come on, let's find out."

He clucked to his horse. It whickered but refused to move. Angry and half-expecting to be shot down by a volley of arrows, Garric kicked his mount hard—harder than he meant to do. It stumbled badly but settled into a walk that took it over the fallen pike.

"Come on," Vascay said gruffly. His horse clopped into motion to follow Garric.

"Hey, but what if they're waiting for us?" Ademos objected.

"If you don't shut your mouth, you'll find the Sister waiting for you and soon!" Vascay snarled. "The monkey thinks it's all right, doesn't she? And by the Sister's eyes, I'll take her word for it after the business back where we landed!"

He cleared his throat. "Sorry, Gar," he said. "Your friend Tint thinks it's clear. And she's all our friend, all of us who're still alive."

Three of the band had died in the ambush, and Alcomm's left arm now ended at the elbow; he rode with his belt tied to the horn of his saddle. They'd have all been killed or captured without Tint's warning, though.

The entrance drive had been gravelled, but grass grew thickly through it except where the feet and wheels of traffic kept the stone clear. The villa ahead had been built for show: its curving, colonnaded wings stretched to either side of a central section whose pillars rose the full three stories to an ornate pediment.

Later owners had converted the structure to more practical purposes. The openings between columns on the wings were bricked up, increasing the internal area considerably. The ornamental plantings on the north side had been removed to make space for ranks of great storage jars under a shed roof, and wagons were parked on the drive and in front of the building.

There were no lights in the villa or its outbuildings, but Garric saw shutters tremble as he and Vascay approached.

He reined up fifty feet from the entrance; Vascay halted beside him.

Tint, who'd been ambling along on all fours, stood upright. "Men *here,* Gar," she said. "Men scared."

Then, hopefully, "We kill men, Gar? Be easy—they *scared.*"

"We're not the Protectors come back!" Garric called. "We're friends of Lord Thalemos. We need to talk to whoever's in charge now, but there won't be any trouble."

He dismounted and walked toward the villa on foot; the gelding whickered thankfully. Garric didn't need the height of a saddle to cow servants who were already terrified; indeed, that'd probably be counterproductive.

His thighs were on the verge of cramping anyway. Gar was exceptionally strong, but he'd never ridden a horse until Garric took over his body. The strain of staying in the saddle was different from anything Gar's great muscles had been called on to do in the past.

Tint loped along beside him with the excitement of a just-unleashed dog. The beastgirl was too pleased to have Garric back on the ground to remember that she'd wanted to sleep.

Garric glanced behind. Vascay had dismounted but remained with the horses. The rest of the band—except for Hakken and an even more distant straggler, still coming down the drive—were climbing out of their saddles with varying degrees of skill and relief.

The horses were blown also. Bad riders were hard on their mounts, as surely as the reverse was true.

Garric stopped under the villa's looming façade, uneasily aware that a nervous potboy on the roof could throw a tile—or a chamber pot—down to brain him. "Somebody come out!" he demanded. "We don't mean any harm, but we need to know what's happened here!"

"Come on out or we'll smoke you out like badgers!" Toster called in his deep bass. "It's been a long hard road getting here, and I'm not in the mood for nonsense!"

Light flared. Ademos had struck sparks into a fireset of straw matting snatched from a wagon. He stepped away from it. The yellow flames threw stark light over the bandits' faces, making them look even harder and more desperate than Garric knew them to be.

The front door opened. The man who came out was middle-aged and heavy—but his weight was more muscle than not, very different from what Garric expected. He had a short beard and a truculent expression, though he hadn't been foolish enough to meet the bandits armed.

"You're the majordomo?" Garric asked.

"I'm Lord Thalemos' stablemaster," the man said. "My name's Orphin. You want the majordomo, you'll likely find him hiding in a clothespress in one of the storage rooms."

He spat. "Not that I can see why you'd want the lazy coward," he added conversationally.

"Who we want is Lord Thalemos," Garric said, "or his advisor Metron. They sent us to find something for them. We've come back and need to talk to them."

Vascay came to join him. He nodded affably to Orphin but didn't intrude on the conversation. Tint scratched her spine with her toes, then yawned and curled up at Garric's feet. Her back was a warm pressure against his left ankle.

"You want Lord Thalemos, you're too late," Orphin said, frowning in mild surprise as he took in the beastgirl's presence. "A gang of Protectors came down on us at dusk and took him away with them. As for this foreign wizard"—he spat again, this time slapping a moth off one of the trumpet vines wrapping the adjacent pillar—"I'd've said he was the one who called the Intercessor's heroes down on the master, but he didn't go off with them. Metron hasn't been around since the Protectors come riding up the drive. One of the girls said she thought it was him she saw running toward the boathouse right before the trumpet blew from the gate, but I don't know. The Protectors searched there too, and they didn't find him."

The stablemaster's grim visage melted into a look of despair. "Shepherd help me, I don't know what's going to happen next. I guess they'll send in an overseer from the Intercessor's staff. Then what'll happen to us?"

"They didn't come out with officials?" Vascay asked. "It was just the Protectors?"

"That was enough, wasn't it?" Orphin said. "There must've been fifty of 'em. We couldn't do anything to stop them, not even if we'd been willing to hide in the woods the rest of our lives."

He spat again, hitting another moth. "Which I'm not, seeing's I've a wife and children, whatever you think about it."

"I think if I had a wife and children," Vascay said quietly, "I might have made the same choice. You'll put us up for now—"

"They'll be coming back!" Orphin said. "You can't stay here, they'll kill us all if—"

"You'll put us up for *now*," Vascay repeated, twitching the bundle of javelins to emphasize his words, "in the stables, and you'll find us food. After you've done that, we'll talk some more. But we're not going anywhere till we've had some food and sleep."

"And something to drink," Hakken called in a frustrated, cracking voice. "A whole lot to drink!"

"Yeah, all right," said Orphin. "Get out of sight in the stables. I'll send over a hamper and a jug."

He shook his head sadly. "Most likely I'll bring the food myself," he corrected himself. "Sister take 'em, they're all scared to so much as lift their heads."

A large death's-head moth flew toward Orphin's eyes, then away. The stablemaster scowled, then spat. His aim was as accurate as usual, but the moth hovered for a flickering instant instead of continuing its path uninterrupted.

The gobbet sailed between Garric and Vascay, then splattered the ground near Toster's foot.

"Sorry," the stablemaster muttered. "Yeah, I'll take you back to the stables. Otherwise, Pusta and Jelf'll think you're coming for them, and the Lady knows *what* they'll do."

The death's-head moth flew toward Garric's eyes. He threw an arm up, startled. It circled his head.

"Come on, brethren," Vascay said over his shoulder. "We've got straw to sleep on and food coming."

Tint, aroused by Garric's sudden movement, came alert. Her head turned upward; her muscles bunched with the lethal certainty of a crossbow cocking.

"No, Tint!" Garric said.

She leaped, her arms outstretched to snatch the big moth. Garric, faster than he'd known he could be, grabbed the beastgirl's throat and held her back.

"*No,* Tint," Garric repeated as he relaxed his grip on the girl. The moth lifted a few feet higher, describing figure-eights between Garric and Vascay.

"Is she all right?" Orphin said uneasily. "She hasn't got hydrophobia, has she?"

"Gar mad?" the beastgirl whimpered, rubbing against Garric's leg. "Gar not mad, please?"

"She's fine," Garric snapped. "We're all fine."

He stroked Tint's back, and in a milder tone said, "I'm not angry, but you've got to do what I tell you. All right?"

Ignoring her moans of appreciation, Garric swept Vascay and the stablemaster with his eyes. "Orphin," he said, "take the men to the stables. Vascay and I have other business."

He crooked a smile at the chieftain. "Brother Vascay," he said. "You and I are going to follow that moth"—he gestured with a casual finger—"and see where it leads. All right?"

Garric knew he was on the verge of hysteria, but he had

to keep going even though everything seemed ludicrously funny. His body was tired, and part of him wanted to break into peals of laughter. What was left of his reason told him that he couldn't drown the scrunch of steel on bone that way, maybe no way. . . .

Vascay frowned, then twitched his javelins toward the puzzled stablemaster. "You heard him, Orphin," he said. "Get the Brethren bedded down."

He turned his attention to his men. "Brother Hame, you'd be a good one to give orders when there's no time to vote. Not so, Brethren?"

Ademos muttered, but the others nodded agreement.

Vascay looked up at the moth. It was lengthening its twisted loops toward the villa's north wing. Moonlight threw the skull on the back of its wings into bright relief.

"Sure, let's go," he said, starting off in the direction the moth was indicating. "This something your friend—"

His javelin butts wagged toward Tint, frisking at Garric's side.

"—told you about?"

"No," said Garric. "Metron's a wizard, though. If he was powerful enough to get away from the Intercessor's men, then he'd find a way to bring us to wherever he's hiding."

"And you think this bug's our guide?" Vascay said.

"I think I've never seen a moth act like this one does," Garric replied quietly. "If it flies off into a redbud and ignores us, then we'll look for some other way to find Metron."

The moon gave good light for the moment, but he and Vascay would be in shadow if they went around the building. He supposed they'd manage.

The moth kept closer. It wasn't worried about being eaten, Garric supposed; not that insects had brain enough to worry, but remained certain that the mind animating this one wasn't an insect's. Moonlight turned the moth's gray wing scales silver and darkened the brown ones to black.

"The Intercessor knew where we'd be landing," Vascay said. He was favoring his left leg. He walked at his normal pace, but he hunched slightly every time the peg came down. "But he didn't know we'd win through. And though the Intercessor knew Lord Thalemos was getting the ring that'd break his power, he didn't know it until just before it happened."

"Eh?" said Garric. Even the brief time he'd been effective ruler of the Isles had taught him that you don't always act immediately on information you've received. Kingship is a complicated business. "He might've known long before he chose to move on Thalemos, mightn't he? To see who'd join the rebel."

"Aye," said Vascay, glancing at Garric with a grin. "But he'd have sent an estate manager out with the troops if he'd been planning this for more than the time it took to alert a company of Protectors. Not so?"

Garric laughed. "So."

Instead of curving back around the north wing of the villa, the moth's flutters and curlicues were leading them through a tract that had once been an ornamental garden but hadn't been kept up for a generation. The tightly planted clump of boxwoods, ragged but still retaining some of their original shape, must have been a maze.

"So," said Vascay, "while I'd sooner not be fighting a wizard, I knew what Echeon was before I started out. It therefore pleases me that he's got limitations despite all his powers."

He looked at Garric, this time not smiling. "And it pleases me that you came to us when you did, Brother Prince," he added. "Because however much help Metron's wizardry may be to us, I put more trust in your wit and your sword."

Garric forced a smile of acknowledgment; he felt embarrassed. "You've honored me with your trust," he said.

As he spoke, he thought of all the others who trusted him, who needed him. One way or another, he *would* get back where he belonged.

"Where Gar go?" Tint asked. "Tint sleep soon?"

"It looks," Garric said, "like we're headed for that copse of willows. There must be something there besides trees or there wouldn't be a path."

"House there," said the beastgirl. "Pond there too. We sleep in house, Gar?"

At least Tint didn't seem to be as hungry as Garric himself was. Though he hadn't let her eat the big moth, she'd been snapping down tidbits as they went along, like a boy walking through a berry patch. In her case it was mostly crickets, though.

"That's the boathouse Orphin talked about," Vascay said. "But he said the Protectors searched it, too. Can a wizard make himself invisible?"

Garric shrugged. "Some can, maybe," he said. "But I don't know why Metron would have to come out here instead of going invisible in the main house."

Vascay nodded. He took the javelins one at a time into his right hand, checking their balance. Tint would've warned them if anybody was waiting for them in the copse, but Garric raised his sword a few fingers' breadth and let it slip back in the scabbard. There was no harm in needless preparation, after all.

The boathouse was an open-sided structure with a peaked tile roof; two small skiffs were stored upturned on the roof trusses. A short dock led from the building into a pond that extended at least a bowshot to right and left; better light might have shown it to be even broader. The water was shallow, though; the moonlight shimmered through cattails well out from the soggy margins.

Vascay rapped a skiff with a javelin butt. The gesture

was pointless, a mere placeholder while the chief's mind tried to puzzle out the problem.

Tint leaped suddenly onto a truss. Vascay jumped back, cocking a javelin. Garric had his sword half-drawn before the men realized the beastgirl had just caught a tree frog. She popped it into her mouth.

The moth was fluttering in tight figures at the end of the dock. "Maybe he's breathing through a reed." Vascay said.

He walked onto the structure—it was less than six feet long—and knelt. At first he fished in the water with his bare hand; then he thrust a javelin butt first under the boards to extend his reach. He brought it up with mud streaming from the ferrule and lower shaft.

"Nothing," Vascay said, rising heavily. "Maybe he was there and then moved when the Protectors had gone, but I don't see them not checking it themselves. Those scum have a lot of experience looking for folks who're trying to hide."

But the moth wasn't over the dock: it circled above the clear water beyond. Garric stepped past Vascay—the boards creaked but held—and walked to the end. All he could see on the water was moonlight.

"Gar?" Tint called. She hopped to the floor of the boathouse with a thump.

Garric lay flat and reached into the water. It was shockingly cold, spring-fed. He couldn't touch the bottom.

He reached behind him. "Vascay, give me one of your—" he began and broke off, because Vascay was already laying a javelin in his hand. The missiles had bodkin points for penetration, so Garric didn't have to worry about cutting himself with an edge.

Garric slid the shaft sideways through the water. It touched something and twisted back in his hand. Maybe a rock, of course: no hollow reed disturbed the pond's surface here. If the wizard was hiding here, he wasn't breathing. . . .

But the moth drew tight circles over Garric's probing arm, fanning his biceps with its great wings.

Garric laid the javelin beside him and rolled onto his back to unbuckle his sword belt. Vascay dried the missile on the hem of his outer tunic. "Find something?" he asked.

"Something," said Garric. "I don't know what."

He swung himself feetfirst into the water. The cold knotted his belly muscles. He bent down and grasped a plump man lying on his back under four feet of water. He lifted, surprised at the effort. When the figure broke surface, Garric saw the fellow had crossed his arms over his chest and was holding an anchor in either hand.

"Got him!" Vascay cried, kneeling to help lift the wizard. "It's Metron all right. That's the clothes he wears!"

They were both strong men, but it was a struggle to flop Metron onto the dock. His dark robe was slashed white across the front. It weighed as much as the body did now that it was waterlogged, but initially the anchors on which his fingers were locked would've been necessary to keep him down.

"Is he dead?" Garric said, gasping in the pond for a moment before he heaved himself up. "I don't see—"

Metron spluttered. His eyelids quivered open, then closed again as he turned his head sideways and vomited water.

Garric lifted himself with a splash; water continued to run from his tunics. He glanced over his shoulder.

The moth had fallen into the pond, lifeless. Its spread wings swirled slowly in the current.

Cashel's skin tingled as the gout of red wizardlight washed him. For an instant he saw the world as a negative image of itself, the shadows bright but moonlight on the sea a streak of blackness.

A sailor cried out in terror, though none of the men Cashel could see were any more injured by the light than he himself was. The fellow screaming wasn't afraid of any *thing*, he was just afraid.

Though there might be plenty of real reasons for fear, of course. Cashel knew *that* from his past experience with wizards.

The gush of light from the beach faded; the stones of the ruined temple now had a rosy glow, as if they'd been soaked with dye. Cashel sensed things happening at the corners of his eyes, but his focus was on the sailors before him.

"Come on, you cowards!" Captain Mounix shouted. "If we're ever going to be safe, we've got to have the girl with us!"

He paused, probably hoping that his men would rush Cashel without him. A sailor threw his club at Cashel's head. Cashel batted it back over the cliff edge with a quick twist of his left hand on the quarterstaff. The club missed Mounix by less than its own spinning width.

"Come on!" the captain screamed. To Cashel's surprise he charged up the steps with his sword held out before him like a spear.

Cashel could've stopped Mounix with a straight thrust; with his full strength behind it, the blunt ferrule would've gone through the captain's breastbone to smash his spine. Cashel killed when he needed to, but he couldn't take the sailors as a serious danger despite their numbers. He spun his staff horizontally, swiping the sword out of Mounix's hand.

The blade rang off a pillar and rebounded. Mounix gave a cry of horror and jumped back, gripping his numbed right hand with his left. Another sailor, drawn to attack with his wooden spear by the captain's example, tried to backpedal also. Cashel reversed his spin and broke the man's knee.

Two sailors pulled their screaming comrade off the temple porch. Cashel waited for the next attempt. He was panting, more to feed the emotions surging through his veins than because he'd really exerted himself.

The temple was changing. The red light didn't just stain the walls, it was rebuilding them. The wear and fractures swelled with a liquid translucence that had the texture of stone when Cashel tested a pillar by brushing it with his elbow.

"Come on, move up," Hook said. "All together, slow and steady. Possin, Ruttal, Wallach . . . with me, all together."

The carpenter slid his right foot ahead a half step, his spear advanced. Instead of waiting this time, Cashel strode forward with his quarterstaff spinning over his head. Hook screamed and jabbed blindly. The quarterstaff cracked the spearshaft in half just ahead of where Hook's left hand gripped it.

The rangy sailor who'd moved up also now tripped over Hook and sprawled toward Cashel. Cashel broke the man's collarbone and stepped back.

"Who's next?" he growled. They'd gotten his blood up by now. "Who wants his head cracked next?"

"Monsters!" shouted a sailor. "There's monsters coming out of the sea!"

"Lady help us!" another man cried. "They're all around! Lady save us!"

Cashel couldn't see what they were talking about. The sailors he *could* see, however, were all turning to look behind them. Cashel took the opportunity to check how Tilphosa was keeping.

The clinging red glow of the temple walls lighted her from all directions, but even its softness couldn't change the girl's stark expression. Tilphosa still held the block of stone she'd taken for a weapon, but despair had subtly eroded her spirit.

"Metra's raised the Archai," she said. "I was afraid that was what she was doing."

The pedestal for the God's image remained empty, but the screening wall behind it, the reredos, had returned to its full majesty despite the fragments of the stone original littering the floor. The carving was complete in solid light: on it insect monsters battled lizard monsters, and in the center with Her arms spread stood the Lady crowned as the Moon. Cashel saw no mercy, no comfort in Her cold visage.

Cashel shrugged. "All right, then," he said. "We'll fight the Archai. Whoever they—"

Around the sides of the temple, pressing the sailors back from both directions, came one set of the monsters from the reredos. The Archai walked upright, and each was each was as tall as a woman, but they weren't remotely human.

The Archai's legs joined their bodies in the middle rather than at the lower end as with men. Their abdomens wobbled beneath, making the creatures look a little like praying mantises. The middle pair of their six limbs ended in fingers, which they now clenched tightly against their chests to keep them out of the way.

The Archai's uppermost arms had sharp, saw-toothed edges with small pincers in place of hands. These were outstretched as they came on.

A sailor shrieked and charged the Archai, swinging his long club in both hands in a desperate attempt to break through. He crushed the wedge-shaped head of the first insect, but others leaped on him from both sides with their arms chopping.

Blood splashed in all directions. The sailor screamed; he continued to scream as his body sank under repeated blows. He must have been dead for some time before his slayers stopped hacking at the quivering corpse. Beside him lay the Archa he'd killed, its limbs twitching in six separate rhythms.

More Archai joined those already confronting the sailors. The men backed slowly. One jabbed his spear at an Archa. The point glanced from the creature's chitinous chest. The Archa grabbed the shaft with its pincered forelimbs.

The sailor jerked back hard, dragging the Archa along with him. The sailor squealed and dropped his weapon, but another man smashed the Archa's shoulder with his club and jumped away before the other monsters could respond. The wounded Archa collapsed and began worrying the spearshaft with its beak.

Shoulder to narrow shoulder, the insectile mass advanced without haste. The sailors backed up the temple steps, still rightly wary of Cashel's quarterstaff.

"Tilphosa, have you got any ideas?" Cashel asked, his eyes on the closing ring of monsters. "Because you know these people, I mean."

"Cashel, they're not *people*," the girl cried. "There's no help for us now!"

Metra came up the track from the beach, swaying on a driftwood litter carried by four Archai. The wizard looked drawn, her plump features more washed out than moonlight alone could explain. Her eyes met Cashel's over the heads of the frightened sailors.

"Barbarian!" she called, her voice cracking. "Master Cashel! Is Lady Tilphosa all right? Show her to me!"

"Tilphosa's fine," Cashel growled. "And she's going to stay that way. You aren't giving orders here, Metra."

The ring of Archai continued its slow pressure, squeezing the sailors inward the way a blacksnake's coils suffocate a vole. Friends had dragged the man with a broken shoulder back from the temple; he lay on the ground, unconscious from pain. As the sailors retreated, the Archai reached him on their spindly legs.

Two of the insects knelt; their legs bent backward like a sheep's, not a man's. Their forearms hammered like cleavers, reducing the victim to a bloody carcass.

A sailor wailed in furious despair as he hurled his club, hitting the chest and one arm of a kneeling Archa. Purple ichor leaked through the chitin, but the remaining forearm chopped three times more before the creature slumped dead over the body of its victim.

"Metra, you've gone mad!" Tilphosa called in a clear voice. "I won't let the Archai take me! I'll die first!"

And how will you manage that? Cashel wondered, because the girl's only weapon was the chunk of stone, which didn't seem like much of a way to commit suicide. Metra might not know that, of course; but it wasn't clear to Cashel that the wizard would care, either. She'd made up her mind to crush everything in her way, and often people who got into that state forgot the goal they'd started out with.

Metra made a strident noise with her tongue close to her palate. Cashel hadn't heard the Archai speak. They seemed to understand the wizard's cry, however, because they stopped where they were.

The insects' narrow chests expanded and shrank with a slight whistling as they breathed. A sailor was crying, and another whimpered in pain.

"Barbarian, I offer you your life!" Metra said in the near silence. "Turn Lady Tilphosa over to me, and I'll spare you. I'll spare the others too, if you like."

Metra's voice was stronger than before, but she still sat upright with difficulty. Raising this army of monsters had drained her badly, despite the assistance the powdered amulet had given her.

"The others are no business of mine," Cashel growled. "Tilphosa is. She says she's not coming with you."

He heard the girl's gasp of relief, though she must know as well as he did that he was no better than bragging. Oh, he'd fight the Archai till they brought him down; but they *would* bring him down, sure as sunrise, and they probably wouldn't be very long about the business either.

What Metra and the Archai did with Lady Tilphosa then—well, Cashel or-Kenset didn't have to worry about that.

Metra's face contorted. She trilled like an angry cicada. A wave of Archai leaped forward, not the whole mass but only half the front rank. Spread out, the insect warriors had full scope to slash into the sailors. There was a bedlam of screams, crackling, and the soft *choonk* of axe-edged forelimbs slicing into meat.

For a moment Cashel poised. If he leaped into the struggle, his staff spinning, he could smash his way through . . . several Archai. Probably a dozen, possibly a score. Metra had raised an army of the monsters that not even a scholar could count.

Cashel turned into the nave of the temple. There was no darkness, because the walls themselves glowed. The Lady of the Moon glared down, merciless and implacable.

"Cashel?" cried the girl.

Cashel swung his quarterstaff butt first with all the strength of his arms and torso, smashing it like a battering ram into the reredos of light. Bolts of red and blue fire ricocheted about the room.

The stone screen had only been three fingers' thick; Cashel's blow would've shattered it. Its ghost in wizard-light stood the shock, numbing Cashel's hands to the wrists. Metra trilled with desperate urgency.

Cashel didn't drop the staff. He stepped back and spun the smooth hickory with the familiar hand-over-hand motion, working feeling into his muscles again. Tilphosa stood in a corner—her eyes open, her expression unreadable.

Cashel brought the staff around again, leading this time with his right hand and the other ferrule. The iron struck on the Lady's sculptured face and headdress.

The reredos flew into shards like sunlight glancing from a windswept pond. Beyond was not the storage room but rather a swirl of pastel colors.

"Come on!" Cashel shouted, but Tilphosa was already jumping through. Cashel followed, his staff thrust out before him like a lance.

For an instant he thought he heard Captain Mounix' voice. Then everything was brightness and a chaotic roar.

Chapter Ten

Sharina's stomach knotted in cold horror.

"Where did she go, wizard?" shouted King Carus, his hand curved like a claw over his sword. He wasn't touching the sharkskin hilt, *quite,* but it was only by an effort of will that he held himself clear. "Where did you send Brichese? What—"

The king's volcanic fury loosed Sharina's muscles. She stepped toward him, her arms raised. In his present madness Carus could cut her down on his way to killing the wizard whom he blamed for what'd happened to Ilna, but Sharina was still thankful for a chance to act instead of standing frozen.

Carus sagged back against the wall, gasping with reaction. "Brichese is a thousand years dead," he whispered. "And I would to the Lady I were with her now!"

Tenoctris sat on the floor again without bothering to speak. She drew out a fresh wand and a stylus of lead pure enough to streak gray lines onto the polished stone.

Sharina knew the wizard would have done the same if Carus' sword were slicing down at her. Tenoctris focused completely on whatever task was before her. Whatever the limitations of her wizardry and the weakness of her frail old body, her mind was as strong and supple as Carus' blade of patterned steel.

"Your highness?" called the captain of the guards from the hallway. The door wasn't barred; it eased a finger's breadth open. "Shall we—"

"Get back where you belong!" Carus said. "One fool with a sword in here's a great plenty already!"

He banged his fist into the wall again, emphasizing his words and—to Sharina—the fact that his hand was empty. The door jerked closed.

"We need you, your highness," Sharina said. She lowered her hands. She'd thought of embracing the man in her brother's flesh, but this wasn't the time for that. "We need you now more than ever."

"Do you?" said Carus with a terrible smile. "Well, perhaps you do. More than Brichese does, that's for certain."

He looked around the room, still smiling. "What I would like," he added in a voice as light as a lute air, "is something to kill. I suppose that'll have to wait for a—"

There was a thump and quick rasping outside the open window. A guard on the ground below cried out.

"Don't throw your spear, you idiot!" another Blood Eagle bellowed. *"Your highness, watch the—"*

A left hand, tanned and as strong as a grappling hook, clutched the bottom of the casement. Sharina reached for her Pewle knife; Carus' great sword was in his hand with no more sound than a snake makes licking the air. Tenoctris continued her soft chant, tapping the figure with her bamboo split.

Chalcus lifted himself, squatting like an ape for an instant on the window ledge, then hopped to the floor. His curved sword was thrust through one side of his bright sash, his dagger through the other. His hands were empty, but his eyes were bright as hellfire.

"I've got it!" Carus shouted, slamming his sword home in its scabbard.

"But your highness . . . ?" a guard below objected.

Carus stepped to the window, passing close to Chalcus. The men neither touched nor seemed to move to avoid one another; their motion was that of vinegar slipping through oil.

The king leaned out. "Did you not hear me? I've got it! Don't bother me again unless you want to go back to following a yoke of oxen!"

He pulled the casements closed as vehemently as he'd sheathed his sword, then walked to the center of the room. He and Chalcus eyed one another.

"So, soldier . . ." Chalcus said in a voice that held the music of swordblades ringing together. "At Ilna's house they told me that there'd been a summons, that her friend Sharina—"

Chalcus nodded toward Sharina. He was smiling, but though she'd always gotten on well with Chalcus, she had at this moment the feeling that a viper was measuring the distance to strike her.

"—had called her to aid Prince Garric in a crisis. And so I came here, thinking to wait politely outside till Ilna had finished her business, not intruding on my betters—"

Carus flared his nostrils at the open scorn Chalcus put into the words "my betters," but his lips continued to smile. His arms were crossed, each big hand on the opposite elbow.

"—until I heard you shout," Chalcus continued. "Where do you suppose I might find Ilna, soldier?"

"I don't know," Carus said, anger clipping the syllables. "Maybe the wizard—"

He gestured with a chop of his chin, then grimaced as though he'd bitten something sour.

"Maybe Lady Tenoctris, that is," he said in correction, "can tell us what I want to know as badly as you do, sailor.

Ilna was here on the bed; then she vanished."

Azure wizardlight puffed above the five-sided figure Tenoctris had scrawled in lead over the mosaic. For a moment Sharina thought it was a tentacled creature, but there was no body—only a mass of lines intersecting like worm-tracks. Several of them lengthened, then faded away; the whole image faded like the stars at dawn, then was gone.

Tenoctris dropped her wand and leaned forward, supporting her weight on her arms. Sharina squatted by the older woman and held her by her shoulders.

The men stared at the old wizard the way wolves sized up a flock: without hostility, but with a merciless desire that made nothing of the object's needs or wishes. They wanted an answer they hoped Tenoctris would give. That she was wrung out with the effort of this and earlier wizardry meant no more to them than their own wounds or weakness would have mattered if they felt they needed to do something themselves.

Tenoctris raised her head, looking from Carus to Chalcus. Her smile was weak, but it was one of understanding.

"I'm sorry," she said. "Ilna's—soul, I'll call it, Ilna's soul returned to the waking world at another point and drew her body to it. I don't know where she went, but I don't think she could have managed that by herself."

Chalcus raised an eyebrow. He was taut as the top string of a lute.

Tenoctris sniffed at the implied question. "Not because I doubt her strength," she said in something closer to irritation than Sharina had generally heard from Tenoctris' lips. "This is a matter of technique, Master Chalcus. Ilna could probably force her own way into the dreamworld, but returning to a place other than where her body lies . . . that I do not believe. Even for her."

"How then?" said Carus in a controlled voice. His left hand had slid down to grip his right, preventing it from drawing his sword as it so clearly wanted to do. "If she didn't do it, who did?"

"I don't know that either," Tenoctris said. "She met someone or something—a wizard, though, not a demon; whoever drew her down did so through art rather than power, but power as well."

Tenoctris struggled to get her feet under her; Sharina helped her rise and guided her back onto the stool. The lead symbols drawn on the floor had a dull sheen like the eyes of a landed fish.

"Now what I'm wondering . . ." said Chalcus, "simple man that I am—"

Sharina watched his expression. There was nothing simple about Chalcus. She wasn't sure that even his two eyes saw the same things when they looked out on the world.

"—is whether it might have been planned that Ilna go off to this dreamworld and not return to trouble the mind of the king who set her the task? Kings are used to dicing with the lives of lesser folk, or so I've heard—eh?"

Carus looked at the smaller man without expression. Chalcus was a cat, but the king was a wolf, or mayhap a dragon.

"Once long ago," Carus said, "there were men who thought I'd do as they said if they took Lady Brichese as their hostage. They could do that, because they were her cousins."

He smiled. It was a terrible expression.

"I led the attack on their castle myself," Carus said. "Some of them I captured, and afterward those lived much longer than they wanted to; but my Brichese died that day in the fire."

The men stared into one another's eyes. Their faces were cold as stone, but their eyes, those eyes . . . Sharina would have shivered, except that she had the hilt of her Pewle knife to steady her.

"I'd have done the same thing again to save the kingdom," Carus said, smiling. "Perhaps I'd still do that. But I don't think that I *am* the kingdom any longer, do you see? And regardless, whatever's happened to Ilna is none of my plan nor my desire."

"So," said Chalcus mildly, liltingly. "So you say. But would you be lying to me, I wonder?"

Carus laughed like boulders slipping. "Don't flatter yourself, sailor!" he said.

Chalcus' lips twisted in a wry smile. "Aye," he said. "I was getting above myself, was I not?"

His expression drew back into its previous taut, feral lines. "So, soldier," he said. "We've a problem. Will our wizard here—"

He nodded to Tenoctris; she acknowledged his glance by raising her chin.

"—be able to solve it?"

"No," said Tenoctris calmly. "I may be able to find where Ilna has gone, but I won't be able to bring her back myself. That's far beyond my powers."

Carus snorted. "Wizardry's never done me much good," he said. "This time wasn't much different from other times. I'll fall back on a cure for the kingdom's ills that I know something about."

He drew his sword a hand's breadth from the scabbard, his thumb and index finger gripping the pommel; demonstrating, not threatening. He grinned at Chalcus. "This," the king said. "What would you like for a command, sailor?"

Chalcus' left index finger traced a scar barely to be seen against the tan skin of the opposite biceps. "I think . . ." he said, and the pause showed that he was thinking indeed, "that I'll carry on as before. Merota and I will go to Tisamur and see what's to be learned about Moon Wisdom."

Sharina thought she was keeping a strait face, but Chalcus must have read the surprise she felt. He grinned at her, and said, "Long odds it was Moon Wisdom she was searching for when she vanished, not so? So it seems to me that other folk searching for Moon Wisdom may find themselves in the place Ilna has gotten to."

He laughed. "Not that she'll need me or Merota, either one," he added. "But we'll be in a place to watch her deal with those troubling our good friend Carus and his kingdom."

"And perhaps," said Carus, "she'll need you. We none of us can have too many friends."

Chalcus merely grinned, but his finger toyed with the eared pommel of his sword. For him, that was a sign of nervousness.

"What help do you need from me, then?" Carus demanded, his thumbs hooked in his sword belt.

"*Need* from you?" said Chalcus. "Don't flatter yourself!"

Whistling a lilting hornpipe, he swaggered to the hallway door. Looking back with a grin, Chalcus said, "I'll see you in Donelle, soldier."

"Aye, or in Hell if we get there first," Carus replied. They were both laughing again until the closing door separated them.

Ilna got to her feet cautiously. Her mind still saw ghost images of Garric's room in the palace, the cracked plaster and her friends watching her worriedly on the bronze bed. That's where her mind *knew* she should have been.

But she wasn't, yet another example of reality being worse than what should have been. The polished marble floor beneath Ilna's bare soles reminded her of how much she disliked stone.

She smiled faintly. That was fair: stone didn't like her either.

The girl, Alecto, glared at the entrance. She was crouching, her athame held low for a disemboweling stroke.

"Have you got a knife?" she demanded. "Maybe we can cut our way through them before they know we're in here!"

Ilna didn't let her sneer reach her lips. She *did* have a knife, a bone-cased sliver of steel that she used for everything from dressing chickens to trimming the selvage from the cloth she wove; she didn't see herself slashing her way through an army of priests and worshippers with it, though. When she'd looked down at the scene earlier, this big circular room had been full of people.

"No," she said looking upward. "We'll hide."

"You can't get out that hole up there unless you can walk upside down like a fly!" Alecto said, but she raised her eyes also.

No, the cast-concrete dome curved up as high as the big room was wide. Though the inner surface was cross-ribbed, not even an acrobat—not even Chalcus!—could have crossed it against the pull of gravity.

The dome rested on pillars, each wider around than Ilna could span with both arms and separated from one another by about the distance of her arms spread. The pillars were only about five or six times a man's height.

A solid wall surrounded the colonnade set out at half the distance of the pillars' height, forming a corridor around the domed area in the center. Overflow from the crowd could stand beneath the corridor's sloping roof, hearing though perhaps not seeing what was going on above the reflecting pool.

Alecto glanced behind a pillar. Her frown showed that she thought—as Ilna did—that if the room filled, there was little chance that the presence of the two interlopers wouldn't be remarked. She started to speak; before the objection reached her tongue she saw Ilna uncoil her sash into a noosed rope. "Ah!" she said instead.

Ilna cast the noose with the skill she displayed in every use of fabric. The heads of the columns mimicked vines growing through a loose wicker basket; complex and delicate for stonework, though nothing to the subtlety of a weaver's art. The silken loop settled over an extended tendril; Ilna pulled it tight.

"Will it hold me?" Alecto said. She took the blade of her dagger in her teeth instead of sliding the weapon back into its sheath.

"The cord will," Ilna said coldly, wondering if the wild woman thought she was going to climb it first. "You'll follow me up. The *cord* will hold an ox. I'm less confident about the stone, but there's nothing better available."

The chanting was growing louder. The interior of the temple was in shadow save for gray light blurring across the west half of the dome as the moon rose, but anyone on the floor would be in plain sight as soon the procession reached the rotunda.

Ilna tugged again, then climbed by the strength of her arms alone. Alecto muttered an objection, but Ilna already knew that Cashel or any other of the village boys who robbed seabird nests on the offshore islands would have used the grip of their feet on the rock as well. She made the choice not out of ignorance but from distaste for the stone.

Each time Ilna's arms hitched her up another level, her body swung against the column. Still, she wasn't *deliberately* touching the fluted marble.

Curves projecting from the column head gave Ilna somewhere to set her feet though they were too smooth to have held the rope. She laid her left arm flat along the vault's lowest rib, gripping as well as she could, and motioned Alecto to follow. The girl did, scrambling like a cat up a fir tree.

It would've been safer for Ilna to loop the cord around a second knob to spread Alecto's weight, but she decided against doing that. As soon as the wild girl saw the cord twitch upward the necessary foot or so, she'd have assumed that Ilna planned to abandon her to the incoming worshippers. She'd have come up in a flying leap that might well have sheared the stone when a more cautious approach did not.

Ilna smiled sourly. Leaving Alecto on the ground would surely lead to Ilna's own discovery as well as being a wholly pointless bit of spite. She'd seen before that what people feared in others generally showed how they'd choose to behave themselves.

Alecto reached the head of the column and braced herself from the side opposite to Ilna. There was at least a chance that anyone glancing upward would mistake them for a pair of statues; though the better hope—and the likelier one—was that nobody would bother to look.

Alecto glanced at Ilna, then took the dagger into her free right hand. The hard set of her mouth didn't change.

Ilna flipped the cord up to her hand, then cleared the noose with a twist that made Alecto's eyes widen. The wild girl had used ropes and snares, that was evident; but she'd never seen anyone use them with Ilna's ease and skill.

Acknowledging the unspoken praise with a slight smile, Ilna tossed the cord into a loop around the pillar, Alecto, and finally herself. The noose itself had been the only weight for the free end. Ilna tugged the cord tight, but instead of tying the loop, she kept the bight in her hands so that she could release it instantly at need.

Close up, Alecto had a strong animal odor compounded of fur and leather garments and her own intense femaleness. Ilna disliked it, but feeling dislike wasn't a new experience for her.

The inner door opened. The worshippers, led by a phalanx of priests in black-and-white robes, entered the cavity of the temple. Their hymn had the rhythms Ilna remembered from Tenoctris' incantations; and also during those of wizards she trusted far less than she did Tenoctris.

Ilna's eyes narrowed as she realized for the first time that there was no statue of the Lady in the great room. Was this a temple after all?

As best Ilna could tell looking down from her perch, the priests, like the worshippers following them, were a mix of men and women in roughly equal numbers. They continued to sing as they filled the room. Two of the leaders carried covered wicker baskets.

The priests took their places around the margin of the reflecting pool, the white slashes of their robes showing up in the dim light like a row of slanting pickets. The laymen moved with solemnity but not precision to stand outside the ring of priests. They'd done this before, but they weren't a military unit marching in formation.

The room continued to fill. Ilna could no more count than she could read, but she was certain that there were more people below her in this room than there were in Barca's Hamlet. They stood at the base of the pillars and moved back into the corridor where Ilna couldn't see them from her perch.

Alecto watched with eyes like a hungry hawk. Her face, already hard despite its curves, grew taut.

The moon was near zenith, reflecting upward from the pool's surface. The last of the worshippers had entered the room. A husky man wearing a sword—a temple servant, distinct both from the priests and from the ordinary towns-folk who made up the worshippers—swung shut the great bronze door.

Priests—one at either axis of the reflecting pool—raised the lids of the round wicker baskets they'd carried in. Their fellows continued to chant. Ilna blinked and would have rubbed her eyes if she'd had a hand free; the rhythms of the hymn were beginning to disturb her balance.

The priests lifted rabbits out of their baskets, tied as though they were going to market. One of the animals was black, the other white. They bawled in terror, a penetrating sound so like a baby's cry that several of the female worshippers faltered in their chanting.

Ilna's lips tightened. She knew what was going to happen. She'd killed her share of poultry in the past with neither qualm nor hesitation; she'd kill more in the future if events spared her to cook more dinners.

Blood sacrifice, *this,* was a waste of meat and a perversion of what every peasant knew was a part—the last and greatest part—of nature. It disgusted Ilna almost as much as the folk performing the ritual disgusted her.

The chant deepened. Even at the first Ilna hadn't been able to make out individual syllables in the echoing cavity of this temple, but now the sound had the groaning weight of the millpond frozen in midwinter.

The kneeling priests held knives; they flashed together in the moonlight. Black blood gouted into the reflecting pool. The reflected moon seemed to swell across the surface of the stained water.

A man cried out, but the chanting of his fellows continued like hollow thunder. A moment before, light had entered through the eye in the dome's center and been reflected from the pool beneath throughout the temple; now the eye was dark, and the moon blazed in full glory where before the water had been.

Ilna's limbs were tight with the strain of holding herself to the column, but her face grew rigid as well. She could see Alecto's lips moving, but she couldn't be sure whether the girl mouthed a curse or a prayer or a spell.

Something formed in the air above the moon. The worshippers' voices were growing hoarse, but the chanting continued with even greater desperation.

At first it was only a blue nimbus, a haze of wizardlight. As the assembly shouted words of power, the ring of priests brought out athames and waved them to the rhythm of the chant; some slashed their own arms. Droplets of blood arced through the air, sinking without trace into the moon's blazing face.

The nimbus shrank into three figures. They were no longer blue; they had no color at all, only a gray sheen as bleak as Ilna's thoughts when she woke in the hours after midnight. They swayed to the rhythm of the chant.

Alecto's face was stark with terror. Her tongue moved slightly, but the sound she made had no more meaning than a death rattle does.

The three creatures were as bonelessly supple as an ammonite's tentacles, but their heads were flat and reptilian. Their conical bodies tapered from two squat, folded legs to the narrow snout. Their arms waved; they ended in cilia rather than fingers or claws.

The creatures were neither evil nor good; they merely *were*, the way the sea *is* or the sun. They were terrible beyond anything Ilna had ever seen.

The chanting stopped. Its echoes rolled about the dome for long moments after, but even that finally stilled. In the silence Ilna heard her companion whisper, "The Pack! These are the ones. . . ."

The three figures faded gradually like fish swimming downward through clear water. There was a crackling that Ilna felt rather than heard; the Pack were gone, and the moon—edging westward past zenith—streamed through the dome's eye again.

The pool was still clear, save for where the rabbits' corpses lay on the coping. The last drops of blood leaking from the severed throats now swirled in dark tendrils through the water.

Gasps, whispers, and sighs of relief echoed through the domed hall. The tension had dissipated as soon as the worshippers below were sure the Pack were gone. The prayer had brought the creatures out of whatever place—whatever Hell—normally held them, but the worshippers were as frightened of the Pack as Alecto was.

Alecto had said only fools would loose the Pack. Ilna didn't see any reason to fault her companion's judgment on *that* point.

The guard threw open the door, sucking in a breeze to purge the warmth of enclosed bodies and the stench of fear. The worshippers drained from the room with a haste just short of panic, jostling at the doorway to the long entrance passage. They'd entered chanting, but there was no pretense of a recessional to put a solemn seal on the proceedings.

This wasn't religion: it was wizardry, and wizardry of a particularly unpleasant sort. Ilna's lip curled. Those who'd performed it were anxious to return to their homes and pretend they had no idea of what was going on.

The priests followed the layfolk, murmuring among themselves. They controlled their fears more carefully, but they too wanted to be gone. The pair—a man and a woman—who'd made the sacrifice carried away the dead rabbits in their baskets instead of leaving them for servants.

Did servants ever enter this room? Now that she thought about it, Ilna thought there'd been smears from previous slaughter on the pool's marble coping before the priests carried out the present sacrifice. This was truly a sanctum, perhaps the more so because it didn't hold the God's image.

Only initiates entered. If they didn't carry out menial tasks like scrubbing blood from the marble, nobody did.

The last of the priests passed from the hall; she didn't bother to close the inner door behind her. Ilna heard the sound of steps shuffling down the passage, fewer and fewer, then the clang of the outer door. The hall was silent, save for the wind sighing softly past the dome's open eye.

"All right, loose me!" Alecto said. She reached for her athame as she spoke, preparing to cut the rope if Ilna didn't release her instantly.

Ilna's hand twitched, curling the noose back around into her hand in a single motion. Manipulating the rope brought her to herself. Strength returned to muscles which her cramped position had reduced to trembling weakness.

Alecto spread her arms wide and gripped the column's flutings between thumb and fingers while her legs circled the shaft. She scrambled down the pillar without waiting for Ilna to snub the rope off for her. She probably couldn't have climbed without Ilna's help, but she could get down again swiftly and safely by herself.

Ilna knew her own limitations. She hung the noose over two separated stone acanthus flowers, drew it tight, and lowered herself hand over hand to the floor. Going down, her body twisted on the rope, but at least she didn't bang into the pillar as heavily as when she'd climbed.

Alecto was already at the inner door. Instead of peering around it, she stood at the hinge side. Her nostrils flared as she sniffed at the gap between the jamb and panel. She held her dagger by her side, the bronze blade concealed against her bare tanned thigh.

Ilna cleared her noose with a flick. She was a little piqued that Alecto didn't notice the trick, and much more irritated to realize that the wild girl's opinion mattered to her.

Alecto looked around. "There's nobody in the hall," she said, speaking in a low voice. She stared at Ilna appraisingly. "So," she continued, "are you going to stick with me, then?"

Ilna frowned despite herself. "If you mean am I willing for us to continue on together," she said, "then I suppose so. For the time being. Do you know where we are?"

"All I know is it's a place I want to be far away from," Alecto said. She glanced back at the air above the reflecting pool, now empty except for moonlight. "Raising the Pack! They're insane!"

She faced Ilna abruptly with her eyes narrowed. "What

were you doing where I found you, eh?" she said. "Are you fooling with the Pack as well?"

"Perhaps," Ilna said, her hands shifting minusculely on the cord that she hadn't yet wrapped around her waist again. "I may have been sent here to drive these creatures back where they belong. If you mean did I have anything to do with raising them, no."

She suspected Alecto would be very quick and very deadly with her bronze dagger. If Ilna herself wasn't quick enough to catch the girl's neck and knife hand in her noose before the blade got home, well, then she deserved to die.

Instead of lunging, Alecto snorted, and said, "You're going to *drive* the Pack? You're crazier than this lot!"

She spat, then rubbed the gobbet into the marble with the ball of her bare foot. "Still, it's no business of mine—*if* you don't try anything so stupid when I'm anywhere around you. Agreed?"

"I'll see to it that you're warned," Ilna said. "Now, shall we leave? Or shall *I* leave?"

The words were empty: Tenoctris had sent Ilna into the dreamworld to search. Ilna—and Tenoctris as well, most likely—had no idea of what to do to prevent those reptilian creatures from invading Carus' sleep. Still, the statement had the desired effect of making Alecto relax and turn her attention to the passageway outside. Ilna supposed that sometimes it was better to mouth foolishness than to have to strangle somebody.

Alecto slipped into the passageway, moving with the silent grace of a cat. The passage was windowless. Some moonlight slipped past the inner door, but she hadn't bothered to swing it fully open.

Ilna followed, wrapping the gathered noose back around her waist as an additional belt. Though . . . the temple faced south, into the full moon. There should be light enough outside the entrance for any guards present to see whatever design Ilna knotted. She took the hank of short cords out of her sleeve, smiling faintly as her fingers worked. "I'll deal with the guards," she said.

Instead of replying, Alecto merely looked back over her shoulder with an expression that was unreadable in the shadows. In a sharper tone Ilna said, "Don't attack them, I mean! I'll take care of anyone out there quietly."

The outer door was heavy, bronze or bronze-covered like the inner one. There were staples and a heavy crossbar to lock it from the inside, but for now all that held it was a spring catch at the upper edge. A drawstring was reeved through a hole in the panel to open it from outside.

Alecto reached for the catch with her free hand. Ilna caught her arm. "I don't want you stabbing somebody," she said, each syllable a needle point. "Put your knife away."

Ilna didn't know why it mattered to her. Perhaps because as she'd watched the rabbits butchered, she realized that her companion was just as quick to offer blood sacrifice as the priests had been.

Alecto tossed her head dismissively. "All right," she said, sheathing her blade with a quick motion. "I won't kill anybody if you're so squeamish."

She tripped the catch and put her shoulder against the door to ease it open. Ilna waited, suppressing her frown. She'd meant to go out first, but it probably didn't matter.

Alecto stepped outside. Ilna couldn't see much except moonlight past the other girl's shoulder, but that meant there wasn't a covered porch that would keep a guard from seeing the pattern knotted into her cords.

"It's clear," Alecto said, stepping out of the building so that Ilna could follow. Then, "What *is* this place? These are houses!"

They were on a hill from which two- and three-story buildings marched down to a harbor. Patches of lamplight, yellower than the moon, shone from windows onto the winding streets; music trembled on the breeze.

Not long ago Ilna too would have been startled, but she'd seen far larger cities in the months since she left Barca's Hamlet. "Come on," she said crisply to Alecto. "We don't want to stay around here."

She shoved the door closed. Its weight resisted her, but the hinges pivoted smoothly. Too late Ilna remembered the bell note with which it had closed behind the crowd of priests and worshippers. She grabbed the long horizontal handle; even so, the door, several times as heavy as she was, bonged against its jamb.

Lamplight flared beside the steps leading down from the entrance. The caretaker's room was built under the staircase. "Who's there?" a man called as he stepped into view.

It was the servant who'd opened and closed the doors for the ceremony. He held his belt in his left hand and was drawing his hook-bladed sword from its scabbard.

"Hey, don't worry," said Alecto, unpinning her wolfskin cape with her left hand. "There's room for you at the party too, handsome."

She swept the cape off her torso, twirling it in a quick figure-eight. Her breasts were full but firm, standing out proudly from her hard-muscled chest. She sauntered down the steps, dangling the cape from the fingers of her left hand.

Ilna was cold with fury, though not even she could have said whether she was angrier at herself or at her companion. The caretaker stared transfixed at the wild girl's naked chest. The spell Ilna had knotted into her cords was as useless as it would have been on a blind man. Of course, the fellow was frozen as rigid now as Ilna's pattern would have left him.

Alecto glanced at Ilna, grinning in a mixture of mockery and open lust. "So, fellow, are you man enough to handle both of us?" she said to the caretaker.

He swung his heavy sword up for a chopping blow.

"Harlot!" he screamed. "Profaning the house of the Mistress! I'll—"

Alecto was just as skilled with the knife as Ilna had expected; her right hand dipped to the ivory hilt and came up to thrust the long blade through the fellow's throat, choking the rest of the words in his blood. He'd only begun his own stroke.

The caretaker stumbled backward, continuing to swing the sword. He was dead but his body didn't realize it quite yet.

Alecto toppled with him, cursing; her dagger was caught in cartilage, and she didn't want to let go of it. Ilna's noose settled over the caretaker's wrist and jerked his arm harmlessly to the side. The sword, a clumsy thing better suited to pruning than war, clanged a sad note against the lowest step.

Alecto set her left foot on the caretaker's chest and tugged her blade free. Blood gushed from both the wound and his mouth. His eyes stared at Ilna as she freed her rope.

Alecto lifted the man's kilt to wipe her dagger. When he guarded the door during the service he'd worn a leather vest and cap as well, but he'd taken them off in his lodgings.

"Too bad," she said, grinning at Ilna again. "He's hung like a pack pony. I wouldn't have minded a little fun with him. First."

Ilna looked at the other woman with a loathing that made her stomach roil . . . but she'd let Alecto lead, and Alecto's actions when the caretaker appeared showed a quick mind—though a disgusting one.

Ilna had alerted the caretaker by slamming the temple door. There was no question of whose fault the sprawled body was.

"Let's get out of here," Ilna said quietly. She nodded toward the countryside visible beyond the squat blocks of houses. "There's woodland out there to the west. We can hide until daylight and then . . ."

Then what?

"Then make plans," Ilna concluded. After all, that was what most of life was about: going on until, she supposed, you couldn't go on anymore.

Cashel heard pipe music, a skirling high-pitched sound very different from the golden tones of the wax-stopped reeds Garric had played to the sheep in Barca's Hamlet. He got to his feet with an easy motion, the quarterstaff crosswise in both hands; close to his chest, not threatening anybody but ready for whatever trouble chose to come.

"Cashel?" said Tilphosa. She was already standing, a pale figure in the shadows. "How did you bring us here? Where *are* we?"

"Mistress, I'm not sure," said Cashel. He was polite by nature, but since he *didn't* have any idea where they were or how they'd gotten there, he thought there were better uses for his time than talking about it.

Three sailors had come through with them: Hook, Captain Mounix, and a stocky fellow named Ousseau whose right arm and chest were bleeding from a deep cut. Ousseau cursed between moans; the two officers lay on the ground, turning their heads quickly in the direction of every noise. Mounix had retrieved the sword Cashel'd knocked from his hand; Hook was unarmed.

The pipe wasn't playing a melody, just sequences of notes that had the same mindless quality as a brook flowing over rocks. Perhaps it was a natural sound, something the wind did in a hollow tree or the song of a night bird.

"Where'd the temple go?" Mounix said, rising to one knee cautiously as if he was afraid that were his head to come up the roof'd fall in on him. "And these trees aren't like what they were on Laut. Where are we?"

"The bark's smooth," Tilphosa said quietly as her left hand stroked the trunk beside her. She still held the block of stone close to her body; the weight must be straining her by this time, but she didn't seem ready to give up her only weapon.

They were in a forest with no sign of the temple or the Archai who'd surrounded it, and the many sorts of trees were different from any Cashel had seen before. None of them were as tall as a crab apple. The trunks were straight, some as thick as Cashel's own body. Large leaves sprayed from the ends of branches that mostly kinked instead of curving. Some limbs carried balls that might be fruit, hanging just above easy reach.

He looked up. The sky was as bright as if the moon was full. The heavens were featureless—a gray-glazed bowl with neither moon, stars, nor the streaking of clouds to give them character.

Hook came over to Cashel; the carpenter's eyes held a new respect. "Did you bring us here?" he asked, glancing around with the nervous quickness of a woodchuck foraging when hawks are about. "Are you a wizard too, Master Cashel?"

"All I did was break a hole in the wall," Cashel said, maybe a bit more harshly than he'd meant to. Tilphosa stood to his side and a little behind, her place and posture showing that she was with him and against the part of the world that included the sailors. "Well, I broke a hole in the light that Metra raised. I don't see any opening from this side, do you?"

"I watched you grow out of the empty air," Tilphosa said quietly. "First you were a shadow, then it was you all whole, and you fell to the ground. And I thanked the Mistress that She'd returned my champion to me."

Cashel glanced at her in surprise. "I don't know . . ." he said; but the truth was, he *didn't* know much about the

Mistress, so there wasn't any point in him talking about Her.

"There's nothing there," Mounix said. He and Ousseau, the latter clutching the torn skin over his right biceps with his left hand, had joined Hook. "I hope to the Lady that means the wizard and her monsters can't come after us."

"I sure don't want to go back there!" Hook said, and even Cashel nodded agreement with that thought.

They were all looking at him. Cashel didn't think he was much of a leader, but the sailors had proved they were no good at trying to think for themselves. As for Tilphosa—well, Tilphosa hadn't any reason to complain about sticking with him.

Cashel cleared his throat. Mounix still held his sword. The blade was twisted sideways, so he probably couldn't have sheathed it if he tried. "Straighten your sword out," he said. "It won't be much good like it is. And we better do something about that cut of yours, Ousseau. Maybe—"

"I've been taught some healing in the temple," Tilphosa said. She dropped her stone and brushed her hands on her tunic. "I wonder if the light's better over . . ."

The sailors turned their attention to the girl. Ousseau allowed her to guide him toward a tall tree whose spindly, needlelike foliage blocked less of the sky's faint illumination.

"Hook?" Cashel said. He didn't raise his voice much, but he spoke loud enough all the sailors had to hear him. "You weren't respectful to Lady Tilphosa back at the other place, on Laut, but I let you live."

"Yes, Master Cashel, we know we were wrong," Captain Mounix said before Hook decided what or whether to reply. "We—"

Cashel shifted the quarterstaff in his hands very slightly. Mounix's mouth shut in mid-babble; Hook said nothing but spread his hands to show, perhaps unconsciously, that they were weaponless.

"That's good," Cashel said. "Because I wouldn't leave you alive a second time."

He turned his back, mostly because he didn't want to look at the sailors for a while, but it was also a good way to end a conversation that had gone as far as he figured it needed to. He was pretty sure there was light ahead through the forest. It wasn't as sharp-edged as a lamp in an open window, just a glow that couldn't be the sky even though it was about the same texture and brightness.

A will-o'-the-wisp, maybe? Cashel worked his big toe into the ground to test it. The soil had a spongy lightness, but in his experience it wasn't wet enough to breed that sort of ghost light.

He didn't know how he felt about the sailors deciding he was a wizard. Ilna always said that what other people thought was their own business; but she really meant "so long as they kept their thoughts to themselves," because she'd always had a short way with anybody she thought was lying about her or Cashel.

Cashel's own concern was a little different: he didn't want it to seem he was claiming credit he didn't deserve, and he knew that he wasn't a wizard the way Hook and the others meant it. He scowled into the forest, trying to grapple with the problem.

There'd be less trouble for Tilphosa if the sailors thought Cashel could turn them into monkeys. He didn't want to kill the trio, which he'd surely have to do if they did try something with the girl again. He guessed he'd let them think what they pleased; but he'd be really glad when he saw the last of them.

"I've done what I can for the wound, Cashel," Tilphosa said from close behind him. "I don't recognize any of the leaves, and I didn't find any spiderwebs to pack the wound, but I made do."

She paused, then added, "What . . . what do you suppose we ought to do now?"

Cashel shook his head slowly, mostly as a way of settling his thoughts. "The woods seem pretty open," he said. "Even though it's night, I thought we'd head toward the light there."

He nodded, suddenly wondering if what he saw was more than imagination.

"Anyway, I think it's a light," he went on. "Maybe we'll find a better place to bed down than here. And I don't feel much like sleeping."

He looked at the sailors. "That all right with you?" he asked.

"Let's go, Cashel," Tilphosa said, touching his elbow. She turned to Mounix again, and in a cold voice said, "Captain, you were told to straighten your sword; do so at once!"

Cashel blinked. He'd started off when Tilphosa told him to, then stopped again when he heard her tell Mounix to fix his sword. Put it on a fallen log and hammer it with the heel of his boot, Cashel wondered? Because there wasn't a proper forge anywhere about, and no flat stones on the ground here either.

"Let's go," Tilphosa repeated, this time murmuring close to Cashel's ear. She gave his biceps a light pressure in the direction of the light.

Cashel stepped off on his right foot, smiling faintly. Now he understood. He'd warned the sailors in his fashion, but Tilphosa—*Lady* Tilphosa—was repeating the message by training them to jump when she whistled. Mounix was hopping around, trying to fix his sword and follow the others at the same time.

It wasn't the way Tilphosa preferred to be, not judging from the way she'd handled herself around Cashel. He'd seen before—when she hauled up Metra—that she could put on the Great Lady when it suited her, though. Of course . . .

In a quiet, apologetic voice, Cashel said, "The thing about reminding people who's boss is, well . . . Metra came back with her own ideas, you know."

"Yes," said Tilphosa cheerfully. "I was glad that you and your staff were there to protect me, Cashel."

She stroked the hickory with the tips of two fingers.

"I'm even more glad that you're still with me," she added.

Cashel cleared his throat but didn't say anything. When he thought about it, there wasn't anything to say.

There were various kinds of trees. Every one of them was a different sort, it seemed to Cashel, but that wasn't something he'd have wanted to swear to till he saw them by daylight.

"How long do you suppose it is before sunrise, Cashel?" Tilphosa asked in a falsely bright voice. In those words he could hear the question she really meant but was afraid to speak: "Do you think the sun ever rises here?"

"I don't know," Cashel said. "I've been wondering if we wound up underground when I went through that wall. But there's light enough to get along by, even if it never gets brighter."

"No," Tilphosa said, the tension gone from her voice. "Things growing in a cave don't have leaves and all these trees do. But you're right, Cashel, we have plenty of light now. I'm sorry to have been . . ."

She didn't finish the sentence. If the word she'd swallowed was "worried," then Cashel didn't see it was anything to have been ashamed of.

The bright blur was close now and the size of a house, but the edges were just as fuzzy as they'd been when Cashel first saw it. It wasn't in a clearing, exactly. The light took the place of trees that should've been there, even though the roots and upper branches showed outside the glowing field.

"Something's moving in the light," Cashel said, speaking a little quieter than he might normally have done. "I don't think it's just the trees."

"Cashel, I see Metra," Tilphosa said. Her voice was calm, but she gripped his arms fiercely. "If you look—"

"Right, I see her," Cashel said.

It was funny: when he squinted just right, it all fell into place. After that he could see the wizard even if he straightened and opened his eyes wide.

She knelt holding her athame on the porch of the temple which Cashel had defended not long ago. She'd spread one of her silk figures on the stones. The scene was washed out and ripply, like Cashel was watching her on the bottom of a pond, but it was Metra all right. Around her stood—

"By the Sister, you fool!" Captain Mounix squealed. "You and the bitch've led us straight back to those monsters!"

Hook took one look at the light and another at Cashel's face as he shifted and brought his staff up. The carpenter grabbed Mounix by the shoulder and clamped the other hand across his mouth.

"Shut up, will you!" he screamed at the captain. "Did you doubt what he told us? *I* didn't! He don't need monsters to finish us if he wants to!"

Ousseau, looking misshapen in the dimness because of his bandaged chest, was still stumbling along after them. His head was lowered; he probably didn't know what was going on.

Mounix's eyes widened. He tried to scramble back. Hook twisted the sword out of his hand and let him go.

Cashel relaxed, taking a couple of deep breaths. He nodded to Hook, and said, "Yeah, she's there with the Archai, just like we left 'em."

"I don't think she can see us," Tilphosa said. She put her hand on Cashel's shoulder the way he himself might've calmed a plow ox who'd startled a wildcat in the stubble.

The thought made him chuckle. "I don't guess they can or they'd be trying to do something about us," Cashel said. "But there's no reason for us to hang around here regardless."

He nodded in the direction they'd been going thus far. "It looks like there's another light up there," he said. "Maybe if we keep going, we'll find a place we want to be, huh?"

"Yes, let's go," Tilphosa said with a grateful smile. The hazy globe didn't make the woods around it any brighter, but Cashel wasn't having any difficulty seeing things by the light of the sky or roof or whatever it was.

Cashel held a hand up to stop her, then called into the darkness, "Hey, Mounix! Give Ousseau here a hand, will you? We're not leaving anybody behind unless they want to stay, got that?"

They started forward. Tilphosa said very softly, "You're a remarkably gentle man, Master Cashel."

He snorted, but he was more pleased than not by the comment. "When you're my size, you better be," he said. "Otherwise, you break things."

The second blur of light was much the same as the first, though this one appeared in a clump of saw-edged grass that Cashel wouldn't have tried to fight through. He cocked his head slightly; the shadows condensed into the image of a man in a green robe, seated on a couch spread with the lush, dappled pelt of some animal. Curtains hung on the wall behind him; the embroidered figures of strange beasts cavorted on the cloth, tossing six-horned heads or screeching from bird beaks on antelope bodies.

Guards stood with their backs to the man on the couch.

He stared at the bowl of water on the table before him, his expression cold and angry.

"Do you know him?" Cashel said. "I don't."

"I've never seen him before," Tilphosa said. "That's a scrying bowl, so he must be a wizard."

After a further moment's consideration, she added, "Is he a eunuch, do you suppose? The way his flesh hangs looks like he is."

"I wouldn't know about that," Cashel said shortly. They didn't geld men in Barca's Hamlet. Cashel had learned things were different in some other parts of the world, but that wasn't knowledge that pleased him.

He frowned at the man in the watery image. "He looks like a guy I saw once," he said. The fellow who'd been talking to Garric on the bridge when he fell over and Cashel jumped in to save him . . . "But it's not the same guy. He's too young, and the fellow I saw was thinner by a lot."

"Are we stopping here, Master Cashel?" Hook asked with nervous politeness.

Cashel turned. Captain Mounix was holding Ousseau. The wounded man looked rather better than he had when Cashel last noticed him. The captain flinched, shifting to put Ousseau's body between him and Cashel.

Cashel nodded. "No," he said, "there's nothing here to hold us."

A fairy glow showed in the farther distance, and just maybe another hung at a slightly higher level beyond that, though the second could've been a patch of the sky itself. The ground was rising, though gradually enough that nobody who hadn't followed sheep for a living would've noticed it. Sheep can find a slope where a drop of water'd hesitate.

Cashel started on. Tilphosa walked with him—the forest was open enough for two side by side most places—and the sailors followed. Cashel smiled. They followed at a *respectful* distance.

"I've never read about this place," Tilphosa said, picking her words carefully to seem, well, not worried. "Have you, Cashel?"

He smiled. "Mistress, I can't read," he said. "I can spell out my name with a little time, that's all."

"Ah!" said Tilphosa. She probably hadn't thought about that sort of thing. Well, she wouldn't, being a lady and all.

"I wasn't educated as a wizard, of course," she said. Cashel wasn't sure if she was changing the subject or if she just needed to talk. "I haven't any talent for it. Some of those who came to the temple did, and they were trained to be Children of the Mistress. They had much reading to do for what they had to learn."

She linked her fingers and clutched them over her stomach, the way she'd have done if she was cold. Cashel didn't think she could be. The air was warm; besides, they'd been walking at a good pace, and there wasn't a breeze.

Cashel saw what she was hinting at. He swallowed and said, "Mistress—"

"Tilphosa," she corrected him.

"Tilphosa," he said, "I'm not a wizard like you think. I can do things, sure, but I don't know how it happens. I just do them."

She gave a little laugh. It didn't sound forced. "I'm told that Metra is very skilled, very powerful," she said. "As a wizard. That's why the Council chose her to accompany me. And you freed us from her enchantment, Cashel."

He smiled. "It looked like a wall," he said. "Sometimes you can break a wall down if you hit it hard enough."

They were close to the light by now. This one seemed to have color, or anyway a different color: a hint of red instead of blue to its silvery grayness. Ilna would be able to say for sure; there was nothing about shape or color that she didn't see.

In the light a man knelt before a pentagram scratched on the narrow deck of a galley. Cashel could see a few of the rowers on the benches beyond the fellow. They leaned into the oarlooms with faces set in a fierce determination not to watch what the wizard was doing.

"I know him!" Cashel said. "This is the guy I asked you about, the one who looks like Metra. He was going to take a piece of statue away from me."

Cashel frowned with a realization. It wouldn't have been the statue the fellow was after, just the ruby ring the statue wore. And that was here in Cashel's purse.

"He's a Son of the Mistress," Tilphosa said, frowning also at some thought of her own. "I don't recognize him, Cashel. He *does* look a lot like Metra."

Cashel glanced back at the sailors. They were keeping up all right. As they should: Cashel was walking at the pace that a herd of sheep would've set.

"Let's go on," he said aloud.

Cashel didn't understand this, but he was used to things he didn't understand and to going ahead anyway. He might not like the scenery on the way, but eventually he'd always gotten to a place where he wanted to be.

There was another fog of light ahead, and Cashel supposed there'd be more after that one. He wondered if they'd ever come out of this forest. He had bread and cheese still in his wallet. With the frugal reflex of growing up poor—and poorer yet—he'd bundled the leftovers away before he started down to deal with Metra's wizardry.

He smiled. That seemed a long time ago, now.

"Do you suppose they're all looking for me, Cashel?" Tilphosa said. "All the wizards whose images we've seen? Metra is, we know that."

"Um?" said Cashel. He thought about the question. "I

don't see how they can be, Tilphosa. That last fellow was somebody I met in Valles. He . . . I mean, that was . . ."

What would Tilphosa say if he told her he came from a time farther in her future than he could imagine himself?

"I'm from a long way away, Tilphosa," he said. "A long way ahead in time."

She turned her head to study him as they walked along. "I see," she said, but Cashel wasn't sure that she meant anything by the words. "Well, I'm glad the Mistress's powers enabled Her to go even through time to bring me a champion."

"I wish you wouldn't talk about the Mistress bringing me, Tilphosa," Cashel said. He looked straight ahead to avoid the girl's eyes, but he flushed regardless. "I mean . . . my sister and I never had much to do with the Great Gods. Well, we couldn't afford to, that was part of it, but with Ilna it was more besides. And, well . . . I just wish you wouldn't say the Mistress is moving me around. I don't feel right hearing that."

"All right, Cashel," Tilphosa said. She didn't sound angry or even hurt. "I'll be more careful about what I say."

Either Cashel had started walking faster in embarrassment or this time the image of light was located closer to the previous one. The scene within was a barn, a big one. There were horses stabled there, so it belonged to rich people. A man sat on an upturned wicker basket, talking to a circle of many other men.

The one talking shared a family resemblance with both Metra and the fellow who'd tried to take the ring back in Valles. He wore a coarse tunic now, but his black-and-white robe was hung to dry on a rafter.

Most of the audience were strangers to Cashel, but—

"That's Garric!" he cried. "That's my friend Garric! But what happened to his head? He's got scars on his scalp!"

"Maybe it isn't really your friend, Cashel?" said Tilphosa. She was frowning when he turned to look at her, but she smoothed her face at once. "I mean . . . the men who look like Metra? Perhaps . . . ?"

Cashel grimaced. One of the beastmen of Bight, a female, fawned at the feet of the fellow he'd thought was Garric. That didn't seem like something the real Garric would've let happen.

The wizard in the center talked urgently, gesturing repeatedly toward the ring held by the older peg-legged man at the side of maybe-Garric. The ring looked a lot like the one in Cashel's purse, but the when the light caught this one right it winked blue.

"I don't know," Cashel said harshly. "Let's get on. There's nothing here for us."

He turned. When the girl didn't follow him at once he reached out—then jerked his hand back.

Cashel's body was cold. Had he been thinking of pulling Tilphosa along against her will? All he knew was that it frightened him to see his friend *changed* that way; frightened him as he'd never feared death.

"Yes, of course, Cashel," Tilphosa said. She stared at his horrified expression with obvious concern. "Let's get away from here. We'll get to the edge of these woods soon, I'm sure."

Cashel wasn't sure of anything except that he was jumpier than he'd been since, well, a long time. "Sorry," he muttered.

"I haven't heard the night bird recently," the girl said brightly, changing the subject for sure this time. "Have you?"

"Um?" said Cashel. "Oh, you mean the music? No, not since just after we got here. These woods are quieter than the ones I'm used to."

"Is that because there's no wind?" Tilphosa asked. She looked about her as they walked along, swaying a little closer to Cashel. She was nervous, but she was keeping it well inside.

"Partly that, I guess," Cashel said. "There's always something happening in the woods, though. Squirrels running about, limbs squealing as they grow. . . . You can hear the trees breathe if you take the time to listen."

"But not here?" said Tilphosa.

"Not that I've noticed," Cashel said; walking steadily forward, but keeping his eyes on the things around him as he always did. He noticed most things, though he didn't generally talk about them.

He cleared his throat. "You can generally tell when there's something wrong with your flock, you know," he said. "Things don't feel right, even if you can't see what it is that's wrong. I don't feel like that here, for what it's worth."

"Thank you, Cashel," the girl said. She laid her fingertips briefly on his arm.

They'd reached the next of the scenes in light. This one was smaller than the others, scarcely the size of the shelter a shepherd might weave for himself from sticks and branches in bad weather. Cashel squinted, waiting for the image in his mind to focus.

"That's Tenoctris!" he said. "It couldn't be anybody else! Oh, if she's looking for us, then everything's going to be all right!"

Tenoctris sat at a table in her cottage in the palace grounds, reading a scroll by the light of a three-wick oil lamp hanging at her side. Most of the room's furnishings were simple, but the lampstand itself was a scaled, sinuous body of gilded bronze. Each wick projected like a breath of flames from a dragon head.

"She's a very powerful wizard, Cashel?" Tilphosa asked. She bent her head as if to read over Tenoctris' shoulder, but of course you couldn't see anything that small in the light here. It was clearer than what you saw through the rounds of bull's-eye glass in the casements of Reise's inn, but not *much* clearer.

The sailors had fallen farther behind, so Cashel figured to wait here for a time anyway. And if there was a way to get into *this* vision, then that'd be a very good thing.

He pushed his quarterstaff into the light. He was careful for fear there might be a spark when the iron touched it or even that the whole scene might vanish with a blaze and crashing.

The metal-capped hickory blurred and vanished; then it hit something and stopped. Cashel pushed harder, but whatever he'd hit was solid. He couldn't see either the end of the staff or anything in the image that ought to be blocking it.

"Cashel?" said the girl, watching him closely.

"Wait," he said tersely. He heard the rustle and whispering of the sailors joining them, but he didn't look around.

Withdrawing the quarterstaff, Cashel thrust his bare left arm into the image of light. His fingers touched—

Cashel laughed and withdrew his hand. "Let's go," he said. "There's nothing here except what we see, and that won't help us."

"But what was it?" the girl said, a trifle sharply.

"Just a tree," Cashel said. "That tree."

He pointed upward. Branches like the stems of ancient wisteria twisted out of the image at about the height Cashel could reach by raising his staff. At the ends were sprays like the whips of a weeping willow, though much shorter.

"Tell him," Mounix whispered.

"You tell him!" Hook snapped back. "I'm all right."

Cashel turned. Tilphosa turned with him but moved a little back. "Tell me what?" he said. His voice was a growl, almost angry; he wasn't pleased to be reminded of the sailors' presence.

"Master," Hook said after a quick glance at Mounix. "The captain wants me to say that Ousseau's pretty well done in. He really means he wants to stop, is what I think."

Cashel looked at them. Ousseau's eyes were open; so was his mouth. There was as much intelligence in the one as the other. Mounix forced a smile that looked like he was dying of lockjaw; Hook tried to lean on the sword he'd taken from the captain and fell sideways when it slid into the soft ground. He barely caught himself.

As for Tilphosa—

"How are you feeling?" Cashel asked, turning to the girl. "Do you want to go on?"

"Yes," she said, though she seemed to be trembling. "We can . . . Maybe a little farther. I'd like to get out of these woods if we could."

Cashel sucked in his lower lip as he thought. "We'll go to the next of these lights," he said after a moment. "The one up there."

He nodded in the direction they'd been heading. "Then we'll bed down if we don't see something better close by. All right?"

"Of course it's all right," Tilphosa said, glaring at the desperate sailors. She touched his arm. "Let's go, Cashel."

Cashel smiled as they trudged on. This one wasn't a girl to get on the wrong side of. He was used to that, of course, since you could say the same thing about his sister Ilna. Despite her being a lady and all, Tilphosa made Cashel feel pretty much at home.

"Cashel?" the girl said. "Are the lights a kind of window that you created when you broke down the barrier around us in the temple?"

Cashel shrugged. He didn't like that sort of question. It was partly that he didn't know the answer, and partly that he was afraid the answer was yes. Like he'd told Tilphosa, he'd always been careful with the strength of his arms because he knew the damage he'd do otherwise. If he was doing things that he didn't know about, then Duzi alone knew the harm he might cause.

"I don't know, mistress," he said. "I didn't mean to, but I don't know."

As they got closer to the pale blur. Alone of the images he'd seen since they came to this place, this was in a real clearing. It hung in the air, in the middle of six straight-trunked trees whose branches wove a kind of arbor over-head.

Cashel hadn't felt anything around the other images. No reason he should, of course, since he'd found that they were only there to his eyes, or maybe to his mind's eye; but this one—

This one didn't frighten Cashel; but he guessed the feeling he got would have frightened a lot of other people.

Tilphosa looked around with a set expression, then picked up a fallen branch and raised it as a club. The wood had rotted to punk, but it seemed to make her feel better to hold something she could at least pretend was a weapon. She must feel something here too.

There was only blackness inside the ball of light. Cashel squinted, then twisted his head to one side and the other, waiting for the image to appear.

"I don't see anything," he said.

"It's dark wherever it is," Tilphosa said. Her voice had a studied firmness. "*Whatever* it is. But it's there. It's watching us, Cashel."

"Yeah, I think it is," he said.

He turned. The sailors had stopped some distance back; they were watching him.

"Come on," he said. "We're not going to stay here after all."

They resumed walking. "Do you think the sky ahead is getting lighter, Cashel?" the girl asked.

"Maybe," he said. "We'll know before long."

Cashel felt the eyes on him long after the blur had vanished from sight behind them.

* * *

"Can't we have a fire?" asked Metron, shivering on bucket upturned in the middle of the stable floor. He wore an ostler's tunic, filthy but dry, while water pooled beneath the stall door from which his own robe of silk brocade hung. "It's not just the cold water, you see. I shut my whole body down when I sent my soul out of it."

Garric smiled. Several of the bandits went grim-faced at the mention of wizardry, but others laughed outright at the absurdity of what they'd just heard.

"Can we have a fire in a barn full of straw?" Vascay mused aloud. "No, we can't. Anyhow, with all the horses in here you'd warm up quick enough even if it *were* cold out. Which it's not."

He coughed to clear his throat. Garric, sitting beside Vascay, glanced at him to judge his expression.

Vascay's face gave nothing away. He opened and closed his left fist; at each movement, the sapphire ring appeared on or disappeared from his little finger. He didn't speak.

"That's the ring I sent you for, isn't it?" said Metron. He'd obviously been taken aback by Vascay's attitude but decided to deal with it by bluster. He held out his hand. "Well done. Now we have to release Thalemos before we can topple the Intercessor."

Tint lay in the straw at Garric's feet, watching Metron intently. At first Garric thought the tremble of her rib cage against his ankle was purring, but after a moment he realized it was an inaudible growl.

"We'll listen to your proposal, wizard," Vascay said nonchalantly. "But right at the moment, I'd say what my Brethren and I have to do is get out of this district by dawn . . . and Thalemos, I'd say, could take care of himself."

"I've been saying that!" Ademos said loudly. "This whole business was a bad idea from the first. We're lucky we didn't all die on Serpents' Isle instead of just Kelbat and Ceto, and now that the Intercessor knows what's going on, well!"

Other men openly agreed with him. From the expressions around the circle, Garric thought more would've called, "Right!" and "The quicker, the better," if they hadn't disliked Ademos too much to willingly identify themselves with his position.

The wizard nodded to the Brethren, his expression bland. If the situation were what Vascay baldly stated, the gang would be gone already and Metron would still be on the bottom of the pond. Vascay was using the legitimate threat to restructure the relationship between him and Metron. If Metron called his bluff . . .

Except that Garric wasn't sure Vascay was bluffing; and if Garric wasn't sure, then Metron would be a fool to take the risk.

Metron wasn't a fool. He spread his hands, and said, "I'm sorry, Master Vascay, I got ahead of myself. This isn't the catastrophe it must seem to your good selves, arriving as you have on the tail of the Intercessor's troops. Echeon is flailing about, but he can't overcome foreordained fate."

"Is fate going to keep the Intercessor's knife from cutting Lord Thalemos' throat?" Vascay said bluntly. "Why won't he do that, Metron?"

"If Echeon kills Thalemos," the wizard said, leaning forward to seem more earnest, "then the *real* Thalemos will appear somewhere else. Echeon has *seen* the future, or at least a portion of it. He *knows* that Lord Thalemos becomes Earl of Laut, so his only hope is to bend him to his will first. When we rescue Thalemos, we'll be able to proceed with the plan."

"Seems to me," Hame said slowly, "that if it's as simple as that, we all oughta go back east where we come from and wait for the happy day. Eh?"

Metron spread his hands again and nodded gravely, his expression studiedly reasonable. "Lord Thalemos will become Earl of Laut," he said. "But he'll surely do so as the Intercessor's puppet if we don't intervene. Echeon is a great wizard, I assure you; but with Thalemos and the power of the ring—"

He gestured toward Vascay's hand, at the moment empty. He wasn't demanding the ring as he had been before.

"—we can overturn him and return Laut to freedom and prosperity."

Metron cleared his throat, and added, "I wonder if you'd be good enough to tell me how you found the ring, Master Vascay? I'm sure it was a difficult task."

Vascay glanced at Garric and raised an eyebrow. The tiny sapphire winked on his finger.

"I found the statue of Thalemos," Garric said. He saw more value in learning where Metron would go with the information than he did in hiding it from him. "It'd been dragged a distance from its plinth and built into a later wall. The ring was on its finger, as you'd said."

Metron's eyes narrowed minusculely. "There was no guardian, then?" he asked.

Instead of answering, Garric let his lips smile. He said, "Why did somebody put up a statue of Lord Thalemos hundreds of years before he was born, wizard?"

Metron's eyes were wary, but he reflected Garric's smile with an unctuous one of his own. "The statue was carved two *thousand* years ago, sir, not mere centuries. This was done by the command of the Intercessor Echea, every bit as powerful a wizard as her distant descendent of today. They both and all of their line wish to bind the fate they know they cannot change."

The wizard turned his hand up; his smile a little harder, a little more real. Answer for answer . . .

"There was no guardian," Garric said. "There was a

poisonous snake, but there's a lot of snakes on the island. And growing near the site were puffballs, which I avoided."

"Did you indeed?" Metron said. "A foolish question, of course: you wouldn't be here otherwise. You're a very clever young man, sir; very clever indeed."

He returned his gaze to the chieftain. "Master Vascay," he said, "Echeon will have placed protections of art over Lord Thalemos; these I can overcome. But there will be physical barriers as well, and against them my arts are useless. Will you help me, knowing that the risk is great but that on the other side of danger is freedom for yourself and your compatriots?"

Men murmured to their neighbors, but for a moment nobody responded directly to the wizard. Vascay kept his eyes on Metron, his own face impassive. At last he said, "So. We'd have to find Lord Thalemos first, I suppose?"

"Lord Thalemos is in the prison in the center of Durassa," Metron said. "The Spike, it's called. It's a tower."

"We bloody well know what the Spike is," Ademos muttered, staring blackly at the pounded-earth floor.

Metron raised a bead of clear quartz, one of several score round beads of various stones which he wore around his neck. "Thalemos had a similar necklace. Echeon took it from him when he arrived at the prison, but this"—he wriggled his necklace slightly, causing light to cascade from the highly polished beads—"has stored all the images it received before that moment."

"He could've been moved," Ademos said.

"To where?" Prada snapped. "Where is there that'd be harder to get into than the Spike, let alone out of? It's all over if Thalemos is in there!"

"I think not, sir," said Metron courteously. The ragged tunic handicapped him, but he still managed to project a degree of dignified authority. "If two of you men are expert climbers, and if you all have the courage of patriots, it will assuredly be possible to rescue Lord Thalemos."

Vascay looked around the circle. Each of the bandits fell silent as his gaze crossed them. "What do you say, brethren?" he asked in an almost teasing tone.

"What do *you* say, chief?" Hame said fiercely.

Vascay tapped his peg leg with an index finger as he paused. "Hakken, you can climb, can't you?" he said to the little ex-sailor.

"Yeah, all right," Hakken said. He didn't look happy about it. "But—oh, Sister take all wizards, I'll go."

Vascay's eyes met Garric's. "Gar," he said, "you used to be able to climb like a monkey. Can you still?"

Garric grinned with anticipation. "I can climb," he said. Regardless of the abilities Gar's muscles remembered, Garric knew that the skills he himself had honed robbing gallinule nests off the coast of Haft would take him any-place a sailor could go.

Tint sat up abruptly and clamped a possessive hand on Garric's knee. "Gar?" she growled. "Me go!"

Garric smiled wider, though his stomach was twitching. "But there'll be three of us, Vascay," he said.

Chapter Eleven

As the councillors filed in from the other end of the big chamber, accompanied by their aides, Sharina saw many expressions go blank. She and Liane were seated to either side of Carus at the round table.

Liane always attended council meetings, but in the past she'd sat slightly back from the table in the capacity of Garric's secretary; Carus had made her an open partici-pant, over her own objection. Princess Sharina of Haft—

Sharina smiled; she wouldn't have minded the style of address she had to use in court if it weren't for the hot, bulky garments that went with it—was sometimes present, but on those occasions she sat at the end of the table among lesser invitees rather than taking the place of honor at Garric's right.

King Carus had placed her there, not Sharina herself. Sharina knew Carus needed the support of both women to carry off his impersonation of Garric, but there was more going on than that. Garric genuinely tried to get along with others; Carus was much more convinced of his own authority. If several of the noblemen found the presence of two young women at his council offensive—so much the worse for the noblemen!

Though Lord Waldron, head of the royal army, was seventy years old, he walked straight as a spearshaft and his mind was as hard as the spear's steel head. He glared through Liane toward Carus as an aide drew out the chair to her left for Waldron to sit on.

Carus looked back at him. The king's face was drawn with sleeplessness and frustration, and the anger in *his* eyes had nothing to do with matters of precedence. Waldron had proved often in his long life that he feared nothing in this world, but Sharina watched his expression grow more guarded now. He wasn't afraid of Carus, but the king's fury showed that this would be no ordinary council meeting.

Chancellor Royhas settled beside Sharina with a murmured, "Princess . . ." If he was disconcerted to find Prince Garric flanked by two women, he concealed the fact with his usual aplomb. Royhas was as wellborn as Waldron, but the soldier was a great landholder from the north of the island while Royhas came from the aristocracy of trade centered in Valles.

Liane leaned to whisper in Carus' ear. The king gave a hard smile, and said in a normal voice—not loud, especially against the shuffle of feet and scrape of chairs, but loud enough all those around him could hear, "The aides need to be present, Liane. Even if we take precautions, what happens here won't be a secret long. It'll be the speed we act with that saves us."

Waldron raised a hand above his shoulder and crooked a finger. An aide—a blond youth with the face of cherub but a swordsman's thick wrists—bent his head close so that Waldron could whisper to him.

The boy nodded and nodded again, then set off for the doorway against the flow of those still entering. He started running as soon he reached the corridor.

Carus had been watching the byplay also. He turned, met Sharina's eyes, and grinned broadly.

Lord Attaper stood just inside the door. He'd arrived for the meeting dressed as commander of the Blood Eagles in gilded cuirass and helmet, studded leather apron, and heavy boots. Attaper even wore his equipment belt, but his ivory-inlaid sword and dagger scabbards were empty.

"Your highness?" he called. He gestured to the doorway, empty now that the last entrants were sitting down. Each councillor's aides stood against the wall behind their principal.

"Right, close us up," Carus said, his raised voice covering the buzz of whispers. Chairs scuffed, but there was dead silence by the time the heavy panel slammed under the pull of Attaper's arm.

Instead of taking the empty chair midway along the right-hand curve of the table, Attaper stood at parade rest beside the doorway. Carus looked at him and grinned again. The Blood Eagle, his feet spread and his hands crossed behind his back, had chosen a place outside the formal seating order to avoid giving superior status to his rival Lord Waldron.

Carus swept his gaze across the council. His eyes had the hard glint of a sea eagle viewing white foam on the wave tops, judging which flecks were wind and which might be made by the fins of fish just below the surface.

"We're being attacked by rogues who call themselves the Confederacy of the West," he said. "They're using wizardry now, though they'll be bringing swords out soon I shouldn't wonder. We're going to cut them off at the knees by moving on them immediately."

Carus paused to let what he'd just said sink in. Aides scribbled in waxed notebooks or on sheets of smooth-planed white birch; the seated principals glanced around to check their colleagues' reaction, but for the most part they kept silent.

Lord Angier, who held a rotating appointment as representative of the united guilds of Valles, was the exception. More puffed up by his presence in the council than daunted by awareness that he was far the most junior person in the room, he said, "What do you mean, 'We're being attacked by wizardry,' your highness?"

Carus pointed his left index finger at Angier. In a voice that was no less terrible for being quiet, he said, "Guildsman, stupid questions wouldn't amuse me even when time wasn't as short as it is today. Shut your mouth and listen."

Angier gaped, first at the king and then at the chancellor, who Sharina knew had acted as his patron. Royhas grimaced and jerked his head in a swift gesture of negation. Angier suddenly understood the enormity of what he'd done; he wilted visibly.

"Right," said Carus softly.

If Garric had been chairing this meeting, there'd have been a babble of voices—some raised in shouts. With Carus at the head of the table, Sharina had a vision of these same men facing a lion in an enclosed space. A hungry lion.

"The Confederates're gathering their forces at Donelle on the east coast of Tisamur," the king said. "Donelle seems to be where the wizards in league with them have their den as well."

Liane opened the parchment codex on which she'd written her notes on the Confederacy, summarizing information from a score of sources. Garric would have asked her to brief the assembly at this point. Carus didn't bother—with an explanation or with Liane, either one.

"I'm going to take the fleet and the army to Tisamur," he continued harshly, "land in the Bight of Donelle, smash the Confederacy's army, and hang every wizard I can catch. Zettin and Koprathu—I'll sail in three days. How many ships will you have ready?"

Zettin, the Admiral of the Fleet, was a nobleman in his late thirties—a former Blood Eagle who'd take any risk for success. Master Koprathu was the elderly Clerk of the Fleet Office responsible for outfitting Admiral Zettin's forces. Both reacted with shock in their different ways.

"Three days?" said Koprathu. He opened a satchel, taking out an abacus and a series of accounts scratched onto potsherds with a stylus. "Oh, that's much too soon, sir, we'll need at least—"

"Your highness," said Zettin, jumping to his feet, "I'm ready to go now with the ten ships of the guard squadron!"

"Koprathu," King Carus said, "I didn't ask for an opinion, I want a number: how many ships can you get ready in three days? Zettin—"

His glance shifted, his face grew harder.

"*Lord* Zettin," he continued, "I could train an ape to caper and do tricks for me. What I need from you isn't noble posturing but hard facts and the readiness to do as you're told. I'll ask you once more: how many ships can be ready to sail in three days?"

Zettin's face didn't change for a measurable instant; the look of noble insouciance remained long after it could possibly have any connection with what was going on in the admiral's mind. Waldron leaned forward, watchful rather than hopeful—though he'd objected at the time, Garric gave the fleet command to Attaper's protégé Zettin.

"There are seventy-six trireme hulls that I trust to swim," Zettin said. "In the arsenal, the builders' yards, and the squadron on duty downriver at the Pool. I have thirty-seven hundred men. That's nominally, but I expect that a sweep of the harbor for sailors will about make up for attrition from sickness and desertion. So, eighteen to twenty ships fully manned, with more in proportion as space is used for cargo and passengers instead of oarsmen. Plus the phalanx, who train with us part of the time but aren't under my command."

"Good," said Carus, gesturing Zettin back to his seat. Zettin sat quickly and gratefully. Without the king's command, he'd have been in a quandary as to whether to sit or stand—and feeling a fool whichever he chose.

Master Koprathu turned over the yellow-glazed shard on which he jotted notes with a fine brush and started working on the back. The shards holding his accounts were spreading in a three-tiered arc before him, encroaching on the space belonging to the councillors to either side. They edged away from the clerk, not least because some of the low-fired pots were crumbling.

Koprathu must have been aware of Carus' gaze—and that of everyone else in the room, drawn by the king's eyes. He continued working with desperate animation, never looking up. Sweat beaded his forehead.

Carus nodded brusk approval. He turned. "Lord Waldron," he said, "what's the status of the army for deployment in three days?"

Another of Waldron's aides, this one a grizzled fellow nearly the general's own age, was trying to offer him a sheaf of paper. It probably held the morning reports of the regiments under his command. Waldron waved the man off impatiently.

"Of the phalanx, cross-trained as oarsmen," Waldron

said, "five thousand, three hundred and seventeen present for duty this morning. Heavy infantry, not cross-trained, two thousand, one hundred and twelve present for duty. Light infantry—"

The archers and javelin men; scouts and skirmishers for the main army and useful as marines in a sea fight.

"—one thousand, eight hundred and seventy-nine present for duty; but I think I can bring that number up by several hundred in three days. They'll come running from their small-holdings if they hear there's a chance for loot and a fight."

Waldron and the king exchanged hard smiles.

"Cavalry," Waldron continued, "only seven hundred and sixteen in and around Valles. Several thousand more if there were time to raise the household troops of my northern neighbors, but three days isn't long enough for that."

"Bring five squadrons south for security in Valles while we're gone," Carus said with a nod. "I doubt we'll have bottoms to transport seven hundred horses anyway, let alone fodder for them."

He paused, then added without raising his voice, "The horsemen will fight as infantry if I order it?"

"They will," said Waldron in the tones a glacier would use if it were very angry. "Or they'll crawl from my camp on their bellies as foresworn cowards."

"*My* camp, Lord Waldron," the king said with a gentle smile, "but I'm fortunate to have a commander who understands that real honor doesn't depend on sitting in a saddle."

He cleared his throat. "You sent your aide out before the council opened?"

Lord Attaper looked from Carus to Waldron sharply, then made his face blank. Placed where he was by the door, he'd missed the interaction between Waldron and the youth.

"I alerted the army for deployment in twenty-four hours," Waldron said, beaming with satisfaction that had nothing soft about it. "If you'd called this council to announce a Founder's Day parade, then the exercise would still have kept my men on their toes."

Attaper grinned at his rival in grudging admiration.

Aides were hunching beside their principals' chairs, whispering numbers and exchanging notebooks or whole files. Everyone at the table save for Liane and Sharina was waiting for the king's hard gaze to spear them; waiting, and dreading the questions that would follow.

"Royhas, how many merchant ships are there in the harbor of, say, fifty tons' burden or better?" Carus demanded.

Instead of looking up from the documents now spread before him on the table, Royhas stabbed a vellum notebook with his index finger and slid it through the litter in front of him. "Forty-seven in Valles, twelve more between Valles and the mouth of the River Beltis," he said. "Some of them are outbound, but we can catch them with a mounted courier."

He flipped back two pages in the notebook, then raised his eyes to meet the king's. "We can expect seven to ten more vessels to arrive in the next three days," Royhas added, smiling with his own tight satisfaction. "Based on normal traffic for this time of year."

"Your highness!" Master Koprathu cried. "Your highness! I've blocks and cordage for forty-seven triremes and oar-sets for thirty-nine—but masts for only twenty-two. I've been trying to get an appropriation for more masts from the treasury, but—"

"Quit while you're ahead, Koprathu!" Carus said before Lord Pterlion, the treasurer, could weigh in with an angry response. The clerk's head jolted up with a look of horror.

Sharina laid her fingertips on Carus' arm; not at all her brother's arm, not at this moment. Carus jerked his head around to meet her eyes. His expression dissolved into a smile.

"Which you are, Master Koprathu, very much ahead," Carus boomed over a bubble of incipient laughter. "If we strip the masts out of the merchantmen we're not using for stores and cavalry mounts, can you get more triremes outfitted? Needs must, we'll row the whole way, but if we can I'd like to save the phalanx for their other work when we land."

"I—" said Koprathu. He was bug-eyed with amazement. "Well, well *yes*, of course, but I'll need men—"

"Lord Zettin?" the king said with an eyebrow raised in interrogation.

"He can have two thousand men in an hour if he needs them," the admiral said. "We'll have every ship you point out down to a bare hull if that's what you want."

Zettin blinked, suddenly aware that he was posturing again. In a rush of decision he blurted, "No, by the Lady! We really can! I mean it!"

Carus nodded dismissal. "Is the City Prefect here?" he demanded. "Lord Putran, isn't it? Where's he?"

A middle-aged, balding, terrified man in a gray robe stood against the wall in a corner; he had a large document case at his feet. He raised his hand, and squeaked, "Milord?" before slapping a hand over his mouth in horror.

"Don't worry about the bloody form of address!" Carus roared. "What have you got to say? Where's Putran?"

Sharina reached for his arm again, but there was no need. The king's sinewy left hand closed over hers affectionately, gave her a pat, and released her while his attention remained centered on the man in gray. Several of the aides along the wall goggled at the way Prince Garric showed his affection for his sister.

"I'm Lord Putran's chief clerk, your highness," the fellow said. "The lord is, well, we're not sure where his lordship is. He, ah, doesn't come to the office very frequently. But I usually handle . . ."

Carus turned his head to glare past Sharina toward the chancellor. Royhas gestured curtly. "I'll take it in hand, your highness," he said. "There'll be three possible candidates for the post before you tomorrow morning."

"Not before me," Carus snapped. "Give them to Liane. But that isn't the business for now anyway."

He crooked a finger toward the clerk. "All right, how much grain is there in the city now? Enough to feed fifteen thousand men for ten days?"

"Not in government warehouses, your highness," the clerk said. His eyes bobbed up and down toward the document case. He wanted to open it, but if he squatted to do so he'd drop out of the king's sight over the table.

He paused, then went on, "Even if we add rye and barley to the stores of wheat, there'd only be full rations for four days."

Carus smiled grimly. "I didn't say 'government warehouses,'" he said, but he didn't snarl. Competence counted with this king, and the clerk's answer had put him on a plane with Lord Waldron. "I said the city. For this emergency, I'll let the residents of Valles eat rats for a week if that's what it takes to supply my troops."

"Oh!" the clerk said. "Well, in that case . . . Yes, that easily, even by the tax declarations. And I know for a fact that those are low, disgracefully low!"

His face grew worried. "But milor . . . ah, but your highness," he said, "these are private property and—"

"Royhas, draft an emergency decree," Carus interrupted. "We'll promulgate it when we leave here."

"Done, your highness," the chancellor said. The aide who'd been kneeling at his side as Royhas whispered hopped back to the wall, scribbling with a blunt stylus on a waxed board.

"Pterlion, they'll be issuing chits on the treasury," Carus

continued, turning his attention to the treasurer. "These will be honored. Do you understand?"

Lord Pterlion, a diminutive man with the manner not of a mouse but a shrew, glared across the table. His lips were pursed into a beak. He dipped his head twice, nodding agreement, but he obviously didn't trust what would come out if he opened his mouth.

"But if there's undeclared goods in the warehouses," Carus added, no longer eyeing his treasurer as a possible next meal, "then the chits come due in a quarter, not at the month. All right?"

Pterlion smiled, an expression his face hadn't practiced often. "*Much* better, your highness," he said. "If I can't find the money in ninety days, then you need another man in this ministry."

"Waldron, they'll need escorts," Carus said. The way his head turned disconcerted Sharina; it was like watching a weathercock in a gusty storm. "Provide—"

He looked at the clerk again. "What *is* your name, anyway?" he snapped. "You from the prefect's office?"

"Hauk, your highness!"

"Right, provide Hauk with however many men he thinks he'll need."

"I am going to use the four regiments of heavy infantry to carry the grain," Waldron said, meeting the king's eyes. Liane, seated between them, leaned back in her chair with the look of someone who'd found herself between duelists. "It'll give them exercise, and it'll show me how they'll react to an order they don't like. Especially their officers."

For a moment Carus was bowstring taut, reacting to the "I am," rather than "May I?" in Waldron's statement. Sharina and Liane reached out simultaneously, their mouths open in fear of the king's reaction.

Carus shrugged them aside, almost angrily, but he said in a growl, "Aye, a good plan, milord. A fine plan."

"Your highness?" chirped Hauk. "I wonder—will you

be wanting dried vegetables, wine, and cheese as well? Because we could get those supplies at the same time."

Liane gasped with relief; Sharina felt herself relax blissfully. She'd been poised to grab the king's arm if he started to slap his army commander, but she didn't think she was either fast enough or strong enough. She wondered what sort of reward would be suitable for the clerk who'd accidentally prevented a crisis.

King Carus laughed with the booming joy of a man who loves life and lives it fully. He rose to his feet, putting his hands on the shoulders of the women seated beside him.

"Yes, Master Hauk," he said, "we'll want those other supplies as well. And by the way"—his gaze, sword-edge hard again, stabbed Royhas—"you've just become City Prefect. Royhas, I won't need those names, but take care of it if Hauk has to be ennobled or some such nonsense. Eh?"

Royhas nodded. Faces—noble faces—around the table showed shock, and some of the aides looked worse than that, but nobody objected aloud. Which was just as well. . . .

"I . . ." said Hauk. He looked like a carp sucking air. "I . . . I . . ."

"Your highness?" said the grizzled aide who'd offered Waldron the morning reports. "Normally the troops wouldn't carry their supplies, they'd—"

He stopped, suddenly aware of what he was saying and who he was saying it to. The man facing him might have a youth's body, but the soul looking out through the eyes wasn't one which had to be told how an army moved.

"Aye, normally we'd land every night on a major island and buy food for the next day," the king said. "We'd reach Tisamur some time next year that way."

He smiled, not a gentle expression, as he swept the room with his eyes.

"Maybe a little sooner?" he went on. "But we're not

going to do that. We're going to strike straight across the Inner Sea, overnighting on islets where nobody lives and nobody can warn that we're coming. We'll carry enough food to get us to Tisamur."

He pointed across the table to a plump man in an immaculate blue robe, his fingers tented before him. Lord Tadai had no formal appointment at the moment, but his presence in the council had surprised no one. He was wealthy, powerful, and *extremely* intelligent.

"Lord Tadai," Carus said, "I want you to go to Pandah and embargo the shipping there."

"Go ahead of the fleet, you mean, your highness?" Tadai said, laying his hands flat on the table. Pandah, the only large island in the Inner Sea, was a stopping point for much of the traffic between distant islands.

"The fleet's not going by way of Pandah," Carus said with a broad grin. "We're striking straight to the Sidera Atoll north of Shengy to regroup. You'll send all merchantmen with cargoes of food to join us there, or stage on to Tisamur if we've left already. I don't care who they are or where they're bound, they're supplying the royal army now."

"For which they'll be paid?" Pterlion asked.

"For which they'll be paid," Carus agreed, nodding, "but Zettin will make sure Lord Tadai has enough marines with him to put a squad aboard every ship he sends south. To remind the citizens of outlying parts of their duty to the Kingdom of the Isles."

Lord Waldron snorted. Like most landowners from Northern Ornifal, he regarded himself and his peers as the upholders of the kingdom and its only *real* citizens. Everyone else, even the merchant nobility of Valles, were on a lower plane. As for the status of mere sailors from other islands—well, indeed!

"Three galleys to Pandah, your highness?" Lord Zettin asked.

Carus frowned. "Four, I think," he said. "Under an officer who's a seaman himself—"

"Because I assuredly am not," said Tadai, smiling comfortably, with his fingers tented again. His oval nails were gilded. "As I've proved, I'm afraid."

The king set his balled fists on the table and leaned onto them. "If anybody doesn't know his job, come to me," he said. "If anybody's trying to do his job and runs into somebody who's getting in the way of that, come to me."

He grinned like a really happy leopard. "But I give extra credit to the folks who *don't* bother me," he added, "because I have my own job to do. Does everybody understand?"

There was no sound save the rustle of documents and the whicker of sandals on the tiled floor as councillors prepared to rise.

"Then, gentlemen, go *do* your jobs!" the king thundered. "And know by my oath on the Lady that I will do mine!"

He gestured to the door. Attaper hauled it open, barely in time to let the first of the hastening councillors out unimpeded.

Carus watched them go. In a voice that only Sharina and Liane could hear, he said, "I sent Ilna into trouble. By the Lady! My sword will get her out again—or I'll die trying!"

Garric awoke to the pressure of a hand on his shoulder. He sat upright, rousing Tint; she *whuffed* at his feet.

Garric half smiled, half frowned at memory of the time he shared his mind with King Carus. In those recent days he'd have come out of his sleep with a drawn dagger in his hand. Carus wasn't with him now, and an innkeeper's son doesn't have reflexes honed by slaughter and assassination.

The ancient king's experiences might have been a better preparation for the life Gar the Bandit was leading now.

Vascay had wakened him. Moonlight trickling through chinks in the wattle-and-daub walls provided the only illumination, but Gar's eyes saw clearly by it.

The other bandits lay sprawled on the straw, snoring or not as their habit was. Alcomm alone seemed wakeful, huddling in a corner and squeezing the biceps of his severed arm with his remaining hand.

"The wizard went out a little bit ago," Vascay whispered. "I waited till he was away before I got you up. I thought you'd want to follow him just to see what's going on. He looks to be heading back to the boathouse, but I guess your ladyfriend—"

He nodded toward Tint. His tone was matter-of-fact, with nothing of a sneer in it.

"—could track him wherever he went, right?"

Garric got to his feet and pulled on the outer tunic he'd been using for a bedcover. He didn't have boots or sandals to worry about. Gar hadn't worn footgear since the seawolf chewed on his skull, so the soles of his feet were as tough as oxhide.

"Yes, all right," Garric said. "Are you coming too?"

Vascay snorted a quick laugh. "It's not worth me putting my leg on, lad," he said. "Not when I've got you to take care of things."

The chieftain grimaced, stroking the stump with hard hands. He'd have been sitting cross-legged if he'd had both legs.

"Clamping to a horse's flank makes the stump swell worse than if I'd hiked the way on the peg all these miles," he said. "Cursed if I know why. One of the mysteries of life, I suppose."

Garric nodded. He glanced at his sword belt, hanging from a tack hook in the empty stall where he and Tint had bedded down. He drew the dagger and thrust the bare blade under the sash of his tunic, then said to Vascay, "I'll borrow a javelin. All right?"

"Aye," said Vascay in a subdued voice. He didn't look up. His hands continued to knead his stump.

The valves of the stable's double door were ajar; Garric glanced through them. Metron was out of sight, and the night was silent. He slipped out with the beastgirl following as smoothly as a stream of oil.

"I want to follow the wizard, Tint," Garric said. "Can you take me the way he's gone?"

Tint ambled off on all fours. "We kill Metron, Gar?" she asked.

Garric lengthened his stride to keep up with the beastgirl, though she wasn't really in a hurry. "No, Tint," he said. "Metron's on our side. Or we're on his. He likes us."

"Metron like Gar?" Tint said. She made a sound with her teeth. "Metron like Gar for food, maybe."

That was pretty close to Garric's own judgment on the wizard, but he didn't say so in case Tint misunderstood it. Garric had known even before he became Prince of the Isles that sometimes you had to ally with people you'd rather not have met.

Metron might not be a trustworthy friend, but the Intercessor was a deadly enemy. If Tint's long jaws tore Metron's throat out, it was hard to see how Garric and his new colleagues would survive the efforts of Protectors of the Peace guided by wizardry.

The trail Tint followed led around the back of the U-shaped villa, past outbuildings and a litter of broken vehicles and equipment. Geese, roosting for the night, quacked nervously awake. Garric expected a watchman to appear, but the only response from the house was the squeak of a shutter being eased open enough for an eye to peer out.

Garric frowned, wondering if the noise would warn Metron. He snorted. No, of course not. The wizard was nei-

she intensely disliked the woman who was performing it.

"*Chphuris on sankiste . . .*" said Alecto.

What if Chalcus were here with them? How would he get along with this wild girl?

Ilna snorted. Well enough, no doubt. Far too well for her own comfort, that she was sure of.

"*Lampse seison souros!*" Alecto cried. She made a final flourish with her knife, an intricate pattern in the air. There was a rustle from above.

The fire was a small one, built from the stems and branches of a wild olive which had sprung up at the base of the great cedar. The wood was green but oily; it caught quickly when Ilna struck sparks from the back of her knife into the wad of milkweed fluff Alecto provided.

The milkweed wasn't ripe either here—wherever "here" was—or in Valles when Ilna went into her trance. Alecto came from a place distant in time; by a season at least, but very likely from farther than that. She eyed Ilna's steel knife with as much fear as envy.

A dove toppled end over end to the ground. It hit with a thump, its beak opening and closing slowly. Alecto snatched the bird's head and broke its neck with a quick jerk.

A second dove flopped down, like the first, stunned but not dead. Ilna killed it, then slipped her paring knife from its case of yellowed bone and began to skin the bird. If they'd had a pot to scald the doves, she'd have plucked them instead, but this would do. Alecto was proceeding in the same fashion, gripping her athame by the end of the blade with a careful gap between the edge and the heel of her hand.

"I was in Valles on Ornifal when I came here," Ilna said, keeping her eyes on her work. "Where did you come from, mistress?"

Alecto shrugged. "I was at home, outside of Hartrag's

village," she said. "I put myself into dreamworld to find a nightmare to send to Brasus."

She chuckled. "He said he was leaving me to go back to his wife and sons," she said. "So I thought fine, I'll let him *dream* about the bitch and her whelps too—with their guts around their necks and their eyes gouged out. See how he likes that!"

Ilna spilled the offal on the bird's skin, then threaded the giblets on a long splinter that she set over the flames. They'd grill more quickly than the rest of the bird, small though it was. Her empty stomach was already twitching in anticipation of the hot morsels.

Alecto shook her head in mingled disgust and disbelief. "I'd never've troubled the Pack," she said. "Oh, sure, I knew I was going into territory close by theirs, but that didn't matter unless they'd already been roused. Who'd've imagined that?"

Ilna thrust a peeled withe the thickness of her little finger through the squab and set it on the supports she'd prepared while Alecto called the birds down. She'd bound straight sticks in a pair of X-frames instead of bothering to find forked twigs of the proper size and angle.

"Yes, Hartrag's village," Ilna said, for the sake of information but also to get her mind off her companion's casual boasts. "But what island are you from? And who's the King of the Isles in your time?"

"Island?" Alecto repeated. "I don't live on an island. I told you, I'm just a bowshot north of Saller's hut, on the path to Queatwa's village."

Ilna's lips tightened in anger. Then she looked at herself with her mind's eye and snorted in disbelief at her foolishness.

A year ago she herself had been only vaguely aware that she lived on the island of Haft. She'd had no idea that there was a King of the Isles and had known little more of the Count of Haft in Carcosa. If Alecto now was as ignorant as Ilna had been so recently, that was no reason to scorn her.

Ilna had much better reason than that to scorn Alecto.

"Ah . . ." she said, thinking about the connections Barca's Hamlet had with the greater world. She turned her spit a notch. She'd squared the withe where it rested on the supports, then beveled the corners to double the number of faces to give her precise control of the way the bird faced the fire. "Do priests come to your village in the spring to collect tithes for the temple in—"

Not in Carcosa, surely.

"—whatever place has the chief temples of the Lady and the Shepherd?"

"I've heard of priests," Alecto said. "Somebody paid to pray for you, you mean? Not in Hartrag's village! Sometimes a hermit comes through and some folks give him a meal. Mostly hermits had better be able to knock over a rabbit or a squirrel for themselves, though."

She'd butterflied her squab with twigs and was holding the skewer in her hand instead of using a frame as Ilna did. The firelight threw harsh shadows onto the planes of her face; despite that she looked tired and, to Ilna's mind, perhaps a little less bestial. Calling doves down to the ground by art was work as surely as climbing the tree to fetch them would have been. Besides, the stress of hiding in the temple must be telling on her muscles as well as Ilna's.

The reason Ilna so disdained Alecto . . . the *real* reason did Ilna no credit, and she was far too honest to hide the truth from herself.

"I was lucky to meet you, I don't mind saying," Alecto said, rubbing her eyes with the back of her free hand. She shifted her legs slightly, then reached under the front of her skirt to scratch herself. "I could run, but I couldn't have run much farther. And the Pack never stop when they've taken up a trail."

"Do you know anything about the people we watched there in the temple?" Ilna said. "If I'm correct, they may call themselves Moon Wisdom and this may be Tisamur. The island of Tisamur."

"Never heard of them," Alecto said. She yawned. "Either one."

She glared at the fire. Ilna turned her squab again, then took the skewer of giblets from the fire and waved it to cool the meat.

"You know it wasn't just the ones we saw in the room who raised the Pack, don't you?" Alecto said unexpectedly, looking directly at Ilna. Her eyes winked like beads of polished chert. "They were just focusing it. There were people outside praying with them, too."

In a softer voice, she added, "More people than I'd ever thought there were. All together."

"I didn't know there were other people," Ilna said. She thought back on the day not so very long ago when she'd entered Carcosa. There were tenements in the city that held more people than lived in all of Barca's Hamlet. "I'm not a wizard, you know."

"Don't give me that!" Alecto snapped. "You wouldn't be here—you wouldn't have been where I found you!—if you weren't a wizard."

"Believe what you please!" Ilna said. She bit the dove's gizzard from the skewer and chewed it. The tough muscle, only half-cooked, gave her an outlet for her irritation.

Alecto lapsed back to staring at the fire. "I suppose they think they control the Pack because there's so many of them," she said morosely. "They're wrong, though. If they keep doing it, eventually they'll let something slip. And then . . ."

She shook her head. In Alecto's voice Ilna heard the tone she herself would have used in describing the craftsmanship of another weaver, one who'd attempted more than her skill would permit her to succeed with. Ilna looked at her companion with new interest.

"The Pack doesn't quit," Alecto said to the fire. "The people we saw, they think they're the Pack's masters. The Pack doesn't *have* a master. All it has is hunger. And if you let the Pack loose, before long it'll come back to feed on you."

Ilna chewed the dove's liver. She said nothing.

She wasn't thinking about the Pack or the nearer dangers of this place in which she found herself. She was thinking about another sort of pattern altogether, a pattern and perhaps a duty.

Chalcus has asked me in every fashion but words, Ilna thought, *and I've pretended that I didn't hear him. This girl, this* woman, *would've said yes to Chalcus before she was even asked.*

And for that I hate her.

"What're you looking at me that way for?" Alecto said in sudden alarm. The keen-edged athame was suddenly in her hand.

"What?" said Ilna. "Sorry, I wasn't looking at you at all. I was thinking about a conversation that I'm going to have when I get home. As I expect to do."

Alecto grinned like a snarling dog. "The guy you're planning to talk to isn't going to like it," she said approvingly. "Or is it a woman?"

"He's a man," Ilna said. "And I think you're wrong."

She bit down on the dove's heart. "More fool him, perhaps," she added. "But I think he'll be very pleased."

"Dawn!" whispered Tilphosa. "Oh, Mistress, You've blessed us with the return of light!"

Cashel staggered. He was just as glad as Tilphosa to have daylight again, but the change from dusk to sunrise caught him in mid-step. Ousseau muttered in the crook of Cashel's left arm, but he didn't wake up.

A waterfall drummed nearby. When he looked for it, Cashel saw edges of white spray through the leaves. That'd be water, which they all needed badly by now.

"Oh!" Tilphosa repeated. She looked at Cashel. Now that there was real light, her face looked almost as gray as it had in the twilit woods they'd come from.

"Ah . . . ?" she said. "Would it be all right to rest now, Cashel?"

He hadn't realized Tilphosa was so close to being done in. She'd kept plodding along beside him, not saying much but never complaining.

"Sure," he said. "I'll be glad to stop myself."

Cashel turned to look over his shoulder. Hook and Captain Mounix were a stone's throw behind. They seemed to be managing all right. Anyway, they had enough energy to complain, though they stopped it quick enough when they saw Cashel's eyes on them.

"We're stopping?" Mounix croaked. "By the Lady, I can't go on any farther! Unless"—his expression grew guardedly hopeful—"you want to give me a hand instead of Ousseau. He's had ease enough, I'd say!"

Cashel squatted expressionlessly and laid Ousseau on the ground. The injured sailor did seem to be doing well. The swelling in his hand and forearm below the bandage was down, and his breathing seemed normal. The touch of cold leaf litter awakened him with a snort.

"You did a good job bandaging Ousseau up," Cashel said to Tilphosa as he rose. "He was lucky to have you around."

Tilphosa smiled and laid her fingers on Cashel's elbow for a moment. "I think we're doing well," she said. Her smile tightened as she looked back at Mounix and Hook. She added, "Even them. For what they are."

The woods back the way the party'd come were still in

shadow. The dawn breaking ahead had to do with more than just the time of day.

Cashel shrugged, working stiffness out of his back muscles. He gave his staff a trial spin, mostly to feel the smooth wood shifting among his practiced fingers. It reminded him of home. That was always a good thing; at times like this, the memory of home was one of the best things there could be.

Mounix and Hook had caught up. Ousseau got to his feet and joined them, standing a staff's length back from Cashel and the girl.

Cashel dipped a ferrule toward where he heard the waterfall. "We'll head that way and likely camp," he said. "We need water, and I figure we ought to walk a ways and get a look at what things're like around here before we bed down."

"What's wrong with it?" Hook said, worried rather than belligerent. His eyes moved nervously. "I thought it looked fine."

"There's nothing wrong that I know about," Cashel said patiently. "It's different, is all, and I thought we best take a look while we're awake."

There hadn't been anything bad even about the woods they'd finally walked out of, but Cashel hadn't recognized a single one of the trees in the whole long time. Around him now were maples and sourwoods, well leafed out. They were well spread apart, maybe because the clay soil was so stony.

Tilphosa drew herself up like a queen. "Come, Cashel," she said. "I'm thirsty."

Her hand on Cashel's arm, she set off toward the sound of water falling. Cashel, warned by the pressure of her fingers, stepped off when she did. He didn't know where Tilphosa had picked up her skill, but he guessed she'd be better than fair at driving a yoke of oxen.

Cashel grinned at the thought as they strode along, but

as they got closer to the falls the smile left his face because his skin had started to prickle again. Oh, there wasn't anything dreadful about that; he'd felt it, kind of an itching like when he'd had too much sun, all the way through the woods they'd just left.

It meant wizardry, or anyway it seemed to. Cashel'd gotten used to being without the feeling for the little while he'd been free of it. He didn't guess he could complain, given the way they'd come to this place. He thought of home again and thought of herding sheep.

"Let me go ahead," he murmured to Tilphosa, taking the quarterstaff in both hands. The sailors were far enough back that they wouldn't be getting in his way.

Tilphosa stopped and knelt. She'd been carrying the half-rotted stick ever since she picked it up. She worked at the clay now with the end of it, digging out a stone the size of her foot. It had a fractured edge.

Good girl. A *really* good girl.

The water draped a sheet of itself over a smooth cliff maybe three times Cashel's height; it pooled, then drained away to the side. A stand of yellow birches grew on the near side of the pool. Cashel stepped through them, his eyes on the water. Because of how the falls roiled the surface, anything could hide in the pool and not be seen till it wanted to be.

"Hello there," said a slurred voice behind him.

Cashel spun, the staff crosswise and his right arm cocked to slam the end forward in a blow that'd bend iron. His mouth was open, but he'd managed to avoid—barely—a shout of surprise. He couldn't see who'd spoken.

"Ooh, he's quick, too," said another voice, again from behind. It was a little clearer than the first. "And so—"

Cashel whirled.

"—big!"

The bark of the nearest birch was stained at head height.

You could imagine a face there if you tried . . . and as Cashel watched in amazement, it was more and more a face. The knot that had squirmed during the last word was now a pair of pouting lips.

"Cashel?" Tilphosa shouted. She'd gotten the rock out of the ground. She held it edge first in her right hand as she ran toward the grove. "I'm coming!"

"Oh, my, he's gorgeous, isn't he?" called another voice. "Oh, it's been so long!"

All the trees were changing. It wasn't fast, nothing you really saw happening. It was more like the water was going down and uncovering the thing that'd been underneath. In place of bark the trunks showed tawny skin and human features.

"Cashel!" Tilphosa said. She put her back to his. "Are they dangerous?"

"Hey, there's girls in there!" Hook said. He trotted into the grove, holding his sword up beside his ear like he wasn't sure if he'd need it or not. The other sailors joined him, Ousseau a step before the captain.

The birches laughed, a musical sound but with something catlike about it. Their faces were continuing to form, taking on human roundness instead of being outlines that might have been drawn on bare wood.

"Dangerous?" said the one who'd spoken first. She had high cheekbones and lips now the color of leaves just before they turn brown. "Not to you, girlie. We're not interested in *you*."

"They shouldn't be interested in her either," said a face whose eyes slanted upward at the corners the way the eyes of Serians did. She winked at Ousseau. "We're much nicer than she is, boys. And she's so skinny!"

Hook touched the cheek of the birch beside him. "It's real!" he said. "It's not wood, it's a real girl!"

The face shifted slightly, and the lips pursed. They kissed Hook's fingertip.

"Of course we're real," the face said. "Real in every way, for a handsome man like you."

"Cashel, I think we ought to go," Tilphosa said in a small voice. "Sometimes nymphs can be . . ."

Cashel glanced at her. Her left hand gripped the crystal lens on her necklace, trying to find comfort in the God she'd been raised to worship. She'd stopped speaking, but her lips continued to move in silent prayer.

Mounix caressed a tree with an expression of wonder and delight. Not only were the faces growing clearer, hinted torsos were beginning to appear on the trunks. Ousseau stood openmouthed, listening to what a nymph whispered into his right ear.

"Come on!" Cashel said in sudden decision. "Drink as much as you can and I'll fill my bottle. Then we'll go on back to sleep where the maples were."

"Leave?" Captain Mounix said. He was fondling the trunk as the face above moaned softly with pleasure. "Not just yet. Look at this!"

Cashel grabbed Mounix by the arm and turned him about. "Now," he said. "Now."

Hook looked over his shoulder as if to protest. Cashel said nothing, but Tilphosa made a curt gesture. "Bring him too," she said, nodding to the wounded sailor.

The carpenter gave her a stricken look but touched Ousseau's elbow. Ousseau ignored him until Hook seized his bandaged upper arm.

"Hey!" Ousseau screamed. He slapped Hook away with his good hand, then glared at Tilphosa with the expression of a child about to cry. "What's it to you?" he demanded.

"Come on," Cashel said bruskly. He shifted Mounix in the direction he wanted him to go and gave him a shove; not hard, but hard enough to get him moving. "We'll go to where the water comes out downstream and get our drink."

Cashel and Tilphosa followed the sailors out of the grove stone-faced. Behind them laughed the bright, cruel chorus of the birches.

Chapter Twelve

W e could go off there somewhere," Alecto said, gesturing toward the relatively open country to the west. "I don't see why we have to hang around this, this—"

Her voice sank to a murmur.

"—city, you call it."

"You *don't* have to hang around," Ilna said coldly as she surveyed the people entering through the gate near which she and the wild girl waited. "Go about your business, and I'll take care of mine by myself."

She didn't—quite—say, "As I'd prefer," because Ilna didn't—quite—want Alecto to leave her. Alecto wasn't the ally Ilna would have chosen, but she was the only ally Ilna had at present. But if the wild girl thought her whim could have the slightest effect on Ilna doing her duty, then she was a fool as well as several sorts of moral failure.

Alecto scuffed the dust with her big toe while muttering something that Ilna chose to ignore. Ilna was looking for a pattern in the traffic. The sun had been up for an hour, and the flow into the city was growing heavy. They didn't close the gates at sunset here, but few chose to travel during the watches of the night.

"Why are there so many people?" Ilna mused aloud.

"There wouldn't be as many coming into Valles at this time in the morning."

Well, the numbers coming though any one gate would have been less; but Valles was entered by three major highways plus a network of minor roads linked to the western suburbs across the River Beltis. Valles was many times the size of this place, however.

The track was bare dirt. The meandering ruts had been made by animals driven to the city, not wheels.

"I never knew there *were* this many people," Alecto said, so morosely that Ilna glanced at her again.

She's afraid, Ilna thought. Alecto was responsible for both of them being here, but she was far more out of place than Ilna was.

Even in the days Ilna expected to spend her whole life within a mile of Barca's Hamlet, she'd been in some way a part of the wider world. Priests and merchants came into the borough, and Ilna sold her textiles for use in the great cities of distant islands. She couldn't have described those cities, not ruined Carcosa and certainly not flourishing Valles, until she saw them; but she'd known they existed.

Alecto had never heard of a city. Ilna frowned in thought. Perhaps even if Alecto had travelled the length of the world of her time, she wouldn't have found a city. A wild girl from a wild time; and for all her powers and ruthlessness, she was frightened of the place to which she had come.

"Look here," said Ilna sharply. "Can you send me back into this dreamworld the way Tenoctris did? You're obviously a powerful wizard, which Tenoctris claims she's not."

Alecto shook her head with a sour expression. "I don't know how she did that," she said. Her expression grew guarded. "Are you lying to me? Did you make the sacrifice yourself and draw the entrance in blood around you?"

"I did not," Ilna said, momentarily so angry that she had

Alecto was now repeating the words she'd used at the start of her chant. The sounds were nonsense to Ilna, but their repetition meant Alecto was ready to act. Ilna watched the travellers with a different intent.

A small flock of sheep ambled past. The beasts were more interested in her than the badger driving them, a solid young man whose full moustache must once have been his pride. There was nothing in his expression now but intent tempered with fear.

Ilna thought of choosing the badger, but following the flock was a well-dressed horseman who seemed frowningly poised to ride either around or through the sheep. Someone garbed and mounted like him should have had attendants, but an impatient man might have pressed on ahead of his retinue.

Ilna stepped aside. "All right," she said in an aside to the girl behind her.

Reflected light flickered across the horseman's eyes. He straightened and stared in the direction of the flash. For a moment the reins slackened, and his body seemed on the verge of slumping from the saddle. Then he jerked his gelding's head to the side and rode directly toward the pentacle.

The horse shouldered to the ground the old woman in its path. She squalled. Turnips spilled from the tapering basket on her back, but the rider paid her no heed. He dismounted in front of the grinning, sweating Alecto and stood with his hands loosely crossed in front of him.

"He's yours," Alecto said to Ilna in triumph. "Ask him anything you please."

She got up shakily, trying to conceal the effort she'd spent in working her art. That was boasting, but it was the sort which Ilna preferred to that of those who'd claim whatever they did was hard beyond the understanding of mere mortals.

"What's this city?" Ilna said crisply, starting with a

question that might arouse suspicion but was innocent in itself. The gelding wasn't trained to stand untethered. When it realized it was loose, it first edged, then walked toward the base of the wall where dew running down the stone watered rank grass.

"This is Donelle," the man said. His eyes were downcast, fixed on the pentacle, and his voice had the slurred lifelessness of one talking in his sleep.

Donelle on Tisamur, much as Garric—probably Liane—had guessed. Ilna's smile would have gone unnoticed except to those who knew her very well. This was where she'd meant to come. She'd just reached the place sooner and in an unexpected fashion.

"Why are you coming to Donelle?" she asked.

"The Mistress has called all Her servitors to Donelle," the man said, "to help with the great work of returning Her to the throne of the world. We will join and pray at midday of the full moon, and She will reascend Her throne."

Ilna frowned. The moon last night was near its first quarter. Seven days, as Garric would say; a handful of days and two days.

"How did the Mistress call you?" she said. "Did a priest tell you to come here?"

"Priest?" the man said. He blinked twice, slowly, as though his numbed mind was trying to find meaning in the word. "The Mistress called me. As I slept, She told me to come to Donelle to aid in the great work."

Dreams, then; but more than just dreams, for the crowd of travellers was too large and too varied to be made up solely of religious fanatics. This fellow wore a cape embroidered in red, and his high leather boots were as well made as the slippers of courtiers in Valles. The band of his broad-brimmed hat was saffron silk and trailed behind him, and he wore a three-tiered gorget of gold and translucent stones.

A wealthy man might drop everything to follow God's call, but Ilna very much doubted that a fop—who remained a fop—would do so.

"Who's in charge of the, the great work?" Ilna said. She didn't know how much help the names of the chief conspirators would be to Garric and the others, but she might as well ask.

"Lord Congin!" a man called from the road. "Where's your horse, milord?"

"There it is!" another called, this time a woman. "Look, it's over by the wall!"

"The Mistress is in charge of the great work," the man said. "We are servitors doing the Mistress's bidding."

Three men and a woman wearing saffron ribbons from their shoulders trotted purposefully toward Ilna and their master. Several more men, coarsely garbed without the ribbon livery, continued to drive a train of packhorses toward the gate. They glanced only occasionally at their superiors.

Alecto wiped the pentacle away with a swift motion of her foot. Lord Congin looked wide-eyed first at her, then Ilna. He would've fallen backward if a retainer hadn't caught him.

"What have you done to his lordship?" shrilled the female servant. "He has no business with an animal like you!"

Ilna caught Alecto's wrist before it came up with the bronze dagger—as it surely would have done. To the servant Ilna said, "Go on your way. Now."

She stepped in front of Alecto so that she could release the wild girl's wrist and take the hank of cords into her hands instead. Her eyes met the servant's. Lord Congin had his color back and was talking in puzzlement to the male retainers. The woman backed to rejoin them, and the whole party resumed their course to the gate.

"Can we leave this city now?" Alecto said.

"No," said Ilna. "We'll go in and see what more we can learn."

She had no money, and Alecto probably didn't know what money was, but it shouldn't be hard to find work with all this influx to care for.

There might not be time before the full moon to get a message back to Garric and Tenoctris in Valles, but that didn't mean Ilna's presence here was useless. Not if this Mistress had a neck that a noose could wrap.

Only six of the bandits besides Garric, Vascay, and Hakken had come out to the boathouse to hear Metron describe his plan for releasing Thalemos from the Spike. The others preferred ignorance to being close to wizardry when they didn't have to be.

Hakken wouldn't have been present either if he weren't one of those who'd be entering the prison.

Metron stood on the dock with the bandits facing him in a semicircle. Tint was splashing in the shallows nearby, pulling up cattails and stripping out the pith to eat. Garric looked around the willow-bordered lake. It was a sad place, even by daylight. He said, "Why here?"

It might be that the reason involved the creature Metron had been speaking to in the night. Garric wore his sword, and Hame carried the signal horn since Halophus was back in the stables.

The wizard shrugged. "To make my task easier," he said. "I worked a great spell here when I hid underwater, and last night I came back while you all slept—"

Did Metron know he'd been watched? He didn't seem to care one way or the other.

"—and worked another, gaining us allies for later in our quest. A place holds some of the power that's evoked in it, so this little demonstration will take less effort."

He seated himself cross-legged at the foot of the dock,

his back to the lake's reed-choked margin, and began scribing the planks with his athame. Vascay looked at Garric; Garric gave a brief nod.

Tenoctris had described power lingering at sites of previous wizardry—and at sites of death and slaughter—just as Metron said. The difference was that Tenoctris had warned it was a danger which could cause a wizard to act in unintended fashions with disastrous results; Metron was concerned only with increasing the power of his spells.

Garric smiled faintly, his hand on the ball pommel of his sword. That didn't change anything; he hadn't trusted Metron's judgment from the first.

"You've got somebody else to break into the Spike so we don't have to ourself?" Hakken said. There was hope in his voice, though he was obviously worried by Metron's preparations.

Without lifting his athame from the soft wood the wizard had drawn a seven-pointed star, then bounded it with a circle. He worked freehand and with a skill that made Garric's lips purse.

"My art will aid you," Metron said. "But not that way."

He sounded condescending to Garric, but Hakken probably found reassurance in the wizard's delivery. "The allies I spoke of will join us after Lord Thalemos is free. They'll help us to establish Lord Thalemos on the throne of Laut."

Garric thought that something else had almost slipped off the wizard's tongue. He was hiding something, though he might simply want to avoid frightening the unsophisticated bandits. Metron must be very tired from the wizardry he'd performed; and he must be a very powerful wizard indeed.

"Go on," Garric said. There was no point in pressing Metron on questions where there was no way of telling what, or which, lies he was telling. "Show us what we're to do."

Metron looked up, meeting Garric's eyes over the figures he'd drawn. The wizard smiled, but his expression only made Garric think about Tint's warning: *He like you for food, maybe.*

Metron took the sapphire ring out of his pouch and set it in the middle of the symbol. The stone was a sparkle too small to have shape.

Without writing words of power around the circle as Garric expected, the wizard said, "*Ammo ammonio hermitaris....*" His athame dipped toward the ring at each syllable, making the ivory blade a suppliant to the jewel's majesty. "*Apa apalla apallasso....*"

Fog lifted from the marshy ground beneath the dock. It grew darker, more solid. It tightened into a column as sinuous as a snake's body, then coalesced in the form of a building in the air above Metron's circle.

Metron's voice sank as he murmured a few words more. His athame continued to beat a fixed rhythm in the air, but his mouth smiled triumphantly as he looked up at the arc of spectators.

"The Spike," he said. "Built in the center of Durassa by the first Intercessor as her palace and workroom . . . and as a prison."

Fog continued to condense into the image. The building, a cylindrical structure in a walled garden, took on texture and the streaky gray/pink color of banded schist. The sheer-sided tower had no doors or windows, but a covered passage ran from the gate in the enclosure wall to the base of the tower.

"The outer wall should be no difficulty for active men like yourselves," Metron said with a greasy laugh. "Even less so for your companion, Master Gar."

Coarse bushes, vines, and—along the low-lying side opposite the entrance passage—bamboo appeared on the image, clothing the outer circuit of the wall. Only the twenty feet or so to either side of the gateway was clear.

Metron's left index finger indicated places where shrubbery completely concealed the stonework; his right hand continued to beat time with the athame. The wizard controlled his breathing carefully, but Garric could see strain in his face and the sweat beading at his hairline.

"They don't keep it up," Vascay said, nodding in recollection. "Occasionally Echeon sends out a squad of Protectors to cut back the worst of it, but he can't hire groundskeepers in the usual way."

"I don't bloody blame them!" Hakken muttered.

"Inside the garden . . ." Metron continued, "are dangers that you could not pass without my art to help you."

Vascay raised an eyebrow. Garric felt his own spirit quiver at the implied challenge.

He grinned at himself. What Metron said was probably true. The wizard might have been foolish to word the matter in quite that fashion in the midst of armed men whose lives had made them hard even if they didn't start out that way; but Garric would be a much greater fool if he let himself react to empty words.

Metron gestured, filling the space between the outer wall and the tower with carefully manicured vegetation. Trees stood in rounds of bright-colored flowers; hedges snaked and branched like water running across flat ground, sometimes encircling more flowers; and one star-shaped bed was of translucent, bell-shaped plants that looked more like jellyfish than anything Garric had seen before on dry land.

Tint wandered back, cleaning her teeth with a fingernail and holding an opened cattail for Garric in case he was hungry. It was probably an exceptionally fine cattail. . . .

Tint rubbed against his leg; he scratched the coarse fur between her shoulder blades in response. The more contact Garric had with the beastgirl the less human she seemed, but he'd have found his wizard-imposed exile much harder to bear without Tint's presence.

"Is that really what the gardens look like over the wall?" Toster said. The big man knuckled his beard with a look of deep puzzlement.

"It is," Metron said. "What I show you here is the thing itself, not an image of the thing."

"Then who keeps them up?" Toster said bluntly. "That's expert work, that is. My old dad would've been proud as could be to have Lord Kelshak's maze come out so neat and no bare holly twigs."

"The garden cares for itself," Metron said. His smile looked strained under its superiority, but the wizard was too proud to suggest an end to idle questions. "No human enters it, nor could a human survive without the help of one such as myself."

Garric didn't speak, but it was one of the times he regretted no longer having Carus in his mind to share a silent comment. A man really confident in his power wouldn't have gone to the lengths Metron did to pose before a gang of bandits.

The wizard cleared his throat, and resumed, "When I've brought you through the gardens—"

"You haven't said just how you *are* going to bring us through the gardens," Hakken said. "Are we supposed to haul you over the wall with us?"

"In a manner of speaking you're correct," Metron said. "I'll provide you—"

His eyes met Garric's.

"I'll provide Master Gar . . ." he went on. He brought a crystal disk on a silvery neck chain out from under his robe. "With this. I will be within it, working my art as required."

Everyone looked at Garric. He shrugged. "Go on," he said.

He closed Gar's callused right hand into a fist, wishing he didn't feel so completely alone and adrift. He wondered how long it would be before he was back with his friends, in his proper world.

How long it would be, and whether it would ever be again.

"When we've reached the tower," Metron said, letting the disk fall against his chest, "we will climb it."

"It'd be easier to go through the wall, it seems to me," Vascay said. "Not easy. But easier."

"Easy, yes, but useless," the wizard said. "The lower floor is a guardhouse. The floor above it holds the kitchen and is guarded as well. The two floors above *that* are the Intercessor's private apartments and workroom . . . and Lord Thalemos is held in the prison levels still higher in the building. Shall we not start where we want to go, my good man?"

"You figure we can throw a line to the top and climb up it?" Hakken said. He squinted in consideration. "We might could at that, but it'd have to be a light grappling hook and a bloody thin line."

"No matter how sharp the hook was, it would find no purchase on top of the tower," Metron said. "There is no parapet, and the stone, as you will see, is smooth as glass."

He tried to sound portentous, but the effort of wizardry was making him wheeze. "Nonetheless," he continued, "my art will enable you to climb to the upper doorway, from which you will enter to release Lord Thalemos."

"Are there jailers up there?" Vascay asked. "There must be."

"There are no jailers," Metron said. "No human enters the upper levels save for prisoners and the Intercessor himself . . . and the Intercessor is no longer fully human. Echea made allies who were not men, and over the centuries her line has swerved closer to the line of those the Intercessors' power depends on."

Vascay looked at his men, his gaze finishing with Garric. "Any more questions?" he asked.

"When do we go?" Garric said.

"Tomorrow at midnight," said the wizard. He stuck his athame point down in the middle of the scribed figure. The image above it dissolved into a bucketful of water, splashing on the dock and draining through the slats.

"Tomorrow at midnight it is," Vascay said. His eyes were still on Garric.

Garric nodded. He rubbed the knot of muscle between Tint's shoulder blades. He wished he understood; but for now it would have to be enough to act.

The high-pitched shriek brought Cashel to his feet from a dream in which he explained to Sharina that he owned all the sheep on the hillside below. "Tilphosa!" he shouted, his staff crosswise before him.

If the sailors'd harmed the girl after he'd warned them, then they could pray to the Sister for mercy. They'd get none from Cashel or-Kenset.

Tilphosa jumped up also. She *eep*ed and threw herself flat as an iron butt cap whistled past her ear. Cashel'd nearly knocked her silly on his way to rescue her.

It was bright day, not much short of noon. The light hadn't kept Cashel from sleeping like an ox after plowing, but it made it easier for him to get his bearings now that he was awake. Tilphosa was fine, just flattened on all fours as she looked up cautiously to judge where the quarterstaff was. The sailors were gone, all three of them.

The scream repeated. Now Captain Mounix was bawling in terror besides. The noise all came from the direction of the waterfall—and the birches. No surprise there.

"Stay—" Cashel said as he started lumbering toward the cries. His mouth closed. *Stay here alone, where who-knows-what might be waiting for a chance to grab you?*

"Duzi!" he said in frustration. "Do as you like!"

Which, being Tilphosa, she was probably going do no

matter what he said. She loped along at Cashel's side, discreetly beyond where she'd be swiped by the staff. She held her chunk of rock up by her shoulder, ready to chop or throw.

Captain Mounix was in the grove, his back to them. He was tight up against a birch, hammering it with both fists and bellowing. The branches weren't holding him or anything like that so far as Cashel could see.

"What's the matter?" Cashel said. Ousseau and Hook were here too, clasping other trees. Hook was the one who screamed like a boar being gelded. "What're—"

He grabbed Mounix by the shoulder and tried to pull him back. Mounix roared in pain and terror.

The nymph he'd been embracing trilled silvery laughter. She'd looked completely human at Cashel's first glance, but her slender body was becoming wood and bark again even more swiftly than he'd watched her form when first he'd entered the grove the previous dawn.

"Don't bother with her, big boy," called the nymph from a nearby birch. Her fully human body stood out from the tree trunk. "She's taken, but I'm not."

She laughed with demonic cruelty. Cashel looked at her, then stared down at the captain, his tunic lifted and groin pressed closed to the bole of the tree.

Oh. It wasn't the nymph's arms that held Mounix; but he was held, and held beyond any easy way of freeing. The captain's eyes closed, and his whole body was going rigid.

Cashel stepped away. He drew his knife while he thought things over. The quarterstaff wasn't going to solve the problem, and even if he'd had a proper axe he wasn't sure he could cut Mounix loose. Not safely, anyway.

Tilphosa stepped close to look. "Don't—" Cashel said, but she paid him no more attention than he'd expected she would. She lifted her rock high in both hands and slammed it as hard as her strength allowed into where the nymph's face had been.

The stone flew out of Tilphosa's grip, bouncing from Mounix's shoulder and falling to the ground. The captain paid no attention to the blow. His body shuddered, then froze; and shuddered again. The dent in the soft birchwood filled and began to re-cover itself with bark.

Cashel could see Hook in profile. He was silent now. His eyes were open but blank, and his arms were limp. The sword he'd taken from the captain lay beside him, its blade broken a hand's breadth below the hilt. He must have been hacking at the nymph who'd trapped him, but any damage to the tree had healed completely. Bark covered the whole trunk and was beginning to grow over Hook as well.

"Cashel?" Tilphosa said in a small voice. "I think that must be Ousseau over there."

She pointed toward the other side of the grove. Cashel could see cloth on the ground, maybe a torn tunic.

"He's just a lump against the tree, now," she said. She closed her eyes. "Cashel, can we leave?"

Cashel put his knife back in its horn sheath and walked over to Hook. He picked up the sword hilt and handed it to Tilphosa.

"Here," he said. "It's not much, but it's better than what you had. Let's get going."

All of the birches had reverted to the look of simple trees, but Cashel heard a tinkle of laughter as he and the girl walked quickly back the way they'd come.

"I don't know where we're going," Cashel said.

"I don't care where we're going," Tilphosa said. "We're going away, Cashel. We're going away!"

"They put this up quickly," Sharina said as she mounted the steps to the wooden platform built out over the south gate into the palace compound. "It seems as solid as the palace wall, though."

The supports were bamboo tied into a lattice as strong and open as a huntsman's net. Reise, Garric's majordomo, had provided tapestries to give a look of luxury to the plank floors and railings. The covered treads made Sharina step carefully, but she couldn't have seen her feet while wearing court dress anyway.

"Builders use the same sort of scaffolding to set keystones," King Carus muttered. "I guess it ought to hold a few people who aren't too badly overweight."

He punched his stomach with the heel of his left hand. Despite Carus' insistence on a daily hour of sword practice, he complained that the round of meetings filling the rest of his time had him as badly out of shape as a calf stalled to provide veal for a banquet.

"We need a proper stand for public announcements, though," he added. "I don't think a thousand people can see me from here, and a king ought to be seen!"

"Perhaps the Customs Tower in Harbor Square?" suggested Liane, the last of their party. "With the booths cleared from the square, most of Valles could gather there."

Lord Attaper stood at the base of the stairs with a platoon of his men. The additional Blood Eagles in full armor outside the gate concealed the heads of their javelins with gilt knobs. They were a guard of honor unless something went wrong, whereupon the knobs would come off very quickly.

"You want to train people to think of me when they see the tax collector?" Carus said with a laugh. "Maybe not, hey? But some sort of tower down by the square might work."

Chancellor Royhas, Lord Waldron, and four attendants already stood on the platform, facing the steps. The nobles bowed to greet the king. In past generations the servants would have knelt, but Garric had decreed that no man in *his* kingdom knelt to another in his public capacity. Today bows—rather deeper than those of the nobles—sufficed for the servants as well.

The crowd shouted and waved as Carus appeared. The cheers started with people sitting on the tiles and in dormer windows, but as quickly as flames crossed a field of stubble it passed to those packing the boulevard below. Ribbons, pennons, and kerchiefs painted with fanciful portraits of the royal household fluttered in hands and on staffs.

Carus might think the crowd was small compared to his memories of the public squares of ancient Carcosa, but then the Isles had been united for a thousand years and the capital's facilities were built to serve the whole kingdom. It amazed Sharina, though, the numbers and the enthusiasm both. Many were crying, "Princess Sharina!" at the top of their lungs, and flailing the air with what they fondly imagined was her painted likeness. . . .

The boulevard leading to the palace gate, and the street that crossed it paralleling the compound's high brick wall, were full of spectators for as far as Sharina could see. The buildings were of two and three stories, with sloped tile roofs and occasionally a dome. Normally thatched or fabric awnings shaded merchandise on display in front of the shops, but these had been taken down—or torn down—when criers went through the city announcing that Prince Garric would speak at midday in front of the palace.

An usher in a black robe with scarlet sleeves stepped to the railing, raising his hands to the crowd. They cheered even louder. He chopped his hands for silence—and most people continued cheering.

Laughing with gusty good humor, King Carus put his left hand on the attendant's shoulder and gently moved the embarrassed man back. Carus hopped *onto* the rail, balancing there on the balls of his feet.

Liane put her fist to her mouth. Royhas cried, "If you break your neck—"

"Relax, chancellor," Carus called over his shoulder. His shout was barely audible over the shrieks of amazement from the crowd. "I've climbed more masts than many who call themselves sailors."

Carus made a megaphone of his hands and bellowed, "Silence!"

Few if any could hear him, but they understood the pantomime. An active quiet, more like the hush of a forest than of a human gathering, fell over the crowd.

"Citizens of the Isles!" Carus shouted. "My people!"

The other three attendants on the platform were scribes, this at Liane's insistence. They began scribbling madly when Carus started to speak, two on wax tablets and the third with an ink-brush on a roll of paper cleverly mounted on the bottom of a thin plank. By nightfall full copies of Carus' speech would be on notice boards in every district of Valles.

The king stood with his fists on his hips, arms akimbo. Though Sharina stood behind him, she'd seen the ancient king's expressions often enough now—so different from her brother's, though wearing the same flesh—to imagine the broad reckless grin he would be wearing. His posture was relaxed. She suspected he could do handstands on the railing if he wanted to.

"There's those who'd bring the kingdom down in blood!" Carus said. "They'll not be permitted to. Lord Waldron—"

He reached his right arm back toward the army commander. Waldron was already as straight and stiff as a swordblade; he quivered noticeably at the recognition, however.

"—and I will see to that, at the head of the forces of the Isles. The kingdom has a sword, now. It's your sons and brothers, not strangers from abroad, who man the fleet and the army."

The crowd cheered again. Sharina suddenly understood where Garric had gotten the skill with which she'd watched him move groups of people since he came to Ornifal. Here was the man who'd taught him, using his voice and his posture with the same practiced ease that whipped his sword through a crowd of enemies.

Carus held his hands up for silence—and got it, while the scribes wrote madly to complete their shorthand accounts of his previous words. The usher on the platform with him, a middle-aged man, watched with undisguised envy.

"The government, under our monarch Valence the Third—"

Carus was as careful as Garric and his ministers to pay lip service to the fiction that Valence remained the King of the Isles. Officially the king's adopted son Prince Garric merely handled day-to-day chores.

"—will remain in the capable hands of our council, headed by Chancellor Royhas."

Again Carus reached back without looking behind him, this time gesturing toward Royhas with his left hand. The chancellor's court robes of creamy silk brocade were hemmed with scarlet in token of his position. He remained almost impassive. The smile that lifted the corner of his mouth could only be seen by someone on the platform with him.

The crowd below was too thick for peddlers to work it. Trays of candies, water jars with cups of varied sizes, and bundles of cloth and metal trinkets were mired in the thick mass of spectators. There'd be time enough for sales when the assembly started to disperse.

Carus silenced the roars with another gesture. He half turned and, with a roguish smile, gestured Liane forward. She looked surprised, but she obeyed.

Carus stepped down backwards as easily as he'd hopped up. He took Liane's right hand in his left and raised it. The crowd had already shouted itself hoarse, but people tried to outdo themselves until Carus lowered his arm and Liane's.

Lord Royhas glanced sideways toward Sharina and lifted an eyebrow. She shook her head minutely. She had no more idea than the chancellor did—or Liane, either one—of what the man in Garric's body intended to do next.

"My people!" Carus said. "My fellow citizens, my friends! There are decisions that only a person, not a government, can make. Here in your presence I announce my betrothal to Lady Liane bos-Benliman and her appointment as my surrogate in all matters that would otherwise have to wait for my return from campaign. Give her your honor and your obedience, for her sake and for my own!"

Liane's mouth was open, but any words she'd intended to speak had dried in her throat. Carus caught her by the waist in both hands, kissed her, and then lifted her above him in a display of strength and agility while the crowd thundered.

He set Liane down. Sharina stepped to the couple's side and embraced both of them. Liane's body was rigid, and her expression was sheer horror.

"Don't worry, child," Carus said, grinning triumphantly. "This won't make any difference to you till Garric comes back, save that you won't have the trouble with the nobility you'd otherwise face when I made you my viceroy."

"But . . ." Liane said, her eyes wide. "But when Garric *does* come back . . ."

"He'll have to go through with the marriage," Sharina said, completing the thought Liane was too embarrassed to articulate. "Which is just as well, *I* think."

"So do I," Carus said. Royhas and Waldron had hesitated; now both men stepped forward to offer congratulations. Carus waved them back, then bent to speak to the women in a voice no one else could hear over the crowd's shouted joyfulness.

"A king *must* marry," the ancient king said. "Your Garric"—he nodded to Liane—"is a brave fellow by any standards, but being raised by a she-wolf like his mother Lora would put anybody off marriage. I'm doing what a good regent ought to do, preparing the kingdom for the rightful ruler who'll succeed me."

Putting an arm each around Sharina and Liane, King Carus stood for a moment looking out over the ecstatic citizenry.

"Besides," he added, barely audible even to Sharina. "I like the lad!"

Chapter Thirteen

That will do for now," Ilna said, turning over to dry the large pottery vessel she'd just scrubbed clean—judging "clean" with her fingertips. The sun had been down for hours, and the innkeeper believed the cookfires gave enough light to work by without the expense of lamp oil.

"Hey!" snarled the cook, the innkeeper's younger sister. "I didn't tell you you could go!"

Cooking for an inn was a hot, brutal job at the best of times, and the huge influx of guests had made it worse. Ilna didn't suppose the woman's temper had ever been good, however.

"No," Ilna said. "I told *you* I was going, back to my bed in the stable for some rest before the ceremony tonight. I've done enough work this day for a week's keep, as you know well."

Thoughtfully she took one of the round loaves of bread which the baker's boy had just delivered. Ilna had been snacking throughout the day's labor, but she didn't know how Alecto was making out in the stables.

Besides, the loaf would be a handy thing to have if she and the wild girl needed to flee.

The cook opened her mouth to snarl but thought better of it. Normally she'd have bullied a girl like Ilna without mercy, but the slim stranger had an air about her that the cook didn't care to push. Instead she said, "If you see Arris, tell him to get his lazy butt in here."

The kitchen was a separate structure at the back of the inn yard, built of stone with a tile roof. The main building, two full stories and a dormer, was half-timbered under shingles, because there wasn't as much risk of fire. Ilna and Alecto were to lodge in the stable loft in return for their labor, though the cook had seemed willing enough to keep Ilna at work till daybreak.

The inn yard was full of coaches, their tongues lifted against the walls to make as much room as possible. The drivers and some of the passengers slept in the vehicles, but all ate food prepared in the inn's kitchen.

The cook's cousin, the ostler, had been glad to hire Alecto. Space for animals in Donelle was as tight as that for humans: a touch and a murmur from the wild girl had calmed a pair of horses restive at being squeezed into the same stall. *One beast knowing another,* Ilna had thought; but whatever the reason, Alecto's skill with animals was remarkable.

"Hey, girl, have a drink with us?" a man called from the group clustered against the oven in the yard for warmth on a cool evening.

Ilna ignored the comment, picking her way between wagons parked so that the wheels nearly interlocked. The man let it drop. Despite Donelle's crowded conditions, there was very little disorder—and less fun. The men packing the inn yard acted like castaways from a shipwreck, not the boisterous, cheerful strangers who filled Barca's Hamlet during the Sheep Fair.

Though the stable door was open, an overflow of horses kept the interior much warmer than the night outside. The animals whickered and occasionally made timbers creak by leaning against the sides of their stalls, but overall Ilna got a feeling of peace when she entered.

The door of the small office and tack room was closed. Snores through the panel proved the ostler was present and undisturbed. Unexpectedly, the light of an oil lamp wavered from the half-loft where Ilna and Alecto were to sleep.

"Alecto?" Ilna called. She didn't speak loudly, afraid to rouse either the horses or the ostler. He wouldn't be pleased to see an open flame in his hayloft; Ilna wasn't happy with her companion's idiocy either. Didn't the folk of Hartrag's village know that dried grass burns?

There wasn't an answer, but Ilna heard the rhythms of a voice chanting. Face set, she took the cords out of her sleeve and began knotting them as she climbed the simple ladder pegged to the stable wall.

The lamp hung from a truss in a loose web made from a bridle and a cord twisted from rye straw. Alecto had placed it so that it gave her the angle she wanted both on the figure she'd scribed on the wooden floor and the blade of the athame she used to reflect the gleam into the eyes of the man clumsily undressing before her.

Alecto was nude. Sweat from wizardry and the stables' warmth dripped down the valley between her breasts. She continued to chant, giving no sign that she saw or cared about Ilna's presence.

She'll run to fat in a few years! Ilna thought. And perhaps she would, but for the time being Alecto's body had a muscular lushness that Ilna could only envy.

The man was Lord Congin, the fellow they'd stopped on his way into the city. He'd given Alecto a look of disgust when he came out from under the spell she'd cast on him. Apparently she'd taken that as a challenge.

Ilna understood the wild girl's reaction. She'd have felt the same way under similar circumstances, not that the circumstances could possibly ever be similar.

"Let him go!" Ilna said. Seeing Alecto do *this* brought back memory of the lives Ilna os-Kenset had destroyed in Erdin in that way, using the skill a demon had taught her in Hell.

The lithe, sweating wild woman stopped chanting and looked at Ilna past Lord Congin's arm. She smiled, breathing hard. "Get your own, girl!" she said. "Or wait till I'm done with this one."

"No," said Ilna. She stepped forward, her hands forming a hollow before her. "Take however many men you want, but I won't let you use your art to do it."

Alecto laughed like a cat wailing. "Fool!" she said. "How will you stop me?" She shifted the athame, sending the lamp's reflection across Ilna's face.

Bronze walls clanged around Ilna's mind. Every surface mirrored Alecto's cruelly laughing face. The walls slid closer, squeezing down on Ilna's selfhood.

She'd expected that from the wild girl, that or worse. Ilna no longer had conscious control of her actions, but her fingers were free. They opened, displaying to Alecto the pattern they'd knotted as Ilna climbed the stairs.

Ilna heard the scream. She tried to open her eyes and found they were already open, peering through a dissolving bronze haze.

Alecto's dagger clattered to the loft's plank floor. She pawed at her groin with both hands, shrieking, "What did you do? I've grown shut! I'm not a woman!"

"What?" bellowed Lord Congin. "Where am—what's going on here?"

He tried to walk and tripped over the linen breeches he'd been taking off when the power of the spell left him. His arms flailed. Only Ilna's quick grab kept Congin from knocking the lamp into the hay still baled around them.

"You—" Alecto cried.

Ilna slapped her, and said, "Be silent!"

Alecto flopped back. Her eyes were open, but she said nothing. She seemed stunned; not so much by the blow as by realizing that Ilna's power had easily overmastered hers.

"Get your clothes on and get out," Ilna to Lord Congin. "No, on second thought, get out and take your clothes with you. Now!"

The half-dressed noble gaped at her, then stumbled to the ladder with his breeches and outer tunic dragging behind him. Ilna thought he was going to plunge headfirst to the stable floor, but he managed to get his feet under him after all. Small loss if he *had* broken his neck, of course.

"As for you," she said to Alecto, "you'll be all right. Listen to what I say next time."

"You said you weren't a wizard," the wild girl whispered. She pressed the back of her hand against her cheek where Ilna had slapped her.

"I said you're not to use your art for *that* purpose," Ilna snapped.

She was breathing hard and her right hand stung. Her fingers picked apart the knots of the pattern she held in her left hand. Her eyes held Alecto's; neither spoke.

"The moon'll be up soon," Ilna said at last. "We'll watch where the leaders, the priests, go when they leave the temple tonight."

"You said you weren't a wizard . . ." Alecto repeated, but her whisper was little more than the movement of her swollen lips.

* * *

Garric waited, smiling faintly and controlling his breathing in order to keep the other bandits calm. A cousin of Hame's was a watchman for this district of Durassa. He'd provided a key to this vacant shop and made sure he was nowhere around when the gang arrived after dark.

A single lamp wick burned in the side room where Metron made his final preparations and Vascay waited. The litter of flaking plaster, packing materials, and unglazed potsherds here in the front of the shop gave no hint of the business which had once been carried on in it.

"The Protectors're probably waiting for us to come out to grab us all," Ademos said, glaring around the circle of his fellows. "If they could wait for us when we didn't know where we were going to land the boat, they'll sure know we're sitting here beside the Spike!"

"Metron said he was going to hide us from the Intercessor," Hame said. He held four equal-sized lengths of bamboo, the ends coned male and female to lock into a continuous rod twenty feet long. He'd loosened the cord binding them so that his fingers could shift one rod over another repeatedly, as though he were plaiting cords into a rope.

Hame was as brave as the next man even in this company, but he knew his cropped ears marked him for execution if he were caught for a second time. That fear was working on him, though he'd volunteered to be one of the pair who waited at the base of the wall for Garric and his companions to return

"*Metron* said," Ademos sneered. "Metron! You trust him?"

Garric reached out. Ademos tried to jerk back but wasn't quick enough: Garric grabbed him by the throat.

"It could be that the world will end in the next moment,

Ademos," Garric said pleasantly. At his side Tint growled like a saw cutting stone.

Garric wasn't squeezing hard, but he knew the red-haired bandit could feel the fingers around his throat trembling with the emotions in Garric's blood. "It will surely end for you if you mouth any more silliness about what the Intercessor will do, or what Metron can do, or any other things of which you know absolutely *nothing*. Do you understand?"

Ademos nodded, his eyes wide. Garric released him.

"We Brethren don't fight amongst ourself," Halophus muttered toward a wall from which the shelf pegs had been pulled.

"Shut up, Halophus," Toster said; not angry, but not expecting an argument either.

Halophus didn't give him one. He forced an embarrassed smile and buffed the curve of his signal horn with a piece of cloth.

"By the *Shepherd*, I wish we was done with the business," Hakken said. As he spoke, his fingers checked the knots of the rope ladder to have something to do.

Red wizardlight bloomed, faded, then vanished in the side chamber. The flash seemed bright for the moment, but it didn't dim the vision of Garric's dark-adapted eyes. Vascay came out of the room, holding Metron's pendant by its silver chain.

"Here it is," Vascay said. Garric couldn't see his face with the light behind him, but his voice sounded tired. "You'd better get moving."

Garric stepped forward and took the pendant. Within the crystal was the tiny figure of Metron. He held his athame in one hand; with the thumb and forefinger of the other, he pinched what could only be the sapphire ring.

"Quickly!" squeaked a voice that Garric heard only in his mind. The image of Metron gestured with his athame.

"I can only remain conscious outside my body for a limited time!"

Garric hung the chain around his neck, his face impassive. The mount was in the shape of a spider whose legs encircled the crystal. The design repelled Garric, but he wasn't wearing it for the looks of the thing.

"Yes, let's go," he said.

Mortised shutters gripped by interlocked iron rods closed the front of the shop. Toster at the pedestrian door put his hands to his mouth and squalled like a cat. Prada, on watch from the rooftop, squalled back a moment later.

Hame slipped out, carrying his rods in one hand and a hog's bladder of narcotic dust in the other. Garric followed with Tint pressing close to his side. In the street he glanced over his shoulder. Beyond Toster and Hakken, he saw Vascay waiting before he returned to watch over the wizard's soulless body in the other room. The chieftain bent sightly forward to massage his stump above the wooden leg.

The shop faced a well-travelled street, but only an alley separated the side from the Spike's ten-foot outer wall. The spot Garric and Vascay together had chosen looked the same in reality as it had when Metron formed the image. The stonework was still solid, but the stems of the wisteria climbing it were strong enough to allow even a clumsy man to reach the top. The vines couldn't hide a man by daylight, but at night they'd break up the outline of Hame and Toster as they waited for Garric's party to return.

Toster laced his hands into a stirrup. Garric stepped into the cup. Toster straightened like a catapult arm, lofting Garric knee high to the top of the wall. He caught himself by his hands, then curled his feet under him and waited.

Tint sprang to Garric's side with a rustle of foliage. She sniffed the garden below, and said, "Bad place, Gar. We leave now?"

Garric heard the piping voice of the wizard in his amulet, chanting words of power that rang as cold as starlight in his mind: "*Dabathaa soumar soumarta max. . . .*"

Hakken came up the wisteria, without Toster's boost but not as easily as Tint had. He looked over his shoulder, then lifted the bladder and bamboo rods by the thin cord tied to his leather belt.

The moon wouldn't rise for another quarter of the night, but stars in the clear sky gleamed from the tower and outlined the garden's varied plantings. Tint gripped Garric's shoulder with her right hand. With the other startlingly long arm she pointed into the clump of giant bromeliads directly beneath them. Her fingers gripped like a stonemason's tongs.

"Gar!" she said. "Gar! There, *teeth*!"

A funnel of red wizardlight formed in the air, pointing down into the bromeliads. For a moment Garric thought the light was the threat Tint warned of; then he realized it was Metron's wizardry duplicating what the beastgirl's nostrils and keen ears had already uncovered.

"A creature waits *there*," Metron squeaked. "It heard you on the other side of the wall. Strike it down before you enter the garden."

Garric reached over his shoulder and touched the hilt of his sword. He wore it across his back tonight, the scabbard's upper set of rings fastened to the top of a bandolier and the lower set lashed tightly to his belt. It was the way Carus had worn his blade on raids and in sea fights, where a scabbard hung in the ordinary fashion might have tangled with his legs. . . .

"Don't be a hero, Gar," Hakken said sourly. He was fitting the bamboo rods together, balancing the whole on his knees as he squatted. "That's what we got this along for."

"Gar go?" Tint said.

Garric lifted her fingers from his shoulder. He'd have

bruises in the morning. "We're going to climb that tower, Tint," he said. "We can't go till we've gotten Lord Thalemos out of the tower."

He'd have bruises if he were *alive* in the morning. What would happen to the soul of Garric or-Reise if the body of Gar the Monkey Boy died here this night?

"Help me hold this," Hakken directed. He'd put the four rods together and now was binding the hog's bladder onto one end with a twist of sinew. "I've never used this from up in the air like this. It's not heavy, but the length makes it seem more."

"Where do you get the poison?" Garric said, holding his right arm out like a branch for Hakken to lay the bamboo across. The thin tube's leverage made it feel like a tree bole.

"Dust from cave mushrooms on the east of the island," Hakken muttered as he adjusted the weapon. "Bloody rare, and *bloody* dangerous to gather, let me tell you. We took this bag from a District Commander of the Protectors. What he used it for I don't know, but he didn't need it after Hame cut his throat."

"Get on with it!" Metron's attenuated voice demanded.

Hakken looked at the crystal. He raised his eyes to Garric's. "Shut him off, will you? Or by the Sister—"

Garric gestured with his free hand. "Get on with it," he said curtly. "And Metron, don't make pointless noise."

Hakken grimaced and sighted along the rod, bringing the free end directly under the cone of light. His eye still close to the slowly wobbling tube, he reached back with his left hand to the bladder and gave it a sharp squeeze.

Nothing seemed to happen. Garric frowned and opened his mouth to speak.

"Don't move!" Hakken snapped. "With the tube this long, it takes—"

A puff of dust, colorless in the starlight, spurted from

the far end of the tube. It spread as it sank into the bromeliads.

"All right, let it go," Hakken said, dropping his end of the bamboo. "And by the Lady's mercy, *don't* stir the stuff up when we get down."

The bromeliads' sword-shaped leaves were so long the points curved back to the ground. They thrashed violently. Garric snatched at his sword hilt.

A creature lurched out. It was the size of a man and walked on two legs, but its lizard tail balanced a head with a seawolf's long jaws. Garric felt Gar's fearful spirit cringe as the boy remembered the fangs that had pierced his brain.

The creature flopped forward. Its hind legs slashed the ground for a moment with claws like sickles; then it was still.

"Don't waste time!" Metron said. "Get me to the ground at once so that I can scry a path for you!"

In miniature, the wizard's voice had the tone and self-importance of an angry wren. Nasty little birds, wrens; egg-thieves and bullies when they could get away with it, though amusing to have around at times.

Hakken grimaced as he set the rope ladder's hooks on the face of the wall. Garric nodded and jumped to the ground without bothering to lower himself by his hands first. The turf was springy, and the modest drop wouldn't have mattered even with rock at the bottom. They didn't need the ladder to enter the garden—or for themselves, to leave it, unless one of them was badly injured—but there was no telling what condition Thalemos would be in if they freed him.

Garric grinned as Tint landed beside him, so lightly that she scarcely seemed to bend the grass. *When* they freed Thalemos; he'd chastened Ademos for negative speculations.

Hakken walked down the wall, gripping the ladder with

his hands to fix the hooks properly. "Now what?" he whispered, looking around them.

Metron was already chanting. "We wait for him," Garric said, curving his left index finger toward the crystal on his breast.

He drew the sword he'd sharpened carefully before the band left Thalemos' villa for the city. He'd wanted to go over it again as they waited in the shop, but he knew the blade was already as keen as he could make it. Further passes on the whetstone would only remove metal that he might need in the coming hours.

The grass curling over his bare feet had a warm, dry texture that surprised him. It didn't seem to be harmful—Tint would have reacted before now if it were—but it was an unpleasant contrast to the coolness he'd expected. Hakken didn't seem to notice, though the sailor'd worn a look of sour worry since they'd set off from the villa at dusk.

Tint rose on her hind legs and sniffed, then lowered her head and snuffled in a narrow arc across the grass. Garric watched her for a moment, then made his own assessment of the garden.

It wasn't the same place as it had seemed from above. A clump of what might be a kind of yucca—spiked heads on smooth woody trunks—nodded slightly. There was no wind that Garric could feel.

To his left, easily within length of his sword, was a plant with drooping sword-shaped leaves in a low stone coping. Huge white flowers grew within the curtain of foliage, but because the bells hung downward it was only now that Garric noticed them.

Were they turning? Surely they *were* turning, the bells lifting slightly on their stems like some many pale faces rising to stare back at the intruders.

Tint noticed Garric's interest. She jumped upright and caught him by both shoulders, pressing him hard. Her head was turned back to watch the flowers.

"Bad, Gar!" she said. "They lie, they hurt Gar!"

"What do you—" Garric began.

A rank odor made him choke in surprise. Something changed, in his nostrils or in his mind itself. He drew in a deep breath and felt himself relax utterly.

Garric couldn't compare the smell with anything he'd known before. Images cascaded from his memory, every joy he'd known in life. Triumphs, kindnesses done him, friendships, and flashes of insight come upon him from all sides: the day he first opened a volume of Celondre, the evening the sky to the east was ablaze with three keystones of rosy light bleeding from the sun setting on the opposite horizon, the moment he took Liane in his arms for the first time . . .

Tint bit his chest.

"Hey!" Garric shouted. If the lizard had heard them coming over the wall, then there wasn't much hope that whispering would hide their intrusion, but Garric still would've kept his voice down if he'd remembered where he was.

That was the point—he hadn't remembered. The flowers' perfume, now a stench like that of eggs rotting, had carried him into a reverie that would have ended . . .

Hard to tell where it would've ended. It wasn't likely to be a place Garric wanted to be, though.

Hakken, his eyes glazed and drool hanging from his mouth, walked slowly toward the clump of flowers. Garric stepped in front of the sailor and slapped his face left-handed. Hakken staggered back, gasping angrily as he groped for the short-handled axe in his belt.

His nose wrinkled. "By the Lady!" he said. "By the Lady! I've not smelled anything that stunk so bad since we raised the *Erdin Belle* with all the rats that'd drowned in the hold when she foundered!"

"Bad!" repeated Tint. The flowers were slumping back on their stems and starting to close. The odor dissipated as suddenly as it had appeared. If it hadn't been for the beastgirl . . .

Garric hugged Tint to his side, her shoulder against the point of his hip. She purred like a big cat. "Thank you, Tint," Garric said. "You saved our lives."

A moth of red wizardlight flew out of the crystal on Garric's breast. It went arm's length ahead of him, just above the grass, then paused to flutter in a tight figure-eight.

"Follow the guide!" Metron squeaked. "Follow it precisely and don't waste time. The Intercessor's enchantments will react to your presence. What was safe before may close in on you."

Hakken drew his axe and looked at Garric. Garric said, "We're going to walk exactly where the moth flies, Tint." He stepped off, suiting his conduct to his words.

Instead of going directly toward the tower through the loose line of yucca-looking plants, the moth led them to the left around the circuit of the outer wall. The course took them close to the lizard—dead or just unconscious?—and the clump of bromeliads where it had hidden.

Hakken, closely behind Garric, hesitated. "The dust . . . ?" he said. "If we stir—"

"Go on, go on!" piped the wizard. "Do you think I can hold this forever?"

Tint padded past Garric on all fours, glancing to either side but showing no concern about the residue of the spores. Her attention was focused primarily on the yuccas to her right. They quivered, but the beastgirl stayed beyond the trunk's height from the base of the nearest. Garric followed, more reassured by Tint's nonchalance than he was by Metron's wizardry.

The moth's quivering path took it over a bed of flowers that looked like red fangs with spiky black tips. Garric hesitated for a moment. Tint, pacing forward nonchalantly, saw his doubt and stopped also.

"Go on!" Metron said. "I've told you, time—"

The moth circled back like a dog trying to lead its master. Tint, her mind never far from the thought of food, tried to snatch it out of the air. Her fingers slipped harmlessly through the creature of light; she opened her hand and peered at its emptiness with a puzzled expression.

"—is short!"

Garric nodded Tint forward and walked on, reminding himself that things weren't always what they seemed. His feet sank into the loose earth of the bed, finding moisture below; the flowers brushed his shins harmlessly.

The moth jogged to the right, following the flower bed for two paces—for the first time directly toward the tower. The building loomed above, a presence in Garric's peripheral vision though his eyes were trained on the ground.

At the end of the flower bed grew a tree whose swollen trunk lay parallel to the ground for most of its length. Only the finger-thick upper stem was vertical, terminating in a spray of whiplike tendrils. They stiffened as the trio approached; Tint shied back.

The moth turned aside, bobbing over lush turf in the direction of a clump of rushes growing in a crystal-edged pool. Again Tint recoiled. She laid the side of her head on the ground, then hopped back and held Garric.

"Bad!" she said. "Teeth, Gar!"

She stroked his thigh and added pleadingly, "Gar, this bad place. We go away, Gar? Go now?"

Garric looked at the empty lawn. There were no bushes big enough to hide another of the lizards, nor was there any other evident danger. The moth circled and returned, insistently.

"Go on!" Metron said. "Follow the guide, and there's no danger. But quickly, quickly!"

"Tint?" Garric said, his sword held low to the side so that the beastgirl wouldn't accidentally fling herself onto its gleaming edge. "Where's the animal? Where's the teeth?"

"Go on, you fools!" said Metron. "The monkey knows nothing!"

"Gar, what are we going to do?" Hakken said. "Because I don't think we oughta just stand here, you know?"

"There, there!" Tint said, pointing furiously at the unmarked grass. Her long face turned quickly back and forth from Garric to the danger only she could see. "Teeth, Gar, bad!"

Garric stepped forward and swiped his sword in an arc at arm's length. The beastgirl's concern was so persuasive that he expected his edge to *thoonk!* into a monster where he saw only empty air. The blade whistled, meeting nothing.

"Must I drive you with my art?" Metron shrilled. "Shall I raise a wall of flame to sear the flesh from your bones if you will not obey?"

Hakken, muttering a curse, leaped onto the lawn with his axe held up in both hands. The moth danced ahead of him, leading him safely to a bed of Dead-Man's Fingers or some similar translucent fungus. "For the Lady's sake, Gar!" he said. "Come on, won't you?"

Garric stepped forward. Two more steps and—

Tint grabbed Garric by the waist and jerked him backward. Small she might be, but the beastgirl's strength was equal to Garric's own. Two pairs of interlocking fangs, each the length of a man's hand, sliced up through the turf and clashed together where Garric's foot had rested a moment before.

Tint shrieked in terror, hopping up and down. Garric lunged, stabbing into the ground with all his weight behind the thrust. Though the blade curved, its point was directly in line with the hilt. It grated along bone, then sank deep.

The turf shivered. The fangs pulled back with the same silent suddenness as they'd slashed upward. Garric gripped his hilt with both hands to keep the force beneath the ground from twisting the sword away from him.

The blade flexed, then sprang free. The tip was wet with blood turned black by the moonlight. Garric straightened. A line of dimples shivered across the sod as the creature thrashed its escape along the tunnel by which it had attacked.

Metron was yammering something; Garric hadn't time to wonder what. Hakken hopped from one foot to the other, gawping down at the ground in fear that another of the creatures was closing on him unseen. If he wasn't careful, he'd lop his own leg off and save the garden the trouble of killing him.

Garric stepped to the sailor's side and grabbed the axe helve above where Hakken gripped it. "Calm down!" he said.

Hakken tried to pull free. Garric had a weapon in either hand; he shouldered Hakken on the point of the jaw. *That* brought the sailor around; he relaxed and forced a smile to show Garric that it was safe to let him go.

"This place is part of the Sister's realm!" Hakken said, as Garric eased back. He massaged his axe wrist with his free hand, looking around with an expression of renewed disgust.

"You can reach the wall now," said Metron's image. He'd had put aside his haughty manner, at least for the time being. "Wait there while I prepare you for the next stage."

They were within a sword's length of the tower, though a quarter of the way around from where they'd faced it when they entered the garden. Garric had been concentrating on each small stage of the moth's course, so it was a surprise to find they'd actually reached their goal.

Because of Tint, they'd reached their goal.

Garric put his arm around the beastgirl again, and said in a mild voice, "Metron? If you call my friend Tint a monkey again, when I next see your physical body I'm going to beat it within a hair of its life. Understood?"

"Please, Master Gar," squeaked the image. "Time is short."

"Let's get it over with," Garric said to Hakken. The wizard was right, of course, but Garric didn't choose to say that in so many words.

They stepped to the tower, cautiously but without further incident. Plants with huge glossy leaves on soft stems grew against the wall. Nowhere did Garric see vegetation actually climbing the stone.

Metron began to chant again. Garric lifted the crystal from his breast to watch for a moment—the angle at which the amulet hung didn't affect the image within it. The wizard sat cross-legged, his athame dipping and rising to the rhythm of the spell. His other hand held the ring over the figure he'd drawn on the blurred surface before him.

Tint squatted beside Garric, rubbing her shoulder against his thigh and purring. She didn't seem concerned, but she remained fully aware of her surroundings. Her hand shot out unexpectedly and snatched a beetle from the wall to her mouth.

Garric looked at his sword. With a reflex gained during the months King Carus had shared his mind, he broke off one of the great leaves left-handed and folded it between his thumb and fingers. With that for a wiping rag, Garric rubbed the smear of blood from the upper hand's breadth of the steel. He kept the back of the blade to his hand and was careful not to slice his fingertips while getting close to the keen edge.

"*Abrasax,*" said Metron. "*Rayasde belhowa hiweh. . . .*"

Hakken turned from eyeing the tower wall. "What do you think, Gar?" he said. "Is he going to float us up there with, you know, his words? Because it doesn't look to me like there's any other way."

"*Sukoka nuriel gatero . . .*" said Metron. The crystal was

filled with rosy color, but it didn't shine onto the tunic of muddy blue that Garric wore for this assault.

Garric touched the wall. There was no need for his sword now, so he sheathed it while he thought.

Like the outer wall, the tower was built of banded gneiss. The striations between layers were the stone's only marking. Though Garric ran his fingers up and down for as high as he could reach, he couldn't feel separate courses. There were no interstices, not even so much as a crack he could have driven a needle into. Either the Spike was really pottery cast to look like stone, or it had been carved whole from a solid outcrop.

"*Naveh!*" Metron cried. "*Badawa! Belhorwa!*"

Garric's skin tingled as though he'd just stepped out of salt water. Hakken must have felt the same and been frightened by it, because he gave a shout, flailing his arms to shake something off him.

"Start climbing," Metron ordered. He sounded tired and his voice was even more distant than usual. "Just put your feet against the wall. But hurry, *please* hurry."

Garric lifted his right leg and set the sole firmly against the stone as if he were pushing off from it. His balance changed. He started to fall forward until he threw up his left foot as well.

"Duzi!" he gasped. He was standing on the tower's side, his body parallel to the ground below. The Spike stretched before him like the trunk of a felled tree, sloping to either side but an easy passage to a youth who'd walked fence rails for fun.

He wasn't *sticking* to the stone; it was as if the Spike had turned onto its side so that gravity held Garric and all his equipment in the normal way. Hakken cried out and fell against the tower. He rose onto his hands and knees, still against the stone, looking at Garric in wonderment.

"Gar!" Tint cried. She leaped to the wall beside him. Her nails scratched for purchase, but the stone was too smooth even for her. She slipped to the ground. "Gar, come back!"

"Wait, Tint!" Garric said.

He turned the crystal up to look at the wizard. "Metron," he demanded. "Why isn't Tint able to climb?"

"Do you think I'm the Mistress herself?" Metron snarled shrilly. "Do you know how much power it takes to shift the cosmos for the weight of just two of you? Get on with it! Don't keep delaying, please!"

Garric felt clammy. He thought his bare skin glowed with red wizardlight. The color was too faint for certainty, and it wasn't something he wanted to think about anyway.

He shivered. "Let's go, Hakken," he said. "Tint, I'll be back as soon as I can. Wait here for me, all right?"

"Gar!" the beastgirl cried. She poised to jump.

"No, Tint!" Garric said, but she leaped onto the smooth stone anyway. When she slipped, she tried to catch Garric's leg. He strode ahead to avoid her grip.

"Come on, Hakken!" he said, speaking loudly to be heard over the wail as Tint slid to the ground. He jogged up—along—the sheer tower, keeping his eyes focused on the sky to avoid seeing that the ground was increasingly far behind him.

Tint continued to jump and wail. There'd been no sign of human guards, but Garric still found the noise disconcerting.

The top, two hundred feet in the air, was as smoothly rounded as a sword pommel. Garric paused, wondering what would happen if he stepped over the end—down, as it felt to him now. Hakken joined him, walking carefully. The tower was broad enough that the two men could have safely stood side by side, but the business was already too uncanny to take further chances.

Metron was chanting. Hakken held his axe in both hands, his elbows close to his sides. His face was set in a rictus, beyond fear and probably beyond hope as well.

Tint still shrieked; the distance wasn't great enough to mute the nerve-wracking cries. Garric felt a surge of anger, which he suppressed in embarrassment. Anger at the beast-girl's inability to understand was as foolish as getting angry at a rainstorm . . . and in this case, a rainstorm that had repeatedly saved his life.

He turned his head to the side and looked out over the darkened city of Durassa. A few yellow glows moved slowly through the streets, lanterns lighting partygoers to their homes. Most of those out at this hour either couldn't afford the price of a linkman or would prefer the dark for their business.

The call of a rattle showed that at least one watchman was alert. Did Hame's cousin wait in a doorway, looking up at the Spike?

Light outlined a score of shuttered windows; the folk in other rooms might be awake as well, staring into the night. Any of them could see Garric and Hakken on the tower, completely exposed.

It probably didn't matter. Human danger wasn't of immediate concern, not now. . . .

"*Chermarai!*" Metron cried. A wedge of the dome's curve turned black and dissipated like mist struck by the full sun. Perfumed air puffed out, warm and damp and green-smelling.

"Inside quickly!" the wizard said. "I'm holding it until you're inside, but hurry!"

"It's dark as arm's length up a hog's ass!" Hakken protested.

"I'll light it after you're in," Metron said. "Please!"

Garric didn't like the dark interior any better than the sailor did, but it seemed to him that this time Metron was doing the best he could. He stepped forward; gravity changed again. Hakken, more afraid of being alone than of what might be waiting inside, jumped after him.

The wedge of sky vanished, at last silencing the beastgirl's cries. For an instant Garric was in darkness that breathed lush odors. The crystal on his breast crackled. Metron's image stood with its left arm outstretched, its fist balled. Azure wizardlight shot from the sapphire ring, spreading into an ambiance which lit a corridor bent into the organic curves of a muskrat's burrow.

Hakken looked about in silent wonder. Though it appeared to have been chewed from the rock rather than being built, the corridor was luxurious beyond the halls of any palace Garric had seen.

Tapestries of thick, lustrous silk hung the walls, showing different pictures depending on the angle Garric's eye fell on them. Between each pair of hangings was a patch of blank wall, a sconce, and a velvet rope attached to the top of the wall.

Metron spoke a word. The sconces lighted one after another, throwing up pale flames like those of the purest olive oil. The blue glow of moments before sucked back into the ring. Wavering lamp flames made the shadows beneath the cords writhe as if they were alive.

The corridor split twenty feet from where Garric stood. Each of the two branches curved off in its own direction; one of them climbing, the other seeming to slope slightly downward.

"Lord Thalemos will be in one of the cells," said Metron. His voice was broken, but the sound of panting didn't reach Garric's mind the way the words did. "I can't tell which. Open the viewslits one at time and look in, but be careful."

"What viewslits?" said Hakken. "I don't see—"

"The cords!" Metron snapped, angry at his own failure to communicate and taking it out, as people generally did, on those they'd failed. "Pull the cords, you fool!"

Garric pulled the nearest cord, a braid of gold-and-scarlet plush. It dipped easily; as it did, the section of wall beside it became transparent. Garric touched the space. He felt stone though his eyes told him there was nothing there. He looked in.

A child of no more than six sat on the floor playing with a pull toy, a painted pottery duck on clay wheels. The room was appointed with an ornate gilt bronze table and a chair inlaid with ivory and mother-of-pearl. There was no bed.

"Go on, go on!" Metron squeaked. "We have to find Thalemos."

"Why—" said Garric.

The child turned to look in his direction. There were pits of orange hellfire where its eyes should have been. Garric dropped the velvet cord and backed away. The stone was again unmarked.

"Hakken, you check the other side of the corridor," Garric said. His voice was hoarse for the first few words. "I'll take these."

He walked quickly to the next pull, this one purple with an ermine tassel on the end. He had to force himself to take the cord in his hand. He tugged it down fiercely to get it over with.

The cell on the other side of the window looked like the interior of a cave covered with the pearly translucence of flow rock. Garric couldn't tell where the light came from. Nothing moved, nothing in the room seemed to be alive. He lowered the cord and moved on.

There were four cells on Garric's side of the entrance corridor. Having gotten his breathing back to normal from the shock of the child's eyes, he opened the third window. Hakken was doing the same across from him.

A demon glared at Garric. It opened long jaws and hissed, its forked tongue quivering only a hand's breadth away. Garric jumped back, snatching at his sword hilt. When the cord slipped from his hand, the demon was a blank stone wall again.

Smiling wryly at his fright, Garric opened the next window. His belly was tight, but nobody watching him would have known how ready he was to flinch. Still, he kept his face as far back from the wall as he could and not be obvious in his fear.

Within, a man lay stretched on a rack. His limbs were taut, but as yet he hadn't quite been disjointed. His body was spare, his face ascetic. His eyes were wide-open, and his expression was patiently resigned despite what must be singeing agony. His gaze met Garric's with neither hope nor fear.

"Metron?" Garric said. "Can we let this fellow out along with Thalemos?"

"This one?" the wizard said. "*This* one? Boy, if I freed him, you would pray the Intercessor to lock him up again—and you would be too late!"

Garric grimaced but closed the window. He started to open the first cell down the left-hand branch but turned to check on Hakken first. The sailor stood transfixed at the window to the second cell on his side.

"Hakken?" Garric said. Hakken seemed paralyzed; only the throb of a vein in his throat proved he wasn't a statue.

Garric walked back and grabbed the man by the shoulder. "Hakken!" he said, glancing through the window as he spoke.

The woman inside was as searingly beautiful as the sun. Garric thought she was nude, but he couldn't be certain even of that. Lust hammered him, crushing his volition.

Reflex was his salvation. He wrenched at Hakken with all his strength, pulling the sailor back. The velvet cord broke; the attached end flopped like a live thing as the window closed.

Garric blinked and rubbed his eyes with his hands. "Duzi help me!" he muttered, still dizzy from the experience. "Hakken, are you all right?"

The sailor had fallen to the floor. He had a stunned look. Rising, he reached again for the broken cord.

Garric caught Hakken's wrist, and said, "Leave it alone! Go on to the next one. We've got to find Thalemos and get out of here!"

"I warned you to be careful," Metron said. "The ones the Intercessors have imprisoned here over the ages are those dangerous to them, but some are dangerous to the cosmos."

"Let me go," the sailor snarled. His eyes were wild with passion. He tried to pull his arm free. When he couldn't, he raised the axe in his other hand.

Garric punched Hakken hard in the pit of the stomach, then wrenched the axe away as the man doubled up. "Check the cells on your side!" Garric said. "Shout if you find Lord Thalemos. And *don't* make me come back for you, Hakken."

The sailor glared at him. He jerked at the next pull in line, glanced within, and let it go. He shambled to the fourth, gave the cell's interior a cursory glance, and looked back over his shoulder at Garric before starting down the branch corridor. Hakken's expression was furious, but he seemed to have recovered from the compulsion he'd felt moments before.

Garric shoved the axe helve under his belt and strode to the branch corridor he'd claimed. He'd return the weapon when they left the prison, though he'd watch his back until he was sure the sailor had buried his wrath. There hadn't been a lot of choice, though.

Garric opened the next window. Unlike previous cells, the only light in this one was a sullen red glow. He thought he saw something flutter within, but as he squinted for a better view he heard Hakken shriek.

"Hakken!" Garric shouted, drawing his sword. He rounded the junction and almost collided with the sailor.

Hakken's face was contorted. He held his right arm out as if he were trying to point. There was nothing in the corridor beyond him. His mouth opened and spewed yellow froth.

Hakken's spine suddenly curved. He pitched backward, dead and rigid before his head hit the floor.

"Metron, what did it?" Garric said, looking behind him and then again down the corridor where Hakken died. There was nothing save for the flaring sconces.

"How would I know?" Metron piped. "It wasn't wizardry, that I swear. Wait and I'll draw the image from his eyes. But it wasn't wizardry!"

Hakken's right arm stuck stiffly into the air. His balled fist and forearm were already black and swollen. There were two raised punctures on the underside of his wrist.

"Don't bother," Garric said tightly, advancing in a shuffle with his sword raised at his side. "I've got it."

The cord that Hakken would have pulled to open the next window was of red-and-black bands separated by thin yellow rings. It hung as still as any of the others—now. Only close examination showed that the two black beads on the end were eyes.

Garric's sword whistled, taking off the serpent's head without touching the stone against which it hung. Fangs glittered in the light of the sconces as the tiny jaws yawned in death.

The body twitched and knotted harmlessly. Garric pulled it, clearing the stone. The reptile continued to squirm, wetting his left palm with its blood.

A young man in silk tunics sat inside the cell, playing with a set of ivory game pieces on a board of inlaid wood. Unlike some of the other prisoners, he showed no awareness of being watched through the solid wall.

"That's him!" Metron said. "Don't move, now!"

The wizard paused, then resumed in a singsong, "*Triskydin amat lahaha. . . .*"

Thalemos—even without Metron's statement, Garric would have recognized the youth from the statue he'd disinterred on Serpent's Isle—rolled an ebony dice cup, checked the throw, and moved a piece. His face was drawn and resigned.

"*Genio gidiba*," Metron chanted. "*Loumas!*"

The blank wall between the hangings dissolved in a vanishing sparkle. Thalemos jumped up, spilling the game board. He grabbed the stool he'd been sitting on but fumbled as he tried to lift it as a weapon.

"Come on!" Garric said, grabbing the youth's sleeve. In terms of years lived, Thalemos was probably older than Garric himself. In all ways that mattered, though, he seemed younger and as malleable as wax. "We're getting out of here!"

"Yes!" Metron chirped. "I've rescued you, Lord Thalemos!"

Which was only one way of putting it, but this wasn't the time to argue. Tugging the boy along with him, Garric sprinted down the corridor. A flash of blue wizardlight touched the curved section of the roof dome at the end. It went black and was gone without the delay and chanting which Metron had required when he won entry.

Hakken's stiff corpse lay behind them. *All men die, and the flesh doesn't matter.* . . . But Garric would have brought the sailor along if he possibly could have.

"You'll have to carry Lord Thalemos," the wizard said. "I don't have time or the power to prepare him. Quickly, quickly!"

"What?" said Thalemos.

Garric caught the youth around the shoulders, knelt to put his left arm behind Thalemos' knees, and toppled him backward. There was no point in explaining; mere action was sufficient. "I've got him."

"*Belhorwa!*" Metron said, only that. Garric felt gravity shift again. He stepped out onto the tower, ignoring Thalemos' cry and clutching fear.

The city was still in night, but the moon had begun to

rise. Garric jogged toward the bushes at the base of the tower, no longer nervous to see the ground so far below. Tint was where he'd left her. She was as still as a statue, now; and, thank Duzi, silent.

"Quickly!" Metron pleaded. No longer was the wizard pretending to be unfazed by the work of wizardry. "Even with the ring I won't be able to hold very much longer."

The bushes quivered. Something rose out of the foliage. *A man's been hiding there,* Garric thought; but as the shadow continued to extend up the wall of the tower, he knew he was wrong.

It was a snake. From the size of the head rising toward him, it was a snake as long as the tower was high.

"Metron!" Garric said. "Stop that thing!"

He tried to draw his sword and almost dropped Thalemos. The youth cried out again and wrapped his arms tightly around Garric's neck. That took care of the problem of dropping him, but trying to fight the creature while burdened with this terrified weight would be an exercise in futility.

Terrified. Garric remembered the effect the viper on Serpent's Isle had on Tint. No wonder she was silent: she was paralyzed with fear!

"Quickly!" the wizard wheezed. "I'm losing you!"

"Gar!" Tint screamed despairingly, and leaped. She touched the sheer wall twenty feet above the ground and got enough purchase from it to spring another dozen feet upward. She grasped the serpent behind the head with all four limbs and bit viciously into the neck.

"Quickly!" said Metron.

Garric felt the beginning of another shift, of *down* preparing to become a plunge of fifty feet to the base of the tower. He sprinted forward, clearing his sword. If Thalemos couldn't hold on by himself, Thalemos was going to have to learn how to fly.

The snake twisted like a straw touched by flame. It

couldn't reach Tint, but it battered her against the side of the tower. She hung on at the first impact, but the second flung her loose. She sailed through the air, already balling her limbs beneath her for a safe landing.

The snake struck, snatching the beastgirl out of the air. Her bleat ended in a crunch of bones. The snake curled its forebody to the ground, lifting its head slightly. It tossed the frail corpse and caught it again, headfirst this time for easy swallowing.

Garric felt the ground rising to meet him. He jumped, flexing his knees, and fell the last ten feet without harm. The shock pulled Thalemos away from him, but that was a side benefit. Garric stepped toward the snake.

"Get over the wall!" Metron was saying. "It won't climb the wall!"

The snake's jaw hinge dislocated, letting its mouth open still wider. Its left eye glittered at Garric beneath spike-scaled brows. A membrane slid sideways, wiping the cornea. Only Tint's feet were still visible.

Garric slashed as though he were splitting wood, striking the small scales on the back of the snake's neck; bone grated beneath his edge. A spasm rippled down the whole long body, throwing distant plantings about as if a tornado had struck the garden.

The snake twisted onto its back, exposing its broad, pale belly scales. Its midbody struck the tower with a *whack* like cliffs meeting. Someone in the street shouted.

Tint's feet vanished. The slight bulge of the beastgirl's body shivered farther down the serpent's throat, drawn by reflexes inexorable even in death. Garric paused with his sword lifted for another blow; he shot the blade home in its scabbard instead.

He turned. Thalemos was watching aghast. Garric caught his arm.

"Follow me!" he said as he started back the way he'd entered the garden. "Put your feet where I do!"

As Garric ran, he wiped his eyes with the back of his hand. If he missed his path for the tears, then Tint would have died for nothing.

Though Sharina stood beside the flutist who blew time for the sailors launching the nearby trireme, even she could scarcely hear the notes over the bedlam of the fleet loading. Either the sailors had better hearing or, more likely, they could have kept pace in their sleep by virtue of their repetitive training.

Across the U-shaped Arsenal, another trireme splashed into the water. The men who'd launched her with block and tackle gave over to a separate crew on tow ropes, drawing the ship to the boarding quay. There most of the hundred-plus crewmen waited, holding their oars upright like a thicket of blighted saplings. Only the helmsman and a dozen rowers were aboard, ready to fend the lightly built vessel away from trouble.

Pulleys squealed; pine keels shrieked in a chorus against the polished limestone draw-ways, despite the buckets of water passed hand to hand up the ramps and poured at the top for lubrication; petty officers snarled commands at men who weren't where they were supposed to be or were sloppy in getting there; and louder than all the rest, the huge crowd of watching civilians chattering provided a deafening susurrus of excitement.

King Carus broke away from his circle of advisors and walked the short distance to where Sharina stood. He wore the field uniform of this day: short tunic, shoulder cloak with hood, and sandals laced to mid calf. He'd wanted to don the breeches and high boots in which he'd campaigned when he was in his own flesh, but Liane had pointed out that the best that would do was puzzle people. Other possibilities started at, "Prince Garric has gone mad," and went downward from there.

"Are you impressed?" Carus said, bending his lips to Sharina's ear.

She didn't know what he expected her to say, so she told the simple truth: "It's confusing. And it's not just me; lots of people are confused, so it's taking a long time."

She didn't point, but the clot of soldiers on the boarding quay across the harbor was self-evident. The two banks of oarsmen had boarded smoothly, but the heavy infantry who'd be riding as passengers in the inboard banks tripped angrily over their fellows and the oarlooms as they tried to reach places in the center of the vessel.

A flash of light made Sharina squint, then shade her eyes with a hand to see better. Lord Waldron himself was on the boarding dock, using his bare sword as a pointer. After she'd seen him, Sharina could even make out the rumble of the old soldier's furious commands.

"Right," said Carus approvingly. "Though they're doing better than I'd expected. If efficiency were all that mattered, I'd have taken the ships downriver with just their crews and boarded the infantry off temporary stages at the Pool."

An officer was trying to get past the Blood Eagles screening Carus; his breastplate was not only gilded but picked out with six very respectable jewels. The fellow's voice was rising.

Carus paused in what he was saying to Sharina and turned his head, glancing toward the guard commander and the irate officer beyond him. The latter cried, "Prince Garric—"

"Lord Ghosli," Carus said, thundering above the general noise, "get aboard the *Lady of Valles* now or surrender your command—and surrender your honor as well, so far as I'm concerned! Do you hear me, milord?"

Sharina blinked. Lord Waldron across the harbor could hear *that* order. Ghosli looked aghast, then furious. He turned and stamped away.

Carus shook his head in disgust. "Shouldn't have said that, should I?" he muttered to Sharina. "Ghosli wants to take his horse aboard, can you believe that? But he uses his own money to buy extras for his men, and his regiment'd follow wherever he led them because of that. I shouldn't have snapped his head off."

Sharina cleared her throat; she didn't have to repeat what Carus had already said, so instead she put her hand on his elbow, and remarked, "It's my duty to remind you to be Prince Garric, your highness, so the fault's mine."

As she'd expected, Carus looked stricken at the thought his outburst had hurt her. Quickly, Sharina went on, "Why *aren't* you boarding at the Pool then?"

The just-loaded trireme moved away from the quay on short strokes by a dozen oarsmen. The slender hull wobbled badly as the infantrymen seated themselves on the cramped inner benches, but the noncoms were sorting matters out. A tow crew slid another vessel into place.

Carus didn't answer for a moment. Instead he put his fists on his hipbones and stood arms akimbo as he viewed the scene. A broad grin spread across his face. Though his laughter didn't boom out the way Sharina half expected, she knew it wasn't far beneath the surface.

Two vessels moving downstream on the push of the current started to converge; their officers' attention was turned to the disorder inboard. The crowd pointed and began to shout at increasing volume. The starboard trireme heeled as its helmsman leaned into the tiller of his steering oar; bellowed warnings from that ship woke the crew of the second to the danger also. Men in the bows of both vessels used oars as poles to fend off the other hull.

An oar cracked under the misuse, but the ships steadied on their separate courses with no greater damage than that. The crowd's concern turned to cheers.

"That's why I'm doing it, Sharina," Carus said, pitching his voice to carry to her but not beyond. "I'm letting everybody, pikeman and swordsman, soldier and civilian, see that it's one army and one kingdom."

He gestured with a sweep of his left arm, fingers straight. "There's men from Haft and Shengy and Seres aboard these ships," he said. "They're going off to deal with a danger that threatens every citizen of the Isles— whether or not they can afford to pay taxes. The people here can see that, and they'll tell the story to others. We're rebuilding the *kingdom* at this moment."

Carus put his great hand on Sharina's shoulder, steadying himself against a sudden surge of emotions. "When I was king in my own name, girl," he said, his voice and arm trembling, "I talked about *my* army and *my* kingdom. As the Shepherd knows, I smashed every foe I faced, smashed them and ground their bones into the mud—until the day I died and the kingdom died with me."

Sharina put her hand flat on the hand of the dead king. She kept her eyes on the harbor so she wouldn't embarrass him with her concern.

"Garric knows better than that, and I know better than that now," Carus said. "It's the army and the kingdom of everybody in the Isles. Kings who remember that don't have to rule with their fists and their swords. And when they die, it doesn't mean chaos for all."

Carus laughed, shakily but still a gusty release of tension. "Mind, girl," he went on, "this skin is a borrowed suit. I intend to return it to your brother with no worse than a scar or two that he might've gotten tripping into the cutlery when he got up from the table. Eh?"

A trumpet blew; the last trireme from the opposite arm of the Arsenal now floated in the harbor, ready to begin boarding. Only *The King of the Isles* remained under the shed roof on the near side, the great five-banked flagship that Sharina and Tenoctris would board along with Carus.

"But until Garric comes back," Carus said, letting his

voice rise more than he probably realized, "while I'm watching the kingdom for him—"

His hand gripped his sword and drew it in a shimmer of sunlight. The crowd bellowed in delight.

"Until then," Carus shouted to his immediate companions over the sound of thousands of throats, "by the *Shepherd!* the kingdom's enemies will die in the mud as surely as they did in my day!"

Cashel stretched, enjoying the light which dappled the ground beneath the tall bushes. He'd awakened at sunrise, but he'd been tired and Tilphosa was worn down to a nub of the girl he'd helped ashore during the storm a seeming lifetime ago. This grove of giant blueberries had been a good place for them to catch up on their rest.

Tilphosa had never been plump, but it bothered Cashel to see the way the girl's cheeks had sunk inward in the time he'd known her. Her alert interest in all around her concealed her condition while she was awake, but she looked like a victim wasted by the flux now when her head was pillowed on springy branches covered by a corner of her cloak.

Cashel rose quietly and began shaking fruit from low-hanging branches. He stretched out the skirt of his tunic as a basket. To avoid the noise he didn't rap the limbs with his staff, but the rustle of leaves woke Tilphosa anyway. She jumped to her feet, her teeth clenched. She was holding the broken sword close to her body ready to stab whatever threat was approaching.

"Oh!" Tilphosa blurted as she lost her balance. She toppled backward, trying to grab a tree for support.

Cashel let the berries spill and lunged to catch her. He caught her all right—when he needed to move, he was a lot faster than people expected—but the jerk he gave her right arm might have hurt as bad as the scrape she'd have gotten on the tree bark.

Tilphosa straightened, and he released her. "I'm sorry," she said. "I'd been having a dream."

She smiled wryly, massaging her right elbow with the other hand. Without meeting Cashel's eyes she continued, "A nightmare, I suppose. About a snake trying to swallow me."

She looked up at him finally, still forcing a smile. Her left hand caressed the crystal disk on her necklace. "I don't think it was sent by the Mistress."

Cashel squatted, thinking he'd pick up the fruit he'd lost when he grabbed for the girl. He had to give it up as a bad job, because most of them had sailed out of the grove when he jumped. He rose and brushed his staff through the tips of the nearest branches. The twigs were heavy with ripe berries; they dropped like a soft hailstorm about Cashel and the girl.

"I haven't seen any snakes about here," he said, popping blueberries into his mouth by the handful. Tilphosa was more ladylike, nibbling each berry individually, but she was hungry too. "There aren't any birds, either, and that's funny. I'd think these trees'd be thick with daws and magpies, but I don't hear a single one."

Tilphosa had put the broken sword—the dagger, you could call it; the blade had snapped into a point of sorts—under her sash, but at Cashel's comment her fingers toyed with the brass hilt again. "Cashel?" she said. "Do these bushes just grow, or were they planted?"

Cashel eyed the grove carefully. "I'd guess somebody was keeping them up, whether or not they planted them," he said. "There's no fruit on the ground except what I knocked down."

He cleared his throat. Blueberries, even very big ones, don't form a solid canopy; the ground should've been covered in grass. Instead he saw ivy and wildflowers. The soft leaves weren't being browsed by animals, neither domestic goats nor voles and rabbits.

"I guess we could get on, now," Cashel said. The sun was halfway to zenith, time and past to be moving; not that there was any clear place to be moving *to*. "If you're up to it, I mean?"

Tilphosa smiled broadly around a mouthful of blueberries; juice trickled from a corner of her mouth, and she wiped it away with the back of her hand. "I'm fine, Cashel," she said. "I was just dizzy from jumping up the way I did."

Cashel wasn't sure that was the truth or, anyway, the whole truth, but if it was what Tilphosa wanted to say, then he wasn't about to call her a liar. "Walking toward the east has got us here," he said, "and it's a better place than some we've seen. I guess we should keep on going."

Tilphosa nodded with determination, her mouth again full of berries. She held the skirt of her outer tunic up awkwardly to carry a further supply. Cashel wondered if the girl—if Lady Tilphosa—had ever used her tunic that way before he demonstrated the method a few moments earlier.

She set off quickly, apparently to show that she was in good shape. Cashel smiled. All it proved was that Tilphosa had a good heart, which he'd known before now. "If you'll slow down, mistress," he said, "I'll be able to keep up with you. I'm used to following sheep, remember."

"Oh," Tilphosa said, looking back in concern. She saw his smile and blushed. "Oh. I'm sorry."

"We'll get there," Cashel said, as they fell into step together. "Wherever there is, I mean."

Tilphosa turned to look at him as they walked. "Where do you want it to be, Cashel?" she asked. "What are you looking for?"

He shrugged as he popped another berry into his mouth. "Well, the way home," he said, his words a little slurred at the beginning. "I'll get there. I've always had a good sense of direction."

He smiled broadly at Tilphosa. "But I guess I'll see you safe to your Prince Thalemos, first, mistress," he added. "We'll find the place you want to be, never fear."

"The place I want to be," Tilphosa repeated without emphasis. Her eyes were on the ground. When she looked up again her expression was hard. Her voice rang as she said, "Cashel, I can't trust Metra. I'm not even sure I can trust . . ."

Her face worked like she'd bitten something sour—or something worse than that. She continued firmly, "I'm not even sure I can trust the Mistress. What if we reach Prince Thalemos and find he's in league with the Archai? They aren't friends to human beings, whatever Metra seems to think!"

Cashel shrugged again. "I guess things'll work out," he said. He didn't know what else to say. This was the sort of conversation that other people liked to have but he'd never seen much use for.

"Do things always work out for you, Master Cashel?" the girl said. "Because I haven't been so lucky myself!"

He'd finished the berries, so he had both hands free again. He wiped his left palm on his tunic and let his fingers find their places on the smooth hickory of his quarterstaff.

"Things pretty much work out, yes, mistress," Cashel said. He started the staff in a slow spin off to his left side to keep it clear of Tilphosa. "Maybe not at first, but after a while I generally find a way."

Tilphosa made a sound, a funny kind of whoop. He looked over in concern, but she waved her left hand at him for reassurance. She was laughing, he guessed, though it still bothered him because he didn't see why.

"It's all right, Cashel," Tilphosa said through her laughter. "I'll just trust things to work out, you see? So long as I'm with you, I'll trust things to work out."

Maybe because Tilphosa had asked if the blueberries had been planted, Cashel began noticing signs of cultivation immediately as they resumed their way eastward. There was nothing overt, no stone walls nor grain growing from plowed furrows, but a mixture of tulips and periwinkles wandered like a stream of red and blue across the landscape in a fashion that Cashel couldn't imagine without cultivation. The boxwoods beyond them, though not trimmed into a hedge, still grew too tightly for nature.

"Cashel—" the girl said. Then, frowning, she went on, "No, I guess not. I thought I saw somebody behind those little trees, but there isn't room to hide."

Cashel looked. "They're pears, it looks to me," he said. The trees were off to the right of the course he'd been setting, but there was no reason not to bend a trifle in that direction. He angled toward them, stepping behind Tilphosa.

"Pear trees that small?" she asked. She fell in with him again, this time on his other side. He noticed her hand rested on the dagger hilt.

The trees were no taller than his shoulder, but they were perfectly formed and full of ripe fruit. The soil had been lightly turned and composted around each one in a circle that would just contain the branches, about where the rootlets would reach. There was somebody here who knew trees, no doubt about that, and who used what he knew.

"I haven't seen them like this before," Cashel said, "but the fruit's full-sized. Here—the juice'll be good till we find a stream to drink from."

He twisted a pear from its branch and handed it to Tilphosa. As he did so, he caught movement out of the corner of his eye. He jerked his head around quickly, but even so he saw only a motion rather than a shape.

"Cashel, what was it?" Tilphosa said, her voice clear. She'd drawn her dagger.

"I don't know," he said, frowning. "It ran into the hollies there. I don't guess it could've been bigger than a rabbit and slip through them like that, but it seemed . . ."

He picked a pear for himself without looking down at the tree. "Well, anyway . . ." he said. "Let's keep on going. I'd like to find water, and chances are there'll be a path or something we can follow."

Cashel looked about them and frowned. He wiped his fingers clean of sticky pear juice on his tunic before he took the quarterstaff in both hands again.

"I don't think there's a tree or bush I can see that people aren't caring for," he said as he considered the landscape. "There must be quite a village close around here. I've seen more wildness in the palace gardens in Valles."

"It doesn't look like a garden to me," Tilphosa said, frowning as well. She wasn't so much arguing as making a comment.

"It's a different sort of taking care," Cashel explained. "It's doing the things the plants want, do you see? Feeding the roots and trimming off dead limbs, but not making things look like *people* want in a garden."

He cleared his throat. "Let's keep going," he said. "I mean, if you—"

"Yes, of course," Tilphosa said, stepping off briskly. She didn't put her dagger away, though Cashel didn't feel anything hostile in the setting. He'd have been hard put to imagine a more peaceful place.

The ground rose slightly; as soon as they came over the rounded crest they saw the village. It was laid out in a circle, more huts than Cashel could have counted on his fingers twice over. They looked like straw beehives, though they were woven of leaves instead of proper straw thatching.

"Have you seen any grass since we woke up this morning?" Cashel asked.

"I don't remember," Tilphosa said. "Does it matter?"

He shrugged. "I don't know," he said. "I haven't seen any myself—nor any grain or reeds either. It's just . . . well, different from what I'm used to."

He cleared his throat. "That's probably why it bothers me," he said. That was true enough: "different" generally meant "bad" to a peasant, whether it was the weather or the way a neighbor offered to pay you for the work you'd done for him last season.

There weren't any animals bigger than bugs in this place either. Not except for the folks who'd built the huts, and he hadn't seen them yet except for maybe a flash in the pear orchard.

He and Tilphosa walked toward the village. There was no sound of people and no woodsmoke either, which was surprising too. Smoke always lingers, especially since Cashel hadn't been around a fire in some days and his nostrils were primed to notice it.

The huts were side by side, as close together as rooms in a city. Houses in Barca's Hamlet weren't big, but there even the poorest people had more space between them and their neighbors than the way these folks lived. There were no windows. The doorways were small—even for the size of the huts—and faced the empty courtyard in the center.

Cashel walked around the curve of the village. The only passage into the courtyard was on the eastern side.

"Is anybody here?" Tilphosa asked. She held her elbows close to her sides as she looked about herself, like she was worried that she'd bump something nasty if she wasn't careful.

Cashel frowned, then let his face smooth. Tilphosa wasn't asking a fool question: she was saying that the silence worried her and that she'd like Cashel to say it was all right . . . which it was, as far as he could tell.

"Somewhere close, I'd guess," he said. He pointed to the drying racks fixed to the back of the huts. They held fruits and vegetables of all sorts, though he didn't see any meat. "Some of those apple slices haven't been cut more than an hour."

Cashel eased through the alley into the courtyard, brushing the hut to either side though he moved sideways. He held his staff high, to clear the domed roofs and just *possibly* so he could swing it if he needed to.

"Given the size they are," he said, "and the size we are—"

He smiled slightly to the girl following him, for she too was a giant compared to the folk who'd built these huts.

"—I don't blame them for being nervous about whether we're friends."

Tilphosa knelt to look into a hut's open doorway. She must not have seen anything to interest her, because she rose with a dissatisfied expression and faced Cashel. Her mouth started to open for another needless question, then spread in a smile instead.

"Those are willows further on the way we've been going," Cashel said, matching her smile with one of his own. He dipped his staff toward the east; not far away a line of trees rose above the shrubbery. "There's likely a stream there; open water anyway. Maybe when the folks here see we're not doing any harm, they'll come out to see us."

They started off again. He hadn't yet seen a path, not even the little tracks that voles made running through a meadow.

"What if they don't, Cashel?" Tilphosa said. "Come out and see us, I mean."

Cashel shrugged. "Then we keep going, like we've been doing anyhow," he said. "It doesn't look to me that they'd be able to give us anything we can't get for ourselves. They don't cook their food, even, that I can see."

Tilphosa smiled cautiously "I'd like a roof if it rains,"

she said. "But sky's clear, and I don't think those huts would be much shelter. They're just dead leaves sewn to a frame of a few sticks."

"I've seen bird nests that were built better," Cashel agreed. Squirrels made that sort of ragged pile, of course. He started to grin at the notion of a village of big squirrels ... and then sobered, because he couldn't be sure that wasn't just what he'd seen.

He chuckled.

"Cashel?" the girl asked.

"I don't guess it was squirrels that made the huts after all," he said. "A squirrel couldn't keep quiet the way the folks around here're doing."

Tilphosa gave him a puzzled look, but she didn't try to follow through on the thought.

Most of the trees ahead were willows the way Cashel had said, but the one in the center of the line had darker foliage than a willow's pale green. It was huge, its branches spreading to cover as much ground as the village they'd just left. The branches dipped close to the ground like the necks of cattle drinking; from some of them hung huge pods.

"Cashel, there's a man," said Tilphosa, pointing with her left hand. Then, her voice rising, she said, "Cashel, he's caught! Cashel, it's—"

"Right!" said Cashel, but he didn't say it loudly because he was already moving and concentrating on what he was going to do next. His staff was crosswise at mid-chest, slightly advanced.

The strange tree had small, rounded leaves, more like an olive's than what belonged on a tree as big as this one. The pods hanging to the ground from the tips of many limbs were bigger than those of any locust or catalpa, though.

Almost big enough to hold a man, Cashel had thought when he first saw them; but he was wrong about the "almost" because he hadn't appreciated quite how stunted the residents of this region were.

Most of the pods were closed and brown. A still-open one off to the right side was the same dark green as the foliage. Cashel could see from the ribbed interior that it was really just a giant leaf, not a seedpod as he'd thought.

A child-sized man, naked and almost hairless, stood as the leaf slowly closed around him. His skin was the color of polished bronze; his eyes glinted like those of a rabbit Cashel had once come upon in the jaws of a black rat snake.

A heavy odor, neither pleasant nor unpleasant, hung in the air. Cashel sneezed as he stepped cautiously closer to the victim, ready to dodge if a limb slashed down at him. He heard leaves rustle or maybe something rustling in the leaves, but the tree didn't move.

Though the little man's eyes no longer focused, a blood vessel throbbed in his throat. The leaf continued to fold, closing from his feet upward. Its deeply serrated edges meshed like the fangs of a seawolf.

It was obviously tough. Cashel's crude knife might cut the pod while it was still green and flexible, but not, he thought, without carving the victim as well.

He paused, letting the range of his senses expand beyond the silent man. Because of the way the branches curved down as they spread from the trunk, he had the feeling of being in a dimly lit vault. He judged the thickness of the limb which kinked where the pod attached, then raised the quarterstaff over his right shoulder.

He punched the staff forward with all his weight behind the blow. If it'd been an oak—or worse, a dogwood— even Cashel's strength could have done no more than bruise the bark. This tree, though, had brittle wood like a pear's; it shattered at the impact of iron-shod hickory.

The tip and half-engulfed victim fell to the ground; the stump of broken branch sprang upward. From the low shrubbery nearby came a many-throated keening like the wind blowing across chimney pots.

Cashel bent and grabbed the little fellow by the shoulder with his left hand. That hand had been leading on the staff and was now in a state of prickly near-numbness. The pod was unfolding the way a cut intestine gapes as its own muscular walls pull it apart. When Cashel threw the man away from the tree, the pod and the scrap of attached branch fell off him.

Cashel scrambled out from under the tree. Tilphosa had come toward him, but she'd carefully stayed beyond the tree's possible reach, where she wouldn't get in Cashel's way. She faced sideways, keeping Cashel in the corner of one eye while the other scanned the bushes around them.

The rescued victim sucked in deep, gasping breaths as though he'd been underwater during the time the leaf wrapped him. He blinked; awareness started to return to his eyes.

"I'll take care of him!" Tilphosa said, kneeling at the fellow's side. She lifted his head with the hand that didn't hold her dagger.

Cashel straightened and surveyed their surroundings for the first time since he'd seen the man being eaten. The limbs of the strange tree were drawing up like the petals of a lotus at nightfall. The odor he'd noticed when he ran close had dissipated and remained only in his memory.

He looked at the stump of the branch; it leaked dark sap. On the ground, the unfolded leaf was crinkling like leather dried near a flame. The bark of the attached bit of limb had already sloughed away.

From a line of viburnum and lilac bushes that couldn't possibly have hidden them, people of the same stunted race as the victim rose into plain view. They were nude, both males and females, the latter often holding babies no bigger than six-week puppies. There were no weapons or tools of any sort in their raised hands as they came toward Cashel and Tilphosa.

Cashel slid his hands apart on the staff as he faced the newcomers. There were a lot of them. If they all came from the village just to the west, then they must crowd more than a handful of themselves into each hut.

"Great lord and lady!" cried an age-wrinkled male. "We Helpers greet you! Welcome to the Land!"

"Welcome to the Land!" chorused all his fellows like frogs in the springtime. Cashel remained tense for a moment, but even he relaxed when the whole mob threw itself down on the ground before him and the girl.

Chapter Fourteen

Sharina stood beside the four-arched fighting tower fixed to the quinquereme's deck between Captain Ceius and the steersmen in the stern and the mast amidships. Ordinarily the wooden tower—painted to look like stone—would've been struck until *The King of the Isles* prepared to go into action. Tenoctris sheltered within it now, working incantations that the sailors preferred not to see.

Waist-high sailcloth curtains covered the lower half of the archways, concealing the seated wizard while allowing her light and air. Sharina was ready to hand Tenoctris anything she called for, though as yet she might as well have stayed in Valles. Occasionally wizardlight dusted the sunlight red or blue as Tenoctris chanted, but those escapes remained faint enough that the crewmen on deck could pretend not to notice.

The captain spoke to the flutist seated on a perch built

into the sternpost. That man lowered the instrument on which he'd been blowing time; at a nod from the captain, a petty officer blew an attention signal on his straight bronze horn.

"Cease rowing!" said Ceius. "Shake out the sail!"

Officers on deck and in the crowded hold beneath relayed the orders in a chorus, generally with the added obscenities that Sharina had learned to expect when somebody was directing soldiers or sailors. The difference between the methods of junior officers and of muleteers, so far as she could tell, was that the former didn't use whips—at least in the royal forces.

While deck crewmen grabbed ropes to unfurl the sail to catch the freshening breeze, the oarsmen released from duty came boiling up from their benches in the hold through the open beams that supported the deck and allowed ventilation below. The first of them, squirming like a snake hunting voles, was King Carus himself. He sprang to the deck beside Sharina.

Captain Ceius stepped forward in greeting, but Carus waved him back. "Carry on, Ceius!" he said. "You've got matters under control."

Petty officers were dipping cups of wine mixed with two parts water from great jars in the bow and stern. Their strikers held waxed rosters to check off the name of each man served. Military personnel didn't have to be scholars, but Sharina had been surprised to learn that even the lowest-ranking officers were able to read at least names or passwords scratched on a potsherd.

Carus winked at Sharina, then took his place in the line forming for the drinks. The men ahead of him immediately scattered in surprise.

"Get back as you were!" Carus roared, speaking so that the ship's whole crew could hear him. "When I'm acting as your commander, I expect you to jump into the sea if that's what I order you. But while I'm pulling an oar, by the Shepherd! I expect to be treated as an oarsman. Does anybody doubt me?"

He raised his big hands, his palms gleaming with the resin he'd dusted on them before gripping the oarloom. Zettkin and his three aides in the bow, all noblemen, stared at the king in amazement, as did several of the nearby Blood Eagles. The bodyguards were recruited from the same class as the aides, though they were generally younger sons and of impoverished houses.

The sailors who'd been in line ahead of Carus drank quickly and stepped away, watching the king sidelong. Carus took the cup offered him—one of four, each chained to a different jar handle—and held it as an officer dipped it full. The striker holding the roster looked at the king in terror, and bleated, "But chief! He's not on the list!"

"As commander," Carus said, "I'm directing that you make an exception in my case."

Laughing in loud good humor, he emptied the cup without lowering it and stepped away, wiping his mouth with the back of his hand. The next man in line dropped the cup against the jar with clang of thin bronze on thick ceramic, then hid his blush as best he could.

Carus grinned at Sharina, rubbing his palms together. "I do it to show that I'm willing to," he said in a low voice. He nodded toward Zettkin and the aides, one of whom still stared as if transfixed. "I won't order them to do manual labor unless I need to, but I want them all to realize that I don't think any man's too good for any job. Some of my nobles may feel otherwise, but they won't dare say so now."

His grin spread even broader. He added, "But I also *like* to row, now and again. It's even better than fencing practice for using every muscle and letting your mind rest."

He sighed, no longer buoyant. "Which I need now even more than most times," he said.

"Have you been able to sleep any?" Sharina asked quietly. There was no real privacy on a two-hundred-foot vessel carrying four hundred men, but the very numbers created a background of noise that made it unlikely that they'd be easily overheard.

Carus shrugged. "No more than usual," he said, which meant scarcely at all. "We'll solve the problem soon, I expect."

Sharina followed the line of the king's gaze out over the sea, a sheet of pale green marked as far as she could see with ships and the white wakes foaming behind them. Most vessels had their mainsail set, though a few were proceeding under one bank of oarsmen and the pull of the small triangular boat sail set from their jib. The sky was clear except for a scatter of tiny clouds on the horizon ahead.

Carus crooked a finger toward the sky. "Clouds like that usually mean land," he said. "They're over the Dandmere Reefs, I'd guess. That was what we called them in my day, anyhow."

He smiled wryly. "I never claimed to be a sailor," he said, "but at the end I was spending half my time on a ship. Some of it stuck, I suppose."

"I suspect Ilna's friend Chalcus knows something about using a sword, even though he *is* a sailor," Sharina said straight-faced.

The king's expression froze; then he realized she was joking. He laughed with the suddenness of a thunderclap, drawing the eyes of everyone aboard.

"Oh, aye, I think Chalcus does indeed know swords," Carus wheezed. "I'd say I wonder how he's getting on— and I do—but I don't worry, you see, the way I'd worry if I cared about any of those who might try to get in his way."

He eyed the fleet again. "We're scattered," he said. "That'd be dangerous if the Confederacy had a fleet, but

we're better off with room between us in a storm, and
that's a greater risk."

Sharina looked at the sky and frowned.

"No, not a *great* risk," Carus said with a smile. "No,
for now I'd say things were as much in proper order as
any operation can be."

He rubbed his temples; as he did so, his face went still
again. Even a man with Carus' spiritual strength and Garric's youthful body needed more sleep than he was getting.

The interior of the fighting tower glittered azure. Sharina winced, hoping the king hadn't noticed it.

He shrugged. "I didn't have a wizard with me the last
time I walked a ship's deck," he said with a grin that
softened with use. "That was when the Duke of Yole's
wizard drowned me along with every man and ship in the
royal fleet. I may have mixed feelings about what our
friend Tenoctris is doing; but not *very* mixed, I assure
you."

Two of the quinquereme's five banks of oarsmen had
been rowing her. Those men, Carus among them, had been
the first released from the benches. Now they dropped
back into the hold through planks removed fore and aft,
while the oarsmen who hadn't been working came up
around the side vents in turn. The oarsmen stayed below
most of the time they were aboard ship: there simply
wasn't enough room on deck to hold them all.

Sharina looked into the eyes that had been her brother's,
and said, "Your highness? Do you . . . that is, are you glad
to be—as you said, walking a deck again?"

Carus met her gaze. He smiled, but this time his expression had the terrible majesty of lightning leaping between cloud banks.

"Will I be sorry to give up the flesh again, girl, when
Garric comes back?" he said. "For that's what you mean,
is it not?"

She nodded and swallowed. Her fists were clenched and her chest tight with fear of the answer.

"Girl," the king said. "I've killed men because I was angry, and there've been times when my blood was up and I killed for no better reason than that I had an excuse and someone was in reach of my sword. But my worst enemy never called me a thief."

He pinched the skin of his biceps with the opposite thumb and forefinger. "I've borrowed this from Garric," Carus said softly. "I'll give it back to him the first chance I have. It doesn't matter whether I want to or not, girl. It's my duty, and I'll do it regardless."

"I'm sorry," Sharina whispered. "I shouldn't have . . ."

Carus laughed cheerfully again. "Do you think you need to apologize for worrying about your brother?" he asked. "Not to me you don't, Sharina!"

He sobered. "Because I'm worried about him too," he added. "And even more worried about what Ilna may be facing."

Ilna thought the rhythmic clacking from the darkness summoned worshippers to the temple, so she touched Alecto's shoulder before sitting up in the straw. She frowned; the light slanting through the loading door at the end of the loft meant that the moon was still well short of zenith.

Alecto was on her feet with the dagger in her hand, as quickly and supply as a cat waking. She didn't try to slash Ilna in half-wakened stupor; her weapon was simply ready if needed, and sheathed again quickly when the wild girl saw that it wasn't.

"What's going on out there?" she said with an undertone of harshness. Ilna bristled, reading into the question an implication that the confusion was somehow her fault. Or not, of course—but everything Alecto did seemed to grate on her.

"I thought it was the call to the temple," Ilna said, "but—"

"Hey!" bawled the stablemaster from the stalls below. "You girls up there! Don't you hear the summons? Get out here now, or I'll come up with a whip!"

"If he likes to hear his voice so much," said Alecto in a deadly whisper as she started for the ladder, "then let's see how he'll sound as a soprano!"

Ilna caught the other woman's knife wrist. Alecto turned, still catlike, and tried to jerk her hand free. Ilna held her, smiling faintly.

"Hey!" the stablemaster repeated.

"We're coming!" Ilna said, her eyes holding Alecto's. "And watch your tongue when you speak to us!"

Alecto tossed her head and relaxed. "All right," she muttered. She gestured for Ilna to precede her down the ladder.

The stablemaster had already gone out into the night, leaving the door ajar behind him. The sharp rapping came again, closer. A horse whickered uncomfortably, as though awakened by the sound and nervous about it. With Alecto just behind her, Ilna stepped into the inn yard.

A priestess in a white-on-black robe stood beneath the archway to the street. Several lower-ranking functionaries accompanied her—clerks, a lantern-bearer, and a brawny man with a flat hardwood block slung from a pole. He'd been hitting the block with a mallet as an attention signal. Ilna hadn't seen that method before, but the sound was distinctive and seemed to carry as far as the blat of the cow-horn trumpet her brother'd used while herding sheep in the borough.

There were half a dozen soldiers in the priestess's entourage. They looked more bored than threatening, but they held their weapons with professional ease. Ilna had seen enough troops to know that these men weren't a militia of shopkeepers and day laborers, armed for the emergency.

"Fellow disciples!" the priestess said. She was a hefty woman; judging by her voice, she might not be much older than Ilna herself. "Evildoers entered Donelle during the past night and have profaned the Temple of the Mistress with the blood of a believer. The Mistress says they're still in the city. They must be caught and punished before they can do further harm."

All the windows facing the inn yard were open. Faces, the staff and guests alike, leaned out to hear the announcement. The servants and hangers-on who'd been in the yard to begin with were quiet and alert as well. Ilna had the impression that the respect they showed was real, not something frightened out of them by the soldiers' presence.

"In order to identify the evildoers," the priestess continued, "the gates have been closed. Everyone in the city will join with at least three other people who have known them for a year or more. Each group will report to a Child of the Mistress, who will mark each person's forehead."

"But I'm from Brange!" called a man who'd been sleeping in the box of one of the coaches. "I don't know ten people here in Donelle!"

"Those who've come as individuals into the city from other communities," said the priestess, "will report to the clerks with me. The Mistress has set gathering places here in the city for each region. Eventually everyone will have others to vouch for them—everyone but the evildoers!"

Men—there were no women in the yard save for Ilna and her companion—shuffled and spoke to one another in low voices. The attendant with the wooden gong cried, "Come along, now! Do you think you've got all night? We have the whole Leatherworker's District to enroll!"

"Yes, and you inside the building come out as well," the priestess called, gesturing toward the faces watching from the windows. "Quickly. It won't take long, but you must get moving!"

"What do we do?" Alecto whispered hoarsely.

"Stand watch while I choose a route," Ilna replied. She eased back toward the stable door, then slipped inside. The bustle in the yard would keep her from being missed for a time, but she and Alecto couldn't hide for long.

The warmth of animal bodies and animal breath enfolded Ilna and calmed her. She wasn't in a panic, but these were dangerous straits. She squatted on the trampled floor, then pulled a handful of straw from a manger and began plaiting it. Ilna rarely used her skill to make decisions for her, but in this case she had no choice. She didn't know how the Mistress had learned the interlopers were still in Donelle, but there was more to it than mere intuition.

Ilna's fingers wove straws in and around their fellows with a swift competence that would have seemed magical to anyone watching. The darkness of the stable didn't affect the work: this was a business for Ilna's soul and hands, not her conscious mind.

Outside an attendant called, "Move along, now, do you hear me? Who's next?" The buzz of voices was louder, some of them now female. Someone shouted back into the inn proper. The words were blurred, but Ilna could identify the cook from her angry tone.

She rose again to her feet, certain that the pattern was complete though she couldn't see it. As she reached for the door, Alecto whispered hoarsely through the crack, "There's a flunky coming this way. The fat pustule of a stablemaster was talking to him!"

Ilna stepped back into the yard. She glanced at the rough straw mat in her hand, then showed it to the wild girl.

"North and then northwest," Alecto said. Her face wrinkled in a thunderous frown.

"How did you do this?" she demanded. "I can see the

directions in it, but there's nothing here really!"

"Hush," said Ilna curtly.

The fat stablemaster had worked his way back through the crowd with a clerk and two soldiers in tow. "There's the other one!" he said to the clerk. "She was trying to hide in the stables!"

Under the gate arch, the inn's residents were giving their names to clerks while the priestess looked on. She pointed to the innkeeper, come from the main building in a nightshirt and cap. "I know Master Reddick by sight," she said. "Stamp him and then the ones he can vouch for."

"I went to get my outer tunic," Ilna said coldly, her eyes on the clerk as if the stablemaster were beneath her notice. "We have nothing to hide."

"Don't you?" the clerk sneered. "That's for me to decide, I think. Now, who are you?"

In his left hand was a notebook made of four thin leaves of birchwood bound with leather straps. The ink-filled tip of a cow horn dangled from a hook in his tunic collar, and he held a short quill between his right thumb and forefinger.

"My name's Ilna," Ilna said. She tossed the straw back into the stable behind her; it had served its purpose, now that she'd read its message. "My kinswoman here is Alecto. We're from Barca's Hamlet."

The soldiers watched Alecto with more than causal interest. One of them shifted his left arm slightly, as if ready to throw his small, round shield in the way of any attack the wild girl made.

"Barca's Hamlet?" the clerk repeated. "I never heard of the place."

Ilna shrugged. The only thing she'd feared was that the fellow somehow *had* heard of Barca's Hamlet—and therefore knew it was on Haft.

"It's north and west of here," she said. "We came to Donelle at the Mistress' summons."

"North and . . ." the stablemaster said. A deep frown furrowed his forehead. He glared at Alecto. "You come from the hills? You didn't tell me that!" .

"You might've known by looking at her," the clerk said, his nose wrinkling. "They're mostly animals up there. And not"—he turned his attention from Alecto back to Ilna—"many worship the Mistress."

"There's some of us," Ilna said, making sure that her tone carried the cold contempt she really felt for this functionary. The Mistress's service had no monopoly on his sort, jumped-up little worms who felt their slight authority made them important people. "Do you object?"

The clerk must have heard a threat in the words—and felt it might be justified. "What?" he said. "Of course not. Well, you'll report to . . ."

He paused, flipping back to the outer leaf of his notebook, then realizing there wasn't enough light to read it by without a lantern. "Well, I know there isn't a gathering place for people from the hills. You'll have to go the temple and ask them there. I'll give you an escort."

Ilna sniffed. "We can find the temple," she said curtly. "We have on past nights, after all."

Before the clerk could object, she added, "Come along, Alecto," and started for the gate across the inn yard. She nodded respectfully to the soldiers as she passed. One of them nodded back, but the men kept their eyes primarily on Alecto.

Someone had lit a stick of lightwood from the oven and stuck its base through the iron harness loop of an upturned wagon tongue. The flame threw a flaring, yellowish light across the inn yard.

A line had formed in the yard's forecourt. Clerks jotted information onto wax or wooden tablets, then divided the people into two groups. Those whose identity wasn't sufficiently guaranteed went out into the street, sometimes pausing first to don clothing for public wear. The others joined a separate group in front of the priestess herself in the gateway.

Ilna didn't want to call attention to herself by making eye contact, but as she neared the gate she saw the priestess touch a stamp to the cook's forehead, then press it into a pot of ochre again. The red pigment outlined a fat-bodied web spider whose forelegs spread in an encompassing arc.

Ilna started, then lowered her eyes and sidled past. She expected the cook to snarl something at her, but the woman wore a nervous expression and didn't seem to have noticed Ilna's presence. She looked as tense as if the mark on her forehead was a real spider.

The waiting soldiers didn't block the gateway, but they narrowed it considerably. Ilna waited for a pair of teamsters to go through ahead of her so that she didn't brush the cuirass of the man to the left. He gave her a speculative look, to which she responded coldly.

The disciples of Moon Wisdom seemed a straitlaced lot; in that at least Ilna felt kinship with them. The soldiers, however, weren't locals and apparently weren't followers of the faith either. They reacted to Ilna in the fashion she'd come to expect from young men with weapons or some other reason to feel full of themselves.

The lantern and burning pine knot hadn't made the inn yard very bright, but the street was darker still, especially where overhanging eaves shadowed the cobblestones. The teamsters turned to the right, the direction that Ilna wanted to go. She stepped away from the gate and paused, letting the others get farther ahead for privacy.

"Did you see that spider?" Alecto said. "Though I suppose it's what you'd expect from people who call out the Pack."

"I saw it," Ilna said without emphasis. She was interested to realize that the spider symbol had affected her companion as well. There was more to it than a smudge of ochre, though she couldn't have said what the added difference was.

In a less distant tone she went on, "I don't think we dare stay in Donelle if they're searching for us this way. We'll get out through the north gate and go on, the way the pattern indicated."

"I still don't know how you did that," Alecto muttered grudgingly. "All it was was a few wisps of straw, but when I looked at it I saw the road through the gates we left by last night."

"You don't need to know," Ilna said. The teamsters had disappeared beyond the jutting corner of the second building down the street. She set off after them.

"Faugh!" Alecto said, glaring at the pavement as she strode along beside Ilna. "The only thing worse would be crossing the lava barrens sunwise of Hartrag's village. The rock here doesn't cut like lava, I'll give it that, but half of it's covered with slime so slick we might as well be walking on ice."

Ilna sniffed. She almost asked what "lava barrens" were, but she decided that she didn't want to give Alecto the satisfaction of knowing something Ilna herself didn't. Instead she said, "If the people in the hills don't worship this Mistress, then we can hope that they'll hide us if the disciples come searching. Though I don't think they'll bother looking for us if we're no longer in Donelle and a direct danger to them."

That left the problem of Ilna getting her information back to Carus and the others in Valles, but she'd learned long ago to take matters one at a time. First she had to avoid being caught and disemboweled by the disciples of Moon Wisdom.

Alecto muttered, out of sorts and perhaps frightened by the twisting streets and stone buildings. In a louder voice she said, "I've hunted in canebrakes where the paths were straighter! How can people live like this?"

Ilna, who hated stone so much that she'd almost have preferred to walk on knives than on these streets, smiled coldly. "We'll be outside soon," she said.

"They closed the gates," Alecto said, her voice sharpened by the undertone of condescension she'd heard in Ilna's words. "We won't be able to walk straight out like we did last night."

"We'll manage," Ilna said. Her fingers were plaiting cords as she walked along. She wished she had some long straws snatched from the stable instead, because for this purpose she was working in a larger scale than she usually did. Her cords were short, no more than two fingers' lengths apiece, so she had to weave several to manage the effect she wanted.

She smiled harshly again. As she'd said to the wild girl: they'd manage.

A family—father, mother, three children, and at the end of the line a servant—passed them going in the opposite direction. At their head was a minor temple official whose lantern lighted his own way, not that of those he was guiding. He looked irritated; they were nervous and uncertain.

Ilna glared at the guide, then found her gaze softening as she met the eyes of the woman carrying her youngest in a sling of coarse cloth. They didn't know anyone in Donelle but one another, so they'd been roused from sleep and led off to a collection center for strangers from their district with no idea of when they'd be released. The children, already tired and whining, would be a shrieking burden long before then.

The Mistress and Her Children didn't care. Ilna supposed she needn't care either, since these people were part of the reason the Pack were loose to hunt in Carus' dreams.

She and Alecto came around a bend in the street which brought them into sight of the wall. The city gate had been closed, apparently with some difficulty. A freshly attached length of hawser ran diagonally from the upper hinge of one of the leaves, lifting the opposite corner so that it didn't sag into the ground and lock the panel open.

A dozen armed men stood in a morose circle in front of the gateway. They were militia, probably members of the night watch called out for this special duty. Close by were a trio of mercenaries, bulky fair-skinned armsmen from Blaise. There was a watchtower, but if its floors were in the same condition as the gate, Ilna understood why the guards weren't in it.

Both groups watched the women approach. The civilians looked worried; the attitude of the soldiers was more generally speculative, though Ilna noticed the senior man lifted his broad-bladed sword a finger's breadth in the sheath to make sure wouldn't bind if he needed to draw it suddenly.

One of the civilians held a lantern hanging from the crossbar of a pole. The lamp had at least two wicks, but the dirty parchment lenses passed only a yellowish glow. Ilna frowned as she walked closer, wondering if there'd be as much light as she needed.

Alecto walked a half step behind. She didn't touch the horned hilt of her dagger, but Ilna could smell murderous tension in the wild girl's sweat. Alecto might fly into berserk slaughter at any moment, driven mostly by fear. Against so many armed men, the result was a foregone conclusion.

"What are you doing here?" said a militiaman in a bronze cuirass, his voice rising a note on every syllable. His full white moustache flared into his sideburns. "You haven't been marked!"

Each of the militiamen had the spider stamping in the middle of his forehead, though the helmets of several of the men partly covered the symbol. The speaker wore real body armor and a number of the others had cowhide vests, which they obviously hoped would turn an edge. They looked more threatened than threatening.

"No, we haven't," Ilna said in a clear voice. The knotted pattern was a ball in her left palm. "Hold that lantern up, and I'll show you why."

The guards were all staring at her. The three professionals moved around to the side so that they had a clear view without being blocked by the militia.

Ilna nodded, gesturing them closer. When she thought everyone could see what she was doing, she reached down with her right hand and pulled the pattern open in the light.

The guards went down like lightning-struck sheep in a clatter of equipment and dropped weapons. They were stunned, not dead, but it would be hours before they regained their senses. The lantern broke on the pavement, spilling oil that blazed into soft flame.

The old man in the cuirass had fallen only to his knees. He pawed his eyes with his left hand and made choking noises. Bad vision had saved him from the pattern's full impact.

Alecto knelt over him, her dagger out. Ilna dropped her cords and caught Alecto's shoulder; she couldn't reach the knife wrist. Alecto twisted and slit the old man's throat to the spine. Blood gouted onto the cobblestones, black in the light of burning oil.

Ilna picked up the pattern and began to unknot it as a way of occupying her fingers. She was afraid of what she might do to her companion if she let her control slip.

"There's a wicket gate in the main panel," Ilna said coldly. "Help me get it open."

She put the cords in her sleeve and stepped to the city gate. A door small enough that she'd have to hunch to pass through it was set in the center of the right leaf. Ilna slid the drawbolt open, but the sagging frame kept her from pushing the wicket open.

Alecto slammed the butt of a watchman's spear into the

panel. It sprang ajar. Alecto stuck the shaft into the crack and levered the door fully open.

She smiled at Ilna. "Are we going out or aren't we?" she said.

"Yes," said Ilna. Her mind was white with fury, but she'd spent most of her life angry, so she knew how to control the emotion. She slipped through the doorway, out of Donelle.

On the pavement behind lay the ring of guards, their eyes open. They were breathing as heavily as sleeping seals; all but the man in the bronze cuirass, whose feet had just ceased to drum the cobblestones.

Garric swung to the top of the wall and found Lord Thalemos squatting there. "Where's the ladder down?" Thalemos cried.

A watchman with a cudgel and a whirling rattle stood calling over his shoulder to people Garric couldn't see around the curve of the wall. Probably it was a detachment of Protectors, summoned from the guardhouse at the front of the enclosure. More Protectors were coming down the street from the other direction, their spears raised to strike.

"Jump, you fool!" Garric snarled. Thalemos goggled at him, then leaped down without looking. He'd have belly-flopped on the pavement if Toster hadn't been there to catch him.

Garric jumped also, angry at the world and particularly at himself. He'd let his fury out at Thalemos, who was guilty of nothing worse than having lived a normal life which hadn't fitted him for slaughter and prison breaks. Between Garric's tone and the bloody sword in his hand, the rescued prisoner had almost broken his neck in fright.

And if that had happened, what would Tint's death have been worth?

A javelin flickered in the air. The leading Protector, still twenty yards down the street, threw up his hands and fell backward. Prada stood on the roof of the building where the gang was hiding. He cocked another missile. The surviving Protectors ducked for shelter in doorways.

Garric followed his group across the street and into the shop. Toster half helped, half carried Thalemos. Garric tried to sheathe his sword, but the curved blade and memory of Tint's cracking bones kept him from finding the mouth of the scabbard.

Metron was jabbering demands in his squeaky mental voice. It was with an effort of will that Garric managed not to smash the crystal between his heel and the cobblestones.

Halophus and Mersrig slammed, then barred the shop door behind Garric, the last to enter. The panel wouldn't withstand a determined burglar, let alone a military assault.

Vascay stood at the door of the inner room, gesturing Garric through tight-faced. The wizard lay on the littered floor, his head pillowed on a rolled-up cloak. Yellow lamplight helped turn Metron's complexion sallow, but Garric had seen corpses laid out for burial with more apparent life in them.

"Put the amulet on my chest!" Metron's voice said. "Quickly, now!"

Garric slipped off the silver chain and set it with the crystal on Metron's chest. He was surprised at how much lighter he felt; the amulet's psychic weight was greater than he'd realized.

The tiny figure of light within the crystal vanished. The wizard's lungs swelled. He lurched upright, snorting like a man saved from drowning. Looking around wildly, he shouted, "Lord Thalemos! Is Lord Thalemos all right?"

Heavy objects hammered the shop door. Wood splintered, followed by a scream.

"Who's next?" Hame cried in a high voice. "Who else wants to die for the Intercessor?"

"He's all right," Vascay snarled, "but he won't be long if we don't get out of here. Come on! You swore you could get us free!"

"Yes, but bring him here," Metron said, crossing his legs shakily. He'd drawn a circle of power on the grimy floor before going into the trance. Now he moved the oil lamp into the center of the figure and took the athame from under his sash.

Garric started for the main room. Vascay waved him back. "Stay with this one," he said. "I'll send the boy in."

Over his shoulder, he muttered, "I've seen enough wizardry for the night—and for a lifetime!"

Metron ignored him. He held the sapphire ring between his left thumb and forefinger, then dipped the athame in his other hand over the words written about the circle.

"*Rexi*," he chanted. "*Thorexi hipporexi . . .*"

The candle guttered—but not, as Garric first thought, because the wizard's movements were fanning it. The flame pinched in and expanded the way ale spurts from a full barrel, sucking the bunghole closed and reopening rhythmically. The light grew brighter but took on the chill red tinge of wizardry.

"*Maskelo*," said Metron. "*Maskelon maskelouphron.*"

Thalemos came into the room, wearing a more settled expression than Garric had previously seen on his face. The boy had been snatched from his cell and carried through a chaos that would've disconcerted anybody facing it cold; no wonder he'd seemed dazed most of the time. Now that Garric looked back on the events of the night, he marveled at the thought he'd really been involved in *that*.

"You wanted me, sir?" Thalemos asked Garric.

Garric hooked his thumb at Metron. "He did," he said. "I think he just wanted to be sure you were safe."

"*Besro, uphro, bolbeoch!*" Metron said. He held out the

ring in his left hand so that the jewel glittered in the wizardlight.

There'd been a pause in the noise from the front room. Now there was a crash that must have been the main shutter giving way, followed instantly by the shriek of steel on steel. A man cried out on a rising note.

Garric turned and started forward. His sword was still in his hand.

"Bring them here!" Metron shouted hoarsely. "I've opened the way, but we've got to leave quickly.

Garric looked over his shoulder. The wizard was trying to get to his feet, still holding up the ring so the candle-flame fell on it. The sapphire's facets scattered light in an oval of bright points against the plaster wall. For a moment Garric thought he was looking at the starry sky; then the pattern blurred into an outrushing void.

"I'll get them!" he said. He stepped into the main room.

The bandits hunched, facing the front wall of the shop. Echeon's men had battered through the center of the shutter, and the dovetailed vertical slats to either side slanted loose. Lanternlight from the street silhouetted the bandits and the men trying to fight their way in.

The Protectors were in half-armor, but the shop's lintel had tripped several of them. Their bodies lay in the opening, a fresh barrier for their fellows, and Mersrig had snatched up one of the fallen shields.

"Metron's got the way open!" Garric shouted.

A Protector gave wordless cry and rushed the opening, his shield held before him at arm's length. Toster met the charge, swinging his axe sideways to clear the low ceiling. The edge split the round of laminated wood with a crash, staggering the Protector. Two spearpoints and Hame's sword bit the man's knee and lower legs, bringing him down in screaming agony. His helmet rolled off; Ademos stabbed him through the back of his neck. None of his fellows had followed.

"The way's open!" Garric repeated. "Head for the back room! I'll hold them off!"

He didn't know why he'd said that, not consciously at any rate; it just didn't cross his mind that he wouldn't be the rear guard in this situation. The bandits were all familiar with weapons, but these tight quarters were sword territory. Garric was the only trained swordsmen among the Brethren . . . and besides, he was Prince Garric of Haft, descendent of Carus, the greatest ruler and man-of-war in the Old Kingdom.

A dozen Brethren looked at Garric, then scrambled toward Metron in the other chamber. They were the men on the fringes of the fight. There hadn't been room enough for the whole band in the opening. The Brethren had sorted themselves into those who wanted to face the first rush of Echeon's minions, and those who preferred someone else take that duty.

The others didn't retreat. Their blood was up, and they knew well that turning their backs now was likely to signal their own slaughter. The Protectors were massing in the street, in great numbers and under the control of officers who'd had time to assess the situation. Overhead, swords hacked at the roofing. Prada had barred the trapdoor when he came back down, but the tiles wouldn't last long under determined assault.

One-handed, Garric tugged the shield from a dead Protector's grip, tossed it up, and caught it by the paired handles in the center. It was a buckler, not a target that would've been strapped to the man's arm.

"Get into the back room!" Garric shouted. "Quickly, for the Lady's sake!"

"Stand clear!" said Vascay. "I'm going to throw out the last of the cave dust! That'll kill everybody in the street, and we can get away!"

"What!" shrieked Halophus. "Are you crazy?"

Vascay flung a bag overarm. The Brethren who faced

the opening now scrambled back in panic. They knew how indiscriminately dangerous the spores were.

The Protectors stood in a double rank, their small shields held forward. As an officer shouted an order, the bag caught the upper edge of a shield and burst in a spray of dust. The men pushed away, screaming in fearful agony. Their serried order disintegrated as though a volcano had just erupted in their midst.

"Go, boy!" Vascay said, clapping Garric on the shoulder. "They'll figure out it was plaster fallen from the ceiling soon enough, and I don't want to be around when they do!"

Only three of the Brethren remained in the side chamber with Thalemos and Metron when Garric followed Vascay through the doorway. Toster stood beside the roiling blur where the wall had been, his face screwed up in terror. He started toward the vortex, then flinched back. His axe trembled; the head and upper helve were slick with Protectors' brains.

"Get through or get out of the way!" Metron screamed. "How long do you think I can hold this?"

Garric tossed down the shield he'd appropriated and sheathed his sword without difficulty. He stepped in front of Toster and backed the big man away, keeping his own body between Toster and the wizard-door.

With a hand behind his back, Garric gestured the other bandits to go. To Toster he said, "You saved my life when I came back over the wall, Toster. I was done up from what happened inside. Without you to take care of Thalemos for me, they'd have had me there in the street."

Prada and Mersrig passed through the vortex, each pausing for a moment before jumping in. The void flashed with rose, then azure, wizardlight as the men vanished.

"Lord Thalemos!" Vascay said. "You're next! Except for you we could've stayed where we belonged."

"I'm afraid," Toster whimpered. "I won't do it! *I won't do it!*"

Thalemos shot Garric a look of uncertainty. Garric waved him fiercely on, afraid to turn away from Toster. Vascay grasped Thalemos by the waistband and the nape of the neck. He half walked, half threw the youth into the vortex ahead of his own entry.

Metron stood and stumbled toward the wall. When the sapphire no longer winked in the candlelight, the portal began to shrink. The wizard disappeared into it with the usual double flash. It continued shrinking.

Toster wore a short cape. Garric twisted the garment, then raised its cowl to blind the big man the way he'd have concealed fire from a terrified horse.

"Come on, Toster!" he shouted, holding the man by the left wrist and shoulder. "Run! With me!"

They lumbered forward, Toster sobbing like a child behind the thick wool. There was still a chance. . . .

"Now duck!" Garric cried, forcing down the big man's head at the same time he lowered his own. "And *jump!*"

It was like diving through a skin of ice over the millpond, hard and cutting and colder than life could bear. Garric tried to scream, but his flesh was a mist of atoms exploding across time and space. *He had no being—*

With a shuddering haste Garric was back in his body: gasping, lying on soft dirt in a forest like none he'd ever seen. He still held Toster. Around them were the other members of the band. Some—those who'd passed through early in the process—stood and looked nervously to their weapons.

Metron lay on his back. His expression was agonized, his eyes screwed shut. The ring was on his left middle finger. Without opening his eyes, he raised his hand so that the sapphire lay against the middle of his forehead. His right hand groped on his chest, then closed on the crystal amulet.

Vascay untangled himself from Lord Thalemos. Both men appeared to be all right, at least as much so as Garric himself was.

Sighing, Garric shoved himself onto his knees, then hunched upright. He could feel every part of himself; not just a finger, say, but every atom of skin and flesh and bone that formed each finger.

The pieces had been separate. Now they were joined again, were *him* again; but in the future Garric would never be able to forget their individual existences.

He looked around. The ground was mostly bare, but arching upward around him were clumps of flat-trunked green vegetation that hid most of the sky.

Something croaked. It sounded like a frog the size of an ox.

"You all right, Gar?" Vascay said. He still had one of his javelins. He used it butt-down as a cane as he got to his feet.

"Yeah," Garric said. He gestured at the forest. "Vascay, these aren't trees. It's grass. We're in a field of grass."

Vascay nodded agreeably, eyeing the landscape as he wiped loam from his javelin's butt spike. "Could be," he said. "Could be. What I'm happiest to see now is that it's not grass full of Protectors, eh?"

Thalemos walked toward Garric and stopped a polite double pace away with his hands crossed behind him, waiting to be acknowledged. Vascay had turned his attention to the long cut along Hame's side.

"Lord Thalemos?" Garric said. "You want something of me?"

All the bandits were up, apparently unharmed by their passage to this place. Toster was using the edge of a giant grassblade to clean his axe. He saw Garric and gave him a shamefaced grin.

Toster had nothing to be ashamed of. Telling him so would only make his embarrassment worse, though.

"Yes, I'm Thalemos bor-Laminol," the youth said. "Actually, what I wanted to do, sir, is introduce myself. And thank you for saving my life."

He smiled shyly, and added, "Saving my life several times that I know of."

"I'm Garric or-Reise," Garric said. "Or you can call me Gar, as the Brethren do."

He looked away as though to survey their surroundings. Thalemos as a person made quite a decent impression. The trouble was that when Garric looked closely at the youth, he saw instead Tint's terror-contorted face as she leaped toward the snake that would kill her.

"I, ah . . ." Thalemos said. "Master Garric, I won't keep you from your duties but, ah, I'm very grateful."

In a rush, he added, "Metron wanted me to go through the portal immediately. I refused to go until you were ready, sir."

Garric met the youth's eyes and managed to smile. "Because you thought Metron might not bother waiting for the rest of us if you were clear?" he said. "I'm glad that possibility occurred to you, milord. And that you chose to act on it."

The strange forest was alive with sounds, none of which proceeded from an obvious source. Most of the notes were very low, more in the order of trembles felt through the ground than ordinary noises.

Vascay came over to Garric and Thalemos. He nodded toward Metron, the only member of the group still on the ground, and said to both men, "Is he all right?"

With a quirked smile he added to Thalemos, "And if he's not, do *you* know what we do next?"

"He'll come around, I guess," Garric said. Metron hadn't moved from where he lay initially, but he'd clearly relaxed. "The art—wizardry—takes a lot out of people."

He stretched mightily, noticing kinks in muscles where he hadn't expected them. He added, "So do other things, of course. I'll be feeling this day's work tomorrow."

Garric grinned and—as King Carus would have—added, "Assuming I'm feeling anything tomorrow, of course."

A sound like that of a cicada, immensely magnified, came from the side where the giant grass gave over to oak-thick briars reaching immeasurably skyward. Metron rose to one elbow, looking in that direction. Garric touched the hilt of his sword, remembering that he hadn't sharpened the blade after the hard service it'd seen carving through the serpent's scales and spine.

The call sounded again, measurably closer. The bandits bunched instinctively, readying their weapons. "Chief, something's coming!" Ademos said.

"Form a line between me and Gar," Vascay said calmly. "Stay close but don't get in each other's way. Hame, you watch our back. This may all be a trick."

He walked to the side, placing himself on the projected left end. Garric drew his sword and strode to a spot ten or a dozen double paces to the chief's right. One of the grass-blades, so large that Garric's spread arms would barely span it, rose behind him. He supposed it'd protect his back, though if the animals living in this place were on a scale with the vegetation . . .

The call sounded a third time. A creature holding a tube with a plunger like an elongated butter churn stepped into sight twenty feet from Garric. It was six-limbed and chitinous, but it stood upright like a short man. It stopped when it saw the humans. Toster raised his axe in both hands and stepped forward.

"No!" cried Metron. "These are our allies. They'll guide and protect us for the rest of the way."

Two more of the creatures minced out of the forest to join the first. These wore gorgets of beaten gold. They didn't speak. Could they speak?

"Wizard, what are you playing at?" Vascay shouted.

"Do you think I don't recognize them? They're the Archai! They're the monsters that brought down the New Kingdom after Prince Garric died on Tisamur!"

"Yes, they're the Archai," Metron said, walking forward shakily. "But that's all in the past, Master Vascay. They're with us against the Intercessor, now. We can't succeed without their help."

Garric looked from the wizard to the gang's chieftain. For the moment he felt nothing, *nothing*.

He couldn't have died on Tisamur: he'd never been on Tisamur in his life. But . . .

"Against the Intercessor?" Vascay said, stalking toward the wizard in the center of the line. His peg dug into the soft ground, causing him to limp. "Of course they're against the Intercessor, you fool! It was the Intercessor that kept the Archai from sweeping over Laut as they did all other islands of the kingdom! What are you *thinking* of?"

"That was a thousand years ago," Metron said, facing Vascay but not raising his voice. "That was a different age, Master Vascay. We have the future of Laut and of the Isles to consider now. And our own future as well."

He made a spreading gesture. The sapphire winked on his middle finger. "How do *you* propose to get out of this place? For myself, I know of no way save through the Archai's help . . . and even then it will be hard, and very dangerous."

The Archa with the tube held it high with one of his middle arms, balancing the upper portion between the saw-edged top limbs. The creatures didn't carry weapons, but their limbs alone were designed to kill.

He—She? It?—jerked down on the plunger. The tube vibrated another raucous shriek. Prada cocked a javelin, in reflex rather than as a conscious threat. Vascay touched the man to calm him.

"Well, Master Vascay?" Metron said, letting a sneer of superiority creep into his tone. "What shall it be?"

"Chief?" said Hame. Vascay looked at him.

"It wasn't these bugs as killed my wife," Hame said. "It was Protectors did that."

Vascay swore into the empty forest, quietly but with a tone and viciousness that Garric hadn't expected to hear from that man's lips. He looked at Metron again.

"All right," Vascay said resignedly. "They're our allies. Now what?"

"It's already in hand, dear man," the wizard said unctuously. "Our transportation is coming now."

"Chief?" Halophus called. "The ground's shaking!"

"It's all right!" Metron said. "This is all planned!"

"By the Lady!" said Thalemos, standing near Garric but a comfortable distance behind and to the left. Since the youth didn't have a weapon, he properly kept back from the line of armed men. "What is that monster?"

It was twenty feet high and walked on more many-jointed legs than Garric could see or imagine. Most of the creature's squirming body was still hidden in the forest when the blunt head halted behind the trio of Archai; it must be hundreds of yards long. Two immense, multifaceted eyes covered most of the front; the mouth parts seemed small for the great body. A net of gold chain gleamed like a saddle blanket on the upper surface.

"It's a millipede," Garric said. He was glad to have Thalemos to answer; otherwise, he'd have been talking to himself, because he needed to get the words out. "That's all it is, a big millipede. They don't bite or sting, they're harmless."

The bandits edged closer together in the giant creature's presence. They weren't seeking so much protection as feeling the need of companionship in the face of the unimaginable. Mersrig had one of the Protectors' sturdy spears. He clutched it in both hands and seemed to be steeling himself for a rush.

Garric strode forward, putting himself in front of the

party. He could smell the millipede, now; the millipede or the Archai themselves. There was a slight astringency, an acid odor similar to that of sour wine.

"It won't hurt us!" Garric said to the Brethren. "They eat compost, that's all!"

It could step on them, of course; that would be as lethal as being in a collapsing building. But there were many ways a man could die. . . .

There were more Archai on the millipede's back, looking down over the smooth black curve of the armored segments. Their heads were triangular and expressionless.

Garric turned to the wizard. "What do we do now, Master Metron?" he asked.

"Do?" said Metron. "Why, mount our steed, of course, my boy. Under my guidance and protection, it will carry us to our destination."

One of the Archai on the millipede's back let down a ladder with center-hung wooden rungs on a chain of gold links. It clanged and clattered against the calcified segments of the creature's shell.

Toster grabbed a rung, then looked back at Vascay. "Yes, go on!" the chief said. "What choice do we have?"

Toster started climbing. Another man took the ladder behind him; the whole band drifted into line to follow. The wizard smirked.

"Master Metron?" Garric said, smiling and speaking in a voice that only Thalemos was close enough to overhear.

"Yes, my boy?" Metron said.

"I'm not your boy, Master Metron," Garric said, still wearing the deceptive smile. "I may be your ally, but I'm not your friend. And I'd like you to keep one thing in mind as we proceed."

The wizard's expression hardened. "Yes?" he said.

"People have died tonight over this business," Garric said. "Some of them were people I liked a lot more than I do you. And if I ever decide that you're sneering at my friends, either the dead ones or the living—I'll kill you. Whatever that does to anybody's plans. Do you understand?"

"Yes," said Metron curtly.

"That's good . . ." said Garric with a smile. His body was trembling with emotions and memories. "Because part of me would really regret it afterward. But it *would* be afterward, you see."

He gestured to the ladder. Vascay, the last of the Brethren, was climbing it. "Go on up, Master Metron. Thalemos and I will follow."

From the look on Metron's face as he turned away, he *did* finally understand.

Cashel cleared his throat. It was hard for him to think properly with the little brown people crying, "Master!" and "Great lord!"

Tilphosa rested a hand on his biceps, looking for reassurance. This wasn't a bad place she and Cashel were in, but it sure was confusing.

"I wish you'd stand straight and just talk to us!" Cashel said. The little people jumped up and stared like bunnies startled in the garden. Cashel supposed he'd spoken louder than maybe he'd needed to. He'd startled Tilphosa too, though she patted him and put her hand back on his arm just as quick.

"Lord?" the oldest of the little fellows said questioningly. Cashel had expected some of the people to fuss over the man he'd saved from the tree, but nobody seemed interested in him. He was sitting up, but his eyes didn't focus yet.

"My name's Cashel," Cashel said. "Just call me that. And this is Tilphosa—"

He frowned and looked at the girl. "Ah?" he said. "Lady . . . ?"

"Just Tilphosa," she said, speaking directly to the little people. "And how are we to address you, sir?"

Of course Tilphosa was used to this sort of thing, meeting people and taking charge. It wasn't something Cashel had ever had to learn about.

He smiled. Everybody in the borough knew who to turn to get their sheep settled down, though.

"We're the Helpers, great lady," the old man said. "My name is Twenty-second. May we feast you at our village, great lord and lady?"

Cashel's belly rumbled at mention of food. The berries had been a long while ago. From what he'd seen in the village he didn't guess there was a chance of bread and cheese, let alone meat, but most anything would go down a treat right now.

He looked at Tilphosa, expecting her to speak. She nodded crisply to him, passing back control: this was *his* job.

"Sure, we'd like that," Cashel said to Twenty-second. He pointed. "Ah, what's his name? The fellow who was being eaten."

"He was Fourteenth," Twenty-second said. "Come, great lord and lady, let us feast!"

The whole troupe fluttered around Cashel and Tilphosa, chattering among themselves. Their voices too high-pitched for Cashel to make out the words—if there were words, not just a sort of birdlike chirping.

Girls no taller than Cashel's waist took his hands. Three of them walked on either side, guiding him in the direction of the village. He held the staff crosswise in front of him while the girls skipped along and behind it like a train of draft animals hitched to a bar.

He glanced over his shoulder. Tilphosa was being conducted in the same fashion, though in her case by a bevy of young males. The rest of the Helpers spread to either side in a loose line. A few adults had run on ahead, vanishing into the immaculate plantings like deer in the forest.

"I'm hungry," Tilphosa called when he caught her eye. "Even if it isn't cooked food."

Cashel grinned in answer, but he was frowning again when he faced the front. He could just make out Fourteenth, still where Cashel had flung him clear. He hadn't moved since he sat up. The rest of the tribe had left him there alone.

Twenty-second walked a few paces to the right, smiling when Cashel looked over to him. "Lord?" the old man said.

Cashel almost asked about Fourteenth, but said instead, "Do you get many visitors here, Master Twenty-second?"

"No, no," Twenty-second replied. "You're the first one in—"

He turned up his palms in uncertainty. "I don't know how long," he said. "My father spoke of visitors, but whether he saw them or his own father did and told the tale, I don't know."

Cashel looked at the little man and looked up at the sun, now nearing zenith. The days and nights here seemed to be the usual length. Even if the years also were the same as Cashel was used to, though, these Helpers might not live as long as folks did—the lucky ones did, anyway— back home. It explained why they were making such a big thing about him and Tilphosa arriving, though.

The girls led Cashel in a gently weaving path. At first he thought it was high spirits and one girl or another tug- ging him more firmly than the girls on the other side. A shepherd learns to note small changes in the land, because sheep do. After a little while, Cashel realized that the girls were taking him by a path that led through the least amount of vegetation.

The Helpers themselves seemed not to trouble even the thickest foliage. Twenty-second walked through a stand of virgin's bower, but the white starry flowers were scarcely waving when the old man reached the outcrop beyond.

Cashel glanced back at Tilphosa. He'd have told her what he'd just figured out, but that might embarrass the Helpers. He decided to watch his own feet as much as he could and whisper to Tilphosa when they were sitting down.

They reached the village again. Quite a number of the tribefolk—a double handful, it looked like—were already at work in the central courtyard and carrying food from the drying racks. Others appeared from the forest, bearing handfuls of fresh fruit and nuts.

The Helpers didn't seem to make baskets any more than they wore clothing. Cashel thought about squirrels again; but they weren't, they were people who were just smaller than the folks in the borough.

The Helpers were too nice to be squirrels. From what Cashel'd seen so far, they were also too nice to be most of the people he'd met thus far in his lifetime. Except for the way they'd ignored Fourteenth after Cashel freed him, and there might be more going on there than an outsider could see.

The girls released Cashel at the passage between the huts. Twenty-second outstretched his hand as a guide without quite touching Cashel and led him into the courtyard.

"Ah, where should we sit?" Cashel asked, checking over his shoulder to make sure Tilphosa was with him.

"Anywhere you please, lord and lady," Twenty-second said with a sweep of his arm. "Wherever you are is the place of honor. Will you have juice or water to refresh you before the meal?"

"Ah, I guess water," Cashel said. He gestured Tilphosa to sit—on bare dirt, but they'd slept on nothing better the night before.

She sat, murmuring, "Water for me as well, thank you," to the older woman who'd entered behind her.

More Helpers were bustling into the courtyard, some carrying food and drink while others merely seated themselves in the open area. Cashel remained standing for a moment, his back to a hut, and he watched. Things didn't seem right; meaning that they didn't seem like anyplace he'd been before, not that there was anything *wrong* exactly about it.

The Helpers wouldn't hurt a fly, he thought. And indeed, maybe they wouldn't; but Cashel hadn't seen any flies or mice or any other animals around since he got up this morning.

Twenty-second took a container from a younger member of the tribe. Instead of offering it directly to Cashel, he pointedly drank from it himself and only then held it out.

Cashel felt his skin go hot; he hadn't realized his suspicions were so obvious to his hosts. He took the cup in his left hand and drank—

Cautiously at first: he might be embarrassed at his suspicions, but he *was* still suspicious. There was nothing but water in the cup, cool but really too flat to do more than cut the dust.

The container was kind of interesting, though. It wasn't pottery, just sun-dried clay. Sap or gum coated the inside to seal it the way Reise tarred the leathern jacks he used for crowds during the Sheep Fair. Unlike tar, this coating didn't flavor the drink. It was soft enough to dent with a thumbnail, but it rose back to a smooth surface afterward.

Tilphosa was being served from a similar cup—and again, the old woman beside her drank first. Tilphosa looked up at Cashel, her blank expression hiding surprise. Cashel squatted beside her, propping his staff against the hut where he could reach it easily if he had to.

The Helpers knelt rather than sitting—like Tilphosa— or squatting. Twenty-second dropped into place on Cashel's other side. Immediately a younger Helper offered the apparent chief several red apples that dwarfed his outspread small hands.

"An apple, lord?" Twenty-second said, taking a delicate bite out of one and holding it out to Cashel.

"Thanks, but I'll have a whole one," Cashel said, taking an apple directly from the servitor. It was pleasantly tart, tasting something like the green-ripening fruit that peddlers occasionally packed into Barca's Hamlet from orchards in the south of the island.

Cashel ate the apple down to the core and paused, wondering what to do. At home he'd have tossed it onto a midden or, if he were with the sheep, seen if he could get it into the sea. A servant plucked the core from his fingers before he was aware of her presence and disappeared with it.

The meal continued, fruits alternating with nuts. Many of the dishes were new to Cashel, but they were mostly good and often excellent. Twenty-second used a sharp stone to bore through the shell of a head-sized nut, drank from the opening, and then gave it to Cashel. The milky contents had flavor that the plain water lacked; Cashel drank the nut empty and was pleased to have more when the old man opened another.

Cashel hadn't expected this food to really fill him, but the nuts surprised him by doing a pretty good job of replacing the bread and cheese he was used to. A servant used a rock to break open the big nut after Cashel had drained it; the meat inside was solid and crunchy, with the same pleasant flavor as the milk.

And the food—not dishes, except the tumblers for water and the juices Cashel now drank cheerfully—kept coming. Each one was different; and each time Twenty-second politely insisted on taking a bite or a sip before the remainder was offered to Cashel.

The older female beside Tilphosa—her name was Seventeenth, if Cashel had heard right—tasted the girl's food also. It wasn't necessary anymore, but Cashel decided it was better just to ignore the business than to make a fuss that probably wouldn't change anything. For all their small size and friendliness, the Helpers were about as stubborn as the nanny goat Squinty Offot used to lead his sheep.

"Lord Cashel?" Twenty-second asked, as Cashel lowered a tumbler of sparkling red juice that he hadn't been able to drain. "Would you and the great lady care to bathe now that you've eaten? You've been travelling far, I can see."

Cashel was glad that his suntan hid the blush that would've returned to his face. "I can see . . ." the old man had said, but he'd probably meant, "smell." Ordinarily back home Cashel had ended his workday by scrubbing off, at least in any weather that didn't mean he had to break ice in the millpond first. He hadn't been able to do that since—well, since he'd dragged Tilphosa out of the surf.

"Down at the creek, you mean?" Cashel said. Down by that tree, was what he was thinking. It'd be a chance to see how things were going with Fourteenth, not that it was exactly his business. . . .

"Oh, no, we have a bath hut here," the old man said. He pointed to the hut on the left side of the passage into the courtyard. It was bigger than the others, but not enough bigger to remark on.

"If you'd like?" Twenty-second said. "Or perhaps your great lady would prefer to be bathed first? There isn't room enough for both of you together, I'm afraid. You're so much . . . so different from us Helpers."

Cashel rubbed his eyes as he thought. Sunlight and a full stomach were making him sleepy. It sure would be nice. . . .

"Tilphosa?" he said. "They're offering us baths in the hut there. Would you like . . . ?"

"Steam baths?" Tilphosa said, frowning. "But that can't be, can it?"

She pursed her lips. "Why don't you go ahead, Cashel?"

she said after consideration. "Then I'll decide."

"Right," said Cashel, rising with a studied control that concealed how full and stiff he was feeling. He had a flash of dizziness before the blood caught up to his brain, but it was gone as quickly as it came. "Master Twenty-second, I'd be pleased to accept."

The girls who'd escorted Cashel to the village clustered around him again. They were childlike; but not children, very definitely young women. Cashel looked at them, then to the chief, and said, "Look, sir, are they the bath attendants? Because I'd rather—"

"Of course, Lord Cashel," Twenty-second said. He made what seemed an idle gesture, but at once the girls disappeared into the crowd and the youths who'd guided Tilphosa stood in their place. Two of them took Cashel's hands.

"Wait," said Twenty-second. He gestured with both hands, palms up, to Cashel's ironbound quarterstaff leaning against the hut behind him.

Cashel snatched it, feeling calmer for the touch of the smooth hickory. It was a piece of his past, of his home. Life had been hard when he grew up an orphan in Barca's Hamlet, but it was a life he knew. Almost nothing Cashel had seen since leaving home had been familiar, and even when it was good it made him uncomfortable inside. It was all confusing, whether people called him Lord Cashel and treated him like a king or when man-sized insects tried to cut him down. . . .

The Helpers walked Cashel straight across the courtyard. Little people who'd been kneeling to eat moments before slipped out of the way without seeming to move. They had a marvelous grace, no matter what they were doing.

Two of the youths entered the hut ahead of Cashel. He squatted, peering inside. The floor had been slightly hollowed out, and the earthen surface was sealed with the same smooth gum as the drink tumblers had been. The door was low, but Cashel could fit on his hands and knees.

"Lord?" said one of the youths.

Cashel leaned his staff beside the hut's door, then hunched forward and crawled through the doorway. The truth was, even bare-handed he'd be willing to match his lone strength against all the little folk who lived in this village. Besides, Cashel's conscious mind couldn't imagine the Helpers being any more hostile than a brood of ducklings.

A tingly, vegetable scent clung to the hut's interior. Little hands loosened Cashel's sash and drew first it, then his tunic, away from him.

The Helpers twittered cheerfully as they worked. One youth measured Cashel's biceps with his fingers, and giggled. "So big, so very strong!"

"Lie down please, Lord Cashel," said a Helper already inside the hut. Cashel obeyed; the floor was slickly cool, pleasant after the morning of direct sun. His eyes adapted easily. Light filtered in through spaces in the flimsy roof as well as by the open door.

Cashel lay on his stomach, his head toward the door and his left cheek cradled on his crossed arms. More Helpers entered the hut, then one still outside passed in a bowl of sun-warmed water and a number of long gourds.

One youth opened the gourds with what looked like a simple twist of the dried stem. They burst outward into balls that looked more like ripe dandelions than they did the loofas Cashel was familiar with. The vegetable scent puffed out fresh and strong as each gourd opened.

A youth sprinkled water on Cashel's back and limbs. The rest of them, four or five at least, began rubbing him down with the gourds. The pods' touch was as warm and soft as raw fleece, but they made Cashel's skin tingle pleasantly.

A Helper worked his gourd over Cashel's neck and

shoulders. The touch of sunburn he'd gotten sitting in the sun vanished as if he'd been daubed with lanolin.

Cashel thought about spending a few more days in the village. He and Tilphosa had only the general goal of getting back to their separate homes, not a hard deadline, but . . .

Though Cashel didn't know of a deadline, there might still be one; this wasn't the place either he or Tilphosa was meant to be. And despite the Helpers' generosity, Cashel knew well how slim the difference between eating through the winter and starving could be in a rural village. Tilphosa ate more than any of the Helpers did, and Cashel ate as much as a whole hutful of the little people. It wouldn't be right to stay even for a few days.

It was nice to think of relaxing for a longer period, though, and the people were so—

Tilphosa shouted.

Cashel lurched to his feet. His head smashed through the hut's roof. He tried to raise his hands to fling away the frame of dried branches, but his arms didn't work. They felt cold—all his muscles felt cold.

Cashel's senses were clear, but he couldn't seem to move. The youths around him in the hut jabbered excitedly. A score of Helpers had brought down Tilphosa and were trussing her with Cashel's own sash torn into strips.

He tried to take a step forward. If he could walk, maybe he could work off the effect of the poison and—

He couldn't walk. He felt himself falling. He couldn't even put his hands out to take his weight, though the impact didn't hurt his numbed body either. "Duzi!" he would have cried, but his throat froze about the word.

Helpers gathered around Cashel in a circle. Twenty-second chirped quick orders. Cashel saw many tiny hands reach down to grasp him, though he couldn't feel their touch. His body swayed upward, lifted on the massed strength of most of the village.

The youths who'd been bathing him walked in front of the procession; their arms dangled loosely at their sides. The poison had been in the gourds, then. He supposed it'd wear off in time.

Cashel met Tilphosa's eyes as his body left the courtyard on scores of tiny feet. She'd been bound but not gagged. "I'll pray to the Mistress for you, Cashel," she called.

Cashel couldn't speak in reply, but there wasn't much to say anyway. It wouldn't have helped to tell Tilphosa to save her prayers for herself, because he figured she was going to need them shortly.

The poison would wear off in time, but Cashel wasn't going to have much time. The Helpers, the whole village of them together, were carrying him down to the man-eating tree.

He was about to replace Fourteenth as the tree's meal.

Chapter Fifteen

Iaeouoi!" Alecto concluded. She tapped her dagger point on the little fireset in the middle of the hexagram she'd scraped in the dirt.

Flame glittered. A line of smoke shot up, then bent at a right angle to drill into the undergrowth beside the two women.

Alecto muttered under her breath and leaned backward. She nodded. "There's the path, then," she said to Ilna. "I wouldn't have known it was there to be found if you hadn't been so sure."

Ilna looked in the direction the smoke pointed: up a rocky slope, toward a notch some considerable distance above them. Dawn was painting the trees on the upper slopes. It wasn't an impossible journey, even in the absence of a visible path; but it wouldn't be an easy one.

"Can you walk?" she said to Alecto. "If you can, we should start now."

The track they'd slept beside wasn't wide enough for wheeled vehicles; nothing passed this way to and from Donelle except pedestrians, pack mules, and herds being driven. That didn't surprise Ilna. Ever since the fall of the Old Kingdom, the only road into Barca's Hamlet had been as slight.

Still, with daylight there was the chance of traffic. The less the two of them were seen, the better their chance of escape.

"Of course I can walk!" Alecto said. "A little direction spell like that is nothing!"

Ilna didn't know whether her companion was posturing or if the effort of the spell really had been trivial. It didn't matter, of course.

"Let's go, then," she said. She ripped off a chunk of the loaf she'd brought from the inn's kitchen. Alecto had already finished her portion: it was wheat bread, something the wild girl had never seen before they entered the city. She'd devoured it ravenously.

Alecto rose to her feet and stretched. "I'll lead," she said. She raised an eyebrow, and added, "Unless you think you're better at following a trail than I am? Because it's no more than that, a trail that one or two people in a year come down to the city by."

"Go on, then," Ilna said with a brusk gesture. She ignored the longing expression Alecto gave the bread.

The slope was covered by mountain laurels, with widely spaced hardwoods where the soil was a little deeper. The shrubs weren't thorny, but their branches interwove in a tangle. Alecto picked as good a route as Ilna could imagine, but it was still hard going.

They paused in the notch. Water dripped from between layers of exposed rock, pooling in a hollow beneath before dribbling down the other side of the ridge. Alecto drank. Ilna tore the remainder of the loaf and gave half to her companion before she knelt to drink in turn.

Alecto was looking north when Ilna straightened, wiping her mouth. The direction they'd come from was wild enough, with only the narrow track—hidden from up here—to show the hand of men. On the far side there was even less to be seen. Enormous chestnuts and pines, bigger than anything Ilna had seen in the managed woodlands of the borough, stretched to the horizon.

Alecto swore bitterly and shivered. Ilna looked at her with a frown of surprise.

"I understand you not liking the city," she said. Indeed, Ilna hated cities almost as much as the wild girl did, and for the same reasons: too many people, too much stone. "I thought you'd be pleased to be back in the wilderness."

"This?" Alecto said harshly. "Trees like this are as bad as buildings! Where's the pastures, where're the farms? This is . . ."

She didn't have a word to finish the sentence, but her tone dripped with despair. Gently, really trying to help, Ilna said, "It's all part of the pattern, Alecto. Here the forest, there the sea . . . and the farms and villages woven through them, every strand in its place."

Alecto looked at her with loathing. "Your patterns!" she said. "You and those fools in the temple there! You bind people, and they bind the Pack. You're just the same as they are!"

"Do you think so?" Ilna said. Her voice was a cold whisper, completely without emotion. She put the remainder of the loaf back in the bosom of her outer tunic. "I think we'd better go on now, mistress."

"I don't like this place," Alecto muttered as she started

down the north slope. That was her idea of an apology, Ilna supposed.

She didn't need to apologize. Alecto was part of the pattern, just as Ilna herself was. Ilna could only wonder—she didn't assume, not when it was something good—whether the Weaver of the world's pattern was as skilled as a mortal might wish.

Instead of going down into the valley, Alecto led them to the west along the slope of the hill to their left. Ilna couldn't see any sign of a trail, but the wild girl gave every evidence of knowing what she was doing. Ilna didn't like her companion, but Alecto's skills were as real as Ilna's own.

Dead leaves and pine straw covered the ground so thickly that there was almost no undergrowth except where a mighty tree had fallen. The slope was steep, often a perfect diagonal, and the patches of visible soil were rocky. Despite that, the trees were of a grandeur beyond anything Ilna had seen or imagined.

She smiled faintly. Her brother would love this forest; wood was to Cashel what fabrics were to her. Of course, Cashel would be planning the best way to begin cutting these giants down.

"They don't come this way often," Alecto said, speaking loud enough to be heard without turning her head. "Once or twice a year is all. Like peddlers coming through Hartrag's village, but here they were going down to the city, not coming up from it."

"Are you following the track with your eyes?" Ilna asked. "Or are you using your art?"

"It's all one," Alecto replied. "It's just finding the path, however you do it."

Ilna scowled, but when she thought about it she decided that Alecto wasn't refusing to give a straight answer. To her, it *was* all the same. Alecto was no more sure of how she found the path than Ilna would know how she recognized a neighbor at a distance too great for eyes alone to make out features.

It was that talent that had taken Alecto into the dream-world without a wizard in the waking world to put her there. The skill the Pack used in hunting down their prey must be similar.

Ahead of them was a narrow gap; a slab of rock had split, and the halves had tilted apart. Ilna stopped. When Alecto looked back at her, Ilna pointed, and said, "It's on the other side of that. The place we're looking for."

Alecto scowled. "How do you know?" she asked.

Ilna shrugged. "The pattern," she said. "It all connects here."

Alecto sniffed. She led the way between the sheer walls of rock. On the other side, straggling across the steep slope, was a village of timber houses and a temple with fluted stone pillars.

Sharina lay with her cloak as blanket and ground sheet, looking at the stars. Tenoctris slept soundly on the sand beside her, her breath whistling in an even rhythm. Sharina was too weary to sleep, but the chance to stretch out at full length was a blessing she wouldn't have appreciated even a few days before.

The royal fleet had beached on a ragged circle of coral sand. Much of the nameless atoll would be underwater at high tide, but the vast array of ships and men was only halting here for a few hours. They'd crossed half the Inner Sea; they would cross the remainder before they got a real rest.

Sharina could have slept under a sail spread on spars, but the night was mild, and she saw no need of shelter. The force carried no unnecessary baggage: King Carus alone had a small tent for privacy. The rest of the assembly thought that was because he was their leader; Sharina and

Tenoctris knew it was because the king's nights were tortured. Morale might have suffered if the troops learned the truth.

Driftwood fires spluttered at a dozen points around the sand. Most of the oarsmen weren't sailors but rather laborers recruited from Valles and the countryside. Among the thousands were many to whom the warmth and sparkle of a fire was more important than sleep.

The Blood Eagles who guarded the women and Carus in the tent beside them stood quietly, leaning on their spears and watching the night. These men had replaced the detachment who'd been on duty earlier; the strain of shipboard was as great on the Blood Eagles as on anybody else, so even they needed a chance to relax before boarding the vessels for the next stage of the voyage.

Carus shouted inside the leather tent. Sharina heard the *sring!* of his blade clearing the scabbard. The side panel bulged as the king thrashed against it.

Sharina jumped up. The guards had heard also, whirling with their weapons ready.

"I'll handle it!" Sharina said to the officer who stood with his sword drawn, reaching for the tent flap with his left hand. "Tenoctris!"

The tent could have slept four if they were good friends, but the roof was too low even at the center pole for Sharina to stand upright. There wasn't much light in the open air— the waxing moon had just risen—and the tent walls were opaque. She opened her mouth to cry, "Your highness— " and Carus had her throat in his big left hand.

A speck of wizardlight glittered in the air, then burst. A faint azure haze clung to the struts that supported the corners of the roof; under the present conditions it lighted the interior as well as a lamp would have done.

Carus relaxed his grip and wiped his hand on his tunic. "Sorry," he said with a wry smile. He shuffled back from the flap. "Come in, won't you? Tenoctris—"

The old woman peered into the tent past Sharina's shoulder.

"—you come too."

He sheathed his sword with a movement Sharina couldn't follow even though she'd watched him do it. She wondered how the king had been able to draw the weapon in the dark confines of the tent.

The glow was fading to blackness. Sharina saw the half gourd with fire-making tools in the corner beside the oil lamp. With the last of the light she struck the steel against the flint, spraying sparks into dried milkweed fluff twisted on a twig. When the tinder blazed up, she touched it to the lamp wick.

"Thanks," said Carus with a kind of smile. "I do better with a flame than with the other kind of light."

The smile grew broader and real. To Tenoctris he added, "Mind, I was glad of anything at all right then, mistress. And I'd guess Sharina was even more pleased to have it."

"Very glad," Sharina said as she hooked the lamp onto the wire hanger attached to a roof strut. She managed to grin so that her face wouldn't give away the fact that she'd thought in the moment Carus seized her that she was about to die.

"More dreams, your highness?" Tenoctris asked. She rubbed her eyes with the back of her hand, looking worn. The wizard had saved Sharina's life—perhaps—by lighting the tent's interior when she did, but the effort required to do that out of a sound sleep had been considerable.

"The same dream," Carus said, quietly but with a murderous scowl. "I thought it was as bad as it could be when it started, but it wasn't."

His smile was real while it lasted, but it slumped after a moment into a blank expression that was without hope or any other emotion.

"There isn't as much of me left as there was before the dreams started, I'm afraid. And the moon's still waxing."

Tenoctris drew a square in the tent's sand floor with her index finger. Sharina couldn't read the words the old woman wrote around the four sides—the white coral sand filled in the marks as she drew them—but the crescent moon in the center of the figure was unmistakable.

She looked up at Carus apologetically. "Your highness?" she said. "Would you rather I go out—"

The king swept the offer away with his left hand. "Do what you need to do here," he said. "It'll take more than a friend's spells to bother me tonight."

Tenoctris looked around her, realizing that her satchel of paraphernalia was outside the tent. Sharina understood her need and offered the spill she'd used to light the lamp. Tenoctris nodded gratefully. Using the burnt twig as her wand, she tapped the four directions, chanting as she did so, "*Nerxiarxin morotho thoepanam iothath. . . .*"

Stabbing the wand down into the crescent she concluded, "*Loulonel!*"

Nothing happened.

Carus frowned. "Did something go wrong?" he asked. He spoke calmly, but Sharina had seen the muscles of his throat and cheeks draw up as Tenoctris intoned her spell.

Tenoctris smiled wearily. "Not at all," she said. "You can go to sleep again, your highness. Nothing more will trouble you tonight."

"Can I?" Carus said. He chuckled. "I think I'll leave the lamp lit, though. Till this is over, I'd better sleep with the lamp lit."

He looked at the two women. His expression was drawn and very tired.

"I wouldn't run if I could, you know," Carus said. "I never did. When somebody made himself my enemy, it was always going to be him or me. I never tried to talk things out, I just went for his throat. And in the end, of course, I met somebody who was better at that game than I was . . . and I drowned, and the kingdom died."

Sharina touched the back of the king's left hand. "You're not going to lose this time, your highness," she whispered.

"No, I'm not," said the ancient king. "Because if I lose this time, dears, I'll spend all eternity in the hands of those gray things in my nightmare. I don't know that I could stand that."

Carus laughed loudly, as though he'd made a joke. To her horror, Sharina found herself laughing also. It was funny, if you were the sort of person who found it so.

The millipede's motion was remarkably soothing. The relatively tiny legs weren't visible from the creature's back. They worked so smoothly that Garric couldn't guess what the two pairs supporting the segment he stood on were doing at any given moment.

The long body curved around obstacles, but its general course was as straight as that of a ship on the open sea. An Archa seated between the compound eyes guided the beast by touching a golden rod to the joint between the head and the first body segment. One end of the rod was spiked, while the other was a stiff fan.

Metron and Thalemos were immediately behind the driver. The wizard sat cross-legged; he'd chalked a pattern on the millipede's calcified armor, but at the moment he was reading in a palm-sized codex instead of working an incantation. Thalemos viewed the moving landscape in silence and with a noble unconcern, but even at this distance Garric could see that the boy was tense.

Vascay was with the remainder of the band several segments up the body from Garric, checking Hame's wound. Finishing there, the chieftain walked carefully back. His peg didn't have as good a grip on the smooth, sloping surface as the bare feet of his Brethren.

The score or more of Archai riding the millipede had

strung a lacework of gold chains across the creature's back, pegging it at intervals to the body armor. A man could grab the chains if he started to slide, but that would be undignified. Vascay couldn't expect to lose his dignity and still retain his position as chief.

The forest wove its patterns above them. The sky was almost never visible, but the giant grasses filtered down much of the light which the leaves and needle-thick limbs of normal trees would have absorbed. Occasionally Garric saw the waggling antennae of an insect on a high stem; and once there was a spider, built on the same scale as the millipede, which watched motionless as they wound their way past.

"So," said Vascay in a normal speaking voice. He and Garric were the only humans on this body segment, though a trio of Archai worked with some golden apparatus of uncertain purpose beside them. "What do you think, lad? Of where we are and what we're doing?"

Garric grinned. "What we're doing," he said, "is waiting for Master Metron to tell us what the next stage is. I can't say I find that a comfortable business, but neither do I see an alternative. And as for where we are—"

He looked around. A beetle bigger than any ox in the borough stared at them through the myriad facets of its eyes.

"—I'd rather it were elsewhere. Though as you said when we arrived here, it's healthier for us than Durassa with a regiment of Protectors trying to lift our heads."

Vascay chuckled. He turned to look toward Metron at the front of the millipede. With a smile as cheerful as if he were sharing a further joke, the chief said, "I've been wondering what we'd learn if we staked out our wizard friend and started touching him up with a hot iron. Eh?"

"We wouldn't learn anything I'd be willing to trust," Garric said. He didn't allow his distaste for the thought of torture to creep into his tone. "And I'm pretty sure we wouldn't learn how to get out of where we are now."

The millipede was crossing low ground; standing water reflected the creature's pale belly plates and the blur of its legs. The color of the forest had become the darker green of sedges. Though the millipede was so steady that it scarcely seemed to be moving, it covered the ground quickly.

"Aye, that's probably so," Vascay agreed. "And of course there's our hard-shelled companions to consider as well—"

He turned his bland smile on the Archai sharing the segment with him and Garric. They'd erected a machine on spiderlike golden legs. One of the creatures turned a lever with its middle pair of arms; the other two watched intently as gears whirred in apparent pointlessness.

"—but if it were no more than that, I'd be willing to take the risk."

"What's that sound?" Ademos called. He was among the dozen or so bandits standing on the third segment forward of Garric and Vascay. Some men were looking around in obvious concern; others just seemed puzzled.

"I don't hear anything," Vascay said to Garric in a low voice.

"I do," said Garric. "It's very high, a squeal or . . . It's like metal rubbing."

Or worse. The instrument the Archai used to announce themselves had grated on Garric's nerves, but this felt like someone drilling behind his eyeballs.

The Archai heard it also. The one cranking the machine worked faster while a companion chittered at him. The third Archa ran toward the rear of the millipede with stiff, jerky strides as though his legs were stilts. He disappeared at last, hidden by the creature's slow curves.

Metron and three Archai at the millipede's head began to argue in the insects' high-pitched form of speech. One of them was the driver, his triangular head rotated to face back over his narrow shoulders.

"Ready your weapons, boys!" Vascay called. "It looks like we're going to have some excitement."

He stepped closer to Garric and gestured toward the millipede's tail with his javelin. "Any more Brethren down that way, lad?" he asked.

"No," said Garric. He drew his sword, wishing he had a whetstone to touch up the blade. Carus—and therefore Garric—had always carried a small stone beside the dagger on the other side of his belt from the sword scabbard, but Ceto hadn't been as careful of his tools.

"Right," said Vascay quietly. "Then let's join the others. I think we'll do better to stay close for the next while."

They stepped forward. Vascay walked easily now, no longer concerned about his footing. He twirled his remaining javelin like a baton between the fingers of one hand, then those of the other.

Two of the Archai stopped arguing with Metron and rushed toward the millipede's hindquarters. The driver faced frontward again; Metron began drawing words around the heptagram he'd already sketched on the creature's glossy black armor.

Thalemos spoke. The wizard ignored him. Thalemos tried again, then straightened stiffly and marched back to join the bandits just as Garric and Vascay arrived. Several of the men eyed him with hostility.

"Lord Thalemos, do you have any idea of what's going on?" Garric asked, speaking in part to make the youth "one of us" in the minds of the Brethren.

"I'm sorry, I don't know any more about this than you do," Thalemos said. "Metron has been too busy to keep me informed."

His voice sounded thin. The young nobleman was irritated at being treated disrespectfully, Garric guessed; but he was too well bred to admit the fact, especially since

Metron probably *was* busy trying to save them. To save Metron's own life, anyway, but the rest of them might benefit.

Something was running beside them in the forest. It stayed parallel to the millipede's course and about a bow-shot distant, a repeated flicker of movement glimpsed through the great grass stems.

"Look there," Garric said, pointing with his left hand.

"They're on the this side too," said Halophus, his voice rising. "They're closing in!"

The shriek at the bounds of audibility sounded again. It seemed closer this time, but Garric couldn't tell which direction it came from. The figure he'd spotted in the near distance finally came into full view.

It looked like a corpse wrapped in its winding sheet; it had neither legs nor arms, but it coursed effortlessly over the broken ground at a pace no man could have matched for long. Two similar figures came out of the forest behind the first, all closing on the millipede.

There was a jangle of gold: an Archa had tossed a boarding ladder over the millipede's side. The links jounced against one another and the creature's armor. The Archa climbed down though the ladder was swinging wildly as the millipede strode forward.

The Archa leaped when it neared the ground, meeting the trio of shrouded attackers with a flurry of its saw-edged forelimbs. The sharp chitin ripped through the skin of the first of the strange creatures, letting out pale ichor and coils of violet intestine.

A fog of light spread from the other pursuers to bathe the Archa, searing the warrior black where it touched. The Archa shrilled in agony, but its forelegs were still chopping into a second shrouded figure when the millipede carried Garric out of sight of the battle.

"There's more of 'em coming," said Toster, rubbing the

flat of his axe on his tunic sleeve as he looked into the forest.

Despairing cries from the other side drew the humans' heads around. Riding the millipede was like being on ship-board: if you were on one railing, you couldn't tell what was happening near the opposite side of the hull. Another of the Archa warriors was gone, presumably over the side to sacrifice itself against their attackers.

"I don't like the bugs," Toster said quietly. "Those things like slime molds're worse, though."

The attackers *did* look a little like slime molds, Garric realized. The disemboweled one had seemed to be an an-imal, but there was nothing in this place Garric would've wanted to swear to.

He smiled with the dark humor he'd picked up when King Carus shared his mind. Silently he added, *Least of all that I'm going to leave it alive.*

A dozen shrouded creatures were approaching from the right side. Across the millipede's back Halophus cried, "Ten! Thirteen! Oh may the Shepherd guard me, the woods're full of them!"

The Archa pumping the levers of the strange machine redoubled its efforts. His fellow rotated his head from one side to the other, then sprang to the left and disappeared over the millipede's side. From the suddenness of the Ar-cha's decision, it was probably committing suicide rather than making a real attempt to solve a hopeless problem.

"I could take one down," Vascay mused, tapping the javelin gently into the palm of his hand. "But I think I'll wait, eh? For a better target."

"Better, sir?" asked Thalemos.

The chieftain smiled. "For a target that might make a difference," he said. "Cheer up, lad. We haven't been hung yet."

Metron shouted, "*Sieche!*" and held the sapphire above the figure he'd drawn. Blue wizardlight flared in sheets, tearing out of the sky and through the waving grass.

The Archa at the machine shrieked. Crackles of azure light enveloped the gold, shrivelling the Archa like an ant dropped on live coals. The gears began to whir at a speed that concealed all but shimmers.

Garric felt the hairs rise on the back of his neck and arms. He wasn't sure whether that was a natural response to what he was watching or if a thunderbolt was gathering to strike.

The millipede continued to pace onward as before, but the surrounding forest shifted. The light went from a wan mixture of browns and greens to a red almost too deep to register on Garric's eyes. The trunks seemed to grow broader, then went gray; the landscape vanished into a moving blur like the flow of a spillway. Bandits cried out, and Garric heard the moaning call of Halophus' horn.

Metron slumped, his right arm under his body and his left with the ring stretched out toward the millipede's head. The forest began to come back into focus; daylight regained its normal hue.

Garric staggered but caught himself. His eyes'd been tricked by the appearance of the landscape slowing down, but his body didn't feel the change in motion. Beside him Hame fell to his knees and cursed.

Vascay touched Garric's arm and nodded toward Metron. The wizard had slipped slightly. His left hand twitched, trying to grip the gold net but unable to close properly.

Garric sheathed his sword and started forward. Thalemos tried to follow him but swayed dangerously. Vascay grabbed the youth's arm and held him despite his attempts to jerk free.

Garric didn't like or trust Metron, but they needed him: he caught the wizard by the shoulders and lifted him upright. Metron's face was blank. His eyes focused on Garric, but there was no understanding behind them.

The driver rotated its head back to stare at the humans for a moment, then faced front again. Garric stayed where he was, feeling the wizard's pulse steady and his breathing slow. Only when Garric was sure Metron had recovered from the ordeal of the incantation did he stand again and look around him.

The landscape through which the millipede strode was much the same as that they'd seen ever since they entered this world. There was no sign of the shrouded monsters who'd attacked earlier.

The Archai machine had slumped into a gleaming mass; its gears had melted together. The only sign of the operator was a smudge against the gold. The creature's arm was fused to the lever it'd been working. That, and the driver, were all that remained of the Archai.

Something called in the distance. The forest stretched on, and the millipede paced forward.

Either the Helpers chanted nonsense syllables just to keep time, or they were singing in a language Cashel didn't understand. They seemed very cheerful, even the youths leading the procession who stumbled occasionally from the effects of the poison they'd rubbed into Cashel's body.

For Cashel it was like floating on his back in a gentle stream. He couldn't move his head, but the tree they carried him toward was generally in his field of view. Its foliage shivered in anticipation, and a branch lowered with the lazy grace of a vulture's wing adjusting to the wind. At its tip, a huge leaf unfolded.

Cashel wondered what the little people would do with Tilphosa. Perhaps they'd let her go; *he* was the one who'd hurt the tree they—what? Tended? Worshipped?

Perhaps; but he didn't believe it. If the tree required human flesh, then the Helpers'd be glad for the girl's presence as soon as Cashel had been digested. Though a slight thing, Tilphosa would make two of the tiny natives.

Except for touch, Cashel's senses were even clearer than usual. He could see and hear perfectly, and he smelled the tree's unfamiliar perfume as they neared it.

Twenty-second called a sharp order, bringing the Helpers to a halt two double paces out from the trunk. Cashel heard a rustling as the great leaf slithered across the soil toward him. He couldn't feel the little people change their grip, but they slanted his feet to the ground and tilted his torso upright. The poison turned him not only numb but stiff as a board.

The Helpers had rotated Cashel's body when they pushed him into position, so he was now looking back the way he'd come. At first he thought the trail of smoke rising from the village was a hallucination from the poison. Then the smoke thinned and bright flames shot up; it was a real fire.

The leaf began to fold about Cashel, starting at his feet. He felt a tinge, the first feeling of any sort that he'd had since the youths had bathed him. The leaf's touch didn't hurt but it tickled, and his frozen throat wouldn't let him laugh.

There was a shower of sparks in the air above the village; a moment later came the crackling roar of flames rising from whatever it was that had fallen. One of the Helpers heard it also. She looked over her shoulder, then began to scream like a leg-snared rabbit. The whole village turned, moving together the way pigeons wheel as a flock.

Tilphosa came out of the blazing village, staggering slightly. She held a torch in her right hand and with the other dragged Cashel's heavy quarterstaff.

Twenty-second pointed to her, trying to force a command through dry lips. Tilphosa slashed her brand through a figure eight. The Helpers screamed and scattered in all directions. The vegetation nearby couldn't hide a vole— but it hid them.

The leaf continued to fold over Cashel, as slowly as the light fails on an autumn evening. It had covered his legs and torso now, and it was beginning to blinker his face. His bare arms tingled, and the darkness coming over his eyes may have been more than just the leaf's steady progress around them from both sides.

Tilphosa stood in front of him and dropped the quarterstaff on the ground. The fire had left smuts all over her head and body, and her wrists were badly burned.

"I'm not strong enough to do what Cashel did to you, tree!" she shouted. "I'll use this instead."

She raised her torch, the ridgepole of one of the huts. The flaming tip was out of Cashel's range of vision. He heard the sizzle of sap bubbling from the bark above him.

The tree made a sound like canvas tearing. The leaf holding Cashel started to unravel from the top down. He tilted forward and tried to stick his hands out in front of him.

"Burn!" Tilphosa screamed. She caught Cashel's arm with her left hand and used him as a brace to jump higher, slashing her torch. "Let him loose or die!"

The leaf crumbled. Cashel toppled outward. He couldn't move his arms quickly enough to get them under him, but he took the shock on his left shoulder. It wouldn't have hurt much even if he hadn't still been half-numb.

Tilphosa grabbed Cashel by the wrist with one hand and tried to pull him away. Her right arm held the torch up, threatening the tree if it tried to snatch them again.

Even with both hands and putting her whole body into the effort, the girl couldn't have lifted Cashel by herself, but he managed to move his own arms enough to crawl forward. His legs were a dead weight dragging furrows in the dirt, though feeling was starting to come back.

When Tilphosa saw that Cashel was moving by himself, she let go of his arm and picked up the quarterstaff. Cashel found that, as he crawled, he gained more control over the muscles. He was properly up on all fours by the time he and the girl'd gotten beyond the circle of the tree's limbs.

"How did you do it?" Cashel wheezed. He could form words again, though his lips didn't bend properly to close some of the syllables. "How did you get loose?"

"I used this," Tilphosa said. She dropped the staff and held up her crystal pendant. The sun glittered dazzlingly on its polished surface. Steadying the disk, she concentrated a white-hot pinpoint of light on a scrap of the leaf Cashel had ripped from the body of Fourteenth when they first saw the tree. Smoke rose, then cleared into a flame that drew the rest of the leaf curling toward it.

Cashel drew a deep breath, then rocked his torso backward so that he was kneeling upright. "Would you give me my staff, please, mistress?" he said politely, pausing to suck breaths deep into his lungs. "I'd feel better to have it."

Tilphosa dragged it to him, apparently unable to lift the iron-shod hickory with her one free hand. Her face looked gray beneath the tan, and her wrists were badly blistered.

Cashel took the staff, feeling strength flood back with the touch of the smooth wood. "The jewel burned through the ties?" he asked. His voice was stronger, too.

"No," said Tilphosa. She managed a smile. "I couldn't point the lens there because of the way I was tied. I lit the hut beside me and used that fire to free my wrists."

Cashel looked at her. She meant she'd held her wrists in the flame till the wool straps burned off her skin.

Cashel planted the staff on the ground before him, then lifted himself to his feet with his shoulder muscles. For a moment he swayed. Cautiously, he lifted the staff, then took a step forward. He lurched like an old man, but he didn't lose his balance. The second step was easier.

He looked around. The Helpers had disappeared like dew in the sun. The tree's branches were drawn up close to the trunk the way a terrified old lady covers her face.

"I wonder what happened to the one I saved?" Cashel said. "Fourteenth."

"I don't care," said Tilphosa venomously. "They all deserve to die. I hope they do!"

Cashel shrugged. "I wish I had some sheep oil to wash your wrists in, mistress," he said. "I guess for now we'll pack them in mud and hope to find better before long."

He turned and looked at the tree again. It was motionless except for a drop of sap falling from the flame-swollen bark.

"Are we going away now, Cashel?" Tilphosa asked.

"Soon," he said. "Tilphosa, did all the houses burn in the village?"

Tilphosa frowned. "No," she said, "I don't think so. The breeze was out of the east, so the eastern half should be still all right."

"Good," said Cashel. "I'm going to bring a couple of them down here."

He made a pass with his quarterstaff, just to be sure everything was working right again. The heavy staff slid through his fingers with greasy ease.

He eyed the tree again. His face was still, but there was a smile of satisfaction in his voice as he added, "I'm going to pile them around the trunk of that thing, mistress. And then you can light them off with your torch."

"Oh," said Tilphosa. Her lips spread into a cheery smile. "Oh, what a *good* idea!"

Her laughter was so infectious that Cashel started chuckling too as they walked the short distance back to the village.

Chapter Sixteen

Alecto brightened visibly at sight of the straggling village. She stood straight and paused to adjust her wolfskin cape to show her breasts to better advantage.

People—women and children, as best Ilna could tell—were working in small plots of corn and vines scattered as widely as the houses. There hadn't been any attempt to terrace the slopes, so the plantings were in whatever bits and pieces of soil that nature offered.

Goats browsing the steeper slopes were the first to notice Ilna and her companion. The animals raised their heads and stared, drawing the attention of a herdboy. He made a trumpet of his hands, and called, "*Yi-yi-yi-yi-yi!*"

His cry carried through the broad valley like a hawk's piercing shriek. Everybody looked at the approaching strangers. Men appeared from the woods, some of them carrying tools. One ran into a house and came out with arrows and a bow, which he proceeded to string.

"Why don't they have dogs?" Alecto wondered aloud. "Still, this is the way people are meant to live. Plenty of room between them, but not just wasteland like between here and that cursed city. We'll be fine here."

"Yes," Ilna said, though the only thing she agreed with was the notion that she'd be able to handle whatever chanced to come up. The villagers looked wary of strangers—as who wouldn't be, off as they were in a place that saw few visitors if any?—but they didn't seem hostile. The bow was the only weapon she saw, though several of the men appeared with iron-headed axes that could split a skull if put to the purpose.

The stone temple was smaller than those Ilna had seen in cities, but the design was similar enough that she was sure of what it was. Four slender columns held up the low-peaked roof of a porch. The building itself was small and squarish, though only a sliver showed from the outside. The rest was carved back into the hillside.

A man came out of the adjacent house, wearing a red robe with gold embroidery and fringe. On his head was a tiara of mother-of-pearl in silver settings, and he was still trying to buckle a matching belt. It had been made for a slimmer man, and the attempt to lengthen it with cords hadn't been very successful.

There was a real path here, though it was rocky and as steep as any other part of the trail they'd been following. Alecto took the lead and, when the trail forked, followed the branch toward the temple.

Ilna said nothing. One of them had to be in front on the narrow track. While the particular choice of leader wasn't the one she'd have made, she didn't have any real reason to object.

Three men, one of them with the bow and an arrow nocked though not drawn, joined the plump old man on the temple porch. That fellow, the priest, finished tugging at his belt and faced the strangers.

"Do you come from the Mistress?" he called. He was trying to be threatening; his voice was powerful, but his appearance wasn't up to the job. "If you do, then go away now! We watch the Gate and want nothing to do with your false God!"

Alecto halted on the path and held up two flight feathers she'd saved from the wings of the grouse she'd charmed down for the past night's dinner. She muttered a spell. There was a gleam of blue wizardlight.

A complete image of the grouse flapped out of her hand and flew toward a giant chestnut growing among the houses. It was an impressive proof of her skill, though

Alecto lost control before the image reached a branch. There was another flash, and the two feathers fluttered slowly down.

Alecto staggered. Ilna stepped around her, and said, "We don't worship any Mistress. Her priests were hunting for us. Our skills tell us we can find safety here."

She gestured back to her companion. Alecto had recovered from the effort of her spell, but she didn't try to push Ilna out of the way again.

"Help us, and we can help you!" Ilna said.

The four leaders held a quick conclave, looking down at the strangers and back to their fellows. The priest tried to meet Ilna's eyes, but only for a moment.

More men had come out of the woods, though the whole population of the village couldn't have been as great as that of Barca's Hamlet. The younger children in the fields now stood close to their mothers; older ones had drifted into pairs and trios. All of them stared at Ilna and Alecto.

The priest turned to Ilna again. The bowman tucked the arrow he'd nocked through his sash, where he carried three others. The men beside him rested the heads of their tools, an axe and a maul, on the ground.

"Greetings, wizards!" the priest said. "We of the Gate are always glad to have visitors, so long as they behave as befits strangers in our land. We'll feast on kid in your honor tonight, and you'll sleep in the temple for as long as you stay with us."

The man with the axe, a cadaverous fellow standing a head taller than anyone else in the village, frowned and muttered in the priest's ear. The priest frowned back and snapped, "This is my decision, Pletnav!"

Bowing apologetically to Ilna, he explained, "Mistress wizard, some of us here at the Gate don't believe in taking the life of any animal. I'm Arthlan or-Wassti, Gatekeeper and Priest of the God, though, and I decree that it's perfectly proper to kill and eat a kid for you."

Arthlan's expression changed to something between concerned and hopeful. "Ah, that is—unless you wizard mistresses refrain from eating meat yourselves?"

"Refrain?" said Alecto with a delighted chortle. "You try me, Arthlan! And you'd better make it *two* kids if anybody else plans to get some. I've been hiking all day, and I'm not half-hungry!"

"Very well," said Arthlan. "Oyra—"

He glanced over to the woman who'd come out of the house beside the temple. She was as plump as the priest but scarcely half his age.

"—take a kid from my own herd. *One* of the kids."

The woman pursed her lips and spoke in a voice too low for Ilna to follow the words. The people here had a nasal accent quite different from the lilt of people in Barca's Hamlet and different also from the clipped tones of Donelle.

"Yes, woman!" the priest said. "The whole village will share!"

He glared around at his neighbors. "After our guests and ourselves have eaten, of course," he added, his tone becoming less agitated with each syllable. By the end of the short sentence, Arthlan sounded as smoothly cheerful as he'd been before the question of expense arose.

"I'm Ilna os-Kenset," Ilna said, "and I'd prefer you call me Ilna in the future. My companion Alecto—"

She wasn't sure whether Alecto's folk didn't use the father's name in their formal address or if the wild girl simply hadn't bothered ever to tell her.

"—and I were driven from Donelle, as I said, by the priests of this Mistress. You're offering to put us up in the temple?"

Maybe Alecto didn't *know* her father.

The villagers were beginning to shift, not dispersing but rather clumping together in groups which whispered with animation among themselves, all the time watching the strangers. Occasionally someone would leave one gathering and trot over to another a furlong away. The scattered nature of the community meant there was no common meeting place like the square in front of the inn in Barca's Hamlet.

"Why yes," Arthlan said. "Would you like to see the building? It's very comfortable, I'm sure you'll find."

"I'll get bedding," said the man with the axe. He shouldered it, and said to the bowman, "You too, Gorlan. You've got a coverlet extra since Magda moved in with Peese, haven't you?"

"Sure, show us this place," Alecto said, eyeing the temple with hesitation. "But it may be I'll sleep in the woods again tonight. I don't . . ."

Her voice trailed off. "I don't like stone buildings," might have been the way she'd planned to finish the sentence; though Ilna suspected that in truth the wild girl had never *seen* a building of dressed stone before she saw Donelle. "Anyway, maybe I'll sleep in the woods."

"Oh, that won't be necessary," the priest said, gesturing them to follow as he waddled to the temple. The trail was broad enough for two people to walk abreast. Most of the other tracks had room for only one set of feet, and those had to be placed carefully to the side of the still-narrower trench goat hooves had worn in the middle over the decades. "You'll see."

"Who do you worship here?" Ilna asked. She didn't believe in the Great Gods, but there were forces with power over men whether or not they were Gods. She'd known that long before she saw the congregation in Donelle raise the Pack. If these folk had similar rites, then she wasn't going to stay to watch them.

"Who?" repeated Arthlan. "Well, God, mistress."

The priest looked back over his shoulder at her with an expression of puzzlement. "God was placed here on Earth to guard the entrance to Hell, preventing the foul spirits of the Underworld from walking among mankind."

The temple had a heavy wooden door with two outward-opening leaves. Both were swung back; they didn't appear to have been closed in years or decades. The porch floor and the threshold slab were worn by the use of ages.

Arthlan stepped inside. The doorway was low; the priest didn't duck, but Ilna—no taller than he but less familiar with the passage—did out of instinct. The only furnishings were the stone benches built into either sidewall. Instead of a back wall, a natural cave plunged into the depths of the hill. It narrowed swiftly, but Ilna couldn't see the end of it as she bent to look in.

"Where's your God?" she asked, doubtful and therefore suspicious. "Don't you have a statue in here?"

Arthlan drew himself up with more dignity than Ilna had thought the plump little man possessed. "Mistress," he said, "we don't worship a statue. There's no place for images here at the Gate of Hell. Our God is real."

"I'm sorry," said Ilna, folding her hands behind her. "I misspoke. It won't happen again."

She *was* sorry; furious with herself, in fact. She believed in very little, and most of that was negative, but she had no business discounting other people's faith simply because she had none of her own.

Alecto entered, scratching her ribs under the wolfskin cape. She ran her left hand over the back wall, smiling at the feel of the natural rock. "Why didn't you say it was a cave?" she said cheerfully. "I've slept in caves before."

Like Ilna, she squatted to peer down the cave's throat. Frowning, she pinched up dust from the floor and released it. The dust fell straight; there were no air currents, in or out of the cave.

"Has anybody gone down that?" Alecto asked the priest as she stood. "It's big enough for a man back as far as I can see."

"It's not a place for men, mistress," Arthlan said with

the same stiff dignity. "Only God and demons can go through the Gate."

"There's water down there," Ilna said, nodding toward the opening because she didn't care to point. "I can smell it in the air."

"Perhaps there is, mistress," Arthlan said, "but I wouldn't know that. We draw our water from the spring beside Taenan's house. We'll provide you with a bucket of it; more, if you'd like."

Ilna stepped back onto the porch. A number of women were coming from both directions, struggling up the slope under loads of bedding and spruce branches.

Ilna frowned at the latter, then realized they must be meant for mattresses. People slept on feather beds in the palace, but what she'd expected here were leather cases stuffed with straw like those of Barca's Hamlet. Springy boughs should be comfortable so long as the blanket over them was thick enough that the needles didn't poke through.

Alecto kicked one of the side benches. The front of it was mortared stone, but the back was cut from the living rock. "Suits me," she said. "Now, how about some of that food you were offering a bit ago?"

Arthlan bowed low. "We'll eat at my house," he said. He gestured the wild girl out of the temple ahead of him. "The goat won't have seethed yet, but we can begin with porridge."

Ilna paused to examine the temple doors. The panels were thick, made of mortised boards. The hinges were hardwood. They hadn't been used in some time, but they were sturdy; so was the crossbar leaning against the interior wall.

She and Alecto should be able to sleep safely tonight, even if the villagers were more hostile than there was any reason to believe.

* * *

Garric rose from where he'd been sitting on the millipede's head. The driver had given no signal that it was aware of Garric's presence; neither did it show that it knew he'd left it to walk back past Metron to the second segment and the others waiting.

Thalemos would have joined him on the head, but Garric had wanted some time alone. He'd faced out over the creature's course, but he was looking into his own mind.

The driver had no more intruded on Garric's thoughts than the millipede itself had. The Archa's middle arms occasionally touched either the spike or the feather of its wand to the thin, flexible chitin connecting the millipede's head to its first body segment. Garric couldn't see any change in the creature's course, but presumably the driver knew its business. It knew better than Garric did, at any rate.

Metron was alert again, sitting cross-legged on the first segment. He looked up from his reading, this time a vellum scroll instead of the codex he'd had out before. His eyes met Garric's; then, with a deliberate lack of expression, he went back to the scroll.

The snub angered Garric more than he'd have expected. Instead of walking past with a nod as he'd expected to, he stopped, and said, "Master Metron. How long are we going to be on this creature's back?"

Metron looked up angrily. Fatigue and danger had taken their toll on the wizard's temper. "That depends on matters I can't be sure of without expending more effort than I choose to do," he said. "I'll inform you when we arrive."

"That's as may be," Garric said, raising his voice slightly. "But since you're ignorant, then we need to stop now to get water and perhaps food. Will you inform the driver, or shall I find a way to communicate with him myself?"

"Are you——" Metron said. He caught himself when Garric shifted his stance. The slight motion, not quite a threat, drew the wizard's attention to the *man* he spoke to. A moment before he'd been taking everyone but himself as mere pawns to be moved at his will.

"That is . . ." Metron covered smoothly, letting the scroll slip closed in his lap. "Master Gar, I don't know precisely how far we must proceed, but we should reach it in a few hours at most. I hope you and your colleagues can do without water for that long."

He gestured with both hands. "I assure you, time is of the essence," he added. "Not only for the success of our endeavors, but for our very survival. We've escaped one set of dangers, but this place has many others. The sooner we're out of it, the better."

Garric said nothing for a moment. Part of him wanted to hang the oily little worm upside down over empty air and listen to him beg for his life. That was pointless, though. It wouldn't remove Echeon from the throne of Laut, and it wouldn't bring back Tint. . . .

"I'll take it under advisement with my fellows and Lord Thalemos," Garric said coldly, turning his back on the wizard. "We'll inform you of our decision."

It was petty to leave Metron worrying about something Garric had no intention of carrying through on, but Garric needed *some* release for his anger. He walked across the quivering, chitinous joint, then up onto the next broad hoop of armor to rejoin the watching Brethren.

Ten of the bandits had made it this far. None of the survivors had wounds that they seemed to regard as serious; not even Hame's slashed arm was incapacitating. They watched Garric's approach with a mixture of fear and hope.

"So, lad," Vascay said. "Any news for us?"

Garric shrugged. "A few hours," he said. "Perhaps less. That one"——he twitched his head back toward Metron——

"wasn't sure." He paused, then added, "I think Metron is telling the truth *that* far, at least."

Thalemos grimaced unhappily. "I've just been telling your, your Brethren, Master Gar," he said, "that I have no more idea than you do about what Metron intends. He told me that I'd wed a noblewoman from Tisamur, and that she and I between us would overcome the power of the Intercessors. This, though . . ."

Thalemos looked momentarily hopeful. "Her name is Lady Tilphosa bos-Pholial," he said. "Perhaps you gentlemen have heard of her?"

"How could we hear about somebody from Tisamur, when nobody's been off Laut in the thousand years since the Intercessors took over?" Ademos said peevishly.

Vascay looked at Garric with a raised eyebrow.

"I've never heard of her," Garric said, answering the unspoken question. "On any of the places I've been."

"As it chances," said Vascay carefully, "I may have heard the name. On Serpent's Isle, where we were looking for the ring our wizard friend has now."

"There wasn't nobody on that place but us, chief," Toster said. The big man furrowed his brow like a fresh-turned field. "And more snakes than the Sister's dungeon has!"

"Yes, but there were statue bases, Brother Toster," Vascay said. "One of them read Thalemos, Earl of Laut"—he nodded to the youth in friendly fashion—"and Brother Gar found the rest of the statue with the ring. Eh?"

"Yes," said Garric, trying vainly to dredge detail from Gar's fuddled memories. Garric or-Reise hadn't been present when the base was found; to Gar it must have been no more than another block of stone in a place that had too many of them already.

"A statue of me on Serpent's Isle?" Thalemos said in amazement. "But . . . I thought everything there was ancient and in ruins?"

"Aye, so it is," Vascay agreed, "and the statue was of

an age with the rest, judging by the way the marble was pitted. But that's neither here nor there."

Which wasn't quite true, Garric thought, glancing in the direction of Metron. The wizard watched intently, obviously fearful that the bandits and his ward were planning to overturn his desires with brute strength. He gave Garric a broad, false smile when their eyes met.

Thalemos was genuinely surprised to hear what the ruins on Serpent's Isle really were. That meant that he was as innocent—as ignorant—of Metron's plans as he claimed to be. Knowing that didn't change the way Garric felt about the wizard, but it gave him reason to trust Thalemos.

Vascay went on, "Across the porch from where we found the one of you—"

He grinned at Thalemos. Garric had seen enough of the bandit chief to realize there really was humor in his expression. In another world, Vascay would have been an excellent schoolteacher. Of course, in another world Garric or-Reise would be managing the family inn in Barca's Hamlet.

"—was a second, the base and the legs besides; though the stone was rotted to a couple sticks. Enough of the base had been protected by clay that I could read the first part of the legend: T-i-l-p-h-o."

He shrugged. "I didn't bother worrying about the rest; it wasn't what Master Metron had sent us to find, that's all it meant to me. But it seems it might've meant something to you, eh, lad?"

Thalemos looked from Vascay to Metron, then beyond the wizard to take in the forest of giant grass and brambles through which the millipede paced.

"Yes," the youth said, "it must. But may the Lady forsake my soul if I know what it is!"

"I don't understand any of this!" said Toster; and Garric

smiled, because he was so perfectly in agreement with the big man.

Tilphosa's wrists were covered with a poultice of mashed comfrey, attached by dock leaves tied on with string twisted from a birch tree's inner bark. It'd given Cashel an extra degree of pleasure to use vegetation the way men were meant to use it, knowing that the Helpers'd be in screaming despair if they could watch him.

Cashel had nothing against plants, any more than he had against the sky or the sea lapping the beach back home. But he knew what a tree's place in the universe was, and he wasn't bragging when he figured that his own place was higher than that.

Tilphosa bent and swept a pebble from between her right foot and her sandal. Cashel had stopped to make bark footgear for her as soon as he figured they'd gotten beyond where the Helpers might be willing to follow them. He wasn't afraid of the little people any more than he was afraid of Meas or-Monklin's kicking ox. They both could be nasty if you weren't careful, though, so Cashel was careful in his dealings with either one.

"Want to hold up here for a while?" Cashel asked.

"No, no," the girl said, skipping to put herself a half step in front to prove her ability to go on. "There's another house just ahead, I see."

"Right," said Cashel, wishing he could put more enthusiasm into his agreement. They'd seen half a dozen huts since they reached this road at midday. Seen the huts and walked onward, at the insistence of the people living there.

"At any rate, they're just folks," Cashel said, going on with his train of thought aloud. He was used to being alone except for sheep most of the time. He'd gotten into the habit of talking to himself, because otherwise he mightn't hear a human voice between sunup and sundown.

"That's right," said Tilphosa. "You can't blame them for being wary of strangers. And the city's right ahead, they say."

She spoke with more enthusiasm than the Cashel guessed she felt, but they were both trying to put a bright face on a tiring day that didn't want to end. It was late in the afternoon. They could sleep rough in this dank land-scape if they had to, but it wasn't something Cashel was going to do for choice.

The road was on top of a causeway, built up arm's length above the surrounding land. It was wide enough for a cart to travel it, but Cashel doubted that any did: there were no wheel ruts in the clay surface, anyhow. Mats wo-ven from the osiers growing in waste patches everywhere about held the sides in place, and pilings rammed down at double-pace intervals on either side anchored the mats.

This wasn't a wasteland, though. The whole route was bordered by terraced fields where an unfamiliar sort of grain grew in neat rows from standing water. A heavy fog lay over the marshes, concealing the dwellings that Cashel was sure must lie on the other side of the fields. That probably didn't matter, because he guessed those folks would've been at least as disinterested in helping travellers as the ones living in the huts he and Tilphosa had stopped at. Like this one, for instance.

It was built up on bamboo stilts to the height of the road a double pace away. The only connection between the two was a tracery of cords anchored to a piling and supporting a bamboo "floor" with spaces wide enough for a foot to slip through between each pair of rods. The hut walls were matting, and the roof was thatch.

In the marsh nearby was a circle of cut bamboo as big around as the hut itself. Cashel had thought of a fish weir when he'd seen one by the first place they'd passed, and that was almost what it was. A shoal of carp came to the surface mouth first when he stopped, hoping that the presence of humans meant somebody was about to throw them a handful of grain.

You couldn't have chickens in a marsh like this: their feet would rot, and they'd die. But you could raise fish and train them to come to be slaughtered at need the same way farmwives back in the borough scattered grain to the hens at the dooryard.

"Hello the house!" Cashel called. Tilphosa waited beside him, balancing on one leg like a stork so she could rub the other foot some more. "We're travellers who need a bite of food. We've got money to pay, but if you'd rather—"

Money wasn't much used between local people in the borough. Many a time Cashel had taken his day's pay in fresh bread or shearings that his sister would turn into finished cloth.

"—we'd be happy to work for it instead."

"Go away!" screamed a voice. It was probably female and certainly angry. "We don't have any work for you. Or food either!"

"Look, we need food!" Cashel said, changing tack from the dignified honesty he'd used before. That had gotten them nowhere in the past, and it obviously wasn't going to work here either. "I'll not harm anyone who treats *me* decent, but I won't be kicked around like a stray dog!"

He reached down and plucked one of the ropes that acted as bridge stringers; it moaned in response. Now that he'd touched it, he wondered whether the flimsy structure would even take his weight. The cords were of some unfamiliar material, maybe bamboo fibers twisted together.

"Look, you can't come in here!" the voice said. "Soong's just up ahead, and there's inns there. They'll feed you and take your money besides."

"Let's go on, Cashel," Tilphosa whispered. "I don't want a fight."

Cashel sighed and turned to the road again. He let the

girl take his left arm; for support, he supposed, but anyway he let her take it.

"There wasn't going to be a fight," he muttered as they strode down the road at a faster pace than usual. Anger was prodding him. "All they had to do was cut the ropes from their side and then drop a storage jar on my head while I was trying to swim in mud."

He cleared his throat, and added, "Besides, I guess it's their house. If they don't want visitors, well, there's plenty people in the borough who'd act just the same."

The mist pooled and streaked. Sometimes it gave a clear view for as much as a bowshot, then went so solid that Cashel put his staff out to bump along the side of the causeway. He didn't suppose they'd drown if they fell in, but he'd been covered with muck often enough to know he didn't like the experience.

"I hear a river," Cashel said. "Soong's on a river, the first fellow said when he ordered us away."

Water has its own range of sounds, from the *plink* of drops falling from the eaves after a rain to the roar of a storm-driven surf. This was a sighing and slapping, slow but powerful. The evening air didn't taste of salt.

A breeze, the first they'd had since midday, swept a channel in the fog. Cashel had taken the glimmers ahead for will-o'-the-wisps. Now they came into focus as lanterns, bright flames haloed by the damp air. Buildings stood out as darker shadows, and sometimes a human figure silhouetted itself against lamplight.

"The city doesn't have walls," Tilphosa noted. "That's a good sign, don't you think?"

Cashel blinked. He hadn't thought about it at all, to tell the truth; he hadn't grown up with fortifications. Since Cashel left Barca's Hamlet he'd lived in places with walls to keep out enemies, but that wasn't a part of the city he cared much about.

Sharina said mostly those walls dated from the very end

of the Old Kingdom. She also said that they hadn't kept
chaos from destroying the places they were meant to protect.

"I guess it's good," he said. "Because it means that people here are peaceful, you think?"

"Yes, even if they aren't very friendly to strangers,"
Tilphosa said. She hugged his arm close, then separated
with only the tips of her fingers on Cashel's elbow to keep
contact.

The road going down toward Soong wasn't steep, but
it had more of a slope than they'd seen before all day. The
last two furlongs into the city were covered with squared
tree trunks, not really paving but better than mud. Some
of the trunks had tilted on their bedding, one end higher
and the other lower than the pair before and beyond. Once
Cashel's weight squelched a raised trunk down like a sluggish teeter-totter, but there was no harm in that beyond his
heart jumping in surprise.

A gust cleared the air, giving them a glimpse of a broad
river which flowed so slowly that starlight could glimmer
on its surface. There were quays along the near bank. On
an island connected by a short causeway stood a temple
whose short fat columns supported a tiled roof. Except for
the façade, the building was as simple and unadorned as
a stone barn.

Cashel looked at the sky; the constellations were unfamiliar. That was what he'd expected, but in his heart
there'd been hope that he'd have at least the Byre or the
seven blue stars of the Axletree to remind him of nights
spent pasturing sheep.

They entered the city. The streets were muddy, but there
were board sidewalks for pedestrians. A hunched man
passed them, driving out of town in a wagon pulled by a
single mule. The contents of the wagon bed rattled under
a coarse mat.

"Excuse me, sir!" Cashel called. The man ignored him, except perhaps for touching the mule's ear with his long bamboo switch.

"It's quite a big city, isn't it?" Tilphosa said. She was trying to sound cheerful, but Cashel noticed that she picked at her tunic in concern to minimize the dirt and damage of the past many days. She touched the dagger hilt, then put her left hand over it—for concealment, not because she was afraid of being attacked. She felt a weapon was out of place in civilized surroundings.

"Big enough to have shops that sell clothes," Cashel said. "In the morning we'll outfit ourselves and . . ."

He let his voice trail off. His mind had run to the planned end of the sentence, ". . . *see if anybody can give us directions* . . ." The foolishness of those words froze his tongue.

The stars above Soong were new to him. Nobody here would know how to get to Valles. Nobody here had *heard* of Valles.

"And we'll decide where we want to go next," Cashel concluded, but without the animation that he'd started the sentence with. He didn't see any path to a place he or Tilphosa wanted to be, and he knew those likely wouldn't be the same places anyway. The only reason he didn't give up was that, well, he wasn't the sort of person who gave up.

They were among the houses now, each of two or three stories. The vacant lots showed that the previous building had collapsed or been torn down. They were more substantial than the huts of the surrounding farms, but all were built of timber with shingle or thatched roofs. The temple out in the river was the only stone structure he'd seen.

Some of the sidewalk planks had rotted through; Cashel walked with a careful shuffle, the way he'd have done on a lake whose ice had begun to soften in the spring weather. Folk bustled by, dressed in baggy trousers and hooded capes. They looked sidelong at the strangers, but none of them spoke.

Cashel made up his mind with a sigh. A shopkeeper had set the bar across his shutters and was fastening it with a bronze padlock. Cashel touched him on the shoulder.

"Pardon me, sir," he said. "Can you direct us to an inn? We're strangers here."

"What?" said the shopkeeper in a female voice. "An inn?"

She raised her head to look them over from beneath her cowl. Judging from her grimace, she didn't like what she saw. "Try the Hyacinth," she said. "Down at the end of the street, where it meets the water."

She wriggled away and disappeared into an alley. Cashel didn't try to hold her. He looked at Tilphosa, and smiled as he said, "I guess even strangers can find the river, huh."

She patted his arm.

Cashel wasn't sure what the shopkeeper meant by "the street," since three roads joined at an intersection close enough to touch with his quarterstaff. He picked the one that headed most directly toward where he knew the river was. That didn't mean a lot in a place where the streets wandered like sheep paths across a pasture, but . . .

"If it doesn't work," Tilphosa said, "we'll try another one. From the way the woman looked at us I'm not sure I'd regret missing the Hyacinth, but I suppose it'll do until we're dressed properly."

She sounded cheerful again. Cashel looked at her and grinned. Tilphosa had adjusted her sash so that the brass hilt of the broken sword was out where anybody could see it. For a little while there she'd gone back to being Lady Tilphosa, concerned about her social position. Now she was Cashel's companion again, the girl who'd come through shipwreck, battle, and anything else the Gods chose to throw at her.

They were getting close to the river. Besides Cashel being able to smell the mudflats, several of the shuttered shops had coarse tunics or ship's stores of one sort and another on their signs.

Prostitutes waited in alley mouths, following Cashel with their eyes. He kept his gaze forward, but Tilphosa glared like a queen at each woman they passed.

Cashel kept his grin from reaching his lips. She was a queen, after all; or anyway she'd be the next thing to a queen after Cashel delivered her to Prince Thalemos.

Tilphosa pointed to the sign hanging from a building at the end of the street. "There it is," she said. "The Hyacinth."

Cashel glanced at her, wondering how she knew. Were her eyes *that* good? The wood was so warped and faded that he wasn't sure he'd have recognized a bunch of purple flowers painted on it even in daylight.

It was an inn, all right, though. During the day there'd even be a counter facing the road, though it was shuttered now. It was on the corner of the street they'd followed and the one fronting the river, so it was the right place beyond question.

He said, "I couldn't have told from the picture."

"Oh, the name's drilled out of the wood below, Cashel," Tilphosa said. "See? Though it's backwards from this way."

She pointed again. He'd taken the design for a cutwork border, not a word.

"I see, mistress," he said. "But I can't read letters either way round."

"I'll read for us, Cashel," the girl said, squeezing his arm again. "You take care of all the other things. And Cashel?"

He met her eyes again.

"Remember that I'm Tilphosa, not mistress. All right?"

"Right," he agreed, giving her a shy smile.

The inn had double doors, but the left panel was latched closed. A pair of men stood in the opening, watching the riverfront as they drank from elmwood masars.

Cashel shrugged, loosening his shoulder muscles as he considered how to tell the fellows that he planned to enter through where they were standing. He'd be polite, of course, and the chances were that they'd respond politely as well; but there was just the least chance that they wouldn't.

"Cashel!" Tilphosa said as she caught his arm.

For a moment Cashel thought she was telling him not to start a fight—which meant walk away from a fight that somebody else had started, and that *wasn't* going to happen to Cashel or-Kenset. Then he followed the line of her eyes out to the river road and saw what she and the men in the doorway both were looking at. Calm again, Cashel watched too.

A tall, hooded figure walked at the head of a procession of men rolling a two-wheeled hand-truck. The corpse on the truck was wrapped in coarse wool. The accompanying men wore peaked hats with black-dyed feathers standing up around the brims, apparently a sign of mourning; the pair of bareheaded females bringing up the rear stroked tambours with muffled sticks.

The figure in the lead was a good seven feet tall. It—Cashel wasn't going to guess sex, not after his mistake with the shopkeeper—wore a robe that was pale green in the glow of the lanterns carried by some of the mourners. The hem brushed the mud, and a veil covered as much of the face as the cowl itself didn't hide. The figure moved as smoothly as the images of the Great Gods brought from Carcosa to outlying boroughs in wheeled carts during the Tithe Processions.

The funeral turned onto the causeway leading to the temple in the river. Cashel saw the click of a spark from the hand-truck's iron tires: the causeway was paved with hard stone.

"Excuse me, gentlemen," Tilphosa said unexpectedly to the men in the doorway. "We're strangers here. Who is that, please?"

The men turned to look at her; the fellow nearer to Cashel jumped back, much as he might have done if he'd glanced up from his drink and found a bull standing at his side.

"By the Shepherd!" he muttered, brushing with his free hand the beer he'd sloshed on the front of his tunic.

The procession reached the temple; its doors opened with only the faintest squeal. Somebody must keep them well greased in this soggy atmosphere. The men pushing the truck stepped back expectantly, and the female musicians redoubled their muted drumming.

"Well, I believe it's Tadbal Bessing's-son the cobbler, mistress," the other man said. "Leastways I'd heard he'd died last night, so if it's not Tadbal, he'll be along shortly."

"No," said Tilphosa in a noticeably sharper tone. "I mean the tall fellow leading them, not the departed. Is he a priest?"

The men looked at each other. Partly to explain Tilphosa's ignorance, and partly to remind the locals to be polite when they spoke to a girl who had a friend Cashel's size, Cashel said, "We're strangers here, you see."

"Right," said the fellow who'd spilled his beer. "That's one of the Nine, you see. They take care of the dead."

"It's the custom here in Soong," the other man agreed.

A figure which could have been a mirror image of the leader came out of the temple. While the mourners stood back, the two of them lifted the corpse from the hand-truck and carried it inside. The temple doors closed behind them.

"There's nine priests?" Tilphosa said.

Cashel consciously kept from frowning. Local customs

were no business of his, unless they involved feeding him to a tree or the like. In Barca's Hamlet people buried their dead in the ground in winding sheets, if they could afford the wool, but every place Cashel had been since he left the borough had a different way of dealing with death. If the people of Soong wanted priests to slide corpses into the river for the catfish to eat, well, that was their business.

"I don't rightly know, mistress," the first speaker said. "Nobody's seen more than three of them together, not that I've heard about. Maybe Nine's just a name."

"Tilphosa, I think we ought to see about food and a place to sleep," Cashel said firmly.

All three looked at him. The man leaning against the closed panel reached down and lifted a pin so that he could pull that half-open as well.

"There you go, master," he said with a sweep of his hand and a friendly smile. "That'll save you having to turn sideways, I guess."

"Yes, of course," said Tilphosa. She stepped into the taproom with her head high; every inch a queen.

Sharina stood at the base of the flagship's forward fighting tower, looking toward the beach two furlongs away. The great quinquereme proceeded along the shore under the thrust of only one bank of oars, giving her just enough way on that she didn't wallow in the surf. The ballistae on the bow and stern towers were cocked and loaded with thick-shafted arrows whose square iron heads could smash a ship's hull at short range or an archer's scantlings half a mile inland.

Carus had transferred from *The King of the Isles* to one of the lightest warships in the fleet, an eighty-oared bireme that had been in service as a revenue cutter before Garric became regent of the kingdom. Earlier in the reign of Valence the Third, the Kingdom of the Isles had controlled

ard
y the
under
ey'd wait
was leisure
ther as they'd

ceably. Oarsmen to
bow swung seaward
ars. The trireme on the
at full power, giving the
of the smaller ship slanted
fect synchrony before lifting to
led chains of diamond-glittering
alongside.

successful?" Sharina asked, giving a
to the possessive. She nodded toward the
ed base where the wizard had been.

d that none of our missing friends are in Do-
noctris said. She offered a minuscule smile, more
an not. "Though I think Ilna may have been there
tly. If I've read the indications correctly. I'm not"—
e smile broadened—"a very powerful wizard, as you
know."

Sharina moved to the opposite rail so that she could
continue to watch the beach. The ships of the squadron
that had landed the initial troops were crawling seaward
again, all but one trireme whose officers stood knee deep
in the water to examine the keel and planking; the captain
apparently thought she'd strained her hull when she
grounded. More ships were backing shoreward, maneu-
vering with difficulty to avoid the stranded vessel.

Sharina hugged Tenoctris. "I've met powerful wizards,"

little more than port duties and the fishing within dory-
haul of Ornifal, but even that slight reach had required
enforcement vessels.

The bireme swept toward the beach at a slight angle,
watched by Sharina and every other person who could get
a view of the proceedings. A score of triremes sculled
along beside *The King of the Isles*—closer than safety permitted—each with its single ballista or catapult aimed
shoreward against a threat as yet invisible.

Admiral Zettkin in the stern of the flagship looked
carved from granite; Lord Waldron on the *Lady of Sunrise*,
a broad-beamed sailing ship that transported his staff and
three days' rations for the whole army, flicked his bare
sword in small, furious arcs at his right side. Everybody
in the fleet was terrified at the idea of Carus—of Garric,
as they thought—making the initial landing on Laut with
only a company of Blood Eagles. It was a comment on
the force of Carus' personality—and on the raging fury
he'd frequently blazed with in the days since he began to
wear Garric's flesh—that none of the strong-minded men
of his army had seriously tried to prevent him from doing
this.

The bireme slid up the beach, first grating and then
grinding slowly to a halt with twenty feet of her bow on
dry land. The little vessel didn't have a ram, so her curving
stem had acted like a sled runner under the rowers' final
efforts.

The bireme tilted to its starboard, inland side. The men,
bodyguards acting as oarsmen only for this last short run-
up, were leaping to the sand even before the hull thumped
down. The first man off, splendid in a silver breastplate
and a gold diadem instead of the helmet every officer had
begged he wear, was King Carus.

A line of Blood Eagles, still juggling the shields on their
left arms, formed in front of him and trotted toward the
straggle of fishermen's huts that were the only buildings

visible. A woman stood in the doorway of one, h⌐
pot in one hand and covering her mouth with th⌐
She threw down the pot and ran inland screamin⌐

The cornicene at Carus' side put his horn to hi⌐
blew a lowing call. A score of triremes, already
to the beach, began backing in. They were mov⌐
than their hulls could accept without straining
hit the sand, but the immediate threat was the
federate army, not a hypothetical fleet that mi⌐
attack the royal force.

Tenoctris came out of her little enclosur⌐
fighting tower, holding the bamboo splint she'⌐
as a wand. She walked to the rail and delibe⌐
it into the sea. "Are things going well, S⌐
asked.

Horns and trumpets blared as nearly a hu⌐
jockeyed for position. Officers on *The Kin⌐*
screamed at crewmen and one another.
needed to turn seaward or she'd run agrou⌐
ern jaw of the broad bay, and there was
than Sharina would've expected about just
avoid that in the shoal of other vessels.
jumped onto the stern rail to bellow at t⌐
trireme within stone's throw to port; a
clung to the admiral's belt with one han⌐
for the mast stays with the other.

"All right, I guess," Sharina said. She found herself
smiling. "The Confederacy of the West seems to be conspicuous by its absence, but right now it looks like half
the royal fleet is in danger of sinking the other half unless
we're lucky."

She paused to watch the shore fill with armed men
climbing out of the triremes, forming under the harsh commands of noncoms, and then advancing in pike-fanged
blocks to the perimeter Carus and his company of Blood
Eagles were marking out. The troops aboard the following

---

blood, and the mud; and the way the pigs squeal . . ."

Tenoctris put her hand on arm Sharina's arm.

Twenty more troop-carrying warships backed tow⌐
shore farther to the east. The first squadron, lighter ⌐
weight of a hundred men apiece, struggled to ge⌐
weigh and clear the beach for later comers. T⌐
offshore until the ships of the fleet as tightly tog⌐
to fit the ships of the fleet as tightly tog⌐
been in the Arsenal.

The King of the Isles slowed not⌐
port had reversed stroke so that th⌐
under the thrust of the starboard
port side was pulling forward
flagship sea room. The oar⌐
back along her hull in pe⌐
surge forward; they sp⌐
droplets into the foa⌐
"Was your wor⌐
slight emphasis
tower's curtai⌐
"I learne⌐
nelle," T⌐
sad th⌐
rec⌐

face him in the field.

Sharina shivered at the thought.

"Is something wrong?" Tenoctris said.

"I was thinking that the war might be over before nightfall if the enemy commander's a fool," Sharina said.
"But—have you ever seen a pig butchered, Tenoctris?"

The wizard shook her head minutely. "My education
was in books, dear," she said.

"I'm just thinking about twenty thousand pigs being
slaughtered at the same time, is all," Sharina said. "All the

she said. "They're all dead, thank the Lady. And thanks to you, the kingdom still stands."

King Carus balanced at the peak of a tripod made by lashing small trees together. From there he could survey both the shore behind him and the hostile countryside beyond the ditched wall his troops were already digging. An aide ran from Carus toward the damaged vessel. The king watched with his hands on his hips, his look of fury visible even at this distance.

"I hope the captain has sense enough to get off the beach before Carus decides to come back personally," Sharina said.

"Yes," said Tenoctris. "They'll do better to take their chance on sinking than what will happen if they disobey the king."

Sharina had been smiling; her face went suddenly grim. "Carus might kill the captain, mightn't he?" she said quietly. "Cut his head off, the way he did the Intercessor's."

Tenoctris nodded. She didn't speak.

The aide and the captain exchanged shouts. The officers began to return to the trireme's deck by climbing oarlooms. The danger was past—this time.

"Tenoctris, he can't behave that way and keep the kingdom together," Sharina said, desperation in her voice. "He knows that, but when he's angry he lashes out at whoever's responsible."

"It's always the real cause, though," the wizard said. "Carus doesn't kick his servant because he doesn't like something the Earl of Sandrakkan has done."

"In the long run it doesn't *matter*," Sharina said. "It's worse! Oh, I know justice is a wonderful thing, but he'd be better off to kick a servant than to knock down a nobleman because he was slow obeying an order. He'd be better off, and the *kingdom* would be better off."

"He isn't sleeping because of the dreams," Tenoctris said, looking at the king who'd now resumed his survey of the landscape beyond the rising wall. "I suppose he was always hasty, but even a saint who gets no sleep . . ."

More ships shuttled toward the beach. A pair of triremes fouled one another, their oars interlocking as the men on deck screamed curses. It would be sorted out, though. For all the seeming chaos, the process continued toward its planned conclusion as inexorably as a storm sweeping onto the land.

"Maybe his way will work," Sharina said softly. "Perhaps Carus will end the dreams and the rebellion with his sword edge. He did that many times in the past, after all."

"Yes," said Tenoctris. "I think I'll . . ."

Her voice trailed off. She walked toward her shelter to resume practicing her art. The old wizard looked so worn already that Sharina almost called her back.

Almost. Because Sharina knew—as Tenoctris did—that the last place haste and reliance on his sword had brought Carus was the bottom of the sea. Without Tenoctris' wizardry to at least warn of such threats, a similar result would occur this time.

And slight though Sharina knew Tenoctris' powers were compared to those of their enemies, it was in those powers rather than the king's flashing sword that the kingdom's best hope lay.

Chapter Seventeen

Cashel set one end of his staff down, not banging it but letting the ferrule rap loudly enough to call attention to him and Tilphosa. The floor was of puncheons, logs halved and set edge to edge instead of being fully squared. The design saved labor and drained better than proper carpentry; in this wet land, the latter virtue might be important. There were rushes on the floor, but they should've been replaced weeks ago.

"We'd like food and a room," Cashel said, as the eyes of the handful of men in the common room turned toward them. There was a small fire on the hearth and a billet of lightwood stuck up on a firedog for the only illumination.

"Food and a bed, you can have," said the woman behind the bar to the left. Cashel hadn't noticed her in the dimness as he entered. "If you can pay for it. Three Reeds for a bed for the two of you. A Reed apiece for porridge, and another Reed if you want it soaked in fish broth."

"How much for a separate room, mistress?" Tilphosa said, her tone that of one demanding rather than begging. Her chin lifted slightly.

The landlady was a largish woman who took care of her looks even though she must be forty years old. She reminded Cashel of Sharina's mother, Lora; though Lora was small and pretended to be "a lady," while this woman was of a much earthier disposition. Instead of an ordinary tunic she wore a sleeved doublet with vertical stripes and the neckline scooped deeply onto her ample bosom.

"I don't have a separate room for anybody but myself, missy," she said, eyeing Tilphosa with disdain. "If you've got a problem with that, you can go back out in the street."

"He looks like a good prospect, Leemay," said one of the men sitting in the fireplace nook with a masar of beer. "Maybe you could find him private room, hey?"

Leemay lifted the gate in the bar and came out into the common room. She wore baggy linen trousers, gathered above the ankles; her feet and those of the men in the room were bare.

"You've got money?" she asked Cashel, no longer hostile. She walked to the hearth where an iron pot hung on a spider.

"Yes," Tilphosa said. She touched Cashel's wrist to silence him. "We've got silver, I mean, and I suppose copper pieces too. It's not stamped with reeds or whatever, though."

Leemay paused, then bent to swing the kettle out to where she could dip from it. She straightened and took one of the wooden bowls hanging from the mantel by riveted leather straps.

"*You've* got silver?" she said, speaking again to Cashel. "You don't look it, if you don't mind my saying."

"We've been shipwrecked," Cashel said. He moved his staff so that it stood vertically before him; the butt rapped the puncheons again, this time a little harder.

Leemay dipped porridge into the bowl, set it on the mantel, and took down a second. "You needn't worry about being robbed here," she said as she filled it also. "And if you didn't have money, well, I've been known to help a likely young man who's down on his luck."

"With the broth," Tilphosa said sharply. "And as I told you, we have money."

The two men at the end of the bar were laughing and nudging one another. Cashel looked at them, just curious. They calmed down immediately, but they still giggled into the cups they quickly lifted to their mouths.

Leemay set the second bowl on the mantel, thrust horn spoons into both, and reached past the seated local to take a pewter cruet from the warming niche in the hearth. She poured a thin fluid into the first bowl and a more generous portion onto the second. After replacing the cruet, she held the first out to Tilphosa, and said, "Come get it, girl—or are you crippled?"

Cashel reached for the bowl. Leemay shifted so that her soft hip bumped him away. Her eyes held Tilphosa's. Tilphosa sniffed and took the bowl.

When the landlady took the second bowl from the mantel, Cashel reached out again. Leemay touched his extended hand with her free one, and said, "Come over to the bar and eat. You'll want ale, won't you?"

She walked across the room, leading Cashel. He shook his hand loose.

"Yes, we'll want ale," Tilphosa said, raising her voice more than the quiet of the inn required. The men at the bar were chuckling among themselves again.

Leemay walked to the other side of the bar but didn't bother to lower the gate again. She set the porridge down and started to draw beer from a tun under the counter.

"Hey, Leemay?" called one of the men warming at the hearth. "You going to do your tricks tonight?"

"I might," said the woman. She eyed Cashel speculatively and smiled. "I just might."

She set full masars in front of Cashel and Tilphosa, then paused and deliberately spilled a little of Cashel's ale on the bar between them. "Eh?" he said.

"I'll show you," Leemay said, still smiling. "Later."

To have an excuse for looking away, Cashel lifted his mug and drank quickly. The beer was all right, though it had an oily aftertaste that'd take some getting used to. He was thirsty, though—thirstier than he was hungry, he found—and he drained it quickly.

Tilphosa opened her sash and took a crescent-shaped silver piece from the purse she carried in its folds. "For our food and lodging," she said crisply. "You'll need to weigh it, I suppose?"

Leemay reached down between her breasts. Grinning, she brought out a wash-leather purse which she opened one-handed.

" 'Atta girl, Leemay!" cried one of the local men.

She set a thin silver coin stamped with a ship's prow on the bar beside Tilphosa's Crescent. She balanced one in either hand, then slipped both into her purse.

"I guess it'll run about the same as a Boat," she said to Cashel. "That's fourteen Reeds to a Boat."

From a cash box under the bar she produced darkened

copper coins and put them on the bar where Cashel's left hand had been resting, one for each finger. "There's your change," she said.

She took his masar and refilled it without being asked. "This is on the house," she said. She nodded toward the pool of beer on the smooth, dark wood. "For what I shorted you."

"Just make sure you don't short her tonight, boy!" called the man in the chimney corner.

"Shut up, Halve!" Leemay said, forcefully though without real anger. She nodded toward Cashel's porridge, and went on, "Eat up, boy. You look peaked."

"Aye, and Leemay wouldn't want that," someone said. Cashel grimaced and took a spoonful of the porridge.

It was a thick mixture of pease and a grain which Cashel hadn't eaten before. The broth was pungent, but it merely added to the bowl's flavors instead of overriding them.

He scooped and chewed steadily, keeping his eyes on his food. Leemay drew beer for others and dished up porridge for the man in the chimney corner, but she kept coming back to the bar across from Cashel.

"Show him, Leemay," said one of the men at the bar. "She's a wizard, boy, and I do mean that."

Tilphosa had been dipping with the corner of her broad spoon instead of taking full gulps as Cashel did, so she'd made only a start on her porridge while he was finishing. Now she leaned back to look at the speaker.

"Oh, don't worry, girlie," he said. "What's a slice off a cut loaf, hey?"

"Here, I'll work with this," Leemay said. Before Cashel could respond, she'd reached up and plucked out a single long hair from where he parted it in the center. She set it on the bar and pinched out one of her own, then twisted the two together. The landlady's hair was black, thick and straight as a spearshaft; Cashel's brunet strand looked thin and light beside it.

"What's your name, lad?" she asked. She set the porridge bowl to the side and began tracing a design about the twined hairs, painting the wood with lines of spilled beer.

"We don't have to tell you our names!" Tilphosa said, clutching her crystal amulet in her left hand.

"My name's Cashel or-Kenset," he said. The landlady'd been free with her own name, and, besides, he didn't care what she knew or didn't about him. "Ah, Mistress Leemay, I know it's early for you, but we've had a hard few days and we'd like to get some sleep. Is there a place my friend and I could bed down now?"

"I may decide to close up early tonight," Leemay said, concentrating on the symbols she'd just drawn. "Wait a bit and we'll see."

She reached under the bar and brought up what Cashel first thought was a stalk of grass, then a splinter of cowhorn . . . and then decided he didn't know. It was no longer than his outstretched hand, slender and grayish green.

Leemay began chanting under her breath. Using the splinter as a wand, she worked her way around the symbols surrounding the entwined hairs. Cashel couldn't hear her words any more than he could see what she'd drawn.

He didn't think anybody could see them, Leemay included. The only light was from the hearth across the room, and the ale had slid back into pools following the wood's natural valleys. The important thing was that she *had* drawn them.

Cashel held his staff upright in his right hand, glad of its feel. He tried not to squeeze the hickory till his knuckles stood out white.

The stool in the chimney corner creaked; the local men were moving to where they could watch also. None of them spoke.

Flecks of wizardlight, both red and the blue that made eyes tingle, appeared above the bar. The snapped alive so suddenly that Cashel's mind supplied a *crackle* to the sparks' silence. Paling, they swelled into interlinked figures the size of a child's straw poppet.

"Hey, *good* job, Leemay!" a local said.

Cashel felt hot. The images were so sharply detailed that he didn't have any difficulty in recognizing his face on the blue figure and Leemay as the red one. There wasn't any doubt about what the images were doing, either.

Tilphosa threw the rest of her beer in Leemay's face. The landlady jerked backward, and the illusion vanished.

Tilphosa picked up the twined hairs, wet with ale, and stuffed them into her purse. "Your exhibition insulted me!" she said in a ringing voice.

Leemay stared at her silently. It'd been a long time since Cashel saw the face of anybody so mad.

"We'll be going now," he said. "We won't trouble you further."

Putting his arm around Tilphosa so he knew where she was, he started backing toward the door. The locals who'd watched the funeral were gone, so worst case Cashel was going to throw the girl out into the street while he and his quarterstaff took care of business in the common room.

None of the men looked like they wanted a problem, though. Three of them crouched, their hands ready to turn the tables over as shields if anything started happening. The two fellows at the bar had backed to the wall, from which they watched Cashel with the expression of rabbits trapped by a fox.

The landlady put down her wand. "My mistake!" she said. "The lady was right to show me that I'd made a mistake. Go if you want—"

She pointed to the door. One panel was closed again; that was going to be a problem for haste.

"—but the nights are dark here in Soong. I'll give you my room."

Nobody spoke. Leemay shrugged, then smiled. "To

make up for what happened a moment ago. Shall we be friends?"

We've already paid, Cashel thought. He knew it didn't matter anymore, but three coppers was more than he'd earned most weeks when he was a boy.

"Cashel?" Tilphosa said in a small voice. He glanced at her. She looked white, and her cheeks were hollow. "Can we stay? I'm really . . ."

She was almost dead on her feet, was what she was trying to say. It'd been a long day, even for Cashel, and he was used to them as Tilphosa was not. Her burns and the hike and now this, the sort of fuss that swallows up all the energy you've got even if it doesn't come to blows at the end after all . . .

"Sure," Cashel murmured. To the landlady he went on, "We'll take your offer, mistress. I, I'm sorry about the mess."

Not that a little splashed beer was going to change this place a lot, but it was polite to say something. Cashel always tried to be polite, especially when it looked like he might be knocking heads in the next instant. That way spectators didn't feel they maybe ought to pile in on the other fellows' side.

Leemay took the stick of lightwood from the firedog, then went back behind the bar. "It's this way," she said to Cashel.

"Hey, don't leave us in the dark," one of the men complained.

"Light another billet, then!" snapped Leemay. She unlatched the door in the end wall. Cashel motioned Tilphosa ahead of him—his body would shadow her if he was in front—and they followed along after the landlady.

Beyond the door was a storage room. Tuns of beer stood along one wall, and lesser items in crates and storage jars were stacked on the other. The aisle between was a tight squeeze for Cashel. He frowned, then realized that Soong was so low-lying that the buildings couldn't have cellars the way Reise's inn did back in Barca's Hamlet.

Leemay opened the door at the far end, then lit the candle in a wall bracket just inside. She gestured Tilphosa through, saying, "There you go, missy. If it suits your ladyship's tastes, I mean."

Tilphosa glanced up at the landlady's renewed hostility, but she didn't rise to the bait. Tilphosa'd seen men killed now, and she was smart enough to understand that she might've seen more die because she'd flown hot at Leemay.

"Thank you, mistress," she said as she entered. "This will be very satisfactory."

Cashel glanced past the landlady and agreed beyond a doubt. The wooden bed frame was big enough for three people Cashel's size, with pillows and at least two feather beds as well as the straw mattress. Tilphosa tested the softness with a hand, less in doubt than as an acknowledgment of the fine bedding.

"Sleep well, then," Leemay said. She started back. Cashel turned sideways and thumped his staff in front of him so it was what the landlady had to squeeze by.

She did that, giving a throaty chuckle as she passed. Cashel didn't hear much humor in the sound, though.

Cashel waited till the door to the common room had closed, then said, "Give me one of those comforters, will you, Tilphosa? Ah, unless you need them both?"

"No, of course not," the girl said. Her face was unreadable. "What do you intend to do, Cashel?"

"I'm going to lie down in the doorway here," he said, nodding. "We'll leave it open, but I don't guess anybody's going to get to you without me waking up. Just in case."

"But the floor's *hard*," Tilphosa said.

He laughed. "Every night I wasn't out in the pasture back home, I slept on the floor of the mill," he said. "That was stone. Don't worry about me, miss—Tilphosa, that is."

She turned her head away. Cashel spread the feather bed on the floor. He'd lie at an angle with his head out in the storage room and his legs slanted past the foot of the bed-frame. Now, should he pinch out the candle or—

"Cashel?" Tilphosa said, still looking away. "I don't have any claim on you, you realize. If you did want to see that woman tonight . . . ?"

"Huh?" said Cashel. He thought hard, trying to fit the girl's words together in a fashion that made sense. "Sleep with *Leemay?* Duzi, mistress! What do you take me for?"

"I'm sorry," Tilphosa said, though she sounded more relieved than apologetic. "Ah, let's get some sleep."

She turned quickly and blew out the candle. Cashel heard the bedclothes rustle as she pulled them over herself.

"Right," he said, settling into his bed as well.

He didn't have any trouble getting to sleep, but he had bad dreams during the night. He kept hearing someone chanting, and Leemay's face hovered over him like a gibbous moon.

Ilna dreamed that she stood on a hilltop as a storm howled about her. Thunderbolts struck close, filling the air with a sulfurous stench. She felt the wind tug her legs and knew that in a moment it would carry her away, rending her apart in the lightning-shot darkness. She opened her mouth to scream but her swollen throat wouldn't allow sounds to pass.

Something flung her violently. She didn't know where she was. There was rock all around her. Moonlight through a transom showed her sharp angles and something thrashing, but her eyes wouldn't focus, and she couldn't get her breath.

Alecto was shouting. She jerked the crossbar out of the

staples holding it and shoved the temple doors open to let in more light. Ilna sucked gulps of the fresh, cool air that flooded in with it. Her throat relaxed, and she could see clearly again.

A creature half out of the cave twisted and flailed four legs that seemed too small for a body the size of a cow's. It slammed the temple walls in its convulsions. Besides the eyes bulging on either side of its huge blunt skull, it had a third orb in the center. The hilt of Alecto's dagger stood up from that middle socket.

Ilna pulled herself onto the temple porch with her hands and elbows, dragging her legs behind her. She had a burning sensation in her right calf, though she thought she'd be able to stand in a moment when the dizziness passed.

People were coming out of the houses scattered along the valley slope. Somebody in each group carried a torch or a rushlight, a pithy stem soaked in grease to burn with a pale yellow flame.

They've been expecting this, Ilna thought. *They wouldn't have been able to rouse so quickly at Alecto's shout if they hadn't been waiting for it.*

She twisted her legs under and sat up, though she wasn't yet ready to squat or stand. She brought the hank of cords out of her sleeve and began plaiting them. No pattern she wove in the light of torches and a partial moon would dispose of all those approaching, but you do what you can.

Alecto shouted, this time in surprise. She jumped out the doorway. An instant later the creature hurled itself onto the porch also, then rolled onto its side. Each of its legs and its thick tail twitched in a separate rhythm. The final lunge had been as mindless as the running of a headless chicken.

The local people's approach had slowed. Ilna took the time to view the monster instead of just reacting to its presence. It was a lizard or—

She prodded the thick neck with one hand. The skin

was slick and moist, that of a salamander rather than a lizard. The lolling jaws were edged with short, thornlike teeth.

Ilna rubbed her right leg, noticing now the line of punctures. Her fingers smeared the drops of blood welling from the holes. Her injuries wouldn't be serious, though, unless the bite was poisoned.

Alecto poised as though steeling herself to snatch coins from a fire. She reached out, gripped the hilt of her dagger, and yanked back with enough strength to have lifted a millstone. The creature's head jerked upward, then slammed against the limestone so hard that bones crunched. It slid a bit farther out so that its head hung off the porch.

"You shouted and woke me up," Alecto said, breathing hard. She tore her eyes away from the quivering monster and scanned the villagers. They'd resumed their approach, though cautiously.

"I woke *you* up?" Ilna said. She was trying to remember what had happened before she crawled out into the air. She'd been dreaming, she knew, but she didn't remember what the dream was.

"Yeah," the wild girl said. "You were staring at it. The air stank so bad it made me dizzy, but I think the eye there in the middle was doing something to you too."

She looked at her dagger; the blade was covered with translucent slime. She swore, and wiped it on her leather kilt, then hurled the garment away.

"Thank you," Ilna said. She lurched to her feet; her right leg felt as though somebody was running a branding iron up and down the calf, but it held her. "For saving my life."

Alecto grunted, her eyes now on the villagers. The priest, Arthlan, had waited till a group of his fellows reached his hut before starting toward the temple with them. The women and children were coming also, mixed in with the adult men. They whispered among themselves, but none of them called to the strangers.

The pain of Ilna's leg subsided to a dull ache. She faced the torchlight coming toward her, expressionless. Alecto had saved her, yes; but the wild girl had waited to strike until the monster was locked onto Ilna's leg and couldn't turn its numbing gaze on her.

Ilna understood the logic. As with much of what her companion did, she didn't care for it.

"Do you suppose we're in trouble for killing their God?" Alecto muttered. "That's what it was, right?"

"I suppose it was," Ilna agreed. "And I, at least, am in less trouble than I'd be if you hadn't killed the thing."

"Are you safe, great wizards?" Arthlan said in a quavering voice from the foot of the porch. He was wearing his diadem and robe of office.

"No thanks to you!" Ilna said. "You put us here to die, didn't you?"

"No, no!" said a woman; the priest's wife Oyra, Ilna thought, but it was hard to tell in the torchlight. Her vision was blurring occasionally besides, probably as an aftereffect of the salamander's third eye or its poisonous breath. She hoped the problem was temporary.

"Mistress wizard," Arthlan said, spreading his hands before him, "we couldn't trouble God, do you see? For many generations He was content with an occasional goat or the cony we smoke out of their lairs. But recently . . ."

"He took my baby ten months back," called a young woman. She held a torch, and her tears glittered in its light. "Came into the hut and tipped him out of his cradle. We were getting ready to name him the very next *day*, and he was gone!"

"And my wife!" said another man. He'd carried an axe when Ilna and Alecto arrived in the village, but he held only a rushlight now. "I woke up when our daughter screamed, but God already had her by the leg. All we could do was watch."

"What do you mean, all you could do was watch?" Alecto snarled. She stood with her arms down but a little out from her sides. The muscles of her legs and bare torso were corded with tension. "You could've took its head off with your axe, couldn't you?"

"Couldn't you have blocked the cave?" said Ilna. She wasn't really angry; the business was too puzzling for a normal emotion like that. "Six or eight of you could slide a slab of rock into the narrow part that this thing couldn't push out again."

She kicked the huge corpse with her bare foot, then regretted the contact. One of the children shrieked in excited horror.

"Mistress wizards," Arthlan said, bowing deeply. "God is God. We couldn't act against Him, do you see? But if He chose to bring your powerful selves to the gateway, then—His will be done."

"His will be done!" cried all the villagers in a ragged chorus. Their voices echoed from the slopes in a diminishing whisper.

"His will?" shouted Alecto. "How about my will, Sister take you?"

Jumping down like a cat, she grabbed Arthlan by the throat and punched the dagger just beneath his breastbone, striking upward for the full length of the blade. The priest gasped and remained standing for an instant as Alecto withdrew the bronze.

Only those closest could see what had happened. Oyra screamed and clawed at Alecto's face. Alecto gave the woman a backhand slash across the eyes.

"They've killed Arthlan!" cried a man. He swiped at Alecto with his torch. "Don't let them get away!"

Torches glittered in all directions. There were villagers on the slope both above and below the temple.

"Inside!" Ilna cried. She jumped over the God-thing's corpse. The shock of her right foot coming down on stone was like a bath in fire, but that didn't matter.

Alecto was inside with her. Together they slammed the panels shut.

"Here's the bar!" Alecto cried, banging it through the staples despite the bad light.

"There!" she added. "That'll hold them."

"Yes," said Ilna. She didn't add, "And then what?" because the question wouldn't have done any good.

At this point, she wasn't sure *anything* would do her and her murderous companion any good.

Garric was saying, "Lord Thalemos, before you met Metron did you—"

The driver jumped to its feet and began screeching like a tortured cricket. Instead of guiding with gentle touches on the millipede's neck, the Archa jabbed the creature violently with the solid end of the rod.

Garric ran forward, though he wasn't sure what he intended to do there. He had his hand on the sword hilt, but he didn't draw the weapon. Vascay trotted with him, as lightly as a one-legged canary.

Thalemos came also. He might as well; there'd be as much safety with Garric and Vascay as there was anywhere in this place.

Metron didn't stand, but he lowered his book and craned his neck to see past the driver's leaping form. The Archa's movements looked wildly spastic to Garric, but they were apparently proper for a six-limbed creature. At any rate, the driver looked to be in less danger of falling from the millipede's back than the seated wizard was.

A pool gleamed through the great grassblades off to the right side. *Water,* Garric thought, *catching the sun. . . .*

And then knew he was wrong, because the pale, pearly

glow wasn't sunlight—and because water wouldn't slosh itself out of its basin and flow in the direction of the millipede.

"It *can't* have been the Intercessor!" Metron said, opening the case which held the instruments of his art. He dropped his scroll carelessly inside and snatched out a small flask; he didn't bother to close the case. "It's chance! It's bad luck!"

The millipede ambled on at its same steady, ground-devouring pace, though it was turning slightly but noticeably leftward. The terrain became furrowed. The creature climbed without difficulty, but the angle and rocking motion made Thalemos wobble.

Garric grabbed the youth and steadied him. They took the millipede's movements the way Garric had learned to ride a ship's storm-tossed deck.

Vascay bent so that he could grip the linked gold netting with his left hand, but he kept his eyes turned to the right. From where Garric stood, the liquid from the pool had disappeared in the trees; perhaps, *perhaps* there was a distant gleam as the millipede started down the far side of the furrow.

Metron's flask was of clear glass with gold-filled etchings on the inside. It held a yellowish powder, too pale to be sulfur. As the wizard spread the contents in thin lines to form a hexagram, the powder darkened to the angry red of dying embers.

The driver squatted again but kept turning its triangular head to look back the way they'd come. Its sharp-edged upper limbs twitched out and in, folding like shears, as if the Archa were slashing something only it could see.

The millipede's foreparts were on level ground; ahead another furrow loomed. Vascay released the safety net and straightened.

"Any notion what the excitement's about, boy?" he asked Thalemos in seeming nonchalance. He gave a minuscule nod toward the crest behind them; the millipede's segmented body was still crossing it.

The youth shook his head vehemently. "I don't know any more about this place than you do!" he said. Then he managed a wry smile, and added, "And I don't like it any better than you do either."

Vascay chuckled. "Maybe so," he said. "Maybe so."

"Chief?" Hame called from the midst of the other men on the third segment. "What's going on?"

"Nothing we need worry ourselves about," Vascay replied in a cheerful tone. "Though I'll tell the *world* I'm going to be glad to get back to a place I've been before, even if there's Protectors in it!"

Turning his face away from the bandits, Vascay added under his breath, "Nothing we need worry about, because there's not a single damned thing we can do about it, eh?"

Metron began chanting in time with the motions of his athame. He'd stoppered the flask again. Around the hexagram the wizard had drawn words in the Old Script, using the brush and bottle of cinnabar as previously. In the center of the figure glittered the sapphire ring.

"Maybe the . . . the glow, maybe it can't get over the hill that we just crossed?" Thalemos suggested.

Garric shrugged, looking toward the rear. The ground was less heavily forested here, but now that they were on the level he'd lost sight of the crest behind them.

"I'm afraid," he said, "that if it were that simple, your advisor there wouldn't be working so busily at . . ."

He nodded toward Metron, chanting words of power over the hexagram.

"Sadly true," said Vascay calmly. He bobbed his javelin's head off to the right. Light glimmered through the trees in that direction, stretching well back the way they'd come.

Driven by a grim need to know the worst, Garric turned his head and looked to the left. As he'd expected—as he'd *known,* for he had known as soon as he saw the gleam coursing them to the other side—the light showed in that direction as well. The pool must have been very deep to be able to form horns about the millipede in the fashion it was doing.

The pearly liquid slid over the ground like beer spilled on a polished bar top. It had no depth, rising only a finger's breadth as it flowed around the giant grassblades and dead vegetation littering the dirt. The horns began to draw in, preparing to circle the millipede.

"Here it comes . . ." Garric said.

"Get ready, boys!" Vascay called. The Brethren had seen the fluid also and held their weapons poised. "I figure our best bet is to cut through it on our own if we lose our ride the way it looks like we're going to."

There's no chance at all, Garric thought. *There's nothing to cut and there'll be nowhere to run.*

He drew his sword, smiling at himself and at mankind's unwillingness to surrender. He wondered what it'd feel like when the glowing liquid flowed over him.

Metron shouted in a crackling voice, *"Akramma chammari!"*

Garric's head jerked around by reflex. The athame poised motionless above the ring. A red spark spat from the ivory tip, merging midway with a blue one from the sapphire.

There was a flicker of white light. The hexagram caught fire with the rushing sound of flame flooding a pool of oil.

Metron jerked his hand and athame back. Saffron fire leaped toward the heavens, then paled and spread outward soundlessly. Ademos cried out.

Garric felt a constriction in his chest as the flash passed through him; then it was gone and he drew in a normal breath again. Vegetation shimmered as if reflected on a wind-ruffled pond.

The yellow tinge had faded so that it was barely distinguishable from air by the time it reached the glowing fluid. Red and azure wizardlight sizzled at the line of contact, dulling the pearly gleam like frost on a silver mirror. Cracks appeared in what had been a surface as smooth as the sky; the rushing encirclement shuddered to a halt.

Metron collapsed over the figure, which had become no more than ash on the purple-black chitin. Garric knelt at his side and held him steady.

"He did it!" Thalemos cried. "Master Metron, you've saved us!"

Vascay didn't speak. Like Garric, he continued to look back at the thing which had pursued them. Before they passed out of sight, Garric saw that the cracks were widening and beginning to leak glowing liquid. The fluid came on again, tentatively at first.

Garric massaged the wizard's cheeks. "Wake up, Master Metron," he said. "We're going to need you again soon."

To Sharina, the walls of Donelle two furlongs away didn't look formidable compared to those of Erdin, Valles, and Carcosa—the latter mighty even in ruin, having served forty generations of builders as a quarry for dressed stone. Donelle's were about twenty feet high, originally built of stone but over the years repaired with brick or even cemented rubble.

Carus, Lord Waldron, their aides, and a dozen Blood Eagles rode up on horses and two mules captured from citizens of Tisamur. Their circuit of the siege works had taken hours. Donelle wasn't large compared to the capitals of major islands, but having to stay out of bowshot of the walls added considerably to the circumference.

Sharina stood up in the shelter of what was now a mantlet; it'd been one wall of a farmer's shed not long ago. A score of officers involved in building the entrenchments, supplying the troops, and goodness knew what all else, descended on the commanders like vultures on a dead ewe. Carus and Waldron didn't even get a chance to dismount.

Sharina relaxed again, looking at Donelle. She didn't need to speak to the king, and his officers did. Her only purpose on Tisamur was to help Carus rein in his temper. Even if she could fight her way to the king through the crowd of armed soldiers, she couldn't restrain him in so confused a setting.

The city's garrison was raising additional towers at intervals along the wall, giving archers on the upper platforms greater range and adding impact to stones flung on those beneath. The new structures were built of wood, wicker, and bull hides. They'd stop an ordinary arrow, but Sharina didn't need a professional soldier to tell her that the heavy missiles from the fleet's catapults and ballistae would shred the towers and everyone inside them.

Carus broke through the mob, shouting orders over his shoulder as he strode toward the mantlet. His bodyguards scrambled to keep up with him, elbowing officers aside with little consideration for rank.

With Lord Attaper and his Blood Eagles as a screen, Carus joined Sharina. He lifted the helmet he'd worn on the tour of inspection and used it to shade his eyes as he surveyed Donelle from this angle.

"Not much, is it?" he said conversationally. "I was half-minded to storm it when we arrived. The trouble is, I don't trust the troops—yet—to stay disciplined when they're not under their officers' eyes. If I'd sent them over the wall—"

His left index finger pointed: here, there, a third spot. The first where the foundations had shifted, forming a crack which, though filled, was a staircase to the battlements. Another where olive trees grew up to the stone as though espaliered; the fruit was ripe. The last the main gate itself, closed but obviously too rotten to withstand the impact of one of the roof beams ripped from a wealthy residence outside the walls and converted to a battering ram.

"—in an hour they'd have been all through the city in packets of half a dozen. And I'd have lost half of them before nightfall, from getting turned around in somebody else's twisting streets and burned when the fire started, as it surely would."

He shook his head with a grimace. "There's always a cookfire kicked over," he said, "or somebody just can't help tossing a lantern onto a thatched roof to prove that they've got a sword in their hand and they can do anything they please. Which, of course, they can."

"What will happen now, your highness?" Sharina asked, smiling deliberately as she looked at her companion.

He'd come to Sharina because only with her and Tenoctris—who was back in camp with the ships—could he talk freely. The Blood Eagles were keeping everyone else at bay by the prince's orders. If they heard what Carus said or Sharina answered, they wouldn't pass it on.

"Siege," Carus said. He shrugged. "It won't take long. The town's packed with people, and prisoners say the whole south end of the island's inside. There can't be enough food within the walls to last for three days, and in six there won't be a rat or a scrap of harness leather to be found."

Soldiers were digging a trench at a bare bowshot from the walls of Donelle; a little closer yet, Sharina suspected. The defenders weren't trying their luck, though, probably because Carus had brought some of his artillery up from the ships already. The catapults and ballistae were cocked and ready to reply to anything the city's bowmen chose to start.

"They'll surrender when the food runs out?" Sharina asked. She looked away from the city, then turned her head quickly so that she wouldn't have to think about what she'd see there.

The countryside around Donelle had been pleasant and prosperous, a mixture of successful farms and the country houses of wealthy townsfolk. In less than a day, the royal army had transformed it into a devastated wasteland.

"The people in control, these Children of the Mistress," Carus said grimly, "they'll have some food. So will the mercenaries they've hired. They'll keep the gates closed for a while yet. But it won't be long, it can't be long."

"And your dreams?" Sharina asked quietly.

"I can stand the dreams longer than the people inside can live on air!" Carus said, though his face went gray at the thought. He added, looking at the city instead of his companion, "I thought about that when we arrived and I was deciding whether to storm the walls. I could've said, 'Kill everybody wearing the black-and-white robe.' I could've said, 'Kill everybody who might have worn the black-and-white robe.' "

His right hand clenched on his sword hilt; the blade rustled against the iron reinforcement at the mouth of the scabbard.

"I could have said, 'Kill everybody!' " Carus said, "and they'd have done it. My men would have done it because *I* said so. Not every man in the army, but enough; and when they were done, the dreams would have stopped."

"Carus?" Sharina said, touching the king's sword hand. He stiffened, then took a deep breath and relaxed at least his body.

The ruin of the countryside wasn't vandalism. Wood is the first thing a siege requires: wood for mantlets, wood to shore trenches and earthen walls, wood for the heavy siege engines to batter through stone. Orchards, sacred groves, beeches planted to shade a house or a bower—all of them fall in a flurry of axe chips, then slide toward the entrenchments behind teams of men and captured oxen.

The quickest sources of finished timber are existing buildings. On the short march from the harbor, Sharina had seen hundreds of houses torn down in a few minutes apiece by squads of troops who'd quickly learned the swiftest ways to convert a home into beams and a pile of rubble.

"I killed people when I wore my own flesh," said the ancient king softly. "Killed them myself and had them killed. I never killed everybody in a city, though."

He knuckled his eyes, then his temples. Sharina had never seen anyone more obviously weary.

Carus lowered his fists and gave her a wry smile. "If I don't get some sleep soon," he said conversationally, "I don't know what I'm going to do. But Donelle'll surrender soon enough."

A trumpet called. The army's first action on reaching Donelle had been to raise a spindly watchtower, a tripod supporting a laddered mast. The basket at the peak put the lookout a good hundred feet in the air. From there he could see most of what went on in the city as well as in the surrounding countryside.

He blew another attention signal, holding the trumpet to his lips with one hand while the other arm pointed south. The eyes of besiegers and those on the city walls both turned in that direction, toward the fleet's encampment.

Sharina glanced at the mantlet. The wattling was of thumb-thick branches woven about saplings of twice the diameter. The hut's corner posts, trimmed cedar trees, now held the mantlet upright against any arrows that got this far.

"What in blazes—" Carus wondered aloud.

Sharina half jumped, half climbed to the top of the mantlet and stood barefoot on its edge. She kept her arms out for balance while her eyes searched the western horizon.

"There's a horseman coming," she said. Nearby soldiers

looked up at her. "He's got a red pennant. He's one of our messengers, your highness!"

"Is he, by the Lady!" Carus said. "So what's Zettkin got that's so important he sends a mounted courier?"

In the excitement, several archers on the nearer gate tower sent arrows toward Carus and Sharina. "Down!" bellowed a Blood Eagle. He grabbed Sharina's ankle and jerked her toward him.

If he hadn't let go, Sharina might have hit badly—on her back or even her head. The bodyguard was satisfied merely to get her down where she didn't draw attention. She landed on her toes and flexed knees, just as the flight of arrows whistled into the ground. The nearest was twenty feet away.

A ballista fired from an earth mound thirty yards behind Sharina. The bow arms slammed forward to their padded stops, sending a bolt screaming overhead to strike in a shower of sparks on the side of a firing slit. The iron projectile glanced through without hitting any of the defenders. Chips the bolt'd shattered from the battlements sprayed stingingly across the platform.

The archers were Tisamur militiamen, not hired professionals. They threw themselves down, then as one rose to look out at the ballista which wouldn't be recocked for another five minutes at the quickest.

The sailors crewing a catapult well down the curve of the siege lines had horsed their weapon around to bear on the gate tower. While the defenders looked in the other direction, the catapult's head-sized stone hit and smashed a section of the battlements inward. The archers went down again; some screaming, the rest unable to. No one showed himself on that tower again while Sharina watched.

The courier charged into the siege lines and slid from his saddle while his horse was still moving. He was a short man, lightly built—a natural jockey in size and with the bantam feistiness of so many little men. Ignoring Lord Waldron and the senior officers around him, he made straight for Carus.

Blood Eagles hunched, lifting their shields into position. Their job was to doubt the goodwill of others—and institutional suspicion aside, a Confederacy assassin could find a pennon to mimic a royal courier.

"Let him through!" Carus ordered.

Attaper turned to eye the king sidelong while keeping the courier in sight. "Stay as you are," he snapped to his men. "You, messenger? You can tell your news from where you are!"

The black-armored guards took their commander's orders, not the king's. The courier made as if to push through; the curve of a shield butted him back. Lord Waldron, glowering like a thundercloud, and the other nearby officers came crowding closer.

"Yes, go on!" Carus said, frustrated but philosophical about it. "What word do you bring from Admiral Zettkin?"

"Your majesty . . ." the courier said. "The Count of Blaise has landed with his whole army in the bay west of us. Admiral Zettkin says there's at least fifteen thousand men, and that he's sure from the equipment that some of the regiments are from Sandrakkan! The admiral is awaiting your orders."

"May the Lady show us mercy!" cried a gray-bearded officer, the adjutant of the regiment building this section of siege works. "They knew we were coming, and they've trapped us! We'll die here as sure as—"

Carus, as swiftly as a stooping hawk, pushed two Blood Eagles aside in his rush. He grabbed the old soldier by the throat and slapped him, forehand and then backhand. His callused hand *cracked* like the ballista's cord.

"Your highness!" Sharina screamed, grabbing Carus' right arm from behind and clinging with all the strength of her supple young body. "Not this! Not here!"

Looking dazed, Carus released the adjutant; he fell as though heart-stabbed. Two of the old man's juniors caught him under the shoulders and drew him back out of sight.

Carus looked around at the shock and fear filling the eyes of the watching officers. He shook himself, then clenched and unclenched his right hand to work feeling back into the numbed fingers.

"No," the king said, "we're not going to die here—and we're not going to give up the siege of Donelle either. Lord Waldron, I'm leaving you here with half the heavy infantry to continue the siege. I'll take the other half, the skirmishers, and the phalanx back to the fleet and size up the situation. And then"—he looked at the gates of Donelle, then around the arc of his officers again—"I'll teach Count Lerdoc what it means to rebel against the King of the Isles. I'll teach him, or the Sister take my soul!"

A few of those listening started to cheer. All Sharina could think of was that the Sister might very well have Carus' soul soon—and the souls of every man of his army as well, if the king's haste led him into yet another misjudgment.

Chapter Eighteen

A lecto leaped onto a bench, then set one foot on the crossbar and braced the other against the sidewall so that she could look out through the small circular window in the transom. A villager shouted a warning.

The wild girl jumped down. A torch smacked the opening, knocking sparks into the temple. Alecto responded with an oath that Ilna—who didn't believe in the Great Gods or much of anything else—found disgusting. Ilna snatched the bedding clear, but the sparks burned out before they landed.

"They're not trying to break the door down," Alecto said quietly. "They're hanging back on the porch, looking at the lizard I killed."

"They probably don't see any reason to hurry," Ilna said, thinking through the pattern which connected the past to the future here at this point. "Hunger will bring us out before long—if they don't decide to block the door from their side"

She smiled with wintry humor. "A pity that the creature ran outside that way," she added. "We wouldn't have lacked for food if it'd died where you stabbed it."

Alecto gave her a look of irritation, apparently uncertain whether Ilna was joking. Since Ilna wasn't sure herself, the confusion was understandable.

Something thumped against the door. Ilna hesitated, deciding between her noose, the hank of cords in her sleeve, and the small bone-cased knife she carried in her sash for general utility. In the end she readied the silken noose. It wasn't a good weapon for these tight quarters, but she liked the feel of it. There wasn't light enough to expect their attackers to see a knotted spell.

Alecto hopped up to the transom again, then dropped back with a grim expression. This time the villagers didn't fling a torch at her.

"They're piling rocks in front of the door," she said. "They're going to block us in."

Ilna nodded without expression. "I'll see where the cave goes, then," she said. It led to somewhere big enough to hold a salamander the size of a horse, after all. And since there were no other options . . .

Alecto didn't seem to have heard her. Outside on the porch, villagers crunched another block of stone down beside the first. With the whole community working, the entrance would very quickly be blocked beyond the ability of the two women to clear.

"I'll kill you all!" Alecto screamed at the door panels. "I'll wipe you off the face of the Earth, you cowards!"

The wild girl knelt and began drawing on the floor with her athame. The blade was covered with the priest's blood, but it had mostly dried by now. She spat on the bronze so that her point left thin red trails of dissolved gore on the stone.

Her face screwed into tight, sour lines, Ilna lay on her belly and crawled cautiously into the narrowing cave. The rock was slimy—from the salamander's skin, she now knew, not water sweating through the limestone as she'd thought when Arthlan first showed them the temple's interior.

Peasants got used to filthy jobs. Ilna smiled: the slime would wash off, if she lived long enough to reach a place with clean water. That didn't seem likely at the moment.

Her body blocked the little light that entered through the temple's transom. She regretted that, but Alecto's chanting also blurred into a dull murmur. Ilna didn't know what the wild girl was attempting, but it probably wasn't anything a decent person wanted to know about.

The tunnel narrowed further. The salamander was thicker through the body than Ilna, but it must be able to squeeze itself down to a degree that a human rib cage couldn't. If she became stuck in the throat of the passage—

Ilna laughed—and regretted it, because the stone didn't let her body shake with laughter as it should. *If I get stuck,* she thought, *I die in a small stone box. Which is exactly what happens to me if I don't find a way out of the temple in the first place.*

Ilna had her arms stretched out in front of her. She squirmed forward by twisting her torso while one elbow or the other anchored her against the stone. It was slow and unpleasant, but—she smiled—not *as* slow or *as* unpleasant as the alternative.

Tight places didn't especially bother her. Stone did, though, but there wasn't anything to do about the fact except ignore it and keep on going. In Ilna's philosophy, going on was the only choice.

The cave started to open up again—not much, but enough for Ilna to reach out with both hands against the stone and pull her hips through the narrowest point. She could smell water close; if nothing else, that meant she and Alecto would starve in three weeks instead of dying of thirst in three days.

She got up on all fours, then lifted her head carefully in hopes that there was room enough to stand. No, the ceiling was still just above her. At least she could keep her torso off the ground.

She reached forward with her right hand and shifted her weight onto it. Her palm slipped down a short, slimy slope into water as cold as charity. She jerked back and just missed lifting her head *hard* into the rock.

Ilna paused for a moment, tasting the water—good, though with a slight tang of iron—and getting her breathing back under control. *Maybe I'm more nervous than I'd thought. . . .* Because of all the stone, she supposed; but that was no excuse, there *were* no excuses.

Alecto's chant echoed down the tunnel, blended into a threatening rumble by its passage. Occasionally a word came clear: "*. . . palipater patrima . . .*" in one moment, "*. . . iao alilamps . . .*" in another.

Ilna explored the edge of the pool with her left hand, hoping she'd find something more promising on the other side than there was in the direction she'd come. There wasn't another side: when Ilna stirred the water, it lapped against a solid stone wall. The pool wasn't much bigger than the tunnel through which she'd crawled to reach it.

She felt as far as she could reach into the water without

finding bottom. There was enough water somewhere to hold the salamander now dead on the temple porch; it was possible, probable even, that this pool was a tunnel like the one that led to the outside; but slightly lower and flooded.

". . . *nerxia* . . ." echoed a voice, no longer identifiable as Alecto's or even as human.

Of course even if there was a larger cavern beyond, it too might be water-filled: an underground sea in which the monster slept motionless in the intervals between crawling to the surface to eat. It didn't come out often, from what Arthlan had said. The salamanders Ilna knew, hiding under the rocks of Pattern Creek or crawling across the leaf mold on damp evenings, had none of the eager liveliness of mice and birds.

She hiked up her tunic to keep it dry—drier than otherwise, at least—and lowered herself feetfirst into the pool. She felt the smooth stone channel curve, but again she didn't find an end. There was no point in trying to go farther unless she was willing to go all the way.

Ilna pulled herself out of the water, a harder task than she'd expected. The monster had polished the rock over the ages of passing to and from the outer world, and Ilna's limbs were already numb from their immersion.

She breathed deeply on her hands and knees, then lay flat again and squirmed through the tunnel in the other direction. It was easier this time. She had a glimmer of moonlight to guide her, and she knew that there *was* an end.

As Ilna worked her way past the tunnel's throat, a flash of scarlet wizardlight blotted the moonglow. Alecto's voice rose into a high-pitched rant: *"Brimo!"*

Another flash, much brighter.

"Ananke!"

Ilna got her legs past the narrowest part of the cave. She thrust her feet hard at the rock walls, at the same time scrabbling forward with her arms. She didn't know why she was in such a hurry, but if the wild girl was bringing matters to a climax, Ilna wanted to be present for good or ill.

Present for ill, probably. Even at better times, Ilna didn't have much confidence in good things happening.

"*Chasarba!*" Alecto screamed.

Ilna squeezed out of the cave. Alecto knelt, holding her dagger point in the center of the figure she'd scribed in human blood. Her face was a study in hellish triumph.

Wizardlight blazed from the blade, penetrating flesh and even rock. For an instant Ilna saw the villagers staring at the temple with expressions of stark horror. Wingless things flew between suns in the void beyond the sky, and creatures swam like fish in the lava beneath the mountains.

The light died, leaving a memory of itself in Ilna's eyes. Alecto laughed like a demon. The ground began to shake.

Outside the temple, villagers screamed. The first tremors were slight, but everyone who lives in a mountain valley knows the danger of landslides.

A violent shock threw Ilna off her feet. The mountainside crackled like sheets of lightning. Slabs of rock broke away, roaring toward the bottom of the valley and sweeping up more debris in their rush.

The tremors lifted dust from the temple floor; Ilna held her sleeve over her mouth and nose so that she could still breathe. The slope was shaking itself like a dog just out of the water.

The temple porch collapsed, blotting out the sheen of moonlight through the transom. Ilna grabbed Alecto's shoulder and dragged her into the natural part of the temple, the funnel in the living rock. It might not survive the violence the wild girl had called down on the whole valley, herself included, but it might. Nothing made by men could possibly—

Cracks danced across the temple roof. "Come on!" Ilna

screamed, pulling Alecto with her as far as she could. She couldn't have explained why she was trying to save her companion, except perhaps that their two lives were the only things Ilna thought she *might* save from the thunder of destruction.

Going on is the only choice. . . .

The cave narrowed. Ilna slid into the throat. "Come on!" she repeated, but she couldn't hear her own voice against the shuddering terror of the earthquake.

The stone squeezed Ilna, battered her. It could close and chew her body like a grass stem in a boy's mouth. No one would ever know that Ilna os-Kenset was a smear of blood between layers of stone.

She worked through, pulling herself into the enlarged chamber. She felt triumphant for the instant before a greater shock threw her against the ceiling, numbing her shoulders and nearly stunning her.

She turned. Water from the pool sloshed across her in icy fury.

"Alecto!" she shouted, knowing she might as well save her breath. She reached back into the tunnel. Her companion's hand was stretched out, still gripping the bronze dagger. Ilna grabbed Alecto's wrist and pulled, dragging her hips through the narrows.

There was nothing to see, nothing to hear but the mountain destroying itself and all the world besides. Guiding Alecto by the hand, Ilna poised on the edge of the pool.

She dived in, headfirst. She couldn't swim, but her hands and feet against the smooth stone would take her as far down as she could go before she drowned or froze . . . or just possibly, she reached a place where a human could live, at least for a little while longer.

No choice. . . .

* * *

Tilphosa screamed. Cashel jumped to his feet, slanting the quarterstaff across his body. He kicked the bedding into the darkness. The shuttered windows blocked all the light that Soong's fog didn't smother to begin with.

Leaning forward, Cashel swept his left hand through the air above where Tilphosa should be lying. His right arm was cocked back, ready to ram his staff's ferrule through anybody he touched who wasn't the girl herself. Nobody was bending over her.

Cashel scooped Tilphosa up one-handed and started for the common room. Rather than strike a light in here, he'd take her to the hearth and blow the coals bright.

Tilphosa's body was as cold as a drowned corpse: colder than the air, colder than mere death.

The door at the far end of the passageway rattled open. Leemay stood back holding an oil lamp, while two of the men who'd slept in the common room stood in the doorway. One held a cudgel and the other, a fisherman, had a gaff with claws of briar root.

"Let me get her out into the light!" Cashel said. He'd let his staff drop in the aisle, but there still wasn't width enough for his haste. His right hip brushed down a hamper of spirits in stoneware bottles; they clattered among themselves without breaking.

"It wasn't a sound!" said one of the men in confusion. "I didn't hear her scream, I thought it!"

The trapdoor into the loft overhead was open at the back of the room. A proper ladder leaned against the molding. In Barca's Hamlet, most people used fir saplings trimmed so that the branch stubs provided steps of a sort. . . .

"Get out of my way!" Cashel said, pushing into the common room. The fisherman jumped out of his way in time; the other fellow didn't and bounced back from Cashel's shoulder. Cashel laid Tilphosa on the bar, cradling her head with his left hand until he found a sponge to use as a pillow.

The fellow's comment about *thinking* the scream made Cashel frown. That's what it seemed to him, too, now that somebody'd mentioned it. He'd been asleep, though, and dreaming—

Leemay held the lamp so that its light fell on the girl's face. The innkeeper was expressionless, scarcely livelier than Tilphosa . . . and Tilphosa might have been a wax statue, her face molded by an artist whose taste was for art that showed bones and ignored the spirit.

"What'd you do to Tilphosa?" Cashel said. Anger deepened his voice. The two men flinched; Leemay did not.

The outside door was already ajar. The left panel opened fully, and more people bumped their way in. Either they'd been summoned by the scream, or somebody'd gone out to call them.

"How could I touch her?" Leemay said. "She was with you; I was up on the roof."

The lamp trembled in the innkeeper's hand. She was weary, weary from the spell she'd just woven on the roof.

The fishermen touched Tilphosa's cheek, then her throat, with the back of his fingers. "She's dead," he said. "Cold as ice. Somebody get the Nine."

"Do you suppose it's plague?" a man asked in concern.

Cashel grabbed for Leemay's throat. She leaned back, too quick for him and a perfect judge of how far he could reach with the bar between them.

"Watch him," she said to the local men around her. "He may have gone mad with grief."

The bar was of heavy hardwood, anchored to the walls and floor, but Cashel would've pushed it over if the girl hadn't been lying on it. He came out through the gate instead, tearing it away instead of folding it up and back.

Two men grappled him. Everyone was shouting; the only light was from Leemay's lamp, though a woman in the doorway held a lantern with lenses of fish bladder.

Cashel caught the two men in his arms and rotated his

torso, hurling them both over the bar and into wall. Somebody grabbed his legs. He brought his right foot back, then kicked hard with his callused heel. The hands released. Cashel lunged forward with his arms outstretched.

He was going to get his hands on Leemay. Then she'd undo whatever it was that she'd done to Tilphosa, or . . .

The crowd milled between him and the innkeeper. More people were coming through the door every moment, but Cashel didn't care about that. The men in front of him struggled, but they could as well have wrestled with an ox as try to stop Cashel in his present rage. He plowed forward, his shoulders hunched.

Leemay backed a step and another step. She was against the wall, now, still holding up the lamp, her flat face passionless.

Somebody threw a net smelling of river mud onto Cashel. Men shouted, twisting it over his torso. It was only a fishnet, but the openwork fabric of tough cords flexed when he pulled at it. It gave against him, never releasing and never allowing his strength a way to break it.

Cashel forced himself another pace onward. An overturned table tripped him; wrapped in the net, he couldn't throw an arm out to keep his balance. He fell, smashing a stool under him.

"I've got a net!" a man cried. "Let me—"

Cashel kicked violently, trying to twist up onto his knees. Several locals shoved him down, and a second net fell over his legs. Willing hands wrapped it tight, trussing Cashel like a hen for market.

Leemay stared down at him. "Don't hurt him," she said, not that anybody seemed disposed to do so. They were just decent citizens, restraining a stranger who'd gone berserk. "He's upset! He'll come to his senses later."

"You killed her!" Cashel shouted.

He squirmed across the puncheon floor, still trying to reach the innkeeper. Cashel wasn't sure he'd even be able to bite her ankles through the fishnet, but at least he was going to try.

Men grabbed the casting ropes and hauled back. The net was made to hold heavy, fiercely struggling prey; it worked as well on land as it would've done with a catch of eels.

"Tie him to the pillar," Leemay said calmly, nodding toward the roughly shaped tree trunk which supported the main roof beam. "Let him sleep off the madness."

Experienced hands slid Cashel across the floor, then lifted his torso upright against the pillar. He twisted, but they were fishermen and used to muscling a writhing netful.

"There you go, lad," one of them said. "Just calm down, and we'll let you loose."

The front door's other panel opened deliberately. The crowd quieted from the back forward as everyone turned to look at the doorway.

Everyone but Leemay. She glanced at the door momentarily, then looked across the room to Tilphosa's still form. She smiled faintly and became expressionless again.

A hooded figure, skeletally thin despite its billowing robes, entered the common room. It had to bend to clear the doorway, but the ceiling between the beams was high enough for it to straighten again.

"Where is the departed?" said a voice. It had to come from under the hood, but it had no more direction than it had life or humanity. It sounded like the wind wheezing through rotten thatch.

"Here," said the man who'd sat in the chimney corner when Cashel and Tilphosa arrived. He gestured toward the bar top.

"You can carry her on one of my tables," Leemay said. "She may have had something contagious, so we need to be quick about taking care of her."

"Tilphosa wasn't sick!" Cashel shouted. "You killed her, woman! You!"

Men took the table that was already upended and knocked out the pins attaching the trestle legs. They carried it to the bar, where two more men lifted Tilphosa's still form onto it. They worked efficiently but with a degree of respect which Cashel noted, though anger was a fire in his throat.

The hooded figure nodded, then bent again and left the inn. Even as close as Cashel now was to the member of the Nine, he couldn't see any sign of legs moving beneath the robe.

The men carrying Tilphosa on the table shuffled out after the priest. The other locals bowed their heads; then, when the impromptu procession was well clear, they began to return to their own homes for the remainder of the night.

Leemay closed the door again; the three guests in the common room muttered quietly as they found their bedding and crawled into it.

Leemay looked at Cashel once more before she pinched out the wick of her lamp. He couldn't see her features through the red rage in his heart.

Ademos, not a man Garric had suspected of being devout, knelt on the millipede's third segment and prayed loudly: first to the Lady, then to the Shepherd, and then back to the Lady. His voice was so loud that Garric—standing with Vascay, Thalemos, and the wizard just behind the creature's head—could hear every word clearly.

The only pause between prayers was however long it took Ademos to draw breath. The other Brethren listened without complaint; indeed, Halophus looked as though he might join in.

Metron lay on the millipede's armor, drained white by the effort of forcing back the pursuing liquid a second time. He was either asleep or comatose; occasionally he snorted like a seal as he struggled to breathe.

"It's catching up with us again," said Thalemos in a tone of aristocratic calm. Indeed, the only hint of the youth's nervousness lay in the fact that he'd bothered to state something so blindingly obvious in the first place.

The living fluid shimmered through the trees to either side. Garric remembered that he'd thought at first it was sun-struck water; he smiled, wishing that he were still so ignorant.

Not long before, a beetle the size of a house had lumbered past the millipede and into the pearly glow. The fluid crawled up the creature's legs like oil soaking a wick. Lines of cobweb-gray traced across the shiny black wing cases; bits of the wings fell away, and the beetle's legs turned to powder also.

The beetle's fat body continued to writhe for as long as Garric's eyes could follow it. The fact that the agony was silent made it all the worse.

"I can't say I'm looking forward to the thing eating me," Vascay remarked conversationally. He glanced sidelong at Garric. "Eh?"

"If you need somebody to kill you now so that doesn't happen," Garric said forcefully, "then look for somebody else."

The chieftain smiled. "I said I wasn't looking forward to it, lad," he said. "I didn't say I wasn't man enough to face it."

"It's coming toward us now," Thalemos said. His voice was still calm, but fear stretched his cheeks tight over the bones.

To the right, a thin tendril slanted from the edge of the liquid sheet. The same would be happening on the millipede's other side. The creature's technique—was it even a creature? Was it as mindlessly destructive as a wind-blown fire?—never changed.

Nor did it need to change. Perseverance was sure to carry the day, if not on this attempt then on the next.

"Time to wake our learned friend," Vascay said, kneeling at Metron's side. He shook the wizard by the shoulder.

He was increasingly firm, but only to rouse the man. Several of the Brethren stared at Metron with obvious hatred, but Vascay knew as Garric did that the wizard was no more responsible for their plight than was any other member of their group.

They'd gambled and apparently lost. The forfeit wouldn't come from a Protector's sword or the gallows in the main square of Durassa, but they'd all known there were risks. Metron would be paying the same price as the rest of them.

"Wakey, wakey," Vascay said, shaking still harder. "Time for your party piece again, Master Metron."

The wizard's eyelids fluttered. He lay with his cheek on his arm. He didn't—or couldn't—lift his head, but he looked at the three men beside him.

"There's no use," he croaked. "I used the last of my True Mercury. You saw that the phial was empty."

"You opened a gate for us into this place from Durassa," Garric said. "Can you open it again so we go back?"

Metron sat up with sudden animation, then gasped with pain. Vascay supported him by the shoulders as if the wizard were a comrade with cracked ribs.

Metron closed his eyes, then opened them with a look of resolution. "Not back, no," he said. "But it may be we're close enough that I can open the passage to, to our destination. We'll need a lamp, a flame—"

"Toster, come here with your lighter!" Vascay ordered. "And Ademos, you're still wearing those clogs. Bring 'em here. I've got a better use for those wooden soles than you walking on them!"

Ademos turned to look, but he didn't get up from his appearance of piety. "What better use?" he demanded.

"Burning them to get us out of this place!" Vascay said. "Move it, Brother Ademos!"

"I don't—" Ademos began.

Toster gripped him by the neck. "Somebody get the shoes and come on," the big man said in a hoarse voice. Calm though he was to look at, Toster was close to the edge also.

Ademos didn't struggle. Halophus snatched off the clogs and followed Toster to the chief.

Metron had moved slightly so that he had an unmarked patch of armor before him. He began to draw, using the brush and pot of vermilion instead of the yellow powder he'd called his True Mercury.

Garric looked into the forest. The glowing liquid lapped alongside, close enough that Vascay could have skewered the tendril with a cast of his javelin. No point in that, of course. It no longer slanted toward them; rather, it was drawing slightly ahead of their course. When the filament gained enough that it could merge with the horn on the other side, there'd be no escape for the millipede or the men riding it.

Vascay trimmed slivers from the wooden shoes; Halophus laid them in a tiny fireset in the middle of the hexagram the wizard had drawn on the purple-black armor.

Metron placed the ring on the tip of his ivory athame. At his muttered instruction, Toster struck the plunger of his fire piston. When he opened the end, a smolder of milkweed fluff spilled onto the fireset and blazed up at the touch of open air.

"*Pico picatrix sesengen . . .*" chanted Metron, holding the sapphire ring up beside the fire. The gem's facets glinted in hard contrast to the muted blur of these forest depths.

The tendrils of fluid slid toward one another again, this time well in front of the millipede. The creature paced forward on its many legs, unperturbed by what was about to happen. The Archa driver stood with a fluting cry. Hurling its wand to one side, it leaped toward the ground in the other direction. It must have fallen under the millipede's pincered feet, but Garric didn't suppose that made much difference in the long run.

Vascay glanced at Garric, though the knife in his hand kept trimming slivers from the clog like a cook peeling a turnip. "Can't say I'm sorry to be shut of him," he said, transferring a palmful of shavings for the waiting Halophus to feed to the fire.

Garric smiled as his ancestor Carus would have smiled, an expression as hard as diamond millstones. There probably wasn't a long run, for the Archa or for the rest of them.

"*Baphar baphris saxa...*" Metron intoned, adjusting the angle at which he held the ring. The jewel refracted the firelight as well as reflecting it, bending some of it back to dance on the next segment of armor.

"*Nophris nophar saxa...*" said Metron.

The arms of glowing liquid met with a gush of pearly light. The thin tendrils broadened swiftly, the way water spreads from a breached dike. The millipede stumped on without hesitation, closing on the fluid as it swelled inward.

"*Barouch baroucha barbatha...*" Metron said. He didn't stop chanting, but his right hand beckoned to the Brethren desperately. A keyhole of light quivered on the second segment of the millipede's back.

"Come on, boys!" Vascay said. "This is it!"

Ademos scrambled to his bare feet. The bandits started forward but stopped in a group, staring at the pattern quivering on the armor.

Vascay's eyes met Garric's. They both knew the dangers: certain death if they stayed here, unknown and perhaps worse horrors on the other side of Metron's passage.

"Lead!" Garric said. "I'll bring up the back like before!"

Vascay leaped into the doorway of light and vanished. Hame and Halophus jostled one another to be next through. Garric touched Thalemos' arm and gestured him forward. The youth hesitated, then followed Prada into nothingness.

Garric stood at an angle, watching Metron with the gateway in the corner of his right eye. He held his sword bare, though he didn't recall drawing it. The Brethren jumped and disappeared, some of them muttering prayers. Toster remained at Garric's side.

The millipede suddenly twisted back, making Garric sway. Metron tried to stand. Garric put his swordpoint at the wizard's throat to hold him where he was. "Toster!" Garric shouted. "Go!"

Toster turned. He jumped toward the ground, his axe swinging.

"I'll kill you!" the big man cried, but then he began to scream. The scream continued, but it no longer sounded like anything that might come from a human throat.

"Please!" Metron said. The fire was burning down. Only an occasional sputter woke glints from the sapphire's facets. "Please, it'll be—"

Garric put his left arm around the wizard. He lunged forward, taking them together into the freezing maelstrom of Metron's gateway.

There was no sound in the passage, but Toster's screams still echoed in Garric's mind.

He supposed they always would.

"Well, my lords—and princess," said Carus, bowing to her as they stood on the ridgeline viewing both the royal fleet and the vast assembly in the bay beyond to the west. "I did Admiral Zettkin an injustice in not believing that Lerdoc could raise fifteen thousand men. He's got that many and more besides, I shouldn't wonder."

Hundreds of ships were grounded on the open coast to the west of the royal encampment. Most of them were sailing vessels, round-bellied merchantmen which could carry some hundreds of men apiece, albeit in great discomfort. Only a score of triremes escorted them; the Blaise fleet was no larger than the royal fleet had been before Garric—guided by Carus—began to rule the kingdom.

You could command an island with soldiers. To command the Isles, you had to have a fleet.

"You didn't say that you doubted him, your highness," said Lord Attaper. Zettkin was a former officer of the Blood Eagles, Attaper's friend and protégé. "Not in my hearing, at least."

"Didn't I?" mused Carus. "Maybe I learned something in the time since—"

Sharina reached out to touch Carus' cheek. The gesture must have looked odd to the high officers standing close and scowling as they gazed at the rebel army, but was better than having the ancient king blurt some variation on "—since I drowned a thousand years ago."

The king's face was warm but as stiff as sun-washed marble. He patted Sharina's fingers, and said, "Since I first came to Valles. I *thought* Zettkin was wrong, though."

If the royal triremes had met the Blaise merchantmen at sea, only surrender could have saved the rebel army from drowning to a man. *If.* Luck or more likely wizardry had given Count Lerdoc perfect weather, perfect timing, and perfect secrecy for his sweep across the Inner Sea. Someone was weaving a plot as complex as one of Ilna's tapestries.

Sharina and the command group were mounted, but Lord Attaper had flatly refused to allow Carus to gallop back to the harbor with only a troop of Blood Eagles to guard him. All four regiments of javelin-armed skirmishers had jogged along with the high officers, the horsemen adjusting their pace to that of their escort. They couldn't fight the whole Blaise army, but they could delay any desperate thrust by the rebels long enough for the rest of the royal army to arrive.

"We could attack them now," said Lord Dowos, previously commander of a cavalry regiment which had remained behind to guard Valles. He pointed at the confused mass of ships and men. "Before they get organized, why, we'll slaughter them!"

Dowos was Lord Waldron's cousin. When he'd demanded to accompany the expedition to Tisamur, Waldron appointed him adjutant of the royal army. Since he and Waldron thought alike, Dowos was a good choice to ride with the king while Waldron sorted out the sudden disruption of the siege.

"No!" said Lord Attaper, to Dowos' right. "That'd be slaughter, all right, but not—"

"Who are you to—" Dowos shouted. He jerked his mount's head to face Attaper. The captured horse, unused to being ridden and too small for the big cavalryman anyway, stumbled to its knees. Dowos jumped clear and reached for his sword.

"If you draw that, Dowos," Carus said in a voice of thunder, "then you'll be the first rebel I kill on Tisamur. Depend on it!"

"Wha—?" said Dowos, turning in amazement at the violence of the words. "Your highness, I'm no rebel! I only—"

"Silence!" Carus said.

Sharina sat transfixed on the king's other side, afraid that any action she took would spark his barely restrained fury. Carus was angry beyond reason at the situation he'd created by bringing the royal army to Tisamur, where the kingdom's enemies could trap it. If Dowos, if *anyone*, did the wrong thing now, the king would unload that anger lethally on an undeserving victim.

Attaper kneed his mount between Dowos and the king.

He caught the reins of the loose horse, and said in a neutral voice, "Let me help you back into the saddle, my lord."

Now Sharina could touch the king's cheek again. "Your highness," she whispered.

Carus threw his head back and laughed. Sharina knew the humor was honest, but at this juncture it disturbed the nearby officers as much as the anger a moment before had done.

"Your suggestion wouldn't be a worse blunder than the way I brought us all to the present pass, Lord Dowos," he said, "but one bad mistake is quite enough for a campaign."

He nodded toward the rebel force. Lerdoc had brought mounts for his cavalry, trusting his wizard advisors for fair winds—if he weren't simply being a nobleman and therefore a fool on the question. At least a squadron of horsemen were with the skirmishers, moving out as the regiments of heavy infantry tried to form on the beach. On the ships stranded when the tide backed, men swarmed like bees from an opened hive.

"Next thing to chaos, isn't it?" the king said with a wry smile. His expression hardened. "How good do you suppose our formation's going to be after we go charging down into them, hey? Especially when their archers start shooting at us from the ships' decks! Every one of those ships is going to be a little fort with its own moat of seawater."

"Your highness . . ." Dowos said, but his voice trailed off. Abruptly he added, "Lord Attaper, my apologies. And my thanks for your assistance with my horse."

Sharina looked over her shoulder. The skirmishers, savage-looking men with bundles of javelins and a broad knife or a hand axe, were spreading into a loose screen on the forward slope of the ridge. Most of these men were hirelings from islands less settled than even the rural parts of Ornifal: hunters, goatherds, nomads of one sort and another. A few wore hide garments, and many were in dressed leather rather than cloth. They were men well used to a hard life, and used also to killing.

In the far distance Sharina could see the leading ranks of the phalanx, moving more slowly because they needed to keep formation if they were to be ready to fight at sudden need. Eighteen-foot pikes waved upright in the air above them like the spines of a poisonous caterpillar. The phalangists wore bronze caps and carried flat, round shields; their real protection came from their tight formation and the hedge of spearpoints that kept enemies from closing with them.

The traditional heavy infantry would be bringing up the rear, but from where Sharina stood they were still out of sight. Those regiments were recruited from Ornifal's yeoman farmers and provided their own equipment, considering themselves socially superior to the oarsmen who formed the phalanx and were the core of Garric's new tactics. They'd be on their mettle to prove themselves better than the phalangists in battle as well as birth.

"Attaper," the king said, "how long do you think it'll take them to get organized enough that Lerdoc would engage of his own accord?"

"Not today," said the Blood Eagle commander. "He's a rash man—he wouldn't be here if he weren't—"

Carus smiled like a curved knife. "True of more than him," he said.

"—so he may not wait to fortify a proper camp, but he'll want to get all his troops ashore and marshalled."

"That's what I'd judge as well," Carus said, nodding. "So . . . What do you suppose he'll do if I withdraw Waldron and those last regiments from Donelle . . . and I bring the whole army together here on this ridge?"

The royal officers looked at one another, dumbfounded by the king's question. "Surely you're joking, your majesty?" said the first who dared speak; Lord Muchon, a former officer of the Blood Eagles and now in command of a division of the phalanx.

He didn't sound sure. Like many of the other officers present, Muchon knew little of Prince Garric beyond the rumor that he'd been a shepherd on Haft a few months before.

"The regiments still in the lines around Donelle are holding ten times their numbers of rebels, mercenaries as well as local militia," Attaper said cautiously. His contact with Garric had been close and of the sort that cements trust. "If you withdraw them, then the rebels will combine their forces and attack us with . . ."

He turned up his palms in a deliberately vague gesture. "Twice our numbers. At least."

There was a general murmur of assent from the command group. The other men looked relieved that Attaper had stated what they all thought was obvious: obvious even to a priestess, let alone to the prince commanding their army.

"Aye," said Carus with a smile like a striking viper's. "The rebels'll march out of Donelle, and we'll hit them while they're marching. Kill the most of them and scatter the rest. If things work well, we'll take the city gates while some of the survivors' try to get back inside, but that can wait if it needs to."

Lord Dowos had been trying to avoid calling attention to himself, choosing to stand holding his horse's bridle instead of remounting. Carus' latest proposition shocked him to speech again.

"But Count Lerdoc!" he said. "It's only three miles to Donelle. Lerdoc'll attack us from behind while we're fighting the troops from Donelle and, and . . ."

"We'll hold the ridgeline here with two regiments of heavy infantry," the king said briskly. "Waldron will. The phalanx has to be moving to be effective. The phalanx to slice through the locals *fast*, the rest of the heavy infantry to watch the flanks, and the javelin men to keep the survivors running far enough that they can't regroup when we turn to deal with Lerdoc."

He slammed his right fist into his left palm. "Crush them!" he repeated. "And then crush Lerdoc, while he's stuck here fighting Waldron."

"May the Lady cast Her cloak about me!" blurted a regimental commander. Nobody else spoke for a moment.

Sharina felt cold. Crush and slice were metaphors when applied to armies, but they and other words—gut, butcher, tear, and every similar term of violence were literal descriptions of what would happen to thousands of the individuals who made up those armies. *Twenty thousand hogs being slaughtered in a morning, squealing and spewing blood on ground already soaked with the blood of others. . . .*

"Your highness," said Lord Attaper, his expression agonized from the effort of what he felt he had to say for the kingdom's sake. "My prince . . . Count Lerdoc is a traitor to you and the Isles, but he's an able general. When he realizes Waldron has only two regiments, he'll bypass them and rush to take the rest of us in the rear."

"We'll have to hope he doesn't move fast enough to do that," Carus said, his tone dismissive but a dangerous glint in his eyes. "It's hard to get an army moving when it doesn't expect to, you know that."

"He's got cavalry," Lord Dowos said, fully animated again. "Maybe not all his infantry at first, but his horse and skirmishers will reach us. They'll hold us long enough for him to get the heavy regiments up too."

"I'll lead my phalanx against anybody you show me, your highness," Lord Muchon said forcefully. "But you said yourself that we have to be attacking. We can't defend against somebody behind us while we're already engaged!"

"Silence!" the king said. His right hand gripped his

sword hilt, and it was with an obvious effort of will that he managed to release it.

No one spoke. The disbelief of the men around Carus was changing to sullen anger.

"We're going to carry out the plan I've outlined," Carus said in a tone of quiet, deadly fury. "Because there's no other choice. Do any of you see an alternative that has a chance of success?"

"Given where we are," said Master Ortron, a commoner and former mercenary leader promoted to command of the other division of the phalanx, "no, there's no chance of anything else working. May the Sister swallow my soul!"

He snorted. With a humor that he might not have been willing to show openly if he'd expected to survive the coming battle, he added, "As she doubtless will."

"See to it, then!" Carus snapped to his officers. He jabbed his mount into a trot in the direction of the fleet encampment.

"Your highness!" Sharina called, prodding her own horse as well. She wasn't a good rider; the only horses in Barca's Hamlet had been those brought by wealthy visitors.

Carus didn't slow down. Attaper, with a face of grim death, gestured forward the platoon of Blood Eagles who formed the king's immediate escort.

"Brother!" Sharina cried.

Carus looked over his shoulder, then reined back so sharply that the hastening bodyguards almost rode into him. The slope was a mixture of brush and turf, but loose rock was exposed on the trail proper; pebbles danced downhill ahead of the king.

"Let me talk privately with my brother," Sharina said as she rode past Attaper.

The Blood Eagles' commander eyed her speculatively. He nodded with the hint of a grim smile. "First section, lead his highness by fifty paces!" he ordered. "Second section, we'll follow at the same interval."

Carus waited for Sharina, then walked his horse down the track beside her. "It isn't what I want, girl," he said quietly, looking at the camp half a mile ahead instead of meeting her eyes. "But there's no choice, the way things are."

He grimaced. "The way I've made things, I'll admit."

The king's eyes swept his surroundings with a sort of wakeful energy that proved to anyone who'd grown up with Garric that some other spirit now animated his form. Garric was an observant youth, but Carus had been a warrior. To him a glint in the forest suggested ambush and slaughter rather than a neighbor cutting wood.

"What's that?" he said, as two Blood Eagles trotted a sedan chair out of the camp. Then, recognizing Tenoctris—who else could it have been?—he added, "If she's found something that couldn't wait till we reached her, then I don't suppose it's good news."

Four more black-armored Blood Eagles accompanied the two with the chair. The squad leader's helmet was marked with a horsehair crest. He kept a cautious eye on the nearby Blaise forces, but Lord Attaper still snarled a loud, angry curse.

Attaper believed he and his regiment had the duty of keeping safe those they were detailed to guard. The fact that the people they guarded might have other priorities—the kingdom's salvation, for example—didn't matter to Attaper, and he was furious that Tenoctris seemed to have convinced some of his men to take a needless risk.

"Carus," said Sharina, speaking so that she would be heard before the wizard arrived. "Even if you win the battle, the *battles*—"

"I will, girl," the king said in a tone that wouldn't brook argument. "I've watched the phalanx training. It all depends on the phalanx going through the mercenaries without a stumble, then turning and double-timing back to face Lerdoc . . . but they'll manage, you watch!"

"Carus, winning that way will be as bad as losing," Sharina said; her expression calm, her voice clear but not raised. "Even if nobody dies tomorrow but rebels—"

Which was as likely as the sun rising in the west.

"—that'll be enough blood shed to drown the kingdom in it. Slaughter like that will fragment the Isles, as surely as it did in your own time."

Carus said nothing. His face showed less emotion than the portrait struck on a coin.

Letting a little of the fear she felt tremble in her voice, Sharina added, "Garric wouldn't do it, your highness. My brother wouldn't choose that way!"

"Sister take you, girl!" the king said. "I didn't choose it myself! There *is* no choice, now that we're here and they're—"

He took his right hand off his sword pommel and swept it through an arc starting with Count Lerdoc's forces and continuing around to point back at the rebel stronghold of Donelle. His face went sour.

"And don't say I should withdraw by sea," he added. "Lerdoc would attack as soon as I started to do that. I'd sacrifice half the army trying to save the rest, and from the moment I've been chased off Tisamur bloody there'll be no kingdom left."

Tenoctris in her sedan chair had reached the contingent of Blood Eagles preceding the king. They'd stopped her and her guards—their colleagues—with as little ceremony as they'd have shown a troop of tattooed savages waving bows.

Carus swore and trotted his horse forward. "If you delay my advisor a moment longer, Undercaptain Atonp," he said pleasantly to the section's commander, "I'll have you mucking out mules for the rest of your life. Which, of course, may not be long, given the circumstances we're in now."

He dismounted and bowed to Tenoctris, motioning her down into her seat when she started to rise. Sharina reached them and slid from her saddle also. It felt remarkably good not to clamp a horse's ribs with her thighs.

The bodyguards were obviously concerned, but Attaper positioned them at a polite distance from Carus and the two women instead of pressing the king to ride the rest of the way to the camp. They were near enough to reach the earthen walls before Lerdoc could organize a force large enough to be dangerous . . . and speaking of dangerous things, the king's mood was obvious to anybody.

"I'm sorry to come rushing to you this way," Tenoctris said, "but there isn't much time. If I'm correct."

The old wizard smiled with a self-deprecating shrug. Her face was pale, and her tongue slurred as she spoke. She looked as though she should be in bed with nurses in attendance.

"I think there's a trap being set for you, your highness," she said. "For all the Isles."

Carus straightened with a frown. "Aye, there is indeed," he said, his voice a little colder than it usually was in speaking to Tenoctris. "There's a Blaise army landed this day already. I'm afraid your warning is late."

His face hardened further. Hatred for wizardry overwhelmed a mind already aflame with frustration. "As you might have seen, were your eyes not so set on your books and spells!"

"What my books and spells *have* shown me, your highness . . ." said Tenoctris in a tone that reminded Sharina that the old woman had been raised a noble "is that there are three springs to the trap. The city you came to take; the army brought from the north to confuse you——"

The king's face blanked at the word "confuse." Its possible accuracy had taken him aback.

"—and the third, the most dangerous, which I can*not* see."

Aristocratic pique had animated Tenoctris during the past brief exchange, but now she slumped against the chair. Her eyelids fluttered but did not close, and she managed a weak smile.

"I'm sorry," she said. "There's a great wizard against us, but that's all I've been able to learn. He or she or *it* is so powerful that my spells show me nothing beyond the fact that there's something to be seen—were I strong enough."

There was commotion at the north gate of the fleet encampment, only a long bowshot distant from where Sharina and her friends were talking. Carus looked up, and muttered, "Zettkin's coming out to see me, since I'm not going to him."

"Not *a* wizard but all the Children of the Mistress together, Tenoctris?" Sharina said. "Couldn't that be what you're seeing?"

The old woman shook her head. "No, child, there's a single mind behind this," she said. "One who's weaving a pattern as subtle as anything our friend Ilna could manage. These Children and their Moon Wisdom are only threads. So are the Confederacy and the Count of Blaise. Human threads."

Carus snorted and put his left foot back in the stirrup, preparing to mount. "I'll bet on Ilna if it's weaving to be done," he said. "And as for those threads you've named—by this time tomorrow they won't be a danger to us or to anybody else!"

"Gar—" Tenoctris began, showing how very tired she was. "Carus, you mustn't act while the third threat still hides. That's what our enemy wants."

"I've never been one to sit on my hands and let the other fellow hit first!" Carus said, turning from his horse with a look of cold fury. "I'm not going to try to learn how to waste my time that way now!"

"Garric wouldn't—"

"Your brother wouldn't do a lot of things!" Carus said. "Your brother is a peasant! What do you want me to do? Challenge Lerdoc to a bout with quarterstaves?"

"I want you to be the King of the Isles," Sharina said, standing straight with her hands clasped behind her back. "Instead of being a petulant boy who throws his book in the fire because he thinks it's too hard for him to understand!"

The Blood Eagles on guard stiffened. They kept their backs to the royal party, but Attaper and the undercaptain turned so they could watch from the corners of their eyes.

Carus could have been carved from an oak tree. Continuing to meet his eyes, her tone still deliberate, Sharina added, "Besides, Lerdoc is old and fat. It wouldn't be a fair bout."

The king stepped forward and hugged Sharina, then lifted her in the crook of his left arm and snatched up Tenoctris with his right. It reminded Sharina of just how strong her brother really was.

"Well," Carus said, laughter bright behind his words, "may the Lady forfend that a King of the Isles should be seen to act unfairly."

He whirled the women in a full circle, then set them down and stepped back so that he could see both together. "The count is a fat old man, as you say, sister," Carus said with continuing good humor. "But he has a son, Lerdain, a likely enough youth from all accounts. The apple of his father's eye."

"I've heard that," Sharina said carefully. "Though Liane is the one who'd have the details."

"I don't need details," said the king. "I need a pretty girl who can swim. Can you swim, sister?"

"Like a fish," said Sharina. She spoke with same flat

certainty that she'd have said her hair was blond, if that had been the question.

"Then between us," King Carus said, "we may be able to save the Isles a battle."

He handed Tenoctris into her sedan chair and gestured Sharina to her horse. As Carus himself mounted, he began to laugh with the amazed jollity of a prisoner just offered a passage to freedom.

Chapter Nineteen

The chill water clamped the muscles over Ilna's rib cage tightly and dulled her need to breathe. The water-filled tunnel wasn't quite as narrow as the passage between the pool and the outer world, but there wouldn't have been room enough to swim properly even if Ilna had known how. She pulled herself along by her hands with an occasional kick against the walls when her toes found purchase.

She didn't know if Alecto was following. She didn't even know if she *hoped* Alecto was following. Ilna had given her companion as good a chance at salvation as she herself had, but she couldn't pretend Alecto's death would trouble her any worse than the wild girl's continuing life would.

Ilna's fingers were numb, and her lungs were a rolling fireball that seemed to be devouring everything around it. Eventually the blaze would absorb her brain and everything would stop, but until then she would keep on going.

Streaks of light pulsed across her eyes. How long could a salamander stay underwater? For hours, certainly; possibly for days. Ilna wasn't sure if the tunnel was still going down; her body rubbed the slick stone, sometimes with her shoulders, sometimes with her hips. The only direction was forward.

Phosphorescence flooded over her—pinks and greens and yellows, all against a background of sickly blue. Ilna blew her lungs out, scarcely aware of what she was doing, and drew in a deep breath. The air didn't have odors in that first moment: it was life, as simple as that. She'd been good as dead, and now she breathed again.

Alecto surfaced noisily, flinging up a spray of rainbow droplets. "Sister take me!" she cried. Then, "May the Pack grind my *bones* if I'm not glad to breathe again!"

Ilna dabbed her feet down, touched rock, and felt the panic in her throat subside. While she could appreciate the irony of escaping all manner of dangers only to drown at the point of safety, that wasn't the story she wanted to be remembered for.

She bobbed—once, twice, and again—to reach the edge of the pool. She was smiling. *I'm not sure I want to be remembered at all; and if I drowned here, there'd be precious little chance of anybody hearing the story anyhow.*

Alecto, who *could* swim and who'd lost the cape, her only remaining garment, in the tunnel, squirmed up onto the shore with the litheness of a cormorant. She'd gripped her dagger in her teeth as she swam; now, ignoring Ilna's struggle to climb out of the pool, she took the weapon in her hand again as she looked around.

There was plenty of light to see clearly, at least for eyes adapted during the long, dark crawl to reach this place. It was a cave, but it was much larger than the one immediately beyond the temple. Ilna looked up. At some points the curving roof was as high as she could've flung a stone.

Mushrooms and lichens covered the cave floor and ran up the walls and ceiling as well. They glowed in muted shades; to Ilna's trained eye no two were precisely the same hue. The faded yellow of one mushroom lacked the green undertone of the otherwise identical bell sprouting beside it.

"How far back do you suppose this cave goes?" Alecto said, trying to keep concern out of her voice. She tapped a wall with her dagger butt; under a finger-thick coating of fungus, the bronze clacked on stone. "Is there a way out besides the way we came?"

"I have no idea," Ilna said, keeping her comments to the literal truth. She supposed—as no doubt the wild girl did—that there wasn't another way out; that there was no way at all now that Alecto's rockslide had buried the temple along with the rest of the village.

It wouldn't do any good to state the obvious, though. Besides, while it was superstition to believe the words might create the grim reality, when Ilna was trapped in a rocky tomb, she found herself closer to superstition than she cared to be.

A cricket scuttled through a grove of knee-high mushrooms, shaking clouds of white spores from the bells. The insect was as big as a mouse; its hind legs were in normal proportion instead of the outsize pair on which its smaller relatives jumped in the world outside the cave.

Ilna ran the coils of the noose through her fingers, squeezing moisture from the silk with firm pressure. She had to decide what to do with her soaked tunics as well. She supposed they'd dry more quickly on her body than if she hung them in the cave's dank atmosphere, but she could speed the process by wringing them out first.

"Well, it doesn't look to me like we're any better off than we were before," Alecto said in a challenging tone. Her words echoed, softened by repetition and the forest of fungus.

"We're a great deal worse off than we were before you murdered the priest," Ilna said. "We can't change the past, though, so I'll begin looking for a way out after I've taken time to rest."

Her voice as she met the wild girl's eyes was very calm, but she held the noose ready to throw. If Alecto chose to attack . . . Ilna didn't know what she'd do with her companion after disarming her, but she supposed she'd think of something.

"Faugh!" said Alecto. She turned and stalked deeper into the cave. Ilna thought the wild girl was simply walking away, but instead she knelt to examine a clump of ball-headed mushrooms.

Ilna grimaced and resumed her survey of the cave. The fungus forest crawled with insects, all of them much larger than similar forms in the upper world. Ilna wondered if there'd be more salamanders like the God-thing Alecto slew, but there was no sign of such. Perhaps now that the giant was dead his lesser kin would move toward the pool, like rams struggling for the flock's leadership after the bellwether dies.

Well, that would mean meat. The omnipresent fungus must be edible; insects at least were able to live and flourish on it. And Ilna supposed that she could eat giant crickets the way she'd eaten crabs caught off the shore of Barca's Hamlet.

The crabs had been stewed, though, and Ilna didn't see much way of building a fire in this place. The notion of raw cricket wasn't appealing.

She snorted, almost a laugh. Very little in the situation was appealing.

"Yes it *is*, by the Sister!" Alecto cried enthusiastically. She stood and turned, holding her dagger out in what Ilna momentarily thought was a threatening gesture.

No: Alecto was using the flat of her blade as a spatula, demonstrating the dark spores she'd shaken from the gills of the mushrooms she'd been looking at. They meant nothing to Ilna. Old Allis fattened the living she scraped from the land in the north of the borough by selling cures to those who trusted her. She picked mushrooms, both spring and fall. Nobody else near Barca's Hamlet did, though. Most people thought any fungus was apt to poison the fool who ate it.

"I've never seen them this big before," Alecto said, "but these are Traveller's Balls as sure as I'm a woman!"

"We can eat them, you mean?" Ilna said. She preferred to be on good terms with her companion instead of at the edge of violence, but she really couldn't understand what Alecto was talking about.

And as for "never seen them this big . . ." Each of these nearly spherical caps was the size of a boar's head. *No* mushroom got that big in the borough.

"Not travelling *that* way," said Alecto, with a half sneer she was unwilling or unable to control in the cause of harmony. Obviously the wild girl felt power had shifted again in her direction. "Travelling like what brought me here. Through the dreamworld!"

"I don't see how that's an improvement," Ilna said. "According to what you told me, our spirits have to come back to our bodies, and they're still here . . . oh."

"Right!" said Alecto in triumph. "I'll find another—"

Her face changed as she realized what she was saying and who she was saying it to. "That is, I'll take you along and we'll both get back to, well, *out* of—"

"We'll go to wherever the next innocent victim happens to be," Ilna said coldly. "Don't bother. I have enough on my conscience without snatching some stranger into the place your luck and judgment puts them. I haven't been impressed by your past successes."

The wild girl's hot fury met the ice in Ilna's eyes—and backed away from it. "Do you think you're better than me?" Alecto shouted. "Do you think I don't know what you are?"

"I don't think a spider is better than a weasel, no," Ilna said, her hands on her noose. "But I think we're different."

"Do as you please!" Alecto said, turning away. "Stay

here and die, then! But I'm going to get out."

Ilna forced herself to relax. She needed rest more than she needed food; perhaps after she slept she'd be better able to follow the strands of this pattern.

And again, maybe she already knew where the pattern led. Maybe it wasn't simply chance that made the web-draped, spider-filled Hell she'd seen in a dead man's eyes quiver constantly at the fringes of her memory.

Alecto had caught a cricket and was opening its body with the point of her knife. *Do insects have blood?* They must, Ilna supposed; and if her companion was determined to use blood magic—let her.

Ilna lay down, resting her head on a clump of broad-capped mushrooms whose firm flesh cushioned her better than a rolled tunic would have done. She still hadn't wrung out her clothing. . . . Well, that could wait; had to wait.

Alecto shook a mushroom cap over herself and the figure she'd scratched on the ground. She began to chant in an angry, hectoring tone very different from the quiet care Ilna was used to hearing in Tenoctris' voice.

It wasn't just that Ilna was exhausted by the effort of worming through narrow tunnels and water almost cold enough to freeze. The rock itself, the whole living mass of it above and around Ilna, was forcing itself onto her soul though for the moment it couldn't crush her body.

Ilna found every moment's existence in this place a battle. The rock wouldn't defeat her so long as she lived, but the struggle was a greater strain than anything her muscles had gone through.

Spores from Alecto's mushroom drifted to where she lay. They had a sharp tang, but the smell wasn't really unpleasant.

Ilna felt herself sliding. Instead of a cave floor as level as those of most houses in Barca's Hamlet, she was on a smooth, steep funnel. She wanted to crawl back, but her limbs didn't move, and nothing she did would make a difference anyway. At the bottom of the funnel was a hole, and she knew what was on the other side of the hole as well.

Alecto chanted. Ilna would've smiled if she'd been able to move the muscles even of her face. She could see the pattern spreading from this point. The wild girl would follow her strand to its end, her end. No one could change that, no one could change any part of what was already woven.

Ilna slid faster. Her eyes were open. They saw the world of the cave as motionless and unchanged: rock and lichen and the insects which ate the fungus and one another.

On the domed ceiling over Ilna's head, a spider the size of a man's spread hand waited in her web for prey. She looked down at Ilna, as still and silent as the rock she gripped.

As the world about Ilna vanished into gray darkness, she felt herself falling upward.

Garric tumbled into sunlight on a landscape of rocks, flowering scrub, and stone boxes. The sea roared against a nearby coastline, and above him birds called.

His face was buried in coarse grass, each stem topped with a tiny white bloom. If he'd come through Metron's passage a hand's breadth farther forward, the spiky leaves of something like a yucca would've been gouging his cheeks. He was too exhausted to feel relief.

At that he was better off than Metron, who lay half under, half beside, Garric's body. The wizard couldn't have been more still if he'd been dead, though Garric found a pulse in his throat when he checked.

He heard voices, Vascay's among them, as the Brethren assessed the situation. Garric braced his hands and levered his torso up so that he could look around. He wasn't quite ready to stand just now.

"There you are, Brother Gar!" Vascay called, waving his javelin in greeting. "How about the wizard? I'd say I didn't care, but this time he brought us to a better place than some I've seen recently."

At a quick glance, it seemed that all the bandits on the millipede's back had made it here. Garric grimaced when he remembered Toster. All who'd dared the wizard's gateway, that is. Well, Toster had the right to make his own decision.

"Metron's here with me," Garric said. "He won't want to move for a while, but he's all right."

He stood carefully, finding as he usually did that he felt better when he started moving again after exertion. Small bees buzzed, trying the flowers. Even the spiky succulent sported orange starbursts that Garric would have guessed were giant asters if he'd seen them from a distance.

Vascay and Thalemos started over to him. Rather than meet them halfway, Garric waited—smiling faintly and looking around to get his bearings. The passage Metron had opened for them twice now seemed to affect some men more than others—and Garric more than most.

It was nearly noon here. Under the sun to the south ranged an arc of craggy hills: rugged, perhaps, but certainly nothing the band couldn't cross if it wanted to. In the middle was the notch of a pass. Garric thought the hills were less than two miles away, though that guess depended in part on how tall the trees sprinkling the slopes were.

The sea battered the shore north of where Garric stood. Near land the water was green, becoming a deep purple-blue toward the horizon. The plain must be eaten away into a steep corniche rather than a sloping beach, but Garric couldn't be sure without getting closer.

All around him, covered by flowers and grasses, were boxes hewn from the same coarse limestone that underlay the soil. Garric frowned as he recognized them: they were coffins.

More precisely, they were ossuaries to hold the bones of the dead whose flesh had decayed during a year or two's exposure on the shelves of common mausolea. That had been the practice in Haft during the Old Kingdom, Garric knew from his reading; though in his own day, the dead were buried in the ground and honored in a general ceremony at the spring equinox.

"We're in a graveyard," he said to Vascay. Thalemos had halted a few paces away, bending to look at an ossuary of alabaster or marble. "All of this."

Gesturing broadly, Garric went on, "It must have served quite a large city, but I don't see any sign of buildings except crypts and these, well"—he touched an ossuary with his foot—"bone boxes."

Vascay shrugged, the gesture nonchalant but his expression guarded. "They might've built their houses of sticks and thatch but buried their dead in stone," he said. "It's a matter of what your priorities are, after all. And this place—"

He carried his glance around the sprawling plain; for as far as a man could see, ruined tombs and ossuaries dotted it. Flowers nodded in the slight breeze.

"—is old, whatever it is."

Magenta flowers that looked like zinnias—they weren't; the plants' leaves were wrong—grew in great profusion where Thalemos knelt and shaded worn lettering with his hand. He looked solemn as he rose to join Garric and the chieftain.

"That ossuary held a Magistrate of Wikedun on the north coast of Laut, washed by the Outer Sea," Thalemos said. He wore a slight frown. "The city doesn't exist anymore."

"I've heard of the place," Vascay said, frowning also. "The rebels of Wikedun fought the Intercessor Echea, back when the Old Kingdom fell two thousand years ago. She defeated the rebels and sank Wikedun under the sea."

"Well," Thalemos said, "the Outer Sea ate away the land, but that was over ages instead of whelming the city suddenly. And the rebels were demon worshippers."

He paused, considering what he'd just said. He added, "According to Ascoin's *History*, they were demon worshippers, I mean. I suppose his stories may be false."

Vascay snorted. "Or they may not," he said. "What I know for a fact"—he looked toward the range of hills—"is that the present Intercessor has half the Protectors on his payroll patrolling the marshes south of here. And they say other guards as well, to keep honest men out of here. Why is that, do you suppose?"

All three men looked down at the wizard, snoring among the flowers at their feet. Presumably Metron knew the answer. He knew the same answer as Echeon did, at any rate.

"I don't think he's faking," Garric said morosely. "The spells Metron has been working would be impossible for anyone but a great wizard, and even then difficult."

"You know wizards, do you, Gar?" Vascay said mildly.

"I've known some," said Garric.

"I'd as soon I never had," Vascay said. He smiled. "But then, I'd as soon a lot of things that turned out differently."

He gestured toward the edge of the plain a furlong away. "Let's walk that way," the chieftain said. "I'd like to take a look at the sea, since I *don't* think we're going back through Echeon's patrols. Regardless of what else might be waiting for us south of the hills."

Thalemos glanced down at the wizard with pursed lips. "He'll be fine," Garric said. "He's just tired. There's nothing we can do beyond letting him sleep."

The remaining bandits were exploring their new surroundings with cheerful enthusiasm, mostly in groups of two or three. Hame stood alone on top of a ruin that might once have been a temple, shading his eyes with his hand searching the plain.

Looking for Toster, Garric realized. *They were friends.* . . . He started to call to Hame, then decided that for the time being he wouldn't do that. For one thing, it'd force Garric to recall the big man's last moments with greater clarity than he wanted to.

Halophus disappeared, then popped back into sight holding a broad armlet. He'd apparently jumped or fallen into a sub-surface tomb; this necropolis held burials of a wide variety of styles. From the bandit's caroling joy and the way sunlight winked, the armlet was made of gold.

"We're all happy to be out of where we were before," Vascay said without emphasis. "I am myself. I don't know that this is a good place—"

He smiled knowingly at his companions.

"—but I know the other was a bad one, at least there at the end."

"Yes," said Garric grimly. They'd reached the edge of the cliff; the sea roared up at them, though it was a calm day. The waves didn't make enough noise against the crumbling rock to drown the screams in his mind, though.

"I've had a lot more money over the past ten years with the Brethren than I did for the twenty before when I was a schoolmaster," Vascay said, his voice barely loud enough for the others to hear him. "Had the money and had more of the things the money could buy. But one of the things I wish turned out differently is that I could've lived my whole life as an honest man."

The corniche was never more than twenty feet above the sea and generally only half that. Green water swirled and foamed about the scree of rocks broken away from the cliff face in the recent past. Garric had led his companions to a notch where the overhang had collapsed perhaps only hours before; the dirt showing at the edges of the fall was still moist and russet in contrast to the grayish yellow where the soil had dried. Standing anywhere else along the edge risked the weight of the spectators bringing down the overhang.

"Doesn't Echeon have ships on patrol off the coast here?" Garric asked. He couldn't see anything but sunlit water all the way to the horizon, but there must be something to prevent interlopers. The gold Halophus had found in practically open sight proved nobody came here.

Garric and his companions might still be able to escape by sea. Even with Echeon's art, the Protectors wouldn't be able to patrol effectively in the middle of a winter storm. Though . . . with a homemade boat and a crew of landsmen, Garric thought he'd rather take his chances walking south through the hills.

"I haven't heard of anything special on this coast," Vascay said. "There's the regular ships watching to keep people here from going out beyond fishing distance and anybody else from getting to Laut. Nothing in particular about this bay or Wikedun, though."

He shrugged. "My gang stayed pretty much in the south and east, that being where we all of us came from," he went on. "But I keep an ear out for what the Protectors're doing, and I'd guess I'd have heard about extra ships the same as I did about the patrols on the land side."

"What's that?" said Thalemos, suddenly pointing seaward.

"That's just a—" Garric said. He shut his mouth on "—*shadow on the water*," because there weren't any clouds in the sky.

It broke surface, or at least several hundred feet of its length did. Its lizardlike head was blunter than that of a seawolf, nor did a seawolf ever reach the size of this creature. The kinship was close, though. Gar's soul, by now buried deep in Garric's mind, begin to whimper.

The serpent looked at the three watching humans, then slid downward again with a sidewise shimmy of its whole long body. The green water covered all but memory of the creature.

"Did it happen to appear now, or were we being warned?" Thalemos asked. He sounded calm, but his clasped fingers writhed like the snake he'd just watched.

"Either way, we can save the effort of building a boat," said Vascay.

He turned. "Come on, lads," he continued. "Master Metron ought to be well enough to speak by now, and I've got some questions to ask the gentleman!"

"If we let you loose, Master Cashel . . ." said the fat, friendly fellow with ribbons dangling from his velvet cap. "Will you behave yourself?"

He'd come into the Hyacinth with four other townsmen: beefy, younger men who carried fishnets like the ones Cashel was already trussed with. No one of the men was Cashel's size, but he was willing to agree that all together the four could handle him. The folk of Soong weren't what he'd call harsh—back home, men preparing to release a maybe-madman would have cudgels to use if the fellow got out of hand—but they didn't take silly chances either.

Leemay came out from the bar and stood beside the man in the fancy hat—the mayor or whatever they called the headman here. "Master Cashel," she said, "I'm sorry about what happened here. There's free food and lodging for you in the Hyacinth this night or however long you want to stay."

She'd lit a lamp shortly before the mayor arrived, and two of the huskies had carried in lanterns of iron and horn. Daylight in this place was somber enough, but Cashel already knew how miserable and dank Soong became after the sun set. . . .

"Let me go and give me what's mine," he said to the

woman. "After that, Duzi grant that you never see me again!"

His voice came out in enough of a growl that the mayor flinched back, and his huskies stiffened as if they might have work to do. Leemay didn't move, just gave a little nod.

"You may change your mind," she said. "My offer remains."

The inn had been open for business during the day. Indeed, the stranger tied to a pillar had probably brought in half the trade. Cashel hadn't spoken to the locals, nor had anybody spoken to him, but all the folk who came through the front door had let their eyes linger on him. Several were still inside, an audience watching from the bar or the tables along the back wall.

Cashel met the innkeeper's eyes, but he didn't speak. He didn't have anything to say beyond what he'd just said.

"Let him go," Leemay said to the mayor.

He looked at her in concern. "Are you sure?" he said. "Maybe tomorrow would be—"

"Let him go," she repeated with an edge in her voice. Cashel had the feeling that though Leemay got along well enough with her fellow townsfolk, nobody wanted to cross her. He could see why that might be.

"All right," the mayor said sharply to the attendant on his right. "Cut him—"

"Sister take you, Jangme!" cried the fisherman who jumped up from a table. "Not unless the Corporation wants to pay me and Long for two new nets!"

He knelt beside Cashel and loosed the tie cords with strong, skilled fingers. Cashel didn't move while the work was going on; if he bunched his muscles in anticipation, it'd just take the fellow longer to finish his job. Cashel knew how to wait.

The fisherman stood, lifting one of the nets with him. Cashel stood also, kicking his legs free of the other net now that the tension was off it. He stretched his arms, over him and out to the sides, arching his back at the same time. The mayor and his attendants watched nervously.

"If you'll give me back my staff," Cashel said, slurring the words because of the anger that he otherwise concealed, "then I'll take myself out from under this roof."

"Ah, Master Cashel," said the mayor, "I think we'd best wait till you leave Soong—in the morning, I suppose?—before we give you that again. While I trust—"

"When I came out last night with the friend the woman there murdered . . ." Cashel said. He spoke slowly, taking a deep breath between each burst of words. "And you tied me up because you thought I'd gone crazy. . . . Then I didn't want to hurt anybody but her"—he nodded to Leemay, who stood impassively—"because the rest of you hadn't hurt me."

Cashel looked around the room. Only one of the mayor's companions would meet his eyes.

"But if you don't give me my staff," Cashel continued in a growl like thunder over the horizon, "then you're all of you no better 'n a gang of robbers. And I'll pull that—"

He pointed to the bar.

"—out of the wall and use it on you before you can stop me."

"What?" said the mayor. He looked around at his attendants. "He couldn't do that! It's pegged top and bottom!"

Cashel stepped over to the heavy hardwood plank. Two of the attendants danced aside instead of trying to stop him.

"Give him his bloody stick!" said the fisherman. "*You* weren't wrestling him this morning, Jangme."

"All right, all right . . ." the mayor said, letting his voice trail off as he turned away. "I just think . . ."

"When did you ever think about anything but how important you are?" the fisherman said.

Leemay stood for a moment, then stepped behind the

bar through the open gate. She reached down and brought up the quarterstaff; it must have been lying all day where Cashel dropped it when he carried Tilphosa out of the bedroom.

He took the hickory. Leemay stroked her fingertips over the back of his right hand. She smiled at him as he jerked away.

"Come back when you decide you want my hospitality, Master Cashel," she said. She laughed from deep in her throat, a sound more like a cat purring than anything Cashel had heard from a human before. "I'll make you very welcome."

The mayor and his huskies were leaving the inn. Cashel had to wait for them to clear the doorway or else shove through; and it was only a lifetime of good manners that kept him from doing that second thing.

When Cashel was finally outside, he banged the double door shut after him. Leemay was still laughing, and he didn't like the sound.

He breathed deeply. It seemed like he hadn't been able to take in a real breath since Tilphosa's cries woke him up this morning. The locals hadn't tied him tight, and there wasn't anything wrong with the air of the inn; but . . .

Well, that was over. If he were his sister instead of himself, Leemay and the whole town would pay more than they might've believed possible in revenge. Cashel wasn't like Ilna in that way or many ways. Funny how different twins could be.

He crossed River Street to the wharfs along the bank. There were still people out, but they seemed to be hastening home. Though Soong was a big place, it pretty much shut down at nightfall the same as country villages did. In Valles the traffic didn't stop from dawn to daybreak, hooves and iron-tired wagons crashing along the cobblestone streets.

Wooden piers reached out into the sluggish river from

a stone-faced embankment which ran the length of the waterside. Some of the boats had places for more oarsmen than Cashel had fingers, but most were relatively small—flat-bottomed and blunt on both ends.

A man was untangling his nets in the belly of a skiff midway down a nearby pier. Cashel walked out, keeping his feet over the stringers. Even so his weight made the structure sway and squeal.

The fellow looked up—and up—when Cashel stopped beside him; the water was a double pace below the level of the pier. "Yeah?" he said.

"Sir, I'd like to rent your boat for the night," Cashel said. "You don't know me—"

"You've got that right!" the local man said. "And I'm not going to rent you the boat I need to put food on my family's table. Maybe—no, I don't know anybody who'd rent a boat to a stranger."

As the man talked, Cashel tugged out the purse he wore on a neck thong. "Sir," he said, "could you buy another boat for three silver pieces?"

"Huh?" said the fisherman. "Three Ships? You don't mean three coppers?"

"These don't have ships on them," Cashel said, holding up the coins so they'd gleam in what wan moonlight filtered through the fog. "There's a man on a horse, I think. But they're silver, and I'll pay them to you for the use of your boat tonight."

The fisherman clambered onto the pier like a monkey. He snatched the coins and held them close to his eyes. Cashel didn't guess the fellow could see much—in this light you couldn't even tell the coins were silver—but they were coins and metal of some kind for sure.

"A deal?" Cashel said.

The fisherman clutched the coins close to his chest. That was fine with Cashel; he didn't want the money back, and if the fellow turned and ran away with it—well, he'd leave his boat behind, wouldn't he?

"You just want the boat?" the man said. "You aren't going to take my net and tackle?"

"The boat and the oars," Cashel said, figuring he'd better make it clear about the oars. "And I hope to give them back when I'm done, but you may have to go search where I left them."

The fisherman nodded in excitement. He hopped into the skiff—water sloshed out to all sides, but his aim and balance were perfect—and grabbed his gear up with one hand, using his left arm as a pole to drape the net on. His left hand wasn't going to let go of the coins for any reason.

Cashel had guessed that values here were the same as back home, where twenty coppers would buy a dory fit to fish out of sight of the land. Thirty coppers—only a few people in Barca's Hamlet would have the amount in silver, even in a good year—was enough to make the owner want to close the deal fast before the buyer came to his senses.

The fisherman climbed to the pier again and started for the quay. "A good evening to you, sir," Cashel called to his back. If the fellow replied, Cashel didn't hear it.

He stepped down into the skiff. It was small, but the way its owner jumped in and out proved it was sturdy and well designed. Cashel slipped his quarterstaff under the single thwart, laying it over where the keel would've been if the flat-bottomed vessel had one. He set the oars into rowlocks of willow root, untied the frayed painter, and shoved the skiff out into the river with his hand against a piling.

The moon gave Cashel light to row by. There were enough snags drifting down the river that he hoped he'd pass unremarked in the fog, but that was a chance he had to take.

He was going into the Temple of the Nine to find Tilphosa. He wasn't sure what he'd do then, but he knew he wasn't going to leave the girl to be fed to the fish or whatever they did in Soong. By going in by the back he hoped to avoid trouble; but he *was* going in.

A peasant without land of his own does a little of everything to keep body and soul together. Cashel had rowed dories in bad weather; he wouldn't call himself a good oarsman, but he could make this skiff serve his purposes easily enough.

A fish slapped the water, nearby but unseen. Apart from that, he seemed to have the river to himself. A few lamps glimmered on shore; Soong must stretch quite a way up and down the river. The lights were blurs in the fog, and an occasional bay of deep laughter was the only human sound that reached him.

Cashel deliberately went out into mid-channel before he angled the skiff back toward the island on which the temple stood. He checked over his shoulder regularly as he rowed, but the lightless temple was completely hidden. Cashel trusted his sense of direction. He figured that if he had to, he could find the place blindfolded.

The skiff grounded sooner than expected. Cashel probed with an oarblade to be sure that he'd actually reached the island instead of colliding with a floating tree. A sheet of mud, glistening a little brighter than the river proper, stretched a long stone's throw up to a dimly glimpsed low wall.

Cashel stepped out and hauled the skiff its own length to a stump around which he wrapped the painter. The muck squelched ankle high, an unpleasant sensation but not a new one. He took his staff into his hands and started toward the wall.

Apparently the temple had an enclosed court behind it. That might even be better for concealment. . . . There was a gate in an archway, but Cashel didn't bother to try it. He set his staff firmly at the base of the wall and reached up with his left hand. He could reach the top, and it was smooth stone with no spikes or sharp flints set into the coping.

He swung himself up, his right arm thrusting against the staff and his left lifting by the wall itself. On top he paused, listening intently. Something plopped in the river behind him, but he heard nothing from the garden. The temple beyond was completely dark. Moonlight showed a tall, narrow door, but there were no windows.

The garden was planted with unfamiliar broad-spreading shrubs, though Cashel couldn't tell a lot in the foggy darkness. A path meandered through them, going from the gate in the wall to the temple's back door.

Cashel swung his staff around, butted it inside the wall, and let himself down by reversing the motion that took him atop the wall. He thought he heard something from the river again, but it didn't matter now.

The ground inside the courtyard was much firmer than the mudflats. Cashel started for the temple, following the path as it wove between the trees. Nuts hung in clusters at the tips of the spiky branches. If Cashel had gone straight ahead, he'd have had to hunch, but the path followed living arches that would have let someone even taller walk upright.

He smiled; well, of course. The Nine were much taller than he was.

In the center of the garden was a large, mossy clearing. The path led to it and then away toward the temple on the other side. He stopped, stretching out his right foot to touch the moss with his big toe. The surface beneath quivered like jelly; it was neither soil nor water.

Cashel grinned. Things had been too easy thus far. He couldn't believe he was the first man to wonder what really went on in the temple, nor that the Nine were so innocent that they had nothing to hide. If he hadn't found a trap, it just meant that the trap was still waiting for him.

As another trap might be, of course.

Cashel backed two steps, then sprang forward. He slammed his staff into the firm ground at the edge of the bog and vaulted with seven feet of hickory as his pivot. He bent over as he came down on the other side so that he wouldn't tumble back. He'd cleared the trap by more than arm's length.

Still smiling but still careful, Cashel made his way to the temple's high, narrow door. It was bronze but had only a simple latch rather than a lock of some kind.

Thinking it might be barred on the other side, Cashel lifted the latch gently, then pulled the door ajar. A pale greenish radiance marked the crack between the panel and its stone jamb; if there were sounds from within, they were lost in the river's faint gurgle.

Cashel opened the door the rest of the way and stepped inside, his shoulders brushing both jambs. He didn't close it behind him.

He was in a shallow room which ran the full width of the temple. It was for storage, he'd have guessed, except that nothing was stored here.

He looked up. Bars crossed the room the short way, spaced along the width. They were thick bronze, polished in the center by wear. Dark robes hung from hooks on the inside wall, one beneath each bar.

Cashel counted them: all the fingers of one hand, and the other hand except for the thumb. Nine.

There was a passage a little longer than a man is tall in the center of the room. Carefully, walking left side forward with his staff slanted across his chest ready to strike, Cashel moved down it toward a light, just bright enough to have color.

There were faint sounds from the room beyond. It wasn't people talking, more like the clicks and slurps of dogs at the carcase of a—

"Duzi!" Cashel shouted. He leaped out of the passage, his quarterstaff raised. The chamber beyond was large and the height of the temple's peaked roof. The ceiling glowed the hue of pond scum in the summer.

The Nine looked up from the corpse they were devouring. Without their robes Cashel couldn't imagine he'd ever thought they were human. Their chitinous bodies had no color but that of the squamous light, and their beaked jaws were toothless.

Cashel stepped forward, spinning the staff. He wasn't sure how this was going to turn out, but he was going to try. The Nine didn't have weapons, and their spindly limbs would shatter under iron-shod hickory.

The Nine curled their abdomens forward beneath the two pairs of legs on which they stood. From their tails squirted sticky fluid that hardened as it splashed over Cashel's head and torso.

Cashel strode forward, willing the staff to spin but feeling the thick hickory bend under the pressure of his arms. The ferrules were glued to his body; the staff *couldn't* move.

Three of the creatures sprayed Cashel's legs. He tried to take another step. Like swimming through molasses . . . and then not even that. Cashel toppled to the stone floor, as helpless as a trussed hen.

The Nine bent over him, chittering among themselves. One of them reached up delicately with a pincered forelimb and pushed a fragment of flesh back into its beak.

Sharina sucked in her stomach as the dory lifted over the crest of an incoming wave. Unatis, the boatman, feathered his left oar and pulled hard with the right one. The rowlock squealed like a rabbit in a hawk's talons.

"Sister take it!" said Carus, sitting in the bow. "You'll wake Lerdoc in his tent with a racket like that!"

"We will not," said Unatis calmly, leaning into both oars now that he had the dory straightened to his satisfaction. "But if the lady would take the tallow block from the basket under my thwart and grease the pin with it, that would quiet the oars."

He grinned at Sharina, facing him from the stern. Unatis was an old waterman from Carcosa harbor; it took more than an angry prince to worry him.

Sharina found the container easily, but in the bad light it took her a moment to open the lid; it was pegged on through loops in the wicker. The tallow was in a wooden block; a screw base drove the column of grease up as it was used. It was a clever device, and a bit of a surprise to find here in a waterman's kit.

Carus laughed. "Aye," he said, "I'm worrying about silly dangers I could change instead of the big ones that I cannot. That's always the way while I'm sitting with nothing to do but wait."

"We'll be to where you told me soon," Unatis said calmly, spacing his speech between strokes of his oars. "A mile off the shore where the Blaise fleet is anchored. After that you'll have no waiting, unless you change your mind and have me take you back to dry land to sleep in a warm bed."

Carus snorted. "That's the last thing I want to think about," he said. "When we've settled this matter, though, I'll sleep for a week."

Sharina had tallowed the port thole pin. She twisted the screw and leaned to her right to daub the other too; if one squealed, the other might soon.

The dory lifted onto another swell. Unatis put the bow into it, then brought them back to the previous heading as they started down the trough.

"There's a westerly current tonight," he said. "Not strong, but a knot or two. If the prince doesn't mind taking a waterman's advice, you'd best start from here unless you plan on swimming to Cordin."

He glanced over his shoulder. "Or I could take you and

the lady closer inshore," he said. "A mile is a long swim for a lady."

"I'll tell that to the next lady I meet," said Sharina. She'd already loosed her sash; now she ducked to pull off the tunic she'd worn for the long pull seaward from the royal encampment. "I'm from Barca's Hamlet, where the only Lady is the one we pray to."

Which I'll be doing tonight, that She may preserve me for the kingdom's sake and my friends' sakes, she thought with a wry smile.

Sharina lifted the oilcloth bundle holding the clothes she'd change into when they reached shore. Wrapped in the center of the silk tunics and embroidered cape was her Pewle knife. In part she'd brought it as a talisman, but the big knife was used to hard strokes and so was the woman who carried it now.

"Ready?" she said to Carus.

The boatman shipped his oars. His bushy moustache fluttered for a moment as he took in Sharina's slim, moonlit body; then he averted his eyes as if from an unexpected horror.

"Aye," said the king, raising his own much larger bundle. He'd stripped off his tunic also, but around his waist was a fabric belt and a dagger enclosed in sheath of leather boiled in wax and lanolin. "Now?"

Sharina slipped over the side, holding her bundle out in front of her. She'd picked her time well, with the dory sliding sideways into a trough that carried it away when she thrust for the shore.

Stretching her body out behind the bundle, Sharina kicked like a frog. Her legs alone would do the work. She could use the clothing to buoy her up if she needed to rest, but unless the current changed unexpectedly, she doubted that would be necessary.

Unatis had been right about the current—of course. The pressure of the water on Sharina's right side was worrying, but her conscious mind knew that it was taking her to where she wanted to be. The awareness she was in the grip of a power greater than her own still made her uncomfortable.

She giggled, snorted seawater, and giggled again.

"Is everything all right, girl?" Carus called. The king was on her left side; she couldn't see him so with her head cocked to the right to breathe, but he sounded close.

"Everything's fine," she said, raising her voice. She was a natural right-hander, so turning onto her right side would be uncomfortable. "I apparently just realized that the sea is bigger than I am. That doesn't say much for my perception, does it?"

Carus laughed—and choked silent on seawater in his turn. They kicked on in companionable silence.

Bonfires and lamplight gleamed for the full arc of the bay holding Count Lerdoc's vessels and army. The fires weren't large enough individually to silhouette a ship, but as Sharina slanted toward the coast she got a feel for the anchorage. Lights vanished and reappeared as her angle to this hull or that one changed.

The camp's size staggered her. From the land, by daylight, she hadn't appreciated just how big it was. She knew that Blaise discipline was loose, so the number of fires was relatively greater than it would've been in the royal army; but she knew also that the count's forces were very great.

The moon was nearly full, gleaming on the swells and turning foam to silver. A watchman in the stern of a moored transport blew his trumpet. He didn't see Sharina and the king; he'd been blowing the same long note at intervals since sundown. What he thought he proved, other than that he was awake, escaped Sharina.

The shore was coming closer. Sharina wasn't tired, but it was time to get a better view. She stopped kicking and lifted her chest onto the buoyant sack of clothing. For a moment she saw nothing but upward-slanting water; then she went over the crest and took in the shoreline less than three furlongs away.

Some of the biggest ships were anchored even farther from the beach than she and Carus—twenty feet to her left—had already penetrated. The shoreline here shelved more gradually than that of the smaller bay just north where the royal fleet had landed, so vessels too large to draw up on land had to stay well out.

Carus came over to her with kicks and three fierce sweeps of his right arm. "They can lighter the cargo and passengers ashore . . ." he said, nodding to the nearest of the thousand-tun vessels. "Those ships won't have a chance if a storm breaks, though."

Sharina glanced up at the clear sky, and said, "Do you think the wizards of Moon Wisdom are still controlling the weather?"

Carus chuckled. "*I* think Count Lerdoc's a neck-or-nothing madman who's praying a storm won't wreck **him** if the danger even crosses his mind," he said. "The problem with an enemy who takes risks is that sometimes he gets lucky."

His moonlit smile was wry, as he added, "Which my enemies have often learned."

The trumpet called again. The *tock! tock! tock!* of wood on wood sounded from the western arm of the bay. Sharina couldn't guess if it were a signal or just late-night carpentry to repair a shelter or a ship.

Carus pointed with his whole arm. "There, we'll come ashore where those boats are beached. The bigger ships might have somebody on board, but those lighters won't have anything but a watchman, if that."

"If there is a watchman?" Sharina said, kicking occasionally to keep her at arm's length upcurrent of the king.

"Then we'll deal with him," Carus said. "One good

thing about a beach is we don't have to worry about how to get the blood off."

Sharina ducked and resumed kicking her way toward shore. In a peasant village, you slaughtered most of the herd at the first touch of frost. That way the remainder would be able to winter over on the fodder you'd stored. In a war it was men you killed, in order that the kingdom itself survive.

Maybe in another age it wouldn't have to be that way. Sharina had enough to do simply trying to save *this* age and the myriads of innocent people who lived in it. If a few rebels died, well, that was the way of the world.

Sailors on watch shouted to one other from ship to anchored ship. Sharina passed close enough to a vessel with a high, rounded stern that she could've thrown a pebble to it; Carus was closer yet. A lantern burned on the deckhouse. Its light didn't illuminate the water, but it would blind a watchman to the blotches on a swell that were swimmers instead of driftwood or flotsam lost when the army disembarked.

The ships' boats were pulled up at the tide line and fastened to oars driven blade first into the sand. Sharina lowered her head and, with her left hand, gripped the cords tying her bundle. She used her right arm and both legs to drive her the rest of the way ashore. The bonfire higher up the beach silhouetted the men around it and the boats below, but if there was a watchman, he was asleep in the belly of one of them.

Sharina's left elbow touched sand. She hunched over her bundle and let the receding surf ground her. When it did, she ran in a crouch to where the bows of a large dory and a smaller boat formed a sheltering V.

Carus was already there, untying his clothing with his left hand. He grinned at her.

At the nearby fire a sailor was shaking time on a tambourine while a comrade sang, ". . . *just another fatal wed-*

ding, *just another broken heart . . .*" No one was on watch at the boats.

That was just as well for him. In the king's right hand, shimmering in the moonlight, was a dagger. Its blade of polished steel would open a man like a trout before he even had time to gasp.

Chapter Twenty

Y ou are staying at the Hyacinth," one of the Nine said to Cashel in a voice no more human than the speaker. The smell of rotting flesh puffed from its beak in time with the words. "You should not have come here."

"I couldn't let you eat my friend!" Cashel said. The spray had hardened on his neck and right cheek; his skin strained painfully when he spoke.

The Nine were right when they said Cashel shouldn't have come here. By Duzi! they were. There was nothing else he could've done, though; and even now, Cashel guessed he'd do it all over again if the only choice was that or doing nothing. He hadn't made any difference, but at least he wasn't going to have to live remembering that he didn't try.

A creature brought its abdomen close to Cashel's right hand. A pore opened. Cashel braced himself mentally for a gush of fluid that would harden over his mouth and nose.

Instead there was a stench of ammonia and the glue holding the quarterstaff to his hand dissolved. Cashel sneezed violently.

The creature tugged. There was still a hardened loop attaching the staff to Cashel's ribs. He couldn't turn his head to watch, but another of the Nine touched its body there and sprayed more ammonia till the staff slipped free.

"Your friend was the woman from the Hyacinth," a creature said.

"The woman from the Hyacinth was entranced, but she was not dead," said another. Their bodies and their voices were identical. Cashel could easily have called every sheep in Barca's Hamlet by name, but the Nine were indistinguishable.

"Our business is with the dead," a third creature said. "We would not harm your friend. We will turn her loose when she has recovered."

The creatures passed the quarterstaff from one to another. Each ran a delicately pincered "hand" along the hickory before giving it to the next. Fresh ammonia bit as one cleaned a last daub of glue from the shaft.

"She has recovered now," said the first of the Nine to speak. "We will turn her loose with you, man from the Hyacinth. But you both must go away."

"What?" said Cashel, trying to understand what he'd just heard. He didn't suppose he ought to be complaining, but . . .

He said, "But you *eat* people!"

The Nine bobbed back and forth on their two pairs of walking legs, looking for all the world like a set of children's dipper toys. They rubbed their beaks sideways, back and forth, to make scraping sounds.

Cashel thought for a moment the Nine were laughing. On reflection, he decided he didn't believe they understood humor.

"We do not eat people, man from the Hyacinth," said a creature who hadn't spoken before. "We eat dead flesh."

Two of the Nine moved away. Trussed as he was, Cashel couldn't see what they were doing. He tried to roll and look back the way he'd come, but he couldn't shift his torso quite enough to overbalance.

"Hold still and we will release you," a creature said. It twisted its abdomen up, brushing Cashel's wrist. The touch was dry and scaly like a snake's skin, not hard.

A cool mist settled over Cashel's arms and torso. He closed his eyes but the ammonia odor set him sneezing again. The glue loosened. When Cashel twisted, chunks of it dropped away like ice from slates in the sunshine.

On either side of the passage were open-fronted alcoves. Stone couches complete with carven pillows were built into all three sides of each. The corpse of an old man lay across the left-hand alcove. Two of the Nine were helping Tilphosa up from a side couch. She wore a dazed expression and kept trying to wipe her eyes with the back of her wrist.

"Well, who . . . ?" Cashel said. He glanced at the meal he'd heard the Nine devouring when he burst in.

The creature who'd first spoken sprayed Cashel's fettered feet tinglingly. He closed his eyes in reflex, but he'd seen more than he wanted to already. The corpse on the floor had been a man; the beard on the half of his face remaining proved that. His body had been emptied, but uneaten coils of intestine lay beside him spotted with attached blobs of yellow fat.

"You will go from Soong, will you not, stranger?" said one of the Nine. "It is better that you should."

"We'll go," Cashel said. "Duzi help me, you *bet* we'll go!"

He wondered if Tilphosa was really fit to travel, then decided that he didn't care. He'd carry the girl on his back if that's what it took to get away from this city and its charnel house.

Cashel stood. His eyes watered from the ammonia, and his stomach was turning. It wasn't just death in the air; he thought the glue was doing something to his lungs also, though the smell of dead meat was bad enough.

Tilphosa stood, wobbly and still supported by the Nine.

"Can I . . . ?" Cashel asked, starting toward the girl before he had an answer.

"Of course," said the creature who'd first spoken. His two fellows stepped aside for Cashel to take their place.

"Cashel, is that you?" the girl said. She clung to him like a spar in a shipwreck. Her flesh still felt cool, but she wasn't a statue of ice as she'd been when he lifted her from the bed this morning.

"Yes," he said. "We're going to leave in just a moment, when you're feeling up to it. I've got a boat. We'll cross the river and then walk a ways to the east."

He looked at the creature who'd spoken first and raised an eyebrow. Did the Nine recognize human facial expressions?

"That is a good plan," said the creature. "We wish you well on your way, but please do not return to Soong."

Cashel's quarterstaff had made it all the way around the Nine. The last to examine the wood held it out horizontally to Cashel. His pincers gripped the staff so gently that they didn't mark the hickory.

With the staff upright in his left hand and his right arm supporting Tilphosa, Cashel felt his stomach settle. Maybe it hadn't been the smell that was bothering him after all.

"Ah, thanks," he said, walking slowly toward the passage. Turning his back on the creatures worried him, though that was pretty silly given the way they'd handled him face on when he'd charged.

One of the Nine stepped out the passage ahead of the humans. He seemed to move by rocking his four clawed feet forward in a motion that reminded Cashel of gears in the millhouse rather than that of any animal he'd seen before walking. The legs scarcely moved at all.

Tilphosa's mind or vision must have cleared enough for her to take in the figure ahead of them. She stiffened, but she continued forward with Cashel's left hand lightly touching her shoulder.

"I thought I was dreaming," she whispered. "I thought I was having a nightmare, Cashel."

"We're fine," he said, words to soothe her. They were probably true, but Cashel himself wouldn't really believe what he'd said till they were across the river and going away.

A breeze had swung the outside door nearly closed. The creature leading them opened it fully and stepped through, holding the panel for Cashel and his companion. The remainder of the Nine followed slowly.

"Sir?" he said to the creature. It rotated its narrow, sharp-edged skull to face him.

"Sir," Cashel went on, "how is it that this . . . I mean, doesn't anybody guess what you're doing here? There's only the few of you. If as many people as there are in the city wanted to come into your temple, you couldn't stop them."

"We were here before humans came to Soong, stranger," the creature said. His voice seemed to come from the center of his chest; it had a buzzing undertone, sort of like a whole chorus of crickets were singing harmony to make the words. "The first settlers knew who we were; they built the temple we live in."

He paused. "Their children, the people of Soong, know also, but they prefer not to think about our necessities and theirs. It is better that you go rather than stay to tell a story that others do not wish to hear."

"But why did they agree to, to feed you this way?" Tilphosa said. As she spoke, her right hand tightened on Cashel's left biceps. He tensed the muscle, because otherwise her pinching was going to hurt. "Did you threaten . . . ?"

The creature scraped his beak again. That *had* to be laughter.

"Woman stranger," he said, "look about you. This valley is marsh up to the ridges. The wood here burns poorly, and every year a flood would float out the contents of the graves."

Cashel nodded. The only real choice for burial was the river. There fish would dispose of corpses in much the same way as the Nine were doing . . . but with the likelihood of bloated, half-eaten bodies bobbing to the surface frequently. Cashel could understand the logic, though that last thought reminded him of the corpse on the floor of the main hall.

"We gave up our fish weirs," the creature said, "and the human settlers gave us privacy to deal with their needs."

"Right," said Cashel. No part of him *felt* it was right, but it was no more his business than some of the things old widowers in the borough got up to with their ewes. He wasn't going to be staying in this region; that was the only important thing. "I guess we'd best be getting on."

The creature nodded like he knew what Cashel was thinking; as he probably did. The Nine were pretty clear about understanding the locals, after all.

He and Tilphosa set out down the path, the creature walking ahead like a pull toy on wheels. As they neared the center of the garden, Cashel heard a woman cry, "Is somebody there? Help me!"

He put his head down and slanted his staff before him, then charged through the hanging branches like a plow furrowing thin soil. The nuts his rush shook off scattered all around.

Leemay was in the bog. Only her head and the tops of her shoulders still showed. "Help me!" she said. "Pull me up!"

Cashel stretched out his quarterstaff. Something gripped it from behind and pulled it back.

He turned. Their guide released the ferrule it had gripped with its deceptively delicate-looking pincers.

"This is not your affair, stranger," the creature said. "Let us go to your boat."

"Help me!" Leemay screamed. "Don't listen to that demon!"

"The Nine aren't demons," Tilphosa said. Her voice was as cold as her flesh had been when her scream roused Cashel this morning. "The Nine saved my life when a human sent me to die."

"Sir," said Cashel, looking from Leemay to the impassive creature, "I can't just . . ."

"We have no business with the living, stranger," the creature said. "But this one will be our business soon, and that is justice."

The rest of the Nine had followed them. They stood now on the path, unmoving and silent. There was no threat in their posture, but Cashel already knew he had no chance if he tried to fight them.

Tilphosa put her hand on his arm. "Come on, Cashel," she said quietly. "I'd like to get away from here."

"Yeah, I guess," Cashel agreed. He followed their guide. There was a path that took them around the bog with just a single screen of branches to brush aside.

Leemay shouted again, then began to scream. When Cashel glanced over his shoulder, he saw the Nine waiting around the bog. They were as motionless as buzzards on a branch.

Cashel was glad to close the courtyard gate behind him and Tilphosa, but Leemay had already stopped screaming.

"Ready?" said Carus, hunching in the shadow of the boats.

"Yes," said Sharina. She grinned. "And honored to accompany such a distinguished young officer as yourself."

Sharina felt as though she was racing down a steep hill. If she ever paused, she'd stumble and maybe break her neck, but for now it felt exhilarating. Running had always been a talent and a delight for her, so the emotions that came with the fancy were good ones.

Carus chuckled, though tightly. *His* mind would view this risky piece of acting in terms of battle, not of a race. He might laugh in the midst of slaughter, but it wouldn't be the same carefree humor as Sharina's when she ran.

Carus donned the bronze helmet he'd carried in his bundle. He'd clipped on a crest of feathers dyed red and white, the colors of Blaise.

"Let's go," he said, rising to his feet with a smooth motion. His left hand rested on the pommel of his long sword to keep it from swinging as he walked. He strode out of the scatter of boats and up the beach. Sharina, covered head to ankles with a caped cloak of blue silk, matched the king stride for stride on his left.

Sharina expected a shout, but nobody noticed them appear. The moon lit only one side of a figure, and beyond a short distance firelight glittered from fittings and equipment rather than illuminating the whole person. Two paces on from where they'd hidden, she and Carus were part of the confusion of a military camp in darkness.

"Watch out!" Carus said as his heel brushed a sagging guy rope that he hadn't noticed till he touched it. "I swear I'm tempted to launch a night attack after all. If nothing else, half these idiots'll break their necks running around the mare's nest they call a camp!"

He chuckled at the thought. Sharina smiled also, though she was glad the king hadn't burst into caroling laughter that would've drawn the attention their appearance did not. She'd never met anyone else who laughed with full-throated humor the way Carus did—except for her brother, even before Garric began sharing his mind with his ancient ancestor.

They tramped on, making their way through the litter and filth. Count Lerdoc's forces hadn't bothered to dig latrines, let alone garbage pits.

"Not here a day and look at the state of this pigsty!" Carus fumed. He wasn't shouting, but neither did it seem to Sharina that he was aware—or that he cared—that they were in the middle of a hostile army. "If I threw siege lines around them, they'd be dying of disease inside a week. . . ."

He sighed. "Which would spread to our troops," he added. "And anyway, we're not going to do it that way."

The mess disturbed Sharina in a different way. Where she grew up, organic waste was composted to become next year's fertilizer. The Blaise camp's disregard for any future beyond the next moment was a metaphor for war itself.

She smiled faintly, wondering if the Old Kingdom historian Tincer had said something like that. It would fit his tersely judgmental prose well enough. If she'd really been with her brother, she'd have asked if he remembered the line; but King Carus hadn't had the time or the inclination for scholarship.

They passed close to a fire. The men drinking around it hunched away from Carus' presence and averted their eyes.

When he was a few steps beyond, Carus murmured in an amused tone, "They think I'm one of their officers, all right. Every common soldier learns that his own officers are going to give him more trouble most of the time than the enemy ever thought of doing."

Besides the helmet, the king wore a waist-length red cloak and a molded cuirass with silver-filled engraving. The cuirass, borrowed from a subcaptain in a regiment of heavy infantry, didn't quite fit him—he'd had to replace the original side laces with longer ones—but junior officers often made do with hand-me-downs. The king's tunic was of good quality wool, and on his feet were an infantryman's heavy sandals instead of high cavalry boots.

They were nearing the camp's central gate. The Blaise forces hadn't thrown up a proper rampart and fighting step the way the royal army had, but a combination of ditches, stockades made from farm buildings and fences, and piled baggage, formed a boundary to the camp. The entrances were angled passages closed with looted carts tilted up on end. It struck Sharina that Count Lerdoc's troops were doing about as much damage to the local countryside as the royal forces were.

A detachment of heavy infantry guarded the entrance. The men didn't seem especially alert, but they were wearing sword belts and full armor; they'd tilted their eight-foot spears against the wall beside them.

"Ready?" Carus said, but it was a warning rather than a question. He strode forward, just as he would've done had Sharina cried, "No!" instead of murmuring, "Ready," as she did.

"Officer of the Guard!" Carus said, not shouting but with a whipcrack in his voice. A youth Garric's age was already rising from the section of tree trunk where he'd sat beneath the lantern.

"Just who are you?" the youth said, trying to sound belligerent. His voice broke on the second syllable.

His men watched without concern. Sharina noticed that most of the interest was for her rather than Carus. She'd have grinned, but that would be out of character; instead she threw her head slightly back so that she could look down her nose.

One of the soldiers, a grizzled fellow with dragons tattooed the length of both forearms, put his fists on his hips and laughed at her. The young officer gave him an angry glance but didn't try to push his authority.

"Carus bor-Rasial," Carus said briskly. "I'm part of the Haft contingent. I'm supposed to escort this lady back to Donelle and return, but that means I'll need the password and countersign to get back through. What is it tonight?"

"Well, I don't know if I should. . . ." said the officer, blurting the truth because he couldn't invent a statement that would make his confusion look any better.

"What's she going to Donelle for?" the grizzled soldier asked. "The king's got siege lines around the city, right?"

"The business of a Child of the Mistress is *not* your business, soldier," Sharina said. In a more appraising tone she added, "If you wish to learn the Moon Wisdom, I can arrange for you to be taught. The Mistress has uses for strong backs."

Unexpectedly the soldier turned his head away and muttered a prayer to the Shepherd. The Blaise army had heard things about Moon Wisdom also, and they must not like the rumors any better than the royal forces did.

"Yes, all right," the officer said. He was standing straighter and speaking in a firm voice after seeing Sharina cow his subordinate. "The password is 'moon' and the countersign is 'stars.' Got that?"

"Right," Carus said, giving a hitch to his sword belt. "Well, I'll be back—"

"Lord Carus," Sharina said, picking up her cue. "I have to return to the count at once."

"What?" said Carus in feigned surprise. "Look, if we don't start now, there isn't going to be enough time for me to get you into Donelle and come back before dawn!"

"Then you'll have to stay in Donelle, won't you?" Sharina said, mimicking an upper-class sneer. It wasn't hard to do: her mother Lora had the temperament—if not the breeding—of the aristocrats she'd once served in the palace at Carcosa.

She turned on her heel, and added, "Come along, sir!"

Carus grimaced. "Yes, milady," he muttered. He followed Sharina toward the heart of the camp, lengthening his stride to catch up. Sharina expected to hear laughter from the guards, but none came. What *did* they know of Moon Wisdom?

"Nicely played, girl," Carus murmured in her ear. "Now, let's see what kind of act you can put on for Lord Lerdain of Blaise!"

* * *

Garric knelt in the graveyard, eyeing an entrance set into a granite ramp that was almost flush with the ground. The bronze doors had warped when the jamb shifted in some past age. Through the crack Garric could see spiderwebs and the glint of eyes.

"He's still . . ." said Thalemos, eyeing Metron with a worried frown. "Still asleep, that is."

Garric translated: *Still unconscious. Still comatose. Still breathing but no more than that.* Aloud he said, "He'll be all right, Thalemos. But staring at him won't make him come around any sooner."

The young nobleman walked around the slab toward his companions, looking unhappy. He may have felt more affection toward the wizard than Garric and Vascay did, but regardless of personal opinion they all wanted him to awaken. Metron was the only person who knew why they were here in Wikedun.

"What do you think?" Vascay said, using his javelin butt to trace the design molded into the doors' surface. "My bet is that it's the catacombs where the priests were buried. Likely there'd be grave goods like you wouldn't believe down there."

The door's decoration was a moon in the grip of a spider whose web spread across the lower portions of both valves. Even distorted, it was artwork of the highest order.

Garric's personal feeling was that melting the cursed thing or throwing it into the sea would be the proper response to it, however.

One of the gang hooted cheerfully. The Brethren were scattered across the plain, though everyone was in sight of the others except when he crawled into a tomb.

"It wouldn't do any good," Garric said. He pointed to the overgrown depression in the ground just behind the entrance. "The passage is blocked just beyond, even if we could get through the door."

He stood. His own guess was that there'd been a small earthquake; the rigid granite block had focused the shocks on the softer limestone through which the catacombs were carved. It'd be hard to open the twisted doors with the tools the Brethren had available, and removing wedged slabs of rock would be next to impossible.

"How would we carry gold back with us?" Lord Thalemos asked. He bent to peer through the opening. Changing the subject, he added, "There do seem to be a great number of spiders here, don't there?"

"Yeah," said Vascay as he turned away with a grimace. He'd been irritated when Thalemos mentioned the difficulty of men on foot carrying any quantity of gold. That was a rich man's point, but the bandit chief knew it was a valid one nonetheless.

Vascay tapped the bronze again with his javelin. "Maybe that's why they worshipped spiders, do you think?"

"No," said Garric. He didn't like the subject. "I think it's the other way around. And Vascay, I think we ought to get out of here. Quickly."

He'd noticed holes in the cliff face; either Vascay hadn't, or he hadn't understood their significance. The chief of the Brethren was both learned and clever, but he hadn't been born and raised a countryman.

Those weren't natural caves: they marked where the sea had sheared back the cliff face and opened tunnels which had been well inland. They'd provide an easy way into the catacombs—and if Vascay didn't realize that, Garric didn't intend to tell him.

An animal squealed. Garric jerked his head around, wondering if a hawk had stooped on a vole when his back was turned.

The victim was a vole, all right, a plump one as long

as Garric's outstretched hand, but it was in a spiderweb instead of a hawk's talons. The vole's hind legs and stubby tail flailed furiously, stretching but not breaking the sticky silk holding its forequarters.

The spider, her orange-and-black body the size of a woman's fist, sidled toward the vole, holding a further loop of silk in her hind legs. She was preparing to bind her victim securely before stabbing her fangs into the warm body.

"Have any of you seen a lizard since we've been here?" Garric asked, watching the spider. Part of him wanted to crush her and free the vole, but nobody who'd kept a garden had much affection for voles, gophers, or any other rodent.

Besides, there were way too many spiders in this sunlit city of the dead for him to kill them all.

"Lizards?" said Vascay. "No, nor any snakes, praise the Lady. I didn't want to show it on Serpent's Isle when we were searching for your ring"—he nodded to Thalemos—"but I'd rather just about anything than deal with a snake."

Garric looked at Vascay sharply. "You *didn't* show it," he said. "I didn't have any idea you felt anything about snakes except not wanting one to bite you."

Vascay smiled faintly. "Couldn't let it show," he said. "The Brethren were spooked enough as it was. If I'd let on *I* was scared . . ."

He shrugged. It struck Garric, not for the first time, that heroes were people who went on no matter how frightened they were; and that everybody was afraid of something.

Metron gave a racking cough and sat up, much as he had after Garric dragged him from the bottom of the pond. Thalemos was closest to the wizard, but Garric and Vascay reached him before the youth did.

Garric put an arm around Metron's shoulders for support. The wizard tried to stand.

"Maybe you'd better rest for a moment, Master Metron," Garric said.

"There's no time for that!" Metron said peevishly. He braced his hands in the coarse soil and pushed, rising to all fours. "The Mistress has been speaking to me. We have very little time, maybe not *enough* time."

He rose, wobbling and suddenly white-faced. Garric helped him get up, since that was what the wizard was determined to do.

"This is Wikedun?" Metron said. He gazed around the plain. "It is, isn't it?"

"Yes," said Thalemos. "I've read enough of the stones to be sure."

"It's Wikedun," said Vascay, "but I want to know why we're here, wizard. And how you propose to get us someplace else that we might *want* to be."

"I said there was no time!" Metron snapped. "Here, there should be a number of animals caught in spiderwebs nearby. Gather up as many as you can find—"

As he spoke, he noticed the vole that'd been trapped moments before. The little mammal was swathed like a corpse for burial, but it still scratched vainly against the silk. The spider had backed to the center of its web without poisoning the helpless prisoner.

Metron bent and scooped up the vole in his left hand, tearing the broad web. The spider watched impassively.

"—and bring them to me," he continued. "I'll be on the edge of the cliff since there's no beach here."

Vascay didn't react, but Garric felt his forehead furrow. Metron hadn't looked over the escarpment to see whether there was a beach or not, but he was quite correct.

Metron walked with quick, mincing steps toward the edge, pausing once to snatch up another victim bound in spider silk. Thalemos started looking around; Vascay did also, though he put his javelin point through a fat-bodied spider before he robbed her web of what was probably a shrew from its small size.

"What're you going to do with the animals, Master Metron?" Garric called. He already knew, knew what the wizard *must* have in mind. Garric knew also that he would have no part of it.

"I'm going to save our lives!" Metron said. "Get on with it! I'll need many more."

"Metron, there's no good that ever came from blood magic!" Garric said.

The wizard ignored him, instead walking to the cliff edge and settling there. He held the vole in his left hand as he scribed on the soil with the athame in his right. The sapphire winked on his middle finger.

"Brethren!" Vascay bellowed. "Brethren!"

The nearer bandits paused in their activities and turned. Halophus put the horn to his lips and blew, then pointed toward the chieftain when the more distant men looked around.

"Search spiderwebs for animals!" Vascay said. "Bring them to the wizard alive! Fast!"

He met Garric's eyes. "Gar," he said, "you live your way, and I respect you for it. For myself, I'm not enough of a philosopher that I won't cut the throats of a few mice if that's what it takes to save my life."

Garric gave him a nod of understanding; his lips were tight. He didn't try to argue.

Vascay stumped off toward Metron. Thalemos gave Garric a shamefaced glance and followed, carrying a silk-wrapped packet in his left hand.

Garric took a deep breath. His throat was dry as sand, and he hadn't seen any water on this plain. "Duzi, help me," he whispered.

He hadn't been alone since he began wearing the medallion of King Carus a seeming lifetime ago. His fingers closed on the breast of his tunic, where the image hung when he was in his own body. Gar had nothing of the sort.

The Brethren were drifting toward Metron, some of them carrying loot they'd found in the tombs. Ademos had been particularly lucky: he had a gold brassard around either arm and a jeweled gold gorget bouncing from a neck chain.

Vascay had delivered his sacrifice and was casting around for more. His eyes met Garric's momentarily, then resumed their quest for prey. The foliage was festooned with silk; sometimes a single coarse bush anchored as many as three webs.

What would Carus do? Not sit around here moping, that was certain. Garric was already convinced they shouldn't stay in Wikedun any longer than necessary; watching Metron begin to pour the blood of little animals over his words of power only reinforced his conviction.

Garric laughed. Fine. If there were swamps on the other side of the hills, then there was water there. It might not be the best water, but the way his throat felt now he wouldn't quarrel with pond scum or even a floating corpse.

Giving his sword belt a hitch to settle it more comfortably, Garric started southward. He'd scout the terrain, get a drink, and then return. Metron's business would've concluded one way or another; hunger and especially thirst would've brought the Brethren into a more reasonable frame of mind than the euphoria at gold and their escape from the millipede had left them.

He turned, and called, "Vascay? I'm going to check the hills. I'll be back, as the Shepherd grants."

The chieftain looked up. He waved his javelin in acknowledgment.

There was a blast of crimson wizardlight. Metron's robes and flesh became momentarily transparent; his bones were eerie shadows against the sunlit horizon.

Grimacing, Garric started walking again. The flash had stopped the Brethren in their tracks. Vascay called in a snarl, "Come on, you fools! Are you going to let a little light scare you out of saving your lives?"

Garric didn't believe Metron's blood magic *would* save them. He'd seen wizards use the power that came from letting lives out, and every time the result had been a bad one for the wizards and those who'd put their trust in the wizards.

He hiked on, heading for the notch in the center of the arc of hills. He'd reach it in half an hour. He wasn't running away from Metron and Metron's magic, but he couldn't stay and watch what he *knew* was evil. Garric wouldn't try to stop Thalemos and the Brethren from making their own choice, but neither would he be a party to it.

Wizardlight continued to flare like sheet lightning, casting its vivid scarlet across the landscape even in this bright sun. Garric's shadow shivered ahead of him, an unstained blur framed by the ruddy touch of evil.

A trumpeter blew a long, silvery note. Garric thought it was Halophus, his call echoing from the hills. He turned his head and saw the Brethren looking south in amazement.

The trumpet sounded again; Halophus hadn't raised his own curved horn to his lips.

In the notch of the hills appeared the first elements of an army. The soldiers were on foot. Their commander hung in a litter between two huge monsters. He was anonymous at this distance, but the dragon banner fluttering above him was the standard of the Intercessor.

The soldiers pouring past into the plain in increasing numbers were lizards. They walked upright and carried bronze weapons, but they weren't men. Their trumpeter called again.

Garric turned back toward his fellows. He held his scabbard with his left hand to keep it from jouncing against his legs as he jogged. It didn't matter now what Metron was doing: Garric's place was with the other humans trapped in this ancient graveyard.

Wizardlight pulsed from Metron's circle of power, leaving afterimages of itself in Garric's eyes between flashes. Most of the Brethren ran east or west, trying to escape from between the lizardmen's hammer and the anvil of the sea. They couldn't possibly succeed.

"Vascay!" Garric called. The peg-legged chieftain wasn't running, and Lord Thalemos stood at his side with his arms crossed in aristocratic disregard for danger. The boy wasn't much use in some ways, but Garric hadn't seen any reason to fault his courage. "Hold where you are! There's a way out!"

He wasn't sure that the catacombs would save them, but a few armed men in a tunnel could hold off a thousand ... for a time. Garric laughed as Carus would have laughed. That's all life was, after all, time added to time until there was no more to add.

Ademos had ducked over the corniche, perhaps hoping to hide among the broken rocks below. He reappeared, flailing his arms in his panic. He'd lost the golden brassards already, and as he stumbled onto the plain he flung away the looted gorget.

Behind Ademos, climbing the cliff like ants making their way up a step, came a score of Archai chittering in metallic voices. They marched past Metron, ignoring Vascay and Thalemos as well, and began to form a line facing the oncoming lizardmen.

The Archai raised their saw-edged forearms, waiting. More of their fellows followed; Metron was raising a whole army of insectile monsters to battle the Intercessor's forces.

Garric drew his sword and ran past the Archai, braced for them to slash at him with their poised arms. They didn't even turn their heads.

"Come on!" Garric shouted. "We've got to get out of here!"

The appearance of Metron's allies hadn't changed Garric's mind about that. He grinned coldly. In fact, that had made him even more sure that this was no place for humans to remain.

Ilna hung in a sea of pearly light. She felt a wrench and found herself lying on a bed of rock like that of the cave.

Like, but not the same. She was in a shallow valley lighted by soft sunlight which something in the sky diffused. The barrier wasn't the solid rock ceiling she'd watched while Alecto chanted, but neither was it the kind of overcast Ilna had seen in normal skies. There was a pattern to these thin streaks and whorls; she thought she could grasp it if she bent her mind to the task in just the right way. . . .

The valley was sparsely forested. Pines and the smaller hardwoods like dogwood and hornbeam had managed to lodge their roots in the thin soil. There were tufts and hummocks of grass, sufficient to keep goats if not sheep like those used to the lush pastures of Barca's Hamlet. At the far end a sheer basalt escarpment closed a trough in the softer limestone.

From the trees and on outcrops of rock hung the webs of spiders whose bodies were as big as a hog's. They stared at Ilna with multiple glittering eyes.

Ilna had come—she'd been brought—to the spider-swathed hellworld which Tenoctris had found in the brain of the dead Echeus. She didn't know how she'd gotten here, and it seemed very unlikely that she'd have time to find a way out.

Ilna stood because it seemed undignified to die lying down. A silver-and-black spider the size of a bull had left its web and was walking toward her on legs as thick as

Ilna's own. The tree which anchored one side of the structure of wrist-thick silk was a hundred and fifty feet high, but it swayed to be free of the spider's weight. Her steps had a mincing precision like those of a crab underwater.

Ilna took out her hank of cords. It was her pride that she could control any living creature which had eyes to read her patterns; were this spider alone, she could hold it till sundown.

It wasn't alone. The valley held more of the creatures than there were people in a Valles tenement. The smallest of them was as big as a dog, and even without poison their fangs could tear her apart.

This wasn't the way Ilna would have chosen to die. She smiled coldly. Well, that was all right; she *hadn't* chosen it.

GREETINGS AND HONOR, ILNA OS-KENSET, said a voice in her mind. WE TO WHOM WEAVING IS LIFE BOW TO YOU, WHO ARE A GREATER WEAVER YET.

SHE FEARS US, said another mental voice. SHE HAS NO REASON TO FEAR. WE ARE HER FRIENDS AND HER DISCIPLES.

WE ARE YOUR FRIENDS AND DISCIPLES, ILNA, agreed a chorus, each tone different but the thoughts all the same.

"You're the spiders," Ilna said. Her gut didn't believe it, but she kept her voice flat because her intellect knew beyond a doubt that she was right.

WE ARE SPIDERS, the first voice said. The black-and-silver giant facing Ilna nodded her fused head and thorax to punctuate the statement. HAVE YOU COME TO OUR WORLD TO TEACH US?

Ilna frowned at the idea. "I didn't mean to come here," she said. "I don't know why I'm here, I don't even know where I *am*."

She'd started to say, "Perhaps I'm here by accident," but before the words came out she realized they were absurd. She didn't know why she was in the place that

Echeus had feared, but it couldn't reasonably have been the result of coincidence. You didn't have to read patterns the way Ilna did to see that.

The giant bowed again, and said, WHATEVER THE CAUSE, WE ARE PLEASED AT YOUR PRESENCE. WOULD YOU VIEW THIS PLACE, ILNA? WE CATCH GLIMPSES OF YOUR WORLD WHERE THE BARRIER IS THIN, BUT WE RARELY HAVE VISITORS LIKE YOU.

"Yes, show me. . . ." Ilna said. She rubbed her eyes; she *hated* spiders. Opening her eyes again and facing the huge spider, she went on, "Where are we? It's not my world, you say; what is it, then?"

TAKE HER TO THE MOUND, said another voice.

TAKE HER TO THE MOUND, the chorus echoed, AND LET HER SEE HER OWN WORLD.

WILL YOU COME WITH ME TO THE MOUND, ILNA? asked the black-and-silver giant. She pointed to the nearby wall of black basalt; all joints of her foreleg sprouted tufts of silver hair. YOU CAN SEE YOUR WORLD AS WE DO.

"Yes, all right," said Ilna. She had to fight an urge to fall to the ground and wrap her arms about herself, moaning. *That* wouldn't do any good. "Can I return to my world from there?"

The great spider set out, climbing the gentle side slope instead of heading directly toward the vertical escarpment. Despite her size, the spider moved with the care of someone to whom walking is not a natural activity; Ilna had no difficulty keeping pace.

I REGRET THAT THERE IS NO WAY TO GO FROM OUR WORLD TO YOURS, ILNA, the spider said. THE ONE WHO EXILED US HERE MADE CERTAIN OF THAT, THOUGH HIS BARRIER OCCASIONALLY ALLOWS HUMANS LIKE YOURSELF TO VISIT US.

Ilna's diaphragm tightened at the words. The spasm forced a gasp from her; she frowned like an angry hawk, embarrassed by the hint of weakness.

Her face still angry, she looked up at the sky. The barrier that dimmed the sun remained there, streaked and twisted. It was as surely a pattern as anything that came from Ilna's loom. More complex, perhaps—

Ilna caught herself and grimaced at the arrogance she'd allowed into her thoughts. More complex *certainly*; but that was only a matter of degree. Given a little time and a certain amount of experimentation, she was sure she could solve the puzzle which the hazy sky set her.

"I don't believe that," she said flatly. "I think there's a way out as surely as my presence here proves there's a way in."

PERHAPS FOR YOU, ILNA, the spider said. There was agreement and an odd satisfaction to the voice in Ilna's mind. WE ARE NOT AS SKILLED AS YOU, SO WE DO NOT SEE THE PATH.

The other spiders were watching her. Sometimes one of the spectators shifted slightly in her web, turning so that she could stare at Ilna with her bank of simple eyes.

"I . . ." Ilna said. "You said you'd been exiled here. How is that?"

The question that most puzzled—and concerned—her was what the spiders ate, but even her willingness to believe the worst didn't compel her to say, "Are you going to devour me?" to a hulking giant like her guide. For the moment she was willing to assume they were as friendly as they appeared to be.

MANY AGES BEFORE YOUR RACE AROSE, the spider said, YOUR WORLD WAS RULED BY A RACE OF MEN SPRUNG FROM REPTILES. WE AND THE LIZARDMEN LIVED IN PEACE FOR COUNTLESS YEARS, BUT AT LAST A WIZARD OF THAT RACE SET HIMSELF AGAINST US. THOUGH HIS POWER WAS GREAT, HE COULD NOT DESTROY US UTTERLY. INSTEAD HE FORCED US INTO THIS PLACE, AN ENCLAVE IN THE COSMOS, WHERE WE HAVE NO COMPANY BUT OURSELVES AND THE PLANTS ON WHOM WE LIVE.

Ilna felt her chest loosen. She believed—and had said—that she didn't care whether she lived or died, but it appeared that death from the fangs of giant spiders wasn't an experience she could manage to look forward to. She grinned in wry amusement at herself.

"I didn't realize spiders ate plants," she said. They were nearing the top of the escarpment. The shallow downslope beyond was more heavily forested than the valley in which she'd arrived. Many of the trees were hardwoods—oaks, hickories, and not far away a black walnut. The webs of huge spiders hung from all of them.

WE DRINK PLANT JUICES, ILNA, said her guide. THERE IS NOTHING HERE BUT THE PLANTS AND OURSELVES. WE ARE NOT AS OUR LESSER SISTERS WHO REMAIN IN YOUR WORLD.

They'd reached the bald dome of basalt that blocked the head of the valley. It was the core of an ancient volcano, frozen into a dense plug that remained when the softer surrounding rock weathered away. No trees or lesser vegetation had found a roothold in the black stone, though where windblown grit had collected in hollows it supported occasional clumps of grass.

Ilna stood, wondering why her guide had chosen this location. The spider climbed to the smooth top of the dome and said, WATCH THE BARRIER, ILNA. WATCH THE SKY.

The spider elevated her rear body and raised her hindmost pair of legs. Spinnerets at the tip of the abdomen writhed, squirting an almost transparent fluid which the hind legs teased into growing coils of silk. The strands wove in and around themselves in a pattern that drew Ilna's eyes.

The creature repeated, WATCH THE SKY!

Ilna looked up. The streaks of haze, never more than hints in the pearly sheen, drew themselves into an imposed pattern less complex than the original: they were forming an analogue of the shape the spider wove in her silk. Instead of a uniform light-struck blur, Ilna saw—

"Garric!" she cried; and in the instant she spoke the word, she knew that she was wrong. She saw Garric's body in the clothes and armor of a common soldier as he walked toward the guards at the entrance of a silk-walled tent, but the woman at his side was Sharina. The man wasn't Ilna's childhood friend, but rather the hard-handed warrior who wore Garric's flesh until his soul could be retrieved.

Ilna curled her lips. Tenoctris had sent her to look for reasons and enemies. She'd found some of both; but she hadn't reported back. She'd failed her friends.

WE WATCHED YOU OFTEN, ILNA, said her guide. THERE IS NONE LIKE YOU IN ALL THE COSMOS. WE BOW TO YOUR SKILL. THERE IS NO PATTERN THAT YOUR WISDOM CANNOT DISCERN.

Ilna sniffed. She knew her own skills, but she knew also what they had cost her to acquire. She had walked in Hell, and on her return to the waking world she'd done more harm than she could repay in a lifetime. She didn't like to hear others praise the things she was capable of, because she knew well what she might do when anger or envy led her.

"You can view any part of our world from here?" she asked.

The spider twisted the pattern in her hind legs. THIS LOCATION IS A WEAK POINT IN THE BARRIER, she said. IS THERE A THING YOU WOULD ESPECIALLY LIKE TO SEE, ILNA?

Other spiders, hanging in webs that could have held a trireme, watched with the rigid patience that Ilna had seen so often among spiders in her garden. Instinct told her they were malevolent, but she had no reason to believe that save her own hatred.

The pearly sky flowed across the view of Carus and

Sharina, then cleared again. Her heart caught again, but this time she didn't speak.

The setting was one she recognized, the sanctum of Moon Wisdom's temple in Donelle. The rites hadn't begun, but several Children of the Mistress made preparations for what was to come.

This time they weren't going to cut the throats of rabbits. The sacrificial animal was trussed and gagged at the edge of the pool. She was a black-haired young girl, naked and trembling from more than the touch of the cold marble on which she lay.

One of the cowled priests was bending over her. When he straightened, Ilna saw the child's face.

This time the victim was Merota.

The spider's legs worked the silk. The image in the sky shimmered, momentarily mirroring the earth below. Ilna frowned. In the reflection she'd seen many long, hairy legs waving skyward in a rhythm that she almost understood.

The image was momentary; the sky re-formed as a window onto her brother Cashel, who stood with a girl Ilna didn't know. They were in a maze formed partly by the braided streams of a river and partly by the stone walls of the city they approached through the fog.

Ilna sensed what her eyes couldn't show her, the danger at the heart of pattern. There was a *thing* at the center of the maze, but outside that—hovering beyond not only sight but the cosmos, unknown even to the one who waited to trap Cashel—was the Pack. Moon Wisdom had loosed them; but as Alecto had warned, the Pack would not stay on any wizard's leash for long.

The spider crossed her hind legs, unmaking the silken pattern and closing the image in the sky. HE WAS YOUR BROTHER, WAS HE NOT, ILNA? she said in Ilna's mind.

"Yes," said Ilna tightly. "That was Cashel. I—"

She'd been about to ask to be left alone to study the sky—study the barrier—without distraction. Before she got the words out, her guide had opened another window onto the world Ilna had left. She saw the real Garric clambering through torchlit gloom with his sword lifted. Ahead of him—

Ahead of Garric was whirling blackness, not the thing itself but a cloak which concealed the thing from Ilna's eyes. All she could be sure of was that the creature was powerful, and that it was hostile to Garric and to all life except its own.

Her guide's legs moved, closing the barrier again. This time the closure was permanent: she bent a hind leg forward, carrying the wad of silk to her mouth. Her jaw-plates chewed the silk methodically before she swallowed it again.

YOUR FRIENDS NEED HELP, ILNA, said the voice in her mind.

"Yes," she said grimly. She held her hank of cords, but her fingers were knotting and unknotting them to settle her mind rather than with any considered purpose. Purpose would come.

"Mistress," she said. *What do you call a giant spider?* "I'd appreciate it if you'd leave me to my own devices for a time. I think it's possible to open the barrier from this side, but it's going to require some thought. Is that agreeable to you?"

WHATEVER YOU WISH, ILNA, said her guide. YOUR SKILL IS GREATER THAN OURS.

Ilna seated herself on the basalt, looking up at the sky. The black-and-silver giant stepped away, picking her path down toward her web.

WE ARE YOUR DISCIPLES, chorused the denizens of this world. WE WILL LEARN FROM YOU.

Chapter Twenty-one

By the time the sun had risen a finger's breadth above the horizon, the fog had burned off. Cashel looked over his shoulder and for the first time saw the other bank of the river. He chuckled.

Tilphosa, curled in the stern of the boat, jerked awake at the sound. "What?" she said. "Cashel, is everything all right?"

"I don't know about everything," Cashel said with a shy grin. "But better off than a little bit ago, sure. See the land, Tilphosa?"

"Yes," she said, squinting into the low sun. She sounded doubtful. "It looks marshy, doesn't it?"

"Right," said Cashel, "but it's land. I've been rowing all night. I was beginning to think it wasn't a river at all but a lake that I wasn't going to get across in this lifetime."

"Oh!" said Tilphosa. She turned and looked west, toward where Soong ought to be. The city was still there, Cashel supposed, but it was long out of sight in their wake. "Cashel, you've been rowing all *night*? What do your palms look like?"

She leaned forward and unwrapped the fingers of his right hand from the oarloom. "I'm fine, mistress," Cashel said in embarrassment. "I'm used to this sort of thing."

That was true enough. His calluses had faced worse than a night of rowing, and the same was true of his shoulder muscles. Even so, Tilphosa looked at him with mingled anger and sympathy.

"Well, stop right now!" she said. "It isn't right that anyone be worked like that!"

"It isn't somebody making me do it, mistress," Cashel said calmly. "It's me doing it. I choose to."

"Well, then choose—" the girl said sharply.

"Mistress," said Cashel, loudly enough to be heard. "I don't want to float here in the middle of a river till we starve. It's that or else me rowing us the rest of the way to land. All right?"

Tilphosa's eyes flashed; then she lowered them, and quietly said, "All right, Cashel. Are you going to take us to the city there?"

"Huh?" said Cashel, looking over his shoulder again. The buildings rising out of the mud and mists were several stories high, gleaming as sunlight struck their wet stone. Granted that the fog was still clearing, he'd have thought he'd have seen them. . . .

"That's funny," Cashel said. "But sure, we'll head for the city. You guide me if the current pulls us off course, all right?"

He resumed rowing. That last was just a way to be friendly to the girl after he'd told her to stop mothering him. The chance of this river's sluggish current drifting him downstream unnoticed was about the same as Cashel sprouting wings and flying to the city.

He smiled at Tilphosa. He'd had his sister to mother him, and Ilna wasn't one to claim hard work was a bad thing for a man—or a slip of a girl like herself, either. Tilphosa was tough and in her way strong, but she didn't have any notion of what was normal for peasants like Cashel.

"I lost my dagger," the girl said suddenly. "I don't have . . ."

She had the tunic she'd worn to bed, period. Well, there hadn't been any time since then to do more than to keep moving.

"Maybe you won't need it," Cashel said calmly. When you really didn't know what was going to happen next, there was no point in deciding it was going to be bad. "Anyway, I've still got my staff."

Tilphosa smiled vividly again, the first time Cashel had seen that expression since they went to sleep in the Hyacinth. "Yes you do, Cashel," she said. "And I've got you."

"Till we get you home," Cashel agreed. His arms and upper body moved with the steady grace of a mill wheel, long pulls that sent the water swirling away each time he withdrew his oarblades. Dimples of foam marked the surface behind them, staying where they were while the wake made a V outward across them. "The Shepherd granting, of course."

"There was a time I'd have said, 'The Mistress granting,' Cashel," Tilphosa said in an odd tone of voice. "Now I think I'll just depend on you. You haven't failed me yet."

She cleared her throat, and went on, "We're getting very close to the quays along the bank. But I suppose you know that."

"Thank you, m-mis . . ." Cashel said. "I mean, thank you, Tilphosa."

He looked over his shoulder, picking the point where he'd land. There were steps down into the water squarely ahead of them. If there'd ever been bollards, they'd rotted away, but he could haul this little skiff up the stairs easily enough. It wouldn't hurt the flat bottom to bump a little.

He *had* known the bank was close, of course. Tilphosa was smart in people ways, not just out of books. Cashel himself was always being surprised by what people did and said, because mostly it didn't make any sense. The best Cashel could do was learn to deal with surprises.

He braked the skiff by reversing his stroke, then turned them so that they drifted stern first to the stairs on the last of their momentum. Mud, poisonously bright with river algae, was slumping away from the stone. Where the sun had dried it, it turned a sickly gray-green.

"If you'll just hop—" Cashel said, but Tilphosa had

already judged her time. She stepped lightly to the stone tread, then bent to hold the boat's transom.

Smiling approval, Cashel paddled the skiff broadside and got out himself. Despite his care, water sloshing from beneath the hull soaked Tilphosa's feet. She didn't appear to notice.

Cashel pulled the skiff up the few steps and set it on the drying mud of the quay. He'd told the fisherman he'd leave the boat when he was through, but now he didn't imagine the fellow would ever see it again. That's what the fisherman had expected, but it still bothered Cashel to reinforce somebody's bad expectations.

A different thought struck him; he grinned. "Cashel?" Tilphosa said.

"The fellow I got the boat from knew how wide the river was even though I didn't," Cashel explained. "I guess when I said I'd leave it for him, he thought I was a fool but not a crook."

Tilphosa frowned, trying to understand what he was getting at. "You see, mistress," Cashel explained, "I'm used to people thinking I'm dumb. That's all right."

"No," said Tilphosa, "it's not. But for now let's see if we can find something to eat."

"Right," said Cashel. "Let me . . ."

He slid his quarterstaff out from under the thwart. Stepping back from the girl, he began to spin it; slowly at first, but building speed as he worked out the kinks rowing had put in his muscles. He whirled the staff in front of him, reversing direction with a skill that only another man familiar with the heavy weapon would appreciate. He brought it over his head, then jumped and let the staff's inertia carry his body around in a full circle.

"There," said Cashel breathlessly. "*There*!"

Tilphosa looked at him with wide eyes, the back of her right hand in her mouth. "Cashel," she said. "That was amazing!"

"Huh?" he said. He seemed to say that a lot when he was around Tilphosa. "It wasn't . . . I mean, I was just loosening up, that's all. Anyway, let's get going."

He really didn't see what the big deal was . . . or maybe he did, and it wasn't flattering.

"Ah, Tilphosa?" he said. "Did you mean that it's amazing somebody as big as me's not clumsy?"

"No, Cashel," the girl said. "I meant you're as graceful as a God when you move. I thought I was . . . inventing memories about how you held off the sailors in the temple. But I wasn't."

Cashel still didn't understand, but he had to say it made him feel good. Prince Thalemos was a lucky man; or anyway he would be, when Tilphosa finally reached him.

They walked into the city. The streets were slimy where the mud hadn't dried yet, but gray-green slabs were cracking off east-facing walls. The stone underneath was pinkish, highly polished, and as hard as granite. The air smelled of slow death, but it wasn't as pungent as that of salt marshes drying at neap tide.

"The river must have covered all this until just now," Tilphosa said. She paused to duck through one of the doorways: low, narrow, and wider at the bottom than the top.

"Nothing there," she said as she returned, still frowning. "Nothing but mud."

"I don't think we're going to find anything to eat here," Cashel said, "unless a carp maybe got stranded. We could go down the river a ways, maybe?"

Tilphosa shaded her eyes with her hand as she looked up. "East was a good way before," she said. She smiled. "At least it was a good enough way, since you were there. I think we ought to keep on as we've started."

Cashel grunted. He was glad to hear her say that, because it was pretty much what he was thinking. He didn't have a reason to go somewhere in particular, but it seemed to him it was important that they anyway went *on*.

The streets twisted worse than the ones in the old part of Valles. When they met, it was always in odd numbers: generally three but sometimes as many streets as the fingers on a man's hand. Cashel tried to keep the sun before him, but he knew he and Tilphosa were doing a lot of backtracking.

They came out into an open courtyard, different from anyplace they'd yet seen. The entrances through the circular wall, instead of being real arches, all had slanting jambs and a big stone across the top. Cashel walked into the clear space and stopped with Tilphosa at his side.

"It doesn't feel like a ruined city," Tilphosa said. "The walls are standing, and the edges aren't even worn."

"I guess the mud covered it," Cashel said, feeling uneasy. "It would've weathered if it had been above ground, but buried . . ."

He started forward, picking the archway that seemed to go more east than the others. The streets into the courtyard all kinked, so you couldn't see down them any distance from inside.

Tilphosa scraped her foot through the soft mud. "The plaza's got a design carved on it, Cashel," she said. She waggled her bare toe. "I wonder what they used it for? Whoever built the city, I mean."

Metra stepped out of the entrance Cashel was walking toward. "The Archai built the city," the wizard said. "They never occupied it, however. Until now."

Archai warriors, their forearms raised, entered the courtyard from all the other entrances. Cashel lunged toward Metra, his quarterstaff outstretched like a battering ram.

Tilphosa shouted in fury rather than fear. Archai swarmed over Cashel from both sides and behind, grasping with their middle limbs instead of hacking him apart with their toothed forearms. He strained forward, but too many Archai held him; it was like trying to swim through an avalanche.

Cashel toppled sideways. He felt chitin crunch beneath his weight, but the grip of countless tiny, hard-surfaced fingers held him beyond the ability to do more than wriggle.

The Archai rolled Cashel over. He fought without any plan beyond wanting to resist whatever the creatures did. His struggles didn't make any difference, except to prove that he wasn't giving up.

They lashed his wrists and ankles together with fibrous ropes, then tied his wrists *to* his ankles. When they had him securely bound they stepped away, chirping among themselves. Cashel rolled sideways so that he could see again.

Four Archai held Tilphosa; she hadn't been tied like Cashel. Metra watched the girl with the grin of a cat over a fish bowl. More Archai than even Garric could have counted stood around the edge of the courtyard and looked down from the surrounding wall.

"You were wondering the purpose of this courtyard, Tilphosa," the wizard said. "It was a temple; it *is* a temple, now that you've arrived."

"*Lady* Tilphosa to you, mistress!" the girl said. Cashel had heard hissing snakes that sounded friendlier.

"I think we can dispense with titles now, Tilphosa," Metra said; a tic at the corner of her mouth showed the insult had gotten home. "The moon will be full tonight, but you and I only have to wait for high noon."

Metra looked down at Cashel. "While I waited . . ." she went on, "I performed a location spell. You had the ring all the time, didn't you? If I'd known that . . ."

She shrugged and made a sound with the tip of her tongue against her palate. Two Archai bent over Cashel. He twisted, but one of them ripped his tunic cleanly with a forearm and the other clipped the silken cord which held the purse around Cashel's neck. The Archa's delicate, three-fingered hand passed the purse to Metra.

She took out the ring and held the tiny ruby to the light. Its facets scattered rosy blurs around the courtyard.

"Yes . . ." she said. "The Mistress has been waiting a very long time, but the wait is over now."

Waiting like a spider in her web, thought Cashel; and he tugged at the ropes, but they were tight and had no more give than steel chains would.

Garric started for the corniche, tugging at the sleeve of Thalemos' tunic to hustle him along. Vascay, his face bleak as Garric had never before seen it, was already moving. His step had a hitch in it; he hesitated each time his peg leg came down on the coarse soil.

"Wait!" cried Metron, looking up from his incantations. A litter of flaccid, bloodless animals lay at his side; his hands and ivory blade were red with the blood that hadn't dripped onto his words of power. "Thalemos, it isn't time yet!"

Thalemos didn't turn at the wizard's voice. His expression was calm, but his face was set.

"It's time and past time, *I* think!" Vascay said. He poised at the edge, waiting for Garric to choose their path downward.

"This way!" said Garric from the notch where the recently fallen bank provided a steep ramp down to the sea which had undercut it. He pointed toward the rectangular shadow to the left where the catacomb lay open. He and his companions could pick their way across the slope, though they'd have to be careful not to slip into the sea.

Archai rose from the water like fishflies hatching. They clambered up the escarpment directly in front of them, regardless of the slope. Occasionally the bank gave way; the ones who'd pulled it down tumbled into their fellows, then rose and crawled upward again.

They brushed past Garric and his companions with no

more regard than a creek has for the men wading in it. Their limbs were slick and cold, like marble statues touched in the evening.

There were hundreds of the chitinous warriors already. Garric supposed more would appear for so long as Metron continued his chant and sacrifices.

The wizard thrust his lips out and gave a fluting call. Archai gripped Garric, three of them before him and more from behind where he couldn't see them. He heard Thalemos shout and Vascay curse.

Garric tried to pull away. The scores of cold fingers held him firmly. He tried to force his way forward, over the cliff in the hope that gravity would tug him free. All he managed to do was to cut his shoulder by shoving it into an Archa's raised forearm.

Relaxing, Garric looked at his companions. Vascay stood with no expression, his head turned back toward Metron. His arms were pinioned, but he still held his remaining javelin. Though the chieftain seemed relaxed, Garric knew that if the Archai relaxed their grip on him for an instant, his javelin would skewer the wizard's throat.

Thalemos was spread-eagled, his feet held off the ground and his arms straight out from his side. His face was set in aristocratic resignation, but a muscle at the back of his jaw pulsed.

Metron resumed his chanting. His athame thrust, then tore. The ivory edge wasn't sharp enough to cut, but the point could pierce a vole's body and a quick twist of the blade let out the little creatures' blood and entrails in a gush.

Wizardlight blazed again. Another wave of Archai emerged from the sea.

The leading ranks of lizardmen spread sideways as they approached the Archai. The insect monsters were individually shorter and slighter than most men, but the reptiles were shorter yet. They had bronze helmets and swords, however, and a few of them carried small wicker shields covered with scaly leather.

The two lines made savage contact. The bronze swords were sharper than the Archai's fanged forearms, but the insects could parry with one arm and hack with the other.

Lizardmen and Archai both continued to chop at their opponents when horribly wounded, their limbs severed or coils of their intestines cascading around their ankles. Even after falling they twitched and tried still to strike. More Archai came from the sea; but the column of lizardmen continued to pour through the distant notch in the hills.

The Intercessor hung in a chair suspended between a pair of reptilian quadrupeds like nothing Garric had ever seen before. The beasts had small heads, long necks, and even longer tails. Each of them was many times the size of the biggest ox in the borough.

Echeon held a long staff of amethyst or purple glass. He chanted, stroking his staff through the air in time with his words of power. The lines of his face had a eunuch's softness, but the features underneath were identical to those of the Intercessor Echeus, whose wizardry had flung Garric's soul forward to this time.

Metron squeezed the corpse of the last vole in his left hand, then tossed it aside. He trilled another order. Garric expected the Archai holding him to react. Instead, a group of warriors seized Ademos, who'd been kneeling in prayer ever since he realized he was trapped between the Archai and their reptilian opponents.

Ademos mewled and flailed like a newborn baby as the Archai dragged him toward the wizard. Vascay said in an expressionless voice, "All those times I thought of cutting the little weasel's throat myself but didn't . . . Maybe I didn't do him a favor after all, eh?"

He chuckled, but it sounded like a death rattle.

Metron gripped Ademos by the hair and twisted the bandit's head back. Garric looked down. He'd seen worse, but it wasn't something he wanted to watch. Ademos' scream became a bubbling gurgle.

Crimson radiance flooded the plain, penetrating stone and sky alike. For an instant all sound ceased. Garric hung in transparent red light, staring into the bowels of the earth where he saw buried treasures and the bones of creatures more ancient than man. Just at the edge of Garric's vision was a moving thing: alive but not of this world. Its jaws slowly devoured the rock in which it swam.

The flash passed, and the images it had shown became dreams rather than memories in Garric's mind. Their reality was specious, the sort of truth into which wizards delved by blood magic.

The sea boiled with Archai, climbing onto the shore for as far as Garric could see to right and left. Once the Archai had ruled the world. Their civilization and race had perished in the distant past, but Metron had the skill to recall the dead in numbers limited only by his power.

The wizard swayed; his efforts had drained him as white as the bloodless corpse of Ademos in the grip of four Archai. They tossed the bandit onto the litter of lesser bodies, all dead in the service of Metron's wizardry.

The lizardmen had been pressing close against the diminishing rank of Archai. Now they gave back again as insectile warriors clambered over the cliff edge beyond both flanks of the Intercessor's troops.

Echeon lowered his staff with a dazed expression. He hooted an order. The beasts carrying his chair had been cropping mouthfuls of grass from among the tombs as they waited. Their heads rose; they gave startled *whuff*s, circled in clumsy unison, and moved twenty paces back from the battle line.

Metron stood swaying with his head bowed, his left hand over his eyes, and his right pointing the athame at the ground. The line of fresh warriors marched by him, mincing on their spindly legs like automatons. They hurled themselves into the lizardmen, driving them back in an orgy of mutual slaughter.

More lizardmen trailed down from the hills, their bronze equipment glinting. Garric didn't know if the Intercessor had an infinite number of troops, but the total of those on or approaching the field was great enough to overwhelm Metron's present forces before long.

Metron raised his head. He pointed his bloody athame at a spiky shrub and spoke a word unheard in the chaos. A spark of scarlet lightning snapped from the ivory, blasting the shrub apart.

The wizard stuffed his athame under his sash, then bent and lifted one of the stems. The base burned with an oily yellow flame.

Holding up the torch, Metron walked toward Garric and his companions; he was wobbling with exhaustion. His left hand made a gesture toward the Archai, who let go of their prisoners. The former guards strutted toward the battle line. The fight was already turning back in favor of the Intercessor's forces.

Vascay shrugged, loosening his shoulder muscles. Garric put a hand on the older man's arm, and said, "No, Vascay. There's still a chance."

He grinned; the excitement made him cheerful. "Though I'm not sure what it is," he added.

"Is there?" Vascay said, but he didn't put his javelin through Metron's throat.

Lord Thalemos looked at his former advisor with an expression more of amazement than loathing, though loathing as well. He turned his back in a deliberate snub, which the wizard was far too tired to notice.

"Come on," Garric said, leading the way down and across the slope. "At least it'll be harder for them to get at us if we're down in the tunnels."

Half-trotting, half-skidding, he reached the mouth of the catacombs. The sea had carved the soft rock back to a burial niche; a coffin of polished granite tilted out over the curling water. There was nothing among the eddies below except boulders. The last of the Archai were already fighting on the field above.

Garric stepped into the tunnel and paused, letting his eyes adjust while his companions joined him. He liked the catacombs even less than he liked the sunlit plain, but these tunnels were the only choice save death.

He grinned. A choice didn't have to be good to be easy.

The four men at the front of Lord Lerdain's tent didn't have uniform equipment like the Blood Eagles, nor was their varied armor as heavy as that of the line infantry they resembled. Most wore iron caps instead of helmets with visors and flaring cheekpieces, and they carried small bucklers instead of targets so heavy that they required a shoulder strap as well as the soldier's left arm for support.

Regardless of their equipment, these were tough veterans. Merchants from one end of the Isles to the other hired Blaise armsmen as bodyguards. That's what these men, now protecting the son of their count instead of acting as hirelings for strangers, were.

Two of the guards had short broad-bladed spears meant to slash rather than throw; the other two had hooked swords bare in their hands. They watched silently as Sharina and Carus approached.

The section leader, a spearman, had a heart tattooed on one cheek and a skull on the other. At the distance of a double pace he dipped his spearpoint toward Carus, and said, "That's close enough. Sir."

"Don't get your bowels in an uproar, soldier," Carus said in a bored tone. "The folks in Donelle sent the count a thank-you gift for arriving, and he's passing her on to the boy."

"Eh?" said the section leader doubtfully.

Carus touched the peak of Sharina's cowl to draw it back. Sharina slapped his hand away. They hadn't discussed this; Sharina was acting as seemed natural for the character she mimicked tonight.

"Hey, temper temper," Carus said with amusement. He waggled his fingers to shake the sting out of them. "Show the boys the goods so they don't think you're some cutthroat out to scrag his lordship, eh?"

Glaring at him, Sharina jerked the cowl down herself. She shook her head side to side, spreading her blond hair in a loose cascade. Moonlight woke as fire from her diamond-studded combs. She'd had to place them herself and hastily, but she thought both her mother Lora and her maid back in Valles would give her efforts qualified approval.

Sharina transferred her disdainful glance to the section leader, then deliberately drew the cowl up to cover her face again. She continued to watch the guards coldly from beneath it.

"By the Lady . . ." the section leader muttered. In a normal voice he went on, "Does Lord Lerdain know she's coming?"

Carus shrugged. "I don't think so," he said. "Ask him. And believe me, if he's not interested, the little lady won't go to waste."

"You have a better chance of feeding the Mistress than you do of knowing me, dog," Sharina said. The contempt in her tone roared straight down from the Ice Capes and the Pole. She turned back to the guards, and added, "Rouse Lord Lerdain and enquire what his will for me may be. This isn't a matter for lackeys."

The other spearman whispered something. The section leader nodded and rapped his spear into the little gong hanging from the tent's ridgepole. A steward in an un-belted silk tunic raised the flap from the inside; he was barefoot but held a lighted lantern.

Sharina walked forward, tossing back her cowl again. No one tried to halt her.

"I am here at your master's service," she said to the steward before the guard could speak. "If he chooses to send me away, well and good; but no other will make that decision."

The silver broach at the throat of Sharina's cape was unpinned; she held the halves closed with her left hand. Now she slid that hand down the seam to grip again just above waist height. The front gaped open; the single tunic she wore under the cloak was of diaphanous silk with panels of lacework.

Smiling like a blond icicle, she closed the cape again.

"Oh!" said the steward. "Yes, of course. Please follow me, ah, mistress . . ."

He turned; Sharina stepped between the guards. Carus called, "Your ladyship?"

Sharina looked over her shoulder. Carus cleared his throat, and said, "Ah—shall I wait? In case, ah, Lord Lerdain doesn't want your company?"

"I scarcely think that's likely," Sharina snapped. She followed the steward into the tent's anteroom, which held clothes chests and an inlaid bed.

As the flap closed, Sharina heard the section leader say, "Not a *bit* likely with that randy bugger, sir. Mind, I'm a little surprised his old man gave her a pass hisself."

A velvet curtain separated the anteroom from the tent's inner chamber. The steward slid it partway open. Without entering, he said quietly, "Your lordship, you have a visitor."

"Huh?" said a sleepy voice.

Sharina pulled the curtain back farther so that she had a good view of the inner chamber—and the reverse. A lighted lantern hung from a trellis anchored to the ridge-pole. Lord Lerdain's bed was of chased and gilded bronze, with a tasseled silk canopy.

The count's son and heir presumptive, a husky youth with fair hair, sat up. He'd run to fat when he was his father's age, but for the moment he was a well set-up fourteen-year-old who looked as if he'd give a good account of himself in a fight.

"Your father sent me, your lordship," Sharina said. She looked at the steward. "I believe your master can handle matters from here. Or"—she glanced at Lerdain appraisingly—"perhaps not. You're rather young, aren't you?"

"By the Shepherd's dick, I can!" Lerdain said, bounding out of bed. His long muslin sleeping tunic bore the lion symbol of Blaise woven in red. He reached for Sharina.

She turned her back and pulled the curtain closed. The steward hopped hastily away. Lerdain fondled her from behind.

Sharina twisted to face the youth. He tried to kiss her. She put the index finger of her left hand on his lips, and said, "Carefully, milord; not a sound."

"What?" he said in puzzlement.

Sharina held his right wrist in her left hand and touched the point of her Pewle knife to the skin beneath his breast-bone, just hard enough to prick. Lerdain jerked at the contact and stared down at the blade she'd hidden under her cloak. It was polished steel and as long as his forearm.

"If you stay quiet, you won't be hurt, and your father won't be hurt," Sharina continued in the same low, pleasant voice as before. "Otherwise, there won't be enough survivors from this army to bury the dead; but that won't matter to you, because I'll have spilled your guts right here and now."

"You?" said the youth. He wasn't shouting, but his voice started to rise from a hoarse whisper. "You can't—"

The trellis was made from thumb-thick ash poles. Sharina held Lerdain's eyes with her own while her right arm slashed sideways, so suddenly that her heavy blade was against the boy's belly again before he could react. The guards and steward must have heard the *whack!* as the keen edge parted the trellis, but the sound wasn't so untoward that it'd bring them rushing into the nobleman's privacy.

"That could've been your spine," Sharina said. It was good that she'd had an excuse to let out some of the emotions surging in her blood. Even so, her voice and the big knife trembled. "You're no good to me or the Isles dead, but I'll still kill you unless you do exactly what you're told."

Lerdain was taller and stronger than she was, but even so Sharina's additional five years gave her more ascendency over the boy than the weapon in her hand did. He might have tried to struggle for the knife, but the firm assurance in Sharina's voice cowed him. He'd have died beyond doubt if he'd grappled with her, but he wouldn't have believed that.

"What do you want me to do?" he said in a husky voice. He probably wanted to turn his face, but Sharina's eyes held him like a vole facing a blacksnake.

"Do you have a long cloak in here?" Sharina said. Garments hung on a rack at the foot of the bed, ready for the steward to offer in the morning; she didn't dare look away from Lerdain to check them, though.

"I guess," the boy muttered. The Pewle knife prodded him a little harder. "Ouch! Yeah, there ought to be a . . ."

He nodded toward the rack. "Can I look?"

"Yes," said Sharina, nodding and drawing the blade back slightly so Lerdain could turn. She put her hand on his right elbow as he rummaged through the shadowed rack, warning the boy that no matter how quickly he turned he wouldn't be able to grab her knife wrist. It would take a braver man than most to lunge at the Pewle knife with open eyes.

"Here," Lerdain said, pulling down a campaign cloak of dark, closely woven blue wool. It was what a common soldier used for blanket and shelter when no other was available. "Is this all right?"

"Yes," Sharina said. The only reason the count's son would have such a garment was to become anonymous in event of disaster. "Put it on, but don't raise the hood yet; and *don't* do anything foolish. There's no reason you shouldn't live for the next half century if you don't make me kill you tonight."

She wondered how she sounded to the boy; like some sort of demon, she supposed. She wasn't angry. She spoke the way the butcher did when he made his rounds through the boroughs north along the coast of Haft. The butcher killed hogs not because he was angry at them, but because it was his job to clamp the beasts' snouts with toothed tongs and to thrust his keen blade into their throats while each owner's wife held a bowl of oatmeal below to catch the blood for pudding.

The boy must have understood that; he shrugged into his cloak, careful not to seem hasty. The Pewle knife's broad blade would slice him from kidneys to collarbone if Sharina needed to kill him.

"I've put the cloak on," Lerdain said, stating the obvious to prod Sharina into giving the next order. She wasn't quite conscious. Rather, the part of her mind in control wasn't her intellect. *That* part of Sharina os-Reise wouldn't have been able threaten to slaughter a boy, even to save the kingdom.

Lerdain was barefoot, but the cloak hid his sleeping garment. In this warm weather, many of the soldiers wouldn't bother with footgear while they were at leisure.

"Step over to the back of the tent," Sharina said, nodding. "I'll open it. Stick your head out and quietly ask the two guards there to come over to you."

"Open it?" the boy said with a frown. "It's—"

"Move," Sharina said. She guided him by her grip on his right elbow. "*Now*."

When Lerdain stood by the tent's smooth silk panel, looking sideways at her, Sharina made another lightning stroke with the Pewle knife. It went in and down, ripping the tough fabric as easily as it could have let out the boy's life.

Lerdain's mouth fell open. He must have had a similar thought.

Sharina gestured curtly with her left hand. Obediently, the boy leaned out through the slit, and said, "Ah—could you . . . ? I mean, would—"

There was a clang like an ironbound chest slamming. "Oh!" said Lerdain as he jerked his head back into the tent.

King Carus forced two dazed-looking guards through the opening, tearing the fabric wider. He held the men by the necks. One had lost his iron cap; the other still wore his, but it'd been displaced when Carus slammed the guards' heads together as they stared at Lerdain. There was enough construction noise, even at this hour, that the risk wouldn't be great.

Carus tilted the latter guard so that his cap fell off also, then crunched their skulls into one another again. Sharina's mouth tightened as though she'd bitten on a lemon.

"Is there time to tie them?" she asked.

"No need," said the king. He'd taken off his helmet and sword belt. He'd waited in the shadows as planned till Lerdain drew the guards' attention, then struck like a leopard.

Blood trickled from the guards' nostrils and ears. Sharina thought of twenty thousand hogs being slaughtered—

except that hogs don't scream, "*Mother!*" and "*Oh, it hurts, it hurts so bad. . . .*"

She was sorry for the guards. She'd pray to the Lady for their souls, if the Isles survived and she survived.

"All right, boy," Carus said to Lord Lerdain. "We're going to walk to the gate. You keep your face hidden and your mouth shut. Understood?"

"What happens then?" the boy said. He was standing very straight, with his eyes focused on the wall past Carus' shoulder.

"Nothing bad," the king said with a shrug. "The wizards of Moon Wisdom decorate a gallows, but that's not something any decent human being ought to regret. Now—does the lady there with the knife scare you?"

"No!" Lerdain lied. "I'm not afraid!"

"Then you're a fool," Carus said with a smile. The smile changed, drawing the boy's eyes and holding them. "And if *I* don't scare you, you don't have the brains of a maggot. Because I'll do anything to save the Isles, do you see? Absolutely anything."

The king's voice had a gentle lilt. A weasel's chittering had more mercy in it.

Carus drew up the boy's cowl and snugged it over his forehead. "Good," he said, still smiling. "I'm glad you understand. Let's go, then."

He left through the slit panel. Lerdain hesitated, then followed when Sharina prodded him with the tips of her left fingers. When she slipped out in turn, Carus already wore his helmet and was belting on his sword and dagger.

The tents crowding the area behind Lord Lerdain's held common soldiers. They weren't marshalled in straight lines, and their guy ropes interlaced as randomly as sticks in a squirrel's nest.

A dice game was going on in one, spilling lanternlight out of the open flap. Carus guided his companions past, paused to check his bearings, and set off in the direction of the east gate at a swinging pace.

He began to whistle. Sharina's memory supplied the words: *Me oh my, I love him so; broke my heart to see him go.* . . .

"They sang that in your day too?" she asked.

Carus chuckled. " 'My True Love's Gone for a Soldier'?" he asked. "Aye, girl, they did. And they'll sing it or a song like it as long as there's women and armies, I shouldn't wonder."

They were nearing the east gate. Several of the men on guard were talking to figures on the other side through gaps in the log gate. They continued their negotiations while their fellows straightened at the approach of Carus and the two cloaked figures a half pace behind.

"Where's your officer?" Carus asked in a mildly irritated voice. The troops wore leather breeches and carried spiked halberds instead of spears; Sharina couldn't guess which island they came from.

"Yeah?" demanded one of the men who'd been chatting through the gate. He wore a bright gold gorget decorated with polished—not faceted—jewels.

Sharina put the fingers of her left hand on Lerdain's spine, just at the base of his neck. The only threat was what the contact implied about her other hand, hidden beneath her cloak.

"Moon," said Carus. He gestured to the gate with his left hand. "We're going out."

"Did the sun addle your brains?" the guard commander said. "Why're you doing that?"

Carus shrugged. "Tomorrow I'll be able to tell you—if I make it back," he said. "But if I make it back, you'll already know. All right?"

Sharina marveled at the easy way the king handled the question: saying nothing but hinting that he was offering a great secret. Her fingers gently rubbed the boy's back as though she were calming a nervous hound.

The commander shook his head in wonder. "Stars, then," he said. "Come on, boys; we'll crack this thing open enough that our loony friends can get out."

The gate was of green wood, boles cut to length but not squared; it was enormously heavy and probably strong as well. Six guardsmen, one of them leaning on a crowbar to lift the end, dragged it narrowly ajar.

"You first, milady," Carus said in a low voice. Sharina didn't argue; she squeezed through at once.

Carus stood behind Lerdain, bracing his hands on the gate leaf and the jamb. He shoved hard, spreading the opening enough for the boy to climb through without having a notch pull his cape off. What would happen then was anybody's guess.

The people outside the gate were all women, old enough that they were probably trying to sell something other than themselves. They backed away when Sharina came through, then stood staring at her.

Carus followed the boy out. He tipped his helmet in salute to the guards, then grinned at his companions.

"Let's go," he said. "There'll be a patrol with horses waiting for us, but if we miss them in the dark, we've got a long walk ahead of us."

He tousled Lerdain's hair under the cowl. "Cheer up, lad," Carus said. "You've saved a lot of lives tonight, not least your own."

They started eastward, feeling the eyes of the camp followers on them as long as the moon allowed. Before that, Carus started whistling again.

There were no Blaise patrols out, so Sharina sang in a cool, clear voice to the king's accompaniment, *"Only time can heal my woe, my true love's gone for a soldier."*

* * *

Ilna's fingers played idly with her cords as she sat on the bare basalt. Occasionally she raised her head toward the barrier in the sky, but her mind already had the information it needed.

She smiled faintly. *Which is as much as to say that I have a loom and a roomful of thread, so the only problem is placing the individual strands where they belong.* What else was there to weaving, after all?

This world was oddly silent. The wind sighed through branches, and she could hear trees creak as they swayed. There were no birds and no animals except the spiders themselves. Were there streams with fish in them? Ilna doubted it, because that wouldn't fit the pattern she was forming of this world.

The spiders watched her. They didn't interfere, they didn't even move for the most part. Occasionally a long, hairy leg adjusted a strand of silk. In the far distance, a green-and-gold monster was decorating her web with a fine silk ribbon midway between the hub and the rim.

Ilna didn't ask herself what purpose the ribbon might have. Everything had a purpose, everything fit into the pattern.

The thought made her pause, then smile wryly. She'd thought—she'd said—that she didn't belong in this world, but of course she did. That was as surely true as every thread in her own simpler patterns belonged where she'd placed it.

She didn't believe in the Great Gods, but she believed in craftsmanship and she *knew* craftsmanship. The pattern someone, Someone—perhaps the cosmos itself, Ilna neither knew nor cared—wove with human threads couldn't be chance.

Ilna looked down at the answer her fingers had drawn in cords. The knotted pattern didn't tell her that something was wrong—she already knew this world was wrong—but it told her where.

Ilna rose with her usual sudden grace and started toward the other side of the Mound. From where she'd sat on the barren rock, she could see only the distant slopes of the valley which the basalt divided. Across the plug she'd be able to view the whole of it.

ILNA OS-KENSET! thundered the mental voice of her black-and-silver guide. DO NOT GO THAT WAY! IT WILL BE FATAL FOR YOU IF YOU LOOK INTO THAT VALLEY!

Ilna strode on, tight-faced. Her fingers were unpicking the knots that had led her to do this. She might—she *would*—need the cords for other purposes shortly.

SHE MUST NOT LOOK! sang the chorus of thousands. IF SHE LOOKS, WE MUST ACT!

Ilna reached the edge of the plug and looked over. The basalt formed an equally sheer wall on this side.

The floor of the valley below seethed with giant spiders. These had left their webs to crawl into a ring surrounding two sheep and an aged man holding a crooked staff. The sheep blatted and bucked, kicking their forehooves into the air. They turned and turned again, looking for a way out. There was no way out.

The man fell to his knees and prayed to the Shepherd; fragments of his words, shouted in a cracked voice, reached Ilna on the Mound above. There was no way out for him either.

SHE HAS SEEN! cried the chorus. WE MUST SLAY HER BEFORE SHE ESCAPES!

The spiders had a facility with patterns second only to the skills Ilna had learned in Hell. Even here at the point of weakness beneath the Mound they couldn't open the barrier some ancient wizard had set around them, but they could *almost* breach it. The combined strength of hundreds of spiders could loosen the mesh of wizardry enough that occasionally they could draw a victim into their world. Then—

The spiders rushed awkwardly forward. Their great legs

weren't made for walking on the ground, so the creatures jerked and stumbled as they jostled one another. They were mad with the need for blood. The few victims cowering below weren't enough to slake the thirst of one of the giants, let alone all of them.

Ilna looked up at the barrier where the sky should be, then again into the valley. She couldn't see the sheep in the maelstrom of fat bodies and long, hairy legs, but two of the largest spiders had risen belly to belly onto their hind legs, struggling for the shepherd's corpse. The frail old body was already flaccid, but the spiders' mandibles chewed on what remained to crush out the last juices.

KILL HER! ordered the black-and-silver monster. SUCK HER BODY DRY!

Spiders who'd missed a share of the three victims below were already climbing the valley sides to reach Ilna on the rock above them. If she went back to where the guide had first displayed the weakness in the barrier, she would see a similar flood of living feculence crawling toward her: huge, colorful bellies dragging, legs like jointed trees feeling their way across the ground.

There was no escape in this world from the spiders' rending, dripping fangs. So—

Ilna seated herself and began to knot her pattern. It was complex, and she doubted whether she'd have time to complete it, but certainty on *that* point could wait on the event.

SUCK ILNA'S BODY DRY! shouted the chorus of minds maddened with bloodlust.

Chapter Twenty-two

Sharina was glad they were going to walk, not ride, to the parley with Count Lerdoc. Though . . .

She smiled at herself. She wasn't a good rider, so the struggle to control her horse would've been something near and common to worry about instead of the formless fears now dancing about her like flies over a sheepfold.

"Your highness . . ." said Attaper. The commander of the Blood Eagles spoke facing Carus with his back to the Blaise army half a mile distant. "I *won't* let you do this! I *must* come with you—at least me if not the whole regiment."

A moment before, Carus had joked with Sharina about whether the Pewle knife would pass unremarked if she wore it in place of one of the pins in her formal coiffeur. With a harshness that didn't seem to come from the same mouth, the king snarled, "Lord Attaper, you're a good man; but if you insist on risking the safety of the kingdom so everything fits your sense of propriety, I'll cut you down where you stand."

"This isn't propriety!" Attaper said. "This is safety, pure and—"

"Milord, I warned—" shouted Carus as he reached for his sword hilt.

The blade came up a finger's breadth from the sheath before Sharina grabbed the king's wrist with both hands. She threw her full weight on Carus' sword arm as though she were working a stiff pump lever. The king's great strength still lifted the sword a hair farther before he relaxed and shot the blade home again.

Lord Lerdain stared as if they'd all gone mad. Sharina suppressed an urge to giggle hysterically. They probably *were* mad to attempt this plan, but what was that balanced against the only chance to save the Isles from chaos?

"Sorry," Carus muttered. He grinned wryly. "I've been saying that a lot. Well, maybe if I'd said it more the first time around, we wouldn't all be where we are now."

"Lord Attaper," Sharina said, stepping back from the man in her brother's body. "Nobody doubts that you're willing to die for your king. Please don't insist on dying *this* way, though. Because you will, you know."

Attaper swallowed hard. His left hand gripped his right with a fierceness that would've broken the bones of a lesser man. "Your highness," he said in a husky whisper. "I was out of line. Forgive me. And may the Lady go with you to this parley, since I cannot."

Carus stepped forward and embraced the chief of his bodyguard. "I'd be honored to have you close my side in any battle, Lord Attaper," he said. "But today I'm making sure there won't be a battle."

He looked at Sharina, then to Lord Lerdain. "Ready to meet your father, boy?" he said.

"Yes sir," Lerdain said. His voice broke; he paused and cleared his throat.

Lerdain wore borrowed clothing, good-quality tunics and a short red cape of fine wool—the latter an officer's garment much fancier than what he'd had when they'd spirited him out of the Blaise camp. His calf-length boots were tooled leather, and the helmet Carus had fitted him with had wings and thunderbolts cast into the bronze. Only the lack of a sword belt distinguished the youth from any young officer in the royal army.

"Let's go, then," the king said. He waved toward the Blaise lines, then stepped forward.

Both armies were drawn up in full array. The Blaise line was longer than that of the royal forces, but it looked like an armed mob compared to the saw-edged weight of the royal ranks.

A cornet blatted an order from the royal line. Sharina and the boy both looked over their shoulders. The phalanx was shifting, each rank advancing while the previous front line countermarched to the rear of the sixteencommand-deep mass. Their pikes waved overhead like a giant grainfield through which serpents slid.

"Just a demonstration," Carus said quietly. "It doesn't mean anything—except it shows they can do it. Will your father understand what *that* means, boy?"

"Yes sir," said Lerdain. "My father is a soldier, sir."

They'd given Lerdain a tour of the royal army during the morning hours, while messengers rode back and forth between the camps to arrange the parley. The boy had been numb with confusion at first, but interest and a genuine aptitude soon brought him around.

"Aye, I'd heard that," Carus said. His voice had a touch of a lilt again, a sign of excitement that made him seem cheerful. "Counted on that, counted on him knowing what a battle would mean. . . ."

He caressed his sword pommel in an eagerness that no one could mistake. Sharina touched her fingertips to the back of the king's hand. "Aye, girl," he said. "I remember."

The ability of the phalanx to march and countermarch in close order meant they had discipline beyond the conception of any troops in the Isles for the past thousand years. Discipline on the parade ground didn't win battles. Five thousand men with the discipline to advance behind eighteen-foot pikes; filling in the places of the men who died in the rank ahead, never slowing, never flinching—*that* won battles.

The only question was whether Lerdoc realized, as his son and Sharina did, that Carus hadn't created an army for the parade ground. If the count misjudged what he saw, he'd learn the truth at pike point; but the Isles wouldn't long survive him.

Two men had set out from the center of the Blaise line. The count, his armor gilded but still functional, was the older template of this boy. His belly sagged beneath his cuirass, and his face was already ruddy with the exercise of walking into the center of no-man's-land, but his left hand kept his scabbard from swinging with an experienced grip.

The man with him was a near giant—seven feet tall and solidly built. He carried a round, ironbound shield broad enough to protect two—as it was meant to do. Bare in his right fist was a sword with a long, hooked blade. The weapon was heavy enough that most men would have gripped it with both hands.

"Lady Sharina?" Lerdain said, leaning forward past Carus so he could meet her eyes. "Why are you coming with us? Instead of your brother's bodyguard, I mean?"

"He doesn't need a bodyguard, milord," Sharina said.

Carus laughed cheerfully. "What *I* need, lad," he said, "is somebody to jump on me when I start to act like a hotheaded fool. I trust Attaper to do many things for me; but not that one, not as quickly as the lady will."

He laughed again. "I've only once been in a place my sword couldn't cut me out of," he continued. "But a lot of those places, it was my sword that put me there to begin with."

They were within easy shout of the count and his bodyguard. The guard stepped in front of Lerdoc and called, "You said bring *one* attendant, but you've brought two!"

He held his great shield out, sheltering the count and not-coincidentally preventing his advance. *Lerdoc's guards aren't any happier about this than the Blood Eagles are,* Sharina thought.

"Father!" Lerdain said.

With a snarl of anger, Count Lerdoc shoved the shield

aside and stumped forward. He was alone for an instant before the guard got his balance and sprinted to catch up. The guard's face was twisted into a silent curse.

Carus, his right hand on the boy's shoulder and Sharina keeping pace to his left, met the count in the middle of the two armies. Carus gave Lerdain a pat, and said, "Go convince your father that you're all right."

The count clasped arms with his son, then stepped aside and glared at Carus. "You don't have any cavalry," he said. His voice was high-pitched with anger, almost like iron squealing. "What if I order my squadrons down on you?"

Carus shrugged. "I'm here to talk, not fight," he said, "just as I told you when we arranged this. If I have to, I can take care of myself and my sister until the skirmishers get within javelin range of your horsemen. Though that won't matter to you, of course."

Lerdoc snorted. "I gave my word," he said, as though that were the last thing to be said on the subject; as perhaps it was. "All right, you want to talk: talk, then!"

Sharina smiled at the huge Blaise armsman who stood beside the count with a furious expression. She hoped both to calm him and to convince him that she was a harmless girl and, therefore, to be disregarded.

Sharina wore the sheathed Pewle knife in the middle of her back, concealed beneath her cloak. If the worst happened, though, she wouldn't draw it: she'd simply grab the guard's sword wrist and hold on like grim death for the instant before the king stabbed through his visor slot.

But nothing like that would happen. . . .

"While Valence my father lives—" Carus said.

"Father by adoption!" Lerdoc said. "You're nothing but a peasant from Haft!"

"While Valence lives . . ." the king continued pleasantly, "he's the King of the Isles. And when he dies, if the Lady has preserved me, I am King of the Isles. You needn't believe I trace my lineage from the rulers of the Old Kingdom, milord, though that's quite true. You *must* believe in my sword and the army I've forged to stretch my sword's reach."

"My men are veterans," Lerdoc snarled. "I'll crush you into the mud unless you surrender now. That's the only thing we have to discuss!"

Still quiet but now with an edge in his voice, Carus said, "There's no one who can overhear us, so let's drop the bluster. It wastes time, and we're short of that. Do you know the wizards who're using you for a pawn? Do you know what Moon Wisdom really is?"

Lerdoc looked uncomfortable. He turned his head to the side as if gazing out to sea, and said, "I'm allied to the Confederacy of the West. If some of my allies have wizards working for them, that's their business."

"You're a pawn," Carus said forcefully. "The worst thing that could happen to you is that you win the battle you came to fight, because then you'd be wearing the yoke of something that isn't human. But you needn't worry about that, because you know full well that my pikemen would carve the heart out of any line you formed against them. . . ."

The king threw his head back and laughed, startling Count Lerdoc and his guard. The boy watched with a look of puzzlement mixed with awe.

"Besides," Carus went on cheerfully, "we're not going to fight, you and I."

"What's your proposal, then," the count said. "Because if you expect me to surrender—"

"Surrender what?" Carus said. "You're the Count of Blaise, my ally and a bulwark of the kingdom against these rebel wizards. We march on Donelle together and call the city to surrender. The mercenaries inside 'll open the gates as soon as they hear there'll be amnesty for everybody but the ones who call themselves Children of the Mistress."

His face was suddenly iron. He said, "*Those* will hang, every one of them."

"What do I get out of this?" the count said. Lerdain's eyes flicked from his to Carus and back again, as though he were watching a game of handball.

"Your life, as a start," the king said softly. "The only thing that has less chance of survival than your army if you face mine is your merchantmen if you try to flee by sea from my warships."

He grinned. "And I'll give you another thing," he said. "I'll make your son my aide."

"What?" said Lerdoc, setting his hand to his sword. His bodyguard lifted his shield so that he could swing it in front of his employer at need. "Take my boy hostage, you mean?"

"Of course he'll be a hostage!" Carus snapped. "But he'll be at my side during every council and meeting of the army command. He'll have a real office, real honor, and if he's as sharp as I think he is, he'll learn real soldiering!"

"You're a boy yourself!" Lerdoc said. "What can you teach Lerdain that I haven't known for thirty years?"

For a moment Sharina thought she'd have to grab Carus again. She couldn't always predict what would ignite the king's volcanic temper, but she'd learned to read the tautness in the face muscles that momentarily preceded the sweep of hand to sword hilt.

Carus caught himself this time. He grinned and in a gentle, rasping voice said, "Let's say that I've been well advised, then, milord."

"Father?" said Lerdain. "The phalanx is—"

"Shut up, boy!" his father said.

"Silence, boy!" Carus said in the same breath.

The two grim leaders faced one another without speaking for a moment. Neither had looked away from the other when they dealt with the interruption.

"Milord," the king said quietly, "you don't need to tell me how dangerous a Blaise armsman is if he gets to close quarters. There's nobody I'd rather have at my back when I went over a city wall or fought through the streets beyond. But your troops won't get closer than pike length to the phalanx, and you know it."

"Pikemen are clumsy," Lerdoc said, but he was arguing for time while his mind weighed the options the king had offered. He looked over his shoulder, reassessing his own troops. "Besides, they've got flanks."

"Which my heavy infantry will hold against anything you throw against them," Carus said, forcefully but not shouting, "for longer than it takes for the phalanx to gut your army and then roll up your line from the middle. And as for clumsy, take a good look at what they're doing now."

"Milord," Sharina said. She thought the two men might shout at her as they'd done the boy, but her they wouldn't silence. She was Princess Sharina of Haft, and she had a right to speak. "We came into your camp and brought out your son—"

She nodded to Lerdain, hugging himself with frustration and embarrassment. A girl waiting tables in a country inn gets used to being bellowed at; the son and heir to a powerful throne does not.

"—to talk peace with you. If we'd wanted simply to end your part in the war, we wouldn't have gone to the *boy's* tent."

"It was the two of *them*, father!" Lerdain burst out. "The prince and princess themselves!"

"You did that?" Lerdoc said to Carus. "And you, girl?"

Sharina nodded. She and the king didn't speak.

"Maybe you've got something to teach me after all," the count said. He sighed and seemed to deflate slightly, like a hog's bladder taken outside in winter. "May the

Lady help me, I *knew* I shouldn't get mixed up with wizards."

Carus clasped arms with the older man. "Let's go to Donelle and cure the mistake," the king said. "And if they *don't* open the gates for us willingly, we'll see how well Blaise armsmen follow their king into the city the hard way, eh?"

"And follow your aide, your highness!" cried Lord Lerdain.

Both the count and his bodyguard gave the boy stricken looks. Carus merely said, "There'll be a time for that, lad. But not, I think, today."

His lifted his face to the sky and boomed his mighty laughter as the armies looked on in wonder.

The sun glinted down into Cashel's eyes. He slitted them, but he didn't want to look away from Tilphosa and Metra even though he couldn't help matters while bound. He wriggled, wishing that he hadn't taken care that his knife fit tightly in its sheath. If he could shake the blade loose, then roll over to pick it up with the hands tied behind his back—

Then the Archai would take the weapon away from him. It was still something to try.

"Did you think you were free, Tilphosa?" the wizard said. "The Mistress guided you here, as surely as She guided me to meet you. She's the Mistress of All; Her web is the whole of present time."

"Not *my* mistress, Metra," Tilphosa said in a tight voice. Her tense arm muscles showed she was struggling against the grip of the two Archai holding her, though neither she nor they moved that Cashel could see. The insect monsters were deceptively strong.

"Your Mistress still, girl," Metra said. "The Mistress of All, whether you choose to believe it or not."

She leaned forward and slipped the ruby ring onto the fourth finger of Tilphosa's left hand. Stepping back, she continued, "You will join Lord Thalemos, as the Mistress planned. And when you do, your rings combined will open the way for Her to return."

Tilphosa clenched and unclenched her fist, trying to work the jewel onto the underside of her finger so that it didn't catch the light. Metra gestured; one of the Archai straightened the girl's hand again and rotated the ring back to where it had been.

"The next time you do that," the wizard said, "they'll break your fingers. That won't affect the spell, you realize."

Cashel squirmed forward. If he got a little closer, he could swing his legs to knock the Archa holding Tilphosa's left hand off its—

One of the creatures behind Cashel gripped his ankle with the pincer of a forelimb and jerked him back. Cashel felt the tickle of blood starting to run down his heel.

Metra's peal of laughter began discordantly and rose to a cackle just this side of madness. "I've been with the Mistress often since you left," she said. "Every night She comes to me, Tilphosa. I'm very close to Her now."

She laughed again, even more wildly than before. Tilphosa watched warily, relaxing her muscles for the moment.

"Did your Mistress make the ring?" Cashel said. He understood Metra, now. She'd taken the Mistress into her mind, and those who the Gods ride don't stay sane or even human. The wizard might decide to do anything; if Cashel got her talking, it might pull her back toward sanity before a whim told her to cut Tilphosa's throat.

"Not Her," Metra said triumphantly. "The Intercessor Echea fashioned the rings, the ruby and the sapphire."

"The Intercessor serves the Mistress?" Tilphosa said. "I don't believe you!"

Cashel didn't care about the answers to the questions—they wouldn't help him get loose, which was the only thing important—but it sounded like the girl did. Either way, it kept Metra talking.

"The pattern can only exist once in the cosmos, girl," Metra said. "Echea hoped to thwart the Mistress by cutting the gems and concealing them, so that we Children of the Mistress could neither find nor form the pattern ourselves. Echea's own wizardry burned her to a husk, but still the Mistress has succeeded!"

Metra's laughter was as brittle as breaking glass. The Archai stood motionless, watching like statues of waxed bronze. Could they understand what the wizard was saying? Now that he thought about it, Cashel wondered if they even heard human speech.

"Echea drove the Archai out of this city, didn't she?" Tilphosa said. "Echea defeated the Mistress."

"Echea is dead!" Metra shouted. "She's dead, and her descendents will be destroyed! Now, shut your mouth, *lady*, or I'll have your tongue plucked out. You won't bleed to death in the time I need for you to remain alive."

"Do as you please, Metra," the girl said quietly. She seemed calm; completely a lady, completely self-assured even under the present conditions. "I don't know what the future will bring, but I know the past brought your Mistress defeat."

Metra stared at her. The expression Cashel saw flit across the wizard's face was fear, unmistakably fear. Though it was gone as quickly as it appeared, it gave Cashel the hope he'd been lacking for the last while.

Somebody who says things with perfect assurance is convincing even if when you step out from the words you can see that they're not really certain after all. It's hard to get away from that kind of spell, especially if you're trussed like a hen on market day.

Metra's fright proved that her heart knew that the Mistress could fail, whatever her mind let her mouth say. Cashel's world brightened by a considerable degree.

It didn't change what Cashel would do, of course. He didn't seem to be making any progress working at the cords holding him, but he didn't have a better idea right now. He continued to strain and twist, then relax, in hope that he'd feel a change in his bonds. Not yet, but maybe the next time. . . .

Metra took her athame from the satchel which held the tools of her art. She looked at it, then put it back and picked up Cashel's quarterstaff instead. The weight made her frown.

"Iron caps," she said with a tinge of anger as she examined the ferrules. "I believed you at first when you said you weren't a wizard. I should have known better. And only a very powerful wizard can work with iron."

"Your eyes are wide, Metra," Tilphosa said. "Even in this bright sun. Have you drugged yourself so you don't have to see the truth?"

The wizard didn't appear to be listening. She began to draw in the courtyard's soft silt with Cashel's staff, making symbols in a circle around Tilphosa.

"Or aren't you really there anymore, is that it?" Tilphosa said, her voice rising with anger. "Is it the Mistress speaking through your body? Your God doesn't care if She leaves you blind after She's done with you!"

Metra dropped the staff without looking where it fell. Even so it was too far away for Cashel to reach, unfortunately. He couldn't have grabbed it anyway, tied as he was, but it would've been good at least to touch the hickory.

Tilphosa glanced down at Cashel. She was emotionally taut and breathing hard. Cashel smiled.

He was proud of his companion: she wasn't giving up even the least little bit. They'd get out of this, he figured;

and if they didn't, well, Garric and the others would take care of things.

Metra gave Cashel a cruel smile. "Your staff was the perfect tool to form the words of power," she said. "You've been a great help to the Mistress."

She giggled uncontrollably, closing her eyes in her delight. When the fit passed she grinned at Cashel again, and added, "Your sister is named Ilna, isn't she?"

Cashel kept his face impassive.

"Yes, Ilna," Metra went on. "The Mistress told me. Your sister is aiding the Mistress in Her works just as you are."

Cashel felt his face growing red. He said nothing, but he strained his arms and legs against each other, trying to snap the cords that joined them. They cut him, but that wouldn't have mattered if he could've felt even a little movement in his bonds.

Metra took a pair of flasks made from sturgeon's bladder from her satchel. They were closed with wooden plugs and tendon overties; she undid the ties and poured pinches of glittering powder from each into the symbols she'd drawn in a circle around Tilphosa. One flask seemed to hold blue vitriol, but the other crystals were the color of cinnabar.

Tilphosa watched with a look of sneering disgust. Though she wasn't bound, the Archai gripped her by both wrist and ankle, holding her as securely as if she'd been nailed to a broad plank.

The sun was at zenith. Metra looked toward it without even trying to shade her eyes. Cashel winced, though the wizard didn't seem to be affected by the blinding glare.

"The time is come," Metra said in a tone of reverent wonder. She didn't seem to be speaking to anyone, even to herself. She tossed down the flasks without bothering to stopper them over the remaining contents.

Cashel expected the wizard either to pick up his quarterstaff or to take out her own athame. Instead Metra raised her arms straight in the air, and cried, "*Noma para sarapamon!*"

A spark of red light snapped from Tilphosa's ring and touched the powdered contents. The crystals flared up fiercer than the sun, dual coils of red and blue wrapping around one another. The twisting column rose higher than the stone walls of the courtyard, waking fresh glints from the tiny ruby.

The blaze thinned, then swelled fiercely again like a great artery pulsing as a heartbeat. "*Pseriphtha misontaik thooth,*" Metra chanted.

Something bellowed in the swamp. There was a splash and a second bellow, this time closer. It sounded to Cashel like the call of a seawolf, the great marine lizards which had sometimes come ashore to snatch sheep from his flock.

Seawolves lived in the salt sea, not the fresh waters of rivers and swamps like those this city had risen from. There must be something similar here, though.

"*Phokensepseu,*" said the wizard, "*erektathous phokentatou!*"

The first flare was beginning to die down. The powder in a deep-dug symbol on the other side of Tilphosa blazed in turn, throbbing in the same rhythm.

"*Ptolema ptolemes origines . . .*" Metra said.

Water spouted high enough that Cashel could see the column above the walls surrounding him. An Archa, or perhaps only the head and torso of an Archa, was caught in it. The screaming roar of some great reptile choked off in blood, though the swamp continued to quiver.

The creature hadn't been powerful enough to penetrate the circle of the city's defenders. Cashel had no reason to trust the Intercessor and his allies, but right at the moment he'd have been willing to give the fellow a try.

He twisted against the ropes. Tilphosa was straining also. It was worth a try. . . .

A third word of power burst into flame as the wizard chanted. The first had sunk to spluttering embers, and the second was a pale ghost of its full glory.

The facets of Tilphosa's ring flashed brighter than reflections should have been in full daylight. They threw a pattern onto the air itself: at first like gnats circling, then more fiercely and spreading into an oval.

Metra was forming a door into another place. Cashel didn't see any way to stop her, but he was pretty sure that somebody'd better do that—and he was closer than other people.

The powder in a fourth word ignited, this time on the side closest Cashel. He braced himself to roll over the flames. An Archa tugged him back with the same brutal efficiency as before; he hadn't even had a chance to move.

"Thiatcha thotho achaipho!" Metra screamed. She staggered with the effort of climaxing her spell. The powder in the three remaining words roared up simultaneously.

Unexpectedly, the Archai holding Tilphosa released the girl. She fell into Cashel when the grip she'd been struggling against no longer held her.

"It's done," Metra said in a wondering voice. She looked at Cashel and Tilphosa. "I didn't even need your blood, stranger. I thought that was why the Mistress had sent you here, but that wasn't the reason after all."

"Nobody sent me here," Cashel said tightly. "Tilphosa, take my knife out and cut me loose."

Metra blinked and rubbed her eyes. She seemed none the worse for looking into the sun, but the power that had ridden her during the past hour had now released her.

"It doesn't matter what you do," Metra said calmly. The wizard's emotions seemed to have burned to ash along with the powder she'd poured into the words drawn in the silt. "Your ring can only close the portal from the other side, Tilphosa; and there the Mistress waits to enter Her kingdom."

Tilphosa tugged Cashel's knife from its sheath of wood battens wrapped and tensioned with rawhide. She sawed the cord tying his hands to his feet, deliberately ignoring Metra and the lens of light forming in the air behind her. Cashel straightened thankfully, then held still for the girl to hack through the bonds holding his wrists.

The Archai didn't interfere. The whole vast crowd of them was staring at the portal as it slowly clarified.

Metra began to laugh. Cashel thought she was having another attack of hysterics; and perhaps it was, but the laughter turned suddenly to tears.

"She is Queen of the World!" the wizard cried. "Her time is come again! Nothing can change Her will!"

The cords broke. Cashel swung his arms forward and flexed them; his wrists were slick with blood.

"Give me the knife!" he said in a husky voice. He'd waited patiently while he had to; now that he could move again, the emotions pumping through his blood threatened to take him over. "I'll get my ankles."

Metra's portal was an oval of solid light above the words of power. Vague shapes moved on the other side. Though it was noonday in the risen city, it was brighter still in the world Tilphosa's ring had opened.

Cashel's knife was a rural blacksmith's product, not a piece of fine cutlery. The iron blade sharpened easily and took a keen edge, but this rope's tough fibers had dulled it. Cashel set his knife carefully, then pulled until he'd severed the tight bonds.

For a moment he thought the blade would snap instead. He'd already frayed the cord, so he'd have finished breaking free by main strength if he'd had to.

Cashel stood, taking deep breaths as he looked for his quarterstaff. He was dizzy from straining against the ropes for so long. The tags of cord still dangled from his bloody wrists and ankles, but they wouldn't get in his way.

"Cashel, look at this," Tilphosa said, her voice rising. She knelt in the soft dirt and stared at the hole opening in the fabric of this world. "Look!"

Cashel hadn't been paying much attention to the portal. He glanced at it, slitting his eyes against the glare. A barrier remained between the worlds, though it was becoming thinner, like a puddle in the sun. On the other side were three figures, reptilian though seemingly boneless.

They were slender but very tall. One held a girl in its tentacle; she looked like a poppet in a child's hand. That creature and its companions had pierced her with their spiked tongues and were rasping out the victim's juices like woodpeckers sharing a grub.

"Is that your Mistress, wizard?" Cashel asked.

He picked up his staff, rolling it through the skirt of his tunic to clean off the dirt. The hickory was smoothed by years of his palms' touch and polished with his body oils. Its touch made him feel at home again.

The assembled Archai keened like the winter wind across chimney pots. Those on top of the wall vanished suddenly, leaping down to scramble through the maze of streets leading away.

The Archai inside the courtyard turned as one and struggled in chittering fury to flee. Warriors jammed the many doorways, hacking at one another in their desperation to escape. The courtyard cleared suddenly; two twitching bodies and a severed forelimb remained on the trampled silt.

Tilphosa rose to her feet. "Metra, what are they?" she said.

Metra stared at the portal; it was clearing as it expanded. Her mouth drooped open, and she seemed to be trying to point with her left hand, but she couldn't get words out.

Tilphosa slapped her hard. "What are they?" she shouted.

"The Pack are loose," Metra said. "The way between the Mistress and this world is open, but the Pack are loose!"

Metra sat down hard, as though her legs could no longer support her. She began to laugh hysterically.

"Loose!" she shrieked. "All life, everywhere in the cosmos, *doomed*! We took the Pack from their cell, but now they're loose!"

The portal continued to expand. Cashel wondered how big it would finally become. Big enough to let the Pack through, he guessed.

Cashel spun his staff out at his right side, then overhead. He started with simple circles, then drew figure eights. He didn't feel the fatigue and stiffness of being tied anymore, and the itching pain where his skin had rubbed off was only a faint memory.

"Metra," Cashel said hoarsely, "how do we close this hole you made?"

The wizard held her sides as she laughed, rocking back and forth. Tilphosa bent and cocked her hand for another slap.

Metra's face cleared. Perfectly lucid and in a tone of cold malevolence, she said, "Shine your ring on the portal from the other side, girl. That's all. It will shrink and close as it's expanding now. Except that the Pack will suck you dry before they devour all the rest of us!"

Tilphosa straightened and looked at Cashel. "Will you guard me?" she said simply.

"Sure," said Cashel. "As long as I can."

The portal was transparent in the center, though the edges had a milky tinge like the membrane inside the shell of a hard-boiled egg. Both the clear portion and the border expanded slowly, like water pooling on a flat surface.

Tilphosa put her hand out to the hole; her flesh passed through unaffected. The creatures on the other side watched; only their tongues moved.

The girl took a deep breath and poised. Cashel stepped between her and the portal. "Guess I'll go first," he said.

He clambered through. The translucent edge had a spongy feeling, but the clear center was plenty big enough for his body.

The sun here was a hammer. The ground was a stony waste with no sign of life or water. He heard Tilphosa's breath catch as she followed him.

The Pack, swaying like monstrous willow trees, glided toward them on short, fat legs.

As they came, the one holding their first victim tossed the emptied body away.

Ilna's fingers knotted cords with a swift ease that kept her calm. For as far down the valley as her eyes could see, giant spiders were leaving their webs and walking toward her. Their spindly legs and cautious pace reminded her of cripples on crutches.

DRINK HER BLOOD. SUCK HER DRY.

Of course, in these numbers even cripples could kill her. She smiled. It was as good an expression as any to wear as you prepared for death.

Ilna looked over her shoulder, just in case the giants behind her had mounted their side of the dome more quickly than those she'd just watching killing the sheep and shepherd. She found that she wanted to face her slayer rather than feel the sudden icy shock of fangs driving into her body from behind.

Was that pride, bragging that she wasn't afraid? Well, there wasn't anybody here to blame her for pride.

Ilna *was* afraid, of course. Not of death, exactly, but while being torn apart by fangs dripping amber poison might be quick, it certainly wouldn't be clean or painless.

She'd failed in her mission for Tenoctris—and for Garric. That was a worse pain still, but it too would end with her death.

Some might say she'd failed the Isles, the kingdom. Ilna had never met a kingdom, so she didn't know. She understood friendship, though, and duty.

DRAIN HER TO A HUSK!

Ilna's fingers wove and knotted, adding cords to a pattern already more complex than anything she'd attempted in the past. Above Ilna the barrier shifted as her fingers moved; and with every change, another layer became clear in her mind.

The spiders picked their way toward her. Ilna frowned. She knew the creatures were clumsy on the ground, but she'd seen them stagger toward their victims a few minutes before. They were awkward, but because of their size and long legs they nonetheless moved as fast as a horse could run. Now . . .

For a moment Ilna thought the spiders were afraid of her. Her patterns could stun, could kill. Spiders whose skills were second only to hers would understand that— but they would also know that their size and numbers could overwhelm her.

Besides, they could see that she wasn't weaving a weapon. They *knew* Ilna was tearing an escape route between their world and the wider cosmos.

SHE MUST NOT ESCAPE! the chorus shrilled; and at last Ilna understood.

For a moment her fingers paused. Oh, the spiders knew what Ilna was doing, all right: she was about to achieve the thing which they in the ages of their exile had never been able to do.

She was going to show these monsters the way back to the world from which some ancient wizard had barred them. The way to Ilna's own world.

Ilna looked up at the barrier. The eyes of her soul

showed her the final pattern, the path for which she'd been searching.

Yes, of course. I was right to trust Her craftsmanship.

Ilna's fingers gathered and knotted, making the last adjustments to her linked cords. Above her the milky barrier cleared in response.

A needlepoint of white light flashed on the hillside before Ilna. It spread jaggedly, a tear racing through the fabric separating the spider world from the greater cosmos.

SHE HAS OPENED THE WAY!

Ilna could close the gap again, but that wouldn't matter. The spiders couldn't create the pattern, but they could duplicate it now that they had seen Ilna's masterpiece.

SHE HAS OPENED THE WAY!

The giants stumbled up the slope, maddened by the thought of the warm blood that waited on the other side to slake their age-long thirst. Ilna thought of the future of webs and monsters she'd glimpsed in the Intercessor's mind. She understood now what he feared.

Ilna stepped through the opening as giant spiders staggered toward her from all sides. She was smiling.

The chamber in which Garric stood had been a burial place for the wealthy and powerful. Three deep niches were cut into either sidewall of an arched vault; in each of them was a sarcophagus of marble or porphyry. The ends of five had floral designs, but the last showed a man in flowing robes gesturing to a crowd which knelt reverently. Behind the central figure, holding a wreath and crescent moon with which to crown him, was a giant spider.

Lord Thalemos followed Garric into the chamber, his hand stretching back to help Vascay. The chieftain's peg didn't grip as well on the slant of crumbling rock as a boot or bare sole.

The three men stared at the delicate carving. "Here's

the wealth Ademos and the others were looking for," Garric said. "Think what carvings this fine would be worth in Valles or Erdin. If you could get them there."

"Would people pay for this?" Thalemos said. "A spider?"

"People will pay for anything," Vascay said, wheezing between his words. "Some people will, boy. After all, it wasn't sand crabs who carved that with their claws."

Metron, sliding and gasping, stumbled into the chamber. His torch waved wildly.

Vascay cursed as the flames whisked close. He touched his javelin point to the wizard's throat. "I've left you alive when maybe I shouldn't have," he said, "but don't push your luck!"

"Lord Thalemos?" Metron said. He steadied the torch, but he gave no other sign that he'd heard Vascay's threat. "Here, take the ring. You have to wear it yourself now."

The wizard held out his left hand with the sapphire on the middle finger. He couldn't pull it off himself because he held the torch in his right, its oily red flames now licking the ceiling. The vault's fresco showed painted webs connecting the moon in the center to the six burial niches. Plaster blackened, and a piece fell off.

"To reach Lady Tilphosa?" the youth said doubtfully. "Is that what you mean?"

"Put the ring on or we'll all die here when the Intercessor comes for us!" Metron said. "It's our only chance!"

Thalemos reached for the ring. Garric watched without expression; he didn't know what the right decision was. He wouldn't interfere with the wizard's direction, but—

He took the torch from Metron's right hand. The wizard resisted momentarily, then gave it up. Garric started down the passageway at the back of the chamber, with Vascay following him closely.

The passage had been used for burials, but in a much more economical fashion than the vault. Instead of niches large enough for a sarcophagus, the deep slots cut in the soft rock here were barely big enough to hold the corpse itself in a winding sheet. The passage was so narrow that Vascay had to walk sideways. To fit bodies into these six-high banks, they must have been bent at the waist and fed through like hawsers being coiled in a ship's hold.

"It's a good place to defend," Vascay observed.

"Echeon would dig down through the roof," Metron called from the end of the line. His voice echoed among graves which the ages had emptied. "He'll know where we are. We must go farther."

Garric continued forward, his sword in his right hand and the torch before him in his left. The passage sloped steeply downward. There were no frescoes in this portion of the catacombs, but prayers and eight-pointed stars scratched in the rock showed that the poor were as pious as their betters.

Even in death they were segregated, though. It was the way of the world, he supposed.

Garric stepped into another large chamber, this one circular and domed instead of being roofed with a barrel vault. From the end of the passage, a flight of seven steps led down to a tessellated pavement. Engaged columns carved from the living rock ornamented the walls; medallions were painted in the spaces between them. An arched doorway led off from the other side.

Garric paused only a moment at the head of the stairs before stepping down to the sunken pavement. The scuff of his bare feet was syncopated by the thump/*tap* of Vascay's boot and peg behind him. Lord Thalemos followed a moment later.

"Yes, that's right!" Metron said. "Thalemos, stand in the center. Move yourself, boy! How long do you think we have?"

Garric turned to eye his companions for the first time since entering the passage of the dead. The wizard had shown a febrile liveliness since his incantations on the cliff's edge. Now he put a hand forward as if to hasten Thalemos with a push.

Garric thought of Ademos, gurgling his life out on the cliff's edge so that more monsters could rise from the sea. "No!" he said. "Don't touch him!"

He raised his sword and strode back toward the steps. "No! by the Shepherd," Garric said. "Thalemos, come here. Wizard, leave us. If you come near this boy again, I'll kill you!"

"We'll go out the other way," Vascay said, stumping past Garric and Thalemos. He held the javelin poised to throw in his right hand.

Metron drew the bloody athame from his sash but remained where he was, midway down the stone stairs. Garric watched him for a moment, then turned to follow Vascay.

"Master Gar?" Thalemos said. "I can take the light to free your hands. Ah, if you'd like?"

"Right," said Garric, grateful but a little irritated not to have thought of that himself without the youth suggesting it. He turned, and as he did so the pattern on the floor caught his eye. He paused, lifting the torch to illuminate the whole area.

From the top of the steps Garric had thought the flooring of stone chips was laid in the matrix randomly. From his present angle these few feet lower, he saw that the polished gray tesserae formed a subtle pattern of radial lines with circular lines crossing them. Spaced at intervals—

"The floor's a spiderweb," Garric said. "There's words in the Old Script around the center. The whole room's been prepared for a wizard's spell."

"Then let's get out, shall we?" Vascay said, his voice loud with tension. His words echoed sullenly from the dome.

Garric handed the torch to Thalemos. His movement

shook a bead of sap from the burning wood onto his wrist; it stabbed like a stiletto, causing him almost to drop the torch instead of passing it.

Vascay looked over his shoulder. "Hey!" he shouted, cocking the javelin to throw. Garric turned to see what the threat was. "Sister take that wizard!"

"*Aphre nemous nothii . . .*" Metron chanted. Using the step for a dais, he gestured with the bloody athame. "*Baphre neou nothii. . . .*"

Torchlight touched Thalemos' ring, waking the sapphire into blue fire. The facets flung brilliant reflections around the walls and dome. Garric's body turned to ice; he could neither move nor speak, though his senses seemed unnaturally acute, and his skin prickled.

"*Lari . . .*" called the wizard. "*Kriphii kriphiae kriphis!*"

The walls blurred into a smooth spinning expanse of blue. The floor was fading, becoming a tunnel that stretched toward infinite distance; overhead was the night sky of some other time. The three men stood like flies trapped on the web-marked stone. The wizard above them chanted triumphantly, "*Phirke rali thonoumene!*"

Garric felt the ground beneath his feet give way. In a rush of gravel and powdered rock, he tumbled into a vaster room a dozen feet below the first. He could move again, but he'd lost his sword and couldn't breathe for the dust. He tugged the front of his tunic over his mouth and sucked air through the cloth.

Vascay had fallen at the same time Garric did. Lord Thalemos had been standing in the center of the upper chamber; he was still there, supported by a pillar rising from the floor of this lower one. The wizardlight was gone, so the only illumination was from the youth's torch flaring through the dust clouds.

"She is come!" Metron shrieked ecstatically. "The Mistress is come into Her kingdom!"

Vascay stumbled over to Garric, breathing through his

sleeve. The fall had broken his javelin, but he still held the half of the shaft with the point.

"I'll lift you," he said in a muffled voice. "We'll heap stones up at the far end, and then I'll lift you."

Garric nodded, his lungs on fire. He couldn't get enough air through his thick tunic. He had to restrain himself from gasping in an unfiltered breath that would suffocate him.

Vascay started toward the mass piled against the wall opposite where Metron stood. Garric followed, feeling the rock shift under his bare feet. *No piece of the previous floor bigger than a walnut remained, so why did it mound so high there in front of them? The dust and gravel should have slipped—*

The mass moved. It was alive, if barely.

"Vascay!" Garric shouted. He was too late. Four huge, hairy legs traced a pattern in the air. Garric had seen Ilna's quickly knotted cords paralyze men bent on murder; now a similar power bound his body in bonds of fire.

"She is come!" Metron repeated.

The dust had settled. Thalemos was locked into a statue on his pedestal, gripped by the same compulsion as held Garric and Vascay. The torch in his hand lighted the scene below. The column under him shielded the wizard from the creature's spell.

The legs shifted the rhythm of their movement slightly. Vascay dropped the javelin. His body stepped forward, controlled by a will not his own.

The thing was a spider, huge beyond nightmare. Millennia of imprisonment left it desiccated, but still it lived. For ages it had spoken in dreams; and when the protecting walls of rock and wizardry had ruptured, it moved.

The Mistress was calling the first of many meals to herself. When she had finished with the victims brought to her chamber here, she would return to the upper world and to lordship over all other life. She was not a god, for all that Metron and the others who lived her dreams thought otherwise, but her mastery over anyone who saw her conferred godlike power.

Vascay walked toward the waiting jaws like a man already dead. The eight eyes glittering in the torchlight watched him. If extended, the Mistress's legs could have spanned Palace Square in Carcosa, where thousands had gathered to listen to the monarchs of the Old Kingdom. Now the limbs were crabbed close together, leaving only enough space for the victim they pulled toward them by their quivering power.

Vascay stepped between the legs. When he could no longer see the pattern they drew, he shouted and managed to half turn before the Mistress sank her fangs in his back. His body stiffened.

The spider's mandibles pumped up and down alternately; a fang stabbed out through the tunic over Vascay's ribs, withdrew, and then penetrated him again a hand's breadth higher than the first time. A drop of venom, orange in the torchlight, dripped to the floor. Powdered rock hissed and steamed.

Garric watched Vascay's body empty like a slashed wineskin. Only when venom had wholly liquified the muscles did the frozen limbs collapse and the head loll forward. Vascay's features had blurred into shadows on the skin, but his skull still kept its shape.

The Mistress flung aside the carcase of her first victim. Her forelegs played the same silent tune but with a greater verve, nourished for the first time in thousands of years. Garric felt his right leg move.

He'd have held it back if he could, but his body was no longer his own. Compulsion pulled like white-hot wires. A step, then a second step.

The waiting mandibles throbbed slowly, up and down. They weren't part of the spider's pattern but rather a sign of her bloodlust. Her hind legs extended with the creaking care of ancient machines beginning to work again.

Garric's right leg took another step. The broken javelin rolled under his foot. His left leg started to move.

Lord Thalemos screamed; reflex hurled the torch from his hand. It shed sparks in an arc that ended when it went out in the dust. Thalemos slapped at the sleeve of his tunic, burning where a drop of blazing sap had fallen onto the cloth. The chamber was again in total darkness.

Garric picked up the javelin. He couldn't see for the Mistress to bind him, but her location was etched onto his mind. He lunged forward.

She wasn't a god. She wasn't immortal. And though there'd be no one to write his epitaph, Garric knew he was about to die a man and for Mankind.

His outstretched left hand touched the right mandible, just above the fang. The spider's hair was as coarse as the bristles of a boar's spine.

The forelegs gripped him from behind. As the mandibles reached for him, Garric stabbed between them—up through the Mistress's mouth and into her brain.

The giant spider's convulsions drove her fangs home. In the midst of the burst of fire that devoured all his nerves, Garric felt the poison-spewing points grate against one another in the middle of his torso.

Then all was blackness.

Chapter Twenty-three

Ilna stepped through the passage she'd opened, into another universe as tightly encysted as the world of the spiders' exile behind her. Sunlight blasted her, glaring from a point in the pale sky and reflected from the bare, rocky soil.

Alecto's corpse lay at her feet. The flaccid skin had no shape but that of the bones it draped, but Ilna recognized the ivory pins still decorating the spill of lustrous black hair.

Alecto's bronze athame glinted some distance away. The wild girl had run for the last time from the danger her anger had called to life.

The Pack turned their heads to view Ilna. Their movements were like those of water or perhaps smoke, a drifting smoothness that seemed to lack volition.

Ilna stepped forward. "You'll feast well today!" she called, bravado in her voice, and in her hands the knotted fabric with which she'd rent the wall between worlds.

She smiled coldly. She'd created a masterpiece in the truest sense, a work which could be fully appreciated by only herself and the One whose craft had formed the fabric of which each universe was a part. To a degree the spiders could understand what Ilna'd done, but their appreciation would be tempered by other emotions.

For a time. For the time remaining to them.

The first spider through the opening was the black-and-silver giant. That was as Ilna expected, and as it should be. The others were allowing their leader to accept the reward she so richly deserved for the plan she had made.

The brilliant sunlight must have blinded the spider's lidless eyes for a moment before they could adapt. When the giant saw what glided toward her and the gap beyond, her mental scream was as shrill as rock shearing. She staggered back, clambering over the bodies of her sisters who packed the hillside leading to the doom of their race.

"Ilna!" called Cashel. He stood partway round the circuit of this world from her. The Pack were confined to a mere bead on the fabric of the cosmos, smaller even than the world which held the great spiders; but like the spiders, they had windows of sorts that allowed them to interact with the greater universe. "Get around behind me! I'll do what I can!"

Ilna gestured toward the gap with her left hand, letting the fabric dangle from her right. She smiled at the Pack. She knew their tentacles would snatch her when they chose, no matter where she stood within the strait confines of their cell. She appreciated her brother's offer, but his strength and courage couldn't bring safety.

Besides, Ilna probably wouldn't have scuttled like a roach caught in the light even if she *had* thought it could save her life. Life had never been that important to her.

The Pack slid toward her. Their size was deceptive— one moment mountainous, the next no more than three slender poplar trees which nonetheless towered above her. She wondered if the Pack had physical bodies at all. In looking up into their faces, Ilna thought she glimpsed worlds of ice and crystal, each as real as Barca's Hamlet had been to her as a young girl.

Was the Pack triple or did her eyes see a single being in three aspects, none of them material in the sense that humans understood matter?

The girl behind Cashel raised her left arm to the white sun. The ruby on her finger sent fire from each facet, painting the otherwise-unseen boundaries of this cyst in the cosmos. It woke lambent flames beyond anything natural light could cause.

The leading member of the Pack leaned over Ilna—and bowed, and passed on through the passage she had torn for them to a larder that could last for ages if they husbanded their bounty.

The second bowed and also entered the world where terrified spiders fled in vain for their lives; then the third. The cell which had held the Pack was now empty, save for three human beings and the empty body of a fourth.

Unknotting her fabric, Ilna walked toward Cashel and the girl. The ruby shimmer fell on her and around her, seeming to pass through Cashel's braced body as easily as it did empty air. Frowning, Ilna turned to look over her shoulder. The gap she'd opened was starting to close.

On the other side, in the world of vegetation and spiders, the Pack ravened like wolves in a sheepfold. The body of the spiders' leader lay just inside the opening; the breeze ruffled the empty black-and-silver shell. A line of similar husks was scattered down the hillside. The Pack could stretch their enjoyment when victims like Alecto were scarce, but abundance drove it wild with bloodlust.

Ilna smiled without humor. And the Pack had spared her. In gratitude? Or did they think at some future time she would release them again to drown a world in slaughter?

She put the hank of loose cords to her sleeve. She might need the cords again, and perhaps she would need the Pack again someday also. The fabric of the universe was too subtle for even Ilna to read its pattern completely.

Cashel stopped spinning his staff and planted it before him. He took a deep breath. "I'm glad you came to rescue us, Ilna," he said. "Because I don't mind telling you, I didn't see any way *I* was going to keep those things back from me and Tilphosa."

The girl, Tilphosa presumably, nodded tightly. She kept her ring raised to the sun. The portals continued to close, the one Ilna had opened and also the one by which she and Cashel must have entered this place.

"Is she a wizard?" Ilna asked, with less warmth perhaps than she'd have shown if Tilphosa didn't seem to think that her trick with the ring was somehow special. Didn't she realize that Ilna could've closed the portal as easily as she'd opened it?

"No, she's just a lady who's been travelling with me," Cashel said. He turned. "Tilphosa, this is my sister Ilna."

Ilna glanced through the hole which slowly closed in back of her companions. On the other side was a city whose stones still dripped with the mud of a swamp.

A lizard covered with bony scutes waddled into view, shouldering massive walls into ruin whenever the way narrowed or twisted sharply. A black-robed woman turned but stumbled in exhaustion as she tried to flee.

The lizard's long jaws slammed on the woman. It jerked its head upward, flinging the victim up to fall back into the waiting maw. Her right arm spun separately, severed by the first crushing impact. The opening winked completely shut.

"Now," Ilna said, "we need to get out of . . ."

As she spoke, the world around her began to go dark. It was only as Ilna fell forward that she realized the dimness was in her eyes, not the sun searing down from above.

Tearing a hole in the cosmos hadn't been easy, of course, even for Ilna os-Kenset. Her last thought before her mind shrank to a point and went black was, *"But it never matters what the task costs, so long as I do it . . ."*

"I want you both to stay well back, now," Carus said to Tenoctris and Sharina as they entered the siege lines around Donelle together. "An archer on that gate tower can double the range he'd get on the flat."

The Blood Eagles marched before and behind Carus and the two women; the section under Attaper immediately about them were mounted, as were the score of aides and couriers who followed closely. Tenoctris, who couldn't very well have walked from the fleet encampment on her own feet, turned out to be an able rider.

That was a bit of a surprise in someone so devoted to scholarship, though Sharina knew it shouldn't have been. Tenoctris' father was a noble. He'd kept up his standards, though the horses may have eaten as well as the family on occasion.

The old wizard sniffed. "Precisely how will my death

harm the Isles worse than yours, your highness?" she said. "And you're planning to go right out under the walls!"

Behind the earthworks and mantlets, Lord Waldron and his officers waited to greet the prince and the returning army. The line of march stretched back to the fleet, even though Carus had left a strengthened garrison with the ships. Tenoctris had warned of danger out of the water, though she couldn't be more precise despite her desperate efforts with an onyx scrying bowl.

"Well, I have to," Carus muttered. "Anyway, there's not much risk when the garrison sees Count Lerdoc's army is with us. Mercenaries have to be willing to die, but that doesn't mean they want to!"

"Yes," Tenoctris said. "And I need to get to the Temple of Our Lady of the Moon whether it's dangerous or not. The risk of a stray arrow isn't nearly as serious as what will happen if we don't hurry."

The Blaise army had been slower to fall into marching order than the disciplined royal troops, so for the most part it followed the royal army. Count Lerdoc himself led the battalion which immediately followed the Blood Eagles in the order of march, however; his lion banner waved in the van. No one on the walls could miss the fact that the force investing Donelle was now twice the size of the royal army alone, nor that there was no chance of outside allies rescuing the city.

Sharina leaned closer to the old woman to speak without being overheard. "Tenoctris, are you feeling all right?" she asked. "You seem—"

"Snappish" was the word that suggested itself. The tendency was common in others, but Tenoctris was a model of gentle humility at most times.

"—worried," Sharina finished. She'd also been raised to be tactful and pleasant.

Tenoctris laughed, suddenly her normal self again. "Dear, I'm quite terrified," she said simply. "For some time I've been sure that these Children of the Mistress don't understand the forces they've put in motion. Now that I'm sensing what it is behind them, using them like game counters, I'm . . . Well, whatever it is, it hasn't the kingdom's good at heart, and I don't imagine that it's thinking of humanity's good either."

Lord Waldron must have started shifting his artillery as soon as the courier informed him of the king's plan. He'd placed in front of Donelle's main gate all the catapults and ballistae he could move in the available time; the remainder of the heavy weapons were on the way also, hunching along the circuit of the walls on carts and sledges drawn by men as well as draft animals. The old noble knew he couldn't prevent his monarch from exposing himself, but he intended to make the risk to an archer in Donelle obvious.

Sharina helped Tenoctris dismount behind the mantlets. Lord Waldron used his position as army commander to greet Carus alone. He didn't try to force his way past the king's guards, but none of his subordinates stepped forward with him.

"Your highness!" Waldron called between the shields of two Blood Eagles. "I've made what preparations I could, but I don't think—"

"On the contrary, milord," Carus said, tapping the guards unwillingly aside, "you've thought things through very well. But it's still me who has to go out there."

Taking off his helmet, he added, "They need to know who's offering them their lives. Now, shift one of these mantlets so that I can get through."

The pulleys which moved the city gate began to squeal. Both heavy leaves lurched open, hand's breadth by hand's breadth each time the men at the capstans took a step. Mercenaries tossed their shields from the gate towers and began to shout. It was a moment before they fell into unison so that Sharina could hear, "We surrender!"

"By the Lady!" Carus said. "It seems it'll take even less to convince them than I'd thought!"

He shoved his way between mantlets which troops had just started to move. Sharina, slimmer and at least as quick, slipped through also before Attaper shouted, "Hey! Don't let her—"

The dozen men coming out the city gate were mostly common soldiers, though a pair of officers in gilded breastplates followed at the end of the delegation. They didn't carry shields or spears, and several had taken off their sword belts as well.

A burly soldier stepped ahead of his fellows to kneel before Carus and Sharina. "Your highness," he said, his face close to the ground, "I'd say, 'Give us terms,' but I'll tell you the truth—"

He looked up, his scarred face twisted in fear and misery.

"—the only thing we really care about is our lives. And if you execute us anyway, well, at least we're out of that hellpit inside the walls!"

"What I planned to offer was to enroll you in the royal army if you'd surrender the city," Carus said cheerfully. "You've already performed your part of the bargain, so you don't need to worry about me keeping mine. But what is it you're so determined to get away from?"

Squads of Blood Eagles were double-timing through the gap they'd torn in the siege works and taking position between the king and the mercenaries. Though they didn't pick up the kneeling spokesman and hurl him back to a safe distance, Attaper and a junior officer planted their legs so close on either side of the man's head that he looked as though he were crawling through a dense thicket.

"They've grabbed up a child," the mercenary said. He hadn't exactly relaxed, but he rose from prostrate to a kneeling position. "We figure they're going to sacrifice her in their temple. It's not like we're a bunch of saints, but—"

"I don't want any part of killing kids like a goose for a feast day," said another soldier. His words were slurred because the same old wound that scarred his cheek had taken out the teeth on the left side of his jaw. "And I *sure* don't want any part of whatever they plan to call up by killing kids!"

There was a general mutter of agreement. Some of it came from the Blood Eagles nearby.

"That's what I was afraid of," said Tenoctris. Sharina jumped. Tenoctris had hobbled up behind her, unnoticed in the noise of heavily armed troops pounding into the clear area around the city walls.

Tenoctris went on, "The spell's been in place for hundreds of years, maybe for millennia. All that remains is to feed it with blood now that the planets are in conjunction. We *must* stop it."

The Blood Eagles, Carus' staff, and the first battalion of Count Lerdoc's forces, came through the siege lines. As they did so, more mercenaries began to pour out of the city. The Blood Eagles were disarming those who hadn't left their weapons behind, but nothing worse than a few harsh commands and complaints passed between the mingling armies.

"Aye, we must," said Carus, drawing his sword. "Which I'd say about any wizards who think to work blood magic in reach of my blade—whatever their purpose for it!"

Raising his blade as a standard, he bellowed, "Lord Waldron, deploy the phalanx at all the gates. Nobody leaves the city till I'm sure we've dealt with all the wizards, the Children. Blood Eagles, skirmishers, and heavy infantry in that order—with me to the temple, where we'll put a stop to whatever's going on!"

Carus pointed to the mercenaries' spokesman. "You're our guide," he went on. "Now!"

The soldier got to his feet. If he had qualms about returning to the city he'd just escaped, he didn't show them.

"Right!" he said as he turned. He paused only to hand Attaper the dagger still in his belt sheath; he'd left his sword, the most expensive part of a soldier's equipment, behind in the city.

"I need to be as close as possible!" Tenoctris cried. Carus and the black-armored bodyguards advancing to the gate ignored her.

Sharina bent, taking Tenoctris' left arm over her shoulders and gripping the wizard around the waist with her right arm. It'd be easier if Cashel were here, but Sharina's own strength had never failed her when she needed to accomplish something.

"I'll help you, Tenoctris," she said. "Just do what you can, and we'll get there!"

Sharina trotted forward, her long legs easily matching the pace of men in armor. The old wizard was an awkward burden, but her weight wasn't a problem yet. It might be later, especially since the temple was on the highest ground in Donelle, but they'd manage.

Cashel was where he was needed. Sharina had to believe that, and it had always been true in the past.

But she needed Cashel very badly herself just now, less for the strength of his arms than his strength of character. Cashel was solid as nothing else in Sharina's world was solid. She supposed Cashel could be worn down, though she'd never seen anything she thought was capable of doing that.

But he wouldn't break. Ever.

The streets of Donelle were eerily empty. The clashing hobnails and rattling equipment of running soldiers echoed because there was none of the usual city noise to blur and dampen it. Ahead of Sharina and Tenoctris were most of the Blood Eagles, with Carus and Attaper in *their* lead. Behind followed the rest of the army with the exception of the phalanx, whose long pikes were useless and dangerous in street fighting.

Not that there was any fighting yet, or any sign of a fight brewing.

The mercenary was taking them by a main street, but it twisted frequently and was never more than twenty feet wide. At an intersection, a well curb blocked half the pavement. The troops shouldered one another and snarled curses.

"Go around to the right!" Sharina ordered the armored men to either side of her and the wizard. "Don't let anybody step on us!"

"Right," said the brawny veteran beside Tenoctris. To the troops crowding him he bawled, "Room for the ladies, curse you!"

Sharina wasn't sure he recognized them, but she'd spoken with authority. When men don't know what's going on—and only the section with Carus at the head of the guard regiment *did* have any idea of what was happening—there's nothing they want more than somebody to tell them what to do.

Sharina opened her mouth to breathe more freely. Tenoctris was a weight on her arm, and though Sharina wore sandals with heavy soles, the shock of her feet against the cobblestones was sure to raise bruises by the morning.

Tenoctris gasped with each stride, her eyes open and her mouth staring. Sharina was taking her weight, but the effort of keeping her legs under her was a great one for the old woman. Occasionally she stumbled, but never did she fail to catch herself before Sharina had to pick her up.

A cat watched from a rooftop, then vanished silently as the troops hammered past. It was the only animal Sharina had seen since they entered the walls. Hunger would have bitten quickly in a city which had been packed with the whole population of the district even before the start of the siege.

The troops came out onto the avenue around the base of the steep hill at the heart of Donelle: the Citadel when the community was founded, but Our Lady's Mount during the past centuries of relative peace throughout the Isles. Though this street was no wider than the one the army had been following, the buildings on the other side straggled up the slope instead of forming a solid wall.

For the first time, Sharina had a good view of the temple. She gasped. The grounds and the sparsely wooded hillside below were crawling with people: sitting on walls and roofs, packing the street that led up to the temple, and clinging to the trunks and branches of trees.

Sharina had never seen so many human beings gathered in one place. It reminded her of termites swarming in spring as a new colony prepared to take wing. The crowd chanted, but its very numbers turned the words into a threatening rumble like distant thunder.

King Carus had paused to assess the situation. The route to the temple was blocked by the vast number of civilians praying to their Mistress. Carus gave an order to the troops nearest to him. They locked shields, braced their spears in their right hands, and prepared to advance.

"Sharina!" Tenoctris cried, her voice clear despite the effort it must take the old woman even to breathe after their run through the city. "Stop the king! Don't let them start killing now or it'll be as bad as the sacrifice the Children intend! The spell feeds on blood, and it doesn't matter whose blood it is!"

Sharina heard the urgency in her friend's voice. She let go of her and sprinted forward. Tenoctris swayed but didn't fall; that didn't matter now.

An armored man couldn't have moved against the press of other armored men. Sharina could and did, slipping through any gap and using her considerable slim strength to shove aside troops who didn't expect to be pushed from behind that way.

King Carus raised his sword, preparing to give the signal for the butchery he considered an unfortunate necessity. He wasn't a cruel man, but he must have been a hard one even before decades of campaigning inured him to slaughter.

Sharina grabbed his wrist from behind as she'd done before, swinging herself around the king's torso to face him. Attaper raised his own blade in furious amazement before he recognized who she was.

"You mustn't!" Sharina said. "No blood, or we'll work the spell ourselves!"

Carus' face cleared from the thunder of the moment before. He shouted, "Shields and spear butts, boys! Shove them out of the way—but no blood!"

Obedient though puzzled, a soldier's usual state, the Blood Eagles reversed their spears and went on. The process was brutal, but it wasn't massacre. The troops advanced, hammering through civilians who chanted and ignored the threat till they were struck down.

Over the chanting came the sound of screams from the temple. The crowd stilled in wonder.

Carus gave a cry like a man stabbed through the heart; he pitched forward. Sharina tried to catch him, but the king's armored body weighed too much. They crashed together onto the cobblestones.

In the temple, the screams grew louder.

Cashel lowered his sister to the ground one-handed. It didn't worry him that she'd collapsed; Cashel knew what wizardry cost, and the thing Ilna did with her weaving was no less wizardry than the words and symbols Tenoctris drew on the ground.

She weighed almost nothing, though. Ilna had never been big, but whatever she'd been through since last he saw her in Valles had worn her to a frame of skin and bones holding up her tunics.

The ruby flared as bright as a crimson sun itself. Tilphosa screamed.

Cashel looked over his shoulder as he rose. "Put it down!" he said. The blazing jewel hurt his eyes to look at. Discomfort made him speak louder than he'd otherwise have done. "Don't let the sun fall on it!"

The walls of the cyst flowed like water over rocks, showing distorted images of what lay beyond. Cashel saw worlds he recognized and worlds he hoped would never be.

"Cashel, I can't move it!" Tilphosa said. She sounded more angry than frightened, but some of both. "I can't move my arm!"

Across the fiery barrier a feathered wizard looked up from its circle of power. It pointed a human thighbone at Cashel's face. Cashel raised his quarterstaff, but the image had blurred into a rocky glen with no animal life before either Cashel or the other acted further.

Cashel cupped his big left hand over Tilphosa's and the ring. His palm exploded in pain worse than the time a gadfly stabbed him in the back of the neck.

Cashel would've said that pain didn't control what he did—but *this* pain was different. If he'd had to stand it, maybe he could have . . . but here he had the choice of snatching his hand away. Cashel's body did that, and his mind couldn't force it not to.

Tilphosa grimaced with anger and frustration. She kept trying to tug her arm down—knowing she couldn't, just the way she'd known she couldn't get away from the Archai who'd held her, but trying anyhow.

"Metra told us that Echea made the ring," she said. "She must have meant this to happen, but I don't know what!"

"It's all right," Cashel said, flexing his hand and finding the hurt was gone as soon as he'd taken it away from the ruby. It'd felt like molten rock boring through him, but there wasn't a mark on his callused palm. He took his staff in both hands, and added, "If it's taking us someplace else, well, we'll handle that."

A nearby patch of the flame-drenched boundary began to clear. Cashel adjusted his stance, ready to act if the lizard they'd seen devouring Metra waited on the other side. Instead they were in a cave lit only by the sunlight pouring from the opening through which Cashel peered.

A young man stood on a pillar of rock. Water foamed about him, rising visibly by the moment. One wall of the cave had collapsed, and the sea was rushing to fill the cavity. Debris swirled on the current: driftwood, seaweed, and a huge mass that Cashel took at first for fabric but which was hairy skin of some sort when it passed directly beneath his vantage point. Trash rolled to the surface, then tumbled under again to reappear farther along the sweeping curve.

The youth had been looking to all sides with the set expression of one who was badly frightened but determined not to show it. When light flooded the cave, he looked up and met Cashel's eyes with desperate hope.

Cashel could hear the roar of the incoming sea, so he figured the stranger could hear him too. He thrust out his staff, gripping the butt with his right hand while his left braced him against the wall of this miniature world.

"Right!" he shouted. The far end of the staff was well short of the pillar, but the fellow might be able ... "Jump for it and I'll pull you in. Jump!"

There was a passage along the wall of the cave to the right. As Cashel shouted, a man in a tattered robe like Metra's came running down it. He stopped at the brink, his eyes and mouth all open with terror.

The youth leaped from the pillar. He caught the end of the staff, though barely, and clung like a barnacle in the surf. He wasn't more than average size, but with seven feet of leverage he dragged down even Cashel's strong arm. He splashed waist deep, but he kept holding on. Cashel started to drag him in.

A figure in bronze armor with the long face of a lizard came down the passage behind the man who wavered on the edge. The lizardman raised his curved sword to strike. The human gave a despairing cry and jumped into the water, striking for Cashel.

Aided by the current he just might have made it, but just as he leaped the tentlike flaccid mass rolled to the surface . . . and rolled under again, taking the swimmer with it. The man's scream ended in a froth of bubbles, indistinguishable from the sea's own dirty foam.

The youth climbed the staff as Cashel pulled. When he was close enough, Cashel leaned back and jerked like he was landing a tuna.

The fellow flopped onto the sun-struck, rocky soil. Seawater sloshed and steamed from his wet robes. His feet, one bare and the other wearing a slipper of embroidered leather, still dangled above the rising water.

"Cashel, I can move!" Tilphosa cried. She and Ilna both grabbed the stranger's hands and pulled him farther in. The ruby on Tilphosa's hand touched the sapphire the youth was wearing. A spark, brighter and whiter than the sun of this place, sprang from the paired jewels.

Tilphosa cried out. The world began to fade, the ground becoming as transparent as the sky and the sun's substance melting away. Another world took shape around them.

Ilna rose from her knees and looked at the scene with which they were about to merge. "That's Merota!" she said. If a voice could have a real edge, throats would be spewing blood. "In the temple in Donelle!"

The noose Ilna'd worn about her waist flowed through her hands smoothly as cream floats on rich milk. She'd overcome the exhaustion that'd struck her down a few minutes before, but Cashel had seen axe blades with softer lines than the angles of his sister's face right now.

Cashel looked out at a large room packed with people except for the long rectangular pool he and his companions hovered over. Those standing at the margin of the pool were cowled priests who wore white-slashed black robes like Metra and the man who'd drowned some moments and worlds apart.

Cashel recognized the priest standing at the head of the pool holding a dagger of green volcanic glass: he was the same fellow who'd tried to take the statue and the ring away in Valles during what seemed now a distant lifetime. He poised the dagger over the throat of the child, whom two of his fellows held for the sacrifice.

Most children would have screamed. Merota, Ilna's ward, waited with a closed mouth and eyes as hard as agates.

Cashel rammed his quarterstaff into the transparent barrier still separating him from the scene he looked out on. Tilphosa and the youth were shouting, and Ilna's expression would have frozen the heart of the sun.

The hickory flexed and the ferrule sparked on nothingness. The staff sprang back, numbing Cashel's hands.

A blade shimmered like sunlight. The priest's head toppled from his severed neck, and the air was full of blood. Another of the robed figures had thrown back his cowl. He held a dagger in his left hand and in his right the long, incurved sword with which he'd beheaded the priest.

He was Chalcus, and as he spun, slashing and stabbing, the walls confining Cashel and his companions dissolved completely. They plunged into a pool of salt water seething with fresh blood and the spastic motions of dying priests.

Cashel bellowed when his feet didn't touch bottom in what he'd thought was shallow water. He grabbed the marble coping with his left hand and pulled himself out, his strength multiplied by the thought of drowning.

Chalcus turned like a dancer. Cashel put his staff up to block the stroke, but the sailor had already switched his aim to a priest whose scream ended in a gout of bright blood from mouth and nostrils. Chalcus was as sure amid slaughter as a trout in the rapids.

The worshippers who filled the big room were trying to get away. There was no place to flee, but Chalcus' blades and the staff in Cashel's hands cleared a space for themselves and their companions.

This wasn't a time for finesse. Cashel struck great, sweeping blows, knowing that whoever the hickory touched would go down. The survivors were howling.

The pool boiled like a surf-swept shore. A figure came out of the bloody water, an Archa whose forelimbs hacked at the nearest worshippers even before its legs and middle limbs had lifted it clear of the pool.

More Archai followed. The midday sun shone through the eye in the center of the domed ceiling. Cashel crushed the head of the insect warrior who slashed at Tilphosa, but its fellows lurched into the crowd of worshippers. They were too surprised and terrified to resist.

"The Mistress is dead!" a priestess screamed. "The Archai will slay all mankind!"

If she'd planned to say more, the saw-edged forelimbs chopping into her back overruled her. There was blood everywhere: in the air and roiling water, and wetting the floor like roof tiles in a thunderstorm.

Chalcus cut a path toward the chamber's rear wall. There was no way out, but at least there'd be safety in one direction. Cashel brought up the rear of the party, occasionally batting a terrified human away but more often smashing Archai limbs and torsos.

Ilna's noose snagged a warrior. As she pulled it toward her, Tilphosa stabbed through the Archa's neck with the athame of some priest now sprawled in death. The youth from the cavern didn't have a weapon, but he held Merota tight as they climbed over twisting bodies which would have tripped a child's legs.

The insects were turning the great room into a slaughterhouse, and still more crawled from the pool in the center.

"*They'll slay all mankind!*" someone cried, or perhaps it was only an echo in Cashel's mind.

Maybe. But he and the friends about him would take some killing yet.

His left hand rubbed gritty cobblestones; his right was wrapped around the hilt of his sword. The sun beat on the back of his neck, and around him everybody in the *world* was gabbling like a flock of frightened chickens—Duzi fly away with them!

He opened his eyes. He was Garric or-Reise. He'd just died in the darkness of a tomb—

"*Welcome home, lad,*" said the voice of the ancestor smiling in his mind. "*Tenoctris says they need us in the temple there, now or a little sooner than that. We're not to slaughter people, but I've never been one to tarry.*"

"Your highness!" Attaper was shouting. "What's the matter? Are you—"

Garric got to his knees; hands lifted him with the desperate haste of bodyguards afraid of having failed the one they were sworn to protect.

"I slipped!" Garric said. "Let's get into that temple and put a stop to whatever Moon Wisdom is planning to do!"

He *had* slipped, after all. He vividly remembered falling backward into darkness as the Mistress's venom coursed through his body. Though the body was that of a boy named Gar. . . .

"Garric, the sacrifice is already complete," Tenoctris called. Two brawny Blood Eagles shoved their way through their fellows, each supporting the old wizard by an axter. "But the Archai mustn't be allowed to spread out from the building. Every human death will summon more of them!"

"Don't kill any people!" Garric bellowed. "But there'll be bugs a-plenty for our swords!"

He started up the hill lithely. His new body—his *own* body—didn't have the bone-deep legacy of hunger and abuse that brain-damaged Gar's did. He was supple and in balance; no stronger than the near-Garric whose form he'd inhabited, but healthy and far more at peace with his flesh.

Lord Attaper clamped his hand on Garric's right shoulder, holding him back a half step. The leading rank of eight Blood Eagles closed in front of them.

When the screams started, the civilians on the hill below had stopped chanting. Those at the back of the crowd turned and noticed the approaching army. Some tried to run, but the hill was so steep that there were as many stairs as ramps on the road to the top. There was no way to get off the pavement without the danger of a long fall.

That wasn't Garric's problem or the Blood Eagles'. The troops used their spear butts as clubs and their shields as battering rams, slamming civilians down or aside. Those who fell on the roadway were trampled or kicked over the side. The troops weren't deliberately cruel, but there was a job to be done. The broken bones of hostile strangers didn't concern them.

The civilians who'd climbed trees or found outcrops on the slopes beside the road began to flee also. The screams had broken the spell that had held a city chanting, and the feeling that replaced it was one of panic. People didn't know what they were running from, but they knew they had to run.

From the volume of the shrieks, the folk inside the temple knew very well what the danger was. They didn't seem to be doing much about it, but that was the problem the royal army had arrived to solve. . . .

Spear butts punched and pounded into the civilians who didn't clear the way of their own accord. Most did, scrambling and sliding down the hill. Some didn't even try to ease their route but simply leaped with their eyes closed, driven to desperation like people trapped on the roof of a burning building. They'd be all right, most of them. Broken limbs, sure; but their fellows inside were facing much worse than that.

"What is it we'll find inside?" Attaper said, shouting into Garric's ear in order to be heard over the din. "Wizards?"

"Maybe wizards," Garric shouted back. "Tenoctris says Archai, bugs that think they're men."

"They'll die like men, anyway," Carus said in Garric's mind.

Garric looked behind him as he mounted the final flight of steps to the temple porch. The army squirmed back to where the city's overhanging roofs hid it, glittering with spearpoints and bronze helmets.

He frowned: a separate column was climbing the south slope, a quarter of the way around Temple Hill from the royal forces. The breeze caught a drooping banner and spread it long enough for Garric to see the lion of Blaise.

"Count Lerdoc's your ally now," Carus said. *"You've made his son your aide. The boy's right behind you in this crush."*

I left the kingdom in good hands, then, Garric thought, half-amused. It'd been bad enough learning to be Gar; now he had to learn to be himself again.

Carus laughed with the joy of a man who had lived to the full when he was alive. He said, *"You left the kingdom in lucky hands, at any rate, lad. And I always told my captains that I'd rather they be lucky than clever."*

The leading soldiers clashed onto the temple porch, their

hobnails sparking on the mosaic of a spider clutching the full moon. The tesserae were harder than the limestone of the ramps and steps below.

The last worshippers inside the temple's sanctum streamed through the bronze doors, their faces pale except for where blood splattered them. All were disheveled, and one middle-aged woman had lost her outer tunic.

The last man down the passage wore priestly robes. "*Kill him!*" Carus ordered in Garric's mind.

Garric wasn't sure what he'd have done if the Blood Eagles had simply knocked the priest out of the way. He'd killed when he had to, but the ease with which Vascay slit a man's throat for expedience was foreign to Garric's nature.

The question didn't arise, because the Archa warrior following the priest caught him in the doorway. The insect's forelimbs chopped down, cutting the neck to the spine in both directions. The priest toppled, his head lolling loose.

The Blood Eagles tried to stop, shocked by the sudden apparition. The man in front of Garric lost his footing. The soldier's legs skidded out in front of him, sending him crashing down on the pavement.

The Archa bent at the joint between thorax and the bulbous abdomen below. A spearpoint glanced off its chitinous chest as the creature slashed at the fallen man's legs. Garric cut off the Archa's head, but its saw-edged forelimbs continued to hack until another spear thrust brought the creature down.

Garric drew his dagger. He leaped the fallen man and the decapitated monster, meeting face on the column of Archai coming up the passage from the sanctum. Attaper and three Blood Eagles were at his side. The warriors made a shrill chirping, so loud as it echoed that the stone walls quivered.

"Leave it to the men, Sister take you!" Attaper shouted,

cutting through the head and half an Archa's thorax with an overhand stroke. Neither he nor Garric carried a shield. "This isn't your job!"

Garric stabbed an Archa through the junction of neck and thorax. It was good to use the straight sword he and Carus had trained with, though the curved blade he'd taken from Ceto had served well enough. His steel grated into the chitin, crushing it like eggshell.

Pale ichor gushed, but the warrior's forelimbs hacked at him anyway. Garric blocked the right with his dagger, but the left arm clanged on his helmet's earpiece, then the shoulder plate of his cuirass. The saw teeth scarred the bronze, and the weight of the blow brought Garric to his knees. His arm was numb, and he wondered if the creature had broken his collarbone.

Attaper sheared off the forelimb and cut deeply into the insect's thorax. It fell sideways. Garric stood, dragged his blade free, and lurched forward again.

Carus wouldn't have let others fight this battle even if Garric had wanted to. The king, tortured every night since he'd taken Garric's place, grinned with a white rage that wouldn't be denied its offered revenge.

But Garric had his own nightmares to appease. He remembered Metron screaming at him while Tint's bones crunched in the serpent's throat. . . . Killing Archai wouldn't give the beastgirl her life back any more than killing the serpent had; but it was something he *could* do, to help cushion the memory of the thing he could not change.

The soldier to Garric's left went down. Another man took his place and fell immediately. The Blood Eagles had never fought the Archai before. They hadn't learned as Carus had in past ages that the insect warriors were much easier to kill than they were to stop.

When the Archai fell, they continued to slash at the soldiers' legs below the studded aprons. A wounded Archa could be more dangerous than one still standing at shield height.

Garric struck the warrior in front of him, then jumped and was saved by a reflex his ancient ancestor had honed. A toothed limb whistled beneath him, the dying stroke of an Archa with a spearpoint all the way through its thorax.

Garric blocked a cut with his sword, brought the ball pommel of his dagger down in a hammerblow on a triangular skull, and then kicked. His hobnails and the thick leather sole of his boot took the stroke that would otherwise have severed his leg. His foot went cold to the ankle, but he could still walk on it.

"There's no room in the world for these and men both!" Carus shouted in his mind. *"They had their time. They will not have ours!"*

Garric took another step. He was out of the passage, into the huge domed vault of the sanctum. For an instant, he and the three soldiers with him faced a score of slashing warriors.

Two men went down. A limb smashed Garric's helmet, breaking the chin strap so that the rim slipped half over his eyes. He struck left and right by instinct, feeling his blades cut deep. Blood Eagles pushed past; Attaper dragged him back against the wall beside the passageway.

Garric gasped, bent forward to draw another breath, and would've toppled onto his face if he hadn't stuck his dagger point down onto the floor to brace him like a steel cane. His cuirass constricted him; he couldn't breathe as deeply as he needed to. A wave of dizzy nausea swept through his body . . . and passed as it always did, as it had many times before when he'd worked in the pride of his strength beyond what mere bones and muscles were meant to stand.

"Are you all right, your highness?" Attaper gasped. Like Garric, he was bracing his buttocks against the wall behind him. Soldiers crowded excitedly into the sanctum, their shields raised.

"They're forcing the bugs back," Carus observed critically, *"but they shouldn't be taking so many casualties. Archai are sword work, not for spears."*

Both Garric's arms and the front of his cuirass were covered with the insects' purplish ichor. It smelled like sour wine and made his skin prickle. When he moved, the dried slime pulled hairs from his arms like a coating of glue.

"I'm all right," Garric muttered to Attaper. He straightened to give himself a better view of the battle. "I should've told the troops to leave their spears outside and go in with swords. Holes in these bugs don't put them down quick enough."

As he spoke, a spear flew from the oculus in the center of the dome. He looked up. The heads of a squad of Blaise armsmen peered down from the thirty-foot opening. One knelt on the edge as Garric watched. He flung a spear and took another handed him by a comrade out of sight.

"Sister take the fools!" Attaper fumed. "They'll be hitting our boys if they keep that up! They're a hundred and fifty feet up!"

A yard-square piece of gilt bronze sailed through the oculus: the soldiers on the roof were tearing off the metal sheathing for missiles. From the way the sheet fluttered, it could have been cloth—but it clanged like a dropped anvil when it hit.

"Hey!" cried a voice from above. "There's people holding out on the back wall!"

"If it's the priests who started this," said Attaper, "the bugs can save us the trouble of killing them. Not that I'd mind the trouble."

"It can't be priests," said Carus, his expression in Garric's mind sharp with surmise. *"Priests wouldn't have survived this!"*

"Hold me!" said Garric, no longer conscious of fatigue. He rammed his sword home in its sheath and used Attaper's shoulder to lift his body, his right foot braced at waist height against the wall. The molding there was very slight, but the marble lip gave his hobnails purchase.

The vault was as wide as it was high, or at least it was too close to tell the difference without a chain. A seething mass of Archai was climbing out of the pool. On the opposite side of them was a wall of warrior bodies, spreading as more Archai climbed to the top and died there.

Even raised a few feet from the floor, Garric couldn't see who was on the other side of the mounded corpses. But—

An Archa reached the top; a quarterstaff slammed it at the junction of thorax and abdomen, breaking off a leg. Garric only knew one man *that* strong.

He dropped to the mosaic floor, drawing his sword again. He knew what he had to do.

"*Let me handle it, lad,*" said the voice in his mind. The king sounded detached and very certain. "*This is a thing I've done before.*"

Then go, thought Garric, surrendering his body to his ancient ancestor. He watched like a man whose horse has taken the bit in its teeth. *Save them, whatever it costs.*

The incoming troops had expanded their hold on the sanctum into an arc wide enough for a dozen men to stand abreast. They fought until they fell and were replaced by fresh troops coming through the passage. The weight of the armored soldiers pushed the Archai back, but the twin forelimbs and suicidal tenacity of the insect warriors made them terrible opponents in a close-quarter fight like this one. The mosaic pavement was slick with blood as well as ichor.

Carus raised his ichor-smeared blade in the air like an oriflamme. "Follow me!" he shouted. He leaped through a space between two Blood Eagles—Garric hadn't believed there *was* a space until it was behind them—and into a wall of Archai milling like ants from a dug-up nest.

Even watching like a spectator at a handball match, Garric couldn't fully understand what happened next. Carus moved like a dancer, using his dagger and the pommel of his sword rather than the blade.

The Archai were quick with their chopping forelimbs; Carus was quicker yet, quicker than thought. He took strokes as he gave them, but even there the king's instinct to duck or turn put his armor under the living blades.

The hammerblows on Garric's helmet and breastplate dented the bronze, but chitin swords weren't dense enough to pierce metal. Some of the strokes were as hard as the one that'd stunned Garric a few minutes before, but Carus operated on a plane in which his whole being was subordinated to the task he'd set himself before beginning.

Like a dancer, Garric thought again; but in Carus' wake lay a swath of twitching bodies as broad as a man's two arms could reach. The air about the king was a fog of ichor and blood, slung in droplets from steel blades and saw teeth.

"Blood Eagles to me!" Attaper roared as he followed Carus into the sudden gap. "Guard your prince or be ready to fall on your swords!"

What had been a battle turned into a sporting event of unbelievable savagery. The bodyguards slashed their way forward, no longer protecting themselves. Their only concern was to keep up with the king and their commander—

And they did keep up, more or less, sweeping their blades into the Archai with the same careless abandon that the insects showed. The insect warriors went down with heads, limbs, even their bodies severed. Men went down also; but not as many as in the opening minutes of the battle when instead of merely killing they'd tried also to protect themselves against unfamiliar dangers . . . and failed in both desires, as often as not.

More troops tramped into the sanctum. Regular infantry and even a few Blaise armsmen mixed with the last of the bodyguard regiment. The king's advance across the floor had opened space for the human army to use its greater numbers, though Archai continued to clamber out of the central pool. The water was murky with blood.

A section of sidewall crashed inward with a cloud of shattered concrete. Iron cast into tight-curled horns to resemble a ram's head poked into the sanctum, then withdrew to smash the hole bigger. Lord Waldron had brought one of the battering rams of the siege train up with his leading battalions.

A good man, Waldron, for all his hot temper and stiff-necked pride in his noble lineage. A flawed man but one who had few equals . . . much like Carus himself.

The king reached the mound of Archai bodies. All Carus saw as he climbed with crunching hobnails were targets and threats, but Garric watching through the same eyes had a better view of the battle than he'd gotten during his brief glimpse from the wall molding.

The troops pouring through the hole they'd battered in the sidewall were dismounted cavalrymen from the regiments of Northern Ornifal; Lord Waldron himself was at their head. There were more men than insect warriors in the sanctum, now.

A huge chunk of the dome fell inward, raggedly doubling the size of the oculus. It carried with it two of the Blaise soldiers who'd chopped it away as a more effective missile than the spears they'd exhausted. Half fell in the bloody pool, crushing several of the Archai who were just climbing out. The creatures still appeared, but in nothing like the numbers they had when the Mistress's plans were being fed by the one-sided slaughter of the civilians she'd gathered as sacrificial animals.

Carus beheaded an Archa atop the mound of bodies. At the same instant, Chalcus' curved blade severed both oddly jointed ankles and Cashel smashed its chest. Purple slime smeared the quarterstaff so thickly that its ferrules were indistinguishable from the hickory pole.

"*We're done, lad!*" King Carus shouted in Garric's mind. "*But by the Lady, so are the bugs!*"

It was Garric's body again, but it was slipping away from him. Thalemos—*what was Lord Thalemos doing here?*—dropped the severed Archa forelimb he'd taken for a weapon. He, Ilna, and another girl braced themselves to catch Garric's slumping figure.

"Prince Garric and the Isles!" someone shouted over the chaos.

"Prince Garric and the Isles!" bellowed the army. The shout grew louder with every repetition as the troops outside the building took it up also.

It was the last sound Garric heard before he sank into the blackness of total exhaustion.

Chapter Twenty-four

When Garric sat very still, the sunlight felt good. The sun was well down in the western sky, though, and "very still" meant without swelling his lungs to breathe. None of his wounds was serious, but there wasn't a palm's breadth of his legs which hadn't been covered by his studded leather apron, or of his arms, which didn't have a slash or a puncture. His chest was bruised front and back, and his face was so battered that he looked out through tunnels in swollen flesh.

"Being around your ancestor . . ." Sharina said, smiling at Garric as she spoke, "was a lot like leading a leopard on a chain. It's a very lovely creature with many virtues, but—"

She snuggled against Cashel in a kittenish fashion that Garric had never expected of his sister.

"*You see your sister,*" said Carus, his image grinning as it lounged against a parapet in Garric's mind. "*Speaking as the man she was close as a shadow to this past week— she's a woman, lad, and I'd guess enough woman for any man she chooses.*"

"—it made me even more pleased to have someone whose strength isn't quite so . . . flashy."

Cashel put his arm around her shoulders. He didn't look at Sharina or say anything, just smiled a little broader than he'd been doing. Cashel no longer blushed at times like this, but you wouldn't say he was perfectly comfortable with it either.

Garric had decided it was important for his troops and the populace of Tisamur to see him up and moving, but he didn't have any intention of tending to real business until he'd recuperated for another day yet. He sat on a terrace of the Citadel, looking down over Donelle to the sea beyond. Cashel, Sharina, and Tenoctris were with him; Ilna was welcome to join them if she cared to; and a line of Blood Eagles kept everybody else at a distance.

All of the bodyguards were battered, and several looked as if they must hurt as much as Garric did. A Donelle aristocrat had been insistent about his *need* to see Prince Garric. Two Blood Eagles had hurled him twenty feet back, across the terrace. The fellow was lucky they hadn't tossed him over the railing instead.

At the nearby temple site, another section of wall toppled inward with a crash and a mushroom of debris. Men were shoveling broken stone and concrete into baskets, dumping them into oxcarts on the west side or giving them to porters to carry away by the steep slope to the east.

Only a fraction of the temple's massive sidewalls remained after a day of concentrated effort.

Tenoctris had been watching the work over her shoulder. She turned to her companions, and said, "I'm always amazed at what people can accomplish when they join together."

She grinned, and added, "Not necessarily for good ends, of course. No single wizard could have opened a passage for the Mistress."

Local civilians were carrying out the demolition. Garric had put Count Lerdoc in charge of the work, so there were a few Blaise officers present to oversee the business. They could've stayed in their billets without decreasing the enthusiasm with which the crews worked.

Lord Lerdain was one of the officers—by choice, Garric had no doubt. The youth strutted like a fighting cock, wearing the helmet that'd been hammered when he followed Garric—followed Carus—through the mass of Archai. The boy was lucky he'd been knocked silly at the start of the rush; otherwise, he'd probably have been killed. But he'd paid his dues, and now he displayed the damaged helmet with rightful pride.

Cashel watched with the professional interest of a man who'd done his share of heavy labor. "They're trying to prove to you that they're loyal," he said, looking amused. "They don't know the tricks of moving big rocks, but they're as willing as any folk I've seen. They'll be lucky if they don't kill themselves, though."

"Convincing me they're loyal is pretty much a lost cause," Garric said. His smile was more cynical than it would have been in the days before he became a prince. "What I *do* believe, though, is that Moon Wisdom's as dead as the Children of the Mistress who were leading it."

He nodded toward the workmen. "They're at least making an effort to *seem* loyal."

"The Children weren't leading Moon Wisdom," Tenoctris said, her eyes focused on a place beyond her present surroundings. "They were just its human face."

Garric remembered the blackness of a cave and the hairy limbs, stiff with age but still living, which held him for the Mistress's fangs. "Sure, that's true," he said.

But if any Children had survived the carnage in the temple, he'd have hanged them as soon as the fighting was over. People who gave themselves over to something so unutterably evil had no business walking the Earth in the company of decent folk.

"Those people have their own reasons for tearing the temple down," Carus noted with a grim smile. *"Having their own allies hack hundreds of them apart for a blood sacrifice makes the rule of a king from Valles seem not such a bad thing."*

Another section of wall came down in a crackling roar that almost drowned the screams of the woman who'd been caught in it. Cashel winced.

"I wouldn't bet it was a woman, lad," Carus said, neither smiling nor frowning. *"When they're hurt bad, anybody's likely to sound that way. Even the brave ones, unless they go numb instead."*

A trumpet sounded in one of the squares below. Men shouted in cadence, then stepped off with a clash of hobnails on cobblestones.

Lord Waldron was re-forming his battalions, mixing four companies of the old royal army with two composed of the mercenaries who'd garrisoned Donelle during the rebellion. Most of the organization took place outside the city walls where there was more room, but . . . loyal or not, it was good for the people of Tisamur to see the highly trained royal army up close.

Garric looked at his sister, smiling faintly at how painful the simple movement was. Every muscle of his neck had been strained by the effort of holding his head straight while blows raining on one side or another of his helmet tried to twist it.

"Sharina, does Lord Tadai have things under control?" he asked. "I should've gone to see him myself, but . . ."

It felt remarkably good to sit with his friends. The days he'd been alone seemed like a lifetime . . . as indeed it had been, for Gar.

"When he arrived with the supply fleet, he went straight to the municipal palace," Sharina said, smiling at the memory. "He didn't even bother getting a night's sleep before he and his aides started going over the accounts from both the city and the temple."

"They had accounts?" said Cashel with a frown. "I thought they were wizards."

"Wizards need to eat too," Tenoctris said. "Though for some of us, that's not much of a priority."

"They were running a rebellion," Garric said. "That means messengers, clerks, supply departments—and the mercenaries themselves, to be paid and billeted."

"None of which happens at the wave of an athame," Sharina agreed. "At any rate, I think Lord Tadai takes more pleasure in that sort of thing than he does in wine and dancing girls."

Carus laughed with an amusement that spread to Garric's own lips. As the others looked at him, Garric explained, "I don't imagine going over financial records will ever replace reading Celondre as the way I like to relax. But my ancestor"—he lifted the cord holding the coronation medallion of King Carus to emphasize it—"was never really as much himself during peace as he was in the middle of a battlefield."

"*And I saw more battlefields than I did days of peace, lad,*" the king's spirit agreed. Suddenly sober, he went on, "*I was so afraid that I'd fail you this time, the way I'd failed the kingdom before in my anger and my arrogance.*"

Thanks to your sister and the Lady, I did not do that quite."

"They're blocking the conduit that fed the temple pool?" Tenoctris asked suddenly. She'd been watching the workmen again. "Not that it was the water itself that . . ."

"Yes," said Garric forcefully. "Blocking the tube and diverting the aqueduct that fed it. I told Waldron to get a squadron of cavalry out to trace the route. We'll block the inlet too when we've found it."

"It was salt water," said Sharina. She nodded eastward over the city. "The sea's well below our level here."

"Yes," said Tenoctris. "It is. And Garric, I'm not sure your men are going to find the inlet."

She smiled. "Though I don't think that really matters, because of what your army did here and what you did where you were."

Garric started to nod toward the demolition work; the pain made him dizzy. Smiling ruefully at his weakness, he instead gestured with a hand. That hurt too, but not nearly as much.

"There'll be a new temple built on the site," he said. "A small one."

"To whom will it be dedicated?" Tenoctris said, suddenly tense. "That is, I don't believe . . . I've never believed in the Great Gods; but sites have power."

"Right," said Garric, "and for that reason I plan to build and endow a temple to the Restoring Shepherd. Whatever's built here will be more than stones and frescoes, so I thought it was important to control where it started at least."

Carus chuckled in Garric's mind. Garric, smiling in harmony with his ancestor, went on, "I'd thought of dedicating it to Duzi, but I decided people wouldn't understand."

"Duzi doesn't belong in a big stone temple," Cashel said quietly. "Though I've called on him in worse places than that, I know."

A platoon of Blood Eagles was marching up from the lower city to replace the detachment now guarding Prince Garric. Garric didn't turn to watch them, but Carus cocked his head and smiled. They were keeping step despite most of them being wounded.

A cheerfully whistled tune drew Garric's eyes and those of his companions. The young Lady Merota approached the line of Blood Eagles, flanked on one side by Ilna and the other by Chalcus.

"*So fare you well, my own true love,*" Merota sang, caroling the chorus of the tune Chalcus whistled. "*So fare you well a while. . . .*"

The sailor wasn't wearing his own weapons, but he carried a long silk-wrapped bundle; the guards stiffened at the sight of it. A reflex Garric borrowed from his warrior ancestor made him reach for his sword.

The sword was gone, missing since healers from both the bodyguard regiment and Lord Waldron's staff cut Garric's armor and equipment away in their haste to get at his wounds. Realizing that, Garric relaxed and started to chuckle. That was very bad for his cuts and strains, but the laughter did wonders for his state of mind.

"*I'm goin' away but I'm comin' back. . . .*"

"Let them pass, Captain Lancar," Garric said, glad he remembered the name of the officer in command of the guard detachment.

The captain turned. He was an old soldier, promoted from the ranks because of courage distinguished even in the company of this regiment of chosen men.

"Yes, *all* of them," Garric said. "And Master Chalcus can bring his package through as well."

"No, your highness," Lancar said. "He can't bring the sword he's got in that wrapper any closer than where I stand."

Ilna snapped, "If I didn't know better, I'd say none of you were older than Merota here. But I suppose being a male and being a child are much the same thing."

Merota looked between her guardians instead of finishing the chorus, "*If I go ten thousand miles.*"

Chalcus laughed and handed the packet to Lancar balanced on two fingers of his left hand. "Here you go, captain."

"These three can pass," Lancar said, motioning his men to step aside.

If the captain was concerned about what Garric would do, or about *anything* other than his duty, his stolid face gave no sign of it. He waited for Merota to lead the adults into the guarded area, then walked around Chalcus and gave the package to Garric.

Chalcus grinned past Lancar's shoulder, and said, "Let him be, your highness. He's a good soldier doing his job, and who can have too many of them?"

"Not me," Garric said, struck grim by the thought. "Not now especially. Attaper's interviewing volunteers to fill at least fifty places in the Blood Eagles, and it may well be a hundred and fifty depending on how lucky we are with gangrene."

"How's Attaper himself?" Sharina asked. "Do the healers think they can save his arm?"

"Yes, they will," said Ilna, drawing eyes to her. Lancar himself looked over his shoulder in surprise, then locked his gaze to the front again.

Ilna drew the hank of cords from her sleeve just far enough to acknowledge them.

"I don't often do fortune-telling," she said. Embarrassment turned her voice unusually cold, even for her. "In this case I thought it might help Attaper if I could truthfully tell him he'd not lose the arm, so I checked."

"She wove a pattern for the warehouse where all the wounded are, too!" Merota said. "They're all going to get better!"

Chalcus tousled the girl's hair. "No, child," he said,

"they're not all going to get better. But more will, I think, than otherwise. Though it's not as a healer I speak, but from the other end of the business."

Garric finished unwrapping his sword and dagger. He'd wondered why Ilna hadn't joined him and the others now that things had settled down. There could have been other reasons, but with Ilna you were usually safe in guessing that duty had determined whatever she was doing.

He pulled the sword an inch from the sheath, saw what he expected, and drew it clear. When he held the blade at a slant to the light, a serpent seemed to squirm up and down the layered steel of the blade.

"*As fine a job of sharpening as I myself could've done,*" Carus noted approvingly. "*And a working edge, too; not something razor thin that'll turn or break on armor.*"

"Thank you, Master Chalcus," Garric said, grinning. He slid the blade home again. He didn't notice his pain and stiffness while he handled the sword. "As good a job of sharpening as the finest warrior I know could have done."

"The least I could do for the man who saved our lives, I thought," the sailor said. With a slight extra brightness in his expression, he went on, "I was wondering one thing as I watched the fellow dancing across the battle to us—was that you, your highness, or the friend you share quarters with?"

Garric laughed. "The friend, sailor," he said. "And I was glad to know him that day, for I don't expect I'd have done as well at the task."

Chalcus nodded pleasantly. "Aye," he said. "You're a brisk lad and very quick for your size; I'd not choose to fight you. But your friend, now—if I couldn't stab him in the back, I'd lay my sword down and hope for mercy. And I say that knowing the hope would be very slight indeed."

He and Garric both laughed, and in Garric's mind, the laughing king said, "*But don't be fooled, lad—he wouldn't want to face me, but face me he would. And we'd neither of us be quite sure of the outcome.*"

The sailor cleared his throat. He looked around the circle, deliberately meeting the eyes of each of the others before saying, "It may be that you think Lady Merota would not have been offered for sacrifice had I not failed my duty to her—"

"You didn't fail, Chalcus!" the child said. "You rescued me!"

"—and you would be right," Chalcus continued. He showed his embarrassment only by the unusual precision of the words; his voice had none of the usual music in it. "I came back from the docks to the room we'd taken at an inn. The child was gone, and everyone there pretended they'd never seen her at all."

"One of the men who took me was a priest!" Merota said proudly. "I could tell from his robes. I cut him with the knife Chalcus gave me!"

"Aye," said Chalcus softly, "and later I cut him worse myself and took his robe, when I'd convinced the innkeeper that he was wiser to fear me than to fear the Mistress. But all that took time; and when I got to where they were holding milady, there was very little time left. Still, I thought since I was there I'd give them reason to wish they'd picked a different victim."

"We can't control results," Ilna said without emotion. "We can only control our own actions."

She looked at Chalcus, and went on, "But if I could have controlled the result, it would have been the same as what occurred."

"Oh," murmured Cashel. He gave Sharina an extra squeeze with his arm and rose gracefully to his feet, holding the quarterstaff close to his body. "That's Tilphosa coming. I'll go . . ."

"And Lord Thalemos," Garric said. "Earl Thalemos now that I've confirmed him as ruler of Laut. He's my old comrade in arms, though he probably doesn't know that."

He looked at Cashel. Sharina was standing now also; her expression was one of ladylike chill. Ilna watched Thalemos and the girl with disinterested assessment, while the grin on Chalcus' face indicated he saw the same thing Garric did but was amused by it.

Well, it wasn't Chalcus' sister and closest friend who were in the middle of this tension.

"Ah," said Garric. "I'll of course pass them through, Cashel, but if you'd rather talk to them privately, that's—"

"We'll talk with them here, I think," Sharina said. Garric had heard winter gales that sounded warmer.

Cashel shrugged, looking more resigned than perturbed. "Sure," he said quietly. "If that's all right with you, Garric."

"Let the Earl of Laut and his lady through, Lancar," Garric said. Even Tenoctris was standing now. He thought about rising from the stone bench, but when he'd tensed his muscles enough to realize what it would cost him, he changed his mind. In a few more minutes, perhaps . . .

Thalemos and Tilphosa were dressed in a style suitable to their station during private functions: overtunics embroidered in gold and silver thread, cutwork sandals of dyed leather. On Thalemos' chest was a gorget knotted from cloth of gold, a placeholder for the ancient regalia of his office which there hadn't been time to cast.

Tilphosa gave Sharina a queenly glance. Thalemos bowed, then stared at Garric in surprise before saying, "Your highness, I, ah . . . did you have a brother on Laut, by any chance?"

"He wasn't my brother," said Garric, "and that was a thousand years in the future besides; but I know who you mean, yes. May the Shepherd guard his soul."

"Yes," Thalemos said. "Ah, I'm honored that you've confirmed me as ruler of Laut, but . . ."

"My chief of staff Lord Tadai will provide some personnel," Garric said, "and Chancellor Royhas in the capital will second some of his clerks shortly as well. You'll have two battalions of the royal army besides, though I don't expect you'll have real problems. The Intercessor, Echeus, died recently—"

Carus chuckled in his mind.

"—and there's been no one in charge since then."

"Yes, ah . . ." said Thalemos. "Your highness, what I actually came to ask . . ."

His voice trailed off and he looked at the girl beside him—Tilphosa bos-Pholial, Garric knew, though he hadn't seen the lady before this moment.

"Your highness," Lady Tilphosa said, "you'll find Laut a loyal bastion of your kingdom henceforth. We have one further favor to ask of you, however: in addition to the troops and staff you've offered, will you send Master Cashel or-Kenset with us? I know by experience that Master Cashel is a sturdier support than any number of soldiers."

Thalemos looked at Garric and tried to smile. He wasn't very successful. Garric knew from his life as Gar that Thalemos was a brave boy; but Tilphosa was very much a lady, not a girl.

So, of course, was Sharina.

Garric cleared his throat, and said, "Milady, I'm not in the habit of telling my friends what to do. Cashel's free to come and go as he pleases. If he—"

"I don't," Cashel said. He didn't look relaxed, exactly, but neither did he look like anything short of an earthquake was going to move him from where he stood. His left hand was on his staff, and Sharina's left hand was on his shoulder.

He nodded to Thalemos and went on, "Mistress—Tilphosa, I mean . . . I said I'd get you to your Prince Thalemos of Laut if I could. That's where you are, near enough. And I'm where I belong too, back with Sharina and my friends."

Tilphosa said nothing for a moment. Then, unexpectedly, she made a deep curtsy to Sharina. Rising, she said, "Milady, I hope you know what you have."

To Garric she continued, "Your highness, I thank you again for your trust and support. You will not find it misplaced."

She turned and strode quickly out of the guarded circle. Thalemos followed, a little awkwardly because Tilphosa's sudden movement had taken him by surprise. He looked greatly relieved.

"An interesting girl," mused Carus. *"Back when I wore flesh, I might have found better use for her than sending her to warm a throne in Laut."*

Fortunately, Garric added in the silence of his mind, *your descendent is more focused on the provision of able leadership for the separate islands of his kingdom.*

Carus laughed in his mind. *"Fortunate indeed, lad,"* he agreed.

Sharina watched Thalemos and Tilphosa go, then looked at her brother. "That's Laut," she said, her voice a little sharper, a little more challenging than usual. "And from what I've seen here, it appears that Count Lerdoc will have no difficulty in ordering matters on Tisamur. What about the other rebels?"

Garric shrugged and wished he hadn't. "I'm planning to make a progress of Cordin and Haft," he said, "putting loyal rulers in place. As soon as I can walk without a pair of canes, that is."

"Will they fight, do you think?" asked Chalcus, the lilt back in his voice. He didn't sound precisely hopeful; rather, he was interested the way one male dog becomes when another walks nearby.

"They're fools if they do," said Garric. "Which, of course, many men are, so I'll be accompanied by as many troops as I brought here to Tisamur; though the mix will be different. It's a good chance to integrate the new companies into their battalions."

Tenoctris had seated herself again, but his younger friends remained standing. After glancing in the direction whence Tilphosa had disappeared, Sharina asked, "Where are you finding the new leaders, Garric?"

"The Tyrant of Cordin ousted the marquis five years ago, Tadai tells me," Garric said. "We're reinstating a nephew of the late marquis, under the guardianship of Tadai's brother-in-law. Here on Tisamur, the Council of Elders will resume the government, with Count Lerdoc's cousin as their liaison with Valles."

"What about Haft, though?" Sharina pressed. "What about our home?"

Garric laughed. "Barca's Hamlet never had much to do with the palace in Carcosa, did we?" he said. "I doubt that will change much, at least at first. Formally the island will be ruled from Valles under a nephew of Lord Waldron as Vicar. I'm giving him an advisor, however; not a local man, exactly, but he lived on Haft for a long time, and I can trust him."

"You're making our *father* the real ruler of Haft?" Sharina said in amazement. Garric smiled and nodded.

"Yes," said Ilna while the others stood silent. "Reise is a very trustworthy man. Carcosa won't warm to him, but I think it will learn to obey."

Cashel laughed loudly. He hugged Sharina, then stepped to Garric and clasped arms with him. Garric braced himself for the pain, but Cashel more than most men knew how to be gentle; he'd have broken other people's bones all his life if he hadn't learned that.

"He'll meet us in Carcosa," Garric amplified as his friend swung away again. "I'm looking forward to that."

Garric looked in the direction Thalemos had gone. "Tenoctris," he said, "Lord Thalemos comes from the future—but in *his* past, Prince Garric died battling the Count of Blaise and waves of Archai conquered all the Isles except for Laut. *His* past never existed."

Tenoctris pursed her lips. Ilna said in the silence, "Events that aren't on the same thread may be knotted together, Garric. The remainder of their length is separate. Which is just as well in this case."

"Tilphosa thought that the Intercessor Echea planned it all," said Cashel. He shrugged deliberately, working the muscles of his shoulders; his hickory staff gleamed softly from its careful polishing with raw wool rich in lanolin. "That she knew everything that would happen when she made the rings."

"Tilphosa is wrong," Ilna said, her tone coldly analytical. Garric suspected Ilna didn't like Tilphosa—putting Tilphosa in with the majority of humanity—but that wouldn't color her judgment. "The pattern was too complex for any human mind to encompass, let alone plan. The . . ."

She paused, searching for a word. You didn't often see Ilna indecisive, even about phrasing.

"The weaver, let's say, Ilna," Tenoctris said quietly. "That name will do as well as any other."

"The weaver, then," said Ilna with a smile so wry it looked bitter, "of *this* fabric wasn't human. Of that I'm sure."

"I'm not sure there really was an Intercessor Echea," Tenoctris said in the same soft voice as before. "Someone, something, may have walked and talked in the flesh of a person named Echea, but I don't believe the animating force was human."

She smiled and rose. "I think it's time we leave Garric," she said. "It's getting dark, and I suspect I understand better than you younger people how easy it is to become overtired when one isn't in the best condition. Which I haven't been for many, many years."

"Right!" said Cashel, smiling at Sharina. His face sobered, and he said, "Ah, Garric? Want me to carry you to your rooms?"

"I'll stay here for a moment to think, if that's all right," Garric said. "I have a litter to ride in. I feel silly, but it's better than crawling—which is the choice."

Laughing, Cashel led them out—Tenoctris between him and Sharina, Merota with Ilna and Chalcus. Ilna looked over her shoulder for a moment, nodded, and walked on.

Does she guess? Garric wondered.

"*If she wants to know, she knows,*" Carus said. His look was far away, on his own past and a woman there who had died. "*Anyway, they'll all know soon.*"

Garric levered himself to his feet, using the stone railing as a brace. He turned and looked eastward, over the city that had returned to the Kingdom of the Isles for the first time in a thousand years.

The sun had almost set. Streaks of cloud on the western horizon cut its swollen redness into three segments. Light flared onto the bank of clouds far to the east, rosy columns mounting from the sea to the high heavens.

Liane would be coming across the Inner Sea on the squadron that brought Reise. A feeling of warmth eased the pain Garric felt from standing.

"I'm not going to move the capital from Valles back to Carcosa," he said, speaking aloud but in a whisper that only he and the ancient king could hear. "But I think it's a good place to hold the marriage."

"*Yes, lad,*" said the grinning Carus. "*It's a fine place for the King of the Isles to wed!*"